P9-BAU-545

LILIAN JACKSON BRAUN

THREE COMPLETE NOVELS

ALSO BY LILIAN JACKSON BRAUN

The Cat Who Could Read Backwards

The Cat Who Ate Danish Modern

The Cat Who Turned On and Off

The Cat Who Saw Red

The Cat Who Played Brahms

The Cat Who Played Post Office

The Cat Who Knew Shakespeare

The Cat Who Sniffed Glue

The Cat Who Went Underground

The Cat Who Talked to Ghosts

The Cat Who Lived High

The Cat Who Knew a Cardinal

The Cat Who Moved a Mountain

The Cat Who Wasn't There

The Cat Who Went into the Closet

The Cat Who Came to Breakfast

The Cat Who Blew the Whistle

The Cat Who Had 14 Tales (Short Story Collection)

LILIAN JACKSON BRAUN

THREE COMPLETE NOVELS

The Cat Who Wasn't There

The Cat Who Went into the Closet

The Cat Who Came to Breakfast

G. P. PUTNAM'S SONS
NEW YORK

G. P. Putnam's Sons
Publishers Since 1838
200 Madison Avenue
New York, NY 10016

Published simultaneously in Canada

Library of Congress Cataloging-in-Publication Data

Braun, Lilian Jackson.
[Novels. Selections]
Three complete novels / Lilian Jackson Braun.
p. cm.
Contents: The cat who wasn't there—The cat who went into the
closet—The cat who came to breakfast.
ISBN 0-399-14127-8
1. Qwilleran, Jim (Fictitious character)—Fiction. 2. Detective and mystery stories,
American. 3. Journalists—United States—Fiction. 4. Cat owners—United States—
Fiction. 5. Cats—Fiction.
I. Title.
PS3552.R354A6 1996 95-25675 CIP

Printed in the United States of America

1 3 5 7 9 10 8 6 4 2

Book Design by Patrice Sheridan

Dedicated to
Earl Bettinger, the Husband Who . . .

CONTENTS

The Cat Who Wasn't There

One

In late August, sixteen residents of Moose County, a remote part of the United States 400 miles north of everywhere, traveled to Scotland for a tour of the Western Isles and Highlands, lochs and moors, castles and crofts, firths and straths, burns and braes, fens and bens and glens. Only fifteen of them returned alive, and the survivors straggled home in various states of shock or confusion.

Among the travelers who signed up for the Bonnie Scots Tour were several prominent persons in Pickax City, the county seat. They included the owner of the department store, the superintendent of schools, a young doctor from a distinguished family, the publisher of the local newspaper, the administrator of the public library, and a good-looking, well-built, middle-aged man with a luxuriant pepper-and-salt moustache and drooping eyelids, who happened to be the richest bachelor in Moose County—or in fact the entire northeast central United States.

Jim Qwilleran's wealth was not the result of his own effort but a fluke inheritance. As a journalist, he had been content to pound a beat, churn out copy, and race deadlines for large metropolitan dailies Down Below. (So Pickax folk called the urban areas to the south.) Then fate brought him to Pickax City (population 3,000) and made him heir to the Klingenschoen estate. It was more money than he really wanted. The uncounted millions hung over his head like a dark cloud until he established the Klingenschoen Foundation to dispose of the fortune philanthropically, leaving him free to live in a barn, write a column for the *Moose County Something*, feed and brush his two Siamese cats, and spend pleasant weekends with Polly Duncan, head of the Pickax Public Library.

When the tour to Scotland was proposed, Qwilleran and his feline companions had just returned from a brief sojourn in some distant mountains, a vacation cut short by disturbing news from Pickax. Polly Duncan, while driving home after dark, had been followed by a man in a car without lights, narrowly escaping his clutches. When Qwilleran heard the news, he had a sickening vision of attempted kidnapping; his relationship with Polly was well known in the county, and his millions made him an easy mark for a ransom demand.

Immediately he phoned the Pickax police chief to request protection for Polly. Then, canceling his vacation arrangements, he made the long drive back to Moose County at a speed that discommoded the two yowling passengers in the backseat and alerted the highway patrols of four states. He arrived home Monday noon and dropped off the Siamese and their water dish before hurrying to the Pickax Public Library.

He went on foot, cutting through the woods and approaching the library from the rear. In the parking lot behind the building he recognized Polly's small gray two-door and an elderly friend's ancient navy blue four-door. There was also a maroon car with a Massachusetts license plate that gave him momentary qualms; he had no wish to encounter Dr. Melinda Goodwinter, who had come from Boston for her father's funeral. He mounted the steps of the stately library in unstately leaps and found the main room aflutter with small children. There was no evidence of Melinda Goodwinter. The youngsters were squealing and chattering and lugging picture books to the check-out desk, on which sat a rotund object about three feet high, like an egg with a cracked shell. The six-foot-two man pushed through the horde of knee-high tots, went up the stairs to the mezzanine three at a time, and barged through the reading room to the glass-enclosed office of the head librarian. None of the persons at the reading tables, he noted with relief, was the young doctor from Boston. Sooner or later he would have to face her, and he was unsure how to handle their reunion: with cool politesse? with lukewarm pleasure? with jocular nonchalance?

The librarian was a dignified and pleasant-faced woman of his own age, and she was eating lunch at her desk, the aroma of tuna fish adding an earthy touch to the high-minded bookishness of the office. Silently she reached out a hand across the desk and managed to smile her delight and surprise while chewing a carrot stick. A fervent and lingering handclasp was as amorous a greeting as they dared, since the office had the privacy of a fishbowl and Pickax had a penchant for gossip. Their eye contact said it all.

"You're home!" she murmured in her gentle voice after swallowing.

"Yes, I made it!" It was a dialogue unworthy of Polly's intelligence and Qwilleran's wit, but under the circumstances they could be excused. He dropped into a varnished oak chair, the keys in his back pocket clanking on the hard seat. "Is everything all right?" he asked anxiously. "Any more scares?"

"Not a thing," she said calmly.

"No more prowlers in the neighborhood?"

She shook her head.

For one uncomfortable moment his suspicious nature suggested that she might have invented the prowler episode to bring him home ahead of schedule; she was inclined to be possessive. He banished the thought, however; Polly was an honorable and loving friend. She might be jealous of women younger and thinner than she, but she had absolute integrity; of that he was sure.

"Tell me again exactly what happened," Qwilleran said. "Your voice was shaky when you talked to me on the phone."

"Well, as I told you at the time, I was returning after dark from the library banquet," she began quietly in her clear, considered manner of speaking. "When I drove into Goodwinter Boulevard—where curb parking is not allowed, as you know—I noticed a car parked the wrong way in front of the Gage mansion, and I could see someone sitting behind the wheel—a man with a beard. I thought that was strange. Mrs. Gage was still in Florida, and no one was living in the main house. I decided to notify the police as soon as I reached my apartment."

"Did you feel personally threatened at this point?"

"Not really. I turned into the side drive of the mansion and was driving back to the carriage house when I realized that the car was following me without lights! And then—*then* I was terrified! I accelerated and parked close to my doorstep with the headlights beamed on the keyhole. As I jumped out of my car, I glanced to the left. He was getting out of his car, too. I was able to rush inside and slam the door before he reached me."

Qwilleran tapped his moustache in an expression of anxiety. "Did you get a further look at him?"

"That's what the police wanted to know. I have the impression that he was of medium build, and when I first pulled up to the drive my headlights picked up a bearded face behind the wheel. That's all I can tell you."

"That narrows it down to forty percent of our male population," Qwilleran said. In Moose County beards were favored by potato farmers, hunters, sheep ranchers, fishermen, construction workers, and newspaper reporters.

"It was a bushy beard, I would say," she added.

"Did Brodie give you a police escort as I requested?"

"He offered to drive me to and from work, but honestly, Qwill, it seemed so unnecessary in daylight."

"Hmmm," he murmured, slumping in his chair in deep thought. Was it a false alarm? Or was Polly really at risk? Rather than worry her unduly, he asked, "What's that absurd egg doing on the check-out desk?"

"Don't you recognize Humpty Dumpty? He's the focus of our summer reading program," she explained patiently. "The children are helping to put him together again by checking out books. After they've taken home a certain number, he'll be well and happy, and we'll have a party . . . You're invited," she added mischievously, knowing he avoided small children.

"How do you know the kids will read the books after they get them home? How do you know they'll even crack them?"

"Qwill, dear, you're so cynical!" she reproved him. "Your stay in the mountains hasn't mellowed you in the slightest . . . By the way, did you see our elevator installation? We're very grateful to the Klingenschoen Foundation. Now the elderly and infirm have access to the reading room."

"You should ask the K Foundation for some chairs with padded seats," he suggested, squirming uncomfortably. "Apart from Humpty Dumpty's great fall, is there any other world-shaking news in Moose County?"

"We're still grieving over the suicide of Dr. Halifax. Dr. Melinda returned for her father's funeral and has decided to stay. Everyone's pleased about that." It was a small-town custom to use the honorific when a local son or daughter had earned it.

Melinda Goodwinter had been Polly's predecessor in Qwilleran's affection—as everyone in Pickax knew—and he was careful not to react visibly. Casually he asked, "Will she take over Dr. Hal's patients?"

"Yes, she's already sent out announcements." Polly spoke of Melinda with studied detachment.

"How about dinner tonight at the Old Stone Mill?" he asked,

changing the subject to conceal his personal concern about Melinda redux.

"I was hoping you'd suggest it. I have something exciting to discuss."

"About what?"

She smiled mysteriously. "I can't tell you right now. It's a wonderful surprise!"

"Where shall I pick you up? And at what time?"

"Shall we say seven o'clock?" Polly suggested. "I'd like to go home to change clothes and feed Bootsie."

"Seven o'clock it is."

"Are you sure you aren't too tired after all that driving?"

"All I need is a strong cup of coffee, and I'll be swinging from the chandeliers."

"I've missed you, dear. I'm so glad you're home," she said softly.

"I've missed you, too, Polly." He started to leave her office and paused on the threshold, from which he could see the reading tables. A white-haired woman sat knitting laboriously with arthritic hands; an elderly man was bent over a stack of books; a younger man with an unruly beard was leafing idly through a magazine. "Who's the fellow with the beard?" Qwilleran mumbled behind his hand as he stroked his moustache.

"I don't know. The woman is Mrs. Crawbanks; her granddaughter always drops her off here while she does errands. Now that we have an elevator we've become a day-care center for grandparents. Homer Tibbitt—you know him, of course—is doing research for the Historical Society. The younger man, I don't know."

Qwilleran strode through the reading room to speak to the thin and angular Mr. Tibbitt, who was in his nineties and still active, despite creaking joints. "I hear you're digging into Moose County's lurid past, Homer."

The retired school principal straightened up, his bony frame clicking in several places. "Got to keep the old brain cells functioning," he said in a cracked voice. "No one's ever recorded the history of the Goodwinters, although they founded Pickax one hundred fifty years ago. There were four branches of the family, some with good blood and some with bad blood, sorry to say. But the clan's dying out in these parts. Amanda's the last of the drinking Goodwinters. Dr. Halifax had two children, but the boy was killed in an accident a few years ago, and if Dr. Melinda marries and produces sons, they won't continue the family name. Of course," he continued after a moment's reflection, "she could do something unconventional; you never know what the young ones will do these days. But at present, Junior Goodwinter is the only hope. He's produced one son so far . . ."

Mr. Tibbitt would have rambled on, but Qwilleran noticed that the bearded man had left the reading room, and he wanted to follow him. Excusing himself, he bolted down the stairs and out of the building, dodging preschoolers, but the car with the Massachusetts plate was pulling out of the parking lot.

From the library he took the back street to the police station, hoping to avoid acquaintances who would question his premature return from the mountains. He found Andrew Brodie, the big, broad-shouldered chief of police, hunched over a computer, distrustfully poking the keys.

"Who invented these damn things?" Brodie growled. "More trouble than they're worth!" He leaned back in his chair. "Well, my friend, you hightailed it back to Pickax pretty fast! How'd you do it?"

"By flying low, bribing cops, and not giving my right name," Qwilleran retorted in the familiar bantering style that Brodie liked. "How's it going, Andy? Have you logged any more reports of prowlers?"

"Nary a one! The incident on Goodwinter Boulevard is hard to figure. Can't say that I buy your theory, Qwill. Kidnapping is something we've never had around here, except once when a father snatched his kid after a custody battle."

"There was a stranger loitering in the reading room outside Polly's office a few minutes ago, a youngish man with a bushy beard and a gray sweatshirt. He was driving a car with a Massachusetts license plate, but he pulled out of the lot before I could catch the number."

"Could it be Dr. Melinda's car? She's back in town."

"This was an old model, and muddy. I'm sure she drives something new and antiseptic-looking."

"If you see it again, get the number and we'll run a check on the registration just for the hell of it. Did you get a description?"

"All I can tell you is that it's a medium-sized car in dull maroon, and it looks as if it's been on dirt roads lately."

"Not hard to do in this neck o' the woods."

Qwilleran looked over Brodie's shoulder toward the coffeemaker. "Could the taxpayers afford a cup for a weary traveler?"

"Help yourself, but don't expect anything like that liquid tar that you brew!"

Qwilleran pushed open the gate into the enclosure, poured a cup of weak coffee, and sat down in another hard institutional oak chair. "Did you play your bagpipe at Dr. Hal's funeral, Andy?"

The chief nodded soberly. "Everybody broke up! Men, women, and children—all in tears! There's nothing sadder than a dirge on a bagpipe. Dr. Melinda requested it. She said her dad liked the pipes." Switching to a confidential tone, he went on. "She thinks she's gonna take over his patients, but the guys around here won't warm up to the idea of stripping and being examined by a woman doctor. I'm squeamish about it myself. I'll find me a male doctor even if I have to go down to Lockmaster. How about you?"

"I'll cross that bridge when I come to it," Qwilleran said carelessly, although he knew the situation would be awkward in his own case. "Our health-care setup will improve when the Klingenschoen Professional Building is finished. We'll be able to lure some specialists up here from Down Below. After all, it's a good place to raise a family; you said so yourself." His effort to divert attention from Melinda was unsuccessful.

Brodie regarded him sharply. "You and her were pretty thick, I understand, when she was here before."

"She was the first woman I met when I came to Moose County, Andy, but that's ancient history."

"I don't know why you and Polly don't get hitched. It's the only way to live, to my way of thinking."

"That's because you're a dedicated family man. Try to get it through your skull that some of us make rotten husbands. I found it out the hard way, to my sorrow. I lost several years of my life—and ruined another life in the process."

"But Polly's a good woman. Damn shame to see her wasted."

"Wasted! If she knew you called her life wasted, she'd tear up your library card! Polly is living a useful and rewarding life. She's the lifeblood of the library. And she chooses to be independent. She has her women friends and her bird-watching and a comfortable apartment filled with family heirlooms . . ."

And she has Bootsie, Qwilleran said to himself as he walked from the police station to the newspaper office. He huffed into his moustache. It was his impression that Polly lavished too much maudlin affection on the two-year-old Siamese. When Bootsie was a kitten, she babied him unconscionably, but now he had outgrown kittenish ways and she still babbled precious nonsense in his ear. In Qwilleran's household, the Siamese were sophisticated companions whom he treated as equals, and they treated him the same way. He addressed them intelligently, and they replied with expressive yips and yowls. When he discussed problems in their presence, he felt their sympathy. He regularly read aloud to them from worthwhile books, news magazines, and—on Sundays—the *New York Times*.

Kao K'o Kung, the male (called Koko as a handy everyday diminutive), was a gifted animal endowed with highly developed senses quite beyond those of humans and other cats. Yum Yum was a female who hid her catly wiles under a guise of affectionate cuddling, purring and nuzzling, often extending a paw to touch Qwilleran's moustache.

From the police station it was a short walk to the office of the *Moose County Something,* as the local newspaper was named. (Everything in mile-square Pickax was a short walk.) The publication occupied a new building made possible by financial assistance from the Klingenschoen Foundation, and the editor-and-publisher was Qwilleran's longtime friend from Down Below, Arch Riker. In the lobby there were no security guards or hidden cameras such as those employed by the large metropolitan dailies for which Qwilleran had worked. He walked down the hall to Riker's office and found the door open, the desk unoccupied.

From the managing editor's office across the hall Junior Goodwinter hailed him. "Arch went to Minneapolis for a publishers' conference. He'll be back tomorrow. Come on in! Have a chair. Put your feet up. I don't suppose you want a cup of coffee."

Recalling the anemic brew he had just swallowed, Qwilleran replied, "I majored in journalism and graduated with a degree in caffeine. Make it black and hot."

Junior's boyish build, boyish countenance, and boyish enthusiasm were now tempered by a newly grown beard. "How do you like it?" he asked as he stroked his chin. "Does it make me look older?"

"It makes you look like a young potato farmer. What's your wife's reaction?"

"She likes it. She says it makes me look like a jolly elf. What brings you home so soon?" he asked as he handed over a steaming cup.

"Polly was frightened by a prowler on Goodwinter Boulevard. I didn't like the sound of it."

"How come we didn't hear about it?"

"She reported it, but there's been no further incident, so far as anyone knows."

"They've got to do something about Goodwinter Boulevard, no kidding," said Junior. "It used to be the best street in town. Now it's getting positively hairy with all those vacant mansions looking like haunted houses. The one where Alex and Penelope lived has been up for sale for years! The one that VanBrook rented is empty again, and it's going begging. Who wants fifteen or twenty rooms nowadays?"

"Rezoning, that's what it needs," Qwilleran said. "It should be rezoned for apartments, offices, good restaurants, high-class nursing homes, and so forth. Why don't you write an editorial?"

"I'd be accused of special interest," Junior said.

"How do you figure that?"

"Grandma Gage has bought a condo in Florida and wants to deed the mansion to me while she's still living. What would I do with fifteen rooms? Think of the heating bills and the taxes and all those windows to wash! I'll own just another white elephant on Goodwinter Boulevard."

Qwilleran's eyes, known for their doleful expression and drooping lids, roamed over the clutter on the editor's desk, the crumpled paper that had missed the wastebasket, the half-open file drawers, the stacks of out-of-town newspapers. But he wasn't looking; he was thinking. He was thinking that the Gage mansion occupied the property in front of Polly's carriage house. If he lived there, he could keep a watchful eye on her. Also, it would be convenient for other purposes, like dropping in for dinner frequently. He smoothed his moustache with satisfaction and said to Junior, "I could use a winter house in town. My barn is hard to heat and there's too much snow to plow. Why don't I rent your house?"

"Wow! That would be great!" the young editor yelled.

"But I still think you should run that editorial."

"The city will never do anything about rezoning. Tradition dies hard in Pickax."

"How about Stephanie's Restaurant in the old Lanspeak house? It was opened a couple of years when I first came here."

"That was the first house on the boulevard," Junior explained. "It faced Main Street and could be legally used for commercial purposes. Too bad it closed; the building's still empty . . . No, Qwill, there are still influential families on the boulevard who'll fight rezoning like tigers. We'll have to wait for some more of them to die off. Dr. Hal lived on the boulevard, you know."

"Do you think Melinda will keep the house?"

"No way! She has an apartment and intends to sell the house and furnishings. Off the record, her dad didn't leave much of an estate. He was an old-fashioned country doctor, never charging patients who couldn't pay and never taking advantage of the insurance setup. And don't forget the expense of round-the-clock nurses for his wife for all those years! Melinda has inherited more problems than property . . . Have you seen her?" Junior asked with a searching look. He knew about Melinda's former pursuit of the county's most eligible bachelor. She was Junior's cousin. All Goodwinters were cousins to a degree. "She's changed somehow," he said. "I don't know how to pinpoint it."

"Three years on the staff of a Boston hospital can do that," Qwilleran said.

"Yeah, they worked her pretty hard, I guess. Well, anyway, can we expect some copy from you this week? Or are you too bushed?"

"I'll see what I can do."

Walking home, Qwilleran recalled his earlier association with Dr. Melinda Goodwinter. He had been a stranger in Moose County at the time, suffering from a fierce case of ivy poisoning. After treating his condition successfully, she offered friendship, flip conversation, and youth. She was twenty years his junior, with green eyes and long lashes and the frank sexuality of her generation. As a doctor, she had convinced him to give up smoking and take more exercise. As a woman, she had been overly aggressive for Qwilleran's taste, and her campaign to bulldoze him into matrimony resulted in embarrassment for both of them. She moved to Boston after that, telling everyone she had no desire to be a country doctor.

When he met Polly, it was he who did the pursuing—an arrangement more to his liking. She was not so thin as Melinda, nor were her lashes so long, but she was a congenial companion and a good cook, who shared his literary interests. They liked to get together and read Shakespeare, for one thing. She made no unacceptable demands, and, more and more, Qwilleran found Polly occupying his thoughts.

On the way home he stopped at Toodles' Market to buy the Siamese something to eat—always a problem because they had fickle palates. Their preferences changed just often enough to keep him perpetually on his toes. There was only one constant: no cat food! As if they could read labels, they disdained any product intended for the four-legged trade. Sometimes they were satisfied with a can of red salmon garnished with a smoked oyster or a dab of caviar, preferably sturgeon. At other times, they would kill for turkey, but he could never be sure. At Toodles' he considered a slice of roast beef from the deli or some chicken liver pâté. Better yet would be a few ounces of tenderloin from the butcher, to serve *au tartare,* but he would have to hand-mince it; ground meat was somehow objectionable. He settled for the pâté.

From there he followed the long way home, just for the exercise, trudging along a back road, then up a gravel trail through an old orchard. He was a hundred feet from the apple barn when he heard clarion voices yowling a welcome. The nineteenth-century barn was an octagonal structure four stories high, with large windows cut into the walls at various levels, and he could see two furry bodies darting about indoors, observing him first from one window and then another. They met him at the door, prancing and waving their tails like flags. It was a ritual that gave him a leap of inner joy in spite of his unsentimental greeting. "What have you young turks been doing since you got home?"

They sensed the liver pâté with quivering whiskers. In spasms of anticipation they dashed up the ramp that spiraled around the interior of the building, connecting the three balconies and ending in narrow catwalks under the roof. Then they pounded pell-mell down the slope to the first balcony, from which they flew like squirrels, landing in the cushioned seating on the main floor. There they washed their paws and whiskers before dinner.

When Qwilleran spread the pâté on a plate and placed it on the floor, he watched them with fascination as they devoured it. They were masterpieces of design: sleek fawn bodies on long brown legs; incredibly blue eyes in seal-brown masks; expressive brown tails tapered like rapiers. To Qwilleran they seemed to have more elegance than Bootsie, who was being overfed to compensate for the loneliness of his solitary life.

At seven o'clock he called for Polly at her carriage-house apartment behind the Gage mansion, and as he climbed the narrow staircase, Bootsie was waiting at the top with ears back and fangs bared.

"Greetings, thou paragon of animals," Qwilleran said, thinking a phrase from Shakespeare would please Polly.

Bootsie hissed.

"You must forgive him," she apologized. "He sensed danger when the prowler was outside, and he's been edgy ever since."

After a warm, silent, meaningful embrace that would have astonished the library patrons and started the Pickax grapevine sizzling, Qwilleran presented Polly with a tissue-wrapped bundle. "Sorry it isn't gift-wrapped," he said. "I brought it from the mountains. It looked like your shade of blue."

Polly was thrilled. "It's a batwing cape! It's handwoven! Who did it?"

"One of the mountaineers," he said, shrugging off the question. "They're all weavers and potters and woodworkers in the mountains." He avoided mentioning that the weaver was an interesting young woman whom he had taken to dinner and who had rescued him twice when he was in trouble on mountain passes.

Polly had shed the drab suit she wore at the library and was looking festive in a summer dress of mixed polka dots, red-on-white and white-on-red. "You're sure it isn't too bold for me?" she asked when Qwilleran complimented her. "Irma Hasselrich helped me choose it."

They drove to the restaurant in the rental car that had brought him from the mountains. "My own car broke down," he explained, "and I left it there." The tale was loosely true; the car had bogged down in mud, and he had given it to the young mountain woman, who would be able to haul it out with her swamp buggy.

The restaurant called the Old Stone Mill occupied a historic gristmill. There was enough affluence in Pickax—and there were enough educated palates—to support one good eatery, and it was owned by a syndicate of businessmen who needed an unprofitable venture for tax purposes. It paid its chefs handsomely and offered a menu worldly enough for local residents who had dined in San Francisco, New Orleans, and Paris.

After Qwilleran and Polly were greeted and seated at their usual table, a six-foot-seven busboy, who towered above customers and staff alike, shuffled up to the table with a water pitcher and basket of garlic toast. His name was Derek Cuttlebrink. "Hi, Mr. Q," he said in friendly fashion. "I thought you were going away for the summer."

"I came back," Qwilleran explained succinctly.

"I'm taking two weeks in August to go camping."

"Good for you!"

"Yeah, I met this girl, and she has a tent. Blue nylon, seven-by-eight, with aluminum frame. Sets up in five minutes."

"Take plenty of mosquito repellent," Qwilleran advised. "Stay away from poison ivy. Watch out for ticks."

Polly asked, "Have you given any more thought to college, Derek?"

"Well, you know, it's like this, Mrs. Duncan. I've decided to stay in the food business. I'm getting promoted to the kitchen, end of the month—in charge of French fries and garlic toast."

"Congratulations!" said Qwilleran.

When the busboy had sauntered away, Polly wondered, "Do you think Derek will ever amount to anything?"

"Don't give up hope," Qwilleran said. "One of these days he'll meet the right girl, and he'll become a famous brain surgeon. I've seen it happen."

He ordered dry sherry for Polly and, for himself, a local product called Squunk water—from a flowing well in Squunk Corners. He always drank it on the rocks with a twist.

Polly raised her glass. *"Slainte!"*

"Ditto," Qwilleran said. "What does it mean?"

"I don't know exactly. It's a toast in Gaelic that Irma Hasselrich always uses." Polly often quoted her new friend.

Personally, Qwilleran had his doubts about Irma Hasselrich. In her forties, she still lived at home with her parents, her father being senior partner in the law firm of Hasselrich, Bennett & Barter. She was the chief volunteer at the Senior Care Facility, and Qwilleran had met her while interviewing an aged patient. At that time, he thought her a handsome woman. She had a Junoesque figure, a polished appearance, and a charming manner. Since Polly was spending the summer in England, he tried to take Irma to dinner, but his invitation was pointedly avoided. He was not accustomed to being rejected, and his reaction was distinctly negative.

Recently the two women had discovered a mutual interest: They often went bird-watching with binoculars and notebooks on the banks of the Ittibittiwassee River or in the wetlands near Purple Point. Furthermore, the well-groomed, well-dressed Irma was influencing Polly to wear brighter colors and touch up her graying hair.

"You're looking especially young and attractive tonight," he remarked as they sipped their aperitifs. "Soon you'll be joining the Theatre Club and playing ingenue roles."

"Not likely," she said with her musical laugh. "But did you hear that the club is doing *Macbeth* in September?"

"That's a surprise!"

"Why? It's a highly dramatic play with witches, ghosts, swordplay, a sleepwalker, and some ghastly murders, and it has plenty to say about temptation, human failure, spiritual evil, and compulsive ambition."

"But according to superstition, it brings bad luck to the company that stages it."

"No one around here is aware of that, so don't enlighten them," Polly advised. "Of course, it's almost certain that Larry will play the title role."

"He'll have to grow a beard again. He won't like that. Who's directing?"

"A new man in town, Dwight Somers, who's taken a position with XYZ Enterprises. He's had theatre experience and is said to be very nice. Auditions have been announced, and it's rumored that

Dr. Melinda is going to read for Lady Macbeth." The Pickax library was a major listening post in the local grapevine.

Qwilleran wanted to ask: Have you seen Melinda? . . . How does she look? . . . They say she's changed a lot. He deemed it wise, however, not to exhibit that much interest, so he asked casually, "Would she be any good in that role?"

"Quite possibly. I saw her at Dr. Hal's funeral and thought she was looking . . . much *older.* The Goodwinter face—long and narrow, you know—has a tendency to look haggard. It doesn't age well."

They ordered jellied watercress consommé and grilled swordfish with pineapple-jalapeño salsa, and Qwilleran asked, "What's the surprise you have for me tonight?"

"Well!" she began with evident relish. "Irma and I had dinner one night while you were away, and we were talking about Scotland. She went to art school there and still has connections, whom she visits frequently. I mentioned that I've always wanted to see Macbeth country, and that started a train of thought. Why not organize a group tour of Scottish Isles and Highlands, with a percentage of the tour cost going to the Senior Care Facility, tax deductible?"

"Sounds okay. Who'd manage it?"

"Irma is plotting the itinerary, and she'll make the reservations and act as tour guide."

"Is she experienced at handling group tours?"

"No. But she's in charge of the volunteer program at the facility, and she's a natural leader, well organized, and certainly knowledgeable about Scotland, especially the Western Isles and Highlands."

"How will you travel in Scotland?"

"By chartered minibus. The Lanspeaks and the Comptons have signed up, and Irma and I will share a room. The price of the tour is based on double occupancy, but singles are available."

Qwilleran said to himself, It's a good idea for Polly to leave the country until the prowler threat blows over. "You'll like the Highlands. I spent my honeymoon there. As I recall, the food wasn't very good, but that was quite a long time ago, and when you're a newlywed, who cares? . . . Would you like me to feed Bootsie while you're away?"

She regarded him hopefully. "We were thinking . . . that you might . . . join the tour."

The suggestion caught him off-guard, and he stared into space for a few moments before answering. "How long is the trip? I've never left the cats for more than a couple of days. Who'd take care of them?"

"Is there someone you could trust to move into your barn for two weeks? My sister-in-law is going to stay with Bootsie."

Qwilleran stroked his moustache with uncertainty. "I don't know. I'll have to think about it. But whatever I decide, the K Foundation will match whatever you raise for the Senior Facility. Will it be advertised?"

"Irma says it's better to make it invitational to ensure a compatible group. We'll go in late August when the heather is in bloom. The tour will start in Glasgow and end in Edinburgh."

"Glasgow?" Qwilleran echoed with interest. "I've been reading about the Charles Rennie Mackintosh revival in Glasgow. My mother was a Mackintosh, you know."

Polly knew, having heard it a hundred times, but she asked sweetly, "Do you think you might be related to him?"

"I know nothing about my maternal ancestors except that one of them was either a stagecoach driver who was killed by a highwayman, or a highwayman who was hanged for murdering a stagecoach driver. As for Charles Rennie Mackintosh, I know only that he pioneered modern design a hundred years ago, and he sounds like an interesting character."

"If you wish to extend your time in Glasgow, you can do that," Polly said encouragingly. "Carol and Larry will go early and see a few plays in London."

"Okay, sign me up for a single," he said. "I'll find a cat-sitter. Lori Bamba would be perfect, but she has kids, and they'd fall off the balconies. The barn was designed for cats and adults."

The soup course arrived, and they savored it in silence as they thought about the forthcoming adventure. When the swordfish was served, Qwilleran said, "I've heard a rumor about Irma Hasselrich, although not from a reliable source. Perhaps you could set me straight."

Polly stiffened noticeably. "What have you heard? And from whom?"

"I protect my sources," he said, "but the story is that she shot a man twenty-odd years ago and was charged with murder, but the Hasselriches bribed the judge to let her off without a sentence."

Drawing a deep breath of exasperation, Polly replied, "Like most gossip in Pickax, it's only ten percent accurate. The motive for the shooting was what we now call date rape. In court, Hasselrich defended his daughter brilliantly. The jury found her guilty of manslaughter but recommended leniency, and the judge was more understanding than most jurists at that time; he gave her probation, plus an order to do three years of community service . . . Does that answer your question?"

Detecting annoyance in the curt explanation, he said, "I'm sorry. I simply repeated what I had heard."

More softly Polly said, "After completing her community service, Irma went on to devote her life to volunteer work. She'll do *anything* for charity! She's raised tons of money for good causes."

"Quite admirable," Qwilleran murmured, but it crossed his mind that "anything" was a strong and suspect word.

He ordered strawberry pie for dessert, and Polly toyed with a small dish of lime sorbet. She had eaten only half of everything that was served. "I'm watching my diet," she explained. "I've lost a few pounds. Does it show?"

"You're looking healthy and beautiful," he replied. "Don't get too skinny."

After dessert they went to her apartment for coffee, and then did some reading aloud. They read two acts of *Macbeth* while Bootsie sniffed Qwilleran's trouser legs with distaste.

It was late when Qwilleran returned to the apple barn, and two indignant Siamese met him at the door. Sensing that he had been associating with another cat, they walked away with a lofty display of superiority.

"Come off it, you guys!" he rebuked them. "I have news for you. I'm taking a trip to Scotland, and *you're not going!*"

"Yow!" Koko scolded him.

"That's right. You're staying here!"

"N-n-now!" shrieked Yum Yum.

"And you're not going, either!"

Two

The day following his evening with Polly, Qwilleran regretted his impulsive decision to go to Scotland and leave the Siamese for two weeks. As he brushed their silky coats—Yum Yum with hindlegs splayed like a Duncan Phyfe table, and Koko with tail in a stiff Hogarth curve—he thought of canceling his reservation, but an inner voice deterred him, saying: *You're a two-hundred-pound man, and you're allowing yourself to be enslaved by eighteen pounds of cat!*

That evening he was reading aloud with the female cuddling contentedly on his lap and the male perched on the arm of his chair, when the telephone rang. "Excuse me, sweetheart," he said, lifting Yum Yum gently and placing her on the warm seat cushion he had just vacated.

It was Irma Hasselrich on the line, speaking with the syrupy, formal charm that was her style. She said, "Mr. Qwilleran, I learn with a great deal of pleasure that you wish to join the Bonnie Scots Tour."

"Yes, it strikes me as an interesting adventure. My mother was a Mackintosh. And by the way, please call me Qwill."

"Needless to say, Mr. Qwilleran," she continued as if she had not heard, "we're delighted that the Klingenschoen Foundation is offering a matching grant. We want to create a park for the patients at the facility, with flower beds, winding paths for wheelchairs, and a pavilion with tables for picnic lunches and games."

"Very commendable," Qwilleran murmured. "How many persons do you expect to enlist for the tour?"

"Our goal is sixteen. That number will fill a minibus."

"Did Polly tell you I want to spend some time in Glasgow?"

"Yes. Several participants want to extend their stay abroad, so I suggest that we all make our own flight arrangements and meet on Day One at a prescribed location in Glasgow."

"How many have signed up so far?"

"Eleven. Perhaps you can suggest other compatible travelers that we might contact."

Qwilleran thought for a few seconds. "How about John and Vicki Bushland? They have a summer place in Mooseville, although they're residents of Lockmaster, where he has a commercial photography studio."

"We would love to have a professional photographer along! May I call them and use your name?"

"By all means."

"As soon as it was known that you were joining the tour, Mr. Qwilleran, I was able to sign up three others: Mr. and Mrs. MacWhannell—he's the CPA, you know—and Dr. Melinda Goodwinter. Aren't we fortunate to have a doctor with us?"

Qwilleran cringed inwardly and combed his moustache with his fingertips. He had visions of the importunate Melinda tapping on his hotel door at a late hour and inviting herself in for a chat. She was a persistent young woman, and, according to Arch Riker, who had met her after her father's funeral, she was still carrying the torch for him, Polly or no Polly.

Qwilleran veiled his distress by inquiring about the weather in Scotland, and Irma assured him that she would send all pertinent travel information in the mail.

When the conversation ended, he immediately phoned Arch Riker at the office of the *Moose County Something.* The two men had grown up together in Chicago and had pursued separate careers in journalism Down Below. Now they were reunited in Pickax, where Riker was realizing his dream of publishing a small-town newspaper.

"Arch, how would you like to knock off for a couple of weeks and go to Scotland with a local group?" Qwilleran proposed. "We could save a few bucks by sharing accommodations." He added a few details and dropped some important names: Hasselrich, Lanspeak, Compton, MacWhannell.

Riker liked the idea, saying that he'd always wanted to play the seventeenth hole at St. Andrews.

"And now the bad news," Qwilleran said. "Melinda Goodwinter is going."

"The plot thickens," said Riker with a chuckle. He was amused by his friend's problems with women. "Does Polly know?"

"If she doesn't, she'll soon find out!"

Complimenting himself on a successful maneuver, Qwilleran called Irma Hasselrich and changed his reservation to double occupancy. The next day it was his turn to chuckle when Riker telephoned.

"Hey, listen to this, Qwill," he said. "I took Amanda to dinner last night and told her about the Scottish tour, and *she wants to join!* How do you like that kettle of fish?"

"She'll have to pay the single supplement. No one will be willing to room with Amanda—not even her cousin Melinda."

Amanda Goodwinter was a cranky, outspoken woman of indefinite age who "drank a little," as Pickax natives liked to say. Yet, she operated a successful studio of interior design and was repeatedly elected to the city council, where she minced no words, spared no feelings, played no politics.

Riker, with a journalist's taste for oddballs, found her entertaining, and for a while the Pickax grapevine linked them as potential mates, but Amanda's prickly personality guaranteed that she would remain single for life. Now he was enjoying the prospect of Amanda disrupting the harmony of a group tour. "I hope everyone has a sense of humor," he said to Qwilleran on the phone. "What's so absurd is that she hates bagpipes, mountains, bus travel, and Irma Hasselrich."

"Then why is she going? Surely not only to be with you, old chum!"

"No, I can't take the credit. She's excited about visiting whiskey distilleries. She's heard they give free samples."

While Qwilleran was relishing this news, Chief Brodie phoned to report that state troopers had spotted a Massachusetts license plate on a maroon car headed south near the county line. "Probably leaving the area," he said. "We ran a check, and it's registered to one Charles Edward Martin of Charlestown, Massachusetts."

"What was he doing here?" Qwilleran asked sharply, a rhetorical question. "In five years I've never seen a Massachusetts car in Moose County. Those New Englanders don't even know it exists!"

"Could be a friend of Dr. Melinda's. Could be he came for her dad's funeral. There were lots of beards there," Brodie said. "Tell you what, Qwill: If he shows up again and we get a complaint, we'll know who he is, at least. For now, we're stepping up the night patrols on Goodwinter Boulevard, and you tell Polly not to go out alone after dark."

Qwilleran's moustache bristled. Whenever he thought of that maroon car, he felt a distinct tremor on his upper lip. His luxuriant moustache was more than a prominent facial feature; it had long been the source of his hunches and suspicions, bristling and tingling to get his attention, and experience had taught him to trust the signals. This peculiar sensitivity was a matter he was loath to discuss with any but his intimate friends, and even they were disinclined to believe it. Nevertheless, it was a fact.

He was not alone in his ability to sense trouble. Kao K'o Kung possessed a unique faculty for exposing evil deeds and evildoers, in the same way that he sniffed a microscopic spot on the rug, or detected a stereo control turned to "on" when the power should be off. When Koko's ears pointed and his whiskers twitched, when he scratched industriously and sniffed juicily, he was on the scent of something that was—not—as—it—should—be!

After the phone conversation with Brodie, Qwilleran turned to Koko, who always perched nearby to monitor calls. "Well, old boy," he said, "the Boulevard Prowler seems to have left town."

"Yow," said Koko, scratching his ear.

"So far, so good. Now, how do we find you a suitable cat-sitter?"

Koko jumped to the floor with a grunt and trotted to the pantry, where he stared pointedly at his empty plate. Yum Yum was not far behind. It was time for their mid-day snack.

Qwilleran gave them a handful of crunchy cereal concocted by the food writer of the *Moose County Something,* Mildred Hanstable. It was the only dry food the Siamese would deign to eat. As he watched them munching and waving their tails in rapture, an idea struck him.

"I've got it!" he said aloud. "Mildred Hanstable!"

Besides writing the food column for the newspaper, she taught home economics in the Pickax schools, and she enjoyed cooking for cats, dogs, and humans. Widowed, she lived alone. Plump and pretty, she had a kind heart, a lively imagination, and an ample lap.

"Perfect!" Qwilleran yelped, so loudly that the Siamese turned to look at him in alarm before finishing the last morsel on the plate.

Mildred Hanstable was the mother-in-law of his friend Roger MacGillivray, and he tracked down the young reporter at Lois's Luncheonette. "What do you think of the idea, Roger? She likes the cats, and they like her."

"It would do her a lot of good—help get her mind off the past," said Roger. "She thinks your barn is sensational, and the chance to live there for a couple of weeks would be like halfway to heaven!"

"One thing I must ask: Is she still drinking heavily?"

"Well, she went through a twisted kind of alcoholic mourning for that no-good husband of hers, but she snapped out of it. Now she's overeating instead. Basically she's lonely. I wish she could meet a decent guy."

"We'll have to work on that, Roger . . . Where are you headed now?"

"I have an assignment in Kennebeck. The Tuesday Afternoon Women's Club is planting a tree in the village park."

It so happened that Qwilleran had brought several handwoven batwing capes from the mountains, and he presented one to Mildred after a staff meeting at the newspaper. It was the kind of voluminous garment that she liked for camouflaging her excess poundage, and the invitation to cat-sit and barn-sit for two weeks thrilled her beyond words.

With that worrisome matter concluded, he now applied himself to other matters. He gave batwing capes to his part-time secretary, the young interior designer who had helped him furnish the barn, and the advertising manager of the *Moose County Something,* making three women deliriously happy. Next, to replace the car that was left mired in the mountains, he found a white four-door on the used-car lot; he never wasted money on new models. All the while, he was cleverly managing to avoid Dr. Melinda Goodwinter, ignoring the reminder that he was due for his annual checkup according to the records of the late Halifax Goodwinter, M.D.

Irma Hasselrich was prompt in mailing tour participants a detailed itinerary as well as information on Scottish weather and appropriate clothing: "Sweaters and jackets are a must, because evenings can be cool, and we'll be traveling to windswept islands and mountaintops. Be sure to include a light raincoat, umbrella, and waterproof shoes or boots." The last was underlined in red. Then: "For special evenings, men are requested to pack a blazer or sports coat with shirt and tie, and women are advised to have a dress and heels for such occasions. Luggage must be limited to *one bag per person,* plus a small carry-on. There will be no smoking on the bus or in restaurants as a matter of courtesy, and no smoking in country inns because of the fire hazard." Enclosed was a brief glossary of Highland and Lowland terms:

loch . . . lake
moor . . . treeless hill
glen . . . secluded valley
fen . . . marsh
ben . . . mountain
firth . . . arm of the sea
burn . . . creek
strath . . . wide river valley
kyle . . . strait
croft . . . farmhouse
crofter . . . farmer
bothy . . . farmhands' barracks
neeps . . . turnips
tatties . . . potatoes
haggis . . . meat pudding
toilet . . . restroom
usquebaugh . . . whiskey
(spelled "whisky" in Scotland)

Included was a suggested reading list: Boswell, Dr. Johnson, Sir Walter Scott, and the like, most of which were in Qwilleran's growing collection of secondhand books.

Nevertheless, he went to Eddington Smith's used-book store and picked up an old travel book with a yellowed fold-out map of Scotland. The bookseller also suggested *Memoirs of an Eighteenth Century Footman.* He said, "It's about Scotland. It was published in

1790 and reprinted in 1927. It's not in bad condition for a sixty-year-old book."

Qwilleran bought it and was on his way out of the store when Eddington mentioned, "Dr. Melinda came in yesterday. She wants me to buy Dr. Hal's library, but she's asking too much money."

That evening, as Qwilleran sat in his favorite lounge chair with *Memoirs,* the cats arranged themselves for a read: Koko on the wide upholstered arm of the chair and Yum Yum on his lap with forelegs extended and paws crossed prettily. Sixty years of assorted household odors made the book fascinating to the Siamese. Qwilleran was enthralled by the incredible account of four motherless children—ages two, four, seven, and fourteen—setting out to find their father, who had left to fight for Prince Charlie. After walking 150 miles, being on the road for three months, begging for food and shelter, they learned that he had fallen in battle at Culloden.

Absorbed in their predicament, Qwilleran was almost too stunned to answer when the telephone rang, until Koko yowled in his ear.

"Uh . . . hello," he said vaguely.

"Hello, lover. Is that you? You sound far away. Do you recognize a voice from your high-flying past?"

"Who is this?" he asked in a flat voice, although he knew.

"Melinda!"

"Oh . . . hello."

"Am I interrupting something important?"

"No. I was reading a book."

"It must be pretty good. What's the title?"

"It's . . . uh . . . *Memoirs of an Eighteenth Century Footman* by John Macdonald."

"Sounds like hot stuff. Someone told me you're collecting old books now."

"I have a few." He was trying to sound like a poor prospect, not to mention a dull and uninteresting person.

"I'm selling my father's library. Are you interested?"

"I'm afraid not. I pick up one book at a time, here and there."

"Why don't you meet me at the house for a look at Dad's library. You might see—something—you like. I'm living at Indian Village, but I could run into town."

"That's a good idea," he said with misleading enthusiasm. "I'll see when Polly Duncan's available, and we'll make an appointment with you. She's my guru when it comes to old books."

There was a pause on the other end of the line. "Okay. I'll get in touch with you later, if the books are still available . . . I hear we're going to Scotland on the same tour, lover."

"Yes, Polly talked me into it."

"Well, don't let me keep you away from your exciting book."

"Thanks for calling," he said in a routine voice.

"Nighty-night."

Melinda never called back about the books, for which Qwilleran was thankful, but her name was frequently mentioned around town. One afternoon he dropped into Amanda's Studio of Interior Design to scrounge a cup of coffee and use the telephone, as he often did when Fran Brodie was in-house. Fran was assistant to Amanda Goodwinter but younger, more glamorous, and better-dispositioned. As a member of the Theatre Club and daughter of the police chief, she had still another attraction: She could always be relied upon for the latest gossip—or local information, as Qwilleran preferred to call it.

Fran greeted him with welcome news: "You've just missed Melinda! She came in to try to sell us her father's books. I don't know what she thought we could do with them . . . Cup of coffee?" She served it in a mug stenciled with the letter *Q*, a mischievous reference to his habitual freeloading. "I'm glad you dropped in, Qwill. I've found something that you simply must have! It's *you!*"

"I should know the free coffee is never free," he said. "What is it?"

She opened a flat box with exaggerated care. "This is an acid-free box, and this is acid-free tissue," she explained, as she unwrapped a drab fragment of cloth.

"What the devil is that?"

"It's a Scottish relic—a fragment of a Mackintosh kilt that was worn by a Jacobite rebel at the Battle of Culloden in 1746!"

"How do you know it is? It looks like a reject from a trash can."

"It's documented. It belonged to an old family in Lockmaster, who came here from Canada. Their ancestors were exiled to the New World during the Scottish Clearances."

"And what am I supposed to do with this faded rag? It wouldn't even be good enough to wash the car!"

"We'd preserve it in a protective frame for you, as they do in museums, and you could put it on display. Of course, we'd have to pick a location without much daylight or artificial light."

"That limits us to the broom closet and the cats' bathroom," he said. "How much is it worth?"

"It's expensive, but you can afford it, considering all the money you save on coffee and phone calls."

"I'll kick it around."

"Do that," Fran said, refilling his coffee mug. "So you're going to Scotland with my boss! I hear they're having trouble filling all the seats. Is that because Amanda is one of the passengers? Or because Irma Hasselrich is the tour director?"

"Doesn't Irma have much of a fan club?" Qwilleran asked.

"I'm afraid people think she's snobbish and bossy, and her perfect grooming frightens some of the casual types around town. Amanda says she looks like a peeled egg . . . One thing I'd like to know: Why did Irma schedule the tour to overlap our rehearsals of *Macbeth?* Our three most important people are taking the trip: the two leads and the director!"

"Is Melinda playing Lady Macbeth?"

Fran nodded with disapproval. "Several women read for it, and Carol was my choice, but Dwight Somers wanted Melinda. He's sort of goggle-eyed about Melinda. She's probably the reason he signed up for the Scottish tour."

Qwilleran thought, Good! I hope he monopolizes her and keeps her out of my hair.

One evening shortly after that, when he and Polly were dining at Tipsy's Tavern in North Kennebeck, Melinda was seated at a table in the same room. He avoided looking in her direction but was aware that her escort was a man with a neat beard.

Polly said it was Dwight Somers. "They're both going on the Bonnie Scots Tour. Melinda is a longtime friend of Irma, you know."

"Is that so?" Qwilleran remarked inanely, wincing at the prick of his vanity; he thought that he himself was Melinda's reason for signing up.

Polly was saying, "I had a physical at her office today. I remember her fifteen years ago when she brought her high-school assignments to the library, and it's difficult to relate to her as a doctor, but Irma says we women must be supportive. My sister-in-law works in the office at the Goodwinter clinic, and I've learned that Dr. Hal's male patients are transferring their records to a man in Lockmaster, an internist and urologist."

Qwilleran said, "If you want my guess, it's their wives who don't want them going to a young . . . *woman* doctor." He was going to say "young attractive woman doctor" but edited his own dialogue.

As if on cue, Melinda passed their table on the way to the restroom. "Hi, lover," she said breezily, pausing for a moment that seemed too long.

Qwilleran rose from his chair and said something trite. "Dr. Goodwinter, I presume." He rose courteously, but he kept one hand on the back of his chair and stood in a semicrouch, ready to sit down again when she moved on, which he hoped would be soon.

"Are you all excited about our trip together?" she asked with a sly glance, addressing him directly.

"Polly and I are both looking forward to it." He nodded graciously to his guest.

"Then I'll see you on the bonny banks of Loch Lomond, lover," Melinda said as she sauntered away, drawing a manicured hand suggestively across their tabletop. The whiff of fragrance that she left behind was the same she had worn three years before.

"Indeed!" Polly said with raised eyebrows. "What was the significance of that pretty performance?"

"She's half-bombed," Qwilleran said with a sense of relief. He had feared he might find Melinda as appealing as before, but the impudent manner that formerly enchanted him now annoyed him; her hair was done in a trendy style he disliked; and she was too thin. His taste had changed. Lest his silence be misconstrued, he quickly said to Polly, "I don't know about you, but I've never traveled with a group, except for a bunch of hyper reporters on a press junket, so I'm hoping for the best and expecting the worst on this excursion."

"We'll enjoy it," she assured him and then said, "Do you remember the bronchitis I had when I spent the summer in England? On this trip I'm taking vitamin C as a preventive. The pharmacist told me about a high-potency capsule, and I respect his advice."

"Did you discuss it with—your doctor?" Qwilleran was dubious of vitamins, broccoli, and anything else said to be salubrious.

"I mentioned it to Melinda, and she said it wouldn't do any harm but probably wouldn't do any good, either. Nevertheless, I intend to try it . . . Have you made your packing list, Qwill?"

"I never make a list. I just throw stuff into my suitcase."

"You're singularly offhand, dear! I make a list and take only basic colors, double-duty garments, minimal accessories, and just enough toothpaste, face cream, and shampoo for fourteen days."

"You're singularly efficient," he retorted dryly. "No wonder the library operates so smoothly."

"Have you done any of Irma's suggested reading?"

"No, but Edd Smith sold me a book with a fold-out map of Scotland. As soon as I opened the map, both cats came running and pounced in the middle of it, tearing it along the old yellowed creases and making a horrible muddle, as Old Possum would say. I hope it was not a prediction that our trip is going to be a horrible muddle."

"With Irma in charge, have no fear!" Polly assured him.

During the summer, following that accidental meeting with Melinda at Tipsy's Tavern, Qwilleran received several phone calls from her, making unacceptable suggestions that he found annoying. He solved that problem by screening calls through his answering machine, but the proximity of two weeks in a minibus could lead to murder, he reflected with testy humor.

Eventually the final orders came from Sergeant Hasselrich, as Lyle Compton called her: "The evening before Day One we shall gather in a private parlor at our Glasgow hotel (see itinerary) for a Happy Hour from six to seven o'clock, after which you will be on your own for dinner. The tour will depart the next morning after a lavish Scottish breakfast (included in your tour package)." There followed a list of participants in alphabetical order:

John Bushland
Ms. Zella Chisholm
Mr. and Mrs. Lyle Compton (Lisa)
Mrs. Polly Duncan
Ms. Amanda Goodwinter
Dr. Melinda Goodwinter
Ms. Irma Hasselrich
Mr. and Mrs. Lawrence Lanspeak (Carol)
Mr. and Mrs. Whannell MacWhannell (Glenda)
James Qwilleran
Archibald Riker
Dwight Somers
Mrs. Grace Chisholm Utley

Qwilleran showed the list to Mildred Hanstable when she arrived at the barn for her briefing prior to cat-sitting with their Royal Highnesses. She arrived in a cloud of fluttering gauze garments that did nothing to minimize her corpulence but gave her the majesty of a clipper ship in full sail. The Siamese greeted her with enthusiasm, knowing her as the source of their crunchy treats.

Mildred perused the list of names and predicted, "Interesting group! Lyle is a certified sourpuss, but nice . . . Amanda has foot-in-mouth disease, which can be very funny at times . . . Irma is so fastidious, she'll probably inspect everyone's fingernails before breakfast . . . Let me know how you like the Chisholm sisters."

"Do they sing?"

"You don't know them, Qwill, because you don't belong to the country club. Grace is a rich widow, and her unmarried sister lives with her on Goodwinter Boulevard. They collect teddy bears."

"May I offer you a drink, Mildred?"

"Make it coffee," she said. "I've brought some cookies. But first show me the ropes."

As he conducted her up the ramp to the three balconies, they were followed by two inquisitive cats with stiffly vertical tails and stiffly horizontal whiskers. He explained, "My bedroom and studio are on the first balcony. The door is closed to keep the cats out, because Koko licks postage stamps and gummed envelopes . . . The guestroom is on the second balcony. I suggest you lock up your toothbrush. Yum Yum has a brush fetish; she'd steal my moustache if it weren't firmly attached . . . I regret that the only television is in the cats' loft on the top balcony."

"Don't apologize. I'll just set up my quilting frame on the main floor and listen to radio," she said. "How often are the cats fed?"

"Morning and evening, plus a handful of your crunchy cereal at noon and bedtime. You'll find canned and frozen delicacies for them in the kitchen."

"To tell the truth, I'd rather cook for them," Mildred said. "I really would! I miss having someone to cook for. What other care do they require?"

"They appreciate brushing once a day, and intelligent conversation, and a little entertainment. Koko prefers activities that challenge his intellect; he's a very cerebral animal." As they both turned to look at him in admiration, Kao K'o Kung rolled over and groomed the base of his tail. "Forget I said that," Qwilleran added. "That scoundrel likes to make a fool of me."

Mildred picked up the female cat, who was now rubbing against her ankles. They were slender and shapely, he noted, for a woman of her weight. "Yum Yum is so huggable," she said.

"Yes, propinquity is her middle name . . . And now let me demonstrate the fine art of policing their commode."

After the briefing they sat in the lounge area with coffee and Mildred's date-nut bars. Massive, square-cut, deep-cushioned chairs and sofas were arranged around a large square coffee table, facing the fireplace cube—a large white monolith with fireplaces on two sides and bookshelves on a third. It was high enough for two Siamese cats to perch like Olympian deities, looking down on the mere mortals below.

"Now, is there anything else I should know?" Mildred asked.

"Mrs. Fulgrove comes in once a week for light cleaning. Mr. O'Dell is our handyman. We have a colony of fruit flies that came with the apple barn, and they come out of hibernation at this time of year. Koko catches them on the wing and munches them as hors d'oeuvres. . . . I guess that's about all."

"And tell me what you're going to do in Scotland."

"Listen to bagpipes, stay in country inns, visit castles, eat haggis—all the usual, I imagine."

"Ugh! Haggis is the innards of sheep, boiled and cut up and mixed with oatmeal and spices, then sewn into a sheep's stomach."

"Sounds delicious."

Mildred's attitude turned suddenly sober. "Before coming over here," she said, "I read the tarot cards for you, and I think you ought to know what they revealed."

"It doesn't sound propitious, but let's hear it." Qwilleran was skeptical about card reading, palmistry, and all the occult sciences that interested his plump friend, but she was sincere, and he always humored her. "Do you mind if I tape this, Mildred?"

"Not at all. I wish you would."

He had already turned on his pocket-size recorder. "What did you learn?"

"Strangely, when I asked the cards about you," she began, "the answers concerned someone else—someone in danger."

"Man or woman?"

"A mature woman. A woman with strict habits and upright values."

That's Polly, Qwilleran thought; someone has told Mildred about the prowler. "What kind of danger?" he asked.

"Well, the cards were rather vague, so I brought the pack with me, and I'd like to do another reading—in your presence."

With mental reservations, he agreed, and they moved to the card table, Qwilleran politely averting his eyes as Mildred struggled to get out of the deep-seated lounge chair. When she asked him to shuffle the pack, Koko hopped to the table with an excited "Yow!"

"Want me to lock him up, Mildred?" Qwilleran suggested.

"No, let him watch." She was laying out a certain number of cards in a certain pattern. "I'm using the Celtic pattern for this reading. This card is the significator." They were colorful cards in fanciful designs, and as she manipulated them she mumbled to herself. There was a thoughtful pause. Then she said, "I see a journey . . . a journey across water . . . with stormy weather ahead."

"Glad I packed my raincoat," he said lightly.

"Stormy weather could stand for dissension, mistakes, accidents, or whatever."

"Too bad I didn't know before I paid my money."

"You're not taking this seriously, Qwill."

"Sorry. I didn't mean to sound flippant."

"This final card . . . is not auspicious . . . You might consider it a warning."

The card showed a scene in a grape arbor, with a woman in flowing robes, a bird perched on her wrist, and a scattering of gold coins. "Looks like a happy card to me," Qwilleran observed.

"But it's reversed."

"Meaning . . ."

"Some kind of fraud . . . or treachery."

"Yow!" said Koko.

"In conclusion . . . I urge you to be prepared . . . for the unexpected." Mildred always became short of breath toward the end of a reading, and her energy flagged, so Qwilleran thought it best not to pursue the subject.

"Very interesting. Thank you," he said as he turned off the tape recorder.

Mildred walked away from the table and took a few deep breaths. When she recovered, she said, "I'll look forward to hearing the outcome."

"So will I!" Qwilleran admitted.

"When do you leave?"

"I catch the shuttle to Chicago tomorrow noon, and the international flight leaves at six P.M. After changing planes at Heathrow and going through the formalities, I should arrive in Glasgow at ten A.M., their time. I'm leaving a list of telephone numbers where we can be reached, and don't hesitate to call if there's an emergency. Mildred, you don't realize how much this is appreciated by all three of us."

"The pleasure is all mine. We'll have a ball, won't we, cats?"

"Yow!" said Koko, squeezing his eyes as if visions of shrimp Newburgh danced in his head.

The next morning Qwilleran said a regretful goodbye to the cats and looked back as he walked out the door to see two pairs of large blue eyes filled with concern. He would have wished for a more cheerful send-off. And when he drove away he was aware of two tiny creatures watching him from an upper level of the huge barn.

At the Moose County Airport he parked his car in the new indoor facility, and the shuttle plane departed without requiring the usual last-minute repairs. The connection in Chicago went smoothly, perhaps too smoothly. Three meals and several magazines later, he arrived in Glasgow on schedule. His luggage was flown, unfortunately, to another city in Western Europe. So began the Bonnie Scots Tour.

Three

By the time the participants in the Bonnie Scots Tour gathered for the Happy Hour on the eve of Day One, Qwilleran had recovered from jet lag, retrieved his luggage, and paid homage to Charles Rennie Mackintosh. Throughout the day other travelers from Moose County had been straggling wearily into the centrally located hotel selected for the jumping-off place.

At six o'clock Qwilleran—dressed in blazer, shirt, and tie according to instructions from Sergeant Hasselrich—reported to the hotel lobby and found it bright with kilts worn by males of all ages; there was a wedding reception in the banquet hall. The Bonnie Scots party was scheduled for the Robert Burns parlor, which was no different from the Sir Walter Scott Parlor or the Bonnie Prince Charlie Parlor or the Robert Louis Stevenson Parlor, except for a portrait of the poet hanging above the bar. When Qwilleran entered, a white-coated young man with red hair was circulating with a tray of champagne and orange juice.

Among the guests already on hand were Larry and Carol Lanspeak, the most likable couple in Pickax. They were civic leaders, owners of the Lanspeak Department Store, and mainstays in the Theatre Club. Qwilleran approached them, saying, "All hail, Macbeth! Hail to thee, Thane of Cawdor!"

"Dammit! It means growing a beard again," said the actor ruefully, rubbing his chin. "First it's Henry VIII, then Abe Lincoln, and now this. How come I never get a chance to play Peter Pan?" He was a mild-mannered man, difficult to imagine as the murderous Macbeth.

Carol said, "Qwill, this is Dwight Somers, who's directing *Macbeth*. I don't think you two have met . . . Dwight, Jim Qwilleran is better known as Qwill. You've seen his column, 'Straight from the Qwill Pen,' in the paper."

"I've heard a lot about you," said the man with the neatly clipped beard, "and I enjoy your column. It's always right on."

"Thanks. You're new in Moose County. Where do you hail from?"

"Most recently, from Iowa. Should I read that line with pride or apology?"

"There's nothing wrong with Iowa that couldn't be fixed with a few Wisconsin lakes and Pennsylvania mountains," Qwilleran said encouragingly. He liked Dwight Somers on sight; the man exuded an inner energy characteristic of theatre people. And his compliments did not go unnoticed; Qwilleran was vain about his writing.

The foursome was joined by the other couple, the Comptons. Lyle was the tall, lanky, saturnine superintendent of schools; Lisa, who worked for Social Services, had dancing eyes and a sense of humor that contrasted with her husband's dour demeanor. She asked, "Who's taking care of your cats, Qwill?"

"Mildred Hanstable. I hope she doesn't overfeed them. They're con artists when it comes to food . . . Are you two ready for a happy adventure in the Highlands?"

With his usual scowl Lyle said, "I'm going to be happy if it kills me!"

A young man with thinning hair walked into the parlor, a camera slung over his shoulder, and Qwilleran introduced him as the photographer from Lockmaster, John Bushland.

"Call me Bushy," he said congenially, stroking his nearly bald head.

"How come you brought your camera and not your wife, Bushy?"

"Well, you see, Vicki started a catering service this summer, and she has bookings she can't cancel. What did you do about the cats, Qwill?"

"They're holding the fort in Pickax, with a live-in cook to cater their meals. I hated to leave them. I left some of my old sweaters lying around, so they can sit on them and not feel abandoned."

"That's thoughtful of you," said Carol Lanspeak, "but I suspect you'll miss the cats more than they'll miss you."

"You don't need to tell me that, Carol. I've been bluffed and bullied by those two opportunists long enough to know."

Gradually the others arrived—the women in skirts and heels, the men in coats and ties. Mr. and Mrs. MacWhannell were a quiet couple, stiffly formal—a tall, portly man and a tiny birdlike woman. Arch Riker and Amanda Goodwinter had obviously had a headstart at a pub. Irma and Polly arrived with a large map of Scotland, which the red-haired waiter hung on the wall. Irma was, indeed, meticulously dressed and groomed, and her statuesque figure had a polished perfection that put the other women at a disadvantage.

The map was an instant attraction, especially the west coast, fringed with firths, lochs, kyles, and isles. "Caused by glacial movement in the Ice Age," the leader explained with authority.

Someone asked, "How big is Scotland?"

Before Irma could answer, a man's voice came from the rear of the group—the chesty voice that goes with a portly figure. "The country is 30,414 square miles, smaller than South Carolina."

Everyone turned to gaze in speechless wonder at Whannell MacWhannell, accountant.

In a small, fearful voice his wife asked him, "Do we have to drive over any mountains, Daddy?"

"Not big ones, Mother," he assured her.

Amanda whispered, "Aren't they a sweet couple? I may throw up!"

The map brought forth a variety of comments:

"Look! There's the famous Loch Lomond!"

"Hope we see the Loch Ness monster."

"Where are the distilleries?"

The deep voice in the rear said, "There's a famous railway bridge over the Firth of Forth, with two spans of 1,710 feet each and two of 690 feet. The tracks are 157 feet above the water."

Amanda groaned. "Big Mac is going to be the official bore on this trip."

Someone said quietly, "Put on your sunglasses, everybody. Here come the Chisholm sisters."

The two women who entered the parlor were older than the others in the group, both having white hair. One walked a few steps behind the other. In the lead was a short, stocky woman wearing a dazzling array of jewelry, her bosomy figure displaying it like a jeweler's velvet tray.

Carol confided to Qwilleran in a whisper, "It's all the real thing! You should see her on Saturday night at the country club! She and Zella also collect teddy bears on a large scale."

He was no connoisseur of jewelry, but he was impressed by the strands of pearls twisted with chunky gold chains and clasped at the left collarbone with a spray of diamonds. Her sister—taller and thinner and plainer—wore a small gold teddy bear with ruby eyes.

The pair headed directly toward him, and the bejeweled sister said in a raspy voice, "You're Mr. Qwilleran! I recognized the moustache from your picture in the paper. We always read your column." She looked up at him brightly. "I'm Grace Utley, and this is my sister, Zella. We're Chisholms. You must have heard of the Chisholms. Our grandfather built the Moose County courthouse . . . yes!"

"How do you do," he said with a gracious bow. "My mother was a Mackintosh."

"We collect teddy bears!" she said, eagerly awaiting a newsman's reaction to this newsworthy credential.

"Very interesting," he said stolidly.

"Yes . . . We have a button-in-ear Steiff that's very rare."

At that moment he was aware that Melinda Goodwinter was entering the parlor; he caught a whiff of her familiar perfume. As a doctor and a Goodwinter she was being greeted with suitable respect, but her eyes wandered around the room until she spotted Qwilleran. Within seconds she was at his side.

"Hello, lover," she said coolly.

"Melinda, have you met Grace Utley and Zella Chisholm?" he asked. "Ladies, do you know Dr. Melinda Goodwinter?"

"We do indeed . . . yes!" said Mrs. Utley. "How are you, dear heart? We were distressed to hear about your father. You have our deepest sympathy."

The waiter reappeared with his tray of champagne and orange juice, and while the older women were momentarily distracted, Melinda managed to draw Qwilleran aside, saying, "Alone at last! You're looking great, lover!"

"How did you like Boston?" he asked, avoiding any lingering eye contact. "It's good of you to come back and take over your father's clinic."

"Boston served its purpose, but I'm glad to be home. I heard you've converted the Klingenschoen barn, and you're living in it."

"For a while, at any rate."

"Do you still have the cats?"

"I provide their bed and board." Koko, he recalled, had not cared for Melinda, always telling her to go home in his subtle, catly way. Trying to keep the conversation impersonal, Qwilleran asked, "How do you like Moose County's new newspaper?"

"Big improvement." Melinda gulped the rest of her champagne. "Aren't you the one who's financing it?"

"The Klingenschoen Foundation is behind it," he corrected her. "Arch Riker is editor-and-publisher. Have you met him? He and I are old friends, and we're sharing accommodations on this tour . . . Arch! Come over here!"

The publisher caught the significance of the situation and rose to the occasion. "We met at the funeral," he said when Qwilleran introduced him. "I'm glad you're taking over your father's practice, Melinda. We need all the doctors we can get. They keep inventing new diseases. I hope you brought your little black bag on this trip, in case anyone chokes on the porridge or gets bitten by a haggis . . ."

Good old Arch! Qwilleran thought. "May I bring you some champagne, Melinda?" he asked. Without waiting for an answer, he slipped away toward the bar and before he could complete his mission, Irma clapped hands for attention, and the group gathered around the map.

"Welcome to Scotland," she said. "I hope you will have a joyous time on the Bonnie Scots Tour. We'll be traveling in Bonnie Prince Charlie country, a region brimming with history and romance."

Qwilleran heard a veiled grunt of protest from Lyle Compton.

"Some of the places we'll visit," Irma went on, "are not open to the average tourist, and most of the inns are off the beaten path, but because of my connections we'll be made welcome. I would like to make one suggestion at this time. For two weeks we'll be traveling as one big happy family, and it would be friendly to alternate seats in the bus and at the table when we stop for meals. Is that agreed?"

There was a vague murmur among the group.

"Day One starts tomorrow morning at seven o'clock when we meet in the hotel coffee shop for breakfast. Your bags should be packed and outside the door of your room not later than six-thirty. I suggest you request wake-up calls for five-thirty to give you ample time."

Five-thirty! Qwilleran huffed into his moustache.

Irma concluded her speech to polite applause, and Qwilleran grabbed Riker's arm. "Round up Amanda and Polly, and let's go to dinner," he said. "I've found a good Indian restaurant. I'll meet you in a taxi in front of the hotel." He made a quick escape.

The restaurant, in true Anglo-Indian style, had white tile floors, tinkling fountains, hanging brass lamps, an assertive aroma of curry, and a background of raga music played on the sarod, tabla, and tamboura. The plucked strings, rhythmic percussion, and hypnotic drone of the instruments provided a soothing background for conversation.

Polly was looking handsome in her blue batwing cape, but Amanda—no matter how carefully she tried to dress—always looked as if she had just washed the car or cleaned the basement. Riker, with his bent sense of humor, thought it was part of her attraction.

"What would it take," she grumbled, "to get them to turn off the music and the fountains?"

"Quiet, Amanda," he said with amusement suffusing his ruddy face. "When in Glasgow, do as the Glaswegians do."

Qwilleran suggested ordering samosas with the drinks, saying they were meat-filled pastries. Then he recommended mulligatawny soup and a main course of tandoori murghi and pulao, with a side order of dal. "All spicy dishes, I don't need to tell you," he warned.

"Why, this is nothing but roast chicken with rice and lentils," Amanda announced when the entrée was served.

Riker nudged her. "Just enjoy it, and don't editorialize." As conversation focused on the forthcoming tour, he remarked, "Compton really knows his Scottish history. He gave a talk at the Boosters Club last month."

"I hope he won't be too argumentative," Polly said with concern. "Irma accepts the romantic version of Scots history, but Lyle is a militant revisionist."

"I like the idea of having a historian on board," Riker said. "Not to mention a professional photographer and a physician."

"Don't you think Melinda is looking rather world-weary?" Polly asked. "Her eyes look strange."

"She's stopped wearing green contacts and three sets of false eyelashes," said her cousin Amanda with tart authority.

"Will someone explain the Chisholm sisters?" Qwilleran asked.

Amanda had the whole story. The Chisholms and the Utleys represented "old money" in Moose County, the former having rebuilt most of Pickax following the fire of 1869. The Utleys, as owners of fisheries, were several rungs down the social ladder but grew rich on trout and whitefish. Grace's late husband invested the family fortune cleverly and, it was rumored, illegally, returning from mysterious business trips with lavish gifts of jewelry for his wife.

Amanda grumbled, "You could buy a fifty-foot yacht with what she's wearing around her neck, but she's slow in paying her decorating bills . . . *Yes!*" she added mockingly.

Over a dessert of gajar halva, which Amanda insisted was nothing but carrot pudding, the conversation turned to Charles Rennie Mackintosh.

"He wore flowing silk ties and had a prominent moustache," Qwilleran reported, preening his own, "and he liked cats."

"How do you know?"

"There was one small clue in the Mackintosh house, which has been reconstructed by the university. The designer and his wife lived there in the early 1900s, and he had the guts to transform a Victorian townhouse into light, airy living spaces! In the drawing room everything is white—walls, carpet, fireplace, furniture, everything—except for two gray cushions on the hearth, for their two Persian cats."

"How charming!" Polly said. "Irma attended the art school he designed."

"I think his most daring innovation was a narrow chair with an extremely high back. He liked to use a grid pattern in wallpaper and furniture—also a small oval shape said to represent the eye of a peacock feather."

Amanda said, "Peacock feathers are bad luck. I wouldn't have one in the house!"

Too bad about that, Qwilleran thought. He had bought several silver brooches based on the Mackintosh peacock feather, to take home as gifts.

The evening ended early; Day One would start at five-thirty.

When the telephones jangled in certain hotel rooms at that hour, disgruntled travelers from Moose County got out of bed and stumbled about their rooms, making tea with their tea-makers. They dressed, packed, put their luggage out in the hall, and reported for breakfast at seven o'clock. No one was really hungry, and they were dismayed by the array of oatmeal, eggs, meat, fish, fruit, pancakes, scones, currant buns, oatcakes, bannocks, jams, marmalade, and more.

"No waffles?" Amanda was heard to complain.

Irma assured them that a full Scottish breakfast would be included with all their overnights. "So take advantage of it," she advised. "For lunch we'll just have a bowl of soup in a pub."

Amanda's grim expression brightened.

At eight o'clock the minibus was waiting in front of the hotel, with the luggage partly loaded in the baggage bins underneath. A red-haired man in a chauffeur's cap was speaking angrily to Irma in a tongue that appeared to be Gaelic, the gist of his argument being that there was too much luggage to fit in the bins. A reassessment of the load indicated that Grace Utley, ignoring the limit on personal luggage, was traveling with three alligator bags plus an alligator carry-on. To make matters worse, she was half an hour late, a fact resented by passengers who had been up since five-thirty.

"There's one on every tour," said Carol Lanspeak philosophically.

Space was found in the passenger compartment for the surplus cases at the expense of rider comfort, and the culprit finally arrived, saying a blithe good-morning to everyone. She was wearing, with her sweater and slacks, some ropes of twisted gold from which dangled a fringe of gold and enamel baubles.

The driver, a sullen man of about forty, was introduced as Bruce, and the bus pulled away from the hotel with Irma sitting on a cramped jumpseat at the front. Using a microphone, she described points of interest as they drove out of the city and into the countryside, while the passengers looked dutifully to right and to left until their necks ached. "In the distance is Ben Nevis, Britain's highest mountain," she would say, and Big Mac's voice would come from the back of the bus: "Elevation 4,406 feet." By the time they stopped for their bowl of soup, they were stunned into silence by the abundance of scenery and commentary.

After lunch, their leader clapped hands for attention. "We shall soon be in Bonnie Prince Charlie country," she told them. "For six months the handsome young prince was trapped like a fox pursued by hounds. After the defeat at Culloden he fled for his life, sometimes betrayed by treacherous friends and sometimes harbored by unexpected supporters attracted by his charisma."

"Charisma? Bunk!" Lyle Compton muttered to Qwilleran. "It was all politics!"

"With a price on his head," Irma went on, "he was trying desperately to escape to France. He slept in the bracken by day and traveled by night, stumbling across moors and through glens. Weary, tattered, and obviously defeated, he kept up his good spirits. After all, he was a prince, and the lovely Flora Macdonald fell in love with him and risked her life to smuggle him out of enemy territory."

Lyle spoke up, his voice crisp with exasperation. "Irma, you've been reading romantic novels and watching old movies! Charles was a liar, an alcoholic, and a fool! He made all kinds of tactical mistakes and had a talent for trusting the wrong aides and taking the advice of idiots. Flora Macdonald had no use for him, but she was pressured into the plot to rescue him—" He stopped abruptly and threw a sharp glance at his wife as if she had kicked him under the table.

Irma's face flushed and her eyes flashed, and Polly rushed in to fill the awkward silence. "What was the date of Culloden?" she asked, although she knew.

"April 16, 1746," Irma said, and big Mac rattled off some statistics.

Later, Amanda said to Qwilleran, "Lyle had better watch his step. She's already shot one man."

On that day, and the next, and the next, Irma herded the group through fishing villages, among ruins, aboard ferries, around rocky islands, across moors covered with purple heather, past granite quarries and peat bogs.

"Where are the people? Where are the farmhouses?" Carol complained. "All we see is sheep!" Flocks of them grazed on the hillsides or crossed the road in front of the bus.

Compton snorted and said to Qwilleran, "I could tell you what happened to the people, but Irma wouldn't like it, and my wife would give me hell again."

At each rest stop the driver assisted women passengers off the bus in solemn silence, then wandered away for a cigarette while the travelers used the facilities and explored the gift shops. Qwilleran bought a tie in the Mackintosh tartan; Larry bought a staghorn cane that he said he might use in the play; Dwight Somers bought a tin whistle.

The family-type seating on the bus and at meals, as suggested by Irma, became a discordant game of musical chairs. Qwilleran avoided sitting with Melinda. No one wanted to sit with Grace Utley or Glenda MacWhannell. Arch Riker was always getting stuck with Zella Chisholm. Both Dwight and Bushy had a desire to sit with Melinda. Melinda kept trying to sit with Qwilleran. And Amanda often ended up with Big Mac.

The bus traveled on single-track roads most of the time, so passengers worried about meeting another vehicle head-on, but Bruce wheeled the bus up and down hills and around endless curves with reckless abandon, causing Glenda MacWhannell to scream at the roller-coaster effect and Zella Chisholm to complain of car sickness.

Hour after hour Irma talked into the microphone, and the monotony of her voice put the riders to sleep, especially after lunch. In the afternoon they would wake up for tea and shortbread at some modest cottage that advertised "Teas" on a modest signboard. Then, at the end of the day, everyone would stumble off the bus, stiff and sore, to check into a quaint inn tucked into a glen or overlooking a loch. In this way Day One, Day Two, and Day Three became a blur.

Qwilleran said to Riker, "I can't remember what we saw yesterday or what we had for dinner last night. If I weren't recording some of this on tape, I'd get home and never know I'd been here."

"I'm not even sure where we are," said his roommate.

The inns, adapted from old stone stables and ruined abbeys, were cozy and rustic, and since there were no room keys—only bolts inside the bedroom doors—Grace Utley had to entrust her jewel cases to the innkeeper's safe. Amanda complained that there were no ice machines, no telephones or TV in the bedrooms, and no washcloths in the bathrooms. Glenda MacWhannell worried about fire.

At the dinner hour, the women reported in skirts and heels, the men in coats and ties, while Mrs. Utley outshone them all with four strands of sapphire beads accented with a chunk of carved white jade, or a necklace of black onyx and gold, clasped at the collarbone with lapis lazuli. Thus arrayed, they dined on fresh salmon or roast lamb with neeps and tatties, served by the jovial innkeeper and his rosy-cheeked daughters.

Come morning, the group would be herded aboard the bus once again, only to wait for the late Grace Utley. There was usually a misty rain at the start of each day, but the afternoon sun made the waters of the lochs and kyles sparkle like acres of diamonds.

On one wet morning they visited a damp and chilly castle with a moat and a drawbridge, a massive gate and a stone courtyard, and a Great Hall hung with armor and ancestral portraits. Here a guide recited a catalogue of battles, conquering heroes, scandals, ghosts, and assassinations, after which the visitors were free to explore regal apartments, dungeons, and staircases carved out of solid rock. Windows were small, passages were narrow, and doorways were low.

"The early Scots must have been pygmies," Qwilleran said as he stooped to maneuver his six-feet-two through a low doorway.

"Look out!" someone yelled.

Turning to check the danger, Qwilleran straightened up and struck his head on the stone lintel above. The blow knocked him to his knees, and he saw blinding flashes of light and heard distant screams and calls for help. Next he was being seated on a bench, and Melinda was checking his pulse and lifting his eyelids, all the while asking questions: "Do you know your name? . . . What day is it? . . . Do you know where you are?"

At this point, Qwilleran was feeling more anger than pain, and he snapped, "Shakespeare wrote *Macbeth*. Moose County is north of the equator. Eli Whitney invented the cotton gin. And if you don't mind, I'd like to go outside and sit in the bus while you people finish your sightseeing and buy your postcards."

Dwight Somers volunteered to go with him.

"I've had enough castle for one day," Qwilleran told him.

"Same here. How did they exist in that damp, gloomy environment?"

"They didn't. If they weren't murdered in their twenties, they died of pneumonia in their thirties."

"I've been wanting to ask you, Qwill: Have you done any theatre?"

"Only in college. At one time I was planning to be an actor, until a wise professor steered me into journalism, and I must admit that a little acting experience doesn't hurt in my profession."

"I was sure you had training. You have a very good voice. I wish you'd take a role in *Macbeth.*"

"What did you have in mind for me?" Qwilleran asked. "Banquo's ghost? One of the three witches? Lady Macbeth?"

"You're not too far off base. In Shakespeare's time she was played by an actor in drag, but he didn't have a moustache. How about doing Macduff? He has a couple of great scenes, and I don't think the guy we've cast is going to work out."

"That's a sizable part," Qwilleran objected. "It would be tough to learn lines after so many years away from the stage . . . No, Dwight, I'd better stick to my role as theatre reviewer for the paper. Have you cast Lady Macbeth?"

"Yes, I gave the role to Melinda. She has a certain quality for Lady Macbeth. She brought a script with her on the trip, and she's been working on her lines."

Members of the party were emerging from the castle and sauntering across the drawbridge.

"Melinda's an interesting woman," Dwight went on. He paused, waiting for an affirmative comment. When none was forthcoming, he said, "We both have apartments at Indian Village, and I've been seeing her quite often but not getting very far." There was another pause. "I'm getting the impression I might be trespassing on your territory."

"No problem," Qwilleran assured him.

"This is the first time I've lived in a town as small as Pickax, and I don't want to violate any codes."

"No problem," Qwilleran said.

When the group started climbing into the bus, everyone expressed concern about his condition, but Melinda examined the bump on his head and announced there was no bleeding.

Their destination that night was a picturesque inn converted from a bothy, with numerous additions, confusing levels, and angled hallways. The beds were comfortable, however, and the furnishings were engagingly old, with a homey clutter of doilies, knickknacks, vases of heather, baskets of fruit, and the ubiquitous tea-maker. Coils of rope were provided under the windows for escape in case of fire.

The Bonnie Scots tourists were booked for two nights, and Irma had promised them a free day, absolutely unstructured, after several days of hurtling around in the bus. They could enjoy the luxury of unpacking their luggage, putting their belongings away in bureau drawers, and hanging clothes in the wardrobes that served as closets.

After a dinner of sheep's head broth, rabbit casserole, and clootie dumplings, Qwilleran excused himself, saying he had a headache and wished to retire early, although the chief reason was a desire to get away from his fellow travelers.

From the main hall he went up half a flight of stairs, turned left into a narrow passage, then to the right and three steps down, through a glass door and up a ramp, and finally to the left, where he bumped into a bewildered Grace Utley, clutching her necklace in panic.

"Are you lost?" he asked. "It isn't hard to do."

"I took the wrong turn somewhere, dear heart," she said. "We're in Number Eight."

"Then you should be in the other wing. Follow me."

After he had conducted her to the hallway leading to Number Eight, she seemed reluctant to let him go. "Mr. Qwilleran," she began in her grating voice, "I shouldn't mention this, but . . . do you think Ms. Hasselrich is carrying on with that bus driver?"

"What do you mean by carrying on?" he asked.

"It's the way she looks at him, and they have secret conversations in a foreign language. Last night, when I looked out my window, I could see them on the moor in the moonlight . . . yes!"

"Could have been ghosts," he said archly. "They haunt the moors all the time. Pay no attention, Mrs. Utley."

"Please call me Grace," she said. "How do you feel after your accident, dear heart?"

"Just a slight headache. I'm retiring early."

Other women in the group had raised eyebrows over Irma's secret nightlife, but Lyle had said, "The woman works sixteen hours a day! She's entitled to some R&R, and ours is not to question where or with whom."

Qwilleran returned to his room and changed into the red pajamas that Polly had given him for a Valentine, hoping for a few hours of solitude. The others were sipping Drambuie in front of the fire, or playing cards, or watching TV in the keeping room.

Lounging in a passably comfortable chair, he began to dictate the day's experiences into his tape recorder: "Today we visited the island where Macbeth was buried in 1057 . . ."

He was interrupted by a knock on the door.

"Now, who the devil is that?" he muttered. He hoped it was not Grace Utley. Worse yet, it was Melinda.

Four

"How do you feel, lover?" Melinda asked as she stood in the passage outside Qwilleran's room. "You seemed rather quiet during dinner."

"After conversing with the same crowd for five days, I'm running out of things to say and also the patience to listen," he said.

"May I come in? I want to check your pulse and temperature. Sit down over there, please." She entered in a cloud of scent that had enchanted him three years ago; now it seemed too sweet, too musky. She inserted a thermometer in his mouth, counted his pulse, raised his eyelids, and looked at his eyeballs. "You're still legally alive," she said as she drew a flask from her official black bag. "Would you like a little nip for medicinal purposes?"

"You've forgotten I can't have alcohol, Melinda."

"Where's your tea-maker? We'll have a nice cup of tea, as they say over here." She filled the pot with water from the bathroom tap. "How do you like the tour so far?"

"There's too much of everything. Too much food, too much conversation, too much bus travel, too many tourists."

Melinda sauntered around the room in familiar fashion. "Your room looks comfortable. The doubles are better than the singles. I'm at the end of the hall in Number Nine—for your future reference—and the furnishings give me gastro-intestinal turbulence. I have a wonderful view of the loch, though. Perhaps Arch would like to exchange with me," she said with a mischievous glance.

"Does anyone know the name of this loch? They all look alike to me," said Qwilleran, an expert at ignoring hints.

"Well, tell me about you, Qwill. What have you been doing for the last three years?"

"Sometimes I wonder. The years speed by." He was in no mood to socialize or particularize.

"Apparently you're not married yet."

"It's fairly well accepted in Moose County that I'm not suitable grist for the matrimonial mill."

Melinda poured two cups of tea and splashed something from the flask into her own cup. "I was hoping we could pick up where we left off."

"I'll say it again, what I've said before, Melinda. You belong with a man of your own age—your own generation."

"I like older men."

"And I like older women," he said with brutal candor.

"Ouch!" she said and then added impishly, "Wouldn't you like a second-string girlfriend for your youthful moments?"

"This is good tea," he said, although he disliked tea. "You must have used two teabags."

"Are you as . . . uh . . . compatible with your present inamorata as you were with me?"

"What is this? The third degree? I think you're exceeding your privilege as a medical practitioner."

She was not easily deterred. "Didn't you ever think you'd like to have sons, Qwill? Polly is a little old for that."

"Frankly, no!" he said, irritated at her intrusion into his privacy. "Nor daughters. I'm a bachelor by chance, choice, and temperament, and offspring are outside my frame of reference."

"With all your money you should have heirs."

"The Klingenschoen Foundation is my sole beneficiary, and they'll distribute my estate for the benefit of the county, the population of which is 11,279, according to Big Mac. So I have 11,279 heirs—a respectable heirship, I'd say."

"You're not drinking your tea."

"Furthermore, I resent suggestions for the disposition of my financial assets."

"Qwill, you're getting to be a grouchy old bachelor. I think marriage would be good for you. I speak as your medical adviser." She transferred to the arm of his chair. "Don't move! I want to check the bump on your head."

"Excuse me," he said and went into the bathroom, where he counted to ten . . . and then a hundred and ten before facing her again. She had kicked off her shoes and was now lounging on the bed against a bank of pillows.

"Won't you join me?" she invited playfully. "I like red pajamas."

He made a point of pacing the floor and saying nothing.

"Let me explain something, Qwill," said Melinda in a reasonable tone. "Three years ago I wanted us to marry because I thought we'd have a lot of fun together. Now I have a couple of other reasons. The Goodwinter clan is dying out, and I want sons to carry on the name. I'm very proud of the Goodwinter name. So I'll make you a proposition—since one has to be conventional in Moose County. If you will marry me, you can have your freedom at the end of three years, and our children will resume the name of Goodwinter. We might even have a go-o-od time together."

"You're out of your mind," he said, suddenly suspecting that the strange look in her eyes was insanity.

"The second reason is . . . I'm broke!" she said with the impudent frankness that he had once found attractive. "All I'm inheriting from my dad is obligations and an obsolete mansion."

"The K Foundation can help you over the rough spots. They're committed to promoting health care in the community."

"I don't want institutional support. I want you!"

"To put it bluntly, Melinda, the answer is *no!*"

"Why don't you think about it? Let the idea gel for a while?"

Qwilleran walked to the door and, with his hand on the knob, said, "Let me tell you something, and this is final. If I marry anyone, it will be Polly. Now, if you'll excuse me, I need some rest . . . Don't forget your shoes."

If Melinda felt the hellish fury of a woman scorned, the Goodwinter pride prevented her from showing it. "Take a couple of aspirin and call me in the morning, lover," she said with an insolent wink as she brushed past him, carrying her loafers.

Huffing angrily into his moustache, Qwilleran dictated a few choice words into the tape recorder before snapping it off. He was reading a booklet about the Mackintosh clan when Arch Riker walked into the room at eleven o'clock.

"You're awake, Qwill! Did you get any rest?"

"Melinda dropped in to take my pulse, and I couldn't get rid of her. The girl is getting to be a nuisance."

"I guessed that would happen. You may have to marry Polly in self-defense. If Polly doesn't want you, how about Amanda? I'll let you have the lovely Amanda."

"This is no joke, Arch."

"Well, I'm ready to hit the sack. How about you? Polly's with the Lanspeaks and the Comptons, playing Twenty Questions. Amanda's winning at cards with the MacWhannells and Bushy; no doubt she's cheating. Dwight is out on the terrace practicing the tin whistle; he'll be lucky if someone doesn't shoot him."

"Once a reporter, always a reporter," Qwilleran commented.

"I haven't seen Irma. Her voice was very hoarse at the dinner table. Too much chatter on that blasted microphone! And her evenings in the damp night air can't do anything for her vocal cords . . . How's the bump on your head, Qwill?"

"It's subsiding, but I'd like to know who yelled 'Look out' and why!"

That was the end of Day Five.

Day Six began at dawn when Qwilleran was awakened by screams in the hall and frantic banging on someone's door.

Riker was sitting up in the other bed, saying, "What's that? Are we on fire?"

There were sounds of running feet, and Qwilleran looked out in the hall as other heads appeared in other doorways. The innkeeper rushed past them and disappeared into Number Eleven, occupied by Polly and Irma.

"Oh, my God!" Qwilleran shouted over his shoulder. "Something's happened to the girls!" As he started down the passageway, the innkeeper's wife was ahead of him.

Her husband shouted to her, "Ring up the constable! One o' the lassies had an attack! Ring up the constable!"

Qwilleran hurried to the room at the end of the hall and breathed a sigh of relief when he saw Polly standing there in her nightgown. She was weeping in her hands. Melinda, in pajamas, was bending over the bed. He threw his arms around Polly. "What happened?"

"I think she's dead!" she sobbed. "I woke up suddenly a few minutes ago and felt that ghastly sense of death. I called Melinda." Polly burst into a fresh torrent of tears.

Still holding her, Qwilleran said to Melinda, "Is there anything I can do?" Others were crowding into the room in their nightclothes.

"Get everyone out of the room—and out of the hall—until the authorities have been here. Out! Out! I'll talk to all of you downstairs, later."

The concerned bystanders wandered back to their rooms, whispering:

"Is Irma dead?"

"What was it? Does anyone know what happened?"

"This is terrible! Who'll notify her parents?"

"It'll kill them! She's their only child, and they're getting on in years."

"She was only forty-two last birthday."

Lyle Compton nudged Qwilleran. "Do you think something happened out on the moor?"

Quickly they dressed and gathered downstairs in the small parlor, and the innkeeper's wife served hot tea, murmuring sympathetic phrases that no one understood or really heard. In everyone's mind the question was nagging: *What do we do now?*

They were aware of vehicles arriving in the courtyard and then departing, and eventually Melinda walked into the parlor in robe and slippers, with uncombed hair and no makeup. She looked wan and troubled. The group fell silent as she faced them and said in a hollow voice, "Irma was the first patient to walk into my clinic—and the real reason for my coming on this trip. And I've lost her!"

When someone asked the cause of death, Qwilleran turned on his tape recorder. At this moment he could feel only compassion for this young doctor; she was so distraught.

"Cardiac arrest," Melinda said wearily. "With her heart condition she should never have undertaken this project. She had this driving ambition, you know, and she was such a perfectionist."

Polly said, "I didn't know she had a bad heart. She never mentioned her symptoms, and we were the best of friends."

"She was too proud to admit to any frailty—and too independent to take my advice or even medication. It could have saved her."

Carol said, "But, Irma, of all people! Who would think—? She was always so cool and collected. She never hurried or panicked like the rest of us."

Melinda explained, "She internalized her emotions—not a healthy thing to do."

"What was the time of death?" Qwilleran asked.

"About three A.M., I would say. Does anyone know what time she came in?"

Polly said, "I don't know. I never waited up for her. She told me not to."

"What happens now?" Larry asked.

"I'm not allowed to sign the death certificate over here," Melinda said. "A local doctor will have to do that. I'll notify Irma's parents and make whatever arrangements are necessary."

Qwilleran offered to call the Hasselriches, since he knew the father well.

"Thanks, but I feel I should do it. I can explain exactly what happened."

"We're certainly grateful that you're here, Melinda. Is there anything we can do for you—anything at all?"

"You might talk it over among yourselves and decide how to handle the rest of the tour. I'll fly back with the body. There'll be some red tape before they release it, the constable said, but they don't anticipate any problem . . . So, if you'll excuse me, I'll go up and get dressed. You can stay here and talk."

When Amanda arrived from the other bedroom wing and heard the news, she said, "I move to cancel the tour and fly home. Anybody second it? Let's cut our losses."

Polly spoke up with conviction. "Irma would want us to continue, I'm sure."

"But do we know what to do and where to go?" Lisa asked.

"Everything is in her briefcase—itinerary, confirmations, maps, and so forth. I'm sure we can follow her plan to the letter. Since we have an extra day here, we'll have time to work it out."

Riker said, "What time is it in Pickax? I want to call Junior and get him started on the obituary. It'll take some digging, because she was a very private person—would never let us do a feature on her volunteer work."

Guests from the other wing straggled into the parlor, and Bushy said, "Why so glum, kids? Did somebody die around here?"

At the breakfast table the members of the Bonnie Scots Tour halfheartedly discussed their options for the day: Go shopping in the village . . . Watch the fishing boats come in . . . Take the ferry to one of the islands . . . Loll around the inn. Larry said he would wander in the hills and study his lines for the play. Amanda thought she would go back to bed. The MacWhannells announced they were leaving the tour and would hire a car to drive to Edinburgh. They gave no reasons for cutting out, and no one bothered to ask why.

After breakfast, Qwilleran and the school superintendent strolled down the winding road to the village below. "Don't forget, Lyle. What goes down must come up," Qwilleran warned. "We have to climb this hill again."

Compton said, "I hope I didn't contribute to Irma's stress by blowing off steam about Scottish history and challenging her statements. Lisa said I should have kept my big mouth shut, but—dammit—Irma drove me up the wall with her sentimental claptrap about the romantic Jacobite Rebellion and her beloved Prince Charlie."

"Don't worry. She was a tough one. She didn't earn the name of Sergeant for nothing. They say she ran the volunteer crew at the Senior Facility like an army battalion."

They stopped awhile to admire the view: the patchwork of rooftops down below, the curve of the harbor crowded with boats, the islands beyond, floating placidly in a silver sea. Behind them the hills rose like Alpine meadows, dotted with sheep and the ruins of stone buildings.

"Lyle, you promised to tell me how the sheep took over the Highlands," Qwilleran said.

"Don't blame the sheep. Have you heard about the Highland Clearances?"

"Only superficially. Okay if I tape this?"

"Go ahead . . . Well, you know," he began, "when the Rebellion failed, the clan system was deliberately destroyed, and Highlanders were forbidden by law to wear kilts or play bagpipes. Instead of clan chieftains they now had rich landlords renting small bits of land to crofters, who shared their one-room huts with the livestock. Then, with the growing demand for meat, the big landowners found it easier and more profitable to raise sheep than to collect rents from poor crofters. Also, sheep could make money for investors in Edinburgh and London."

"Agribusiness, eighteenth-century style," Qwilleran remarked.

"Exactly! To be fair, though, I should say that not all the landlords were villains; some of the old families tried their best to help their people, but overpopulation and old-fashioned farming methods combined to keep the crofters in a state of near-starvation."

"What happened to them when the sheep took over?"

"They were driven off the land and forbidden to hunt, fish, or graze livestock. Their pitiful crofts were burned before their eyes."

"Where did they go?"

"They were sent to live in destitution in big-city slums or in poor coastal villages. Many were transported to North America, and that's another story! They were exploited by ship owners and sent to sea in leaky tubs overcrowded and without sufficient food and water . . . I shouldn't be telling you this; it shoots up my blood pressure."

The two men wandered around the waterfront and watched the fishing boats coming in, surrounded by screaming seagulls. Crewmen in yellow slickers were slinging prawn traps onto the wharf, laughing and joking. Facing the docks were freshly painted, steep-roofed cottages huddled in a row, with flowers around the door-steps and seagulls on the chimney pots. Some of the cottage windows had cut-off curtains that allowed cats to sit on the windowsills.

Lyle said, "The Scots today are nice people—sociable, hospitable, and slyly witty—but they have a bloody history of cutting throats and pouring molten lead on their enemies."

They lunched at a pub before returning to the inn. There they learned that Melinda had checked out and was on her way to Glasgow in a hired car, leaving a message: "Don't feel bad about my giving up the rest of the tour. This is my responsibility as Irma's friend and physician."

Lisa reported to Qwilleran, "Polly and I packed Irma's belongings to ship home. Polly's all broken up. She's in her room, saying she doesn't want to be disturbed by anyone."

"I guess that means me," he said.

For him the death of their leader was an excuse to phone Mildred Hanstable and inquire about the Siamese. They were often on his mind, although he refrained from talking about them to anyone except Polly. Grace Utley showed pictures of her teddy bears to anyone who sat next to her on the bus. Nevertheless, Qwilleran often looked at his watch, deducted five hours, and visualized the cats having their breakfast or taking an afternoon nap in a certain patch of sun on the rug. He wondered how they were hitting it off with Mildred. He wondered if they were getting fat on her cooking. He wondered if they missed him.

When he telephoned Pickax, it was eight o'clock in the morning, their time, and Mildred had heard the news of Irma's death on the radio. "They didn't give any details on the air," she said. "There'll be more in the paper when it comes out, I hope."

"It was a heart attack. She'd been under a lot of stress. Conducting a tour is a big job for an amateur guide—with a bunch of Moose County individualists in tow. The obituary will probably be in today's paper. Please save it for me . . . How are the cats behaving?"

"We get along just fine! Yum Yum is adorable. When I'm quilting she sits on the frame and watches the needle go in and out. Koko helps me read the tarot cards."

"If the Siamese were humans," Qwilleran explained, "Yum Yum would win prizes at the county fair, and Koko would discover a cure for the common cold . . . Is he there? Put him on."

Mildred could be heard talking to the cats. There was a faint yowl, then some coaxing, and then a louder response.

"Hello, Koko!" Qwilleran shouted. "How's everything? Are you taking care of Yum Yum?"

It took the cat a while to understand that the voice he knew so well was coming out of the instrument held to his ear, but then he wanted to do all the talking, delivering a series of ear-splitting yowls and even biting the receiver.

Wincing, Qwilleran shouted, "That's enough! Take him away!"

There were sounds of scuffling and arguing, and then Mildred returned to the line. "There's one unusual thing I'd like to report," she said. "Last night while I was quilting, I heard an unearthly howl coming from one of the balconies. Koko was in my bathroom, howling in the shower. It made my blood run cold. I went up and talked to him, and finally he stopped, but it really gave me a scare."

"What time did it happen?"

"Between nine-thirty and ten, when that crazy DJ was on WPKX. I turned off the radio, thinking Koko objected to the program."

"I don't blame him," Qwilleran said. "That guy makes me howl with pain, too."

After hanging up the phone, he realized that Koko had howled between two-thirty and three, Scottish time. That cat knew the moment that Irma died! . . . He had a sense of death that spanned the ocean!

Only eleven of the original sixteen travelers reported for dinner that evening, and they were quieter than usual. The meal started with cock-a-leekie soup served with small meat-filled pastries called bridies, followed by lamb stew with barley and neeps, as well as a dish of tatties and onions called stovies.

Lyle Compton asked, "Has anyone seen Bruce today?"

No one had seen the bus driver. They all agreed he deserved a day off, and they wondered if he even knew about Irma's death.

Lisa said, "According to the Bonnie Scots game plan in Irma's briefcase, Bruce is not to smoke on the job or mix with the passengers, and he must be clean and presentable at all times. For this he's getting $1,000, plus meals and lodging and whatever tips we give him. He was paid $100 up front."

"We should tip him generously when the tour ends," Larry said. "He's an excellent driver. He picks up the luggage unobtrusively while we're at breakfast and has the bus packed for departure on time. He's not friendly, but he's courteous in a businesslike way." Everyone agreed.

After dinner, Lisa said to Qwilleran, "Polly and I decided that Larry should manage the tour."

"Why? You two are completely capable, and you've studied the contents of the briefcase."

"That's the problem," she said. "If a man is in charge, he'll be considered well informed, well organized, and a good leader. Because Irma was a woman, she was called fussy, bossy and a know-it-all."

"That's preposterous, Lisa!"

"Of course it's preposterous, but that's the way it is in Moose County, and it'll take a couple of generations to change the attitude. I just wanted you to know why Larry will be calling the plays."

The next morning, Amanda was absent from the breakfast table, and Riker explained to Qwilleran, "She has a dental problem. She broke her upper denture, and she's too embarrassed to open her mouth. Until we reach Edinburgh and get it repaired, she'll have to live on a soft diet, like porridge and Scotch."

Arch Riker was wrong. At that moment, Amanda was arranging for transportation to Glasgow; she was canceling the rest of her tour.

Carol said, "We're like the Ten Little Indians. Who's next?"

After breakfasting on a compote of dried apple slices, prunes, and figs, followed by creamed finnan haddie and oatcakes, the group shook hands with the innkeeper and his wife and prepared to board the bus in the courtyard of the inn. The baggage was loaded in the bin, but Bruce was not there to help the women aboard. Neither could he be found smoking a cigarette on the grounds, nor passing the time with a cup of coffee in the kitchen. At nine o'clock there was still no driver. In fact, they never saw Bruce again.

Five

The events of the last twenty-four hours bewildered the members of the Bonnie Scots Tour as they switched from sadness at the loss of their leader to indignation at the loss of their driver. Obviously Bruce had been there earlier, picking up the luggage in the hall and loading it properly in the waiting bus. The assistant cook said she had given him his breakfast in the kitchen at six o'clock.

Some of the passengers sat in the bus waiting hopefully for his return, while others trooped back into the inn for another cup of coffee. Mrs. Utley, who had been late in rising as usual, reported that she looked out her bedroom window while everyone was at breakfast and saw a car pull into the courtyard. It left again immediately and went downhill in a cloud of dust. No one paid any attention to her.

Eventually the innkeeper called the constable, and Larry gave the constable a rough description of the missing driver. No one knew his last name, and a quick check of Irma's briefcase failed to fill in the blank. The nearest hospital also was called, but no red-haired forty-year-old male had been admitted.

Larry addressed the group seriously. "How long do we sit here, wondering if he'll show? We have a reservation at another inn tonight and a lot of traveling to do in the meantime."

"Let's not hang around any longer," Riker advised. "It's our bus, not his. Let's hit the trail."

"That is," said Larry, "if anyone is comfortable with driving on the wrong side of the road."

Qwilleran volunteered to drive, if someone else would navigate, and Dwight was elected. Larry offered to read Irma's travel notes en route, and Lyle said he would fill in the historical facts. With this arrangement in effect, the bus pulled away from the inn for Day Seven: another castle, another loch, another stately garden, another pub lunch, another four o'clock tea with shortbread.

Qwilleran was a good driver. Everyone said he was better than Bruce. "Cheaper, too," he boasted.

At lunchtime, Carol said to him privately, "I feel terribly sorry for Melinda. My father was a surgeon, and even after thirty years in the operating room he was absolutely crushed if he lost a patient. So Irma's death was a terrible blow for Melinda, coming right on top of her father's suicide and the rumors about her mother's death. She has no immediate family now. She lost her only brother while she was in med school. She and Emory were only a year apart and grew up like twins. His birth was a difficult one, and that's what started Mrs. Goodwinter's decline into complete helplessness."

Why is she telling me this family history? Qwilleran wondered.

"You know, Qwill, it's none of my business, but I wish you and

Melinda had gotten together. You always say you're not good husband material, but the right woman makes a difference, and you don't know what you're missing by not having children. Forgive me for saying so."

"No offense," he said, but he suspected that Melinda had coached her.

"All aboard!" came the commanding voice of their leader. The mild-mannered Larry Lanspeak could project like King Lear on the stormy moor.

During the afternoon drive through Glencoe, with its wild and rugged mountain scenery, Lyle entertained the passengers with the story of the Glencoe Massacre in the late 1600s.

"King James had fled," he began, "and the Scottish chieftains were forced to pledge allegiance to William of Orange—by a certain date. There was one chief who missed the deadline: Macdonald of Glencoe. When his oath finally arrived at government headquarters—late—a high official suppressed it and gave orders to exterminate the clan. A Captain Campbell was dispatched to the glen with 128 soldiers, and they lived there for a while on friendly terms with the Macdonalds, presumably accepting the chief's hospitality. Suddenly, one day at dawn, the treacherous attack took place. Campbell's men put more than forty members of the clan to the sword, including women, children, and servants . . . I never trust a Campbell," Lyle concluded.

"Don't forget, dear," said his wife, "you married one."

"That's what I mean. They make great apple pie, but I don't trust 'em." Then he went on. "The order for the attack was supposedly written on a playing card, and ever since that time, the nine of diamonds has been called the Curse of Scotland."

That night they checked into a rustic inn that had been a private hunting and fishing lodge in the days when upper-class sportsmen came up from London for grouse-shooting and fly-casting. The Bonnie Scots group entered through massive oak doors, iron-strapped and green with mold, and walked into a lobby hung with hunting trophies. An ancient leather-bound journal recorded the names of sporting notables who had bagged 86 grouse and 33 pheasant on a certain weekend in 1838.

Larry picked up the room keys and distributed them. "Hey, look! We have locks on our doors!" he announced. "We're back in the civilized world!" Then, while the other men unloaded the bus, he telephoned the previous inn to inquire about the missing driver. There was still no clue to his defection.

When the luggage was marshaled in the center of the lobby,

Bushy announced, "Grab your own bags, folks, and if you can't lug 'em upstairs yourself, we'll help you."

Piece by piece the luggage was identified and removed.

"Where's mine?" Mrs. Utley demanded. "You left it on the bus!"

A quick check proved that the baggage bin was empty.

Qwilleran said, "Are you sure you placed it outside your room this morning, Mrs. Utley?"

"My sister took care of it while I was in the shower! Where is she? Somebody go and get her! Bring her down here!"

The shy Zella, acting as if under arrest and stammering in self-defense, insisted she had put the bags in the hall along with her own suitcase. Hers had arrived safely. "I always packed for Grace while she was dressing," she explained in a tremulous voice. "I brought up the jewel cases from the safe and packed them. Then I stayed in the hall with the luggage until it was picked up."

"And Bruce picked it up?" Qwilleran asked.

"I saw him."

He exchanged knowing glances with Bushy, who was now official baggage handler as well as official photographer.

"They've been stolen!" Mrs. Utley screamed. "That man! That driver! He stole them! That's why he ran off! Somebody picked him up in a car! I saw them speed away from the inn!"

Other members of the group, hearing the commotion, came down to the lobby, and the hysterical Mrs. Utley was assisted to her room.

"Does anyone have a tranquilizer for the poor woman?" Carol asked.

"At least she has her carry-on bag, so she can brush her teeth," said Lisa, "and I imagine she's well covered with insurance."

"Where did Irma hire that guy?" Compton kept saying.

Larry phoned the previous inn, describing the missing luggage, and after a search the innkeeper called back to say that no alligator bags could be found anywhere. Larry also phoned the constable in the fishing village and learned that a report of the missing articles would have to be filed in person.

Larry said, "We'll hire a car and drive tomorrow. I'll go back there with Grace."

"That's really noble of you," said Lisa.

Qwilleran asked Bushy, "Do you think you may have taken a picture of Bruce?"

"No, he'd never let me shoot him—always turned his back. I thought he was camera-shy, but now I'm beginning to wonder . . ."

The Chisholm sisters had a tray sent up to their room, while the others gathered in the dining room for a five-course dinner of smoked salmon, lentil soup, brown trout, venison, and a dessert flavored with Scotch whiskey—or whisky, as it said on the menu card. Afterward they assembled in the lounge, where hot coals were glowing in the fireplace, and the Lanspeaks organized an impromptu revue to bolster morale. Carol and Lisa harmonized "Annie Laurie" and Larry read Robert Burns's poem "To a Mouse," with a passable Scots accent. Then Dwight played "The Muckin' o' Georgie's Byre" on the tin whistle, one of the Scottish tunes in the booklet that came with his purchase.

"It didn't take you long to become a virtuoso," Polly remarked.

"I've been playing since I was a kid," Dwight explained. "I won second place in an amateur contest when I was ten."

"Amanda says a tin whistle sounds like a sick locomotive," said Riker.

"It's weird, all right. I'm thinking of using it in *Macbeth* whenever the witches are on stage."

Lisa asked, "Are any of you fellows going to buy kilts? We're scheduled to visit a woolen mill tomorrow."

"Not I," said Qwilleran promptly, although secretly he thought he would look good in one.

"I think men look sexy in kilts . . . but they've got to have sturdy, good-looking legs," she added with a telling look at her lanky husband.

Bushy said, "I heard a good story from the innkeeper this morning. There was this newspaper woman from the states, attending some Highland games over here. Men were swinging battle axes and tossing the caber, which is something like a telephone pole, and half the male spectators were wearing kilts. This was her chance, she thought, to get an honest answer to the old question: Is it true they don't wear anything underneath? So she went up to a congenial-looking Scot with red hair, who wore his kilt with a swagger. 'Excuse me, sir,' she said. 'I'm from an American newspaper. Would you mind if I asked a bold question? Is it true that—ah—*nothing is worn under your kilt?*' He answered without hesitation. 'Yes, indeed, ma'am, it's true. Everything is in perfect working order.' "

Lyle grunted, and his wife giggled. He said, "When the English Redcoats ridiculed the Scots for fighting in 'short skirts' during the Rebellion, they didn't know the reason for the national costume. It was for walking through a dense growth of heather. When the English soldiers tried it in full uniform, they bogged down."

Larry said, "Tomorrow we visit the battlefield at Culloden. Why don't you brief us, Lyle?"

"How much do you want to know? It was one of the bloodiest military mistakes ever made!"

"Go ahead," everyone insisted.

"Well . . . Prince Charlie wanted to put his father back on the throne, and the English marched north to put down the uprising. They had 9,000 well-equipped, well-trained professional soldiers in scarlet coats. They had competent officers in powdered wigs, as well as a full complement of cannon, muskets, horses, and supply wagons. The Rebels were 5,000 hastily assembled, poorly commanded Scots with broadswords, daggers, and axes."

Qwilleran had turned on his recorder.

"It wasn't just Scots against the English. There were Highlanders against Lowlanders, Rebels against Loyalists, clans against clans, brothers against brothers.

"When the Rebels fought at Culloden, several mistakes had already been made by their commanders. They chose a battlefield that gave the advantage to the enemy; their food had run out; they had marched their troops all night in a maneuver that didn't work; the men were exhausted from hunger and lack of sleep; even their horses had died of starvation.

"Then the battle started, and they received no order to advance but stood in ranks while the enemy cannon mowed them down. Desperate at the delay, some of the clans broke through in rage, blinded by smoke, screaming and leaping over the rows of their dead. Then the cannon changed to grapeshot, and there was more slaughter. Still they attacked like hungry wolves. The muskets fired at them point blank, and they rushed in and hacked at the bayonets with swords. Some discarded their weapons and threw stones like savages. When the battle was lost, the survivors fled in panic, only to be chased down by the dragoons and butchered."

Lyle stopped, and no one spoke. "Well, you asked for it," he said.

Dwight put another shovelful of coal in the grate. Then members of the group started drifting away, saying they'd step outside for a breath of air, or they'd go up to bed, or they needed a drink.

It rained on Day Eight when they visited the battlefield at Culloden, and they found it depressing. It still rained when they visited a distillery, and even the wee dram served at the conclusion of the guided tour failed to cheer them. The Bonnie Scots Tour was winding down fast. Polly blamed it on the loss of their leader. Qwilleran thought it was a let-down after the enchantment of the Western Isles and Highlands.

On the bus, Bushy grabbed the microphone and tried to elevate the general mood with stories that fell flat. "Did you hear about the Scotsman who went to visit a sick friend with a bottle of Scotch in his pocket? It was a dark night, and on the way he tripped and fell on a sharp rock, but he picked himself up and went on his way. Soon he felt a trickle of something running down the outside of his leg. It was too dark to see, but he dabbled his fingers in it and tasted it. 'Thank God! It's only blood!' he said."

Later that evening, when Larry and the Chisholm sisters returned from the scene of the crime, he said to Qwilleran, "That woman is impossible, but we got everything taken care of. What did I miss?"

"Not much. A historic battlefield is all in your head. There's not much to see."

"And the distillery?"

"Everything was spic-and-span and absolutely sterile. Too bad Amanda wasn't there for the wee dram . . . Tell me, Larry, how valuable was the stuff stolen from Grace Utley?"

"According to her, one necklace alone was worth $150,000. Some of the stone-set brooches and bracelets were estate stuff, valued up to $50,000 apiece. It was a nice haul for someone. Do you suppose the theft was impromptu on Bruce's part . . . or what?"

Day Nine was devoted to museums and shopping. Mrs. Utley bought clothing and luggage enough to see her back to Pickax. The other women shopped for sweaters and kilts. Even Arch Riker found a cashmere cardigan that he considered a bargain. And then they checked into their last inn before Edinburgh, a stately, ivy-covered mansion on extensive landscaped grounds, furnished with antiques and chintz. The bedrooms were large, with ornate plaster ceilings, lace curtains, and telephones!

"I'm expecting Junior to phone," Riker said. He was trying on his new sweater when there was a knock at the door.

Qwilleran opened it to find a young man with a tea tray. "You've got the wrong room. We didn't order tea," he said.

"Compliments of the house, sir." The waiter marched into the room and set the tray on a lace-covered tea table in front of a stiff little settee. The tray was laden with porcelain cups and saucers, a rosebud-patterned china teapot, a silver milk and sugar service, a plate of shortbread, and dainty embroidered napkins in silver rings.

"Just what I wanted. More shortbread," Riker remarked as he sat on the settee and awkwardly poured tea into the eggshell-thin cups. Qwilleran pulled up a small chair opposite.

At that moment the telephone rang. "That's Junior!" said the editor, jumping to his feet. "He's really on the ball!"

As he started toward the phone, a button of his sweater caught on the lace cloth and dragged it off the table along with the tea, milk, sugar, shortbread, and china. With the tablecover trailing from his sweater button, he answered the phone with the composure of a veteran news editor. Then he turned to Qwilleran. "It's the desk clerk downstairs. Wants to know if everything's all right."

"Tell him to send up a mop and a shovel," Qwilleran said.

It was the final calamity of the Bonnie Scots Tour, but there was one more surprise in store for Qwilleran. The telephone rang in the middle of the night, and he jumped to a sitting position before his eyes were open. He turned on the bedside lamp. It was three o'clock.

"Something's happened to the cats—or the barn!" he said to Riker, who showed signs of stirring.

As he expected, it was an overseas call, and Mildred Hanstable was on the line. "Hope I didn't take you away from your dinner, Qwill."

"Dinner! It's three o'clock in the morning!"

"Oh, forgive me!" she cried in chagrin. "I deducted five hours instead of adding. I'm so sorry!"

"Is anything wrong? Are the cats all right?"

"They're fine. We've just had a little snack."

"When is Irma's funeral? How are the Hasselriches taking it? Have you heard?"

"That's why I'm calling, Qwill. The funeral's been postponed—for family reasons, it said in the paper. Actually, the body hasn't arrived yet."

"*Hasn't arrived!* It left here with Melinda four days ago!"

"Yes, Melinda is home. She said the body was flown cargo . . . but it's lost."

"How do you know?"

"Roger was at the funeral home, asking why there were so many flowers and no body, and the Dingleberry brothers told him it had gone astray."

"Is there any trace of it?"

"Oh, yes. It arrived from Scotland and went to Chicago all right, but then it was shipped to Moose Jaw in Canada, instead of the Moose County Airport."

"Is that where it is now?"

"No, it's been traced to Denver, and they think it's on the way back to Chicago, by way of Atlanta."

Qwilleran groaned. "This is absurd, Mildred. Does Junior know what's happened?"

"Roger told him, but it's being suppressed to keep from upsetting Irma's parents."

"Hold the line," Qwilleran told her. Turning to Riker, he said, "Irma's body hasn't arrived. It's being shipped all over North America. Junior is withholding the news."

The two men stared at each other, both thinking what a headline it would make. All their training and experience and instincts as newsmen told them to go for the headline, but Pickax was a small town, and the *Moose County Something* was a small-town newspaper, and attitudes were different.

Riker nodded assent.

"Well, thank you, Mildred," said Qwilleran. "Is everything else okay? How about the cats?"

"One of them has been chewing holes in your old sweaters and throwing up."

"That's probably Koko. He hasn't done that for years! He's lonely."

"I'm terribly sorry I disturbed you, Qwill."

"That's all right. I'm glad you called. I'll be home soon—perhaps sooner than I planned."

Six

On the morning of Day Ten the members of the Bonnie Scots Tour placed their luggage in the corridor at seven-thirty instead of six-thirty, having voted unanimously to amend Irma's orders and start sleeping an extra hour. Qwilleran walked down the hall to Polly's room and knocked on the door. "May I come in?" he asked.

"Good morning, dear. I was about to plug in the tea-maker. Would you like a cup?"

"No, thanks. I simply want you to know I'm leaving the tour as soon as we reach Edinburgh."

"Has something happened at home?" she asked anxiously.

"No. I simply have a strong desire to get back to Pickax, that's all." He fingered his moustache significantly. "I'm changing my flight."

"Would you like company, Qwill?"

"Don't you want to see Edinburgh? It's a magnificent city. I've had many newspaper assignments there."

"Frankly, my heart isn't in this tour since Irma died, and it may seem foolish, but . . . I'm lonesome for Bootsie."

"Give me your ticket and I'll phone the airline," he said.

In changing their flights, he also upgraded their reservations to first class. Even though he was reluctant to spend money on transportation, he needed the extra space for his long legs and wide shoulders, and—after ten days of small talk with the heterogeneous Bonnie Scots family—he wanted privacy for a sustained conversation with Polly.

Twenty-four hours later they had said goodbye to their traveling companions and were airborne—Qwilleran stretching his legs luxuriously, Polly sipping champagne, and both of them enjoying the pampering of VIPs.

"I wonder if Bootsie has missed me," Polly said. "I've never left him for more than a weekend. My sister-in-law takes good care of him, but there isn't the rapport that he has with me."

"Mildred says Koko's been chewing my sweaters. That means he's lonely, even though she's feeding him haute cuisine and perverting him with dubious diversions, like tarot cards."

The champagne bottle made the rounds again, and delectable hors d'oeuvres were served, prompting Polly to say, "Do you realize we were never offered any haggis in Scotland?"

"We never heard any bagpipes, either," he added.

"Or saw anyone dancing the hornpipe."

"In fact, we never really met any Scots. We were always with our own group, a little bit of Moose County on foreign soil."

This was followed by a regretful silence until Polly said, "On the credit side, I survived the trip without bronchitis, although I decided not to take my vitamin C. The capsules were too large and hard to swallow."

"Your bronchitis in England last year was all psychological, because I wasn't with you."

"What a sweep of vanity comes this way!" she said, quoting Shakespeare with glee.

"A little vanity is a good thing," he retorted.

"That's a questionable aphorism, if I ever heard one! Who said that?" she demanded.

"I did."

Polly lapsed into a sentimental reverie induced by the champagne. At length she said, "I've missed you, darling. We haven't had any time to ourselves on this trip."

"I've missed you, too, Polly."

"I feel so sad about Irma, and I couldn't even attend her funeral. She was probably buried two days ago."

"I don't think so," Qwilleran said slowly and soberly. "There's been a complication."

"What do you mean?" Polly snapped out of her brooding mood, then gasped as he reported the bizarre odyssey of Irma's casket. "Well," she said after a while, "I have something surprising to report, too."

"Let's hear it."

Polly hesitated, as if pondering where to begin. "Well . . . when I turned over Irma's briefcase to Larry, I withheld one small personal file and put it in my luggage, thinking to give it to her parents. Then Bruce disappeared, and no one knew his last name, so I searched this file without finding a clue. But there was one letter that I think you should see." She rummaged in her carry-on bag and extracted a document envelope tied with tape. In it was a folded sheet of notepaper that she handed to Qwilleran. "Read this."

Dear Irma,

Thank you from the bottom of my heart! Bruce will do a good job for you. He's an excellent driver, no mistake. He's had an awful time finding work since he got out, but he's promised to stay clean now. Do give him a proper talking to. He'll listen to you. I know you two meant a lot to each other when we were young. My brother is a good sort really, and I expect he's quite learned his lesson. Bless you! Don't forget to ring me when you reach Edinburgh.

For auld lang syne,
Katie

Qwilleran read the note twice. So that was the way it was! he thought. Irma and Bruce were—what? Youthful sweethearts? Former lovers? And Bruce had been in prison—for what? Larceny? A narcotics violation? Irma apparently knew about his record. Did she hire him in spite of it? Or because of it? Qwilleran's cynicism was close to the surface where Irma was concerned. There was more to this story, he suspected.

Polly was waiting to hear his reaction to the letter. "What do you think, Qwill?"

"Did the envelope have her full name and return address?" he asked.

"There was no envelope."

"There was gossip throughout the tour about Irma's nightly excursions with Bruce. Did she ever explain to you?"

"Not a word, and I was determined not to mention it. She was a responsible adult, and it was none of my business. She always came in after I was asleep, apparently creeping around in the dark without turning on the lights or making a sound. It was considerate of her, I thought."

"If Bruce stole Mrs. Utley's luggage, he wasn't as 'clean' as Irma was led to believe."

"It would seem so," Polly agreed.

"Did she ever mention this Katie person to you?"

"No, she was secretive about her Scottish connections, but that was characteristic of her. We never knew how much was bottled up in that cool exterior."

Qwilleran said, "If we could identify Katie, the police would have something to work with, at least. One would expect Irma to carry an address book in her briefcase—or a list of phone numbers if she planned to call friends in Scotland."

"Perhaps it was in her handbag," Polly suggested. "I packed it without examining the contents and sent it home in her luggage. Melinda was to turn everything over to the Hasselriches."

"Her parents might know Katie's name and whereabouts. If not, you could ask them for the address book on the pretext of notifying Irma's Scottish friends about her death . . . In fact," he added, "Bruce might be listed."

There were signs that dinner was about to be served. Individual tables were unfolded from the chair arms, and white tablecloths were whisked across them, followed by linen napkins, wineglasses, tiny vases of fresh flowers, and four-page menu presentations.

Qwilleran said, "We can assume that turbulence is not in their flight plan."

They ordered vichyssoise, tournedos of beef, and Caesar salad.

After a while he asked, "What will happen at the Senior Care Facility? Will they be able to replace Irma?"

"The administrators always said they'd have to hire a professional if Irma retired. Lisa wants to apply for the job."

"She'd be pretty good, I think."

"Before we left for Scotland," Polly said, "Irma was working on a project called Pets for Patients, with volunteers bringing their cats and dogs to the facility on certain days to boost morale. If it goes through, I'd be willing to take Bootsie. How about you, Qwill?"

"I'd take Yum Yum, but I doubt whether Koko would cooperate. He has his own ideas and doesn't always do what cats are supposed to do."

They ordered crème caramel for dessert, and after coffee Qwilleran presented Polly with a small white box bearing a monogram: CRM. It was a handmade silver brooch in the form of a peacock feather, combined with blue-green enamel and a smoky quartz crystal mounted in the eye of the feather.

"It's beautiful!" she cried. "I love peacock feathers! What is the stone?"

"A cairngorm from the Cairngorm mountains in Scotland. This is one of the designs being made in the Charles Rennie Mackintosh style."

"It will be perfect on my batwing cape. Thank you so much, dear."

"Are you going to watch the movie?" he asked. The screen was being lowered at the front of the cabin.

"I'd rather take a nap," she said.

"I'm going to look at this magazine, if my reading light won't disturb you."

Window shades were drawn to shut out the brilliant sunlight, while passengers either put on their earphones to watch the film, or went to sleep, or both. He held the magazine open to a feature on Tlingit art, but he was thinking rather than reading. If he could discover the bus driver's identity, he would turn the information over to the Pickax police chief and let him follow through. Reviewing the Scottish tour in his mind, Qwilleran searched for clues in the behavior of Irma as well as Bruce. The tapes he had recorded might reveal forgotten details. Their content was intended as material for "Straight from the Qwill Pen," but it could serve another purpose now . . . His magazine dropped to his lap, and he fell asleep until the cabin was again flooded with light and another meal was served.

By the time the plane landed in Chicago, and by the time they claimed their baggage and went through Customs and Immigration, it was too late to continue to Moose County. They stayed overnight at an airport inn and caught the shuttle flight in the morning. At the Moose County Airport Qwilleran's white four-door was waiting in the long-term parking structure, a new building made possible by a grant from the K Foundation.

Polly said, "I remember when the terminal was a shack without chairs or indoor plumbing."

"I remember when we had to park our cars in a cow pasture and be *very careful,*" Qwilleran said, "and that was only five years ago."

"I can hardly wait to see Bootsie," she said on the way to Pickax.

"I'm looking forward to seeing my two rascals also."

When they arrived at Polly's carriage-house apartment, she ran up the stairs while Qwilleran followed with her luggage. "Bootsie!" she cried. "How's my little boy? Did you miss me?"

The husky Siamese approached with curiosity, appraised her coolly, then turned abruptly and walked away, leaving his adoring human crushed.

Qwilleran said, "That's your punishment for abandoning him. After he thinks you've suffered enough, he'll smother you with affection. I expect the same treatment when I get home."

After two weeks of picturesque inns and impressive castles, he had forgotten that the converted apple barn was such a wondrous bit of architecture. The octagonal structure had a rough stone foundation that looked like thirteenth-century Scotland, and the weathered shingle siding was crowned by a slate roof. There were no furry creatures spying on him from the windows, however. They were in the kitchen, sitting contentedly on top of the refrigerator, watching Mildred Hanstable as she slid a casserole into the oven. They looked down on Qwilleran with condescension.

"Welcome home!" she greeted him. "How was the trip?"

"No one ever said traveling is easy."

"How about a cup of coffee?"

"As soon as I dump this luggage. I've been living out of it for two weeks." He carried his bags up the ramp to the balcony, and when he returned he had a small white box in his pocket, with CRM on the cover. The Siamese were still sitting sphinxlike on the refrigerator. "Did they ever find Irma?" he asked as he slid onto a seat at the snack bar.

Mildred poured two mugs of coffee. "Yes, she finally arrived, and they buried her yesterday, although there was some further unpleasantness. The Dingleberry brothers told Roger—off the record, of course—that the Hasselriches disagreed violently about burial versus cremation."

"Did the obit run?"

"Yes. On the front page. I left it on the coffee table. It's a lovely write-up . . . Well, apart from the tragedy, Qwill, how was your adventure?"

"I'll know better after I've spent a night in my own bed and recovered from tour trauma."

"Did you buy yourself a kilt?"

"No, just a couple of ties in the Mackintosh tartan. Speaking of Mackintosh, here's a memento of Glasgow." He pushed the small white box across the bar.

"Oh, Qwill! Thank you so much!" she exclaimed when she saw the peacock feather pin in silver and enamel. "What's the name of this stone?"

"It's a cairngorm, found only in Scotland, I believe."

"It was sweet of you to think of me."

"It was generous of you to take care of the Siamese, Mildred."

"Not a bit! It was a thrill to live in this barn, and the cats were enjoyable company. I wouldn't mind having one just like Koko."

"There's no such thing as just-like-Koko," he informed her. "He's the Shakespeare of cats, the Beethoven of cats, the Leonardo of cats!"

Hearing his name mentioned favorably, Koko rose and stretched his rear chassis, then extended his forelegs with spreading toes, after which he jumped down from the refrigerator with a thump and an involuntary grunt and ambled over to Qwilleran to sniff the foreign aromas. Who could say what scents were registered by that twitching nose? Old castles? Heather? Scotch broth? Fishing villages? Sheep? A distillery? The bones of ancient kings? A battlefield soaked with blood 250 years ago?

"Did the cats misbehave in any way?" Qwilleran asked.

"Well, one of them stole my emery boards—a whole pack of them, one at a time."

"Petty larceny is Yum Yum's department. I owe you a pack. I'll take it out of her allowance. How about Koko?"

"He did one naughty thing that gave me a scare," Mildred said. "I was getting ready to take my diet pill, and he swooped in and snatched it. I was afraid he'd eat it and get sick, but he just punctured the capsule with his fangs."

"Yes, he likes to sink them in soft, gummy things, like jelly beans," Qwilleran explained. "Do I smell macaroni and cheese in the oven? All the time I was eating nettle broth, mutton pie, boiled sheep's tongue, and tripe and onions, I was dreaming about macaroni and cheese."

"That's for our lunch," she said. "I'm leaving some leftovers in the refrigerator for the cats—meatloaf, codfish cakes, terrine of turkey—and there's beef stew for you in the freezer. I've been cooking up a storm while you were away and having a wonderful time."

After lunch, Mildred packed and moved out, and Qwilleran shut himself in his balcony suite until an operatic chorus outside his door reminded him it was time for dinner. The three of them snacked informally on the leftovers, and then he sprawled listlessly in his favorite lounge chair with no desire to read the newspaper or play the stereo or write a letter or take a walk or call anyone on the telephone. It was post-vacation lethargy. When the Siamese crowded around, having forgiven him for his unexplained absence, he stroked Yum Yum halfheartedly and told Koko without much conviction that he was a handsome fellow.

Impulsively, Koko jumped from the arm of the chair and walked deliberately to the large square coffee table, where Mildred had left a copy of the *Moose County Something*. Hopping to the tabletop, he stared down at the newsprint with a nearsighted gaze. Then, arching his back and bushing his tail and sweeping his ears back, he commenced a slow prance around the lead item on the front page. He circled it again and again in a hair-raising ritual that Qwilleran had seen before. It meant that Koko's extra senses were detecting a discrepancy that escaped human perception.

Qwilleran felt the familiar crawling sensation in the roots of his moustache. There on page one was the three-column photo of Irma Hasselrich and the half-page obituary. Koko, he remembered, had howled at the exact moment of her death. Without benefit of satellite he had known what was happening in a remote Scottish hamlet. Was it possible that the cat sensed more than that? Was Koko the source of the subliminal message urging him to return home early? Polly thought she had a remarkable rapport with Bootsie, but it was nothing compared to the mutual understanding that existed between Qwilleran and Koko.

But no, he finally decided; it was all absurd imagining. "I'm punchy from jet lag," he said to the Siamese. "Let's turn out the lights and call it a day."

Seven

Back home in his own bed Qwilleran enjoyed a good night's sleep, but in the morning he was disoriented. He didn't know what day it was. He knew only that it was Day Thirteen. After living in a tour-induced limbo, where days had numbers instead of names, he had not adjusted to the standard calendar week. Consequently, the morning after Koko's macabre dance around Irma's obituary was Day Thirteen in Qwilleran's book.

The sound of church bells ringing on Park Circle suggested that Day Thirteen might be translated into Sunday. On the other hand, it might be Saturday if the bells were celebrating a wedding. He thought of phoning the city desk at the *Moose County Something* and asking, "Is this Saturday or Sunday?" He had answered stranger questions than that when he worked for metropolitan newspapers Down Below. The local radio station was of no help; the announcer gave the time, the temperature, the wind velocity, and the relative humidity, but not the day of the week. As for the WPKX brand of daily newscasting, it was a half hour of what Qwilleran called mushy news—no less mushy on Saturday than on Sunday.

If the day proved to be Saturday, that meant he had arrived home on Friday. Yet, would Mildred Hanstable have been there on a Friday morning? She taught school and would have been in the classroom unless, of course, it was a Teacher-Optional Workday, in which case she might have opted to stay home and prepare macaroni and cheese, although that was extremely unlikely for one as conscientious as Mildred. Ergo, this had to be Sunday, and the church bells were calling the faithful to worship. That was Qwilleran's cue to walk to the drug store and pick up the out-of-town Sunday papers.

The cats were relaxing in a patch of sunlight on the rug without a thought in their sleek brown heads. What matter to them that it was Sunday—or even Thursday? Every day was Today in their scheme of things, and there was no such thing as Yesterday or Tomorrow.

"I'm going downtown," he announced to them. "Is there anything you want from the drug store?"

They looked at him as if he were demented. Or *daft,* as they said in Scotland. (Qwilleran had bought a glossary of Scottish terms at the Edinburgh airport.) The Siamese knew very well when he was talking nonsense. Or *blethering,* as they said in Scotland.

A brisk walk downtown had the effect of clearing the stupefied brain he had brought home from the Bonnie Scots Tour. He did his best thinking while walking alone. Now he resumed his ruminations begun on the plane: Irma knew about Bruce's past record . . . She might have relived her youthful passion on the moor . . . She might have vented some hidden bitterness caused by her own conviction for manslaughter . . . She might have been Bruce's accomplice in the jewel theft!

This wild scenario brought forth not so much as a tickle on Qwilleran's upper lip, but when he tried another avenue of brainstorming, his moustache bristled slightly: Irma might have been Bruce's victim. If he planned to steal the jewels, wouldn't it be logical to eliminate the one person who knew his identity? Could he have slipped her some kind of drug that would stop her heart? This was a technical detail he would have to check with Dr. Melinda—an undertaking he hardly relished. To phone her on a Sunday afternoon would give rise to sociable invitations, such as, "Come over for a drink, and we'll discuss it," or "Let's have dinner." To visit her clinic on Monday would lead to other undesirable developments, such as, "Remove everything except your socks and shoes, and the doctor will be right with you." No, he decided, it would be safer to meet her "accidentally" in some crowded or busy place, where they could exchange a few words without getting involved in anything personal.

Qwilleran found himself walking with clenched teeth. It annoyed him to be in this awkward position with Melinda after three years of an easy relationship with Polly. He resented being hounded by an overzealous female. He had terminated other liaisons without embarrassment, and he had been jilted himself without creating a rumpus. Somehow he had to get rid of that woman! Koko had never liked her. Did the cat's uncanny prescience foretell this course of events? It was not beyond the realm of imagination.

At the drug store, Qwilleran picked up several out-of-town newspapers—his way of keeping in touch with the turmoil Down Below.

"How was Scotland, Mr. Q?" asked the cashier.

"Okay."

"I heard about Ms. Hasselrich."

"Yes, it was too bad."

"Did you see the Loch Ness monster?"

"No, we were there on his day off."

On the way home Qwilleran's mind turned to the subject of Irma's address book. If he could learn the whereabouts and/or phone number of the pivotal Katie, he could turn the whole matter over to Andrew Brodie and let him make a case of it, if he wished. Andy would be interested in Koko's startling reaction to the obituary, being one of the few who knew about the cat's sensitivity to the scent of crime. A detective from Down Below had told him about it in all seriousness. To the Pickax police chief, Koko was the town psychic.

Qwilleran walked home with his newspapers via the back road, hoping to avoid questions from well-meaning townsfolk. There was little traffic on Trevelyan Road, but eventually a car stopped and the driver called to him, "Want a lift, Qwill?" It was Scott Gippel, the used-car dealer.

"No, thanks. I'm walking for my health," Qwilleran said with a comradely salute.

"How was Scotland?"

"Fine."

"Sorry about Irma Hasselrich."

"Very unfortunate."

"Bring back any Scotch?"

Arriving home with several pounds of newsprint under his arm, Qwilleran all but stumbled over a moving hump in the foyer rug. It was a familiar occurrence, meaning that a cat had hidden stolen goods and was trying to retrieve the loot. He threw back a corner of the rug and exposed Yum Yum huddled over a playing card. It was face down, and when he turned it over, he recognized a card from Mildred's tarot deck. He also recognized the two perforations in the corner. Koko had been the thief; he always left his mark, like the Black Hand.

The picture on the card was a pleasant scene: a grape arbor with a woman in flowing robes, a bird perched on her wrist. They were surrounded by nine gold circles, each with a five-pointed star in the center. Qwilleran remembered the card from Mildred's reading prior to the Scottish venture. Dropping his stack of newspapers, he found his recording of the episode and slipped it into a player. The following familiar dialogue unreeled:

"Do you mind if I tape this, Mildred?"

"Not at all. I wish you would."

"What did you learn?"

"Strangely, when I asked the cards about you, the answers concerned someone else—someone in danger."

"Man or woman?"

"A mature woman. A woman with strict habits and upright values."

"What kind of danger?"

"Well, the cards were rather vague, so I brought the pack with me, and I'd like to do another reading—in your presence." (Pause.)

"Yow!"

"Want me to lock him up, Mildred?"

"No, let him watch. (Pause.) I'm using the Celtic pattern for this reading. This card is the significator. (Pause.) I see a journey . . . a journey across water . . . with stormy weather ahead."

"Glad I packed my raincoat."

"Stormy weather could stand for dissension, mistakes, accidents, or whatever."

"Too bad I didn't know before I paid my money."

"You're not taking this seriously, Qwill."

"Sorry. I didn't mean to sound flippant."

"This final card . . . is not auspicious . . . You might consider it a warning."

"Looks like a happy card to me."

"But it's reversed."

"Meaning . . ."

"Some kind of fraud . . . or treachery."

"Yow!"

"In conclusion . . . I urge you to be prepared . . . for the unexpected." (Pause.)

"Very interesting. Thank you."

Click.

As the tape slowly unreeled, the Siamese were alerted, having heard another cat inside the black box, and both of them circled the player with curiosity. Perhaps they also recognized the voices of Qwilleran and Mildred. It was significant that Koko had yowled at her mention of treachery. At the time of the reading, Qwilleran had thought the cards referred to Polly. Now it was obvious that Irma was the woman in danger; it was she who would be the victim of treachery . . . That is, Qwilleran reminded himself skeptically, if one took the cards seriously.

He looked up Mildred Hanstable's number. It was Sunday morning, and she would probably be at home, cooking or quilting. "Good morning," he said. "The meatloaf was delicious. The Siamese let me have some of it for dinner last night."

"There's beef stew in the freezer for you, don't forget," she said.

"I feel twice blessed. I'm calling, Mildred, to ask if you've lost one of your tarot cards. I'd hate to see you playing with a short deck."

"I don't know. Let me check." In a moment she returned to the phone. "You're right. There are only seventy-seven."

"I'm afraid Koko stole one. He left his fang marks in it. I hope that doesn't affect the—ah—authority of the deck."

"Where did you find it?"

"Hidden under a rug. It's a card I remember from your reading before I left for Scotland." He described the woman in the grape arbor.

"Yes, I recall. It was reversed when I read for you, and I predicted treachery."

"And you were right! Grace Utley's jewels were stolen by a trusted bus driver." He avoided mentioning his suspicions about Irma's death.

"Grace was crazy to take them on the trip," Mildred said, "but no one ever said that woman was in her right mind."

"Shall I mail the card to you?" he asked. "Or shall we have dinner some evening—soon."

"I'd love it!" Her voice rang with pleased surprise.

"We'll include Polly and Arch," he added hastily, "and the three of us will tell you all about Scotland."

"Say when. I'm always free. Just hang on to the nine of pentacles until then."

"What is the significance of pentacles?" he asked.

"They correspond to diamonds in regular playing cards."

An odd coincidence, Qwilleran thought as he hung up. The nine of diamonds! The Curse of Scotland!

Now he was impatient to talk with Polly about the address book. He waited until he thought she would be home from church, but there was no answer when he called. She might have gone to Sunday brunch with her sister-in-law, or she might be visiting the Hasselriches.

A few hours later Polly called in great excitement. "I have it! I have the address book!" she cried.

"How did the family react to your request?"

"When I phoned about it, they were most appreciative and invited me to dinner after church. It was a painful occasion, but we talked about Irma lovingly, and they said they consider me their surrogate daughter now. I was deeply touched."

"Did they know anything about Katie?"

"Only that she and Irma had been in art school at the same time. When I brought the book home, I searched it for a Katie with an Edinburgh address and discovered one Kathryn Gow MacBean. It looks as if MacBean might be her married name, in which case Bruce would be a Gow." Polly sounded excited about her first attempt at detection and deduction.

"Good work, Polly!" Qwilleran said. "Give me the Edinburgh phone number, and I'll see what I can find out." He avoided mentioning Koko's death dance around the obituary or his own murder theory.

She said, "I'd invite you over for coffee or something, but I need to do some laundry and get myself together for work tomorrow. Let me know what luck you have."

After hanging up, Qwilleran checked his watch. It was too late to call Edinburgh, but the next morning he took his first cup of coffee to the telephone desk, locked the meddlesome Koko in the loft, and placed a call to Katie. He said, "This is Jim Qwilleran, a friend of Irma Hasselrich." He used a sincere and cordial tone of voice intended to inspire confidence.

"Yes?" the woman replied warily.

"I'd like to speak to Kathryn Gow. Or is it Kathryn MacBean?"

"I'm Mrs. MacBean."

"I'm phoning from the States—from Irma's hometown of Pickax."

"Where is she?" came a sharp reply. "I mean, I expected her to ring me up."

"She never reached Edinburgh, I'm sorry to say," Qwilleran said, introducing a grieved note to prepare his listener for bad news. "I was a member of her Scots Tour, and while we were still in the Western Highlands, she suffered a heart attack and died."

"*Died!* . . . That's perfectly awful!"

"It pains me to break the news, but her family felt you'd want to know."

There was a blank silence.

"Hello? Hello?" he said.

In a softer voice Katie said, "I do declare, this is a bit of a shock! I mean, she was fairly young."

"Her body was flown back here, and she was buried two days ago. We're notifying a list of her friends."

"Was the rest of the tour canceled? My brother was the driver. Odd that he didn't notify me."

"Bruce Gow! Is he your brother?"

"Ah . . . yes."

"He's an excellent driver, and he was very courteous to a busload of crotchety American tourists."

"Yes, he's . . . very good. What is your name, did you say?"

"Jim Qwilleran. My mother was a Mackintosh. We're branches of the same clan. There was a MacBean, a giant of a man, who fought at Culloden and killed thirteen English with his broadsword, fighting with his back to a wall." This was intended to proclaim his Scottish sympathies and win her good will.

"Ah . . . yes . . . there's a fair number of Mackintoshes about." Her attention was wandering as if she were concerned about her brother. "When did it happen?"

"Almost a week ago."

"Honestly, I'm in a state! I'm not sure I know quite what to say, Mr. . . . Mr. . . ."

"Qwilleran. It would help to console Irma's parents if you would write them a note. How long had you known her?"

"More than twenty years. We met in art school. In Glasgow." She seemed to be speaking in a guarded way.

"Do you have any snapshots or other memorabilia that you could part with? I'm sure her parents would welcome any little memento."

"I expect that's the least I can do, isn't it?"

"Do you have the address?"

"Goodwinter Boulevard? Yes, of course."

"I'll send you a clip of the obituary that ran in the local newspaper. It has a very good photo of Irma."

"That would be kind of you. If you could spare two cuttings . . ."

"Glad to do it, Mrs. MacBean."

"And thank you for calling, Mr. . . ."

"Qwilleran."

He verified her address before concluding the conversation and hung up with a strong feeling of satisfaction. Now he was ready to talk with Chief Brodie.

He walked briskly downtown to the police station, and the sergeant at the desk nodded him into the inner office before a word was spoken.

Brodie looked up in surprise. "When did you get back, laddie?"

"Saturday. Did you hear the bad news?"

The chief nodded. "I played the bagpipe at her funeral."

"You probably heard that she had a fatal heart attack, but there's more to the story than that, and I'd like your advice." Qwilleran glanced toward the outer office and closed the door.

"Pour a cup of coffee and sit down. How was Scotland, apart from that?"

"Beautiful!"

"Get your fill of bagpipes?"

"Believe it or not, Andy, we didn't hear so much as a squeal, all the time we were there."

"You went to the wrong places, mon. You should come to Scottish Night at my lodge. We'll show you what piping is all about . . . So, what's buggin' you?"

Qwilleran pulled up a chair. "Well, there were sixteen of us on the bus traveling around Scotland," he began, "and our driver was a Scot named Bruce, a sullen fellow with red hair who spoke only to Irma. They conversed, I believe, in Gaelic."

"She knew Gaelic? That's a tough language."

"They seemed to communicate all right. Then one morning she was found dead in bed by her roommate, Polly Duncan. Cause of death: cardiac arrest, according to Dr. Melinda, who was traveling with us. The next day the bus driver disappeared, and so did Grace Utley's luggage, containing a small fortune in jewels. I suppose you know about her spectacular jewelry—and the way she flaunts it."

"That I do! She's a walking Christmas tree!"

"We notified the village constable and gave a description of Bruce, but no one knew the guy's last name except Irma, and she was dead!"

"And Scotland is full of redheads by the name of Bruce. So what's the advice you want?"

"I have reason to believe," and here Qwilleran smoothed his moustache proudly, "that the heart stoppage was drug-induced. We hear of young athletes dropping dead because of substance abuse. If it can happen to them, it can happen to a forty-year-old woman with an existing heart condition."

"You can't tell me that Irma was doing drugs. Not her! Not that woman!"

"Listen, Andy. Every night after dinner she went out with Bruce. There was a lot of gossip about it."

"Why would a classy dame like her hang around with a bus driver?"

"We've since found out—from correspondence in her briefcase—that he was an old flame. Also, it appears, an ex-con. If he was plotting a jewel heist, wouldn't he get rid of the one person who could identify him? I suspect he slipped her some kind of drug."

Brodie grunted. "Do the police over there know that you suspect homicide?"

"No, it's a new development. But here's the good news, Andy." Qwilleran waved a slip of paper. "We've found the name, address, and phone number of Bruce's sister in Edinburgh, and through her we learned his last name is Gow."

"Give it here," said the chief, reaching across the desk. "Also the name of the town where you reported the larceny. Do you know what we're getting into? They'll want to exhume the body!" Then he added, partly in jest and partly because he believed in Koko's extraordinary gifts, "If Scotland Yard can't find the suspect, we'll assign your smart cat to the case."

"Yes," said Qwilleran, going along with the gag. "Too bad Koko wasn't there!"

He left the police station with a light step, knowing he had contributed vital information to the investigation, and he treated himself to a good American breakfast of ham and eggs at Lois's Luncheonette, with a double order of her famous country fries.

His elation was short-lived, however. When he returned home, the barn was a scene of havoc: torn newspapers everywhere, books on the floor, the telephone knocked off its cradle, and the rest of Qwilleran's morning coffee spilled on the desk and floor, while Koko was in the throes of a catfit. He raced around and around the main floor, almost faster than the eye could see, then up the circular ramp to the catwalk under the roof, where he screamed like a banshee before pelting down the ramp again, rolling on the floor, and fighting an imaginary adversary.

Qwilleran watched in helpless astonishment until the cat, having made his point, sat down on the coffee table and licked himself all over. He had staged catfits before, and it was always a desperate attempt to communicate.

"What's it all about, Koko?" Qwilleran asked as he cleaned up the mess. "What are you trying to say?"

It was Irma's obituary that had been shredded, and he was trying to convey that she had not died of natural causes; of that Qwilleran was sure. He had learned to read Koko's body language and the nuances of his yowling. The varying inflections and degrees of intensity—like the subtleties of Oriental speech—registered affirmation or negation, approval or disapproval, excitement or indifference, imperious demand or urgent warning.

Now, as Qwilleran watched that rippling pink tongue grooming that snowy white breast, an idea flashed through his head. It was a wild shot but worth trying. He would interrogate Koko! He waited patiently until the fastidious toilette was finished, then sprawled in the roomy lounge chair where the three of them always gathered for enjoyment of quality time. Yum Yum hopped onto his lap, landing weightlessly like a squirt of whipped cream, while Koko settled on the wide arm of the upholstered chair with perfect composure.

Solemnly, Qwilleran began, "This is a serious discussion, Koko, and I want you to give it your personal best."

"Yow," the cat replied, squeezing his eyes agreeably.

The man turned on the tape recorder, which was never far from his trigger finger. "Are you aware of the death of Irma Hasselrich?"

"Yow!" came the prompt reply, an obvious affirmative.

"Was she murdered?"

Koko hesitated before saying "Yow!" in a positive way.

"Hmmm," Qwilleran said, patting his moustache. "Did the bus driver cause her to ingest a substance that stopped her heart?"

Koko gazed into space.

"I'll rephrase that. Did the bus driver slip her a drug that killed her?"

Koko was mute. He looked from side to side, and up and down, with convulsive movements of his head.

"Pay attention!" Qwilleran rebuked him, and he repeated the question. "Did the bus driver—"

"Yow," Koko interrupted but without conviction.

It was not the definitive response that Qwilleran had hoped for, and he thought it wise to ask a test question: "Koko, is my name Ronald Frobnitz?"

"Yow!" said the town psychic as he leaped to catch the fruit fly he'd been tracking.

Eight

After the unsatisfactory interrogation of the redoubtable Koko, Qwilleran decided that the cat was a charlatan. Or he was a practical joker who delighted in deluding the man who gave him food, shelter, respect, and admiration. Despite Koko's past record, there were moments when Qwilleran seriously doubted that he was anything but an ordinary animal, and his so-called insights were all a matter of coincidence.

The telephone rang, and Koko raced him to the instrument, but Qwilleran grabbed the handset first.

"Qwill! You're home!" said the pleasant voice of Lori Bamba, his part-time secretary. "How was Scotland?"

"Magnificent! How's everything in Mooseville?"

"Same as always. We're all very sorry about Irma Hasselrich. She was a wonderful woman."

"Yes, that was a sad happening . . . Did you have any problems with my correspondence?"

"Nothing that I couldn't handle. Did it rain a lot while you were there?"

"Mornings were misty. That's what keeps the Scottish complexion so fresh and the Scottish landscape so verdant—just the way it looks in the whiskey ads."

"Do you think the cats missed you while you were away?" Lori asked.

"Not much. Mildred Hanstable cat-sat, so they ate well."

"There are several letters for you to sign, Qwill, and Nick can drop them off this afternoon. Will you be home around three-thirty?"

"I'll make it a point to be here," Qwilleran said. He found the Bambas an attractive young couple—Lori with her long, golden braids, Nick with his dark, curly hair and alert, black eyes. The best of the next generation, Qwilleran called them. Lori had been Mooseville postmaster before retiring to raise a family and work out of her home. Her husband, trained as an engineer, worked for the state prison near Mooseville, and since Nick shared his interest in crime, Qwilleran looked forward to seeing him and relating the case of the missing bus driver.

Meanwhile, he had a cup of coffee and listened to one of the tapes he had recorded during the tour. The Siamese listened, too, with Koko making an occasional comment from the top of the fireplace cube.

> "Tonight we are comfortably lodged and extremely well fed in another historic inn. I suspect Bonnie Prince Charlie slept here 250 years ago. One can hardly buy anything without his picture on it. Irma likes to talk about the heroic women who aided the prince's cause. Flora Macdonald dressed him in women's clothing and passed him off as her maid as they trav-

eled through enemy lines. And then there was Lady Ann Mackintosh, who raised regiments to fight for the prince, while her husband was off fighting for the other side."

Koko responded to the sound of a familiar voice with a happy gurgling sound, but as the tape unreeled he seemed to hear something else.

"Bushy is taking hundreds of pictures on this trip. At first, when Irma stopped the bus for a spectacular view, we all piled out with our cameras, but now Bushy and Big Mac are the only ones who take pictures. The rest of us, jaded with spectacular views, remain in our seats. Occasionally Bushy photographs members of our group in different settings, especially Melinda. He seems to think she's a good model."

Koko jumped on and off the desk when he heard this segment, and Qwilleran recalled Lori Bamba's theory—that cats respond to the palatal *shhhh* sound. (Her own cats, for that reason, were named Sheba, Shoo-Shoo, Natasha, Trish, Pushkin, and Sherman.) Evidently "Bushy" was the trigger sound here.

"Today I was talking to Lyle Compton about the famous medical school at Glasgow University, and he mentioned that the infamous Dr. Cream was a Glaswegian. He was the nineteenth-century psychopath who became a serial killer in England, Canada, and the United States—not as legendary as Jack the Ripper but noted for 'pink pills for pale prostitutes,' as his M.O. was described."

Koko reacted excitedly to this reference, leading Qwilleran to assume that he heard the word "serial" and confused it with the crunchy "cereal" that was his favorite treat.

In mid-afternoon Qwilleran walked downtown to the offices of the *Moose County Something*, to pick up a few more copies of Irma's obituary. He also left a small white box with a CRM monogram on the desk of Hixie Rice, the advertising manager, who had been his friend and neighbor Down Below. Then he dropped into Junior Goodwinter's office.

"You're back early," the managing editor said. "We don't expect Arch till tomorrow or Wednesday. Tell me about Scotland. What did you like best?"

"The islands," Qwilleran answered promptly. "There's something wild and mystic and ageless about them. You feel it in the stones under your feet—the ancient presence of Picts, Romans, Saxons, Gaels, Angles, Vikings—all that crowd."

"Wow! Write it up for the 'Qwill Pen' column!" Junior suggested with his boyish enthusiasm.

"That's my intention eventually, after I've had a chance to sort out my impressions. But I came in to compliment you on the obit, Junior. A beautiful piece of copy! We're sending clips to Irma's friends in Scotland . . . How about the local scene? Any momentous news in Moose County?"

"Well, we're carrying a series of ads on the liquidation of Dr. Hal's estate. Melinda's selling everything in a tag sale. I hope she rakes in some dough, because she needs it. After that, the house will go up for sale, and we'll have another empty mansion on Goodwinter Boulevard."

"Did you attend Irma's funeral?" Qwilleran asked.

"Roger covered it, but I didn't go. The cortege watchers counted forty-eight cars in the procession to the cemetery."

"I hear there was some kind of argument about the disposition of the remains."

"Oh, you heard about that? Melinda said they'd had a doctor/patient discussion about living wills. She said Irma preferred cremation and no funeral. Mrs. Hasselrich wanted to go along with her daughter's wishes, but her husband—with his legal mind-set, you know—said it wasn't in writing. So Irma was buried in the family plot with full obsequies—eulogies, bagpipe, tenor soloist, and marching band. You know how Pickax loves a big funeral production!"

Qwilleran said, "I ought to write a column on living wills."

"Can you rip off a piece on Scotland for Wednesday? Your devoted readers are waiting to hear about your trip."

"We saw a lot of castles. I'll see if I can write a thousand words on castles without having to think too much," Qwilleran promised as he started out the door.

Walking home from the newspaper office, he let his mind wander from castles to the baronial mansions on Goodwinter Boulevard. The only solution to the local problem, as he envisioned it, would be rezoning . . . or a bomb . . . or an earthquake, and the old-timers in Pickax would prefer either of the latter to rezoning. He was walking along Main Street toward Park Circle when a car in a southbound lane caught his attention. It had what he thought was a Massachusetts license plate, its light color like a white flag among the dusky, dusty local plates. But it was not the old maroon car he had seen and suspected at the time of the prowler scare. It was a tan car, and it was soon lost in traffic. He thought, It could be the same guy in a new car; it could be the same car with a new paint job.

Qwilleran felt it wise to alert Polly, if he could do so without alarming her, and when he reached the library he went in, nodded to the friendly clerks, and climbed the stairs to the mezzanines. She was sitting in her glass-enclosed office, listening sympathetically to a young clerk who was pregnant. The young woman left immediately when her boss's special friend appeared in the doorway.

"Anything new?" Polly asked eagerly.

"I had a long telephone conversation with Katie," Qwilleran said, "and it appears her brother's name is in fact Gow. She was surprised he hadn't notified her of Irma's death—or so she said . . . By the way, did you and Irma ever discuss living wills? Or last wishes? Or anything like that?"

"No. She never mentioned death or illness. Why do you ask?"

"I thought I might write a column on living wills. It's a hot topic right now. When you two got together, what did you talk about, anyway? Besides me," he added to give the discussion a light touch.

Her smile was mocking, but her reply was serious. "We talked about my problems at the library . . . and her work at the facility . . . and clothes. She had a great interest in fashion. And naturally we talked about birds. Irma's life list included the Kirtland's warbler, the red-necked grebe, and the white-winged scoter. She had traveled around the country on bird-counts."

Polly stopped and regarded him wistfully, and he squirmed in his chair, knowing she would expect him to go birding in Irma's place. Clearing his throat to signal a change of subject, he asked casually, "Have you noticed any more suspicious characters around town since we returned?"

"Well . . . no . . . I haven't really been looking."

"In times like these a woman should keep her eyes open and her wits about her, no matter where she is."

"Oh, dear! I suppose you're right, but it sounds so threatening!"

He avoided pursuing the unpleasant subject but tossed off a parting reminder to be careful, with no mention of the tan car with a Massachusetts plate. Later in the afternoon he reported it to Nick Bamba, however. Nick had an eagle eye for anything automotive: car makes and models, license plates, bumper stickers, drivers, and even the driving habits of individual motorists.

When Nick arrived to deliver his wife's typing, his first words were, "I see you've got a new car."

"Not new, just different," Qwilleran said. "My old one conked out, and I hate to let Gippel skin me on a new model. The prices are outrageous. My first car, when I was sixteen, was $150."

"How come you got a white one?"

"Does it look like a diaper service? It's all they had on Gippel's lot—that is, the only car where the floor of the backseat would accommodate the cats' commode . . . Nick, how would you like a wee dram of Scotch, hand-carried from the distillery for a moment such as this?"

"Sure would, but don't make it too wee."

They sat in the lounge area, Nick sipping Scotch on the rocks, Qwilleran sipping white grape juice, and both of them dipping into bowls of Mildred Hanstable's homemade sesame sticks. Then the Siamese started parading in front of them. Whenever the Bambas visited the barn, Koko and Yum Yum made themselves highly visible, walking back and forth languorously, pivoting and posing like models on a fashion-show runway.

"So what did you think of Scotland?" Nick asked.

"The Western Isles and Highlands are fascinating," Qwilleran told him. "The landscape is almost spooky, with a haunting melancholy in spite of all the tourists and backpackers."

"How were the country inns?"

"Pleasant, hospitable, comfortable. The food was different, but good. Have you and Lori given any more thought to opening a bed-and-breakfast?"

"We talk about it all the time. With the tourist business increasing, we think we should act now and get in on the ground floor, but it'll take a lot of nerve to quit my good job with the state."

"Is the tourist season long enough to make it worthwhile?"

"Right now there's a seven-month season for boating, camping, hunting, and fishing, and there's talk about developing a winter sports program."

"May I touch up your drink, Nick?"

"No, thanks. One's enough. It's really smooth. Did you see them making it?"

"Not exactly. This stuff has been lying around in a cask for fifteen years."

The Siamese were still making themselves conspicuous, and Yum Yum carried something in her jaws and laid it at Nick's feet.

"Hey, what's this?" he asked.

Qwilleran said, "It's an emery board. She was stealing them from our cat-sitter, and I keep finding them around the house. You should be flattered that she's parting with one of her treasures."

"Thanks, baby," Nick said, leaning over to scratch her ears. "If we open a country inn, Qwill, we're going to permit pets. I don't know how practical it'll be, but we'll work it out somehow."

"Good for you! When I drove to the mountains earlier this year, I stopped at a motel that actually provides an overnight cat for guests who don't have their own. They do a brisk business at two dollars per cat, per night."

"Lori and I never knew why you canceled that trip," Nick said.

Confidentially, Qwilleran explained the prowler episode. "I don't want this to go any further," he said, "but I had reason to believe he wanted to grab Polly and hold her for ransom."

"No! You don't mean it! Did the police do anything about it?"

"Brodie offered her protection, and I came home immediately. The prowler had a wild beard, and I saw a young man of that description at the library, acting suspiciously. He drove an old maroon car with a Massachusetts plate. Later, the state police saw him leaving the county, and there's been no further sighting—until today."

"What happened today?"

"I saw a car with a Massachusetts plate, and they're rare around here, if not virtually unknown."

"You're right about that," said Nick. "I hardly ever see a New England car. Funny, isn't it?"

"This was not the original maroon car, but it had the original bushy beard behind the wheel. I didn't catch the license number."

"I'll watch for it." Nick's eye had been sharpened by his job at the prison.

"It's a tan car. Try to get the number. Brodie ran a check on the previous vehicle. It's registered to one Charles Edward Martin."

"Will do, Qwill. Now I've got to get home to dinner. Here are your letters to sign. Anything to go?"

"Only this." Qwilleran handed him a small white box with CRM on the cover. "A souvenir of Scotland for Lori."

"Gee, thanks. She really likes that cape you brought her from the mountains." Nick had to wade through a tangle of legs, tails, and undulating bodies on his way to the door. "And thanks for the Scotch. It's good stuff!"

Qwilleran had still another gift to deliver that day, and he walked downtown for the third time. The three commercial blocks of Main Street constituted a stone canyon. In the nineteenth century, the surrounding countryside had been quarried to pave Main Street and build the stores and civic buildings. Squeezed between the imitation forts, temples, and castles was the Old English storefront housing Amanda's Studio of Interior Design. When he walked into the studio, he was greeted by Fran Brodie, who was always as chic and personable as her boss was dowdy and cranky.

"How's Amanda?" he asked. "Did she recover from the tour?"

"Oh, yes," Fran replied with an airy wave of the hand. "Dr. Zoller repaired her denture, and she's once more her old, sweet, smiling self. She left on a buying trip this morning. What did you think of Scotland?"

"Ask me what I think of tourists! We travel to a foreign country and never really leave home. We take our own egos, preferences, hobbies, dislikes, and conversation and never really appreciate what we see and experience. In Glasgow I went exploring at my own pace and enjoyed it more. You'd like the Charles Rennie Mackintosh exhibits, Fran." He handed her a small white box. "Here's what the contemporary artists are doing in the Mackintosh tradition. I thought you'd like it."

"It's lovely! It's Art Nouveau! What is this unusual stone?"

"A Scottish cairngorm."

She pinned it on the lapel of her bronze-toned suit and gave him a theatrical kiss. "You're a darling! Will you have coffee?"

"Not this time, thanks. It's late, and you're probably ready to close up. I just wanted to ask when you start rehearsals for *Macbeth*. How are you going to get the show on the boards by the last week in September?"

"We're used to chaos in community theatre, Qwill, but it always works out by opening night. Dwight did the casting and blocking before he left, and I worked with the supporting cast while you were away—the witches, the bleeding captain, the porter, and so forth. Derek Cuttlebrink is doing the porter in act two, scene three. *Knock, knock, knock! Who's there?* He'll provide our comic relief."

Before leaving, Qwilleran said, "About that fragment of the Mackintosh kilt—I'll take it. Now that I've seen the battlefield at Culloden, it has some meaning. Go ahead and have it framed . . . and I may see you at one of the rehearsals," he said as he left the studio.

On the sidewalk he stopped abruptly. Parked at the curb was a tan car that had not been in evidence when he arrived a few minutes before. He walked behind it and wrote down the license number. Then, hurrying back into the studio just as Fran was preparing to lock the door, he demanded, "What's that tan car parked out in front?"

"Is he there again?" she said indignantly. "He's supposed to park in the rear. I'm going to complain to the hotel."

"Who is he?"

"The new chef they've just hired. God knows they needed one! The menu hadn't been changed for forty years."

"Where did they get him? Where's he from?"

"Fall River."

"Fall River, Massachusetts? That's not exactly the gourmet capital of the east coast!"

"No, but he's offering things like chicken cordon bleu instead of pig hocks and sauerkraut, and that's an improvement."

"Does he have a beard?" Qwilleran asked.

"Yes, a shaggy one. He wears it in a hairnet to cook."

"What does he give as his name, do you know?"

Fran said hesitantly, "I think it's Carl. I'm not sure. You seem unusually curious about him."

"May I use your phone?"

"Sure. Go ahead. We'll put it on your bill," she said archly.

"As we say in Scotland," he admonished her, "don't be *pawky!*"

He called the police station.

Nine

The telephone at the apple barn rang constantly Tuesday morning, keeping Koko in a frenzy; he considered it his responsibility to monitor all calls. The barrage started with thank-yous from Lori Bamba and Hixie Rice, each of whom had to be told the significance of CRM, the Art Nouveau background of the peacock feather, and the name of the semiprecious stone.

Then came a report from Chief Brodie: The tan car with the Massachusetts license was registered to one Karl Oskar Klaus of Fall River. He spelled the name. Klaus was the new chef at the hotel, he said.

"Do you know anything about him?" Qwilleran's attitude was challenging.

"Only that he hasn't robbed the bank yet," Brodie quipped. "What do you have against Massachusetts?"

"Nothing. In fact, my mother was born there. I'm a second-generation codfish."

Next, a weary traveler phoned from Lockmaster.

"Welcome home, Bushy," Qwilleran said. "How was your flight?"

"Not too bad. As soon as I catch up on my sleep, I'll start developing my black-and-white film. I think I've got some good shots."

"Hear any news about the jewel theft before you left?"

"Nope. Nobody was feeling too sorry for Grace Utley. It's hard to shed tears over lost diamonds when all you have is a $50 watch."

Qwilleran said, "I'm looking forward to seeing your pictures, Bushy. When will you have prints? Bring them up here and I'll buy lunch."

"In a couple of days, okay? And Qwill . . . I'll be wanting to talk to you about a problem."

"What kind of problem?"

"Personal." He sounded discouraged for a young man who was usually so exuberant.

The next call came from Arch Riker. "When did you get in?" Qwilleran asked him.

"Three o'clock this morning! How long have you been home? Three days? And you haven't written a line of copy!"

"Sounds as if you're at the office. Go home and go to bed, Arch. Everything's under control. Junior's saving me a hole on page two for tomorrow. Have I ever missed a deadline?"

"Another thing!" Riker shouted into the phone. "I came home on the same flight with Grace Utley—in the same row, for God's sake! And I wish you'd call her and get her off my back." For a veteran deskman, usually so placid, this was a surprising outburst.

"What does she want?"

"She wants to publish a book about her teddy bear collection, and she wants someone to do the writing and editing. You could do it. You don't have anything else to do."

"You must be kidding, Arch."

"She'll pay. You could pick up a few bucks."

"Sure. Just what I need," Qwilleran said. "Go home and sleep it off, chum. You're pooped after that long flight, or *ramfeezled,* as the Scots say."

"At least talk to her and get me off the hook. I've got a paper to publish."

Qwilleran muttered a protest but agreed to follow through, after giving her a day to recover from jet lag. He promised to get rid of her in one way or another.

"Try murder!" Riker said and slammed down the receiver.

Before writing his column on castles, Qwilleran refreshed his memory by listening to a tape that he recorded after bumping his head on a stone lintel.

"There are said to be more than a thousand castles in Scotland, some with very low doorways. They were first built in medieval times by conquerors of Scotland, as fortresses from which to rule the rebellious natives. A livable castle consisted of an impregnable wall as much as fourteen feet thick, a ditch or moat, a tower called a keep, an iron gate called a yett, an inner courtyard, and housing for the conqueror's family, retainers, and soldiery. This stronghold also had a pit for prisoners, and gun-loops and battlements from which defenders could hold the fort, as the saying goes, and pour boiling oil on attackers.

"Many of these historic castles now lie in ruins. What is more stirring to the imagination than a noble ruin on a mountaintop, silhouetted against the sky . . . or on a cliff overlooking the sea . . . or on a lonely island, reflected in the silvery water of a loch? Other castles have been restored as museums or palatial residences whose owners admit the public for a fee.

"Today we visited the island where Macbeth was buried in 1057" . . . (Sound of knocking.) "Now who the devil is that?"

(Pause.)

"How do you feel, lover? You seemed rather quiet during dinner."

"After conversing with the same crowd for five days, I'm running out of things to say and also the patience to listen."

"May I come in? I want to check your pulse and temperature. Sit down over there, please."

As soon as Melinda's voice issued from the player, Koko began protesting in a piercing monotone. After three years' absence, she still aroused his antagonism, the cause of which had never been clear. Had he objected to her perfume? Did he detect her hospital connection? Anything associated with a hospital was on Koko's hate list. No, more likely he had sensed her motives; Koko was dedicated to keeping Qwilleran single.

Qwilleran retired to his studio to write a thousand words on castles, and the Siamese retired to some secret hideaway. Before he left the barn to deliver his copy, however, he made a routine check. He never left home without knowing their whereabouts. This time they were not sleeping on the chairs in the lounge area, not huddled on the fireplace cube or the refrigerator, not hiding under a rug or behind the books on the shelves. They were in one of those voids in another time warp into which cats are able to vanish at will. It happened frequently, and the only way to rout them out was to shout the secret password: *Treat!* Then they would materialize from nowhere to claim their handful of crunchy cereal or morsel of cheese. It was the only guaranteed method, and to ensure its efficacy he never used the T word unless he meant to deliver.

So Qwilleran yelled "Treat!" and they suddenly appeared in the kitchen. "I'm going out," he told them as he dispensed their snack. "Don't answer the phone if it rings."

Being on a short deadline, he used the quick route downtown, through the woods that gave the apple barn its countrified seclusion, and he was able to deliver his copy to Junior Goodwinter in time for Wednesday's edition.

"Is this your piece on castles?" the editor asked. "I've been waiting to read it. Everyone likes castles."

"While churning it out," Qwilleran said, "I figured out how to solve the Goodwinter Boulevard problem. Turn it into an avenue of castles and sell tickets to tourists. The owners can reserve seven or eight rooms for their families, while the public tramps through the other ten or fifteen at $5 a head. The revenue from admissions will take care of taxes and maintenance."

"I wish you weren't only kidding," Junior said.

"Do you know anything about the new chef at the hotel? Have you eaten there since they hired him?"

"No, but I hear he's pretty good, although *anyone* would be an improvement."

Using Junior's phone, Qwilleran called Polly at the library. "Are you feeling adventurous? Would you like to have dinner at the hotel? They have a new chef."

"That's what I heard. Is he good? What is his background?"

"He's from Fall River, Massachusetts." Facetiously he added, "They say he's a legend in Fall River."

It had to be an early dinner, because Polly had scheduled one of her frequent committee meetings at the library, and the members were gathering at seven-thirty. He often wondered how a small library in a small town could keep so many committees busy with whatever it was they did. Meanwhile he killed time by listening to a few more of his Scottish tapes. The Siamese listened, too. When their dinner hour was approaching, their empty stomachs stimulated their interest in everything that Qwilleran did.

One tape launched him on a new train of thought and aroused certain suspicions. It was a conversation with Lyle Compton toward the end of the tour. Lyle was saying:

"Too bad we didn't see any smugglers' caves. I used to read about Dick Turpin, the notorious smuggler and highwayman, but Irma never mentioned smuggling at all. I wonder why. At one time in history it was a national industry. The ragged coastline, you know, with all those hidden coves and sheltering islands, was ideal for bringing in contraband by ship."

"What did they smuggle, Lyle?"

"Luxury items like rum, wine, tea, tobacco, lace, diamonds, and so on. From Scottish coastal villages they were transported to major cities in Britain by wagon and stagecoach—disguised as something else, of course. It drove the government crazy, but it must have been an exciting operation. They had a network of tunnels and hiding places, including caves along the shore. A whole string of inns was involved."

"With a great natural resource like the coast of Scotland, you can't tell me that they're not exploiting it today."

"You're right, Qwill! Probably for drug smuggling."

Click.

There was no vocal response from Koko during this tape, although his ears twitched whenever he heard Qwilleran's voice. Then it was five-thirty and time to pick up Polly at the library.

Qwilleran was wearing his new suede sports coat ordered from Scottie's Men's Store before the tour. He had never spent that much money on any item of clothing, but Scottie had assumed his Scots brogue and talked him into it. It was camel beige, and he wore it with brown trousers. Polly said he looked wonderful. She was wearing a black and yellow kilt purchased in Inverness.

"It's a MacLeod tartan, but it goes with my black blazer," she explained.

"So much for clan loyalty," he said.

The "New" Pickax Hotel had been built in 1935 after the Old Pickax Hotel burned down, and now the locals were saying that it was time for another fire. In 1935 the public rooms had been furnished in Early Modern—not comfortable, not attractive, but sturdy. Recently a runaway snowplow had barged into the front of the building, demolishing the lobby but not the sturdy oak furniture.

Qwilleran and his guest were the first to arrive in the dining room, and the hostess seated them at a window table overlooking Main Street. He remarked, "I hear you have a new chef."

"He's completely redone the menu," she said. "It's very exciting! Would you like something from the bar?"

After ordering dry sherry for Polly and Squunk water with a twist for himself, Qwilleran scanned the menu card. Only a diner familiar with the hotel for the last forty years would consider the selection exciting: French onion soup instead of bean, grilled salmon steak instead of fish and chips, chicken cordon bleu instead of chicken and dumplings, and roast prime rib instead of swiss steak.

When the waiter brought the drinks, Qwilleran asked, "Is the chicken cordon bleu prepared in the kitchen, or is it one of those frozen, prefabricated artifacts shipped in from Ontario?"

"No, sir. The chef makes it himself," the waiter assured him.

Qwilleran decided to try it, but Polly thought the ham and cheese stuffing would violate her diet; she ordered the salmon.

The previous cooks had merely dished up the food; the new chef arranged the plates: parsley, boiled potatoes, broccoli, and a cherry tomato with the salmon; broccoli, a cherry tomato, and steamed zucchini straws with the chicken cordon bleu.

"I see they've gone all-out," Qwilleran commented.

Surveying the neat bundle on his plate, he plunged his knife and fork into the chicken, and a geyser of melted butter squirted fifteen inches into the air, landing on his lapel and narrowly missing his left eye.

"This isn't what I ordered!" he said indignantly as he brushed the greasy streak with his napkin. "Waiter! Waiter!"

"It's chicken Kiev!" Polly cried.

Qwilleran said to the young man, "Is this supposed to be chicken cordon bleu?"

"Yes, sir."

"Well, it's not! It's something else. Take it back to the kitchen and tell Karl Oskar I want chicken cordon bleu."

"Your coat is ruined!" Polly said in dismay. "Do you think the cleaner can get it out?"

The waiter soon returned with the plate. "The chef says this *is* chicken cordon bleu, like it says on the menu."

Blowing furiously into his moustache, Qwilleran said, "It may be so described in Fall River, but it's chicken Kiev in the rest of the civilized world! . . . Come on, Polly. We're going to the Old Stone Mill." To the bewildered hostess he said, "I'm sending you the bill for a new suede coat, and if I hadn't ducked, you'd be paying for an eye, too."

Over dry sherry and Squunk water at their favorite restaurant, the pair tried to relax, but Qwilleran was in a bad humor, and he plunged recklessly into a subject that had been on his mind for a couple of days, his suspicions augmented by the tape he had heard before coming to dinner. "You know, Polly," he blurted out, "I'm beginning to wonder if Irma's death could have been murder."

Polly recoiled in horror. "Qwill! What makes you say that? Who would do such a thing? And why?"

"How well did you really know Irma?"

She hesitated. "She was just a casual acquaintance until recently, when we started to go birding together. Out there on the riverbank or in the wetlands, where it was quiet and peaceful, it was easy to exchange confidences—"

"Did she ever tell you what she did on her frequent trips to Scotland?"

"Not in detail. I know she went birding in the islands. She always mentioned puffin birds and the red-necked phalarope—"

"Hmmm," he murmured cynically, thinking that bird-watchers on the islands would make good lookouts, especially if equipped with radios. "I hate to say this, Polly, but I always received the impression that Irma was hiding something behind a somewhat artificial facade, and now it occurs to me that the Bonnie Scots Tour may have been a cover for something else—a scam that backfired."

"*What!*" Polly's throat flushed. "What in God's name are you talking about?" She pushed her sherry away in an angry gesture.

"For centuries the Scottish coastline has lent itself to smuggling. Today the contraband is probably drugs."

Shocked, Polly demanded, "Are you suggesting that Irma was involved in *smuggling drugs?* Why, that's unthinkable!"

Qwilleran thought, Irma was fanatically devoted to raising money for charity, and fanaticism makes strange bedfellows. He said, "She never told you anything about her friends in Scotland. What about this man she sneaked away with every night—always in wild, secluded country where the inns had no names? What were they doing? And did something go wrong? He could have slipped her a drug because she became a threat. He had a police record. Obviously he was planning to steal the jewels. Did Irma know about that?"

Polly snatched the napkin from her lap and threw it on the table. "How can you make such malicious assumptions when she's not here to defend herself? It was a heart attack! Melinda said so!"

"Melinda could be wrong."

"I refuse to listen to this assault on Irma's integrity!"

"I'm sorry, Polly. Perhaps Irma was an innocent victim, murdered because she could identify Bruce after he committed his crime . . . Finish your drink, and we'll ask for the soup course."

"No!" she said bitterly. "You have your dinner. I'll wait in the lobby."

He signaled the waitress. "Check, please, and cancel our order."

They drove back to town in silence, but he could feel the waves of anger emanating from the passenger seat. When they reached the library, Polly stepped out of the car and said a curt thank you.

At the barn, he was met by two alert Siamese with questioning tails, as if they felt the tension in the air. Now Qwilleran felt hungry, as well as uneasy about the scene with Polly and indignant about his suede coat. He threw it on a kitchen chair and searched the refrigerator for the makings of a sandwich. Yum Yum, as if she wanted to comfort him, presented him with an emery board.

"Thank you, sweetheart," he said.

As he swallowed his sandwich and gulped his coffee, he admitted to himself that he had been tactless in linking Polly's friend with illegal activity. Yet, there was something about the events in the Highlands that made his moustache bristle, and he was floundering in his search for a clue.

He played some more tapes, hoping for enlightenment:

> "At the inn where we're lodged tonight, the fireplace mantel is draped with a fringed scarf; the lamp shades are fringed; and there are rugs thrown over the sofas—all very cozy. Blankets are used for draw draperies over the windows, which should say something about winters in the Highlands. The mantel shelf is adorned with the usual clock, some pieces of china, and a live but apathetic cat. The cats in the Scottish Highlands are not as nervous as American cats. They walk in slow motion, stretch lazily instead of purposefully, and spend their time resting on wharf pilings, fences, doorsteps, windowsills, rooftops, or fireplace mantels."

It surprised Qwilleran that the Siamese failed to respond to this segment of the tape. There was something about the sound of the word "cat" that usually commanded their immediate attention. When they were sleeping, he had only to whisper "cat" and their ears would twitch. The tapes rolled on:

> "Today I did my neighborly duty on the bus, sitting with Zella in the morning and Grace in the afternoon. When we're on the road, Zella looks out the window and enjoys the scenery. Grace never stops talking about life back home. She's an encyclopedia of Pickax scandal, and what she doesn't know, she invents. That, at least, is her reputation. It appears that the only Moose County families without skeletons in the closet are the Chisholms and the Utleys, and even the Utleys have a few bones rattling under the stairs."

Qwilleran kept glancing at his watch. He half expected Polly to phone and say, "Qwill, I'm afraid I overreacted." He thought she would call about nine o'clock, after the committee meeting, but the telephone was exasperatingly silent.

> "After dinner tonight Irma did her usual vanishing act, and Larry, Melinda, and Dwight went into the garden to work on *Macbeth*. I'd hear Larry's magnificent voice: *'Is this a dagger which I see before me?'* He'd repeat it several times with different emphasis. Or I'd hear Melinda screaming, *'Out, damned spot! Out, I say!'* How do these intrepid actors endure the midges that swarm up out of the bushes in millions?"

It was a disappointing session for Qwilleran, with no clues on the tapes and no pertinent comments from Koko. Neither cat, he now realized, had been in evidence for some time—not, in fact, since he had returned home. Where were they? Reluctant to overdo the T word, he wandered about the barn, searching all levels, calling their names, hoping to find one or the other. No luck! And where, he asked himself, was his suede coat?

Ten

When Qwilleran found his suede sports coat, he had a wild impulse to phone Polly and relate the incredible circumstances: how he had found it under a kitchen chair . . . how the suede surface was furred with cat hair . . . and how the streak of melted butter had completely disappeared. There was not even a trace of it! The left-hand lapel was now more roughly sueded than the right, but the grease spot was gone.

Before he could pick up the phone, however, he thought about their disagreement at the restaurant. They'd had spats in the past, which were always resolved when one or the other decided the triumph was not worth the battle. This time he was in no mood to wave the white flag. She should have been more understanding, he thought. She should have known he was blowing off steam after the infuriating chicken episode. She was well acquainted with his reckless surmises when faced with unanswered questions. Furthermore, he had apologized—somewhat—in the restaurant, and he was in no hurry to make further amends.

Perhaps there was an element of suppressed guilt lurking under his rationalizations, calling for atonement, and that was why he telephoned the Chisholm sisters the next morning with such a pretense of bonhomie. Grace Utley answered.

"Good morning," he said in his most ingratiating tone. "This is your erstwhile traveling companion, Jim Qwilleran. I trust you two lovely ladies had a pleasant journey home."

"Oh, Mr. Qwilleran! It's so nice of you to call!" she said, with excitement heightening the rasp in her voice. "We had an enjoyable flight. Mr. Riker was our seatmate, and he's a most interesting man."

"He enjoyed your company, too. That's why he asked me to call. He says you have an idea for a book that you want to discuss."

"About our teddy bear collection . . . yes! He was quite excited about the idea. Would you be willing to help us? I know you're a very busy man . . ."

"Not so busy that I'd turn down a stimulating challenge! I'd like to explore the possibilities—perhaps this afternoon."

"So soon?" she crowed with delight. "Then you must come for lunch, dear heart. Zella is a wonderful cook."

"I'm sure she is," he replied, "but I have a previous engagement. How about two o'clock?"

"Then we'll have tea," she said with finality. "We brought some shortbread from Edinburgh. Do you like Scotch shortbread?"

"My favorite treat!" If Qwilleran was atoning, he was doing it with panache.

To fortify himself for the appointment he had a good lunch at the Old Stone Mill—crab bisque, a Reuben sandwich, pumpkin pie—and before driving to Goodwinter Boulevard he picked up a bunch of mums at the florist shop. Mums were Moose County's all-purpose flower for weddings, funerals, and table centerpieces. On second thought, he bought two bunches, one rust and one yellow.

The sisters lived in one of the larger stone mansions on the boulevard, next door to the residence of the late Dr. Halifax Goodwinter. The Chisholms and the Utleys had been among the founders of Moose County. Yet, like many of the old families, they were disappearing as the later generations stayed single or remained childless or moved away after marrying outsiders from such remote areas as Texas and the District of Columbia. It was said that Grace Utley had two daughters Down Below, who would have nothing to do with her. So the widow and her unmarried sister lived by themselves in the big house. According to Junior Goodwinter, they were among the old-timers who would fight rezoning to their last breath.

Upon arriving, Qwilleran had hardly touched finger to doorbell before the door was flung open.

"Welcome to Teddy Bear Castle!" cried Grace in her abrasive voice, while Zella hovered in the background, wringing her hands with excitement. She was wearing her gold teddy bear with ruby eyes. Grace, bereft of everything but what she had on her person at the time of the theft, was reduced to a few gold chains and a frog brooch paved with emeralds.

With a courteous bow Qwilleran presented his flowers, rust for Grace and yellow for Zella, who squealed as if she had never before received a floral token.

"So good of you to come!" said Grace. "Zella, dear, put these in water." Then grandly she waved an arm about the foyer. "How do you like our little friends, Mr. Qwilleran?"

Being familiar with boulevard architecture, he knew what to expect: grand staircase, massive chandelier, carved woodwork, stained glass, oversize furniture. But he was unprepared for the hundreds of shoe-button eyes that stared at him—charmingly, impishly, crazily—

from tabletops, cabinets, chairseats, and even the treads of the wide staircase.

"We're collectors," Grace explained with pride.

"So I see." Feeling a presence behind him, he turned to find a plush animal somewhat larger than himself.

"That's Woodrow, our watch bear," said Grace.

"How many do you own?"

"Zella, dear, how many do we have now?" she shouted toward the kitchen.

"One thousand, eight hundred, and sixty-two," came the small voice.

"One thousand, eight hundred, and sixty-two . . . yes. Zella has them catalogued for insurance purposes." She led Qwilleran to a locked vitrine in the drawing room. "This is Theodore, our button-in-ear Steiff. One just like him sold for $80,000."

Other bears sat on chairs, windowsills, the fireplace mantel, and the grand piano.

"That's Ignace on the piano bench—Zella's special friend. She took him to Scotland. I took Ulysses, the one on the rocking horse," Grace said. "Fortunately Ulysses was traveling in Zella's luggage."

Other bears sat at the dining room table with a full setting of china, crystal, and silver at each place and a napkin on each lap. Several, wearing eyeglasses, were reading books in the library or working at the desk. Throughout the house they were arranged in tableaux: playing croquet, trimming a Christmas tree, sailing toy boats in a tub of water, wheeling a baby bear in a stroller, gardening with a toy wheelbarrow. Although they all seemed to have the same perky ears, felt snout, stitched mouth, and shoe-button eyes, they had individual facial expressions and personalities. Many were in costume. Some squeaked, or laughed, or blinked battery-operated eyes.

Qwilleran, who had seen everything as a newsman Down Below, had never seen anything like this.

"Zella, dear, you may serve the tea now," Grace said as the tour ended.

A few distinguished bears were invited to join the party. They had their own tiny cups and saucers, and Zella poured tea for them.

Grace said to Qwilleran, as sweetly as she could with her rasping voice, "We're going to name our next little friend after you, and you must attend the christening party."

Asking permission to use a tape recorder, he asked the routine questions: Why do you collect bears? When did you start? Which have you had the longest? Where do you find them? Who makes the costumes? How do you keep them from catching dust? Do you have a good security system?

"The best!" said Grace. "We also have a watchman living in the caretaker's apartment over the garage, and his wife vacuums the bears in rotation."

Meanwhile, Qwilleran drank tea without pleasure and ate shortbread dutifully, asking himself, What am I doing here? . . . Are the women crazy? . . . Are they pulling my leg?

With his third cup of tea he made a desperate effort to change the subject. "Well, it looks as if you're going to have some excitement next door—the liquidation sale."

Grace erupted in indignation. "It's absolutely dreadful! Zella and I are leaving town until it's over. No one should be allowed to have a tag sale in a neighborhood like this! How will they handle the crowds? Where will they park? Everyone in Moose County adored Dr. Hal and will want to buy something as a memento. I'll tell you one thing: Dr. Hal would never have permitted such a sale! But his daughter is another breed. She does as she pleases without regard for anyone else. The entire contents of the house should have been moved to the Bid-a-Bit auction barn."

"Why didn't Dr. Melinda do that?" he inquired.

"Why? Because she can make more money with a tag sale on the premises!"

"Did you know the Goodwinter family well?"

"All my life! . . . Zella, dear, this tea is cold. Would you bring a fresh pot?" When her sister had left the room, she said in a hushed voice, "Zella could have married Dr. Hal, but she missed her chance by being too meek, and he had the misfortune to marry a woman with bad blood. Mrs. Goodwinter's father died of a disease that the family never mentions, and her brother embezzled money in Illinois and went to prison. Melinda was their firstborn, spoiled from the cradle. Their son—we always knew he'd be the black sheep of the family. He finally left town and was later killed in a car accident. Everyone said it was a blessing in disguise because he was an embarrassment to his father and a worry to his mother, who was a chronic invalid."

Before making his escape, Qwilleran asked, "Would you ladies allow the *Moose County Something* to photograph your collection for a feature story?"

"We'd be flattered, wouldn't we, Zella? That is, Mr. Qwilleran, if you'll promise to write the article yourself. You write so well!"

"I think that could be arranged. And now, thank you for a memorable adventure and delicious tea."

Blushing furiously, the shy sister stepped forward, saying, "This is for you!" She handed him a brown velvet teddy bear, hardly three inches high.

"Oh, no! I wouldn't think of robbing your collection," he said.

"But we want you to have it," Grace insisted. "Please accept it."

"His name is Tiny Tim," Zella said.

With Tiny Tim in his pocket, Qwilleran left the house, saying to himself, *Whew!*

Back home at the barn, his first move was to phone Riker at the office. He said, "Arch, you owe me one! I've just spent a tedious afternoon with the Chisholm sisters, drinking tea and eating shortbread, and they want me to be godfather to their next teddy bear."

"What about their idea for a book?"

"They never mentioned a book. They just wanted someone to visit and be impressed by their collection, but I think we should do a story. Send a good photographer over there, like John Bushland, and I'll bet the wire services will pick it up!"

While he was on the phone, the Siamese were rifling his jacket pocket. They knew instinctively that something new had arrived.

"Oh, no, you don't!" he scolded when he finished the phone call. They were sinking their fangs into the spongy body. He hid Tiny Tim in the kitchen drawer where he always tossed his car keys.

Then he checked the answering machine; there was still no call from Polly, all the more reason why he wanted to consult Melinda. If she agreed that Irma's attack could have been drug-induced, he would be in the clear. The entire cast was scheduled to rehearse that night; he could get an answer from her during a break, without personal complications.

The K Theatre, built within the fieldstone shell of the former Klingenschoen mansion, was small—only 300 seats—but it was large enough for the Pickax Theatre Club. The auditorium was a steeply raked amphitheatre with a thrust stage, and there was a gracious lobby. When Qwilleran arrived there Wednesday night, he found Larry Lanspeak in the lobby, bent over the drinking fountain.

"Your beard looks promising," he told the actor.

Larry rubbed his chin. "In two more weeks it should be good enough for an eleventh-century Scottish king."

"How's the play shaping up?"

"Not bad. Not bad at all! When we were away, Fran worked with the supporting cast in the eleven scenes where Melinda and I don't appear, and she did a good job. This is our first full-cast rehearsal."

Larry returned to the stage, and Qwilleran slipped into the back row. Some of the actors were draped over the front seats, awaiting their scenes. Dwight was in front of the stage directing performers who were running lines without the book. One of them, playing a messenger, was making his exit, and Lady Macbeth was saying, *"Unsex me here, and fill me from the crown to the toe top full of direst cruelty!"*

"Hold it!" the director said. "Bring the messenger back, and take it again, Melinda, from *Thou'rt mad to say it!* Give it some *fire!"*

They repeated the scene. Then Larry made his entrance. *"My dearest love, Duncan comes here tonight!"*

Melinda replied, *"And when goes hence?"*

"Tomorrow—" Larry interrupted his own line, saying, "Dwight, how do I play this? Is Macbeth honored that the king is going to stay under his roof? Or is he already planning to kill him? What is he thinking at this moment?"

The director said, "Lady Macbeth plants the idea of murder in his head with her line, *And when goes hence?* That means, Melinda, that you've got to give her question some powerful innuendo. *And—when—goes—hence?* The audience should feel a chill up the spine . . . Got it, everybody?"

"Got it," said Larry. "She plants the idea, and I pause before *Tomorrow.* In that split second the audience realizes the king will never leave the castle alive."

Qwilleran was impressed with Dwight's direction and told him so during the break, intercepting him on the way to the drinking fountain.

"Thanks," he said. "Larry's a joy to direct, let me say that. Now I know why he has such a great reputation in community theatre. I'd heard about him in Iowa before I knew there was any such place as Pickax."

"Will the show be ready by the last Thursday in the month?"

"It's got to be! The tickets are printed."

Carol walked up the aisle to get a drink of water, and Qwilleran said to her, "Why don't you ask the K Foundation to give you a drinking fountain backstage?"

"Not a bad idea. It would save wear and tear on the aisle carpet . . . Did I hear someone mention tickets?" she asked. "We could use some help in the box office, Qwill. Are you available?"

"If it doesn't require any rare skills or mental acuity."

To Dwight she said, "Qwill lives right behind the theatre—in an apple barn!" Then she went on her way to the lobby.

"I've heard about your barn," the director said. "I'm partial to barns."

"Stop in for a drink some night after rehearsal."

"I'll do that. I'll bring my tin whistle, and you can tell me how you react to my witch music."

There was a whiff of perfume, and Melinda sauntered up the aisle en route to the drinking fountain. "Hi, lover," she said with surprise and pleasure. "What are you doing here?"

Dwight gave a quick look at both of them and drifted away to the lobby.

"Just snooping," Qwilleran said, "but since you're here, I'll ask you a couple of questions. If I write about the liquidation of your father's estate in the 'Qwill Pen' column, will that be okay with you?" He knew it would be, but it was an opener.

"God, yes! Every little bit helps," she said. "I need to sell everything. The preview will be a week from Friday. Would you like a preview of the preview?" she asked teasingly. "Hang around, and I'll take you over to the house when we finish here."

"Thanks, but not tonight," he said.

"Wouldn't you like to see *everything*—without people around?"

He employed the journalist's standard white lie. "Sorry, I have to do some writing on deadline. But before I go, here's one more question. It's about Irma's death. As you probably know by now, the bus driver disappeared after you left, along with Grace Utley's jewels, and Irma was the only one who knew his name or anything about him. It occurred to me that Bruce could have given her some kind of fatal drug to conceal his identity."

"No, lover, it was cardiac arrest, pure and simple," she said with a patronizing smile, "and considering her medical history and the pace of her life, I'm surprised it didn't happen sooner."

Qwilleran persisted. "The police now know the driver has a criminal record, so murder is not beyond the realm of possibility, considering the size of the haul."

Melinda shook her head slowly and wisely. "Sorry to disappoint you, Qwill," she said with a tired, pitying look. "It would have made a good story, and I know you like to uncover foul play, but this was no crime. Trust me." She brightened. "If you would like to go somewhere afterward and talk about it, I could explain. We could have a drink at my apartment—or your barn."

"Another time, when I'm not on deadline," he said. "By the way, your Lady Macbeth is looking good." He turned and was halfway across the lobby before she could react to the weak compliment.

He walked home through the woods, swinging a flashlight and thinking ruefully, So it wasn't murder! Now I suppose I should square things with Polly.

The telephone was ringing when he unlocked the door, and Koko was racing around to inform him of the fact.

"Okay, okay! I'm not deaf!" he yelled at the cat as he snatched the receiver. "Hello? . . . Hi, Nick. I just got in the house. What's up?"

"You know the Massachusetts car you told me about? I saw it!" said Nick triumphantly.

"The tan car? Forget it! It belongs to the new chef at the hotel. He's from Fall River."

"No, not the tan job, Qwill. The original maroon car! It's back in town."

"Where did you see it?"

"I was driving north on the highway to Mooseville, and I saw this car turn west on the unpaved stretch of Ittibittiwassee Road. You know where I mean? The Dimsdale Diner is on the corner."

"I know the road," Qwilleran said. "It leads to Shantytown."

"Yeah, and the car was beat-up like the kind you always see turning into that hell hole."

"Did you follow it?"

"I wanted to, but I was driving a state vehicle and didn't think I should. He'd get the idea he was under surveillance. But I thought you should know, Qwill. Tell Polly to be careful."

"Yes, I will. Thanks, Nick." Qwilleran hung up slowly, his hand lingering on the receiver. So the Boulevard Prowler was back in town! He punched a familiar number on the phone.

It was ten-thirty P.M., and Polly would be winding down, padding around in her blue robe, washing her nylons, doing something with her face and hair. He had been a husband long enough to know all about that routine.

She answered with a businesslike "Yes?"

"Good evening, Polly," he said in his most seductive voice. "How are you this evening?"

"All right," she said stiffly without returning the polite question.

"Was I an unforgivable bore last night?"

After a moment's hesitation, she replied, "You're never a bore, Qwill."

"I'm grateful for small compliments, and I admit it was bad form to bring up a painful subject at the dinner table."

"After what happened to your new coat, I believe you could be excused." She was softening up. "Did you take it to the cleaner?"

"That wasn't necessary. It was chicken-flavored butter, and the cats took care of it. You'd never know anything happened!"

"I don't believe it!"

"It's true."

There was a pause. It was Polly's turn to say something conciliatory. Qwilleran thought he was handling it rather well. Finally she said, "Perhaps I overreacted last night."

"I can't say you weren't justified. It was my fault for pursuing the subject so stubbornly. Blame it on my Scots heritage."

"I know. Your mother was a Mackintosh," she said, adding a light touch to the sober conversation. The Mackintosh connection was a running joke between them.

"Did you have a good day?" he asked.

"Interesting, at best. One of my clerks was rushed to the hospital in labor, and Mr. Tibbitt pressed the wrong button and was trapped in the elevator. We checked out 229 books and 54 cassettes, collected $3.75 in overdue fines, and issued 7 new-reader cards . . . Did you have a good day?"

"I did an assignment for Arch, and earlier this evening I audited a rehearsal at the theatre. Were you out at all tonight?"

"No, I had dinner at home and spent the evening reading and putting my wardrobe in order."

"If you have occasion to leave your apartment after dark, Polly, I'd rather you didn't drive alone. These are changing times. We have to face the fact that strangers are coming into Pickax. If you have an evening engagement, call me and I'll provide chauffeur service."

"Why this sudden concern, Qwill? Has anything happened? If it's because of that prowler last June . . . that was three months ago!"

"It's your neighborhood I worry about," Qwilleran said. "There are so many vacant houses. It behooves you to be careful. Meanwhile, would you like dinner tomorrow night? I'll be on my best behavior."

"The library will be open, and it's my turn to work."

"How about Friday?"

"The Hasselriches invited me to dinner. They're having Irma's favorite rolladen cooked in red wine."

Qwilleran huffed into his moustache. That was twice in one week! Now that she was their "surrogate daughter," they would be monopolizing her time. "Then how about Saturday? We could drive to Lockmaster and have dinner at the Palomino Paddock," he said, one-upping the Hasselriches' rolladen. In a state-wide dining guide the Paddock was rated **** for food and $$$$$ for price.

Polly gasped as he hoped she would. "Oh, that would be delightful!"

"Then it's a date."

There was a pause.

"All's well, then?" he asked gently.

"All's well," she said with feeling.

"À bientôt, Polly."

"À bientôt, dear."

He immediately phoned the Paddock to reserve a good table. It was short notice for the celebrated restaurant, but the mention of his name commanded special consideration even in the next county, the K Foundation having recently funded a swimming pool for the youth center in Lockmaster.

Then he started up the ramp to change into pajamas and slippers. He was halfway to the first balcony when Koko rushed up behind him at a frantic speed and lunged at his legs, throwing him off balance and nearly knocking him to the floor.

"Say! Who do you think you are?" Qwilleran yelled. "A Green Bay linebacker? You could break my neck, you crazy cat!"

Koko, who had bounced off his target, picked himself up and sat on his haunches with head lowered as he licked his paw and passed it over his mask, stopping between licks to stare at the forehead of the man who was scolding him.

Qwilleran passed his own hand over his moustache as he thought, Can he smell Melinda's perfume? I spent two minutes with her, and he knows it! . . . And then he thought, Or is he trying to tell me something? I'm following the wrong scent; he's trying to push me back on track. *What does he want me to do?*

Eleven

The morning after Koko's flying tackle, there was no more domestic violence in the apple barn, but Koko stared at Qwilleran pointedly, as if trying to communicate. Over coffee and a thawed breakfast roll, the man tried to read the cat's message, thoughtfully combing his moustache with his fingertips. Could it be, he wondered, a warning about the Boulevard Prowler? Precognition was one of Koko's rare senses.

In sheer uncertainty mixed with curiosity, Qwilleran drove his car north that morning, turning left at the Dimsdale Diner onto the unpaved extension of Ittibittiwassee Road. This neglected stretch of gravel dead-ended at the abandoned Dimsdale Mine, with its rotting shafthouse and red signs warning of cave-ins. Nearby, where the thriving town of Dimsdale used to stand, there was only an eyesore called Shantytown.

It was a slum of shacks and decrepit travel trailers, rusty vehicles, and ramshackle chicken coops. They were scattered in a patch of woods, and the transients who lived there were actually squatters on Klingenschoen property. Shantytown was known as a hangout for derelicts, but poor families also lived there, and children played in the dust that surrounded the substandard housing. Efforts by the county and the K Foundation to "do something about Dimsdale" never achieved much. As soon as families were helped to move on to a better life through skill-training, employment, and a healthy environment, more families moved in to take their dreary place.

On this occasion, Qwilleran chose not to drive into the Shantytown jungle, thinking that his white car would be too conspicuous, but he peered through the woods with binoculars for a glimpse of a maroon vehicle and saw nothing that fitted that description. Leaving the area, he stopped for lunch at the diner, chiefly to confirm that it was as dismal as he remembered. The windows were still opaque with grime; two more seats had fallen off the stools at the counter; and the coffee lived up to its reputation as the worst in the county. Nevertheless, he recalled one dark and anxious night when he was stranded on the way home from North Middle Hummock with his car upside down in the ditch; the cook at the diner had sent him hot coffee and stale doughnuts on-the-house, a gesture that was much appreciated at the time.

A chalkboard announced the diner's Thursday specials: TOM SOUP, TUNA SAMICH, AND MAC/CHEEZ. Qwilleran, who had never encountered a plate of macaroni and cheese he didn't like, ordered the special with sanguine expectation but found the pasta cooked to the consistency of tapioca pudding. As for the sauce, library paste could have tasted no worse.

When he returned to the barn, ill-fed and somewhat ill-tempered, Koko was hopping up and down like a puppet on strings, a performance that signified a message on the answering machine. The call was from John Bushland in Lockmaster: "Qwill, it's Bushy.

Making a delivery in Pickax this afternoon. Will drop by. Hope you're there. Got some good pix."

The photographer's van pulled into the barnyard about two o'clock.

"How come you're making a delivery in the backwoods?" Qwilleran asked. Lockmaster, with its horse breeders and golf courses, considered itself more civilized than its rural neighbor to the north, where potato farms and sheep ranches were the norm, and feed caps and pickup trucks were high fashion.

Bushy said, "Arch wanted to know if I had any shots of the Bonnie Scots gang with Scottish landmarks or local color. He said he'd run a spread, maybe a double-truck."

"Could you help him?"

"Oh, sure. I delivered more than a dozen prints, and I brought a set to show you, plus some scenics that are kind of different. Where can we spread them out?" There were three yellow boxes filled with 8x10 black-and-white glossies. "I'll have the color later," he said. "Here we are when we had lunch at Loch Lomond . . . and in this one we're waiting for the ferry at Mull. Here are some of the gals on the bridge at Eilean Donan Castle. The only complete group is around the bus at Oban; I even jumped into the picture myself."

"Wait a minute," Qwilleran said as he went to the desk for a magnifying glass. "Isn't that the bus driver in the background?"

Bushy studied the print with the glass. "You're right! He didn't duck his head for this one! I can blow it up and make a mug shot for the police."

"This calls for a celebration! How about Scotch with a splash of Squunk water?"

The photographer followed Qwilleran to the serving bar. "I know how it happened, Qwill. I was using the tripod, and I set the timer so I could run and get in the picture, and because I wasn't behind the camera, Bruce didn't realize he was being photographed . . . Hey! The cat's licking the prints!"

"Koko! Get away!" Qwilleran clapped his hands threateningly, and Koko darted guiltily from the vicinity.

"It must be the emulsion he likes," Bushy said. "Maybe I should put them back in the boxes . . . Guess what!" he said with more incredulity than enthusiasm. "Arch wants me to photograph the teddy bears for a story you're writing!"

"Be prepared for a wacky experience!"

"I know. Grace hired me to shoot her jewelry for insurance purposes before we left on the trip, and she hasn't paid me yet!"

Qwilleran huffed into his moustache. "What do you bet she's

giving us the teddy bear story so she'll get free photos for the same purpose?"

The photographer sipped his drink moodily for a while and then said, "Do you think Pickax could support a photo studio, Qwill?"

"Why? Do you want to open a branch?"

"I'm thinking of moving my whole operation up here," Bushy said morosely. "That's the problem I told you about. Vicki and I are breaking up. My studio and darkroom are in the house, and I've got to get out. She's turning it into a restaurant."

"Sorry to hear about that, Bushy. I thought everything was going great with you two."

"Yeah . . . well . . . it looks like we won't have a family, so she's been hot for a career, which is okay with me, but she's gone crazy over her damned catering business! And now some guy at the riding club wants to back her financially if she'll open a restaurant. He comes on pretty strong, if you know what I mean. He's not just interested in food."

Qwilleran shook his head sympathetically. "I've been through that kind of mess myself, and let me offer some advice: Whatever you do, don't let them grind you down. *Illegitimi non carborundum,* as they say in fractured Latin."

"Yeah, but not so easy to do," Bushy said grimly. "Anyway, do you think a photo studio would go up here?"

"With the right kind of promotion . . . definitely! Pickax could use your talent and energy. If you don't mind working for a paper, the *Something* could give you plenty of assignments. And with your kind of enthusiasm, I predict you'll be president of the Boosters Club within a year!"

"Thanks, Qwill, I needed that! Those are the first upbeat words I've heard since I got back from Scotland . . . And now I've got work to do. I'll bring the mug shot of the bus driver tomorrow when I come up to shoot the bears."

"Deliver it to Andy Brodie," Qwilleran advised. "Start making points with the police chief."

When the photographer had left, he opened the yellow boxes on the dining table, where he could spread the prints out, and he was astounded at what he saw. Bushy had used unorthodox camera angles and different lenses and exposures to produce a startling kind of travel photography: impressionist, partially abstract in some shots, surreal in others. He went to the phone to call Arch Riker.

"Got an idea for you," he told the publisher. "I've just been talking to Bushy."

"Yes, we're running his Bonnie Scots pix Monday. How about writing some cutlines? We'll need them by noon tomorrow."

"Do I get a by-line?"

"Depends on how good they are. We'll go with the teddy bears Tuesday. That means copy's due Monday morning . . . Now what's your idea?"

"I've been looking at Bushy's scenic photos, and that guy definitely has a different way of looking at castles, mountains, sheep, fishermen, and all the other stuff. They're exhibition quality, Arch! Why couldn't the *Something* sponsor an exhibition of his travel photos?"

"Where?"

"In the lobby of the K Theatre, to tie in with the opening of *Macbeth*. He also has interesting shots of Larry and Melinda rehearsing in the courtyards of old inns."

There was a pensive pause before Riker said, "Once in a while you come up with a good one, Qwill."

As Qwilleran returned to the dining area, feeling pleased with himself, he was abashed to hear a telltale sound that was not good; Koko was slurping photos.

"NO!" he yelled. "Bad cat!"

Koko leaped from the table with a backward kick, scattering prints in all directions.

"Cats!" Qwilleran grumbled as he segregated the damaged glossies. Several had been deglossed in spots by the cat's sandpaper tongue and potent saliva.

He mentioned Koko's aberrant behavior to Polly as they drove to Lockmaster Saturday evening. "It's not the first time he's done this."

"Bootsie never does anything like that," she said.

Sure, Qwilleran thought. Bootsie never does anything—but eat.

The exclusive Palomino Paddock was located in lush horse country, and they found a parking place between an Italian sports car and a British luxury van. Eight o'clock guests in dinner jackets and long dresses were beginning to arrive—one pair in a horse-drawn surrey. The building itself, in purposeful contrast to the exquisite food and elegant customers, resembled an old horse stable—which it may well have been—and the interior was artfully cluttered with saddles, bales of hay, and portraits of thoroughbreds. Informality was the keynote, and the waitstaff—all young equestrians—were dressed like grooms. Early diners in hunting pinks, sipping their exotic demitasses, sprawled in their chairs with breeched and booted legs extended stiffly in the aisles.

Qwilleran and his guest were conducted to a cozily private table in a horse stall, where a framed portrait of a legendary horse named Cardinal was enshrined, with credit given to the Bushland Studio.

When a young wine steward wearing the keys to the cellar on heavy chains presented the wine list, Qwilleran waved it away. "The lady will have a glass of your driest sherry, and you can bring me Squunk water with a slice of lime. That is," he added slyly to test the young man's education, "if you have a recent vintage."

With perfect aplomb and a straight face the steward said, "I happen to have a bottle dated last Thursday and labeled Export Reserve. I think you'll find it exciting, with a mellow bouquet and distinctive finish." In reference to Squunk water, "bouquet" was a flattering term.

The waitress had the breezy self-confidence of a young woman who keeps her own horse, wins ribbons, and looks terrific in a riding habit. "I'm your waitperson," she said. "We love having you here tonight. My name is Trilby."

"May I guess the name of your horse?" Qwilleran asked.

"Brandy. He's a buckskin. No papers, but beautiful points! I'll bring you the menus."

To Polly he said, "The woman in a red dress over there is Bushy's wife, Vicki. Her escort is someone I don't know."

"Vicki's my aunt," said Trilby, presenting the menus, "and he's an officer of the riding club. They're going to open their own restaurant." She dashed away again.

In a lower voice, Qwilleran said, "The Bushlands are having marital problems."

"Oh, I'm sorry to hear that," she said. "He's such a congenial and thoughtful young man."

"Talented, too. Wait till you see his pictures of Scotland. They have nothing to do with postcard art. Arch is going to start giving him assignments."

"That's good news! The photos in the *Something* are so unimaginative."

"We use amateurs with smart cameras. What we need is a smart photographer. For starters, Bushy is going to photograph Grace Utley's teddy bears."

"Are you interested in teddy bears?" asked Trilby, who had returned to discuss the evening's specials. "We have a teddy bear club in Lockmaster."

"Good for you!" Qwilleran said. "What do you recommend this evening?"

"We have a new chef, and he's prepared some very exciting things: for an appetizer, a nice grilled duck sausage with sage polenta and green onion confit. Our soup tonight is three-mushroom velouté."

"Is your chef from Fall River, by any chance?"

"I don't think so. Our specials tonight are a lovely roasted quail with goat cheese, sun-dried tomatoes, and hickory-smoked bacon and also a pan-seared snapper with herb crust and a red pepper and artichoke relish."

"Oh, dear!" Polly said in dismay. "What do you think I would like?"

"My personal favorite," said Trilby, "is the roasted pork tenderloin with sesame fried spinach, shiitake mushrooms, and garlic chutney."

Polly decided on plain grilled swordfish, and Qwilleran ordered fillet of beef for himself. Raising his glass of Squunk water he proposed, "*Lang may your lums reek,* as they say in Scotland."

"That sounds indecent," Polly replied as she raised her glass uncertainly.

"I believe it means 'Long may your chimneys smoke.' In the old days they weren't concerned with pollution. They just wanted to keep warm and cook their oatmeal."

They talked about the Chisholm sisters' teddy bear collection (incredible!) . . . the prospect of a tag sale on Goodwinter Boulevard (deplorable!) . . . the forthcoming production of *Macbeth* (ambitious!).

Qwilleran said, "I've promised Carol I'll work in the box office next week."

"You have? There'll be a run on tickets," Polly predicted teasingly. "Everyone will want to buy a ticket from a handsome bachelor who is also a brilliant journalist and fabled philanthropist."

"You're *blethering,* as they say in Scotland," he protested modestly, although he knew she was right. He had enjoyed semicelebrityhood while writing for major newspapers Down Below, but that was nothing compared to his present status as a billionaire frog in a very small frog pond.

She said, "I hear that Derek Cuttlebrink is playing the porter, and Dwight has him telescoping his six-feet-seven into a five-foot S-curve that will probably steal the show."

"I know Derek," said Trilby swooping in with the entrées. "He's a sous chef at the Old Stone Mill."

"Very sous," Qwilleran muttered under his breath.

"I'll bring you some hot sour-dough rolls," she said as she whisked away.

"Quick!" he said to Polly. "Do you have anything private to discuss before Mata Hari brings the rolls?"

"Well . . . yes," she said, taking him seriously. "My sister-in-law does the bookkeeping at the Goodwinter Clinic, you know, and she told me in strict confidence that the staff is beginning to worry about Dr. Melinda."

"For what reason?"

"She's made at least two mistakes on prescriptions since returning from Scotland. In both cases the pharmacist caught the error—it had to do with dosage—and phoned the nurse at the clinic."

Qwilleran smoothed his moustache. "She has too many irons in the fire: worrying about the liquidation sale, rehearsing the lead in the play, running off to Scotland—"

"All the while carrying a full load of appointments," Polly reminded him.

"I thought her patients were deserting her."

"Most of Dr. Hal's male patients transferred, but women are flocking to the clinic in droves."

The hot rolls came to the table, and Qwilleran applied his attention to enjoyment of the food, but his imagination was flirting with the idea of Melinda's mistakes. Doctors are not always right, he told himself. She could have been wrong about Irma's death. Wisely, he refrained from mentioning it to Polly.

The house salad, served after the entrée, was a botanical cross section of Bibb lettuce surrounded by precise mounds of shredded radish, paper-thin carrot, and cubed tofu, drizzled with gingered rice wine vinaigrette dressing and finished with a veil of alfalfa sprouts and a sliver of Brie.

"And for dessert tonight," Trilby recited, "the chef has prepared a delicate terrine of three kinds of chocolate drenched in raspberry coulis."

"I'm fighting it," Polly said wistfully.

"I surrender," said Qwilleran.

After a demitasse that smelled like almonds and tasted like a hot fudge sundae, they drove back to Pickax in the comfortable silence of a pair of well-fed ruminants. Finally Qwilleran asked, "How was your dinner with the Hasselriches last night?"

"Rather depressing. They're going through a bad period."

"Do you know if . . . uh . . . Irma's medical records were returned to them?"

"I don't know. Is that customary?"

"I have no idea," he said, "but one would think they might be turned over to the family by the attending physician."

"Why do you ask, Qwill?"

"No particular reason. As a matter of curiosity, though, why don't you ask your sister-in-law, discreetly, what happens to the records of a deceased patient?"

"I suppose I could do that. I'll see her at church tomorrow." They had arrived at Polly's carriage house. "Will you come up for a little reading?"

"Is that all?" he asked. "I could use a large cup of real coffee."

He had brought *Memoirs of an Eighteenth Century Footman* for reading aloud. "It's a true story," he explained, "about the orphan of a Scottish gentleman, who became a veritable prince of servants, with gold lace on his livery and a silk bag on his hair."

With its Scottish background and unbowdlerized style, it proved to be more interesting than they expected, and it was late when Qwilleran returned to the barn.

The Siamese were prancing in figure eights, demanding their overdue bedtime snack, and he gave them their crunchy treat before checking his answering machine. There was a message from Nick Bamba: "Got some good news for you. Call whenever you get in. We'll be watching the late movie."

It was two o'clock when he called the Mooseville number. "Are you sure I'm not calling too late?" he asked.

Lori assured him, "With all the commercials they throw in, the movie won't be over till four. I'll let you talk to Nick."

"Hey, Qwill!" said her husband. "I saw the maroon car again tonight!"

"You did? Where was it?"

"Parked on Main Street in Mooseville. He could have been in the Shipwreck Tavern or he could have been in the Northern Lights Hotel."

"More likely the tavern."

"And that's not all. Lori went to a baby shower in Indian Village, and she saw the same car leaving the parking lot."

"What do you suppose he was doing among all those yuppies?"

"I dunno. Maybe looking for a victim . . . Sorry, I shouldn't kid about it."

"Well, there's nothing we can do until he makes an overt move," Qwilleran said. "I'll tell you one thing: I'm not letting Polly go out alone after dark!"

Nick had barely hung up when the phone rang again, and Qwilleran assumed he was calling back; no one else in Moose County would call at that hour. He picked up the receiver. "Yes, Nick."

"Nick? Who's Nick?" asked a woman's voice. "This is Melinda. Hi, lover!"

Annoyed, he said stiffly, "Isn't that epithet somewhat obsolete under present circumstances?"

"Ooh! You're in a beastly mood tonight! What can we do about that . . . huh?"

"You'll have to excuse me," he said. "I'm expecting an important call."

"Are you trying to brush me off, lover? My feelings are hurt," she said with coy petulance. "We used to be such good *friends!* Don't you remember? We were really attracted to each other. I should have trapped you three years ago—"

"Melinda," he said firmly, "I'm sorry but I must hang up and take another urgent call." And he hung up. To Koko—who was standing by as usual, with disapproval in his whiskers—he said, "That was your friend Melinda. She's over the edge!"

Twelve

It was a peaceful Sunday morning. The church bells were ringing on Park Circle as Qwilleran walked downtown to pick up the out-of-town newspapers. At the apple barn, the Siamese huddled in a window to count the leaves that were beginning to fall from the trees. Their heads raised and lowered in unison, following the downward course of each individual leaf. In another week there would be too many to count, and they would lose interest.

At noon, Polly phoned. "I forgot to tell you, Qwill. The Senior Care Facility is trying the Pets for Patients idea this afternoon. I'm taking Bootsie. Would you be willing to take Yum Yum?"

"I'll give it a try. What time?"

"Two o'clock. Report to the main lobby."

"Did you speak to your sister-in-law, Polly?"

"Yes. She said doctors usually keep the records of deceased

patients for a few years—for their own protection in case of dispute."

"I see. Well, thank you. And thank her, also."

Shortly before two o'clock he brought the cat carrier out of the broom closet. "Come on, sweetheart," he said to Yum Yum. "Come and have your horizon expanded."

Koko, usually ready for an adventure, jumped uninvited into the carrying coop, but Yum Yum promptly sped away—up the ramp, around the balcony, and up the next ramp with Qwilleran in pursuit. On the second balcony he was able to grab her, but she slithered from his grasp, leaving him down on all fours. She stopped and gazed at his predicament, but as soon as he scrambled to his feet, she raced to the third balcony. He lunged at her just as she started to crawl along a horizontal beam that was forty feet above the main floor. "Not this time, baby!" he scolded.

It was no small endeavor to evict the stubborn male from the carrier with one hand and install the squirming, clutching, kicking female with the other, and they were the last to arrive at the Senior Care Facility. There was a high decibel level of vocal hubbub, barking, snarling, growling, and hissing in the lobby, which teemed with pet lovers, dogs on leashes, cats in carriers, and volunteers in yellow smocks, known as "canaries" at the facility. Lisa Compton was there with a clipboard, assigning pets to patients.

Qwilleran asked her, "Are you the new chief of volunteers?"

"I've applied for the job," she said, "but today I'm just helping out. It's our first go at this project, and there are some wrinkles to iron out. Next time we'll stagger the visitors. Who's your friend?"

"Her name is Yum Yum."

"Is she gentle? We have an emphysema patient who's requested a pet, and the doctor has okayed a cat, thinking a dog would be too frisky. Yum Yum seems quite relaxed."

Qwilleran peered into the carrier, where Yum Yum had struck the dead-cat pose she always assumed after losing an argument. "Yes, I'd say she's quite relaxed."

Lisa beckoned to a canary. "Would you take Mr. Qwilleran and Yum Yum up to 15-C for Mr. Hornbuckle? The limit is twenty minutes."

In the elevator, the volunteer remarked, "This old gentleman was caretaker for Dr. Halifax on Goodwinter Boulevard until a couple of years ago. The doctor kept him on even though he couldn't work much toward the end. Dr. Hal was a wonderful man."

The occupant of 15-C was sitting in a wheelchair when they

entered—a small, weak figure literally plugged into the wall as he received a metered supply of oxygen through a long tube, but he was waiting eagerly with bright eyes and a toothy grin.

The canary said loudly, "You have a visitor, Mr. Hornbuckle. Her name is Yum Yum." To Qwilleran she said, "I'll come back for you when the time's up."

Yum Yum was relaxed to the consistency of jelly when Qwilleran lifted her from the carrier.

"That's a *cat?*" the old man said in a strange voice. The nasal prongs made his voice unnaturally resonant, and ill-fitting dentures gave his speech a juicy sibilance.

"She's a Siamese," Qwilleran said, putting the limp bundle of fur on the patient's lap blanket.

"Purty kitty," he said, stroking her with a quivering hand. "Soft, ain't she? Blue eyes! Never seen one like this." He spoke slowly in short sentences.

Qwilleran made an attempt to entertain him with anecdotes about Siamese until he realized that the patient would rather talk than listen.

"Growed up on a farm with animules," he said. "Barn cats, hunt'n' dogs, cows, chickens . . ."

"I hear you used to work for Dr. Halifax."

"Fifty year, nigh onto. I were like family. Mighty fine man, he were. What's your name?"

"Qwilleran. Jim Qwilleran."

"Been here long?"

"Five years."

"Y'knowed Dr. Halifax? I were his caretaker. Lived over the garage. Drove 'im all over, makin' calls. Many's a time they'd call 'im middle o' the night, and I drove 'im. Saved lives, we did. Plenty of 'em."

Yum Yum sat in a contented bundle on the blanketed lap, purring gently, her forepaws folded under her breast. Occasionally an ear flicked, tickled by a spray of saliva.

"Sittin' on her brisket, she is! She's happy!" He had a happy grin of his own.

Qwilleran said, "I know Dr. Halifax worked long hours, taking care of his patients. What did he do for relaxation? Did he have any hobbies, like fishing or golf?"

The old man looked furtive as if about to reveal some unsavory secret. "Painted pitchers, he did. Di'n't tell nobody."

"What kind of pictures?" Qwilleran asked, envisioning something anatomical.

"Pitchers of animules. Thick paint, it were. Took a long time to dry."

"What did he do with them?" Melinda had never mentioned her father's hobby; in fact, she had avoided talking about her family.

"Put 'em away. Di'n't give 'em to nobody. Warn't good enough, he said."

"What did you think of them, Mr. Hornbuckle?"

With a guilty grin he said, "Looked like pitchers in the funny papers."

"Where did he go to paint them?"

"Upstairs, 'way in the back. Nobody went there, oney me. We got along good, him and me. Never thought he'd go first, like he did."

Yum Yum was stirring, and she stretched one foreleg to touch the oxygen tube.

"No, no!" Qwilleran scolded, and she withdrew.

"Minds purty good, don't she?"

"Mr. Hornbuckle, do you know that Dr. Hal's daughter is a doctor now? She's following in her father's footsteps."

The old man nodded. "She were the smart one. Boy di'n't turn out so good."

"In what way?" Qwilleran had a sympathetic way of asking prying questions and a sincerity that could draw out confidences.

"He were into scrapes all the time. Police'd call, middle o' the night, and I'd drive the doctor to the jail. It were too bad, his ma bein' sick and all—always sick abed."

"What happened to the boy finally?"

"Went away. Doctor sent 'im away. Paid 'im money reg'lar iffen he di'n't come back."

"How do you know this?"

"It were through a bank in Lockmaster. Drove down there reg'lar, I did. Took care of it for the doctor. Never told nobody."

Qwilleran asked, "Wasn't the young man eventually killed in a car accident?"

"That he were! Broke the doctor's heart. Di'n't make no difference he were a rotten apple; he were his oney son . . . Funny thing, though . . ."

"Yes?" Qwilleran said encouragingly.

"After the boy died, the doctor kep' sendin' me to the bank, reg'lar, once a month."

"Did he explain?"

"Nope."

"Didn't you wonder about it?"

"Nope. 'Twarn't none o' my business."

There was a knock on the door at that moment, and the canary entered. "Time for Yum Yum to go home, Mr. Hornbuckle. Say goodbye to your visitors."

As Qwilleran lifted the cat gently from the lap blanket, she uttered a loud, indignant "N-n-now!"

"Likes me, don't she?" said the old man, showing his unnatural dentures. "Bring 'er ag'in. Don't wait too long!" he said with a cackling laugh. "Mightn't be here!"

Downstairs in the lobby, Lisa asked for comments to chart on her clipboard.

"A good time was had by all," Qwilleran reported. "Yum Yum cuddled and purred, or *croodled,* as they say in Scotland. Is Polly Duncan here?"

"No, she and Bootsie came early. They've gone home."

Arriving at the barn, Qwilleran released Yum Yum from the carrier, and she strolled around the main floor like a prima donna, while Koko tagged after her, sniffing with disapproval. He knew she had been to some kind of medical facility.

Later, Qwilleran phoned Polly and asked, "How did the macho behemoth perform this afternoon?"

"The visit wasn't too successful, I'm afraid. We were assigned to an elderly farm woman who had lost her sight, and she complained that Bootsie didn't feel like a cat. Too sleek and silky, I imagine. She was used to barn cats."

"We had an emphysema patient, and I thought Yum Yum might turn into a fur tornado when she saw the oxygen equipment, but she played her role beautifully. She croodled. She's a professional croodler."

"Cats know when someone needs comforting," Polly said. "When Edgar Allan Poe's wife was dying in a poor cottage without heat or blankets, her only sources of warmth were her husband's overcoat and a large tortoiseshell cat."

"A touching story, if true," Qwilleran commented.

"I've read it in several books. Most cats are lovable."

"Or *loosome,* as the Scots say. By the way, I promised Mildred we'd tell her all about Scotland. How will it be if we take her to dinner at Linguini's next Sunday? We'll invite Arch Riker, too."

Polly thought it would be a nice idea. Actually, the following Sunday was her birthday, but he pretended not to know, and she pretended not to know that he knew.

The next morning he walked downtown to buy her a birthday gift, but first he had to hand in his copy at the newspaper. In the city room he picked up a Monday edition and read his Bonnie Scots cutlines to see if anyone had tampered with his carefully worded prose. Then he read the large ad on page three:

TAG SALE

Estate of Dr. Halifax Goodwinter
At the residence, 180 Goodwinter Boulevard
Sale: Saturday, 8 A.M. to 6 P.M.
Preview: Friday, 9 A.M. to 4 P.M.

Furniture, antiques, art, household equipment, books, clothing, jewelry, linens, china, silver, crystal, personal effects. All items tagged. All prices firm. All sales final. No deliveries. Dealers welcome. Curb parking permitted.

Managed by:
Foxy Fred's Bid-a-Bit Auctions

"Did you see the ad for the Goodwinter sale?" Carol Lanspeak asked him when he went to the Lanspeak Department Store to buy a gift. "Melinda hasn't said a word to the Historical Society. One would think she'd give the museum first choice—or even donate certain items."

"I suppose she has a lot on her mind," Qwilleran said. "How's her Lady Macbeth progressing?"

Carol, who had been arranging a scarf display in the women's department, steered him away from the hovering staff who were eager to wait on Mr. Q. He was a regular customer, and they all knew that Polly wore size 16, liked blue and gray, preferred silver jewelry, and avoided anything that required ironing.

Before answering his question, Carol said, "This is off the record, I hope."

"Always."

"Well, Larry finds her very hard to work with. She never looks at him when they're acting together, and there's nothing worse! She acts for herself and doesn't give him anything to play against. Very bad!"

"Is Dwight aware of this?"

"Yes, he's given her notes several times. Granted we have another ten days to rehearse, but . . . I don't know about Melinda. Did you hear that she lost another patient? Wally Toddwhistle's grandmother. Perhaps you saw the obituary."

"What can you expect, Carol? She inherited all of Dr. Hal's octogenarian and nonagenarian patients with one foot in the grave."

"Well . . ." Carol said uncertainly, "our daughter got her M.D. in June and is interning in Chicago. Melinda wants her to come back and join the clinic. Naturally, Larry and I would love to have her living here rather than Down Below, but we're not sure it's the wise thing to do, considering . . ." She shrugged. "What do you think?"

"What does your daughter think?"

"She wants to stay in Chicago."

"Then let her stay there. It's her decision. Don't interfere."

"I guess you're right, Qwill," Carol admitted. "Now what can we do for you?"

"I need a birthday gift for Polly. Any ideas?"

"How about a lovely gown and robe set?" She showed him a blue one in size 16.

"Fine! Wrap it up," he said. "Nothing fancy, please." He was a brisk shopper.

"White box with blue ribbon?"

"That'll do . . . Now, what do I need to know about the box office job tomorrow?"

"Just report a few minutes early," Carol said. "I'll meet you there and explain the system."

At one-thirty the next day, Qwilleran said to the Siamese, "Well, here goes! Let's hope I don't sell the same seat twice." He had sold baseball programs at Comiskey Park and ties at Macy's, but he had never sold tickets in a box office. He walked to the theatre, through the woods and across the parking lot, where there appeared to be an unusual profusion of cars for a Tuesday afternoon. In the lobby, the ticket purchasers were milling about as if it were opening night.

"Hi, Mr. Q," several called out as he pushed through to the box office. The window was shuttered, but there was a light inside, and Carol admitted him through the side door.

"Can you believe this crowd?" she remarked. "Looks like we've got a hit show! . . . Now, here's what you do. When customers first come up to the window, ask them what date they want, and pull the seating chart for that performance. Seats already sold have been x-ed out on the chart."

The chart of the auditorium showed twelve rows of seats on the main floor and three in the balcony—twenty seats to the row, divided into left, right, and center sections.

"Next, ask them how many tickets they want and where they

want to sit. All seats are the same price. Then you take the tickets out of this rack; they're in cubbyholes labeled according to row. Be sure to x-out the seats they're buying . . . Then take their money. No credit cards, but personal checks are okay. Any questions?"

"What's that other rack?"

"Those are reserved tickets waiting to be picked up. You probably won't have any pickups so early in the game, but you'll get phone orders. When you sell tickets by phone, put them in the pickup rack, and don't forget to x-out the seats on the chart." Carol pulled out a drawer under the counter. "There's the till, with enough small bills to make change. Lock it when you're through, and lock the box office when you leave."

"What do I do with the keys?"

"Put them in the bottom of the tall-case clock in the lobby. It's all very simple."

The hard part, Qwilleran discovered, was on the other side of the window. He opened the shutters and faced his public. They had formed a queue, and there were about forty in a line that snaked around the lobby.

The first at the window was a small, nervous woman with graying hair and wrinkled brow. "Do you know me?" she asked. "I'm Jennifer's mother."

"Jennifer?" he repeated.

"Jennifer Olson. She's in the play."

"No doubt you'll want tickets for opening night," he guessed, reaching for the Wednesday chart.

"Yes, ten tickets. Our whole family is going."

"Here's what's available, Mrs. Olson. Do you want them all in the same row, or a block of seats?"

"What would a block be like?"

"It could be two rows of five, one behind the other, or three shorter rows bunched together."

"I don't know. Which do you think would be best?"

"Well, it's like this," Qwilleran explained. "If you take a block, it can be closer to the stage. To get a full row you'll have to sit farther back."

"Why is that?"

"Because," he said patiently, "tickets have already been sold in various rows at the front of the auditorium, as you can see by this chart." He pushed the seating plan closer to the glass and waited for Mrs. Olson to find her reading glasses.

Frowning at the chart, she said, "Which is the front?"

"Here's the stage. As you can see, the entire front row is still available, if you don't mind sitting that close."

"No, I don't think we should sit in the front row. It might make Jennifer nervous."

"In that case, the next full row available is H. That's the eighth row."

"I wonder if Grandma Olson will be able to hear from the eighth row."

"The acoustics are very good," he assured her.

"What are those?" Mrs. Olson asked.

The customers standing in line were getting restless. The man behind her kept looking at his watch with exaggerated gestures. A young woman had a child in a stroller whose fretting had escalated to screams. An older woman leaning on a quad-cane was volubly indignant. And the front doors opened and closed constantly as frustrated ticket purchasers left and new ones arrived.

Qwilleran said, "Mrs. Olson, why don't you walk down into the auditorium and try sitting in the various rows to see how you like the location? Meanwhile, I can take care of these other customers . . . Take your time, so that you're sure."

There was a groan of relief as she left, and Qwilleran was able to serve the entire lineup by the time she returned. The selection had dwindled considerably, but he could offer her an irregular block of seats in the center section.

"But we need three aisle seats," she said. "My husband is with the volunteer fire department and will have to leave if his beeper goes off. My sister has anxiety attacks and sometimes has to rush out in a hurry. And Grandpa Olson has a bad leg from the war and has to stretch it in the aisle."

"Left leg or right leg?" Qwilleran asked.

"It's his left leg. He took shrapnel."

"Then you'll have to take the left of the center section or the left of the right section."

"Oh, dearie me! It's so confusing. There are so many people to please."

Helpfully Qwilleran suggested, "Why not let me select a block of tickets for you, and if your family decides they're not right, bring them back for exchange."

"That's a wonderful idea!" she cried gratefully. "Thank you, Mr. Q. You have been so helpful. And I must tell you how much I enjoy your column in the paper."

"Thank you," he said. "That will be sixty dollars."

"And now I need eight more for Saturday night," she said. "They're for Jennifer's godparents and her boyfriend's family."

It crossed Qwilleran's mind that Jennifer probably had two lines to speak, but diplomatically he asked, "Is your daughter playing Lady Macbeth?"

"Oh! How strange you should mention that!" Mrs. Olson seemed flustered. "She's really doing Lady Macduff, but . . ."

"That's a good role. I'm sure you'll be proud of her."

The woman scanned the lobby and then said confidentially, "Jennifer has learned all of Lady Macbeth's lines—just in case."

"Was that her own idea?" Qwilleran was aware that understudies were a luxury the Theatre Club had never enjoyed.

In a near-whisper she said, "Mr. Somers, the director, asked her to do it and not tell anyone. You won't mention this, will you?"

"I wouldn't think of it," he said.

When Jennifer's mother had left, he thought, So! Dwight is doubting Melinda's capability to play the lead! And she's already making errors in prescriptions! What is happening to her?

Despite Qwilleran's desire to be rid of Melinda, he could hardly ignore her plight. They had been good friends once. Quite apart from that, he had a newsman's curiosity about the story behind the story.

The towering clock in the theatre lobby finally bonged four, and he counted the money, balanced it against the number of tickets sold, locked up, hid the keys, and walked home slowly. Ambling through the cool woods he began to think about Bushy's photographs, particularly three Highland scenes.

There was a lonely moor without a tree or a boulder or a lost sheep—totally empty and isolated except for a telephone booth in the middle of nowhere, and Bushy had added a woman digging for a coin in the depths of her shoulder bag.

One was a haunting scene of a silvery loch in which floated an uninhabited island with a ruined castle reflected in the still water. In the background a gray, mysterious mountain rose steeply from the loch, and in the foreground a woman sat on a stone wall reading a paperback with her back to the view.

Then there was a riot of flowers behind a rustic fence and garden gate, on which hung the sign:

Be ye mon or be ye wumin,
Be ye gaun or be ye cumin,
Be ye early, be ye late,
Dinna fergit tae SHUT THE GATE!

In Bushy's picture there was a woman in the garden, and the gate stood open.

The series ought to be titled "Tourism," Qwilleran thought, and as soon as he reached the barn he hunted up Bushy's yellow boxes and pulled out the three photos. Each one had its surface defaced by Koko's rough tongue, and in each photo the woman was Melinda.

Thirteen

That was the week that Moose County was discovered by the media. Overnight it became the Teddy Bear Capital of the nation. Qwilleran's story and Bushy's photographs ran in the *Moose County Something* with a teaser on the front page and the full treatment on the back page. It was picked up by the wire services and published in several major newspapers around the country, and a television crew flew up from Down Below on Thursday to film the collection and interview the collectors.

During the week there was also a series of break-ins in the affluent Purple Point area, but this untimely happening was played down while the TV people were around. It was also the week of the Goodwinter tag sale, and on Friday afternoon Qwilleran attended the preview.

Goodwinter Boulevard was a broad, quiet avenue off Main Street with two stone pylons at the entrance to give it an air of exclusivity. A cul-de-sac with a landscaped median and old-fashioned street lights, it extended the equivalent of three blocks, ending at a vest-pocket park with an impressive monument. The granite monolith rose about twelve feet and bore a bronze plaque commemorating the four Goodwinter brothers who founded the city. Their mansions—and those of other tycoons who had made fortunes in mining and lumbering—lined both sides of the boulevard. Qwilleran usually found it a pleasant place for a walk, having interesting architecture and virtually no traffic—only an occasional car turning into a side drive and disappearing into a garage at the rear.

Friday afternoon was different. The ban on curb parking was lifted, and both sides of the street were lined with parked cars bumper-to-bumper, while other vehicles cruised hopefully and continually, waiting for someone to leave. Many had to give up and park on Main Street. As for the sidewalks, they teemed with individuals going to and from the preview, with a large group gathered in front of No. 180.

Qwilleran approached a woman on the fringe of the crowd and asked her what was happening.

She squealed in delight at recognizing his moustache and said, "Oh, you're Mr. Q! They won't let us in until some of the others come out. I've been out here since eleven. Wish I'd brought my lunch."

No one showed impatience. They chatted sociably as they edged closer to the entrance of the mansion. Qwilleran slipped around to the rear and used his press card for admittance, although the well-known overgrown moustache would have accomplished the same end.

He entered a kitchen large enough to accommodate three cooks, where a Bid-a-Bit employee at the coffee urn offered him a cup. He accepted and sat down on a kitchen chair just as Foxy Fred walked in from the front of the house, wearing a red jacket and his usual western hat. Qwilleran, turning on his tape recorder, asked him, "How do you size up this collection?"

"Four generations of treasures going at give-away prices!" said the auctioneer, who was not known for understatement. "Most prestigious sale in the history of Moose County! Fifty or seventy-five years from now, our grandkids will be proud to say they own a drinking mug or a pair of nail clippers that belonged to a great twentieth-century humanitarian!"

"But Fred, this kind of sale raises havoc with a quiet neighborhood," Qwilleran said. "Why didn't you cart the goods away and hold an auction in a tent out in the country?"

"The customer requested a tag sale, and the customer is always right," said Foxy Fred, gulping down a cup of coffee. "Well, I gotta get back where the action is."

In the large rooms on the main floor the ponderous heirloom furniture had been pushed back and rugs had been rolled up. Long folding tables were loaded with china, crystal, silver, linens, and bric-a-brac. The interior had the sadness of a house that had not seen a formal dinner, afternoon tea, or cocktail party for twenty-five years, the span of Mrs. Goodwinter's illness.

Curious crowds moved up and down the aisles, examining the items, checking the prices and muttering comments, while red-jacketed attendants announced repeatedly, "Keep moving, folks! Lots more waiting to get in." There were also three roving security guards, making themselves highly visible and looking seriously watchful.

Qwilleran dodged from aisle to aisle, asking viewers, "Why are you here? . . . See anything you like? . . . How are the prices? . . . Will you come back tomorrow to buy? . . . Did you know the Goodwinter family?" He himself spotted a silver pocketknife he wouldn't mind buying; engraved with the doctor's initials, it was priced at $150.

Upstairs, the crowds were less dense. Chests and dressers and disassembled beds were pushed back, and long tables were piled with blankets, towels and such. Clothing filled portable racks. One room, which was empty, had obviously been Melinda's; she had removed her furnishings to her apartment, but her distinctive fragrance lingered.

At the rear of the second floor there was a large room that no one entered, although an occasional viewer would poke a head through the doorway and back away quickly. It was two stories high and had three large north windows. This had been Dr. Hal's studio. Hanging in every wall space and filed on floor-to-ceiling shelves like books were brightly colored paintings on stretched canvas or rectangles of wallboard, and hundreds more were stacked on the Bid-a-Bit tables. It was the output, Qwilleran surmised, of twenty-five lonely years. None was bigger than an ordinary book. All were flat, two-dimensional depictions of animals against unrealistic landscapes of kelly green and cobalt blue. Red cats and turquoise dogs stood on hind legs and danced together. Orange ducks with purple beaks faced each other and quacked sociably. Tigers and kangaroos flew overhead like airplanes. These were the "animules" that had caused old Mr. Hornbuckle both wonderment and amusement.

A sign saying "Pictures $1.00" prompted Qwilleran to run downstairs to the kitchen and phone the high school where Mildred Hanstable taught art as well as home ec.

"She's in class at this hour," said an anonymous voice in the school office.

"This is urgent! Jim Qwilleran calling! Get her on the phone!" He was willing to throw his name around when it served a good purpose.

"Just a minute, Mr. Q."

A breathless art teacher came on the line.

"Mildred, this is Qwill," he said. "I'm at the Goodwinter house previewing the tag sale, and there's something here that you must definitely see! How fast can you make it over here?"

"I'm free next hour, but the period's just started."

"Cut class! Get here on the double! You'll be back before anyone misses you. Come in the back way. Use my name." Meanwhile he went upstairs and closed the door to Dr. Hal's studio.

When Mildred arrived, they climbed the servants' stairs from the kitchen, Qwilleran explaining, "Dr. Hal had a secret hobby. He painted pictures."

"My God!" Mildred gasped when she saw them.

"My words exactly! They're marked a dollar apiece, and no one is interested. A hundred dollars would be more appropriate. They might sell for a thousand in the right gallery. I don't know anything about art, but I've seen crazier stuff than this in museums."

"It's contemporary folk art," she said. "They're charming! They're unique! Wait till the art magazines get hold of these!"

"Wait till the psychologists get their claws into them! It's the Noah's Ark of a madman."

"I'm weak," Mildred said. "I don't know what to say."

"Go back to your class. I simply wanted an opinion to corroborate my own hunch."

"What are you going to do about it, Qwill?"

"First, take the decimal point out of that sign. Then notify the K Foundation."

Reluctantly the art teacher tore herself away from the bizarre collection, and Qwilleran went back to asking questions downstairs: "Do you collect antiques? . . . Are you a dealer? . . . Have you ever seen a sale to equal this? . . . What do you plan to buy?"

It was while taping their uninspired answers that he caught a glimpse of a bushy-haired, bushy-bearded young man in jeans and faded sweatshirt, wearing a fanny pack. He was browsing among odds and ends on a table toward the rear of the main floor.

Qwilleran's moustache bristled; he remembered that shaggy head from the reading room at the public library. It had been three months before, but he was sure this was the person who drove away in a maroon car with a Massachusetts plate and who was later identified as Charles Edward Martin. The man was reading labels on old LP records and fingering household tools. He examined the initials on the silver pocketknife. He picked up a cast-iron piggy bank and shook it; there was no rattle.

Sidling up to him, Qwilleran asked in a friendly way, "Quite a bunch of junk, isn't it?"

"Yeah," said the fellow.

"Find anything worth buying?"

"Nah."

"What do you think of the prices? Aren't they a bit high?"

The young man shrugged.

Hoping to hear him say a few words with an eastern accent, Qwilleran remarked, "I have a feeling we've met somewhere. Ever go to the Shipwreck Tavern in Mooseville?"

"Yeah."

"That's where I've met you! You're Ronald Frobnitz!" Qwilleran said.

The subject was supposed to say, "No, I'm Charles Martin," or better yet, "Chahles Mahtin." Instead he shook his head and scuttled away.

Noting that the silver pocketknife had scuttled at the same time, Qwilleran followed him to the front door, hindered by the crowds. The man was moving fast enough to make good time but not fast enough to arouse the suspicion of the security guards. Qwilleran thought, That Chahles Mahtin is smaht! He followed him through the milling hordes on the sidewalk—all the way to Main Street, where the suspect drove off in a maroon car with a Massachusetts plate.

Qwilleran, who was without his car at the moment, jogged to the police station, hoping to catch Brodie in the office, but the chief was striding out of the building. "Do you have a minute, Andy?" Qwilleran asked urgently.

"Make it half a minute."

"Okay. I attended the preview of the Goodwinter sale and saw someone who is undoubtedly Charles Edward Martin."

"Who?"

"The guy I suspect of being the Boulevard Prowler. I tried to get him into conversation, but he was closemouthed. When Polly was threatened three months ago, you checked the registration and came up with the name of Charles Edward Martin. The same car has been spotted three times in the last few days: headed for Shantytown, parked near the Shipwreck Tavern, and pulling out of the parking lot at Indian Village."

"Probably selling cemetery lots," Brodie quipped as he edged toward the curb. "I can't pick him up for driving around with a foreign license plate. Has Polly been threatened again? Has he been hanging around the boulevard after dark?"

"No," Qwilleran had to admit, although he pounded his moustache with his fist. How could he explain? Brodie might accept the idea of a psychic cat, but he'd balk at a moustache that telegraphed hunches.

"Tell you what to do, Qwill. Get your mind off those damned license plates. Come to the lodge hall for dinner tonight. It's Scottish Night. Six o'clock. Tell 'em at the door you're my guest." Brodie jumped into a police car without waiting for an answer.

Qwilleran went for a long walk. While he walked, he assessed his apprehensions in connection with the Boulevard Prowler. As a crime reporter and war correspondent he had faced frequent danger without a moment's fear. Now, for the first time in his life, he was experiencing that heart-sinking sensation—fear for the safety of another. For the first time in his life, he had someone close enough to make him vulnerable. It was a realization that warmed his blood and chilled it at the same time.

As for Brodie's patronizing invitation, he was inclined to ignore it. He knew many of the lodge members, and he had passed the hall hundreds of times—a three-story stone building like a miniature French Bastille—but he had never stepped inside the door. True, he had a certain amount of curiosity about Scottish Night, but he decided against it. Brodie's cheeky attitude annoyed him. And how good could the food be at a lodge hall?

In that frame of mind he returned to the apple barn, expecting to thaw some sort of meal out of the freezer. The Siamese met him at the door as usual and marched to the feeding station, where they sat confidently staring at the empty plate. Well aware of priorities in that household, Qwilleran opened a can of boned chicken for the cats before checking his answering machine and going up the ramp to change into a warmup suit. And then it happened again!

He was halfway to the balcony when Koko rushed him. This time he heard the thundering paws on the ramp and braced himself before the muscular body crashed into his legs.

"What the devil are you trying to tell me?" he demanded as Koko picked himself up, shook his head, and licked his left shoulder.

In the past Koko had thrown irrational catfits when Qwilleran was making the wrong decision or following the wrong scent. Whatever his present motive, his violence put Brodie's invitation in another light, and Qwilleran continued up the ramp—not to change into a warmup suit but to shower and dress for Scottish Night.

He drove to the lodge hall on Main Street, and as he parked the car he saw men in kilts and tartan trews converging from all directions. At the door he was greeted by Whannell MacWhannell, the portly accountant from the Bonnie Scots Tour, who looked even bigger in his pleated kilt, Argyle jacket, leather sporran, tasseled garters, and ghillie brogies.

"Andy told me to watch for you," said Big Mac. "He's upstairs, tuning up the doodlesack, but don't tell him I called it that."

Most of the men gathering in the lounge were in full Highland kit, making Qwilleran feel conspicuous in a suit and tie. As a public figure in Pickax he was greeted heartily by all. "Are you a Scot?" they asked. "Where did you get the W in your name?"

"My mother was a Mackintosh," he explained, "and I believe my father's family came from the Northern Isles. There's a Danish connection somewhere—way back, no doubt."

The walls of the lounge were hung with colorful clan banners—reproductions, MacWhannell explained, of the battle standards that were systematically burned after the defeat at Culloden.

"What tartan are you wearing?" Qwilleran asked him.

"Macdonald of Sleat. The MacWhannells are connected with that clan, somewhere along the line, and Glenda liked this tartan because it's red. Why don't you order a Mackintosh kilt, Qwill?"

"I'm not ready for that yet, but I've been boning up on Mackintosh history—twelve centuries of political brawls, feuds, raids, battles, betrayals, poisonings, hangings, assassinations, and violent acts of revenge. It's amazing that we have any Mackintoshes left."

At a given signal the party trooped upstairs to the great hall, a lofty room decorated wall-to-wall with weaponry. Six round tables were set for dinner, each seating ten. At each place a souvenir program listed the events of the evening and the bill of fare: haggis, tatties and neeps, Forfar bridies, Pitlochry salad, tea, shortbread, and a "wee dram" for toasting.

"We'll sit here and save a seat for Andy," said Big Mac, leaning a chair against a table. "He has to pipe in the haggis before he can sit down."

Looking around at the ancient weapons on the walls, Qwilleran remarked, "Does the FBI know about the arsenal you have up here? You could start a war with Lockmaster."

"It's our private museum," said his host. "I'm the registrar. We have 27 broadswords, 45 dirks, 12 claymores, 7 basket hilts, 14 leather bucklers, 12 pistols, 21 muskets, and 30 bayonets, all properly catalogued."

Politely Qwilleran inquired about Glenda's health. "Has she recovered from the stress of the tour?"

"Frankly, she should have stayed in Pickax. She doesn't like to travel," her husband explained. "She'd rather watch video travelogues. I took eight hundred pictures on this trip just for her. She gets a kick out of putting them in albums and labeling them. How about you? Did you stick it out to the end?"

"All except Edinburgh, but I'd like to go back there with Polly someday."

"We spent a couple of days in Auld Reekie before catching our plane. I left Glenda in the hotel and went out taking pictures. You can get some good bird's-eye views in Edinburgh. I climbed 287 steps to the top of a monument. The castle rock is 400 feet high. Arthur's Seat is 822 feet. Funny name for a hill, but the Scots have some funny words. How about 'mixty-maxty' and 'whittie-whattie'? Don't ask me what they mean."

Big Mac was more talkative than he had been with the nervous Glenda in tow, and he had statistics for everything: where 300 witches were burned and who died from 56 dagger wounds. He was interrupted by the plaintive wail of a bagpipe.

The rumble of male voices faded away. The double doors burst open, and a solemn procession entered and circled the room, led by Chief Brodie. Normally a big man with proud carriage, he was a formidable giant in full kit with towering feather "bonnet," scarlet doublet, fur sporran, and white spats. With the bag beneath his arm and the drones over his shoulder, he swaggered to the slow heroic rhythm of "Scotland the Brave," the pleated kilt swaying and the bagpipe filling the room with skirling that stirred Qwilleran's Mackintosh blood. Behind the piper marched a snare drummer, followed by seven young men in kilts and white shirts, each carrying a tray. On the first was a smooth gray lump; that was the haggis. On each of the other six trays was a bottle of Scotch. They circled the room twice. Then a bottle was placed on each table, and the master of ceremonies—in the words of Robert Burns—addressed the "great chieftain o' the puddin' race," after which the assembly drank a toast to the haggis. It was cut and served, and the marchers made one more turn about the room before filing out through the double doors to the lively rhythm of a strathspey.

Brodie returned without bagpipe and bonnet to join them at the table.

"Weel done, laddie," Qwilleran said to him. "When a Brodie plays the pipe, even a Mackintosh gets goosebumps. That's an impressive instrument you have."

"The chanter's an old one, with silver and real ivory. You can't get 'em like that any more," Brodie said. "I'm a seventh-generation piper. It used to be a noble vocation in the Highlands. Every chief had his personal piper who went everywhere with him, even into battle. The screaming of the pipes drove the clans to attack and unnerved the enemy. At least, that was the idea."

When dinner was served, Big Mac leaned over and asked the chief, "Are you related to the master criminal of Edinburgh, Andy? I saw the place where he was hanged in 1788."

"Deacon Brodie? Well, I admit I've got his sense of humor and steel nerves, but he wasn't a piper."

Qwilleran said, "We've had a lot of excitement on Goodwinter Boulevard this week, with the TV coverage and the mob that turned out for the preview."

"It'll be worse tomorrow," Brodie said with a dour look.

"Why is the sale being held at the house?"

"Too many ways to cheat when it's trucked away for an auction. I'm not saying Foxy Fred is a crook, you understand, but Dr. Melinda's a sharpie. Never underestimate that lassie!"

"Tell me something, Andy—about those break-ins on Purple Point. We never had break-ins when I first came here, but since they've started promoting tourism, the picture is changing."

"You can't blame the tourists for Purple Point; that was done by locals—young kids, most likely—who knew when to hit. They knew the cottages are vacant in September except on weekends. Besides, they took small stuff. An operator from Down Below would back a truck up to the cottage and clean it out."

"What kind of thing did they take?"

"Electronic stuff, cameras, binoculars. It was kids."

The emcee rapped for attention and announced the serious business of drinking toasts. Tribute was paid to William Wallace, guerrilla fighter and the first hero of Scotland's struggle for independence.

MacWhannell said to Qwilleran, "He was a huge man. His claymore was five feet four inches long."

Then the diners toasted the memory of Robert the Bruce, Mary Queen of Scots, Bonnie Prince Charlie, Flora Macdonald, Robert Burns, Sir Walter Scott, and Robert Louis Stevenson, the response becoming more boisterous with each ovation. Qwilleran was toasting with cold tea, but the others were sipping usquebaugh.

The evening ended with the reading of Robert Burns's poetry by the proprietor of Scottie's Men's Store and the singing of "Katie Bairdie Had a Coo" by the entire assembly with loud and lusty voices, thanks to the usquebaugh. That was followed by a surprisingly sober "Auld Lang Syne," after which Brodie said to Qwilleran, "Come to the kitchen. I told the catering guy to save some haggis for that smart cat of yours."

Many of the members lingered in the lounge, but Qwilleran thanked his host and drove home with his foil-wrapped trophy. When he reached the barn the electronic timer had illuminated the premises indoors and out. "Treat!" he shouted as he entered through the back door, his voice reverberating around the balconies and catwalks. The cats came running from opposite directions and collided head-on at a blind corner. They shook themselves and followed him to the feeding station for their first taste of haggis.

As Qwilleran watched their heads bobbing with approval and their tails waving in rapture, an infuriating thought occurred to him: Is this why Koko wanted me to go to the lodge hall? The notion was too farfetched even for Qwilleran to entertain. And yet, he realized Koko was trying to communicate.

Qwilleran wondered, Am I barking up the wrong tree? . . . Am I suspecting the wrong person? . . . Are my suspicions totally unfounded? And then he wondered, Am I working on the wrong case?

He considered Koko's reaction to Melinda's voice on the tapes . . . the licking of photographs in which she appeared . . . the whisker-bristling when she called on the phone . . . his hostile attitude after Qwilleran had spent a mere two minutes with her at the rehearsal. It could be Koko's old animosity, remembered through sounds and smells. It could be a campaign to expose something reprehensible: a lie, a lurking danger, a guilty secret, a gross error.

That was when Qwilleran dared to wonder, Did Melinda make a mistake in Irma's medication? Could it be that she—not the bus driver—was responsible for Irma's fatal attack?

Fourteen

On Saturday morning, in the hours between midnight and dawn, residents of Goodwinter Boulevard sleeping in bedrooms insulated by foot-thick stone walls became aware of a constant rumbling, like an approaching storm. If they looked out the window, they saw a string of headlights moving down the boulevard. Several of the residents called the police, and the lone night patrol that responded found scores of cars, vans, and pickups parked at the curb, leaving a single lane for moving traffic. The occupants of these vehicles had brought pillows, blankets, and thermos jugs; some had brought children and dogs. The more aggressive were on the front porch of the Goodwinter mansion, lined up on the stone floor in sleeping bags.

When the officer ordered the motorists to move on, they were unable to comply, being trapped at the curb by incoming bumper-to-bumper traffic. Both eastbound and westbound lanes were clogged with the constant stream of new arrivals, and when the curb space was all occupied, they pulled into private drives and onto the landscaped median. The patrol car itself was unable to move after a while, and the officer radioed for help.

Immediately the state police and sheriff's cars arrived, only to be faced with a vehicular impasse. Not a car could move. By this time lights were turned on in all the houses, and influential residents were calling the police chief, the mayor, and Foxy Fred at their homes, routing them out of bed and into the chill of a late September morning.

First, the police blockaded the entrance to the westbound lane and started prying vehicles from the eastbound lane until the traffic flow was restored. Motorists who had parked in private drives or on the grassy median were ticketed and evicted.

By that time, dawn was breaking, and legal parkers were allowed to stay, since the city had lifted the ban on curb parking for the duration of the tag sale. As for the evicted vehicles, they now lined both sides of Main Street, while more traffic poured into the city from all directions.

Qwilleran heard about the tie-up on the WPKX newscast and called Polly. "How are you going to get out to go to work?" he asked.

"Fortunately it's my day off, and I'm not leaving my apartment for anything less than an earthquake. Besides, my car is at Gippel's garage . . . You can imagine that Bootsie is quite upset by the commotion."

"What's wrong with your car?"

"It's the carburetor, and the mechanic is sending away for a rebuilt one. It won't be ready until Tuesday. But that's no problem; I can walk to and from the library."

"I don't want you walking alone," he said.

"But . . . in broad daylight?" she protested.

"I don't want you walking alone, Polly! I'll provide the transportation. Is there anything I can do for you today? Need anything from the store?"

"Not a thing, thank you. I plan to spend the day cleaning out closets."

"Then I'll pick you up at six-thirty tomorrow night," he said. "We have a seven o'clock reservation at Linguini's."

Qwilleran lost no time in hiking to the tag sale. It was his professional instinct to follow the action. The action was, in fact, all over town. The overflow from Goodwinter Boulevard and Main Street now filled the parking lots at the courthouse, library, theatre, and two churches, as well as the parking space that business firms provided for customers only.

On the boulevard excited pedestrians who had parked half a mile away were swarming toward No. 180, while others were leaving the area with triumphant smiles, carrying articles like bed pillows, boxes of pots and pans, and window shades. Foxy Fred had organized the crowd in queues, admitting only a few at a time, and the lineup extended the length of the westbound sidewalk and doubled back on itself before doing the same on the eastbound sidewalk. Persons with forethought had brought folding camp stools, food, and beverages.

Across from the doctor's residence there was another stone mansion that Amanda Goodwinter had inherited from her branch of the family, and when Qwilleran arrived on the scene she was standing on her porch with hands on hips, glaring at the mob.

"The city council will act on this at our next meeting!" she declared when she saw him. "We'll pass an ordinance against disrupting peaceful neighborhoods with commercial activities! I don't care that she's my cousin *and* a doctor *and* an orphan! This can't be allowed! She's a selfish brat and always has been!" Amanda looked fiercely up and down the street. "The first person who parks in my drive or on my lawn is going to get a blast of buckshot!"

Qwilleran pushed his way through the crowd and around to the back door, flashing his press card, and entered through the kitchen, where he scrounged a cup of coffee. In the front of the house Foxy Fred's red-coated helpers were expediting sales and handling will-calls. Portable items were carried to the row of cashiers in the foyer, and purchasers of furniture and other large items were instructed to haul them away on Monday, or Tuesday—no later.

The Comptons were there, and Lyle said to Qwilleran, "If you think this is a mess, wait till the trucks start coming to pick up the big stuff next week."

"We've got a will-call on that black walnut breakfront," Lisa said. "I'd love to have the silver tea set." She glanced at her husband hopefully.

"At that price we don't need it," he said. "There are no bargains here. Melinda's going to make out like gangbusters on this sale. I saw a lot of vans and station wagons with out-of-county plates, probably dealers willing to pay the prices she's asking."

Lisa said, "I loved your story on the teddy bears, Qwill, and we saw Grace Utley on television. I wonder what she thinks of this madhouse."

"She was smart enough to leave town on the eve of the preview."

"Any news about the jewel theft?"

"Not to my knowledge."

Lyle said, "I'll bet she wanted them stolen so she could spend the insurance money on those damned teddy bears!"

On the way home Qwilleran caught up with Dwight Somers, walking empty-handed toward Main Street. "I'm getting out of here," said the director. "The line is the equivalent of twelve blocks long!"

"Would you like to come over to the barn for a drink or a cup of coffee?"

"I'd sure like to see your barn. I'm parked in the theatre lot."

After he picked up his tin whistle from his car, they started out on foot through the woods. "A hundred years ago," Qwilleran explained, "this barn serviced a large apple orchard."

"Larry told me about the murder in the orchard following a Theatre Club party. That was quite a story!"

"That was quite a party! Have you been lucky enough to plug into the Pickax grapevine?"

"I'm not a full subscriber yet. I think I'm on probation."

"The barn was used for storing apples and pressing cider originally, and even after it was renovated we could smell apples in certain weather. The orchard suffered a blight at one time, and the dead wood has been removed, but when the wind blows through the remaining trees, it sounds like a harmonica and frightens the cats."

"How many do you have?" Dwight asked.

"Two cats. Forty-seven trees."

Dwight was properly impressed by the octagonal shape of the barn and the interior system of ramps and balconies surrounding the central fireplace cube. The Siamese, who usually disappeared when a stranger entered, did him the honor of approaching within ten feet, and Koko struck a pose like an Egyptian bronze.

"Beautiful animals," said the visitor. "I used to have a Siamese—when I was married. Why is the little one staring at me like that?"

"She's fascinated by your beard. She likes beards, moustaches, toothbrushes, hair brushes—" Qwilleran said. "What'll you have to drink?"

"It's early. Make it coffee."

While they waited for the promising gurgle of the computerized coffeemaker, Qwilleran asked, "What brought you to Moose County, Dwight? Most people don't even know it exists."

"To tell the truth, I'd never heard of it until the placement agency sent me up here. The company I worked for in Des Moines merged with another, and I was outsourced. XYZ Enterprises was looking for a PR rep who could contribute to the community in some useful way and improve their corporate image, which is pretty grim right now."

"I know. Developers frighten people. The general public doesn't like to see changes in the landscape, for better or worse."

"That's the truth! My chief asset was that I'd acted and directed in community theatre, so here I am, and I like it! Never thought I'd like living in a small town."

"This is not your average small town," Qwilleran pointed out as he served the coffee.

"I can see that! Our basic idea is to make our presence felt in a positive way through participation. For example, we're collaborating with the hospital auxiliary on the first annual Distinguished Women Awards next Friday. A couple of your friends are on the list."

"How's the play shaping up?"

"On the whole I'm pleased with it. Wally Toddwhistle built some fabulous sets out of junk. Fran Brodie designed the costumes, and Wally's mother is making them. Fran is codirector—a very talented girl! Attractive, too—with those race-horse legs! Has she ever been married?"

"I don't think so. Do you know she designed the interior of this barn?"

Dwight glanced at the square-cut contemporary furniture, the Moroccan rugs, the large-scale tapestries. "She did a great job! She did Melinda's apartment, too. That girl must have spent a mint on it!"

"Melinda has expensive tastes."

Dwight had put his tin whistle on the coffee table, and Yum Yum was stalking it. With her body close to the floor she was creeping in slow motion toward the shiny black tube. Just before she pounced, Qwilleran shouted a sharp "No!" and she slunk away backwards as slowly as she had advanced. "She'll steal anything that weighs less than two ounces," he explained.

Dwight said, "I brought the whistle to get your opinion, Qwill. I'm going to tape some weird tunes to play during the witches' scenes." He picked up the whistle and tootled some wild, shrill notes that sent Koko and Yum Yum hurtling up the ramp and out of sight, with their ears back and their tails bushed.

"I think you've hit it right," Qwilleran said. "Even the cats' hair is standing on end . . . How did your Macduff turn out?"

"Better than I expected, especially in his scene with Macbeth. When he has Larry to bounce off, he's really with it. Larry is a superb actor."

"And Lady Macbeth?"

"Well . . ." the director said with hesitation. "I have to tell you her performance is erratic. At one rehearsal she really gets inside the character, and the next night she seems diffused. Frankly, I'm disappointed. She says she hasn't been sleeping well."

"Do you think she's worrying about something?" Qwilleran asked, smoothing his moustache.

"I don't know. Another thing. She doesn't take direction very well," Dwight complained. "Is that because she's a doctor? You can't tell them anything, you know. Was she difficult when she lived here before?"

"No, she was fun to be with, and she had a great zest for life. When I inherited the Klingenschoen mansion, she staged a formal dinner party for me—with a butler, footmen, two cooks, musicians, sixteen candles on the table, and a truckload of flowers. She had unbounded energy and enthusiasm then. Something must have happened to her in Boston."

"I hate to mention this, Qwill, but I wonder if she's on drugs. I know there are hard-driving physicians who take diet pills to keep going, then downers so they can unwind. They become addicted."

Qwilleran recalled the new strangeness in Melinda's eyes. "You could be right. One reads about health-care professionals becoming chemically dependent, as they say."

"What can anyone do about it? She might get into serious trouble."

"There are treatment centers, of course, but how would one convince her to get help? Assuming that's really her problem."

The director said, "I'm concerned enough that I've coached someone to do Lady Macbeth in case Melinda doesn't make it on Wednesday night. Keep your fingers crossed!" He pocketed his tin whistle and stood up. "This is all between you and me, of course. Thanks for the coffee. You've got a fabulous barn."

After he had left, the Siamese ambled down the ramp cautiously, and Yum Yum looked in vain for the tin whistle. Koko alarmed Qwilleran, however, by sniffing one of the light Moroccan rugs. With his nose to the pile, he traced a meandering course as if following the path of a spider. Qwilleran dropped down on hands and knees to intercept it, but there was nothing but an infinitesimal spot on the rug. Koko sniffed it, pawed it, nuzzled it.

"You and your damned spots!" Qwilleran rebuked him. "You just like to see me crawling around! This is the last time I'm going to fall for it!"

The next day, when Qwilleran went out for the Sunday papers, he walked past the entrance to Goodwinter Boulevard and was appalled at the condition of the exclusive enclave. Food wrappers and beverage containers littered the pavement and sidewalks. Lawns had been trampled and the landscaped median was gouged by tires. Melinda had made no friends among her neighbors. It would be Monday before the city equipment could undertake the cleanup, and the cartage trucks were yet to come.

When Qwilleran picked up Polly for their dinner date that evening, she said, "For two days trucks will be backing into the Goodwinter driveway, running over curbs, ruining bushes, and knocking down stone planters."

"Why did the city let them do it?" he asked.

"In the first place, no one asked permission, I suppose, and even if they did, who would speak up against the estate of the revered Dr. Halifax? This is a small town, Qwill."

To reach Linguini's restaurant they drove north toward Mooseville, and Qwilleran was describing Scottish Night at Brodie's lodge when his voice trailed off in mid-sentence. They were passing the Dimsdale Diner, and he spotted a maroon car with a light-colored license plate in the parking lot.

"You were saying . . ." Polly prompted him.

"About the haggis . . . yes . . . It's not bad. In fact, it's pretty good if you like spicy concoctions. Even the cats liked it!"

The Italian trattoria in Mooseville was one of the county's few ethnic restaurants—a small mama-and-papa establishment in a storefront with a homemade sign. Mr. Linguini cooked, and Mrs. Linguini waited on tables. There were no murals of Capri or Venice, no strings of Italian lights, no red-and-white checked tablecloths or candles stuck in antique chianti bottles, no romantic mandolins on the sound system—just good food, moderate prices, and operatic recordings. Mr. Linguini had made the tables from driftwood found on the beach, and they were covered with serviceable plastic, but the napkins were cloth, and diners could have an extra one to tie around the neck. Qwilleran had chosen Linguini's because . . . well, that was the surprise.

Mildred Hanstable was still living at her cottage on the beach, so they stopped to pick her up, Arch Riker choosing to meet them at the restaurant. There was a reason why he wanted to drive his own car, Qwilleran suspected; they had not been lifelong friends without developing a certain transparency. The paunchy, ruddy-faced publisher was Mildred's boss at the *Moose County Something,* for which she wrote the food column, and when the three of them arrived, he was already sitting at the four-stool bar sipping a tumbler of Italian red. The opera of the evening was *Lucia di Lammermoor.*

Mrs. Linguini gave them the best of the eleven tables and then stood staring at the four of them with one fist on her hip. That was Linguini body language for "What do you want from the bar?"

"What are you drinking tonight?" Qwilleran asked Mildred.

"Whatever you're having," she said.

"One dry sherry, two white grape juice," he told Mrs. Linguini, "and another of those for the gentleman."

Mildred said, "Dr. Melinda wants me to lose weight, so I'm off alcohol for a while, and I'd like to ask you a personal question, Qwill, if you don't mind. When you first went on the wagon, how did you feel about going to parties?"

"Well, all my partying was done at press clubs around the country—"

"And Qwill was a hell-raiser when he was young," Riker interrupted.

"When I first stopped drinking, I stayed away from press clubs and felt sorry for myself. That was phase one. In phase two, I found I could go to parties, drink club soda, and have a nice time. *Not a good time,* but a nice time . . . Now I realize that a good time depends on the company, the conversation, and the occasion—not a superficial high induced by a controlled substance."

"I'll drink to that!" said Riker.

There were no menu cards, and everyone in the restaurant had to eat what Mr. Linguini felt like cooking on that particular evening.

Accordingly, when Mrs. Linguini brought the drinks, she also plumped down four baskets of raw vegetables and a dish of bubbling sauce kept hot over a burner. *"Bagna cauda!"* she announced. "You dip it. Verra nice."

Riker, a meat-and-potatoes man, looked askance at the vegetables, but when he tasted the anchovy and garlic sauce, he ate his whole basketful and some of Mildred's.

"Zuppa di fagioli!" Mrs. Linguini said when she brought the soup course. "Verra nice."

"Looks like bean," he observed.

"And now tell me about Scotland," Mildred requested. "Were you pleased with the tour?"

"Scotland is haunting and ingratiating," Qwilleran replied, "but when a tour guide is telling me what to look at, I don't absorb the scene as much as I do when I make my own discoveries."

"Hear! Hear!" said Riker.

"The four of us should go back there next year, rent a car, stay at bed-and-breakfasts, meet some Scots, and discover Scotland for ourselves. Of course, it's more work that way, and takes more time, and requires research."

The soup bowls having been removed, the pasta course appeared. Mrs. Linguini could hardly be said to serve; she delivered, banging the food on the table without ceremony. *"Tortellini quattro formaggi.* Verra nice."

"Four cheeses! There goes my diet," Polly complained.

"I adore tortellini," said Mildred, "even though they're known as bellybuttons. The legend is that they were inspired by Venus's navel."

"If you like legends," Polly told her, "you'll love Scotland! They have kelpies living in the lochs, ogres in haunted graveyards, and tiny fairies dressed in moss and seaweed who weave tartans from spiderwebs."

"We didn't see any," Riker said. "Probably went at the wrong time of year."

"How do you like tonight's pasta?" Qwilleran asked.

"Verra nice!" they chorused in three-part harmony.

Then Mildred wanted to know about the jewel theft, and they all pieced together the story, with Qwilleran concluding, "Scotland Yard is looking for the bus driver."

"Does anyone know why it's called Scotland Yard?"

No one knew, so Polly promised to look it up at the library the next day. Next they talked about the tag sale and Dr. Hal's secret hobby.

Riker said, "We're breaking the story on Monday's front page. The K Foundation is buying the whole collection for $100,000."

"Wonderful!" said Mildred. "Melinda needs the money."

"I wouldn't say she's hurting. I see her $45,000 car parked on the lot at Indian Village."

Qwilleran mused over his pasta as Mildred extolled the paintings. He wondered if the saintly Dr. Halifax had yet another secret in his life. Perhaps his monthly payments through a Lockmaster bank had not gone to his profligate son, else why would they continue after the young man's death? "Did either of you know the doctor's son?" he asked the two women.

"He never came into the library," Polly said.

"He wasn't in any of my classes," said Mildred, "but I know he was a problem at school and a worry to his parents."

"And yet I suppose they gave him a big funeral and pulled out all the stops."

"No, just a memorial service in the home for the immediate family. His mother was bedridden, you know."

Skeptical as always, Qwilleran thought, Perhaps the car crash was no accident; it could have been planned. He remembered another such scandal in Pickax, involving a "good family." If such were the case, the doctor's payments were extortion money, going to a hired killer.

"Here she comes again," Riker mumbled.

The entrée was delivered. "*Polpettone alla bolognese!* Verra nice."

"It's meat loaf," he said after tasting it.

"But delicious! I'd love to take some home to Bootsie," Polly said.

That prompted Qwilleran to describe Koko's reaction to the Scottish tapes—how he responded to certain voices and certain sounds. Then Polly told how she liked to tease Bootsie when he was on her lap by reciting "Pickin' up paw paws, puttin' 'em in a basket." She said, "The implosive *P* tickles the sensitive hairs in his ears, and he protests."

"Now I'll tell one," Qwilleran said. "On one of my tapes, Lyle Compton tells about the Scottish psychopath who poisoned prostitutes in three countries. As soon as he mentions 'pink pills for pale prostitutes,' Koko protests forcibly, although the implosive *P* is coming from a recorder and can't possibly tickle his ears!"

"We all know that Koko is an extraordinary animal," Riker said mockingly. "He gives new meaning to the word 'cat' . . . Ye gods! Here comes dessert!"

"*Zuccotto!* Verra nice," said Mrs. Linguini.

As the overstuffed diners gazed at the concoction of cream, chocolate, and nuts, the coloratura aria coming from the speakers was the Mad Scene from *Lucia*.

"How appropriate!" Polly remarked.

Abruptly the music stopped, and diners at all the tables looked up as Mr. Linguini in long apron and floppy white hat burst through the kitchen door. Going down on one knee alongside Polly, he flung his arms wide and sang in a rich operatic baritone:

"Hoppy borrrthday to you,
"Hoppy borrrthday to you,
"Hoppy borrrthday, cara mia,
"Hoppy borrrthday to you!"

Everyone in the room applauded. Polly clasped her hands in delight and looked fondly at Qwilleran, and *Lucia di Lammermoor* resumed.

Mildred said, "No one told me it was your birthday, Polly. You must be a Virgo. That's why you're so modest and efficient and serene."

The evening ended with espresso, and with difficulty the party pushed themselves away from the table. Riker volunteered to drop Mildred off at her cottage, since it was right on his way to Indian Village. Uh-huh, Qwilleran mused; just what I expected.

He and Polly drove home in silence. She was a happy woman who had had too much food; he was purposely holding his tongue. He wanted to say, I still think your friend didn't die of natural causes; I suspect Melinda made an error in Irma's medication. But it was Polly's birthday, and he refrained from spoiling it with another conjecture. One should be able to say anything to a close friend, he reflected, and yet part of friendship was knowing what not to say and when not to say it, a bit of philosophy he had learned from recent experience.

When they turned into Goodwinter Boulevard, the old-fashioned streetlamps were shedding a ghastly light on the scene of Saturday's nightmare, and their car headlights exposed piles of litter in the gutter. As they approached the Gage mansion and slowed to turn into the side drive, their headlights picked up something else that should not have been there: a car parked the wrong way, with a bearded man at the wheel.

"There he is again!" Polly screamed.

Fifteen

When Polly screamed, Qwilleran opened his car door and stepped out, facing the parked car.

"Don't!" she cried. "He may be dangerous!"

Immediately the other car went into reverse, then gunned forward, swerving around Qwilleran and narrowly missing his elbow. It headed for Main Street, traveling the wrong way in the westbound lane, traveling without lights.

"Let's get to the phone," Qwilleran said as he jumped back in the car and turned up the drive to the carriage house.

The patrol car responded at once, followed by the police chief himself, wrenched away from his Sunday night TV programs.

Qwilleran told Brodie, "This is the same prowler who was hanging around last June—the same M.O., the same beard—although he pulled the visor down when he found himself spotlighted. Last June you ran a check. He's Charles Edward Martin of Charlestown, Massachusetts."

"Did you get the number tonight?" Brodie asked.

"He drove away fast without lights, although I'd guess it was a light-colored plate—the kind we've seen before. His taillights didn't go on until he reached Main Street and turned right . . . I told you the car had been seen in Dimsdale, Mooseville, and Indian Village, and you made some quip about selling cemetery lots."

The chief's grunt was half recollection and half apology.

"Since we pried you out of your comfortable recliner, Andy, would you take a cup of coffee? . . . Polly, do you feel like brewing a pot?"

She was sitting on the sofa, hugging her cat and looking upset. "Certainly," she said weakly and left the room.

In a lower voice Qwilleran said, "Why does this guy lie in wait for Polly? I've told you my suspicions. Whoever this creep is, he knows her connection with me, and he's plotting abduction. Believe me!" He massaged his moustache vigorously. "Incidentally, he's the same guy I saw shoplifting at the Goodwinter sale."

Brodie was not interested in coffee, but he gulped it, promised full cooperation, and went home to catch the eleven o'clock news.

Polly paced the floor nervously. "Why does he loiter around here, Qwill?" She had the intelligence to know the answer, and Qwilleran knew she was aware of the reason, yet neither of them wanted to put it into words. Instead, he assured her that three police agencies would be working on it.

"But it will call for intensive vigilance on your part, Polly. I don't want you going anywhere alone! I'll drive you to and from work, take you shopping, deliver you to evening meetings. It will be a bore for you, but it won't last long. The police know exactly what they're looking for, and they'll soon pick him up for questioning."

Qwilleran refused to abandon her until her equanimity was restored, so it was late when he left the carriage house. He almost forgot the birthday gift in the trunk of the car. The sight of the blue gown and robe ensemble did much to cheer her—or so she made it seem. It was unclear who was trying to reassure whom.

The next morning, after driving Polly to the library, he took his white car to Gippel's garage. "Give this crate the once-over, will you?" he asked the head mechanic. "And let me have a loaner for the day."

Gippel's loaners had decent engines, but the paint was dull, the fenders were bent, the springs were worn out, the interior was dirty, and the upholstery was torn—exactly the kind of vehicle Qwilleran wanted for a tour of Moose County. His first destination was Dimsdale, where his loaner looked quite normal in Shantytown. There was no maroon car there. Next he drove to Mooseville and checked the Shipwreck Tavern, the eatery called the Foo, and the shabby waterfront where he had once made the mistake of chartering a boat. From there he proceeded east along the lakeshore to the affluent resort area called Purple Point, which was completely deserted on a September Monday. Next came the village of Brrr, coldest spot in the county. Already it was in the throes of November winds from the northeast, and the scene was bleak. Even the parking lot of the Hotel Booze was empty, but Qwilleran went into the Black Bear Café to see Gary Pratt, the proprietor. With his shaggy hair and beard he resembled the mounted black bear at the entrance. Gary was puttering behind the bar.

"Where's everybody?" Qwilleran asked.

"It's early. They'll be in for burgers at noon. What brings you up here?" Automatically he poured a glass of Squunk water on the rocks.

"Just moseying around before snow falls. What kind of winter do you expect?"

"Lots of snow but an early thaw. I see by the paper that you went to Scotland. How'd you like it?"

"Nice country. Reminds me of Brrr. Did you do much sailing this summer?"

"Not as much as I'd like to. Business was too good."

"If you guys are going to promote tourism," Qwilleran said, "you can kiss your summer loafing goodbye . . . but then you can afford to go to Florida in the winter."

"That's not for me. I like winters up here. I'm into dogsledding."

"Are you getting more out-of-state customers these days?"

"Yeah, quite a few."

"Have you run into a guy from Massachusetts called Charles Martin? Wears a beard like yours. Drives a maroon car."

"There was a bearded guy in here, trying to sell cameras and watches to my customers—obviously hot. I threw him out," Gary said.

Two other bartenders reported similar incidents. Otherwise, no one knew a Charles Martin. Qwilleran visited Sawdust City, North Kennebeck, Chipmunk, Trawnto, and Wildcat and drank a lot of Squunk water that day.

After returning the loaner he picked up Polly at the library and took her to dinner. Eight hours in the real world of the Dewey decimal system had helped her recover from the fright of the night before, but not from the dinner of the night before. All she wanted to eat, she said, was a simple salad and a bran muffin.

"What did you do all day?" she asked, as they settled in a booth at Lois's Luncheonette.

"Just cruised around, looking for ideas for my column. It was a good day to get out of the house because Mrs. Fulgrove was coming to clean and complain about cathair. I pay her extra for cathair, but she complains just the same."

Polly said, "I looked up the origin of Scotland Yard. It was an area in London with a palace for visiting Scottish kings in the twelfth century. It later became headquarters for the CID."

"Polly, you're the only person I know who follows through."

"That's what libraries are all about," she said with professional pride. "By the way, Gippel called to say the supplier sent the wrong part, so I won't have my car until Friday."

"You have a full-time volunteer chauffeur, so that's no problem," he said. At the same time he was thinking, If no car is parked at her carriage house, the prowler will wait for her to drive in; the police can set a trap. He made a mental note to pass this information along to Brodie.

Driving Polly home, he noted that the trucks were still carting purchases away from the Goodwinter mansion, and he pointed out the breakfront that the Comptons had bought. At her apartment he stayed just long enough for a piece of pie and then went home to feed the Siamese. The conscientious Mrs. Fulgrove was driving away as he pulled into the barnyard, and he waved to her; the woman's scowl indicated that she had worked overtime because of the vast amount of cathair *everywhere*.

He unlocked the back door, expecting to be welcomed by the usual clamor and waving tails, but the cats surprised him by their absence, and when he went to the kitchen to stow his car keys in the drawer, he was surprised to find it open—just enough for an adroit paw to reach in and hook a claw around a small brown velvet teddy bear.

"Oh-oh!" he said and went looking for Tiny Tim. All he found was a pair of debilitated animals lying on the rug in front of the sofa, apparently too weak to jump on the cushioned seat. They were stretched out on their sides, their eyes open but glazed, their tails flat on the floor. He felt them, and their noses were hot! Their fur was hot!

He rushed to the telephone and called the animal clinic, but it was closed. Anxiously he called Lori Bamba, who was so knowledgeable about cats.

"What's the trouble, Qwill?" she asked, responding to the alarm in his voice.

"The cats are sick! I think they've eaten foreign matter. What can I do? The vet's office is closed. Shouldn't they have their stomachs pumped out?"

"Do you know what they ate?"

"A stuffed toy, not much larger than a mouse. It was in a kitchen drawer, and I think Mrs. Fulgrove left it open."

"Was it catnip?"

"No, a miniature teddy bear. They act as if they're doped. Their fur is red hot!"

"Don't panic, Qwill," she said. "Did Mrs. Fulgrove use the laundry equipment?"

"She always puts sheets and towels through the washer."

"Well, the cats probably slept on top of the dryer until they were half-cooked. Our cats do that all the time—all five of them—and the house smells like hot fur."

"You don't think they would have eaten the teddy bear?"

"They may have chewed some of it, in which case they'll throw it up. I wouldn't worry if I were you."

"Thanks, Lori. You're a great comfort. Is Nick there? I'd like to have a word with him."

When her husband came on the line, Qwilleran reported the return of the Boulevard Prowler and his own scouting expedition around the county, adding, "None of the bartenders had heard of Charles Martin, so he might not be giving his right name—that is, if he gives any name at all. He's an unsociable cuss. Anyway, it would be interesting to know where he's holing up."

"I'll still put my money on Shantytown," Nick said. "Anyone can shack up there. Or if he thinks the police are after him, he could hide out in one of the abandoned mines. He could drive his car right into the shafthouse, and no one would ever know."

"Okay, we'll keep in touch. Would you and Lori like to see *Macbeth* on opening night? I'll leave a pair of tickets at the box office in your name."

"I know Lori would like it. I don't know much about Shakespeare, but I'm willing to give it a try."

"You'll like *Macbeth,* Nick. It has lots of violence."

"Don't tell me about violence! I get enough of that at work!"

Next, Qwilleran called Junior Goodwinter at home and said, "You left a message on my machine. What's on your mind?"

"I have news for you, Qwill. Grandma Gage is here from Florida to sign the house over to me. Are you still interested in renting?"

"Definitely." Now Qwilleran was even more eager to live on the property where Polly had her carriage house.

"It has a subterranean ballroom," Junior said to sweeten the deal.

"Just what I need! Can I move in before snow falls?"

"As soon as I have the title."

"Okay, Junior. Are you and Jody going to opening night?"

"Wouldn't miss it!"

By the time Qwilleran had changed into a warmup suit and had read a newsmagazine, the Siamese started coming back to life—yawning, stretching, grooming themselves, grooming each other, and making hungry noises.

"You scoundrels!" he said. "You gave me a fright! What did you do with Tiny Tim?"

Ignoring him, they walked to the feeding station and stared at the empty plate, as if to say, "Where's our grub?"

While Qwilleran was preparing their food, a loud and hostile yowl came from Koko's throat, and he jumped to the kitchen counter, where he could look out the window and stare into the blackness of the woods. Standing on his hind legs he was a long lean stretch of muscle and fur, with ears perked and tail stiffened into a question mark.

"What is it, old boy? What do you see out there?" Qwilleran asked.

There were lights bobbing between the trees—headlights coming slowly along the bumpy trail from the theatre parking lot. He checked his watch. It was the hour when the rehearsal would be over and Dwight would be dropping in for another confidential chat about his problem with Melinda. But why was Koko so unfriendly? He had shown no objection to Dwight on the previous visit, and it was not the first time he had seen mysterious, weaving lights in the woods. Qwilleran turned on the exterior lights.

"Oh, no!" he said. "You were right, Koko."

The floodlights illuminated a sleek, silvery sportscar, and Melinda was stepping out. He went to meet her—not to express hospitality but to steer her around to the front entrance. If she insisted on intruding, he wanted to keep it formal. He approached her and waited for her to speak, bracing himself for the usual brash salutation.

She surprised him. "Hello, Qwill," she said pleasantly. "We just finished our first dress rehearsal. Dwight told me about your barn, and I couldn't wait another minute to see it."

"Come around to the front and make a grand entrance," he said coolly. It was the barn that was grand—not his visitor. She wore typical rehearsal clothes: tattered jeans and faded sweatshirt, with the arms of a shabby sweater tied about her shoulders. Her familiar scent perfumed the night air.

"I remember this orchard when we were kids," she said. "My brother and I used to ride up that trail on our bikes, looking for apples, but they were always wormy. Dad told us never to go into the barn; it was full of bats and rodents."

Opening the front door, he reached in and pressed a single switch that illuminated the entire interior with uplights and downlights, dramatizing balconies, catwalks, and beams.

"Oooooooh!" she exclaimed, which was what visitors usually said.

Qwilleran was aware that the Siamese had scampered up the ramps and disappeared without even waiting for their food.

"You could give great parties here," she said.

"I'm not much of a party giver; I simply like space, and the cats enjoy racing around overhead." He was trying to sound dull and uninteresting.

"Where are the little dears?"

"Probably on one of the balconies." He made no move to take her up the ramps for sightseeing.

Melinda was being unnaturally polite instead of wittily impudent. "The tapestries are gorgeous. Were they your idea?"

"No. Fran Brodie did all the furnishings . . . Would you care for . . . a glass of apple cider?"

"Sounds good." She dropped her shoulder bag on the floor and her sweater on a chair and curled up on a sofa. When he brought the tray, she said, "Qwill, I want to thank you for buying my dad's paintings."

"Don't thank me. The K Foundation purchased them for exhibition."

"But you must have instigated the deal. At a hundred dollars apiece it came to $101,500. Foxy Fred would have sold them for a thousand dollars."

"It was Mildred Hanstable's idea. Being an artist, she saw their merit."

The conversation limped along. He could have sparked it with questions about the play, the tag sale, the clinic, and her life in Boston. He could have turned on a degree of affability, but that would only prolong the visit, and he hoped she would leave after a single glass of cider. She was being too nice, and he suspected her motive.

Melinda said, "I'm sorry I was a nuisance on the telephone last week, Qwill. I guess I was sloshed. Forgive me."

"Of course," he said. What else could he say?

"Do you ever think of the good times we had together? I remember that crazy dinner at Otto's Tasty Eats . . . and the picnic on the floor of my apartment when the only furniture I had was a bed . . . and the formal dinner with a butler and musicians. Whatever became of that pleasant Mrs. Cobb?"

"She died."

"Knowing you, Qwill, was the highlight of my entire life. Honestly! Too bad it had to be so short." She looked at him intently. "I thought you were the perfect man for me, and I still do."

Qwilleran's naturally mournful expression was noncommittal as he recalled his mother's sage advice: When there's nothing to say, don't say it. During his calculated silence Melinda gazed into her glass of cider, and he studied the framed zoological prints on the wall. At the end of the wordless hiatus he asked, "How did the dress rehearsal go tonight?"

She roused from her reverie. "Dwight said it was bad enough to guarantee a good performance on opening night. Will you be there?"

"Yes, I always take a group of friends on opening night."

"Will you come backstage after the show?"

"Unfortunately," he said, "I'm reviewing it for the paper, and I'll have to rush home to my typewriter."

She glanced around the barn. "Why don't the cats come around? I'd love to see them before I go. I always adored little Yum Yum." As Qwilleran recalled, the two females ignored each other. "And I thought Koko was really smart, although I don't think he liked me."

Gratefully Qwilleran sensed that the end of her visit was in view, and to speed the departing guest he summoned the Siamese. "Treat!" he shouted toward the upper regions of the barn. The rumble of eight pounding paws was heard, and two furry bodies swooped neck-and-neck down the ramp to the kitchen. He explained to Melinda, "The T word always works, but I'm honor-bound to deliver, or the strategy loses its effectiveness. Excuse me a moment."

She took the opportunity to browse around, asking about the antique typecase that hung over his desk and remarking about the collection of Scottish tapes, labeled Day One, Day Two, etc. "I'd love to hear them sometime, and your kitchen is so grand, Qwill! Have you learned to cook?"

"No," he said without explanation or apology.

"I've become a pretty good cook. My specialty is Szechuan stir fry with cashews."

Koko polished off his five-eighths of the treat and left the room with purposeful step as if he knew exactly where he was going—and why. Yum Yum lingered, however, and allowed herself to be picked up and cuddled in Melinda's arms.

"Look at her gorgeous eyes! Isn't she a darling?"

"Yes, she's a nice cat."

"Well, I guess I'd better head for home. I have appointments all day tomorrow, starting at seven o'clock at the hospital. And then tomorrow night is the final dress rehearsal."

"Drive carefully," he said.

She picked up her shoulder bag and looked for her sweater. "*What's that?*" Her face wrinkled with disgust. Alongside her sweater was something brown and slimy.

"Sorry about that," Qwilleran said, gingerly removing the chewed remains of Tiny Tim. "Koko was presenting you with a parting gift—his favorite toy." Courteously he walked his uninvited guest to her car and said, "Break a leg Wednesday night!"

He watched the silver bullet wind through the woods and then returned to the barn. Koko was sitting on the coffee table, looking proud of himself; there were times when his whiskers seemed to be smiling. "You're an impertinent rascal," Qwilleran told him with admiration. "Now tell me why she came here tonight."

"Yow," said Koko.

Qwilleran tugged at his moustache. "It was not to see the barn . . . not to see you . . . not to talk about old times . . . What was her real motive?"

Sixteen

The morning after the impromptu visit from Melinda, Qwilleran drove Polly to work. She said, "The trucks were still hauling things away until late last night, but thank goodness they're required to have everything out by tonight. It's been nerve-wracking. Bootsie is very unhappy."

After dropping her at the library, Qwilleran continued on to the police station to see if they had picked up a prowler suspect, but the normally quiet headquarters bristled with activity. Phones were busy; the computer was working overtime; officers were bustling in and out. Brodie, between phone calls, waved Qwilleran away and said, "Talk to you later."

Mystified by the unusual dismissal, Qwilleran backed out of the station and went to the office of the *Moose County Something*. Even the unflappable city room reflected the excitement of breaking news.

"What's happening at the police station?" he asked the managing editor.

"This'll floor you, Qwill," said Junior. "Roger just came from headquarters. You know all those trucks hauling stuff from the Goodwinter sale? One of them backed up to the Utley house last night and cleaned out all the teddy bears! They used the tag sale as a cover. Sounds like professionals from Down Below. By now the stuff is probably on a plane headed for California."

"Where were the women?"

"Still in Minneapolis."

"They had a watchman. Where was he?"

"Threatened at gunpoint and then tied up. His wife was visiting relatives in Kennebeck, came home late and found him bound and gagged."

Qwilleran said, "It would be interesting to know how they transported 1,862 teddy bears."

"They bagged them in leaf bags—those large black plastic ones. That's according to the caretaker."

"I wonder if they got Theodore. He was worth $80,000. No doubt the women had Ulysses and Ignace with them in Minneapolis. Doesn't it sound like an inside job, Junior? I'd question the caretaker. I'd find out if the local supermarkets had a run on black plastic leaf bags in the last few days. Have you talked to Grace Utley?"

"Roger tracked her down in Minneapolis. She's furious, and her sister is under a doctor's care. They're not coming back. They're going to live down there and sell their house, so we'll have one more haunted house on the street. They should change the name to Halloween Boulevard."

A brief bulletin about the theft appeared in the Tuesday paper, ending with the usual statement: "Police are investigating."

Qwilleran spent Tuesday and Wednesday writing copy for his column, when not chauffeuring Polly or helping out at the box office. The house was sold out for opening night, and there was a great ferment of anticipation in Pickax; everyone who was not in the cast knew someone who was. Comments from ticket purchasers were varied: "Dr. Melinda is playing the female lead . . . The director is a new man in town, unmarried . . . That funny Derek Cuttlebrink is in the show."

As Qwilleran and Polly drove to the theatre on opening night, he said, "I think we'll like what Dwight has done with this play. For one thing, he's cut out Hecate's long, boring scene."

"Good decision," she agreed. "It wasn't written by Shakespeare anyway."

Excited and well-attired townfolk were gathering under the marquee of the theatre and milling about the lobby, where the Bonnie Scots photographs were on exhibit. It was a big occasion in a small town, an occasion for dressing up. Polly wore her dinner dress and pearls; Qwilleran wore his suit. When they took their seats in row five on the aisle, Jennifer Olson's family was already there—all ten of them—and Grandma Olson kept waving her program at occupants of surrounding seats and saying, "My granddaughter is in the play!"

The house lights dimmed, and after a moment of breathless silence the haunting notes of a tin whistle filled the theatre—no melody, just sounds from another world.

Polly whispered, "It gives me shivers."

There were rumblings of thunder and flashes of lightning, and three shadowy, gray, ugly creatures whished onto the dimly lighted stage, their bodies bent in half, their voices cackling, "*When shall we three meet again?*" One looked like a cat, another like a toad. "*Fair is foul, and foul is fair!*"

The mood was set, and the story unfolded with the entrance of the king and his sons, the report from the bleeding captain, and praise for brave Macbeth. Then the tin whistle again chilled the audience, and the three witches sidled on stage to celebrate their evil achievements, dancing in an unholy circle as drumbeats were heard off stage. "*A drum, a drum! Macbeth doth come!*"

A murmur rippled through the audience when Larry made his entrance, proclaiming in his great voice, "*So foul and fair a day I have not seen.*" Two scenes later, when Melinda entered as Lady Macbeth, the audience gasped at her costume—sweeping robes of what looked like fur, and a jeweled wimple. When she began her monologue, however, Qwilleran and Polly exchanged brief glances; her delivery lacked energy. Still, act one kept the audience on the edge of their seats: the king murdered by Macbeth . . . the two grooms murdered as a cover-up . . . alarm bells and bloody daggers. There was a moment's comic relief when Derek Cuttlebrink telescoped his youth and height into the arthritic shape of an ancient porter. "*Knock, knock, knock! Who's there?*" At intermission it was the French fry chef from the Old Stone Mill who was the topic of conversation in the lobby.

When Qwilleran spoke to the Comptons, Lyle said, "I think *Macbeth* was written for bumper stickers: *What's done is done! . . . Out, out, brief candle . . . Lay on, Macduff!*"

Lisa said, "Qwill, how do you like Melinda? I think she's dragging."

Her husband agreed. "The sleepwalking scene is supposed to come in act two. She played it in act one."

Most of the audience, while waiting for flashing lights to signal them back into their seats, spoke of other things, as small-town audiences do: "Hey, what did you think about the teddy bear heist?" . . . "Everybody on Goodwinter Boulevard is blowing their stack after that sale!"

Nick and Lori Bamba were there, and Nick whispered something in Qwilleran's ear that he remembered later.

In the second act the weird music accompanied the witches' dance around the cauldron. *"Thrice the brinded cat hath mew'd!"* Macbeth, suffering from strange diseases and seeing ghosts, was going mad. Lady Macbeth walked in her sleep, plagued by visions of bloody hands. *"Out, damned spot! Out, I say!"* To make matters worse, their castle was besieged by an army of ten thousand soldiers.

While waiting for his favorite line—*Tomorrow, and tomorrow, and tomorrow, creeps in this petty pace from day to day*—Qwilleran began to feel uncomfortable. He found himself staring at the stage without seeing it. Then a chilling shriek of women's voices came from the wings. He clapped his hand to his moustache and half rose from his seat, whispering to Polly. "Tell Arch to drive you home!" A second later he was walking quickly up the aisle.

On the stage, Macbeth was saying, *"Wherefore was that cry?"* And an attendant replied, *"The Queen, my lord, is dead!"*

Neither line was heard by Qwilleran. He was running across the theatre parking lot to his car. He drove through the woods at the rear, and as he approached the barn, he could see the long orchard trail and red taillights receding at the far end of it.

The barn's automatic lights were on, indoors and out, but he beamed his headlights on the rear entrance and found the glass panel in the door shattered. Jumping out of his car he hurried into the kitchen. The first thing he saw was blood on the earthen tile floor. "Koko!" he shouted.

The cat was sitting on top of the refrigerator, methodically licking his paws with toes spread wide and claws extended. For one moment, Qwilleran thought he had attacked the intruder and driven him away. Yet, there was too much blood for ordinary cat scratches. More likely the housebreaker suffered gashes from broken glass. He phoned the police from the kitchen, and the patrol car reported immediately, with the state police not far behind. A B&E at the Qwilleran barn had top priority.

By the time they arrived, he had assessed the damage: "Broken window, forced entry, two items missing," he reported. "One is a combination radio and cassette player. The other is a carrying case of cassettes—all spoken tapes from my trip to Scotland plus interviews conducted around Moose County. The tapes would be of no value to anyone, unless he wanted to suppress the material contained, and that's highly unlikely."

Or is it? he wondered, almost at the same moment.

One of the officers said, "They thought it was country music or rock. Cassettes are like candy to the kids."

"You think it was a juvenile break-in?" Qwilleran asked. "It happened just before I arrived home. I saw a car leaving through the orchard and turning right on Trevelyan. Either I interrupted them, or they had taken what they came for. The equipment was on my desk, visible through the windows. The interior lights came on automatically at dusk."

"You should keep the shades pulled when you go out," the officer advised. "Lotta nice stuff here."

"I guess you're right. What's happening to Pickax? Petty thieves . . . master burglars . . . prowlers . . ."

"The town's growing. New people coming in. We were on TV last week."

Koko was watching the police stoically from the top of the refrigerator, and one of them, feeling eyes boring into the back of his head, turned suddenly and asked, "Is that the cat Brodie talks about?"

As soon as they were off the premises, however, Koko's cool behavior changed. He uttered a loud wail from the pit of his stomach, ending in a falsetto shriek.

"For God's sake! What's that about?" Qwilleran gasped. And then he shouted in alarm, "*Where's Yum Yum?*"

She had a dozen secret hiding places and was known to evaporate when strangers came to the house.

"TREAT!" Qwilleran shouted and then listened for the soft thumps meaning a cat had jumped down from a perch. There was a hollow silence.

"TREAT!" His voice reverberated among the beams and balconies, but there was no soft patter of bounding feet. Even Koko was ignoring the irresistible T word; he sat on the refrigerator as if petrified.

Qwilleran peeled off his coat and tie, grabbed a high-powered flashlight from the broom closet, and raced to the upper level to begin a frantic search of every known hiding place, every crevice in the radiating beams, under and over every piece of furniture, inside every drawer and closet . . . all the while calling her name.

He didn't see the headlights approaching the barn through the woods, but he heard the pounding on what remained of the back door. Looking over the balcony railing, he saw Nick and Lori Bamba wandering inquisitively into the kitchen.

"Is this blood on the floor?" Nick was asking.

"What's wrong with Koko?" Lori was saying.

As Qwilleran walked down the ramp, flashlight in hand, Nick called up to him, "I picked up the B&E on my police band when we left the theatre. How bad is it?"

Qwilleran could hardly force himself to say what he was thinking. "It looks . . . as if . . . they've stolen Yum Yum."

"Stolen Yum Yum!" they echoed in shocked unison.

"The police were here, and I reported the theft of a radio and cassettes. I didn't know then that she was missing. I've searched everywhere. I'm convinced she's gone. There's an emptiness when she's not here." He stooped and picked up a stray emery board and snapped it in two. "Koko knows something's radically wrong. He knows she's gone."

"Why would they take her?" Lori wondered.

That was something Qwilleran preferred not to contemplate. He walked aimlessly back and forth, pounding his moustache.

Nick headed for the phone. "I'm going to call the police again."

Qwilleran and the cat on the refrigerator had been staring at each other. "One minute, Nick!" he said. "At the theatre you mentioned you'd seen the prowler again."

"Yes, today. His car was parked outside the Dimsdale Diner, so I went in and sat at the counter next to this bearded guy. The cook called him Chuck. I talked about fishing and baseball, but he didn't respond. I got the impression he wasn't tightly wound, or else he was stoned. I'm sure he hangs out in Shantytown."

"Let's go out there," Qwilleran said impulsively, reaching for a jacket.

"D'you think he's the one who broke in?"

"I'm getting ideas. Everything's beginning to mesh." He combed his moustache vigorously with his fingertips.

"Okay. We'll take my car. It's got everything we need."

Qwilleran said, "Lori, talk to Koko. He's acting like a zombie."

The road north from Pickax ran straight, and Nick drove fast. At Ittibittiwassee Road he turned left into the wooded slum, the car bouncing slowly along the rutted road between the trees, the headlights picking up glimpses of shacks and junk vehicles.

"If his car isn't here," Nick said, "we'll try the site of the old mine."

At the mention of the abandoned mine, and all it implied, Qwilleran felt nausea in the pit of his stomach. "There it is! That's the car!" he said.

Nick turned off his lights and parked in a patch of weeds behind a junk truck. "If he's the right one, I can radio the police."

"How shall we work this?"

"I'll get him to open up. You stand back out of sight, Qwill, until I get my foot in the door."

"Let me go first."

"No. Your moustache is too well known. Hand me the gun from the glove compartment, in case he gives us any trouble."

"Easy with the car door," Qwilleran said, as they stepped out into the weeds.

The maroon car was pulled up to a ramshackle travel trailer with a dim light showing through the small window. A radio was playing. By approaching the window obliquely, the two men could see parts of the interior while avoiding the meagre spill of light into the yard. They saw a heavily bearded man lying on a cot, fully clothed, taking swigs from a pint bottle. Although the face was hairy, red gashes could be seen on the forehead. Another gash crusted with dried blood trailed from the corner of one eye, which was swollen shut.

Qwilleran thought, To get those wounds from glass, he'd have to go through the door headfirst; he was clawed! He whispered to Nick, "I can see my radio and cassettes in there."

They crept forward. Then Nick banged on the door and called out in a friendly voice, "Hey, Chuck! I've got some burgers and beer from the diner!" After a slight delay, the door opened cautiously. It opened outward, and Nick yanked it all the way. "Jeez, man! Wha' happened? You been in a fight—or what?"

"Who're you?" the bearded man mumbled.

"You know me—Harry from the diner." Both men barged through the door as the fellow stepped back uncertainly.

"You're cops!"

"Hell, no! I'm Harry, don't you remember? This is my uncle Bob."

There was a foul odor in the littered trailer, also a large collection of electronic equipment, also a silver pocketknife alongside a small sink.

"Wotcha doin' here?"

"Just wanna warn you, Chuck. The cops are on your tail. You gotta get out of here."

"Where's the beer?"

Qwilleran said with avuncular concern, "Forget the beer, son.

You need a doctor . . . Harry, can we take him to a doctor? . . . Yes, son, you could lose an eye if you don't have it taken care of fast. Where'd you get those bloody gashes?"

"Uh . . . in the woods," was his fuzzy-minded reply.

"You must have been attacked by a wildcat! You can get blood poisoning from something like that. We've got to get you to the hospital for a shot, son, or you're dead! Was it a wildcat? . . . *Or was it a housecat?"* Qwilleran gave it a threatening emphasis.

The wounded man looked at him suspiciously.

Qwilleran, who had been sniffing the fetid air of the trailer like a connoisseur, suddenly bellowed, "TREAT!"

"NOW!" came a piercing shriek from behind a small closed door.

He yanked it open. It was a closet-size toilet, and Yum Yum was perched precariously on the rim. She was wet. She had slipped into the rusty bowl.

Ripping off his jacket, he wrapped it around her, crooning reassurances in her ear. "Take her to the car," he said to Nick, "and stay with her. You know what to do. I want to talk to Chuck for a minute."

Yum Yum knew Nick, and she was purring as he carried her from the trailer. As an afterthought, he took the gun from his pocket and laid it on the sink.

Casually picking it up, Qwilleran said, "Sit down, son. You look sick. The poison's getting into your bloodstream. I want to give you some advice before the police get here. They're going to ask a lot of questions, and you'd better be ready with some good answers."

The fellow sat down on the cot, looking bewildered.

"Where did you get all these radios and cameras?" Qwilleran began. "Where did you get that pocketknife? What brought you here from Massachusetts? Do you know someone in Pickax? Do you have a partner here? Why did you break into my barn and take my cat? Did you think I'd pay a lot of money to get her back? Who told you I had a valuable cat? Was it your partner's idea? What was your name before you changed it to Charles Edward Martin?"

Headlights and flashing blue lights were approaching through the woods.

"Here comes the popcorn machine! Better tell the police the whole truth, or you'll be in bad trouble. And tell them the name of your partner, or they'll throw the book at you, and your partner will go scot-free . . . Here they are! And now, if you don't mind, I'll take my radio and cassettes."

* * *

On the way back to town, Qwilleran held Yum Yum tightly. Only her nose projected from the enfolding jacket as she looked up with trusting eyes and contemplated his moustache. He said, "That guy's not very sharp. He has the instincts of a criminal, I think, but not the capabilities."

"He's punch-drunk," Nick said, "from booze or drugs or both. I've seen a lot of 'em. What I don't understand—how did he manage to grab Yum Yum? She's always leery of strangers."

Qwilleran was not ready to tell the whole story as he perceived it, not even to Nick. He said, "She likes beards. She's a pushover for anything resembling a brush. I think he broke in primarily to abduct one of the cats for ransom. After he had grabbed her and taken her out to the car, he came back for the radio he'd seen on my desk. That's when Koko sprang on his head from the top of the refrigerator and drew blood."

"Mmmmmmmmmm," Yum Yum murmured.

"Yes, sweetheart, we'll soon be home, and you can have a bath."

Nick said, "How did you know she was in that john?"

"The pervading stink in that place had a distinct overtone of cat—nervous cat! I know it well! And there were cat hairs everywhere. I can imagine her flying around that trailer, shedding hair like a snowstorm and finally seeking refuge in that foul closet. My poor little sweetheart!"

Before the Bambas left the apple barn that night, Lori gave Yum Yum a bath, and Qwilleran supplied warm towels, while Nick nailed something over the broken window in the door.

"I feel guilty about keeping you people out so late," Qwilleran said. "Do you have a baby-sitter?"

"Nick's mother is staying overnight," Lori said. "Thank God for mothers-in-law!"

"How could you be so sure, Qwill, that Yum Yum's kidnapper was the Boulevard Prowler?" Nick asked.

"Just a hunch." Qwilleran pounded his moustache with his fist.

After they had gone, he still had to write a review of the play for the Thursday paper, but the Siamese needed comforting, so he touched a match to the combustibles in the fireplace and made a lap for them. Both cats climbed aboard, Yum Yum sinking like a lead weight with her chin on his wrist. Even Koko, who was not a lap-sitter, huddled close to his ribcage.

Only then could he think objectively. He could visualize the headline in the next day's paper: *Goodwinter Heir Alive and in Jail.* He tried to recall when he had first suspected the Boulevard Prowler to be Dr. Hal's son. Absurd though it might seem, it was Yum

Yum's cache of emery boards that steered his mind in that direction. Someone had told him—Carol Lanspeak, he thought—that Melinda's brother was named Emory. Emory spelled with an O was a fairly common name in the Pickax phone book. Every time Qwilleran found a stray emery board on the floor, his mind went to the stray son who was killed in a car crash . . . Then the old gentleman at the Senior Care Facility had talked about the doctor's monthly payments. Emory wasn't Moose County's first remittance man; local historians wrote that wealthy families had often deported undesirable members to areas Down Below to avoid embarrassment to the family name. As for the payments continuing after Emory's death, Qwilleran could invent several explanations but accepted the most credible: Emory was still alive . . . A few days later he met the bearded suspect at the preview of the Goodwinter sale, lingering over a table of family memorabilia: old LP recordings, a much-used piggy bank, the doctor's monogrammed pocketknife, a photo in a silver frame. Upon talking to him, Qwilleran realized that the beard disguised a long narrow face, known in Moose County as the Goodwinter face.

Then, Qwilleran tried to recall, when did I first suspect he had a partner?

The fellow could carry off a solo operation like pilfering a silver pocketknife. And, being a native of Moose County, he would know the best time to break into the Purple Point cottages. But he wasn't smart enough to plot a kidnapping; that was obvious. Furthermore, having lived Down Below for a decade or so, how would he know about Qwilleran's wealth and his relationship with Polly? How would he know about the renovated barn in the orchard and Qwilleran's obsessive concern for his pets? How did he know that Qwilleran would be attending the play on Wednesday night?

When it had become clear to him that the prowler was the resurrected Emory Goodwinter, all the questions were answered, including, "What was the maroon jalopy doing in the elite Indian Village?" and "Why did Melinda drop in so sociably after the rehearsal Monday night, and why was she working so hard to be sweet?"

She dropped in, Qwilleran now believed, to case the premises, and he had played right into her hands, giving her the T word and demonstrating how it worked. He mentally kicked himself, thinking, God, what a fool I was! He remembered her interest in the Scottish tapes, which she probably instructed Emory to grab—just in case they contained information that might be incriminating.

The blaze in the fireplace burned out, and Qwilleran carried the

Siamese to their loft apartment, limp with sleep, and wrote his review of *Macbeth.*

Seventeen

As the Siamese and the rest of Pickax slept, Qwilleran wrote his review of *Macbeth,* praising Larry and being kind to Melinda. Kindness, he had learned, was a large consideration in writing drama criticism for a small town. To maintain some semblance of integrity, however, he expressed his opinion that it was redundant to project the image of a dagger on the back wall of the stage when Macbeth said, *"Is this a dagger which I see before me?"* He wrote, "It distracts audience attention from Shakespeare's great words, although modern grammarians—with their rules about whiches and thats—may be uncomfortable with the famous line."

Convinced that his review was sufficiently charitable, he retired for the night, taking care to set his alarm clock. He had to drive Polly to the library the next morning. Even though the Boulevard Prowler had been apprehended, her car was still at Gippel's garage, awaiting a rebuilt carburetor.

"I was concerned about your sudden exit last night," she said when he called for her, "but Arch said it was a bit of theatricality indulged in by drama critics."

"There's an element of truth in that," he replied evasively. "I'll tell you the whole story when we both have more time. Meanwhile, I'd like you to do me a favor—with no ifs, ands, or buts. Yours not to reason why! Just do it!"

"Well!" she said warily. "Is it so very terrible?"

"Ask your sister-in-law to sneak a look at Irma's medical records in the clinic office. I'm curious about her heart condition and the prescribed medication."

"You're like a dog with a bone, Qwill; you simply won't let go of the matter. I'm not sure it would be ethical, but I'll ask her at church Sunday."

"Ask her today. Phone her and take her to lunch at Lois's. Charge it to me . . . But don't eat too much," he added to lighten the serious aspect of his request.

"I'm overwhelmed by your generosity!"

"Are you going to the women's banquet tonight? I'll take you there and pick you up, and you can tell me her reaction. If it's unethical, ask her to do it anyway. I won't tell."

"Under protest, dear," she sighed as she stepped out of the car. "Have a nice day. Issue lots of new-reader cards!"

From there he drove to the *Moose County Something* to hand in his breathlessly awaited copy, and Arch Riker beckoned him into his private office. "Man, have we got a story!" said the publisher, waving a galley proof. "It's set up in type and ready to go, and we'll break it as soon as your burglar is arraigned. Is this why you ran out of the theatre last night? You must have some kind of burglar alarm implanted under your skin! Or did Koko alert you via mental wireless?" Riker never missed a chance to make a mocking reference to the cat's remarkable abilities, which were beyond his understanding. He handed over the galley:

BREAK-IN EXPOSES
GOODWINTER HOAX

A suspect has been charged with breaking into the Pickax residence of James Qwilleran Wednesday night, bringing to light a six-year-old hoax. The suspect, Charles Edward Martin of Charlestown, MA, is in fact Emory Goodwinter, allegedly killed six years ago in a car crash on the New Jersey Turnpike. Records show his name was legally changed at that time. He is the son of the late Dr. Halifax Goodwinter.

Articles stolen from the Qwilleran residence have been retrieved. The cost of damage is not yet known. Stolen articles in the suspect's possession have been identified as those taken from Purple Point cottages in the last week, total value $7,500. Loitering and shoplifting charges also have been brought.

The suspect is a police prisoner at the Pickax Hospital, where he is being held for treatment of injuries incurred during Wednesday night's break-in.

Qwilleran taunted Riker in return by saying scornfully, "Is that all the information you were able to get?"

"Why? Do you know something we don't?"

"Plenty!" he said, looking wise.

Junior appeared in the doorway. "How'd you like my headline, Qwill? I hated to do that to cousin Melinda, but this is the biggest news since VanBrook. We've been trying to reach her for further details. Can't find her. Emory had a police record before he left town, so the burglaries won't surprise her."

Uh-huh, Qwilleran thought.

"He was running with a gang of vandals from Chipmunk while he was still in high school. The big surprise was to find him alive after his father insisted for six years that he was dead. Do you think she was a party to the hoax, or an innocent dupe like the rest of us?"

Riker said, "Do you have something you want to tell your old buddies, Qwill?"

"Not yet." He had no desire to relive the painful moments of Yum Yum's abduction. As for the identity of Emory's partner, that was something for Emory to disclose. "See you later!" he said with a debonair wave intended to confound them. He was eager to talk to the police chief.

Brodie hailed him as soon as he crossed the threshold at headquarters. "I see you're gonna get your name in the paper again!"

"You should be thanking me for doing your work!" Qwilleran retorted.

"How'd you find him?"

"Nick Bamba, who has an eye like an eagle, had tracked the Boulevard Prowler to the Dimsdale area, and I'd already decided he was Emory. When he broke in and kidnapped my female cat—"

"What! You didn't report anything like that!"

"I didn't know it when I gave the report to the officers. As soon as I learned she was missing, Nick and I found Emory in Shantytown, rescued her, and radioed you. Did Emory identify his accomplice?"

The chief looked at him sharply. "You know about that?"

"I knew he had to have an accomplice, and Melinda was the only person who qualified. Her behavior has been irrational ever since she returned from Boston. Some of us suspect drugs."

"I'm glad the good doctor isn't alive to face this mess. It'd kill him!"

"What are you going to do about her?" Qwilleran asked.

"That'll be up to the prosecutor . . . If you ask me, there was bad blood on her mother's side."

"I assume Emory answered questions cooperatively."

"Best damned suspect we've ever had! Answered questions before we asked 'em. His sister knew about the hoax; they were in touch all the time she was in Boston, and after Dr. Hal died, she sent Emory money once a month. He didn't come for his dad's funeral last

June; he came expecting to collect his inheritance in instant cash. When that didn't work out, Melinda told him another way to get rich quick: Get rid of Mrs. Duncan."

So that was the plot! Qwilleran realized in horror. Murder, not ransom!

His expression caused Brodie to say, "Sit down. Have a cup of coffee."

Qwilleran took his advice. "Melinda had always wanted to marry into the Klingenschoen fortune. She hounded me all summer and halfway across Scotland. Last Sunday, Emory again failed to grab Polly, as you know. The next night, Melinda showed up at the barn after rehearsal, and she was playing America's Sweetheart, without the curls. I couldn't fathom her motive. Now I know. She was plotting with Emory to kidnap one of my cats! For ransom! That woman needs help!"

After his visit with Brodie he stopped at the drug store to buy a few items and chat with the pharmacist, a young man more congenial than the crabby old pill counter who used to be on duty in the prescription cage. Then he went home to brush the cats. Only then did he realize what it would have been like to lose Yum Yum—not to have her pawing his pant leg, reaching up for his moustache, and croodling—worse still, not to know her whereabouts or her fate. Koko himself had not fully recovered from the trauma of the night before; he prowled incessantly and muttered to himself.

"Shall we listen to some tapes?" Qwilleran asked, and Koko ran to the desk, yowling with anticipation. Either he had added "tape" to his vocabulary or he was reading Qwilleran's mind. Of the tapes recorded before Melinda left Scotland, one segment in particular caught Koko's attention—a brief exchange between Polly and Melinda:

> "I didn't know she had a bad heart. She never mentioned her symptoms, and we were the best of friends."
>
> "She was too proud to admit to any frailty—and too independent to take my advice or even medication. It could have saved her."

Qwilleran thought, If Irma refused to take medication, there would be no prescription to foul up; we'll know more about this when Polly's sister-in-law checks Irma's records.

Farther along on the same tape were the voices of, first, the Lanspeaks and then the MacWhannells:

"Do you realize, folks, how lucky we are to have Melinda along on this trip?"

"Irma was coming down with something at the castle today. I told Larry it sounded like laryngitis."

"I knew someone who dropped dead of a sore throat. It's a freak disease—some kind of syndrome."

"Daddy, you suspected something was wrong last night, didn't you?"

"You're right, Mother . . . It so happened we were playing a table game with Polly and Dwight, and I went upstairs to get a sweater for Glenda. We had room No. One, and the girls had Nine and Eleven at the end of the hall. I saw Melinda come out of Eleven and scoot right into her own room. I started to speak to her, but she was preoccupied. I told Glenda right then that Irma must be ill."

Qwilleran thought, Yes, but . . . Irma was out on the moor with Bruce and came in late, according to Polly, so Eleven was empty, because Polly was in the lounge.

"Yow!" said Koko, who seemed to enjoy MacWhannell's chesty voice.

The time came to drive Polly to the Distinguished Women's banquet in the New Pickax Hotel, an event subsidized by XYZ Enterprises with proceeds going to the Pickax Hospital for an intensive care unit. She looked stunning in her blue batwing cape and peacock feather brooch, and he told her so. She wanted to know more about the burglar and the hoax, but he assured her that everything had been reported in the newspaper. The loitering charge, he said, indicated that Emory was the Boulevard Prowler.

After dropping her off, he went to the theatre to have another look at *Macbeth*. He wanted to see if the actors felt more comfortable in their roles and whether Dwight had taken his advice about the dagger. Aware that he could not stay for the entire performance, he slipped into an unsold seat in the back row.

The lights dimmed, and an unwelcome voice came through the speakers—the anonymous voice that announces changes in the cast, usually to everyone's disappointment. "In tonight's performance the role of Lady Macbeth will be played by Jennifer Olson, and the role of Lady Macduff will be played by Carol Lanspeak. Thank you."

There were murmurs in the audience and at least one squeal of delight from some friend of Jennifer's. To Qwilleran the substitution raised an urgent question, and at intermission he went backstage to hunt down Dwight Somers. "Where's Melinda?" he asked.

"I don't know," said the director. "When she didn't report by seven-fifteen, I called her clinic, and the answering machine said they were closed until nine tomorrow morning. Then I called her apartment; no answer. We both live in the Village, you know, and there's an elderly neighbor who knows everything that goes on. I phoned her, and she said that Melinda's car had been in and out of the parking lot all day, but now it was gone again. I even called the police about a possible accident. Nothing! So I decided to go ahead with Jennifer. How's she doing?"

"Not bad, under the circumstances."

"I heard about Melinda's brother. She must be really upset. That's the only reason I can imagine why she wouldn't show, but she should have notified us."

The stage manager was calling "Five minutes," and Qwilleran returned to the auditorium. He stayed through the sleepwalking scene, then slipped out. The banquet would be over.

When he picked up his passenger, she was carrying a large flat box. "I received an award for public service," she said. "It's a very tasteful plaque."

"Congratulations! Recognition is long overdue," he assured her. "What did they serve for dinner? Not chicken cordon bleu, I hope."

"No, some other kind of chicken. It wasn't bad. Of course, the sole topic of conversation was the return of Emory Goodwinter."

"Naturally. How many awards were presented?"

"Ten. It was a tearful moment when Mrs. Hasselrich accepted Irma's posthumous award for volunteerism. Melinda received the health-care award, and a hospital official accepted it, since Melinda had to be at the theatre."

"Correction. She was not at the theatre," Qwilleran said. "Her role was filled by the Olson girl."

"Oh, dear!" Polly said sympathetically. "Melinda must be devastated by the unpleasant publicity!"

"Mmmm," he agreed without conviction. "Who else won a plaque?"

"Oh, let me tell you the sensation of the evening," she said, laughing. "Lori Bamba, as secretary of the auxiliary, was the presenter, and she was wearing a batwing cape just like mine, but in violet. When Fran Brodie went up for the arts award, she had the same thing in green! Mildred Hanstable received the education award, and she was wearing one in royal blue. Finally, Hixie Rice had it in taupe. We stood on the platform in a row looking like a malapropos chorus line—tall, short, plump, thin—but all with batwing capes and peacock brooches! The whole room was in a screaming uproar that simply wouldn't stop until the hotel manager rang the fire bell."

"It just proves," Qwilleran said, "that I know a lot of distinguished women."

Polly invited him up to her apartment for coffee and cake, and they were welcomed by Bootsie, who had the brassy voice of a trumpet.

"How's old Gaspard?" Qwilleran greeted him.

"Really, Qwill, you treat him with such disrespect," she complained.

"He treats me with disrespect. I think he's jealous."

"I think you're jealous, dear." She started the coffee brewing and cut a large wedge of chocolate cake for him and a sliver for herself.

After the first few bites he asked casually, "How did your sister-in-law feel about my request?"

"She said it was highly irregular, but she agreed to bring Irma's records to me at the banquet, provided she could return them early in the morning."

"And?"

"Tonight she informed me that the folder has been removed from the filing cabinet."

"Perhaps they have a special drawer for deceased patients."

"They do, but it was neither there nor in the active file. Why are you interested, Qwill?"

"Just curious . . . Did Mrs. Hasselrich ever mention any disagreement about Irma's funeral?"

"Good heavens, no!"

"She was buried, but Melinda said she wanted to be cremated. How come no one else knew Irma favored cremation?"

"Qwill, dear, I'm afraid to ask what's on your mind."

"Nothing. Just talking off the top of my head. Is there any more cake?"

"Of course. And may I fill your cup?"

After a period of silence, which his hostess attributed to gustatory bliss, he said, "They say vitamin C is good for fighting colds. What kind did you take to Scotland?"

"High-potency capsules, but they were too large for me to swallow comfortably."

"Want me to take them off your hands?"

"I'm afraid I didn't keep them, but you can buy them at the drug store," Polly said. "Irma was complaining of a sore throat, so I offered them to her."

"Did she take them?"

"I don't know. I left them in the bathroom for her and never saw them again. Do you think you're catching cold, dear?"

"I have a slight cough." He coughed slightly. "This is very good cake. Did you make it?"

"I wish I had time to bake. No, I bought it at Toodle's . . . By the way, you didn't tell me how well the Olson girl performed."

"She was scared stiff, but she knew her lines. She'll be better tomorrow night if Melinda doesn't make it." He noticed Polly glancing at her watch. "Well, I'll pick you up tomorrow morning, same time. . . . *What's that?*"

They heard sirens speeding down the boulevard, and they caught glimpses of flashing lights.

"Sounds like an accident," he said, moving toward the door like the veteran reporter that he was. "I'll go and check . . . See you tomorrow!" He ran down the stairs, jogged the length of the driveway, and found neighbors standing on porches and looking westward. Walking rapidly toward the end of the street, he met a couple standing on the sidewalk—the city attorney and his wife.

"We were just coming home," said the woman, "and this car was speeding down the boulevard. There was a terrible crash."

"Going eighty, at least," her husband added. "The driver must have been crocked. Obviously didn't know this is a dead-end street, although it's posted."

"Here comes the sheriff's wagon," Qwilleran said. "They've got to cut someone out of the wreckage." He hurried toward the scene of the accident. Police floodlights were beamed on the small park, the granite monument, and the car crumpled against it.

Running back to his car, he drove home to call the newspaper. He could hear the phone ringing as he unlocked the door, and he caught it before Riker hung up.

"Qwill, I'm phoning from a gas station. If you can rustle up some Scotch, I'll be right there—with some breaking news."

"Come on over," Qwilleran said. "I've got news, too."

Within minutes, Riker walked in, his ruddy face unusually flushed, and he was beaming. The drink was waiting for him, and the two men took their glasses to the lounge area. "What do you think about Mildred Hanstable?" the publisher asked.

"Nice woman."

"She doesn't like living alone, and neither do I. We get along very well. What do you think?"

"I'd like to see you two get together," Qwilleran said with sincerity. "It would be good for both of you."

"Amanda was only a divertissement."

"That's a good word for her. Mildred is more your type."

"Glad to have your blessing, Qwill . . . Now what's your news?"

"A suicidal car crash!"

"Who?"

"Melinda. I recognized the silver bullet she drives. She raced it down Goodwinter Boulevard and rammed it into the Goodwinter monument at the end of the street. She may have been drinking; she may have been stoned. Whatever, I'm positive it was intentional. She grew up on the boulevard; she knew it's a dead end with a speed limit of thirty-five."

"Let me use your phone." Riker tipped off the night desk in his newsroom, then said, "Any idea of the motive, Qwill? Don't tell me she died for love of you, old chum!"

"I don't kid myself that it was anything like that. No, she had personal problems. Lady Macbeth was a metaphor for what was happening in her own life, in my opinion." He declined to divulge the rest of the story to the press, even though Riker was his best friend. If he discussed it with anyone, it would be with Brodie.

The next morning, the opportunity presented itself. The only person in Moose County who would dare to phone Qwilleran before eight A.M. was the police chief. He seemed to take sadistic pleasure in rousting his slow-starting friend out of bed.

"Rise and shine!" Brodie shouted into the phone. "It's daylight in the mines! I'm on my way over to see you."

Groaning and spluttering a few comments, Qwilleran pulled on some clothes, ran a wet comb through his hair, and started the coffeemaker.

In short order the chief strode into the barn, looking bigger than ever as the importance of his mission added to his stature. "Weel, laddie," he greeted his reluctant host in familiar Scots style, "the dead is risen and the mighty is fallen! Did you hear about Dr. Melinda?"

"I heard, and I saw. I was on the boulevard when the ambulance arrived. How about some coffee?"

"Tell you what, pour half a cup and fill it up with hot water, and I'll be able to drink it without having a stroke . . . Got some more news, too. They picked up your bus driver in London, but the loot was smuggled out of Scotland—gone to chop shops on the continent. He admitted the theft but not the murder. Do you still think he drugged her?"

"No, I think Melinda was responsible for Irma's death. It was guilt that drove her over the edge."

"Hmmm, interesting notion," Brodie mused. "She left a suicide note in her apartment that didn't make much sense—all about the smell of blood and a damned spot she could never wash out."

"Those were her lines in the play. It's a confession of murder."

"What did she have against Irma?"

"It was an accident, but she lied to cover up, saying Irma died of natural causes. She wanted the body cremated to conceal the evidence. Then it appears that she destroyed Irma's medical records. No doubt they'd indicate that Irma did not have a heart condition."

"Did you figure this out yourself? Or did your smart cat stick his nose in the case?"

"Andy, you wouldn't believe what he's been doing!"

"I'll believe anything after what Lieutenant Hames told me Down Below."

"First, Koko let out a bloodcurdling howl at the exact moment Irma died in Scotland, and he wasn't even there! Then he shredded her obituary—another indication that something was wrong—and kept pointing his paw at Melinda. He threw a fit when he heard her voice on tape and also destroyed photographs of her. There's something else remarkable, too. Let me play you a tape if I can find it."

Koko, having heard his name, came ambling out from nowhere and stationed himself between the recorder and the police chief, with an ear cocked in each direction.

Fast-forwarding the tape, Qwilleran picked up fragments of his own voice: "another historic inn. I suspect . . . hundreds of pictures on this trip . . . medical school at Glasgow . . ." He said, "Okay, Andy. Listen to this:"

> ". . . the infamous Dr. Cream was a Glaswegian. He was the nineteenth-century psychopath who became a serial killer in England, Canada, and the United States—not as legendary as Jack the Ripper but noted for pink pills . . ."

Koko interrupted with a stern "Yow-w-w" like a yodel, and Qwilleran snapped off the recorder, saying, "Now let me play another tape recorded on the eve of Irma's death, when Melinda came to my room, uninvited." After a few stops and starts, the following dialogue was heard:

> ". . . So I'll make you a proposition—since one has to be conventional in Moose County. If you will marry me, you can have your freedom at the end of three years, and our children

will resume the name of Goodwinter. We might even have a go-o-od time together."

"You're out of your mind."

"The second reason is . . . I'm broke! All I'm inheriting from my dad is obligations and an obsolete mansion."

"The K Foundation can help you over the rough spots. They're committed to promoting health care in the community."

"I don't want institutional support. I want you!"

"To put it bluntly, Melinda, the answer is *no!*"

"Why don't you think about it? Let the idea gel for a while?"

"Let me tell you something, and this is final. If I marry anyone, it will be Polly. Now, if you'll excuse me . . ."

Qwilleran pressed the stop button, relieving Koko's anguish. He had accompanied the dialogue with a coloratura obbligato particular to Siamese vocal cords.

"On this same evening," Qwilleran told Brodie, "while Polly and Irma were occupied elsewhere, Melinda was seen going into their empty room. It's my theory that she tampered with some vitamin capsules that Polly had taken to Scotland, substituting a drug that would stop the heart. I checked with our pharmacist here, and he said it could be done—in several ways. Melinda didn't realize that Polly had stopped taking the vitamins and had turned them over to Irma, who was catching cold. Inadvertently, Melinda killed one of her best friends."

Brodie grunted a wary acceptance of the story, but Qwilleran had not finished. From a desk drawer he produced a small bottle, uncapped it, and poured a few capsules into the palm of his hand. "These are similar to the vitamins Polly took to Scotland. They're pink, Andy! Pink pills!"

The chief shook his head. "The rest of Koko's shenanigans I'm willing to buy, but this . . . I don't know. It's a little hard to swallow."

"Lieutenant Hames would swallow it."

"That he would! Hook, line, and sinker!" He stood up and groped in his pockets. "I'm forgetting what I came here for . . . Here! This is for you." He handed over a square envelope with Qwilleran's name in a familiar handwriting. "It was in Melinda's apartment along with the suicide note. I've got to get back to the station."

Glancing at the envelope with a mixture of curiosity and dread, Qwilleran dropped it on his desk while he accompanied Brodie to the police car parked at the back door, and after the chief had driven away with a wave of the hand, he walked around the barn three times before going indoors. He was in no hurry to read Melinda's last missive. No matter what the gist of it—remorse, apology, passionate outburst, or bitter accusation—it would be painful reading.

As he walked he pondered Koko's incredible involvement in the case. There was no knowing how much of it was coincidence, how much was serendipity, and how much was his own imagination. The cat's tactics in revealing clues ranged from the significant to the purely farcical. Even Qwilleran had to admit that the pink-pill business was farfetched. So was Koko's sniffing of the spot on the rug, as if he knew Shakespeare and, more particularly, *Macbeth*.

And then he thought, I owe Irma an apology. She was a wonderful woman—unapproachable, perhaps, and annoyingly private, but she had her reasons, and she did a tremendous amount of good for the community. She went out on the moor with Bruce every night to try to straighten him out, the way Katie wanted her to do. It didn't work.

Suddenly he remembered he had to drive Polly to work. But first he would read Melinda's farewell note, his curiosity having overcome his apprehension. He let himself in the front door, and the moment he stepped into the foyer he sensed complications. He experienced that oh-oh feeling that always swept over him when bad news was impending—when a cat had thrown up on the white rug, or had broken a tray of glasses, or had stolen the shrimp Newburgh. There was a guilty stillness in the place.

Slowly he moved through the foyer, looking to left and right. In the lounge area his experienced gaze skimmed every surface, every corner, in search of disaster. In the kitchen, scene of many a catly crime, everything was in order. Then he turned toward the area where he had his desk and telephone, his bookshelves and comfortable reading chair. There, on the desktop and the floor beneath, was a shower of confetti. Minute scraps of paper, some of them chewed into tiny wads, were all that remained of Melinda's note.

"Koko!" he shouted. "You did this, dammit! You fiend!" Qwilleran glanced quickly around. "Where the devil are you?"

Yum Yum was on top of the fireplace cube, looking down on the scene like an innocent bystander, sitting on her brisket, her whiskers upturned as if smiling . . . but Koko wasn't there.

The Cat Who Went into the Closet

One

The WPKX radio announcer hunched over the newsdesk in front of a dead microphone, anxiously fingering his script and waiting for the signal to go on the air. The station was filling in with classical music. The lilting "Anitra's Dance" seemed hardly appropriate under the circumstances. Abruptly the music stopped in the middle of a bar, and the newscaster began to read in a crisp, professional tone that belied the alarming nature of the news:

"We interrupt this program to bring you a bulletin on the forest fires that are rapidly approaching Moose County after destroying hundreds of square miles to the south and west. Rising winds are spreading the scattered fires into areas already parched by the abnormally hot summer and drought conditions.

"From this studio in the tower of the courthouse in Pickax City we can see a red glow on the horizon, and the sky is hazy with drifting smoke. Children have been sent home from school, and businesses are closed, allowing workers to protect their families and dwellings. The temperature is extremely high; hot winds are gusting up to forty miles an hour.

"Traffic is streaming into Main Street from towns that are in the path of the flames. Here in the courthouse, which is said to be fireproof, preparations are being made to house the refugees. Many are farmers, who report that their houses, barns, and livestock are totally destroyed. They tell of balls of fire flying through the air, causing fields to burst into flame. One old man on the courthouse steps is proclaiming the end of the world and exhorting passersby to fall on their knees and pray."

The newscaster mopped his brow and gulped water as he glanced at slips of paper on the desk. "Bulletins are coming in from all areas surrounding Pickax. The entire town of Dry River burst into flames an hour ago and was completely demolished in a matter of minutes . . . The village of New Perth is in ashes; thirty-two are reported dead . . . Pardon me."

He stopped for a fit of coughing and then went on with difficulty. "Smoke is seeping into the studio." He coughed again. "Pineytown . . . totally destroyed. Seventeen persons running to escape . . . killed as the flames overtook them . . . Volunteer firefighters who went out from Pickax are back. They say . . . the fire is out of control."

His voice was muffled as he tried to breathe through a cupped hand. "Very dark here! Heat unbearable! Wind is roaring! . . . Hold on!" He jumped to his feet, knocking his chair backward, and crouched over the mike with a gasping cry: "Here it comes! A wall of fire! Right down Main Street! *Pickax is in flames!*"

The lights blacked out. Coughing and choking, the announcer groped for a doorknob and stumbled from the studio.

Music blared from the speakers—crashing chords and roaring crescendoes—and the studio audience sat motionless, stunned into silence until a few started to applaud. The initial clapping swelled into a tumultuous response.

Someone in the front row said, "Gad! That was so real, I could feel the heat!"

"I swear I could smell smoke," another said. "That guy is some actor, isn't he? He wrote the stuff, too."

Most of the onlookers, gripped by emotion, were still speechless as they glanced once more at their programs:

The Moose County Something
presents
"THE BIG BURNING OF 1869"

- An original docu-drama based on historic fact
- Written and performed by James Qwilleran
- Produced and directed by Hixie Rice

The audience is asked to imagine that radio existed in 1869, as we bring you a simulated newscast covering the greatest disaster in the history of Moose County. The scene on the stage represents a broadcasting studio in the tower of the county courthouse. The action takes place on October 17 and 18, 1869. There will be one intermission.

PLEASE JOIN US FOR REFRESHMENTS
AFTER THE PERFORMANCE

The audience, having struggled back to reality, erupted in a babble of comments and recollections:

"I had an old uncle who used to tell stories about a big forest fire, but I was too young to pay any attention."

"Where did Qwill get his information? He must have done a heck of a lot of research."

"My mother said her great-great-grandmother on her father's side lost most of her family in a big forest fire. Makes you want to hit the history books, doesn't it?"

More than a hundred prominent residents of Moose County were attending the performance in the ballroom of a mansion that Jim Qwilleran was renting for the winter months. Most of them knew all about the middle-aged journalist with the oversized moustache and doleful expression. He had been a prize-winning crime writer for major newspapers around the United States. He was the heir to an enormous fortune based in Moose County. He wrote a much-admired column for the local daily, *The Moose County Something*. He spelled his name with a Qw. He liked to eat but never took a drink. He was divorced and thought by women to be highly attractive. His easy-going manner and jocose banter made him enjoyable company. He was a close friend of Polly Duncan's, the Pickax librarian. He lived alone—with two cats.

The townspeople often saw the big, well-built man walking or biking around Pickax, his casual way of dressing and lack of pretension belying his status as a multi-millionaire. And they had heard remarkable stories about his cats. Now, sitting in rows of folding chairs and waiting for Scene Two, the spectators saw a sleek Siamese march sedately down the center aisle. He jumped up on the stage and, with tail importantly erect, proceeded to the door where the radio announcer had made his frantic exit.

The audience tittered, and someone said, "That's Koko. He always has to get into the act."

The door, upstage right, was only loosely latched, and the cat pawed it until it opened a few inches and he could slither through. In two seconds he bounded out again as if propelled by a tap on the rump, and the audience laughed once more. Unabashed, Koko licked his left shoulder blade and scratched his right ear, then jumped off the stage and walked haughtily up the center aisle.

The house lights dimmed, and the radio announcer entered in a fresh shirt, with another script in his hand.

"Tuesday, October 18. After a sleepless night, Pickax can see daylight. The smoke is lifting, but the acrid smell of burning is everywhere, and the landscape is a scene of desolation in every direction. Only this courthouse and a few isolated dwellings and barns are miraculously left standing. The heat is oppressive—110 degrees in the studio—and the window glass is still too hot to touch.

"Crews of men are now fanning out through the countryside, burying bodies that are charred beyond recognition. Because so many families lived in isolated clearings, we may never have an accurate count of the dead. More than four hundred refugees are packed into the courthouse, lying dazed and exhausted in the corridors, on the stairs, in the courtroom and judge's chamber. Some have lost their feet; some have lost their eyes; some have lost their senses, and they babble incoherently. The groans of badly burned survivors mingle with the crying of babies. There is no medicine to ease their pain. Someone has brought a cow to the courthouse to provide milk for the youngest, but there is no food for the others . . ."

Before the dramatic presentation of "The Big Burning of 1869," the historic calamity had been quite forgotten by current generations intent on land development, tourism, new sewers, and the quality of TV reception. Qwilleran himself, playwright and star of the production, had never heard of the disaster until he rented the old mansion on Goodwinter Boulevard and started rummaging in closets. The furnishings were sparse, but the closets were stuffed to the ceiling with odds and ends—a treasure trove for an inquisitive journalist. As for his male cat, he was cat enough to risk death to satisfy his catly curiosity; with tail horizontal he would slink into a closet and emerge with a matchbook or champagne cork clamped in his jaws.

The mansion was constructed of stone and intended to last down the ages, one of several formidable edifices on the boulevard. They had been built by lumber barons and mining tycoons during Moose County's boom years in the late nineteenth century. A pioneer shipbuilder by the name of Gage had been responsible for the one Qwilleran was renting. One feature made the Gage mansion unique: the abundance of closets.

Shortly after moving in, Qwilleran mentioned the closets to his landlord. Junior Goodwinter, the young managing editor of the *Moose County Something*, had recently acquired the obsolete building as a gift from his aging grandmother, and he was thankful to have the rental income from his friend and fellow-staffer. The two men were sitting in Junior's office with their feet on the desk and coffee mugs in their hands. It was three weeks before the preview of "The Big Burning."

Junior's facial features and physical stature were still boyish, and he had grown a beard in an attempt to look older, but his youthful vitality gave him away. "What do you think of Grandma's house, Qwill? Does the furnace work okay? Have you tried lighting any of the fireplaces? How's the refrigerator? It's pretty ancient."

"It sounds like a motor boat when it's running," Qwilleran said, "and when it stops, it roars and snarls like a sick tiger. It frightens the cats out of their fur."

"Why was I dumb enough to let Grandma Gage unload that white elephant on me?" Junior complained. "She just wanted to avoid paying taxes and insurance, and now I'm stuck with all the bills. If I could find a buyer, I'd let the place go for peanuts, but who wants to live in a castle? People like ranch houses with sliding glass doors and smoke detectors . . . More coffee, Qwill?"

"Too bad the city won't re-zone it for commercial use. I've said it before. You could have law offices, medical clinics, high-class nursing homes, high-rent apartments . . . Parking would be the only problem. You'd have to pave the backyards."

"The city will never re-zone," Junior said. "Not so long as old families and city officials live on the street. Sorry about the lack of furniture, Qwill. The Gages had fabulous antiques and paintings, but the old gal sold them all when she relocated in Florida. Now she lives in a retirement village, and she's a new person! She plays shuffleboard, goes to the dog races, wears elaborate makeup! On her last trip here, she looked like a wrinkled china doll. Jody says she must have met one of those cosmetics girls who drive around in lavender convertibles."

"She may have found romance in her declining years," Qwilleran suggested.

"Could be! She looks a lot younger than eighty-eight!"

"Answer one question, Junior. Why are there so many closets? I've counted fifty, all over the house. It was my understanding that our forefathers didn't have closets. They had wardrobes, dressers, highboys, china cabinets, breakfronts, sideboards . . ."

"Well, you see," the editor explained, "my great-great-grandfather Gage was a shipbuilder, accustomed to having everything built-in, and that's what he wanted in his house. Ships' carpenters did the work. Have you noticed the woodwork? Best on the boulevard!"

"By today's construction standards it's incredible! The foyer looks like a luxury liner of early vintage. But do you know the closets are filled with junk?"

"Oh, sure. The Gages never threw anything away."

"Not even champagne corks," Qwilleran agreed.

Junior looked at his watch. "Time for Arch's meeting. Shall we amble across the hall?"

Arch Riker, publisher and CEO of the *Moose County Something*, had scheduled a brainstorming session for editors, writers, and the effervescent promotion director, Hixie Rice. None of the editorial staff liked meetings, and Qwilleran expressed his distaste by slumping in a chair in a far corner of the room. Hixie, on the other hand, breezed into the meeting with her shoulder-length hair bouncing and her eyes sparkling. She had worked in advertising Down Below—as Pickax natives called the major cities to the south—and she had never lost her occupational bounce and sparkle.

Similarly Qwilleran and Riker were transplants from Down Below, having grown up together in Chicago, but they had the detached demeanor of veteran newsmen. They had adapted easily to the slow pace of Pickax City (population 3,000) and the remoteness of Moose County, which claimed to be 400 miles north of everywhere.

Riker, a florid, paunchy deskman who seldom raised his voice, opened the meeting in his usual sleepy style: "Well, you guys, in case you don't know it, winter is coming . . . and winters are pretty dull in this neck of the woods . . . unless you're crazy about ten-foot snow drifts and wall-to-wall ice. So . . . I'd like to see this newspaper sponsor some kind of diversion that will give people a topic of conversation other than the daily rate of snowfall . . . Let's hear some ideas from you geniuses." He turned on a tape recorder.

The assembled staffers sat in stolid silence. Some looked at each other hopelessly.

"Don't stop to think," the boss admonished. "Just blurt it out, off the top of your head."

"Well," said a woman editor bravely, "we could sponsor a hobby contest with a thrilling prize."

"Yeah," said Junior. "Like a two-week all-expenses-paid vacation in Iceland."

"How about a food festival? Everyone likes to eat," said Mildred Hanstable, whose ample girth supported her claim. She wrote the food column for the *Something* and taught home economics in the Pickax school system. "We could have cooking demonstrations, a baking contest, an ethnic food bazaar, a Moose County cookbook, nutrition classes—"

"Second it!" Hixie interrupted with her usual enthusiasm. "And we could promote neat little tie-ins with restaurants, like wine-and-cheese tastings, and snacking-and-grazing parties, and a Bon Appetit Club with dining-out discounts. *C'est magnifique!*" She had once studied French briefly, preparatory to eloping to Paris.

There was a dead silence among the staffers. As a matter of newsroom honor they deplored Hixie's commercial taint. One of them muttered a five-letter word in French.

Junior came to the rescue with an idea for a Christmas parade. He said, "Qwill could play Santa with a white beard and a couple of pillows stuffed under his belt and some flour on his moustache."

Qwilleran grunted a few inaudible words, but Hixie cried, "I like it! I like it! He could arrive in a dogsled pulled by fifteen huskies! Mushing is a terribly trendy winter sport, you know, and we could get national publicity! The networks are avid for weatherbites in winter."

Riker said, "I believe we're getting warm—or cold, if you prefer. Snow is what we do best up here. How can we capitalize on it?"

"A contest for snow sculpture!" suggested Mildred Hanstable, who also taught art in the public school system.

"How about a winter sports carnival?" the sports editor proposed. "Cross-country skiing, snowshoe races, ice-boating, ice-fishing, dog-sledding—"

"And a jousting match with snow blowers!" Junior added. "At least it's cleaner than mud wrestling."

Riker swiveled his chair around. "Qwill, are you asleep back there in that dark corner?"

Qwilleran smoothed his moustache before he answered. "Does anyone know about the big forest fire in 1869 that killed hundreds of Moose County pioneers? It destroyed farms, villages, forests, and wildlife. About the only thing left in Pickax was the brick courthouse."

Roger MacGillivray, general assignment reporter and history buff, said, "I've heard about it, but there's nothing in the history books. And we didn't have a newspaper of record in those days."

"Well, I've found a gold mine of information," said Qwilleran, straightening up in his chair, "and let me tell you something: We may be four hundred miles north of everywhere, but we've got a history up here that will curl your toes! It deserves to be told—not just in print—but before audiences, young and old, all over the county."

"How did you discover this?" Roger demanded.

"While snooping in closets, hunting for skeletons," Qwilleran retorted archly.

Riker said, "If we were to put together a program, what would we do for visuals?"

"That's the problem," Qwilleran admitted. "There are no pictures."

The publisher turned off the tape recorder. "Okay, we've heard six or eight good ideas. Kick 'em around, and we'll meet again in a couple of days . . . Back to work!"

As the staff shuffled out of the office, Hixie grabbed Qwilleran's arm and said in a low voice, "I've got a brilliant idea for dramatizing your disaster, Qwill. *C'est vrai!*"

He winced inwardly, recalling other brilliant ideas of Hixie's that had bombed: the Tipsy Look-Alike Contest that ended in a riot . . . the cooking demonstration that set fire to her hair . . . the line of Frozen Foods for Fussy Felines, for which she expected Koko to make TV commercials . . . not to mention her aborted elopement to France. Gallantly he said, however, "Want to have lunch at Lois's and tell me about it?"

"Okay," she said. "I'll buy. I can put it on my expense account."

Two

The atmosphere at Lois's Luncheonette was bleak, and the menu was ordinary, but it was the only restaurant in downtown Pickax, and the old, friendly, decrepit ambiance made the locals feel at home. A dog-eared card in the window announced the day's special. Tuesday was always hot turkey sandwich with mashed potatoes and gravy, but it was real turkey sliced from the bird; the bread was baked in Lois's kitchen by a white-haired woman who started at five A.M. every day; and the mashed potatoes had the flavor of real potatoes grown in the mineral-rich soil of Moose County.

Qwilleran and Hixie ordered the special, and she said, "I hear that you're not living in your barn this winter." He had recently converted a hundred-year-old apple barn into a spectacular residence.

"There's too much snow to plow," he explained, "so I'm renting the Gage mansion on Goodwinter Boulevard, where the city does the plowing." He neglected to mention that Polly Duncan, the chief woman in his life, lived in the carriage house at the rear of the Gage property, and he envisioned cozy winter evenings and frequent invitations to dinner and/or breakfast.

"All right. Let's get down to business," Hixie said when the plates arrived, swimming in real turkey gravy. "How did you find out about the killer fire? Or is it a professional secret?"

Qwilleran patted his moustache in self-congratulation. "To make a long story short, one of Junior's ancestors was an amateur historian. He recorded spring floods, sawmill accidents, log jams, epidemics, and so on, based on the recollections of his elders. In his journals, written in fine script with a nib pen that blotted occasionally, there were firsthand descriptions of the 1869 forest fire in all its gruesome detail. The man was performing a valuable service for posterity, but no one knew his accounts existed . . . So what's your brilliant idea, Hixie?" Qwilleran concluded.

"What would you think of doing a one-man show?"

"Isn't a one-man show based on a three-county forest fire a trifle out of scale?"

"*Mais non!* Suppose we pretend they had radio stations in the nineteenth century, and the audience sees an announcer broadcasting on-the-spot coverage of the disaster."

Qwilleran gazed at her with new respect. "Not bad! Yes! Not bad! I'd go for that! I'd be glad to organize the material and write the script. If Larry Lanspeak would play the announcer—"

"No! If we're going to sponsor the show, we should keep it in our own organization," she contended. "Actually, Qwill, I was thinking about you for the part. You have an excellent voice, with exactly the right quality for a radio announcer . . . Stop frowning! You wouldn't have to learn lines. You'd be reading a script in front of a simulated mike." She was talking fast. "Besides, you're a local celebrity. Everyone loves your column! You'd be a big attraction, *sans doute.*"

He huffed into his moustache. At least she had the good taste to avoid mentioning his local fame as a multi-millionaire, philanthropist, and eligible bachelor.

She went on with contagious enthusiasm. "I could take care of production details. I could do the bookings. I'd even sweep the stage!"

Qwilleran had done some acting in college and enjoyed working before an audience. The temptation was there; the cause was a good one; the story of the great fire cried for attention. He gave her a guarded glance as his objections began to crumble. "How long a program should it be?"

"I would say forty-five minutes. That would fit into a school class period or fill a slot following a club luncheon."

After a few seconds' contemplation he said grimly, "I may regret this, but I'll do it."

"*Merveilleux!*" Hixie cried.

Neither of them remembered eating their lunch. They discussed a stage setting, lighting, props, a sound system, and how to pack everything in a carrying case, to fit in the trunk of a car.

Hixie said, "Consider it strictly a road show. My budget will cover expenses, but we'll need a name for the project to go into the computer. How about Suitcase Productions?"

"Sounds as if we manufacture luggage," Qwilleran muttered, but he liked it.

Returning home from that luncheon with a foil-wrapped chunk of turkey scrounged from Lois's kitchen, Qwilleran was greeted by two Siamese who could smell turkey through an oak door two inches thick. They yowled and pranced elegantly on long brown legs, and their blue eyes stared hypnotically at the foil package until its contents landed on their plate under the kitchen table.

With bemused admiration Qwilleran watched them devour their treat. Koko, whose legal title was Kao K'o Kung, had the dignity of his thirteenth-century namesake, plus a degree of intelligence and perception that was sometimes unnerving to a human with only five senses and a journalism degree. Yum Yum, the dainty one, had a different set of talents and qualities. She was a lovable bundle of female wiles, which she employed shamelessly to get her own way. When all else failed, she had only to reach up and touch Qwilleran's moustache with her paw, and he capitulated.

When the Siamese had finished their snack and had washed their whiskers and ears, he told them, "I have a lot of work to do in the next couple of weeks, my friends, and I'll have to shut you out of the library. Don't think it's anything personal." He always addressed them as if they understood human speech, and more and more it appeared to be a fact. In the days that followed, they sensed his preoccupation, leaving him alone, taking long naps, grooming each other interminably, and watching the autumn leaves flutter to the ground. The grand old oaks and maples of Goodwinter Boulevard were covering the ground with a tawny blanket. Only when

Qwilleran was an hour late with their dinner did the cats interrupt, standing outside the library, rattling the door handle and scolding—Koko with an authoritative baritone "Yow!" and Yum Yum with her impatient "N-n-now!"

Qwilleran could write a thousand words for his newspaper column with one hand tied behind his back, but writing a script for a docu-drama was a new challenge. To relieve the radio announcer's forty-five-minute monologue, he introduced other voices on tape: eye witnesses being interviewed by telephone. He altered his voice to approximate the bureaucratese of a government weather observer, the brogue of an Irish innkeeper, and the twang of an old farmer. With their replies sandwiched between the announcer's questions, Qwilleran was actually interviewing himself.

Once the script was completed, there were nightly rehearsals in the ballroom of the Gage mansion, with Hixie cueing the taped voices into the live announcing. It required split-second timing to sound authentic. Meanwhile, Polly Duncan returned home each evening to her apartment in the carriage house at the rear of the property and saw Hixie's car parked in the side drive. It was a trying time for Polly. As library administrator she was a woman of admirable intelligence and self-control, but—where Qwilleran was concerned—she was inclined to be jealous of women younger and thinner than she.

One evening Arch Riker attended a rehearsal and was so impressed that he proposed a private preview for prominent citizens. Invitations were immediately mailed to local officials, educators, business leaders, and officers of important organizations with replies requested. To Riker's dismay, few responded; he called an executive meeting to analyze the situation.

"I think," Hixie ventured, "they're all waiting to find out what's on TV Monday night."

"You've got it all wrong," said Junior Goodwinter, who was a native and entitled to know. "It's like this: The stuffed shirts in this backwater county never reply to an invitation till they know who else is going to be there. You've got to drop a few names."

"Or let them know you're spiking the punch," Qwilleran suggested.

"We should have specified a champagne afterglow," Hixie said.

Junior shook his head. "Champagne is not the drink of choice up here. 'Free booze' would have more impact."

"Well, you should know," said Riker. "The rest of us are innocents from Down Below."

"Let me write a piece and splash it on the front page," the young editor said. "I'll twist a few political arms. They're all up for re-election next month."

Accordingly, Friday's edition of the paper carried this news item:

MOOSE COUNTY DESTROYED BY FIRE . . . IN 1869

History will come to life Monday evening when civic leaders will preview a live docu-drama titled "The Big Burning of 1869." Following the private premiere at the Gage mansion on Goodwinter Boulevard, the *Moose County Something* will offer the show to schools, churches, and clubs as a public service.

There followed the magic name of Jim Qwilleran, who was not only popular as a columnist but rich as Croesus. In addition, the mayor, council president, and county commissioners were quoted as saying they would attend the history-making event. As soon as the paper hit the street the telephones in Junior's office started jangling with acceptances from persons who now perceived themselves as civic leaders. Furthermore, "live" was a buzz word in a community jaded with slide shows and video presentations. Hixie went into action, borrowing folding chairs from the Dingleberry Funeral Home, renting coatracks for guests' wraps, and hiring a caterer.

On the gala evening the Gage mansion—with all windows alight—glowed like a lantern among the gloomy stone castles on the boulevard. Flashbulbs popped as the civic leaders approached the front steps. The publisher of the newspaper greeted them; the managing editor checked their wraps; the political columnist handed out programs; the sports editor directed them to the marble staircase leading to the ballroom on the lower level. The reporters who were providing valet parking carried one elderly man in a wheelchair up the front steps and wheeled him to the elevator, which was one of the mansion's special amenities.

Meanwhile, Qwilleran was sweating out his opening-night jitters backstage in the ballroom—a large, turn-of-the-century hall with Art Deco murals and light fixtures. More than a hundred chairs faced the band platform, where musicians had once played for the waltz and the turkey trot. The stage set was minimal: a plain wood table and chair for the announcer with an old-fashioned upright telephone and a replica of an early microphone. Off to one side was a table for the "studio engineer." Cables snaked across the platform, connecting the speakers and lighting tripods to the control board.

"Do they look messy?" Qwilleran asked Hixie.

"No, they look high tech," she decided.

"Good! Then let's throw a few more around." He uncoiled a long yellow extension cord that was not being used and added it to the tangle.

"Perfect!" Hixie said. "It gives the set a certain *je ne sais quoi.*"

A sweatered audience filed into the ballroom and filled the chairs. Pickax was a sweater city in winter—for all occasions except weddings and funerals. The house lights dimmed, and the lilting notes of "Anitra's Dance" filled the hall until the announcer rushed onstage from a door at the rear and spoke the first ominous words: "We interrupt this program to bring you a bulletin . . ."

Forty-five minutes later he delivered the final message: "No one will ever forget what happened here on October 17, 1869." It was an ironic punch line, considering that few persons in the county had ever heard of the Big Burning.

Climactic music burst from the speakers; the audience applauded wildly; and the mayor of Pickax jumped to his feet, saying, "We owe a debt of gratitude to these talented folks from Down Below who have made us see and hear and feel this forgotten chapter in our history."

The presenters bowed: Hixie with her buoyant smile and Qwilleran with his usual morose expression. Then, as the ballroom emptied, they packed the props and mechanical equipment into carrying cases.

"We did it!" Hixie exulted. "We've got a smash hit!"

"Yes, it went pretty well," Qwilleran agreed modestly. "Your timing was perfect, Hixie. Congratulations!"

A small boy in large eyeglasses and a red sweater, who had been in the audience with his father, stayed behind to watch the striking of the set. "What's that yellow wire for?" he asked.

Qwilleran replied with overblown pomposity, "That, young man, happens to be the major power conduit used by our engineer for operating our computerized sound and light system."

"Oh," the boy said. Then, after a moment's puzzled contemplation, he asked, "Why wasn't it connected?"

"Why don't you go upstairs and have some cookies?" Qwilleran countered. To Hixie he muttered, "Kids! Always asking questions! Not only that, but they're notorious carriers of the common cold. If we're taking this show on the road, I can't afford to be laid up."

"I predict we'll be swamped with bookings," she said.

"Undoubtedly. Moose County can't resist anything that's free."

"Should we extend our territory to Lockmaster County?"

"Only if they pay for it . . . Now let's go upstairs and get some of that free grub." After the excitement of a first night and after forty-five minutes of intense concentration on his role, Qwilleran felt empty and parched.

On the main floor the guests were milling about the large, empty rooms, admiring the coffered paneling of the high ceiling and the lavishly carved fireplaces. They carried plates of hors d'oeuvres and glass cups of amber punch. The Siamese were milling about, too, dodging feet and hunting for dropped crumbs. Koko sniffed certain trousered legs and nylon-clad ankles; Yum Yum eluded the clutches of a young boy in a red sweater.

Qwilleran pushed through the crowd to the dining room, where a caterer's long table was draped in a white cloth and laden with warming trays of stuffed mushrooms, bacon-wrapped olives, cheese puffs, and other morsels too dainty for a hungry actor. There were two punch bowls, and he headed for the end of the table where Mildred Hanstable was ladling amber punch into glass cups.

"Cider?" he asked.

"No, this is Fish House punch made with two kinds of rum and two kinds of brandy," she warned him. "I think you'll want the other punch, Qwill. It's cranberry juice and Chinese tea with lemon grass."

"Sounds delicious," he grumbled. "How come no one is drinking it?"

Polly Duncan, looking radiant in a pink mohair sweater, was presiding over the unpopular bowl of pink punch. "Qwill, dear, you were splendid!" she said in her mellow voice that always gave him a frisson of pleasure. "Now I know why you were so totally preoccupied for the last two weeks. It was time well invested."

"Sorry to be so asocial," he apologized, "but we'll make up for it. We'll do something special this weekend, like bird watching." This was a gesture of abject penitence on his part. He loathed birding.

"It's too late," she said. "They've gone south, and snow is predicted. But I'm going to do roast beef and Yorkshire pudding, and I have a new Brahms cassette."

"Say no more. I'm available for the entire weekend."

They were interrupted by a cracked, high-pitched voice. "Excellent job, my boy!" Homer Tibbitt, official historian for the county, was in his nineties but still active in spite of loudly creaking joints. He was pushing a wheelchair occupied by Adam Dingleberry, the ancient and indestructible patriarch of the mortuary that had lent the folding chairs.

Homer said to Qwilleran, "Just want to congratulate you before going home to my lovely young bride. Adam's great-grandson is on the way over to pick us up."

"Yep, he's bringin' the hearse," said old Dingleberry with a wicked laugh.

Homer delivered a feeble poke to Qwilleran's ribs. "You son-of-a-grasshopper! I've been scrabbling for information on that blasted fire for thirty years! Where'd you find it?"

"In some files that belonged to Euphonia Gage's father-in-law," Qwilleran replied. He neglected to say that Koko pried his way into a certain closet and dragged forth a scrap of yellowed manuscript. It was a clue to a cache of hundred-year-old documents.

A valet was paging them. "Car for Mr. Dingleberry! Mr. Tibbitt!"

As the elderly pair headed for the carriage entrance, Qwilleran was approached by a cordial man in a black cashmere sweater. "Good show, Mr. Q!" he said in a smooth, professional voice.

"Thank you."

"I'm Pender Wilmot, your next-door neighbor and Mrs. Gage's attorney."

"Too bad she couldn't be here tonight," Qwilleran said.

"I daresay this old house hasn't witnessed an event of this magnitude since Harding won the presidential election. How do you like living on the boulevard?"

"I find it somewhat depressing. There are seven for-sale signs at my last count."

"And I'd gladly make it eight," the attorney said, "but our property has been in the family for four generations, and Mrs. Wilmot is sentimental about it, although she might be swayed by a juicy offer."

"There'll be no juicy offers until the boulevard is re-zoned."

"It is my considered opinion," Wilmot said, "that the city will approve re-zoning in the year 2030 . . . Mr. Q, this is my son, Timmie." The boy in the red sweater, having failed to catch the slippery Yum Yum, was now clutching his parent's hand.

"And how did you like the show, young man?" Qwilleran asked him.

Timmie frowned. "All those houses burned down, and all those people burned up. Why didn't the firemen get a ladder and save them?"

"Come on, son," his father said. "We'll go home and discuss it."

They walked toward the front door just as Hixie dashed up, followed by the owner of the Black Bear Café. Gary Pratt's muscular hulk and lumbering gait and shaggy black hairiness explained the name of his restaurant. Excitedly Hixie announced, "Gary wants us to do the show at the Black Bear."

"Yeah," said the barkeeper, "the Outdoor Club meets once a month for burgers and beer and a program. They have a conservation guy or a video on the environment. They've never had a live show."

"How many members?" Qwilleran asked.

"Usually about forty turn out, but it'll be double that if they know you're coming."

"Okay with me. Go ahead and book it, Hixie."

Qwilleran moved through the crowd, accepting congratulations.

Susan Exbridge, the antique dealer, gave him her usual effusive hug. "Darling! You were glorious! You should be on the stage! . . . And this house! Isn't it magnificent? Euphonia gave me a tour before she sold the furnishings. Look at the carving on that staircase! Look at the parquet floors! Have you ever seen chandeliers like these? If you'd like a live-in housekeeper, Qwill, I'll work cheap!"

Next the Comptons paid their compliments. "You were terrific, Qwill," said Lisa, a cheerful, middle-aged woman in a Halloween sweater. "Everything was so professional!"

"It's my engineer's split-second timing that gives the show its snap," Qwilleran said.

"You guys ought to do the show for grades four to twelve," said Lyle Compton, superintendent of schools. "It would be a great way to hook the kids on history."

Qwilleran winced, having visions of a schoolful of carriers circulating respiratory diseases.

"Believe it or not," Lisa said, "I used to come to this house to take 'natural dance' lessons from Euphonia. She had us flitting around the ballroom like Isadora Duncan. It was supposed to give us grace and poise, but we all thought it was boring. I really wanted to take tap."

Her husband said, "You should have stuck with Euphonia. She's in her late eighties and still has the spine of a drum major, which is more than I can say for any of us."

"I met her only once," Qwilleran said. "I came here to interview her for an oral history project and found this tiny woman sitting on the floor in the lotus position, wearing purple tights. She had white hair tied back with a purple ribbon, I recall."

Lisa nodded. "She used to tell us that purple is a source of energy. Junior says she still wears a lot of it and stands on her head every day."

"When she lived in Pickax," said Lyle, "she drove a Mercedes at twenty miles an hour and blew the horn at every intersection. The police were always ticketing her for obstructing traffic. All the Gages have been a little batty, although Junior seems to have his head on straight."

As Junior Goodwinter joined them, Lisa changed the subject. "Have you ever seen an autumn with so many leaves on the ground?"

"According to hizzoner the mayor," said Junior, "Lockmaster County is shipping truckloads of leaves up here every night under cover of darkness and dumping them on Pickax."

"I'll buy that," Lyle said. "We should send them some of our toxic waste."

They discussed the forthcoming football game between Pickax High and their Lockmaster rivals, and then the Comptons said goodnight.

Junior gazed ruefully at the empty rooms, faded wallcoverings, and discolored rectangles where large paintings had once hung. "Grandma had some great stuff! Susan Exbridge can tell you how valuable it was. Everything was sold out of state. Sorry there's no TV, Qwill. Why don't you bring one over from your barn before snow flies?"

"I can skip TV. It amuses the cats, but they can live without it. Would your grandmother have liked our show tonight?"

"I doubt it. She never likes anything that isn't her own idea."

"She sounds a lot like Koko. Is it true she used to give dancing lessons?"

"Way back, maybe forty years ago," Junior said. "Before leaving for Florida she asked me to videotape one of her dances. Yikes! It was embarrassing, Qwill—this woman in her eighties, in filmy draperies, cavorting around the ballroom like a woodland nymph. She was limber enough, and still kind of graceful, but I felt like a voyeur."

"What happened to the video?"

"She took it to Florida. Do you think she plays it on a VCR and dreams old dreams?"

"It's not a bad idea," Qwilleran said. "When I'm her age I'd like to watch myself sliding into first base."

"I saw you talking to Pender Wilmot. How did he like the show?"

"He was quite enthusiastic. By the way, Junior, I'm surprised your grandmother doesn't take her legal work to Hasselrich Bennett & Barter."

"They're too stuffy for her taste. She likes younger people. She feels young herself. It's my guess that she'll outlive us all . . . Well, it looks like everyone's leaving. Sure was a success! I can't believe, Qwill, that you did all those voices yourself!"

Only a few members of the hungry and thirsty press remained to drain the two punch bowls. They mixed the contents of both and declared it tasted like varnish, but good!

Qwilleran said to Hixie, "Did you see the guy in a suit and tie? He was with a blonde—the only ones not in sweaters."

"That was a wig she was wearing," Hixie informed him. "Who were they?"

"That's what I was going to ask you."

"I say they were spies from the *Lockmaster Ledger,*" she said. "They steal all our good ideas. Do you suppose she had a tape recorder under that big wig? I'm glad we copyrighted the script; we can sue."

Arch Riker and Mildred Hanstable were almost the last to leave. The publisher was beaming. "Great job, you two kids! Best PR stunt we could spring on this kind of community!"

"Thanks, boss," said Qwilleran. "I'll expect a raise."

"You'll be fired if you don't start writing your column again. The readers are screaming for your pellucid prose on page two. Consider your vacation over as of tomorrow."

"Vacation! I've been working like a dog on this show! And I haven't seen anything that looks like a bonus!"

This sparring between the two old friends was a perpetual game, since the *Moose County Something* was backed financially by the Klingenschoen Foundation, established by Qwilleran to dispose of his unwanted millions.

Riker drove Mildred home, and Qwilleran told Polly he would escort her to her carriage house in the rear. "I'll be right back," he told the Siamese, who were loitering nearby and beaming questioning looks in his direction.

"I've missed you, dear," Polly said as they walked briskly hand in hand through the chill October evening. "I thought I had lost my Most Favored Woman status. Bootsie missed you, too."

"Sure," Qwilleran replied testily. He and Polly's macho Siamese had been engaged in a cold war ever since Bootsie was a kitten.

"Would you like to come upstairs for some real food and a cup of coffee?"

Qwilleran said he wouldn't mind going up for a few minutes. When he came down two hours later, he walked slowly despite the falling temperature, reflecting that he was happier than he had ever been in his entire life—not that the pursuit of happiness had concerned him in his earlier years. What mattered then was the excitement of covering breaking news, working all night to meet a deadline, moving from city to city for new challenges, hanging out at press clubs, and not caring about money. Now he was experiencing something totally different: the contentment of living in a small town, writing for a small newspaper, loving an intelligent woman of his own age, living with two companionable cats. And, to cap it all, he was on the stage again! Not since college days, when he played Tom in "The Glass Menagerie," had he known the satisfaction of creating a character and bringing that character to life for an audience.

At the side door of the mansion he was greeted by the scolding yowls and switching tails of two indignant Siamese, whose evening repast was late.

"My apologies," he said as he gave them a crunchy snack. "The pressure is off now, and we'll get back to normal. You've been very understanding and cooperative. How would you like a read after I've turned out the lights? The electric bill is going to be astronomical."

Despite his affluence, Qwilleran was frugal about utilities. Now he went from room to room through the great house, flipping off switches. The Siamese accompanied him, pursuing their own special interests. In one of the large front bedrooms upstairs he noticed a closet door ajar and a horizontal brown tail disappearing within. Minutes later, Koko caught up with him and dropped something at his feet.

"Thank you," Qwilleran said courteously as he picked up a purple ribbon bow and dropped it in his sweater pocket. To himself he said, If Euphonia's theory is true, Koko sensed a source of energy. Cats, he had been told, are attracted to sources of energy.

The three of them gathered in the library for their read, a ritual the Siamese always enjoyed. Whether it was the sound of a human voice, or the warmth of a human lap and a table lamp, or the simple idea of propinquity, a read was one of their catly pleasures that ranked with grooming their fur and chasing each other. As for Qwilleran, he enjoyed the company of living creatures and—to be perfectly honest—the sound of his own voice.

"Would anyone care to choose a title?" he asked.

In the library there were a few hundred books that Mrs. Gage had been unable to sell, plus a dozen classics that Qwilleran had brought from the barn along with his typewriter and computerized coffeemaker. Koko sniffed the bindings until his twitching nose settled on *Robinson Crusoe* from Qwilleran's own collection.

"Good choice," Qwilleran commented as he sank into a leather lounge chair worn to the contours of a hammock. Yum Yum leaped lightly into his lap, settling down slowly with a sigh, like a motor vehicle with hydraulic suspension, while Koko arranged himself on a nearby table under the glow of a 75-watt lamp bulb.

They were halfway through the opening paragraph when the telephone on the desk rang. "Excuse me," Qwilleran said, lifting Yum Yum gently and placing her on the seat he had vacated. He anticipated another compliment on "The Big Burning" and responded with a gracious "Good evening."

Arch Riker's voice barked with urgency. "Hate to bother you, Qwill, but I've just had a call from Junior. He's flying to Florida first thing in the morning. His grandmother was found dead in bed."

"Hmmm . . . curious!" Qwilleran murmured.

"What do you mean?"

"A few minutes ago Koko brought me one of her hair ribbons."

"Yeah, well . . . that cat is tuned in to everything. But why I'm calling—"

"And everyone at the party tonight," Qwilleran went on, "was mentioning how healthy she was."

"That's the sad part," Riker said. "The police told Junior it was suicide."

Three

The news of Euphonia Gage's suicide was surprising, if not incredible. "What was her motive?" Qwilleran asked Arch Riker.

"We don't know yet. We'll run a died-suddenly on the front page of tomorrow's paper and give it the full treatment Wednesday. Junior is drafting an obit on the plane and will fax it when he arrives down there and gets a few more details. Meanwhile, will you see if you can dig out some photos? Her early life, studio portraits—anything will be useful. She was the last of the Gages. Junior says she left some photo albums in the house, but he doesn't know exactly where."

As Qwilleran listened to the publisher's directive, he felt a fumbling in his pocket and reached down to grab a paw. "No!" he scolded.

"What'd you say?"

"Nothing. Yum Yum was picking my pocket."

"Well, see what you can find for Wednesday. Usual deadline. Sorry to bother you tonight."

"No bother. I'll give you a ring in the morning."

Before resuming the reading of *Robinson Crusoe,* Qwilleran added the purple ribbon bow to what he called the Kao K'o Kung Collection in a desk drawer. It consisted of oddments retrieved by one or more cats from the gaping closets of the Gage mansion: champagne cork, matchbook, pocket comb, small sponge, pencil stub, rubber eraser, and the like. Yum Yum left her contributions scattered about the house; Koko organized his under the kitchen table, alongside their water dish and feeding station.

As the day ended, Qwilleran felt a welcome surge of relief and satisfaction; "The Big Burning" had been successfully launched and enthusiastically received. He slept soundly that night and would not have heard the early-morning summons from the library telephone if eight bony legs had not landed simultaneously on tender parts of his supine body.

Hixie Rice was on the line, as bright and breezy as ever. "*Pardonnez-moi!* Did I get you out of bed?" she asked when Qwilleran answered gruffly. "You sound as if you haven't had your coffee yet. Well, this will wake you up! We have two bookings for our show, if the dates are okay with you. The first is Thursday afternoon at Mooseland High School. That's a consolidated school serving the agricultural townships."

"I'm not keen about doing the show for kids," he objected.

"They're not kids. They're young adults, and they'll love it!"

"Of course. They love anything that gets them out of class, including chest X-rays," he said with precoffee cynicism. "What kind of facility do they have?"

"We'll be doing the show in the gym, with the audience seated in the bleachers. The custodian is constructing a platform for us."

"What's the second booking?"

"Monday night at the Black Bear Café. It's the annual family night for the Outdoor Club, and they were going to have a Laurel and Hardy film, but Gary urged them to book 'The Big Burning' instead."

"Maybe we can play it for laughs," Qwilleran muttered.

"At the high school we're scheduled for the sixth period, and we should get there at one o'clock. I'll be out in the territory, so I'll meet you there. It's on Sandpit Road, you know . . . And would you be a doll, Qwill, and glue my cuesheet on a card, *s'il vous plaît?* It'll be sturdier and easier to handle . . . See you Thursday afternoon. Don't forget to bring the complex computerized sound and light system," she concluded with a flippant laugh.

A grunt was his only reply to that remark. As he hung up the receiver he felt certain misgivings. Performing for a hand-picked audience of civic leaders had been a pleasure, but a gymful of noisy, hyperkinetic "young adults" from the potato farms and sheep ranches was a different ballgame. He pressed the button on his coffeemaker and was comforted somewhat by the sound of grinding beans and gurgling brew.

Meanwhile, he fed the cats, and whether it was the soothing sight of feline feeding or the caffeine jolt of his first cup, something restored his positive attitude, and he tackled Riker's assignment with actual relish.

It was not as easy as either of them supposed. There were no photos of Euphonia Gage in the desk drawers. The closet in the library was locked. In the upstairs bedroom where Koko had found the purple ribbon, the closets were stuffed with outdated clothing, but no photographs. Returning to the library he surveyed the shelves of somber books collected by several generations of Gages: obsolete encyclopedias, anthologies of theological essays, forgotten classics, and biographies of persons now unknown. Sitting in the worn leather desk chair, he swiveled idly, pondering this mausoleum of the printed word.

It was then that he glimpsed a few inches of brown tail disappearing behind a row of books at eye level. Koko often retired to a bookshelf to escape Yum Yum's playful overtures. He failed to appreciate aggressive females, preferring to do the chasing himself. So now he was safely installed in the narrow space behind some volumes on nutrition, correct breathing, vegetarian diet, medicinal herbs, Hindu philosophy, and similar subjects of interest to the late Mrs. Gage.

Qwilleran smoothed his moustache, suspecting why Koko preferred these books to the Civil War histories on the same shelf. Could it corroborate the theory about cats and energy? Could Euphonia's innate verve have rubbed off on these particular bindings? In earlier years he would have scoffed at such a notion, but that was before he knew Koko. Now Qwilleran would believe anything!

Out of curiosity he opened the book on herbs and found remedies for acne, allergies, asthma, and athlete's foot. Hopefully he looked under F but found nothing on football knee, which was his own Achilles' heel. He did find, however, an envelope addressed to Junior and mailed from Florida, casually stuck between a new book on cholesterol and an old book on mind power. He opened it and read:

> Dear Junior,
>
> Ship all my health books right away. I teach a class in breathing twice a week. These old people could solve half their problems if they knew how to breathe. Also send my photo albums. I think they're on the shelf with the Britannica. I'll pay the postage. Thank you for sending the clippings of Mr. Q's column. I like his style. No one down here has the slightest knowledge of how to write. Perhaps you should start a subscription to the paper for me. Send me the bill.
>
> —Grandma

The letter, dated two weeks previously, hardly sounded like a potential suicide, and Qwilleran wondered, Had something drastic happened to change her lifestyle or her outlook? It could be sudden illness, sudden grief, personal catastrophe . . .

Two photo albums were exactly where she had said they would be, and he turned the pages to find the highlights of her life, all captioned and dated as if she expected some future biographer to publish her life. He found a tiny Euphonia in a christening dress two yards long, propped up on cushions; a young girl dancing on the grass in front of peony bushes; a horsewoman in full habit, with the straightest of spines; and a bride in a high-necked wedding dress with an armful of white roses. In none of the photos was there a glimpse of her bridegroom, daughter, parents, or grandchildren—only an unidentified horse.

Qwilleran narrowed the collection down to ten suitable pictures and telephoned Riker at the office. "Got 'em!" he announced. "How about lunch?"

At noon he walked downtown and tossed the photos on the publisher's desk. Riker shuffled through the pack, nodded without comment, and said, "Where shall we eat?"

"First I want to use your gluepot," Qwilleran said. "Do you have a five-by-seven index card?"

"No. What for?"

"Never mind. Just give me a file folder, and I'll cut it down. I want to paste Hixie's cuesheet on a card for durability."

"Apparently you're expecting a long run," the publisher said with satisfaction.

"Yes, and I'm charging the paper for mileage."

They drove in Riker's car to the Old Stone Mill on the outskirts of town, the best restaurant in the vicinity.

"Have you heard from Junior?" Qwilleran asked.

"Give him a break! His plane left only an hour ago." They were passing the impressive entrance to Goodwinter Boulevard. "How do you and the cats enjoy rattling around in that big house?"

"We're adaptable. Actually, I live in three rooms. I sleep in the housekeeper's old bedroom on the main floor. I make coffee and feed the cats in a huge antiquated kitchen. And I hang out in the library, which still has some furniture—not good, but not too bad."

"Is that where you found the dope on the forest fire?"

"No, it was in an upstairs closet. The house is honeycombed with closets, all filled with junk."

"That's the insidious thing about ample storage space," Riker said. "It sounds good, but it turns rational individuals into pack rats. I'm one of them."

"But Koko is having a field day. Old doors in old houses don't latch properly, so he can open a closet door and walk in."

Riker—who had once had a house and wife and children and cats of his own—nodded sagely. "Cats can't stand the sight of a closed door. If they're in, they have to get out; if they're out, they want in."

"The Rum Tum Tugger syndrome," Qwilleran said with equal sagacity.

In the restaurant parking lot they crossed paths with Scott Gippel, the car dealer. "I heard on the radio that old Mrs. Gage died down south. Died suddenly, they said. Is that true? Suicide?"

"That's what the police told Junior," Riker said.

"Too bad. She was a peppy old gal. I took her Mercedes in trade on a bright yellow sports car. She had me drop-ship it to Florida."

When they entered the restaurant, the hostess said, "Isn't that sad about Mrs. Gage? She had so much style! Always came in here wearing a hat and scarf. The barman kept a bottle of Dubonnet just for her . . . Your usual table, Mr. Q?"

The special for the day was a French dip sandwich with skins-on fries and a cup of cream of mushroom soup. Riker ordered a salad.

"What's the matter?" Qwilleran inquired. "Aren't you feeling well?"

"Just trying to lose a few pounds before the holidays. Do you have plans for Christmas Eve?"

"That's two months away! I'll be lucky if I survive Thursday afternoon at Mooseland High."

"How would you like to be best man at a Christmas Eve wedding?"

Qwilleran stopped nibbling breadsticks. "You and Mildred? Congratulations, old stiff! You two will be happy together."

"Why don't you and Polly take the plunge at the same time? Share the expenses. That should appeal to your thrifty nature."

"The chance to save a few bucks is tempting, Arch, but Polly and I prefer singlehood. Besides, our respective cats would be incompatible . . . Have you broken the news to your kids?"

"Yeah, and right away they wanted to know how old she is. You know what they were thinking, that she'll outlive me and collect their inheritance."

"Nice offspring you begot," Qwilleran commented, half in sympathy and half in vindication. For years Riker had chided him for being childless. "Are they coming for the wedding?"

"If the airport stays open, but I doubt it. Fifty inches of snow are predicted before Christmas."

The two men talked about the forthcoming election (the incumbent mayor had a drinking problem) and the high cost of gasoline (when one lives 400 miles north of everywhere), and a good place for a honeymoon (*not* the New Pickax Hotel).

When coffee was served, Qwilleran brought up the subject that was bothering him. "You know, Arch, I can't understand why Mrs. Gage would choose to end her life."

"Old folks often pull up stakes and go to a sunny climate away from family and friends, and they discover the loneliness of old age. My father found it gets harder to make new friends as years go by. Mrs. Gage was eighty-eight, you know."

"What's eighty-eight in today's world? People of that age are running in marathons and winning swimming meets! Science is pushing the lifespan up to a hundred and ten."

"Not for me, please."

"Anyway, when Junior phones, ask him to call me at home."

The call from Junior came around six o'clock that evening. "Hey, Qwill, whaddaya think about all this? I can't believe Grandma Gage is gone! I thought she'd live forever."

"The idea of suicide is what puzzles me, Junior. Was that just a cop's guess?"

"No, it's official."

"Was there a suicide note?"

"She didn't leave any kind of explanation, but there was an empty bottle of sleeping pills by her bed, plus evidence that she'd been drinking. Her normal weight was under a hundred pounds, so it wouldn't take much to put her down, the doctor said."

"Did she drink? I thought she was a health nut."

"She always had a glass of Dubonnet before dinner, claiming it was nutritious. But who knows what she did after she started running with that retirement crowd in Florida? If you don't sow your wild oats when you're young, my dad told me, you'll do it when you're old."

"So what was the motive?"

"I wish I knew."

"Who found the body?"

"A neighbor. Around Monday noon. She'd been dead about sixteen hours. This woman called to pick her up for lunch. They were going to the mall."

"Have you talked with this neighbor?"

"Yes, she's a nice older woman. A widow."

"Yow!" said Koko, who was sitting on the desk and monitoring the call.

"Was that Koko?" Junior asked.

"Yes, he's always trying to line me up with a widow who'll make meatloaf like Mrs. Cobb's . . . So, what happens now, Junior?"

"I'm appointed as personal rep, and Pender Wilmot has told me what to do. She'd sold her condo and was living in a mobile home in a retirement complex called the Park of Pink Sunsets."

"Very Floridian," Qwilleran remarked.

"It's a top-of-the-line mobile home. She bought it furnished from the park management, and they'll buy it back, so I don't have that to worry about. I have to get some death certificates, round up her personal belongings, and ship the body to Pickax. She wanted to be buried in the Gage plot, Pender says."

"When do you expect to be home?"

"Before snow flies, I hope. Sooner the better. I don't care for this assignment."

"Let me know if you want a lift from the airport."

"My car's in the long-term garage, but thanks anyway, Qwill."

Qwilleran replaced the receiver slowly. No known motive! The news was a challenge to one who was tormented by unanswered questions and unsolved puzzles. He had known suicides motivated by guilt, depression, and fear of disgrace, but here was a healthy, spirited, active, well-to-do woman who simply decided to end it all.

"What happened?" he asked Koko, who was sitting on the desk, a self-appointed censor of incoming phone calls. The cat sat tall with his forelegs primly together and his tail curved flat on the desktop. At Qwilleran's question he shifted his feet nervously and blinked his eyes. Then, abruptly, he jerked his head toward the library door. In a blur of fur he was off the desk and out in the hallway. Qwilleran, alarmed by the sudden exit, followed almost as fast. The excitement was in the kitchen, where Yum Yum was already sniffing the bottom of the back door.

Koko's tail bushed, his ears swept back, his whiskers virtually disappeared, and a terrible growl came from the depths of his interior.

Qwilleran looked out the back window. It was dusk, but he could make out a large orange cat on the porch, crouched and swaying from side to side in a threatening way. The man banged on the door, yanked it open and yelled "Scat!" The intruder swooshed from the porch in a single streak and faded into the dusk. Yum Yum looked dreamily disappointed, and Koko bit her on the neck.

"Stop that!" Qwilleran commanded in a gruff voice that was totally ignored. Yum Yum appeared to be enjoying the abuse.

"Treat!" he shouted. It was the only guaranteed way to capture their immediate attention, and both cats scampered to the feeding station under the kitchen table, where they awaited their reward.

Returning to the library, Qwilleran phoned Lori Bamba, his freelance secretary in Mooseville, who not only handled his correspondence but advised him on feline problems. He described the recent scene.

"It's a male," Lori said. "He's a threat to Koko's territory. He's interested in Yum Yum."

"Both of mine are neutered," he reminded her.

"It makes no difference. The visitor probably sprayed your back door."

"What! I won't stand for that!" Qwilleran stormed into the phone. "Isn't there some kind of protection against marauding animals, invading and vandalizing private property—an ordinance or whatever?"

"I don't think so. Do you have any idea where he lives?"

"When I chased him, he headed for the attorney's house next door. Well, thanks, Lori. Sorry to bother you. I'll see my own attorney about this tomorrow."

Blowing angrily into his moustache, Qwilleran strode through the main hall and glared out the front window, where autumn leaves smothered sidewalks, lawns, pavement, and the median. Then, smashing his fist in the palm of his hand, he returned to the library and phoned Osmond Hasselrich of Hasselrich Bennett & Barter. Only someone with the nerve of a veteran journalist would call the senior partner at home during the dinner hour, and only someone with Qwilleran's bankroll could get away with it. The elderly lawyer listened courteously as Qwilleran made his request concisely and firmly. "I want an appointment for tomorrow afternoon, Mr. Hasselrich, and I want to consult you personally. It's a matter of the utmost secrecy."

Four

While waiting for his Wednesday afternoon appointment with Mr. Hasselrich, Qwilleran tuned in the WPKX weather report several times, hoping for an update—hoping to hear that dire atmospheric developments in the Yukon Territory or Hudson Bay would close in on Moose County, depositing eighteen inches of snow and closing the schools. No such luck! The meteorologist, who called himself Wetherby Goode, had a hearty, jovial manner that could make floods and tornadoes sound like fun, and on this occasion he was actually singing:

"Blow, blow, blow the leaves/ Gently in the street./ Merrily, merrily, merrily, merrily,/ Fall is such a treat! . . . Yes, folks, the mayor—who is running for re-election—has promised leaf pickup before Halloween. The vacuum truck will be operating east of Main Street on Friday and west of Main Street on Saturday. So lock up your cats and small dogs, folks!"

By the time Qwilleran walked downtown to the office of Hasselrich Bennett & Barter, the whine of leaf blowers paralyzed the eardrums like a hundred-piece symphony orchestra playing only one chord.

At the law office he sipped coffee politely from Mr. Hasselrich's heirloom porcelain cups, inquired politely about Mrs. H's health, and listened politely to the elderly attorney's discourse on the forthcoming snow—all this before getting down to business. When Qwilleran finally stated his case, Mr. Hasselrich reacted favorably. As chief counsel for the Klingenschoen Foundation, he had become accustomed to unusual proposals from the Klingenschoen heir, and although he seldom tried to dissuade Qwilleran, his fleshy eyelids frequently flickered and his sagging jowls quivered. Today the august head nodded without a flicker or a quiver.

"I believe it can be accomplished without arousing suspicion," he said.

"With complete anonymity, of course," Qwilleran specified.

"Of course. And with all deliberate haste."

Qwilleran walked home with a long stride.

That evening, when he took Polly Duncan out to dinner, she asked casually, "What did you do today?"

"Walked downtown . . . Made a few phone calls . . . Ran through my script . . . Brushed the cats." He avoided mentioning his meeting with Hasselrich.

They were dining at Tipsy's, a log cabin restaurant in North Kennebeck, Polly with her glass of sherry and Qwilleran with his glass of Squunk water. "Guess what's happening on Christmas Eve!" he said. "Arch and Mildred are tying the knot."

"I'm so happy for them," she said fervently, and Qwilleran detected a note of relief. He had always suspected that she considered Mildred a potential rival.

"Arch suggested we might make it a double wedding," he said with a sly sideways glance.

"I hope you disabused him of that notion, dear."

He gave their order: "Broiled whitefish for the lady, and I'll have the king-size steak, medium rare." Then he remarked, "Did you read the obituary in today's paper?"

"Yes. I wonder where they found those interesting pictures."

"Did you know Mrs. Gage very well?"

"I believe no one knew her very well," said Polly. "She served on my library board for a few years, but she was rather aloof. The other members considered her a snob. At other times she could be quite gracious. She always wore hats with wide brims—never tilted, always perfectly level. Some women found that intimidating."

Qwilleran said, "I detect a lingering floral perfume in one of the upstairs bedrooms at the house."

"It's violet. She always wore the same scent—to the extent that no one else in town would dare to wear it. I don't want to sound petty. After all, she was good enough to rent the carriage house to me when I was desperate for a place to live."

"That was no big deal," Qwilleran said. "No doubt she wanted someone around to watch the main house while she was in Florida."

"You're always so cynical, Qwill."

"Were you surprised that she'd take her own life?"

Polly considered the question at length before replying. "No. She was completely unpredictable. What was your impression when you interviewed her, Qwill?"

"She came on strong as a charming and witty little woman, full of vitality, but that may have been an act for the benefit of the press."

"What happens now?"

"Junior is in Florida, winding up her affairs and trying to get home before snow flies."

"I hope the weather is good for the trick-or-treaters. Are you all ready for Halloween?"

"Ready? What am I supposed to do?"

"Turn on your porch light and have plenty of treats to hand out. Something wholesome, like apples, would be the sensible thing to give, but they prefer candy or money. They used to be grateful for a few pennies, but now they expect quarters."

"Quarters! Greedy brats! How many kids come around?"

"Only a few from the boulevard, but carloads come from other neighborhoods. You should prepare for at least a hundred."

Qwilleran grunted his disapproval. "Well, they'll get apples from me—and like it!" He was quiet when the steak was served; Tipsy's specialized in an old-fashioned cut of meat that required chewing. Eventually he said, "We put the show on the road tomorrow. Mooseland High is our first booking, unless we're fortunate enough to have an earthquake."

"You don't sound very enthusiastic, dear. Do they have a good auditorium?"

"They have a gym. They're building a platform for us. Hixie made the arrangements. I've practiced packing the gear, and I can set up in nine minutes flat and strike the set in seven."

The afternoon at Mooseland High School was better than he expected, in one way; in another, it was worse. In preparation for the show he packed the lights, telescoping tripods, cables, props, and sound equipment in three carrying cases and checked off everything on a list: script, mike, telephone, extension cords, double plugs, handkerchief for the announcer to mop his sweating brow, and so forth. In college theatre there had been a backstage crew to handle all such details; now he was functioning as stage manager, stagehand, and propman as well as featured actor. It was not easy, but he enjoyed a challenge.

Everything on the checklist was accounted for, with one exception: Hixie's cuecard. He unpacked the three cases, thinking it might have slipped in accidentally, but it was not there. He remembered gluing the cuesheet on a card in the newspaper office; could he have left it there? He phoned Riker.

"You took it when we went to lunch," Riker said. "I saw it in your hand."

"Go and see if it's still in the car," Qwilleran said urgently. "And hurry! We have a show in half an hour! I'll hold." While holding he appraised the calamitous situation. How could Hixie operate the sound system and lighting without her cuecard? There were six cues for music, eight for voices, five for lights—all numbered to correlate with digits on the stereo counter. With more experience she might be able to wing it, but this was only their second performance.

Riker's search of the car was fruitless. Without even a thank you Qwilleran banged down the receiver and returned to the ballroom, where he paced the floor and looked wildly about the four walls.

The Siamese watched his frantic gyrations calmly, sitting on their briskets and wearing expressions of supreme innocence.

Their very pose was suspect. *"Did you devils steal the card?"* he shouted at them.

The thunder of his voice frightened them into flight.

Now he knew! It was the glue! He had used rubber cement, and Koko had a passion for adhesives.

In desperation Qwilleran figured it would take twenty minutes to drive to the school, nine minutes to set up; that left eleven minutes to find the cuecard in a fifteen-room house with fifty closets, all of which looked like dumpsters. Impossible!

Take it easy, he told himself; sit down and think; if I were a cat, where would I . . . ?

He dashed upstairs to the kitchen. It was their bailiwick, and the six-foot table was a private baldachin sheltering their dinner plate, water dish, and Koko's closet treasures. Among them was the cuecard with two perforations in one corner.

Muttering words the Siamese had never heard, Qwilleran raced back downstairs and repacked the equipment while keeping one eye on his watch. He was cutting it close. He had to drive to the school, find the right entrance, unload the suitcases, carry them to the gym, set up the stage, test the speakers, focus the lights, change clothes, and get into character as a twentieth-century radio announcer in a nineteenth-century situation. Hixie would be waiting for him, worried sick and unable to do anything until he arrived with the equipment.

He exceeded the speed limit on Sandpit Road and parked at the front entrance where a yellow curb prohibited parking. As he was opening the trunk of the car, a short, stocky man in a baggy business suit came running from the building, followed by a big, burly student in a varsity jacket.

"Mr. Qwilleran! Mr. Qwilleran!" the man called out. "We thought you'd forgotten us! I'm Mr. Broadnax, the principal. This is Mervyn, our star linebacker. He'll carry your suitcases. It's a long walk to the gym."

The three of them hustled into the building and walked rapidly down one long corridor after another, and all the while the principal was saying, "Will it take you long to set up? Mervyn will help. Just tell him what to do . . . The classes change in eight minutes. Everyone's looking forward to this. Lyle Compton raved about it . . . Don't give up! We're almost there. The custodian built a special platform. Is there anything you need? Is there anything I can do?"

Qwilleran thought, Yes, shut up and let me figure out how to set up in eight minutes.

"Is Miss Rice going to be here today?" the principal asked.

"Is she *going to be here?* She's half the show! Hasn't she arrived? I can't go on without her!" Qwilleran's forehead started to perspire profusely. What could have happened to her? Why hadn't she phoned? He'd give her ten minutes. Then he'd have to cancel. It would be embarrassing.

They finally arrived at the gym—Mr. Broadnax chattering and waving his arms, Mervyn lugging the three suitcases, Qwilleran mopping his brow. The custodian had constructed a platform—rough wood, three feet high, plywood surface supported by two-by-fours and reached by a short flight of wooden steps at the rear. On it were two small folding tables and two folding chairs.

"Now, is everything all right?" asked Mr. Broadnax. "Are the tables big enough? Would you like larger ones from the library? Mervyn will bring them in . . . Mervyn, go to the library—"

"No! No! These are fine," Qwilleran said absently. He was worrying about other things.

"Shall we help you unpack? Where do you want the tripods? Do you need a mike? We have a good PA system . . . Mervyn, get Mr.—"

"No! No! I don't need a mike." He pointed to a door behind the stage. "Where does that lead? I need a door for entrances and exits."

"That's a tackroom for gym equipment. It's locked, but I'll get the key . . . Mervyn, go to the office and bring me the key to the tackroom. Hep!"

Mervyn plunged out of the gym like a linebacker blitzing a quarterback. Meanwhile, Qwilleran mounted the shaky steps to position the furniture and speakers. The floor of the stage, he discovered, bounced like a trampoline. Walking gingerly, he placed the speakers at the front corners of the stage, beamed the two spotlights on the announcer's table, and situated the engineer's table at one side so that Hixie—if she ever arrived—would have more stability underfoot. Where, he asked himself, could she possibly be? Glancing frequently at his watch, he tested the two speakers, tested the two lights (one white, one red), and tested his own voice.

Just as Mervyn returned with the key to the tackroom, a bell rang, and there was instant tumult in the hall.

"May we stall a few minutes?" Qwilleran asked the principal. "I don't know what's happened to my partner. I'm seriously concerned."

The uproar in the hall grew louder, like the roar of a rampaging river when the dam has broken. The double doors burst open, and a flood of noisy students surged into the gym. The two men went into a huddle behind the stage.

"I can't do the show alone. We'll be obliged to cancel," Qwilleran said.

"Could you just give the students a talk about the fire and answer questions?"

"It wouldn't work."

"Maybe a talk on journalism as a career choice."

"I'm sorry, but we'll have to cancel, Mr. Broadnax."

At that moment a side door was flung open, and a distraught Hixie rushed on the scene. "Qwill, you'll never believe what happened!"

"I don't want to know," he snapped. "Everything's been tested. Get up there and take over. Walk carefully. The floor bounces." He ducked into the tackroom, leaving the door ajar in order to hear his cues.

The principal was saying, "These people from the newspaper have come out here to present an exciting show for you, and I want you to give them your complete and courteous attention. There will be no talking during the program and no moving around!"

Great! Qwilleran thought; they hate us already, and they're going to be bored out of their skulls; I should have brought a guitar.

Mr. Broadnax went on. "The show is about a radio broadcast during a great forest fire in 1869, when your great-great-great-grandparents were alive. It's all make-believe, because radio hadn't been invented in those days. I want you to sit quietly and pretend you're the studio audience."

The students became miraculously quiet. A moment later they erupted in cheers and whistles as Hixie, a young and attractive woman, mounted the platform and went to the engineer's station.

"Students!" came the sharp voice of the principal, and they were silenced as if by some secret weapon.

After a few bars of "Anitra's Dance," Qwilleran emerged from the tackroom, climbed the shaky steps, and walked across the stage with knees bent to minimize the bounce. "We interrupt this program to bring you a bulletin . . ."

Perhaps it was the size and magnificence of his moustache or the knowledge that this was the richest man in the northeast central United States. Or perhaps Qwilleran did indeed have a compelling stage presence. Whatever it was, the young people in the bleachers were spellbound, and they were entranced by the other voices coming from the speakers, especially that of the old farmer. Fleeing the flames in a horse-drawn wagon, he had brought his family to safety in a lakeport town, where he was being interviewed by telephone.

"Tell me, sir," said the announcer, "is the fire consuming everything in its path?"

"No," said a parched and reedy voice, "it's like the fire was playin' leapfrog, jumpin' right over one farm and burnin' the next one down to the ground. I don't know what the Lord is tryin' to tell us! We picked up one ol' feller wanderin' around, blind as a bat. Didn't even know where he was! His clothes, they was all burned off. He was stark naked and black as a piece o' coal. We sure had a wagonload when we come into town. We was lucky. They was all alive. Some wagons came into town full o' corpses."

There were gasps and whimpers in the audience as flames were reported to be sweeping across the countryside and consuming whole villages. Suddenly red light filled the stage, and the announcer jumped to his feet.

"Pickax is in flames!" he yelled. Knocking over his chair, he ran gasping and choking from the stage. In his panic he bounced the plywood floor, and both speakers fell over, facedown, while one leg of the folding table collapsed, sliding the telephone and mike to the floor.

"Oh, God!" Qwilleran muttered as he dashed into the tackroom and slammed the door. How would Hixie set up the stage again? Would the audience consider it slapstick comedy? There was an excited uproar in the bleachers, rising above the crashing Tchaikovsky fire music. By opening the door an inch, Qwilleran thought, he could get an idea how Hixie was coping, but the door refused to open. He was locked in!

"Oh, no!" He pounded on the panels with both fists, but the crescendo of the music and the student pandemonium drowned out his appeal for help. His face was already flushed by the emotion of the scene, and now he could hardly breathe in the airless, sweaty closet. He found a dumbbell and hammered on the door; no one heard. Soon the music would signal him to make his entrance, and if he failed to respond on cue, the tape would run out of music, and the disembodied voice of the Irish innkeeper would come from nowhere, answering questions that were not being asked—unless Hixie had the sense to stop the tape. But how would she know he was locked in?

The music ended, and Hixie realized something was wrong; she pressed the button. The hubbub in the audience subsided. In the momentary silence, Qwilleran pounded on the door frantically with the dumbbell, bringing Mr. Broadnax with the key. It was an overheated but poised radio announcer who mounted the flimsy steps—to deafening applause.

As the voice of the Irish innkeeper came from the speakers, the students were shocked to hear him say, "There's plenty o' sad tales they're tellin'. One poor man tried to rescue his two children—both of them half suffocated—but he couldn't carry both of the little ones because his right arm was burned off. Burned clean off, mind you! He had to *choose between them,* poor man!"

When it was over, the performers took cautious bows to vociferous applause. Then the audience piled out of the gym, and Hixie said, "They loved it when everything fell over. They thought it was part of the show."

"Best program we've ever had!" the principal told them as they packed their gear. "Even the troublemakers liked it, especially the part where the man's arm was burned off . . . Now, what can we do for you? Mervyn will carry your suitcases. Would you like a cold drink in our cafeteria?"

Qwilleran and Hixie were both glad to get out of the building. "Okay, chum, what happened to you?" he asked peevishly.

"You'll never believe this," she said. "I had lunch at Linguini's, and the parking lot was full, so I parked in the weeds behind the restaurant. When I came out, it was getting chilly, so I put on the coat that was on the backseat. As soon as I pulled onto the open highway, I felt something crawling inside my sleeve. I screamed, ran the car off the road, and jumped out. At the same time a mouse ran out of my coat."

"But that doesn't explain why you were so late," he objected with a lack of sympathy.

"I had to wait for a farmer to come with a tractor and pull me out of the ditch."

"Well . . . if you say so," Qwilleran said dubiously. "But I'll tell you one thing: I'll never set foot on another platform unless I've personally tested it."

"And I'll never park in the weeds behind Linguini's again! *Je le jure!*"

Upon returning home from Mooseland High School, Qwilleran's first move was to phone Gary Pratt at the Black Bear Café. "Gary," he said, "I'd like to run up there tomorrow afternoon and see where we're going to present our show for the Outdoor Club. I don't want any surprises Monday night."

"Sure thing. What time tomorrow?"

"How about two o'clock?"

"I'll be here," said the barkeeper. "There's somebody I want you to meet, too—a nice little girl who comes in quite often."

"How little?"

"Well, I mean, she's in her twenties, but a heck of a lot smaller than your other farm girls around here. She has a problem you might be able to help her with."

"If it's a financial problem, tell her to check with the Klingenschoen Foundation," Qwilleran said. "I don't get involved with anything like that. I'm lucky to be able to balance my checkbook."

"It's nothing like that," Gary said. "The thing of it is, it's a family problem, and it sounds kind of fishy to me. I thought you might give her some advice."

Qwilleran said he would listen to her story. He had little interest in a young farm girl's family problems, however. What really piqued his curiosity was the suicide of a woman with no apparent motive. He was glad when Junior phoned him on Friday morning.

"Turn on the coffeemaker," the young editor ordered. "I'll be right there with some doughnuts from Lois's. I have some things to report."

Lois's doughnuts were freshly fried every morning, with no icing, no jelly, no chopped nuts—just old-fashioned fried cakes with a touch of nutmeg. The two men sat at the kitchen table, hugging coffee mugs and dipping into the doughnut bag.

Qwilleran said, "I've figured out why nineteenth-century tycoons built big houses and had fourteen kids. Eight of them were girls and considered a total loss. Two of the sons died in infancy; another was killed while stopping a runaway horse; one was deported Down Below to avoid local scandal; one became a journalist, which was even worse—halfway between a cattle rustler and snake oil salesman. They were lucky to have one son left to run the family business."

"That's just about what happened in the Gage family," Junior said. "Grandpa was the last male heir."

"When did you get back from Florida?"

"Around midnight. Almost missed the last shuttle out of Minneapolis."

"Did you get everything wrapped up?"

"To tell the truth," Junior said, "there wasn't that much to do. Grandma had sold her car; the furniture went with the house; we gave her clothes to charity; and the only jewelry she had was seashells and white beads. She'd unloaded her good jewelry, antiques, and real estate early on, to simplify the probate of her will, she said. The only property she couldn't dump was Lois's broken-down building. If anyone bought it, the city would make them put in a new john, widen the front door, fix the roof, and bring the electricity up to code. Don Exbridge was interested in buying the building, but he'd want to tear it down, and the public would be outraged."

Qwilleran agreed. "There'd be rioting in the streets and class-action lawsuits."

"You know, Qwill," said Junior, "I don't care about getting a big inheritance from Grandma Gage, but it would be nice if she established an education trust for her great-grandchildren. Jack has two kids; Pug has three; and Jody and I have one and seven-eighths, as of today."

"How is Jody feeling?"

"She's fine. We're starting the countdown. It's going to be a girl."

Qwilleran said, "Didn't you tell me that your grandmother put all three of you through college?"

"Yeah, my dad was broke. She despised him, so paying our tuition was a kind of put-down, not an act of generosity. At least, that's what my mother told me."

"More coffee, Junior?"

"Half a cup, and then I've got to get to the office. Golly, it's good to be home! There were two things that sort of shocked me at the Park of Pink Sunsets. One was that the management will buy Grandma's mobile home back again—for one-fourth of what she paid them for it! Wilmot advised me to accept the offer and cut my losses."

"What was the other shocker?"

"Grandma had developed a passion for the greyhound races! Can you picture that sedate little old lady stepping up to the pari-mutuel window and putting two on number five in the sixth?"

"Who told you this?"

"Her neighbor, the one who found the body."

"Did you talk much with her?"

"She wanted to gab, but I didn't have time. I just wanted to get home to my family and my job."

Qwilleran patted his moustache thoughtfully. "I've been thinking, Junior, that I could write an interesting profile of Euphonia Gage. There are plenty of people around here who knew her and would like to reminisce. I could also phone her neighbor at the mobile home park. What's her name?"

"Robinson. Celia Robinson."

"Will she be willing to talk?"

"She'll talk your ear off! Brace yourself for a large phone bill."

"Don't be naive! I'll charge it to the newspaper."

Before leaving, Junior said, "Qwill, I've decided why Grandma did what she did. She believed in reincarnation, you know, so maybe she was bored with shuffleboard and was ready to get on with another life. Is that too far out?"

A strange sound came from under the kitchen table.

"What's that?" Junior asked in surprise.

"That's Koko," Qwilleran explained. "He and Yum Yum are both under the table waiting for doughnut crumbs."

Five

When Junior mentioned his reincarnation theory as a motive for Euphonia's suicide, the chattering under the kitchen table had a negative, even hostile sound.

"You didn't care for the idea," Qwilleran said to Koko after Junior had left for the office. "Neither did I. I don't know what it is, but there's something we don't know about the lady."

Three doughnuts and two cups of coffee had only whetted Qwilleran's appetite, and he walked to Lois's for buckwheat pancakes with Canadian bacon, maple syrup, and double butter. Lois herself was waiting on tables, and when she brought his order, he thought the pancakes looked unusual. He tasted them cautiously.

"Lois," he called out, "what's wrong with these pancakes?"

She stared briefly at the plate before snatching it away. "You got Mrs. Toodle's oat bran pancakes!" She took the plate to another table and returned with the right one. "Do these look better? She put margarine and honey on 'em, but she hadn't started to eat."

That's the way it was in that restaurant—informal. Lois was a hard-working woman who owned her own business, labored long hours, enjoyed every aspect of her job, and jollied or insulted the customers with impunity. She had been feeding downtown Pickax for thirty years, and her devoted clientele regularly took up collections to finance building repairs, since the "stingy old woman" who owned the place would do nothing about maintenance. Twice Qwilleran had dropped a twenty-dollar bill into the pickle jar.

"So you lost one of your good customers!" he said to Lois when he paid his check.

"Who?"

"Euphonia Gage."

"That old witch? You gotta be kidding! She was too hoity-toity to come in here," Lois said with lofty disdain. "She sent her housekeeper to collect the rent. When her husband was alive, he came in himself, and I fixed him a thick roast beef sandwich with horseradish. Nice man! If I was short of cash, he didn't mind coming back the next day."

"For another sandwich?" Qwilleran inquired.

"You men!" Lois snapped with a grimace that was half rebuke and half fondness.

Walking home, Qwilleran began to formulate his profile of Junior's grandmother. He would call it "The Several Hats of Mrs. Gage." She was dancer, snob, health nut, and "purplist," a word he had coined. She was generous, stingy, elegant, aloof, witty, unpredictable, gracious, and hoity-toity.

Later, he was sitting at his desk, making notes for the profile, when Koko trudged past the library door with something in his mouth. The plodding gait, lowered head, and horizontal tail suggested serious business. Kao K'o Kung was not a mouser—he left that occupation to Yum Yum—but his behavior was suspiciously predatory, and Qwilleran followed him stealthily. When within tackling distance, he grabbed Koko around the middle and commanded, "Drop that filthy thing!"

Koko, who never took orders gladly, squirmed and clamped his jaws on the prey, shaking his head to prevent the forcible opening of his mouth. Realizing it was no mouse, Qwilleran coaxed in a gentler voice, "Let go, Koko. Good boy! Good boy!" And he massaged the furry throat until Koko was induced to lick his nose and lose his grip.

"What next!" Qwilleran said aloud, snatching the trophy. It was a partial denture—left and right molars connected by a silver bridge—and it was destined for the collection site under the kitchen table.

The objects that Yum Yum charmingly pilfered from pockets and wastebaskets were toys, to be hidden behind seat cushions for future reference. Koko was the serious treasure hunter, however. Qwilleran thought of his excavations as an archaeological dig for fragments that might be pieced together to reconstruct a social history of the Gage dynasty. In fact, he had started a written inventory. Now he confiscated the denture and carried it to the library, while Koko followed in high dudgeon, scolding and jumping at his hand.

"It's only an old set of false teeth," Qwilleran remonstrated as he dropped it into the desk drawer. "Why don't you dig up a Cartier watch?" He added "partial denture" to the other recent acquisitions on the inventory: leather bookmark, recipe for clam chowder, purple satin bedroom slipper, man's argyle sock, 1951 steeplechase ticket, wine label (Bernkasteler Doktor und Graben Hochfeinst '59).

On Friday afternoon Qwilleran drove to the Black Bear Café, wearing his new multicolor sweater. Although his prime purpose was to inspect the staging area for "The Big Burning," he was also slated to meet a young farm woman who needed advice, and the sweater made him look ten years younger—or so he had been told.

Gary's bar and grill operation was located in the Hotel Booze in the town of Brrr, so named because it was the coldest spot in the county. The hotel had been a major landmark since the nineteenth century, when sailors, miners, and lumberjacks used to kill each other in the saloon on Saturday nights, after which the survivors each paid a quarter to sleep on the floor of the rooms upstairs. It was a boxy building perched on a hilltop overlooking the harbor, and ships in the lake were guided to port by the rooftop sign: BOOZE . . . ROOMS . . . FOOD.

When Gary Pratt took over the Hotel Booze from his ailing father, the bar was a popular eatery, but the upper floors violated every building regulation in the book. Yet, the banks refused to lend money to bring it up to code, possibly because of Gary's shaggy black beard and wild head of hair, or because he had been a troublesome student in high school. Qwilleran had a hunch about Gary's potential, however, and the Klingenschoen Foundation obliged with a low-interest economic development loan. With the addition of elevators, indoor plumbing, and beds in the sleeping rooms, the Hotel Booze became the flagship of Brrr's burgeoning tourist trade, and Gary became president of the chamber of commerce. Wisely he maintained the seedy atmosphere that appealed to sportsmen. The mirror over the backbar still had the radiating cracks where a bottle had been flung by a drunken patron during the 1913 mine strike.

When Qwilleran arrived on that Friday afternoon he slid cautiously onto a wobbly barstool, and Gary, behind the carved black walnut bar, asked, "Squunk water on the rocks?"

"Not this time. I'll take coffee if you have it. How's business?"

"It'll pick up when the hunting season opens. I hope we get some snow. The hunters like a little snow for tracking."

"They say we're in for a lot of it this winter." It was one of the trite remarks Qwilleran had learned to make; local etiquette called for three minutes of weatherspeak before any purposeful conversation.

"I like snow," said Gary. "I've been dog-sledding the last couple of winters."

"Sounds like an interesting sport," Qwilleran said, although the idea of being transported by dogpower had no appeal for him.

"You should try it! Come out with me some Sunday!"

"That's an idea," was Qwilleran's carefully ambiguous response.

"Say, I've been meaning to ask you about the different characters in your show. It must have been hard to change your voice like that. I sure couldn't do it."

"I've always had a fairly good ear for different kinds of speech," Qwilleran said with a humble shrug. "The big problem was recording the voices. When I played them back, the tape was punctuated with the yowling of cats. So I locked them out of the room and tried again. This time the mike picked up a trash impactor and the sheriff's helicopter. I finally recorded at three o'clock in the morning and hoped no one in my neighborhood would require an ambulance."

"Well, it sure was impressive. Where did you get all your information? Or did you make some of it up?"

"Every statement is documented," Qwilleran said. "Do you know anything about the Gage family? One of them was an amateur historian."

"All I know is that this woman who just died—her husband used to hang around the bar when my father was running it. Dad said he was quite a boozer. Liked to swap stories with the hunters and fishermen. Never put on airs. Just one of the guys."

"Did you ever meet him?"

"No, he died before I took over—struck by lightning. He was horseback riding when a storm broke, and he made the mistake of sheltering under a tree. Killed instantly!"

"What about the horse?" Qwilleran asked.

"Funny, nobody ever mentioned the horse . . . Another cup of coffee?"

"No, thanks. Let's go and see where we're going to present our show."

"Okay. Just a sec." Gary picked up the bar telephone and called a number. "Nancy, he's here," he said in a low voice. "Okay, Qwill, let's go. The meeting room's across the lobby." He led the way to a large room that was barren except for a low platform and helter-skelter rows of folding chairs. "Here it is! What do you need? We can get you anything you want."

Qwilleran stepped up on the platform and found it solid. "We need a couple of small tables, preferably noncollapsible, and a couple of plain chairs . . . I see you have plenty of electric outlets . . . What's behind that door?"

"Just a hall leading to the restrooms and the emergency exit."

"Good! I'll use it for entrances and exits. Hixie says there'll be families attending, so I suggest seating the kids in the front rows.

They'll have better sight lines and be less fidgety, I hope . . . And now I'll take that second cup of coffee."

Back in the bar Gary said, "Hey, there's Nancy, the girl I want you to meet."

Seated on one of the tilt-top barstools was a young woman in jeans, farm jacket, and field boots. She was slightly built, and her delicate features were half hidden by a cascade of dark, wavy hair. In dress and stature she might have been a seventh grader on the way home from school, but her large brown eyes were those of a grown woman with problems. She turned her eyes beseechingly on Qwilleran's moustache.

"Nancy, this is Mr. Q," Gary said. "Nancy's a good customer of ours. Burgers, not beer, eh, Nancy?"

She nodded shyly, clutching her bottle of cola.

"How do you do," Qwilleran said with a degree of reserve.

"Nice to meet you. I've seen your column in the paper."

"Good!" he said coolly. Had she read it? Did she like it? Or had she just *seen it?*

Gary served Qwilleran a fresh cup of coffee. "Well, I'll leave you two guys to talk." He ambled to the other end of the bar to visit with a couple of boaters.

The awkward silence that followed was broken by Qwilleran's uninspired question. "Are you a member of the Outdoor Club?"

"Yes," she said. "I'm going to see your show Monday night."

He huffed into his moustache. Had she heard good things about it? Was she looking forward to it? Or was she simply going to *see it?* Again it was his turn to serve in this slow-motion game of Ping-Pong. "Do you think we'll have snow next week?"

"I think so," she said. "The dogs are getting excited."

"Dogs? Do you have dogs?"

"Siberian huskies."

"Is that so?" he remarked with a glimmer of interest. "How many do you have?"

"Twenty-seven. I breed sled dogs."

"Are you a musher?"

"I do a little racing," she said, blushing self-consciously.

"Gary tells me it's becoming quite a popular sport. Do you breed dogs as a hobby or a vocation?"

"Both, I guess. I work part-time at the animal clinic in Brrr. I'm a dog-handler."

"Do you live in Brrr?"

"Just outside. In Brrr Township."

How long, Qwilleran wondered, can this painful dialogue continue? He was determined not to inquire about her problem. If she had a problem, let her state it! They both wriggled on the ancient barstools that clicked noisily. He tried to catch Gary's eye, but the barkeeper was arguing heatedly with the boaters about the new breakwall.

"Nancy, I'm afraid I don't know your last name," Qwilleran said.

"Fincher," she said simply.

"How do you spell it?" He knew how to spell it, but it was an attempt to fill the silence.

"F-i-n-c-h-e-r."

Fortunately Gary glanced in their direction, and Qwilleran pointed to his empty cup and Nancy's half-empty bottle.

Gary approached with his bearish, lumbering gait. "Did you tell him about your problem?" he asked Nancy.

"No," she said, looking away.

Gary poured coffee and produced another bottle of cola. "The thing of it is, Qwill, her dad disappeared." Then he went back to the boaters.

Qwilleran looked inquiringly at the embarrassed daughter. "When did that happen?"

"I haven't been able to find him since Sunday." She looked genuinely worried.

"Do you live in the same house?"

"No, he lives on his farm. I have a mobile home."

"What kind of farm?"

"Potatoes."

"Where did you see him on Sunday?"

"I went over to cook Sunday dinner for him, the way I always do. Then he watched football on TV, and I went home to my dogs."

"And when did you first realize he was missing?"

"Wednesday." There was a long, exasperating pause. Qwilleran waited for her to go on. "The mail carrier stopped and told me that Pop's mailbox was filling up, and his dog was barking in the house, and there was no truck in the yard. So I drove over there, and Corky was so starved, he almost took my arm off. He'd wrecked the house, looking for something to eat. And the place smelled terrible!"

"Did you notify the police?"

Nancy looked at her clenched hands. They were small hands, but they looked strong. "Well, I talked to a deputy I know, and he said Pop was most likely off on a binge somewhere."

"Is your father a heavy drinker?"

"Well . . . he's been drinking more since Mom died."

"Did you do anything further?"

"Well, I cleaned up the mess and took Corky home with me, and on the way I stopped at the Crossroads Tavern. That's where Pop goes to have a beer with the other farmers and chew the rag. They said he hadn't been around since Saturday night. They figured he was working in the fields."

"Has your father ever done this before?"

"Never!" Her eyes flashed for the first time. "He'd never do such a thing at harvest. The weather's been wet, and if he doesn't dig his potatoes before the first heavy frost, the whole crop will be ruined. It's not like him at all! He's a very good farmer, and he's got a lot invested in his crop."

"And this deputy you mentioned—does he know your father?"

"Yes," she said, shrinking into her burly jacket.

"What's his name?"

"Dan Fincher."

"Related to you?"

She turned away as she said, "We were married for a while."

"I see," said Qwilleran. "What's your father's name?"

"Gil Inchpot."

He nodded. "The Inchpot name goes back a long way in the farming community. The farm museum in West Middle Hummock has quite a few things from early Inchpot homesteads."

"I've never been there," Nancy said. "I never cared much for history."

"What kind of truck does your father drive?"

"Ford pickup. Blue."

"Do you know the license number?"

"No," she said, pathetically enough to arouse Qwilleran's sympathy.

"Let me think about this matter," he said, pushing a cocktail napkin and a ballpoint pen toward her. "Write down your address and telephone number, also the address of your father's farm."

"Thank you," she said simply, turning her expressive brown eyes toward him.

He thought, Beware of young women with beseeching brown eyes, especially when they look twelve years old. "If you learn anything further, ask Gary how to get in touch with me."

"Thank you," she said again. "Now I have to go back to work. I just ran over from the clinic."

She left, lugging a shoulder bag half her size. Qwilleran watched her go, smoothing his moustache like the villain in an old melodrama, but the gesture meant something else. It meant that he sensed an element of intrigue in this country tale. The reaction started with a tingle on his upper lip—in the roots of his moustache—and he had learned to respect the sensation.

Gary returned with the coffee server.

"Please! Not again! It's good coffee, but I'm driving."

"Nice little girl, isn't she?" the barkeeper remarked.

"I don't visualize her racing with a pack of sled dogs. She looks too delicate."

"But she's light, like a jockey, and that makes a good racer. What do you think of her story?"

"It bears a closer look."

"Yeah, that ex-husband of hers is a jerk! Imagine brushing her off like that!"

"If she wants to talk to me, you dial the number for her, Gary."

"Sure, I understand. I'll bet you're pestered by all kinds of people."

Qwilleran threw a ten dollar bill across the bar. "Keep the change for a down payment on some new barstools. And I'll see you Monday night."

From the Hotel Booze he drove directly to the police station in downtown Pickax, where his friend Andrew Brodie was chief.

Brodie waved him away. "If you're looking for free coffee, you're too late. The pot's dry."

"False deduction," Qwilleran said. "My prime objective is to see if you're doing your work, issuing lots of parking tickets, and arresting leaf burners. Did you blow your leaves into the street, Andy? The vacuum truck will be on your side of town tomorrow."

The chief shot him a veiled look. "The wife takes care of that."

"Oh, ho! Now I understand why you're always advocating matrimony! I knew there was some ulterior reasoning."

Brodie scowled. "What's on your mind, besides leaves?"

"Do you know a guy named Gil Inchpot?"

"Potato farmer. Brrr Township."

"Right. His daughter's worried about him. He's disappeared. His truck's gone. He abandoned his dog. And he decamped when the potatoes were ready to harvest."

"That's the sheriff's turf," Brodie pointed out. "Did she report it to the sheriff's department?"

"She talked to a deputy named Dan Fincher."

"That guy's a lunkhead! I used to work for the sheriff, and I have firsthand evidence."

"Well, the lunkhead laughed it off, said Inchpot was off on a binge somewhere."

"The daughter should notify the state police. They cover three counties. Do you know the license number of the missing vehicle?"

"No, but it's a blue Ford pickup, and I have Inchpot's address, in case you want to run a check on it—with that expensive computer the taxpayers bought for you."

"Seeing as how it's you," Brodie said, "I'll run down the number and turn it over to the state police post."

"That's decent of you, Andy. If you ever want to run for mayor, I'll campaign for you."

The chief scowled again. "It would do me good to give Dan Fincher a swift kick in the pants, that's all."

Six

When Qwilleran returned home after his discussion with the police chief, Goodwinter Boulevard was transformed. All the leaves had been blown from the front lawns and sidewalks into the gutters, in preparation for the vacuum truck on Saturday. He found a lawn service vehicle parked behind the house, and three industrious young men with backpack blowers were coaxing the backyard leaves into heaps.

"Did Junior Goodwinter hire you?" Qwilleran asked one of them, feeling guilty that he had failed to take care of it himself. "Send the bill to me, but first, answer one question: What happens to these huge piles of leaves?"

"We'll be back tomorrow to finish up. We've run out of leaf bags," said the boss of the crew. "It's been a busy day. Everybody's in a rush to get rid of the leaves before snow flies."

"What happens if a big wind comes up tonight and blows these piles all over the yard?"

"We get another day's work, and you get another bill," the lawnman said with a guffaw.

As the backpackers went on their merry way, Qwilleran walked about the yard through rustling leaves—a joyous activity he remembered from boyhood. Suddenly, through the corner of his eye, he saw something crawling through the shrubs that bordered the property. He was prepared to yell "Scat!" when he realized it was the attorney's son. He called out sternly, "Is there something you want, young man?"

Timmie Wilmot scrambled to his feet. "Is Oh Jay over here?"

"I don't know anyone of that name."

"He's our cat. A great big orange one with bad breath."

"Then he'd better not hang around here," Qwilleran said in a threatening voice.

"I'm afraid he'll go out in the street and get sucked up in the leaf sucker." The boy was looking anxiously about Qwilleran's yard. "There he is!" He ran across the grass to a pile of leaves that effectively camouflaged a marmalade cat. Grabbing the surprised animal around the middle, he staggered back across the yard, clutching the bundle of fur to his chest, the orange tail dangling between his knees and the orange legs pointing stiffly in four directions. The pair reached the row of shrubs on the lot line and crawled through the brush to safety.

Indoors, the Siamese were concerned chiefly with Qwilleran's recent association with a dog-handler who also raised Siberian huskies. Their noses, like Geiger counters detecting radiation, passed over every square inch of Qwilleran's clothing, their whiskers registering positive.

He arranged some roast beef and boned chub from Toodle's Deli on a plate and placed it under the kitchen table. Then, turning on the kitchen radio for the weather report, he heard the following announcement instead:

"The hobgoblins will be out tomorrow night, which is official Beggars' Night in Pickax. A resolution passed by the city council limits trick-or-treating to one-and-a-half hours, between six o'clock and seven-thirty. Children should stay in their own neighborhoods unless accompanied by an adult. In all cases, two or more children should go together. The police department makes the following recommendations in the interest of safety:

"Stay on the sidewalk; don't run into the street. Don't go into houses if invited. Avoid wearing long costumes that could cause tripping. Don't eat treats until they have been inspected by a parent or other responsible person. Discard unwrapped cookies and candies immediately. Happy Halloween!"

Qwilleran turned to the cats, who were washing up. "Did you hear that? It would be more fun to stay home and do homework."

Saturday morning, after he had heard the announcement for the third time, he went back to Toodle's Market and bought a bushel of apples. When he arrived home, his phone was ringing, and Koko was announcing the fact by racing back and forth and jumping on and off the desk.

"Okay, okay!" Qwilleran yelled at him. "I can hear it, and I know where it is!"

Junior's voice said, "Where've you been so early? Did you stay out all night? I've been trying to reach you."

"I was buying apples for trick-or-treat."

"Apples! Are you nuts? They'll throw 'em at you! They'll soap your windows!"

"We'll see about that," Qwilleran said grimly. "What's on your mind? Are you at the office?"

"I'm going in later, but first: How would you like to take a little ride?"

"Where?"

"To the Hilltop Cemetery. Grandma was buried there yesterday—privately."

"How come?"

"Her last wishes, on file in Wilmot's office, specified no funeral, no mourners, no flowers, and no bagpipes."

"That will break Andy Brodie's heart," Qwilleran said. The police chief prided himself on his piping at weddings and funerals.

"It was Grandma's revenge on the police for all the traffic tickets she got, not that she ever paid them."

"Then why are you going to the cemetery this morning?"

"Somehow," said her grandson, "it isn't decent to let her be buried with only the Dingleberry brothers and a backhoe operator in attendance. Want to come along? I'll pick you up."

"I'll bring a couple of apples," Qwilleran offered.

The Hilltop Cemetery dated back to pioneer days when the Gages, Goodwinters, Fugtrees, Trevelyans, and other settlers were buried across the crest of a ridge. Their tombstones could be seen silhouetted against the sky as one approached.

On the way to the cemetery Junior said, "Pickax lost to Lockmaster again last night, fourteen to zip."

"We should give up football and stick to growing potatoes," Qwilleran remarked.

"How's everything at the house?"

"Koko just came out of a closet with a man's spat. I haven't seen one of those since the last Fred Astaire movie. He was dragging it conscientiously to the collection site in the kitchen, staggering and stumbling. His aim in life is to empty the closets, ounce by ounce."

"They'll have to be cleaned out sooner or later."

"Watch it!" Qwilleran snapped. Junior had a friendly way of facing his passenger squarely as he spoke, and they narrowly missed hitting a deer bounding out of a cornfield. "Keep your eyes on the road, Junior, or we'll be residents of Hilltop ourselves." They were passing through farm country, and he asked Junior if he knew a potato farmer named Gil Inchpot.

"Not personally, but his daughter was my date for the senior prom in high school. She was the only girl short enough for me."

"You're no longer short, Junior. You're what they call vertically challenged."

"Gee, thanks! That makes me feel nine feet tall."

They parked the car and walked up the hill to a granite obelisk chiseled with the name Gage. Small headstones surrounded it, and there was one rectangle of freshly turned earth, not yet sodded or marked.

"There she is," said her grandson. "I was supposed to ship her books to Florida, but I had too many other things on my mind—my job, and the baby coming. I promise, though, she's going to get a memorial service exactly how she wanted it."

"Has her will been read?"

"Not until my brother and sister get here. Jack has to come from L.A., and Pug lives in Montana. Grandma wrote a new will after moving to Florida. It was in the manager's safe at the mobile home park, all tied up with red ribbon and sealed with red wax. It will be interesting to know what changes she made."

"You told me once that you were her sole heir."

"That's what she said at the time, but I think she was just cajoling me into doing something for her. A world-class conniver, that's what she was!"

"When Pug and Jack arrive," Qwilleran suggested, "I'd like to take all of you to dinner at the Old Stone Mill."

"Gee! That would be great!"

"Would you like an apple?"

The two men stood munching in silence for a while, Junior staring at the grave and Qwilleran gazing around the horizon. "Pleasant view," he remarked.

"Pallbearers always hated burials up here. No access road. They have to carry the casket up that steep path . . . Wish I had a flower to throw on the grave before we leave."

"We could bury our apple cores. They'd sprout and produce apple blossoms every spring."

"Hey! Let's do it!" Junior exclaimed.

They scooped out some soil and buried the cores reverently, then drove back to town without saying much until Qwilleran ventured, "You never told me anything about your grandfather."

"To tell the truth, my grandparents are closer in death than they ever were in life," Junior said. "She was into arts and health fads; he was into sports and booze. The Gage shipyard had folded, and he spent his time manipulating the family fortune, not always legally. Grandpa spent two years in federal prison for financial fraud. That was in the 1920s."

"If they were so mismatched, why did they marry? Does anyone know?"

"Well, the way my mother told me the story, Euphonia's forebears were pioneer doctors by the name of Roff. They'd deliver a baby for a bushel of apples or set a broken bone for a couple of chickens, so the family never had any real money. Somehow Euphonia got pressured into marrying the Gage heir. The Roffs, being from Boston, had a certain 'class' that Grandpa lacked, so it seemed like a good deal all around, but it didn't work."

"Was your mother their only child?"

"Yeah. She called herself a Honeymoon Special."

Qwilleran asked to be dropped off at the variety store, where he bought a blue light bulb and a Halloween mask. Then he spent an hour with his recording machine taping weird noises. The Siamese watched with bemused tolerance as their human companion uttered screeches, anguished moans, and hideous laughs into the microphone.

The performance was interrupted by the telephone, when Gary Pratt called. "Nancy's here. She wants to tell you something. Okay?"

"Put her on."

In a breathless, little-girl voice Nancy said, "The state police found Pop's truck!"

"That was fast. Where was it?"

"At the airport."

"In the parking structure?"

"No. In the open lot."

He nodded with understanding. There was a charge for parking indoors, and most locals preferred to park free in the cow pasture. "Is there any clue as to his destination?"

"No . . ." She hesitated before continuing in a faltering way. "He never . . . he doesn't like to travel, Mr. Qwilleran. He's hardly been . . . out of Moose County . . . except for Vietnam."

"Still, some unexpected business transaction may have come up—suddenly. What did the police say?"

"They told me to report a missing person, and they'll check the passenger list for flights."

"Let me know what they find out," Qwilleran said. He was beginning to feel genuinely sorry for her, and in an effort to divert her from her worries he said, "You know, Nancy, I'd like to write a column on dog-sledding. Are you willing to be interviewed?"

"Oh, yes!" she said. "The mushers would love the publicity."

"How about tomorrow afternoon?"

"Well, I want to go to Pop's house after church to clean out the refrigerator, but I could be home by two."

"By the way, what's the situation in the potato fields?"

"No severe frost yet. I'm praying he comes back before the crop's ruined."

"Could you hire someone to do the harvesting in an emergency?"

"I don't know who it would be. They're all busy with their own work."

"It won't hurt to ask around, Nancy. And I'll see you tomorrow afternoon."

The hour of hobgoblins approached. Qwilleran tried on his death's-head mask and prepared a sheet to shroud his head and body. The tape player was set up near the entrance, and at six o'clock he turned on the blue porch lamp that cast an eerie light on the gray stonework. He was ready for them.

The first squealing, chattering trio to come up the front walk included a miniature Darth Vader, a pirate, and a bride in a wedding dress made from old curtains. They were carrying shopping bags. Before they could ring the bell, the front door opened slowly, and unnatural sounds emanated from the gloomy interior. "Oooooooooh! Oooooooooo!" Then there was a horrifying screech. As the pop-eyed youngsters stared, a shrouded skeleton emerged from the shadows, and a clawlike hand was extended, clutching an apple. The three screamed and scrambled down the steps.

Later groups were scared stiff but not stiff enough to run away without their treats, so the supply of apples diminished slightly. Many beggars avoided the house entirely. They trooped down the side drive, however, to the brightly lighted carriage house where Polly was distributing candy.

The last intrepid pair to brave the haunted house were a cowboy with large eyeglasses and a moustache glued on his upper lip, accompanied by a tiny ballerina with a white net tutu and sequined bra over her gray warmup suit. The cowboy pressed the doorbell, and Qwilleran pressed the button on the player: "Oooooooooh! Oooooooooh!" The spooky wail was followed by a screech and a cackling laugh as a ghostly figure appeared.

"I know you!" said the cowboy. "You told us about those people burning up."

In a sepulchral drone Qwilleran said, "I . . . am the . . . scrofulous skeleton . . . of Skaneateles!"

The boy explained to his small companion, "He can talk so you don't know who he is. He's that man with the big moustache."

"What . . . do . . . you want?" the apparition intoned.

"Trick or treat!"

The clawlike hand dropped apples into the outstretched sacks, and Timmie Wilmot turned to his sister. "Apples!" he said. "Cheapo!"

At seven-thirty Qwilleran was glad to turn off the blue light and shed his mask and sheet.

Soon Polly phoned. "Did you have many beggars?"

"Enough," he said. "I have some apples left over, in case you feel like making eight or nine pies. How about going out to dinner?"

"Thanks, but I couldn't possibly! I'm exhausted after running up and down stairs to answer the doorbell. Why don't you come to brunch tomorrow? Mushroom omelettes and cheese popovers."

"I'll be there! With apples. What time?"

"I suggest twelve noon, and don't forget to turn your clocks back. This is the end of Daylight Saving Time."

Before resetting his two watches, three clock radios, and digital coffeemaker, Qwilleran added several new acquisitions to the collection in the desk drawer: swizzle stick, stale cigar, brown shoelace, woman's black lace garter, handkerchief embroidered "Cynara," and box of corn plasters.

On Sunday morning it was back to Standard Time for the rest of the nation but not for Koko and Yum Yum, who pounced on Qwilleran's chest at seven A.M., demanding their eight o'clock breakfast. He shooed them from the bedroom and slammed the door, but they yowled and jiggled the doorknob until he fed them in self-defense. He himself subsisted on coffee and apples until it was time to walk back to the carriage house. He used his own key and was met at the top of the stairs by a husky Siamese who fixed him with a challenging eye.

"Back off!" Qwilleran said. "I was invited to brunch . . . Polly, this cat is much too heavy."

"I know, dear," she said regretfully, "but Bootsie always seems to be hungry. I don't know how Koko stays so svelte. When he stretches, he's a yard long."

"I suspect he has a few extra vertebrae. He walks around corners like a train going around a curve; the locomotive is heading east while the caboose is still traveling north . . . Do I smell coffee?"

"Help yourself, Qwill. I'm about to start the omelettes."

When he tasted the first succulent mouthful, he asked in awe, "How did you learn to make omelettes like these?"

"I prepared one every day for a month until I mastered the technique. That was several years ago, before we were all worried about cholesterol."

"I'm not worried about cholesterol," he retorted. "I think it's a lot of bunk."

"Famous last words, dear."

He helped himself to another popover. "Junior's siblings are coming to town for the formalities, and I'm taking them to dinner. I hope you'll join us."

"By all means. I remember Pug when she used to come into the library for books on horses; she married a rancher. Jack went into advertising; he was always a very clever boy."

"Did you know that Mrs. Gage owned Lois's building?"

"Of course. The Gage family has had it for generations."

"Did you ever meet Euphonia's husband?"

"No, our paths never crossed."

"They say he and his wife didn't get along."

With a slight stiffening of the spine Polly said, "I'm not in a position to say, although they never appeared in public together."

"He and Lois seemed to hit it off pretty well."

"Qwill, dear, for someone who deplores gossip, you seem to be wallowing in it today."

"For purely vocational reasons," he explained. "I'm planning an in-depth profile of Euphonia."

Polly nodded knowingly, being familiar with his ambitious writing projects that never materialized.

He went on. "No one has come up with an acceptable motive for her suicide. Junior thinks it has to do with her belief in reincarnation, but I don't buy that explanation."

"Nor I . . . May I fill your cup, Qwill?"

"It's superlative today. What did you do to it?" he asked.

"Just a touch of cinnamon."

They sipped in contented silence, as close friends can do, Qwilleran wondering whether to tell her about Koko's latest salvage operations. Besides the purple hair ribbon and purple bedroom slipper, there had been an empty vial of violet perfume, an English lavender sachet, and a lipstick tube labeled "Grape Delish." Koko had chosen these mementoes out of an estimated 1.5 million pieces of junk. Why? Could he sense Euphonia's innate energy in purpleness? Or was he trying to communicate some catly message?

"What are you reading these days?" Polly asked.

"For myself, a biography of Sir Wilfred Grenfell, but the cats and I are going through *Robinson Crusoe.* That was Koko's choice. The opening sentence has 105 words—a maze of principal and subordinate clauses. It's interesting to compare with the staccato effect of simple declarative clauses in *Tale of Two Cities,* which opens with 120."

Polly smiled and nodded and asked if he would like to hear a Mozart concerto for flute, oboe, and viola. Qwilleran had always preferred a hundred-piece symphony orchestra or thousand-voice choir, but he was learning to appreciate chamber music. All in all, it was a cozy Sunday afternoon until he excused himself, saying he had to interview a breeder of Siberian huskies.

He avoided mentioning that the breeder was a woman—a young woman—a slender young woman with appealing brown eyes and a mass of dark, wavy hair and a little-girl voice.

Half an hour later, when he arrived at the address in Brrr Township, he knew he was in the right place. A twenty-seven-dog chorus could be heard behind the mobile home. The excited huskies were chained to a line-up of individual posts in front of individual shelters. Nancy's truck was not in the yard, and when he knocked on the door there was no answer, except from Corky within. He strode about the yard for a while, saying "Good dogs!" to the frenzied animals, but it only increased the clamor. He was preparing to leave when a pickup with a boxy superstructure steered recklessly into the yard, and Nancy jumped out.

"Sorry I'm late," she said excitedly. "The police came to Pop's house while I was there. They checked the airline, and he never bought a ticket!"

Or, Qwilleran thought, he bought a ticket without giving his right name.

"I don't understand it!" she went on. "Why would he leave his truck there? I was worried about the potatoes, but now I'm worried that something has happened to Pop!"

Sympathetically Qwilleran asked, "Was he having trouble of any kind? Financial problems? Enemies he was trying to avoid?"

"I don't know . . . I don't see how . . . He was well liked by the other farmers—always helping them out. When I lived at home, I remember how stranded motorists would come to the house to use the phone. They were out of gas, or their car had broken down. Pop had his own gas pump, and he'd give them a gallon or stick his head under the hood of their car and fix what was wrong. He could fix anything mechanical and was proud of it . . . So now I'm worrying that he was helping someone out and they took advantage of him. You never know who's driving on these country roads nowadays. It used to be so safe! Everyone was honest. But now . . . someone could come along and stun my dogs and make off with the whole pack. They stole a big black walnut tree from a farm near here." The dogs were still barking until she silenced them with a command.

"How old is your father?" Qwilleran asked.

"Fifty-seven."

"When did your mother die?"

"She passed away three—no, four years ago. Pop changed a lot after that."

"Could there be anything new in his lifestyle that you don't know about?"

"You mean . . . like women? Or drugs?" She hesitated.

A reassuring manner was his stock in trade. "You can tell me, Nancy. I may be able to help."

"Well . . . he used to be very tight-fisted, but lately he's spending a lot of money."

"Extravagance can be a way of coping with grief. How is he spending the money?" Qwilleran asked.

"On farm improvements. Nothing wrong with that, I suppose, but"—she turned frightened eyes to him—*"where is he getting it?"*

Seven

Qwilleran and the dog-handler were standing in the farmyard. "Well, you don't want to listen to my troubles all day," Nancy said with a gulp. "Do you want to go and see the dogs?"

"First, let's sit down and talk for a while. I've seen them, and I've heard them," he said dryly.

"You should hear them before a race! They love to hit the trail, and they go wild when they're waiting for the starting flag."

They entered a small mobile home where they were greeted by a large, friendly, all-American, farm-type, cork-colored mongrel whose wagging tail was wreaking havoc in the tight quarters.

"Good boy!" Qwilleran said while being lashed by the amiable tail.

"This is Pop's dog," Nancy said. "Where would you like to sit?" She brushed debris from a couple of chair seats and hastily picked up litter from the floor.

"Is it okay if I tape this interview?" He placed a small recorder on a nearby table, and a swipe of the tail knocked it off.

"I'd chain him outdoors, but he'd drive the other dogs crazy," she said apologetically. "Corky! Go in the other room!" She pointed, and obediently he walked six feet away and stretched out with his chin on his paw.

"You have a way with dogs," Qwilleran complimented her. "How did you get into this specialty of yours?"

"Well, I spent a couple of years in Alaska, and when I came home I bought a sled and a pair of huskies—Siberians. They're smaller than Alaskans but stronger and faster." Her small, wavering voice became stronger as she warmed up to her subject.

"Then you're the one who started the sport here?"

"It was easy. When somebody tries dog-sledding on a beautiful winter day, they're hooked! I'll take you for a ride after we get some snow."

"How do you accommodate passengers?"

"You ride in the basket, and I ride the runners."

"Hmmm," he murmured, thinking he'd feel foolish sitting in a basket pulled by a pack of dogs. "Are all sled dogs as frisky as yours?"

"If they're good racers. A high attitude is what they should have. Mine are born to be racers, not pets, but I love them like family."

"What else makes a good racer?"

"Hard muscles in the right places. A good gait. And they have to like working in a team."

"Training them must be a science," Qwilleran said.

"I don't know about that, but it takes a lot of patience."

"I believe it. How many dogs make a team?"

"I've seen as many as twenty in Alaska. I usually run eight."

"How do you drive them?"

"With your voice. They learn to take orders. Would you like a cola, Mr. Qwilleran?"

He said yes, although it ranked with tea at the bottom of his beverage list.

Nancy went on with enthusiasm as she opened a can. The shy, inarticulate, almost pathetic young woman became self-possessed and authoritative when talking about her vocation. "Each dog has a partner. They're paired according to the length of their stride and their personality. They become buddies. It's nice to see."

"Isn't it a great deal of work?"

"Yes, but I love feeding them, brushing them, socializing, cleaning up after them. Do you have dogs?"

"I have cats. Two Siamese. When do the race meets start?"

"After Christmas. We're training already. You should see us tearing around the back roads with the dogs pulling a wheeled cart! They know snow is on the way. They're getting so excited!" She showed a picture of a dog team pelting down a snowy trail; out of a total of thirty-two canine feet, only four seemed to be touching the ground.

"I believe they're flying!" Qwilleran said in amazement.

His willingness to be amazed, his sympathetic manner, and his attitude of genuine interest were the techniques of a good interviewer, and Nancy was relaxing and responding warmly. He could read her body language. Take it easy, he told himself; she's vulnerable. In businesslike fashion he asked, "Did you attend veterinary school?"

"I wanted to, but I got married instead—without telling my parents."

"How did they react?"

She looked at the tape recorder, and he turned it off.

"Well . . . Pop was furious . . . and Mom got cancer. I had to be nurse for her and housekeeper for Pop." Shrugging and wetting her lips, she said, "Dan didn't want a part-time wife."

"And that led to your divorce?"

She nodded. "When Mom died, I went to Alaska to get away from everything, but dog-sledding brought me back."

"And your father—how did he react to your return?"

"Oh, he was getting along fine. He had a housekeeper three days a week and a new truck and a harvester with stereo in the cab and half a million dollars' worth of drain tile. He was a lot nicer to me than before, and he gave me a piece of land for my mobile home and kennels . . . I don't know why I'm telling you all this. I guess it's because you're so understanding."

"I've had troubles of my own," he said. "One question occurred to me: Is your father a gambler?"

"Just in the football pool at the tavern. He never even buys a lottery ticket . . . Would you like another cola?" Corky had just rejoined the group, and a swish of his tail had swept Qwilleran's beverage off the table.

"No, thanks. Let's go out and see what a sled looks like."

The seven-foot sled, like a basket on runners, was in a small pole barn, where it shared space with a snowplow, snow blower, and other maintenance equipment.

"It's made of birch and oak," Nancy said. "This is the handrail. That's the brake board down there. It's held together with screws and glue and rawhide lacing. I varnish it before each sledding season."

"A work of art," Qwilleran declared. "Now let's meet your family."

The dogs anticipated their coming. Puppies in a fenced yard were racing and wrestling and jumping for joy. The adults raised a high-decibel clamor that Nancy quieted with a secret word. They were lean, handsome, high-waisted, long-legged animals in assorted colors and markings, with slanted blue eyes that gave them a sweet expression.

"These two are the lead dogs, Terry and Jerry. They're the captains, very brainy. Spunky and Chris are the wheel dogs, right in front of the sled."

Both Qwilleran and Nancy turned as a police vehicle pulled into the yard. It was a sheriff's car, and an officer in a wide-brimmed hat stepped out.

She shouted, "Hi, Dan! This is Mr. Qwilleran from the newspaper."

Qwilleran, recognizing the deputy's reticent and almost sullen attitude, said, "I believe we've met. You rescued me after a blizzard a couple of years ago."

The deputy nodded.

"Mr. Qwilleran is going to write up my dog team, Dan."

"But we'll hold the story until after snow flies. I'll work on it and call if I have any more questions . . . Beautiful animals. Interesting sport. Good interview." He moved toward his car.

"You don't have to leave," she protested.

"I have to go home and feed the cats," he explained, making an excuse that was always accepted.

Nancy accompanied him to his car. "Gary says you're living in Mrs. Gage's big house."

"That's right. I'm renting it from Junior Goodwinter, her grandson." He noticed a flicker in her eyes, which he attributed to memories of the high school prom, but it was something else.

"I've been in that house many times," she said. "It's huge!"

"Did you know Mrs. Gage?"

"Did I! My mother was her housekeeper for years and years. Every year Mom took me there for Christmas cookies and hot chocolate, and Mrs. Gage always gave me a present."

"That was gracious of her," Qwilleran said. "What did you think of her?"

"Well, she didn't fuss over me, but she was . . . nice."

Now he had one more adjective to describe the enigmatic Euphonia Gage, and another reason to call Florida and quiz her talkative neighbor.

"Do you like apples?" he asked Nancy before leaving. He handed her a brown paper bag.

Back at the mansion he submitted to the Siamese Sniff Test. After an afternoon with Corky and twenty-seven Siberian huskies, he rated minus-zero. Their investigation was cut short by a ringing telephone.

"Hey, Qwill!" said an excited Junior Goodwinter. "Can you stand some good news?"

"It's a boy," Qwilleran guessed.

"No, nothing like that; Jody's still here, getting antsy. But somebody wants to buy the Gage mansion! I just got a long distance phone call!

"Congratulations! Who's making the offer?"

"A realtor in Chicago."

"Is it a good offer?"

"Very good! What do you suppose it means? The house wasn't even listed for sale. And why should they pick mine when there are seven for-sale signs on the street? I'll bet Grandma Gage tipped someone off before she died."

"Don't ask questions," Qwilleran advised. "Take the money and run."

"I'm going to tell them it's rented until spring, so don't worry about having to move out, Qwill."

"I appreciate that. And let's not tell Polly until the deal's closed. She'll be upset about losing the carriage house."

"Okay, I won't. Golly! This is the best news I've had since I-don't-know-when."

"Good things come in threes," Qwilleran said. "Maybe Jody will have twins. By the way, was there a woman in the Gage family by the name of Cynara?"

"I don't think so. How do you spell it?"

"Like the poem: C-y-n-a-r-a."

"Nope. Doesn't ring a bell."

At a suitable hour—late enough for the fifty-percent discount but not too late for a Pink Sunset resident—Qwilleran placed a call to Florida, and Koko leaped to the desk in anticipation. "Arrange your optic fibers," Qwilleran advised him. "This may be enlightening." The cat's whiskers and eyebrows curved forward.

When a woman's cheery voice answered, he asked in a rich and ingratiating tone, "May I speak with Celia Robinson?"

There was a trill of laughter. "I know it's you, Clayton. You can't fool your old grandmother. Does your mother know you're calling?"

"I'm afraid I'm not Clayton. I'm a colleague of Junior Goodwinter, Mrs. Gage's grandson. I'm calling from Pickax. My name is Jim Qwilleran."

She hooted with delight tinged with embarrassment. "Oh, I thought you were my prankish grandson, changing his voice. He's a great one for playing practical jokes. What did you say your name was?"

"Jim Qwilleran. Junior gave me your number."

"Yes, he was here for a few days. He's a nice boy. And I know all about you. Mrs. Gage showed me the articles you write for the paper. What's the name of the paper?"

"*The Moose County Something.*"

"I knew it was a funny name, but I couldn't remember. And I loved your picture! You have a wonderful moustache. You remind me of someone on TV."

"Thank you," he said graciously, although he preferred compliments on his writing. Clearing his throat he began, "The editor has assigned me to write a profile of Euphonia Gage, and I'd like to talk with someone who knew her in Florida. Were you well acquainted with her?"

"Oh, yes, we were next-door neighbors, and I sort of looked after her."

"In what way? I'm going to tape this if you don't mind."

"Well, I checked up on her every day, and I'd always drive her where she wanted to go. She didn't like driving in the bumper-to-bumper traffic we have around here. She was eighty-eight, you know. I'm only sixty-eight."

"Your voice sounds much younger, Mrs. Robinson."

"Do you think so?" she said happily. "That's because I sing."

"In nightclubs?" he asked slyly.

Mrs. Robinson laughed merrily. "No, just around the house, but I used to sing in a church choir before I moved down here. Would you like to hear me sing something?"

Qwilleran thought, I have a live one here! "I was hoping you'd suggest it," he said. He expected to hear "Amazing Grace." Instead she sang the entire verse and chorus of "Mrs. Robinson" in a clear, untrained voice. Listening, he tried to visualize her; it was his custom to picture strangers in his mind's eye. He imagined her to be buxom and rosy-cheeked, with partly gray hair and seashell earrings. "Brava!" he shouted when she had finished. "I've never heard it sung better."

"Thank you. It's Clayton's favorite," she said. "You have a nice voice, too . . . Now, what was I telling you about Mrs. Gage? She didn't like to be called by her first name, and I don't blame her. It sounded like some kind of old-fashioned phonograph."

"You said you did the driving. Did she still have her yellow sport coupe?"

"No, she sold that, and we took my navy blue sedan. She called it an old lady's car. I thought she was being funny, but she was serious."

"And where would you two ladies drive?"

"Mostly to the mall—for lunch and to buy a few things. She liked to eat at a health food place."

"Would you say she was happy at the Park of Pink Sunsets?"

"I think so. She went on day trips in the activity bus, and she liked to give talks at the clubhouse."

"What kind of talks?"

Mrs. Robinson had to think a moment. "Mmmm . . . diet and exercise, music, art, the right way to breathe . . ."

"Were these lectures well attended?"

"Well, to tell the truth, they weren't as popular as the old movies on Thursday nights, but a lot of people went because they didn't have anything better to do. Also they had tea and cookies after the talk. Mrs. Gage paid for the refreshments."

Qwilleran said, "I met Mrs. Gage only once and that was for a short time. What was she like?"

"Oh, she was very interesting—not like the ones that are forever talking about their ailments and the grandchildren they never see. The park discourages young visitors. You have to get a five-dollar permit before you can have a visitor under sixteen years of age, and then it's only for forty-eight hours. Clayton likes to spend the whole Christmas week with me, because he doesn't like his stepmother. She's too serious, but his granny laughs a lot. Maybe you've noticed," she added with a giggle.

"How old is Clayton?"

"Just turned thirteen. He's a very bright boy with a crazy sense of humor. We have a ball! Last Christmas he figured out how to beat the system. When I picked him up at the airport, he was wearing a false beard! The sight of it just broke me up! He said I should introduce him to my neighbors as Dr. Clayton Robinson of Johns Hopkins. I went along with the gag. It's lucky that none of our neighbors have very good eyesight."

"Did he have his skateboard?" Qwilleran asked.

"Yow!" said Koko in a voice loud and clear.

"Do I hear a baby crying?" Mrs. Robinson asked.

"That's Koko, my Siamese cat. He's auditing this call."

"I used to have cats, and I'd love to have one now, but pets aren't allowed in the park. No cats, no dogs, not even birds!"

"How about goldfish?"

"Oh, that's funny! That's really funny!" she said. "I'm going to ask for a permit to have goldfish, and see what they say. They have no sense of humor. Last Christmas Clayton brought me a recording of a dog singing 'Jingle Bells.' Maybe you've heard it. 'Woof woof woof . . . woof woof woof!' "

"Yow!" Koko put in.

"Was Mrs. Gage amused?" Qwilleran asked.

"Not exactly. And the management of the park threw a fit!"

"Who are these people who issue five-dollar permits and throw fits?"

"Betty and Claude. He owns the park, and she's the manager. I don't think they're married, but they're always together. Don't get me wrong; they're really very nice if you play by the rules. Then there is Pete, the assistant, who takes over when they're out of town. He's handy with tools and electricity and all that. He fixed my radio for nothing."

"How did Mrs. Gage react to all the restrictions?"

"Well, you see, she was quite friendly with Betty and Claude, and she got special treatment, sort of. They took her to the dog races a lot. She enjoyed their company. She liked younger people."

"Including Dr. Clayton Robinson?"

His grandmother responded to the mild quip with peals of laughter. "Clayton would love to meet you, Mr. . . ."

"Qwilleran. Did he get away with the beard trick?"

"Oh, we didn't hang around the park too much. We went to the beach and movies and video arcades and antique shops. Clayton collects old photos of funny-looking people and calls them his ancestors. Like, one is an old lady in bonnet and shawl; he says it's his great-grandfather in drag. Isn't that a hoot?"

"Your grandson has a great future, Mrs. Robinson."

"Call me Celia. Everybody does."

"Talking with you has been a pleasure, Celia. You've given me a graphic picture of Mrs. Gage's last home. Just one serious question: Does anyone have an idea why she took her life?"

"Well . . . we're not supposed to talk about it."

"Why not?"

"Well, this isn't the first suicide we've had, and Claude is afraid it'll reflect on the park. But Mr. Crocus and I have whispered about it, and we can't figure it out."

"Who is Mr. Crocus?" Qwilleran asked with renewed interest.

"He's a nice old gentleman. He plays the violin. He had a crush on Mrs. Gage and followed her around like a puppy. He misses her a lot. I hope he doesn't pine away and die. There's a big turnover here, you know, but there's always someone waiting to move in. They've already sold Mrs. Gage's house to a widower from Iowa."

"Considering all the restrictions, why is the park so desirable?"

"Mostly it's the security. You can call the office twenty-four hours a day, if you have an emergency. There's limousine service to medical clinics, although you pay for it. They recommend doctors and lawyers and tax experts, which is nice because we're all from other states. I'm from Illinois. Also, there are things going on at the clubhouse, and there's the activity bus. Would you like to see some snapshots of Mrs. Gage on one of our sightseeing trips? Maybe you could use them with your article."

Qwilleran said it was an excellent suggestion and asked her to mail them to him at the newspaper office.

"What was the name of it, did you say?"

"*The Moose County Something.*"

"I love that! It's really funny!" she said with a chuckle. "I'll write it down."

"And do you mind if I call you again, Celia?"

"Gosh, no! It's fun being interviewed."

"Perhaps you'd like to see the obituary that ran in Wednesday's paper. I'll send two copies—one for Mr. Crusoe."

"Crocus," she corrected him. "Yes, he'd appreciate that a lot, Mr. Qwilleran."

"For your information, I'm usually called Qwill."

"Oh! Like in quill pen!"

"Except that it's spelled with a Qw."

"Yow!" said Koko.

"I'd better say goodnight and hang up, Celia. Koko wants to use the phone."

The last sound he heard from the receiver was a torrent of laughter. He turned to Koko. "That was Mrs. Robinson at the Park of Pink Sunsets."

The cat was fascinated by telephones. The ringing of the bell, the sound of a human voice coming from the instrument, and the mere fact that Qwilleran was conversing with an inanimate object seemed to stimulate his feline sensibilities. And he showed particular interest in the Florida grandmother with lively risibility. Qwilleran wondered why. He thought, Does he know something I don't? Koko's blue eyes were wearing their expression of profound wisdom.

"Treat!" Qwilleran announced, and there was the thud of galloping paws en route to the kitchen.

Eight

On Monday morning Qwilleran was weighing the advantages of staying in bed versus the disadvantages of listening to a feline reveille outside his door. The decision was made for him when the telephone rang in the library. He hoisted himself out of bed, put his slippers on the wrong feet, and padded down the hall.

"Hey, Qwill!" came the familiar voice of Junior Goodwinter. "I need help! Tomorrow's election day, and we're gonna do a rundown on the candidates in today's paper. Would you handle one for us? It's an emergency. Everyone's pitching in, even the maintenance guy."

"Now's a helluva time to think of it," said Qwilleran in the grumpy mood that preceded his first cup of coffee. He looked at his watch and computed the length of time before the noon deadline.

"Don't blame me! Arch came barging in half an hour ago with the idea, and he's the boss."

"What's he been doing for the last two weeks, besides courting Mildred?"

"Listen, Qwill, all you have to do is question your candidate on the list of issues, but not on the phone. Personal contact."

Qwilleran growled something inaudible. There were three candidates for the mayoralty, seven for two vacancies on the city council, and six for one post on the county board. "Okay," he said, "of the sixteen incumbents, outsiders, nobodies, and perennial losers, which one is assigned to me?"

"George Breze."

"I might have known you'd give me an airhead."

"Stop at the office first to get a list of the issues. Deadline is twelve noon, so you'd better get hopping."

Fifteen minutes later, Qwilleran—unbreakfasted, unshaved, and only casually combed—reported to the newspaper office. Junior handed him a list. "Just tape the interview. We'll transcribe it."

"By the way," Qwilleran said, "I phoned Celia Robinson in Florida last night."

"Tell me about it later," the editor said as both phones on his desk started to ring.

George Breze was a one-man conglomerate who operated his sprawling empire from a shack on Sandpit Road, surrounded by rental trucks, mini-storage buildings, a do-it-yourself car wash, and junk cars waiting to be cannibalized. Usually there was merchandise for sale under a canvas canopy, such as pumpkins in October, Christmas trees in December, and sacks of sheep manure in the spring. His parking lot was always full on Saturday nights. Teens were admonished not to stop there on the way home from school.

Breze was one of two candidates opposing the incumbent mayor, the well-liked Gregory Blythe. On the way to interview him, Qwilleran stopped for breakfast at the Dimsdale Diner, where the number of pickups in the parking lot assured him that the coffee hour was in full swig. Inside the decrepit diner the usual bunch of men in feed caps gathered around a big table, smoking and shouting and laughing. They made room for Qwilleran after he had picked up two doughnuts and a mug of coffee at the counter.

"What's the latest weather report?" he asked.

"Heavy frost tonight," said a sheep rancher.

"Light snow later in the week," said a farm equipment dealer.

"The Big Snow is on the way," a trucker predicted.

"Who's our next mayor?" Qwilleran then asked.

"Blythe'll get in again. No contest," someone said. "He drinks a little, but who doesn't?"

"Do you see George Breze as a threat?"

The coffee drinkers erupted in vituperation, and the county agricultural agent said, "He's exactly what we need, a mayor with wide experience: loan shark, ticket fixer, ex-bootlegger, part-time bookie, tealeaf reader . . ."

The last triggered an explosion of laughter, and the group broke up.

Qwilleran caught the ear of the ag agent. "Do you know Gil Inchpot?"

"Sure do. He shipped out a week ago without harvesting his crop or fulfilling his contracts. He must've cracked up."

"Is there any chance of hiring fieldhands to dig his potatoes? The K Foundation has funds for economic emergencies."

"Don't know how you could swing it," said the agent, removing his cap to scratch his head. "Everybody's short of help, and they're racing to get their own crops in before frost."

"Inchpot always helped other people in a pinch," Qwilleran argued.

"That he did; I'll give him credit. Gimme time to think about it, Qwill, and pray it doesn't freeze tonight."

With this scant encouragement Qwilleran drove to the Breze campaign headquarters on Sandpit Road and found the candidate seated behind a scarred wooden desk in a ramshackle hut. He was wearing a blue nylon jacket and red feed cap.

"Come in! Come in! Sit down!" Breze shouted heartily, dusting off a chair with a rag he kept under his desk. "Glad you called before comin' so I could cancel my other appointments." He spoke in a loud, brisk voice. "Cuppa coffee?"

"No, thanks. I never drink when I'm working."

"What can I do you for?"

"Just answer a few questions, Mr. Breze." Qwilleran placed his tape recorder on the desk. "Why are you running for office?"

"I was born and brought up here. The town's been good to me. I owe it to the people," he answered promptly.

"Do you believe you'll be elected?"

"Absolutely! Everybody knows me and likes me. I went to school with 'em."

"What do you plan to accomplish if elected mayor?"

"I want to help the people with their problems and keep the streets clean. Clean streets are important."

"Would you favor light or heavy industry for economic development in Pickax?"

"Light or heavy, it don't matter. The important thing is to make jobs for the people and keep the streets clean."

"What do you think about the current controversy over sewers?"

"It'll straighten out. It always does," Breze said with a wave of the hand.

"There's talk about township annexation. Where do you stand on that issue?"

"I don't know about that. I don't think it's important. Jobs—that's what matters."

"Do you support the proposal to install parking meters in downtown Pickax?"

"Is that something new? I haven't heard about it. Free parking is best for the people."

"What do you think of the education system in Pickax?"

"Well, I went to school here, and I turned out all right." The candidate laughed lustily.

"Do you think the police department is doing a good job?"

"Absolutely! They're a good bunch of boys."

"In your opinion, what is the most important issue facing the city council?"

"That's hard to say. Myself, I'm gonna fight for clean streets."

Qwilleran thanked Breze for his cogent opinions and delivered the tape to the paper. "Here's my interview with the Great Populist," he told Junior.

"Sorry to brush you off this morning," said the editor. "What did you want to tell me about Celia Robinson?"

"Only that I talked with her for half an hour and didn't get a single clue to your grandmother's motive."

"I know you like to get to the bottom of things, Qwill, but frankly, I've got too many other things on my mind. Jack and Pug are flying in tomorrow. The reading of the will is Wednesday in Wilmot's office. The memorial service is Thursday night. And every time the phone rings, I think it's Jody, ready to go to the hospital."

"Then I won't bother you," Qwilleran said, "but count on dinner Wednesday night, and let me know if there's anything I can do. I could drive Jody to the hospital if you're in a bind."

After stopping for lunch, he went home and parked under the porte cochere. Even before he approached the side door, he could hear the commotion indoors, and he knew he was in trouble. Two indignant Siamese were yowling in unison, pacing the floor and switching their tails in spasms of reproach.

"Oh, no!" he groaned, slapping his forehead in guilt. "I forgot your breakfast! A thousand apologies! Junior threw me a curve." He quickly emptied cans of boned chicken and solid-pack tuna on their plate. "Consider this a brunch. All you can eat!"

That was his second mistake. All the food went down, but half of it came up.

Qwilleran spent the afternoon preparing for his third performance of "The Big Burning," and when he drove to the Hotel Booze at seven o'clock, the parking lot was jammed. The Outdoor Club was in the café, enjoying boozeburgers, when he set up the stage in the meeting room. There were extra chairs, he noted, the front row being a mere six feet from the platform.

"Largest crowd they've ever had!" Hixie Rice exulted as she tested the sound and lights, "and I've got bookings for three more shows!"

A rumble of voices in the lobby announced the approaching audience, and Qwilleran ducked through the exit door, while Hixie shook hands with the officers of the club and seated the youngsters in the front rows.

With his ear to the door he heard the first notes of "Anitra's Dance" and counted thirty seconds before making an entrance and mounting the stage. "We interrupt this program to bring you a bulletin on the forest fires that are rapidly approaching Moose County . . ."

In the first three rows eyes and mouths were wide open. A small girl in the front row, whose feet could not reach the floor, was swinging them back and forth continuously. Her legs, in white leggings, were like a beacon in the dark room. When the old farmer's voice came from the speakers, the legs swung faster. The old farmer was saying:

"I come in from my farm west o' here, and I seen some terrible things! Hitched the hosses to the wagon and got my fambly here safe but never thought we'd make it! We come through fire rainin' down out of the sky like hailstones! Smoke everywhere! Couldn't see the road, hardly. Hay in the wagon caught fire, and we had to throw it out and rattle along on the bare boards. We picked up one lad not more'n eight year old, carryin' a baby—all that were left of his fambly. His shoes, they was burned clean off his feet!"

The white legs never stopped swinging, back and forth like a pendulum: left, right, left, right. Qwilleran, aware of the movement through the corner of his eye, found himself being mesmerized. He had to fight to maintain his concentration on the announcer's script:

"Here in Pickax it's dark as midnight. Winds have suddenly risen to hurricane fury. Great blasts of heat and cinders are smothering the city. We can hear screams of frightened horses, then a splintering crash as a great tree is uprooted or the wind wrenches the roof from a house. Wagons are being lifted like toys and blown away! . . . There's a red glare in the sky! . . . *Pickax is in flames!"*

The red light flicked on. Coughing and choking, the announcer rushed from the studio.

In the hallway beyond the exit door Qwilleran leaned against the wall, recovering from the scene he had just played. A moment later, Hixie joined him. "They love it!" she said. "Especially the part about the boy with his shoes burned off. The kids identify."

"Did you see that one swinging her legs in the front row?" Qwilleran asked irritably.

"She was spellbound!"

"Well, those white legs were putting a spell on me! I was afraid I'd topple off my chair."

"Did you hear the girl crying when you told about the little baby? She created quite a disturbance."

"I don't care if the whole audience cries!" Qwilleran snapped. "Get those white legs out of the front row!"

When he made his entrance for Scene Two, an instant hush fell upon the room. Surreptitiously he glanced at the front row; the white legs had gone.

"After a sleepless night, Pickax can see daylight. The smoke is lifting, but the acrid smell of burning is everywhere, and the scene is one of desolation in every direction. Only this brick courthouse is left standing, a haven for hundreds of refugees. Fortunately a sudden wind from the lake turned back the flames, and Mooseville and Brrr have been saved."

Qwilleran had not seen the last of the white legs, however. Halfway through Scene Two he was interviewing the Irish innkeeper by phone: "Sir, what news do you hear from Sawdust City?"

A thick Irish brogue came from the speakers: "It's gone! All gone! Every stick of it, they're tellin'. And there's plenty of sad tales this mornin'. One poor chap from Sawdust City walked into town carryin' the remains of his wife and little boy in a pail—a ten-quart pail! Wouldja believe it, now?"

At that tense moment, Qwilleran's peripheral vision picked up a pair of white legs walking toward the stage. What the devil is she doing? he thought.

The girl climbed onto the stage, crossed to the exit door at the rear, and went to the restroom.

The radio announcer went on. "Many tales of heroism and fortitude have been reported. In West Kirk thirteen persons went down a well and stood in three feet of water for five hours. In Dimsdale a mother saved her three children by burying them in a plowed field until the danger had passed . . ."

The white legs returned, taking a shortcut across the stage. It didn't faze the audience. At the end of the show they applauded wildly, and the president of the Outdoor Club made Qwilleran and Hixie honorary members. Then she fielded questions while he packed the gear, surrounded by the under-ten crowd. They were fascinated by the tape player, lights, cables, and other equipment being folded into compact carrying cases.

"I liked it when you talked on the telephone," one said.

"How do you know all that stuff?" another asked.

"Why didn't everybody get in a bus and drive to Mooseville or Brrr to be saved?"

"How could he get his wife and little boy in a pail?"

"I liked the red light."

One three-year-old girl stood silently sucking her thumb and staring at Qwilleran's moustache.

"Did you like the show?" he asked her.

She nodded soberly before taking the thumb from her mouth. "What was it about?" she asked earnestly.

He was relieved when Nancy Fincher came to the stage. "Mr. Qwilleran, it was wonderful! I never liked history before, but you made it so real, I cried."

"Thank you," he said. "As soon as I put these cases in my car, may I invite you for a drink in the café?"

"Let me carry one," she said, grabbing the largest of the three. Delicate though she seemed, she handled the heavy case like a trifle.

When they were established on the wobbly barstools, he asked, "Will you have something to eat? I'm always famished after the show. 'The Big Burning' burns up a lot of energy."

"Just a cola for me," she said. "I had supper here, and half of my burger is in a doggie bag in my truck."

Qwilleran ordered a boozeburger with fries. "You mentioned that potatoes are a complicated crop to raise," he said to Nancy. "I always thought they'd be a cinch."

Nancy shook her head soberly. "That's what everybody thinks. But first you have to know what kind to plant—for the conditions you're working with and the market you're selling to. Different markets want large or small, whiteskins or redskins, bakers or boilers or fryers."

"You seem to know a lot about the subject."

"I grew up with potatoes."

"Don't stop. Tell me more." He was concentrating on the burger, which was enormously thick.

"Well, first you have to have the right kind of soil, and it has to be well drained. Then you have to know the right time to plant and the right kind of fertilizer. Then you worry about crop diseases and weeds and insects and rain. You need enough rain but not too much. And then you have to gamble on the right time to harvest."

"I have a new respect for potato farmers . . . and potatoes," he said.

A soft look suffused Nancy's face. "When Mom was alive, we used to dig down with our fingers and take out the small new tubers very carefully, so as not to interfere with the others. Then we'd have creamed new potatoes with new peas."

Gary Pratt shuffled up to them. "Are you folks ready for another drink or anything?"

"Not for me," she said. "I have to stop and check Pop's mailbox and then go home and take care of my dogs. I've been working at the clinic all day."

The two men watched her go, lugging her oversized shoulderbag.

"Quite a gal," Gary said. "She has that tiny little voice, and you think she doesn't have much on the ball, but the thing of it is, she's a terrific racer, and she really knows dogs. I tried to date her when she came back from Alaska, but her old man didn't like my haircut. So what? I didn't like the dirt under his fingernails. Anyway, Nancy still had a thing for Dan Fincher. Women think he's the strong, silent type, but I think he's a klutz."

"Interesting if true," said Qwilleran, making light of the gossip. "What's the latest on the weather?"

"Heavy frost tonight. Snow on the way."

On the trip back to Pickax Qwilleran drove through farming country, where the bright headlights of tractors in the fields meant that farmers were working around the clock to beat the frost. He felt a twinge of remorse. If he had acted sooner, the Klingenschoen clout might have saved Gil Inchpot's crop.

He was carrying a sample of boozeburger for the Siamese. "After my faux pas this morning," he told them, "I owe you one." Later, the three of them were in the library, reading *Robinson Crusoe,* when the sharp ring of the telephone made all of them jump.

Qwilleran guessed it would be Junior, announcing that Jody had given birth; or it would be Polly, inquiring about the show in Brrr; or it would be Arch Riker, saying that Breze was suing the paper because the other candidates sounded better than he did.

"Hello?" he said, ready for anything.

"Mr. Qwilleran," said a breathless voice, "Gary gave me your number. I hope you don't mind."

"That's all right."

"I discovered something when I got to Pop's house, and I notified the police, but I wanted to tell you because you've been so kind and so interested."

"What was it, Nancy?"

"When I got to the farm, I cut my hand on the mailbox pretty bad, so I went indoors for some antiseptic and a bandage. And in a medicine cabinet I saw Pop's dentures in a glass of water. He would never leave home without his dentures!"

Qwilleran combed his moustache with his fingertips as he thought of the partial denture in the desk drawer. He glanced at the Siamese. Yum Yum was pedicuring her left hind foot; Koko was sitting there looking wise.

Nine

There was heavy frost in Moose County that night. The tumble-down hamlet of Wildcat, the quaint resort town of Mooseville, the affluent estates of West Middle Hummock, the condominiums in Indian Village, the vacation homes in Purple Point, the stone canyons of downtown Pickax, the mansions of Goodwinter Boulevard, the abandoned mineshafts, the airport . . . all looked mystically hoary in the first morning light. Qwilleran felt moody as he drank his morning coffee. There was the usual letdown after the excitement and challenge of doing a show, plus a gnawing regret about the Inchpot crop. Hundreds of acres of potatoes had been lost—after being scientifically planted, fertilized, weeded, sprayed, and prayed over. And now, after hearing Nancy's grim news about the dentures, Qwilleran felt real concern about Gil Inchpot himself.

He was somewhat gladdened, therefore, when Lori Bamba called to ask if her husband could deliver some letters and checks for signing. Nick Bamba was an engineer at the state prison; he shared Qwilleran's interest in crime and the mystery that often surrounds it. Whenever Qwilleran mentioned his suspicions and hunches to his friends, Polly remonstrated and Riker taunted him, but Nick always took him seriously.

He was a young man with alert black eyes that observed everything. "Someone ran a truck over your curb," he said upon arrival.

"Those blasted leaf blowers! They're a slap-happy crew!" Qwilleran complained. "Did you vote this morning?"

"I was first in line. There was a good turnout in Mooseville because of the millage issue. The voters don't get excited about the candidates; one's no better than another. But propose increased millage, and they're all at the polls to vote no. Why don't you run for county office, Qwill? You could make waves."

"I'd rather see Koko's name on the ballot . . . Will you have coffee or hot cider?"

"I'll try the cider." Nick handed over a folder of correspondence. "Lori says you're getting a lot of fan mail since your 'Big Burning' preview. The Mooseville Chamber of Commerce wants to book the show after the holidays."

"I trust the members are all over eight years old," Qwilleran said testily.

They carried their cider mugs into the library, and Nick remarked, "I see you've got an elevator. Does it work?"

"Definitely. We used it at the preview of our show. Adam Dingleberry was here in his wheelchair."

At that point Koko walked into the library with deliberate step and rose on his hind legs to rattle the closet doorknob.

"What's old slyboots got on his mind?" Nick asked.

"This is the only closet in the house that's locked, and it drives him bughouse," Qwilleran said. "All the closets are filled with junk, and Koko spends his spare time digging for buried treasure."

"Has he found any gold coins or diamond rings?"

"Not as yet. Mostly stale cigars and old shoelaces."

"Want me to pick the lock for you? I'll bring my tools next time I'm in town."

"Sure. I'm curious about this closet myself."

"I suppose you heard on the radio about the missing potato

farmer, Gil Inchpot. Police are investigating his disappearance ten days ago."

"I heard something about it," Qwilleran mentioned.

"He's quite a successful farmer, you know. I never met the guy, but his daughter was married to a deputy sheriff I know, Dan Fincher. It didn't last long; her father broke it up."

"Why? Do you know?"

Nick shrugged. "Dan isn't very big on particulars. I know that Gil Inchpot is well liked at the Crossroads Tavern and at the farm co-op, but Dan says he's a bully at home."

Qwilleran reached for Nick's cider mug. "Fill 'er up?"

"No, thanks. I've got errands to do—prison business."

"Do you like apples at your house? I've got some you can take home to the kids."

Nick left, carrying a brown paper bag, and after Qwilleran had signed his letters and checks, he took another sackful to the newspaper office.

"I'll trade these for a cup of coffee," he told Junior. "How's everything going?"

"Jack and Pug have arrived. They're staying at the New Pickax Hotel. Jody doesn't feel like having company."

"That's wise. Will she come to dinner tomorrow night? Polly is joining us."

"Why don't you make the reservation for six?" said the expectant father, "and we'll see how she feels."

"When is the will being read?"

"Ten-thirty tomorrow morning. Keep your fingers crossed."

While the will was being read in Pender Wilmot's office, Qwilleran was at home, eating an apple and estimating the extent of Euphonia Gage's estate. No doubt she had cashed in heavily when she liquidated her jewels, real estate, fine paintings, and family heirlooms. No doubt her late husband, being financially savvy and not entirely honest, had left her some blue-chip securities. Her recent economies, such as living in a mobile home and wearing seashell jewelry, were no more peculiar than his own preference for driving a used car and pumping his own gas. And, nearing the end of her life, she may have been moved by a nobly generous impulse to provide handsomely for her six great-grandchildren and the one yet unborn.

That evening, his guests were late in arriving at the Old Stone

Mill. He and Polly sat waiting and talking about the election results. As everyone expected, Gregory Blythe had been re-elected. He was an investment counselor, a good administrator, and a former high school principal with Goodwinter blood on his mother's side. The public had forgotten the scandal that ousted him from the education system in Pickax, and he was always sober when he conducted city council meetings.

After half an hour Polly asked, "What do you suppose has happened to them? Junior is always so punctual. Perhaps he's taken Jody to the hospital."

"I'll phone their house," Qwilleran said.

To his surprise, Jody answered. "He left about half an hour ago to pick up Pug and Jack," she said. "I decided not to go. I hope you don't mind." She sounded depressed.

"Do you feel all right, Jody?"

"Oh, yes, I'm all right, considering . . ."

When the hostess conducted the tardy guests to the table, Qwilleran rose to greet three unhappy faces: Pug as distraught as a Montana rancher who has had to shoot her favorite horse; Jack as glum as a California advertising executive who has lost his major client; Junior as indignant as an editor who is being sued for libel.

Introductions were made, chairs were pulled out, napkins were unfolded, and Polly tried to make polite conversation: "Are you comfortable at the hotel? . . . How do you like Montana? . . . Have you adjusted to sunny California?" Her efforts failed to elevate the mood.

"What would you like to drink?" Qwilleran asked. "Champagne? A cocktail? Pug, what is your choice?"

"Bourbon and water," she said, pouting.

"Scotch margarita," said Jack grimly.

"Rye on the rocks," said Junior, fidgeting in his chair.

While they were waiting to be served, Qwilleran talked about the weather for five minutes: the weather last month, the outlook for the rest of this month, the prediction for next month . . . all of this to fill the void until the drinks arrived. Then he raised his glass. "Would anyone like to propose a toast?"

"To bad news!" Junior blurted.

"To a royal rip-off!" said Jack.

"Oh, dear," Polly murmured.

"Sorry to hear that," Qwilleran said.

Scowling, Jack said, "Pug and I flew thousands of miles just to be told that she left us a hundred dollars apiece! I'm damned mad! She was a spiteful old woman!"

"Surprising!" Qwilleran turned to Junior for corroboration.

"Same here," said the younger brother, "only I didn't have to cross the continent to get the shaft."

"I had the impression," Qwilleran remarked, "that your grandmother was a generous person."

"Sure," said Pug. "She put us all through college, but there were strings attached. We didn't know it gave her the privilege to direct our lives, dictate our careers, choose our hobbies, approve our marriages! She was furious when Jack went to the coast and I married a rancher. For a wedding present she sent us a wooden nutcracker."

Polly asked, "Can anyone explain the reason for her attitude?"

"If you're looking for excuses, I can't think of any."

Junior said, "Here's a typical example of her thoughtlessness. Her ancestors were pioneer doctors here, and she inherited a beautiful black walnut box of surgical knives and saws and other instruments, all pre–Civil War. Why didn't she give them to the Museum of Local History, where they'd mean something? Instead she sold them with everything else."

"She was a selfish egocentric, that's all," said Jack.

"How about your grandfather?" Qwilleran asked. "What was he like?"

"Kind of jolly, although he wasn't around much."

"Our paternal grandmother was different," said Pug. "She wasn't rich, but she was warm and cuddly and loving."

"And she made the best fudge!" Jack added.

There was a nostalgic silence at the table until Qwilleran cleared his throat preparatory to introducing a sensitive subject. "If you're all left out of the will, who are the beneficiaries?"

The three young people looked at each other, and Junior said bitterly, "The Park of Pink Sunsets! They get everything—to build, equip, and maintain a health spa for the residents. She revised her will after she got to Florida."

Polly said, "It's not unusual for the elderly to forget family and friends and leave everything to strangers they meet in their final days. That's why wills are so often contested."

"Well, if it's any consolation," Qwilleran said in an effort to brighten the occasion, "Junior owns the contents of the locked closet in the library, which may be full of Grandpa Gage's gold coins and Grandma Gage's jewelry."

No one was amused, and Junior replied, "There's nothing in that closet but her private papers, and I'm instructed to burn them."

Then Jack said, "If anyone thinks we're sticking around for the memorial service tomorrow night, they can stuff it! We've changed our flight reservations."

"That hotel," Pug said, "is the worst I've ever experienced! I can't wait to get out of this tank town!"

Qwilleran said, "I think we should all have another drink and order dinner." He signaled for service.

"I second the motion," Junior said. "Enough gnashing of teeth! Let's enjoy our food, at least . . . How are your cats, Qwill?" To his sister and brother he explained, "Qwill has a couple of Siamese."

Polly said, "Qwill, dear, tell them about Koko and the cleaning closet."

He hesitated, trying to recollect the incident in all of its absurdity. "Well, you see, where I live in the summer, there's a closet for Mrs. Fulgrove's prodigious collection of waxes, polishes, detergents, spray bottles, and squirt cans."

"Is that woman still cleaning houses?" Pug asked. "I thought she'd be dead by now."

"She's still cleaning and still complaining about cathairs. I always leave the house to avoid her harangues. One day I came home after the dear lady had left and found the male cat missing! But the female was huddled in front of the cleaning closet, staring at the door handle. I yanked open the door, and out billowed a white cloud. It filled almost the whole closet, obliterating shelves, cans, and bottles. And above it all was Koko, sitting on the top shelf, looking nonchalant. Mrs. Fulgrove had accidentally shut him in the closet, and he had accidentally activated the can of foam carpet cleaner."

"Or purposely," Junior added.

"I reported the story in my column, and the manufacturer sent me enough foam cleaner to do all the rugs in Moose County."

After that interlude, everyone was somewhat relaxed though not really happy, and Qwilleran was relieved when the meal came to an end. As the party was leaving, Junior handed him an envelope.

"Forgot to give you this, Qwill. It came to the office today, addressed to you."

It was a pink envelope with a Florida postmark and the official logo of the Park of Pink Sunsets. He slid it into his pocket.

On the way home to Goodwinter Boulevard, Qwilleran said to Polly, "Well, the mood at our table was not very favorable for the consumption of food. I apologize for involving you."

"It could hardly be called your fault, Qwill. How were you to know? The entire situation is regrettable."

"I don't suppose you want to attend the memorial service tomorrow night."

"I wouldn't miss it!" Polly's tone was more bitter than sweet.

Qwilleran dropped her off at her carriage house, saying he would pick her up the next evening. He was in a hurry to open the letter from Florida.

Sitting at his desk he slit the pink envelope—a chunky one with double postage—and out fell some snapshots as well as a note. Celia had remembered how to spell his name; that was in her favor.

Dear Mr. Qwilleran,

I enjoyed talking to you on the phone. Here are the snaps of Mrs. Gage with some other people from the park. We were on a bus trip. I'm the giddy-looking one in Mickey Mouse ears. That's Mr. Crocus with Mrs. Gage and a stone lion. Hope you can use some of these with the article you're writing.

Yours very truly,
Celia Robinson

Spreading the snapshots on the desk, Qwilleran found the diminutive Euphonia neatly dressed in a lavender pantsuit and wide-brimmed hat, while her companions sported T-shirts with the Pink Sunset logo splashed across the front. Also conservatively dressed in tropical whites was an old man with a shock of white hair; he and the stone lion could have passed for brothers.

The Siamese, always interested in something new, were on the desktop, sitting comfortably on their briskets and idly observing. Then, apparently without provocation, Koko rose to his feet with a guttural monosyllable and sniffed the pictures. There was something about the glossy surface of photographs that always attracted him. Studiously he passed his nose over every one of the Florida pictures and flicked his tongue at a couple of them.

"No!" Qwilleran said sharply, worrying about the chemicals used in processing.

"Yow!" Koko retorted in a scolding tone of his own and then left the room. Yum Yum trailed after him without so much as a backward look at the man whose lap she so frequently commandeered.

An uneasy feeling crept across Qwilleran's upper lip, and he patted his moustache as he examined the snapshots the cat had licked. Sandpaper tongue and potent saliva had left rough spots on the surface. In both of them Euphonia looked happy and pert, posed with a yellow sports car in one shot and with the Pink Sunset tour bus in the other. More important than the damage, however, was the realization that two of her companions looked vaguely familiar. He had no idea who they were or where he had met them or under what circumstances.

Ten

Thursday was bright and clear, although Wetherby Goode reminded his listeners that November was the month of the Big Snow, a threat that annually hung over the heads of Moose County residents like a Damoclean icicle.

Qwilleran said to Koko, "Would you like to take a walk? This may be your last chance before snow flies. I'll get the leash."

Yum Yum, whose vocabulary included the word "leash," immediately disappeared, but Koko purred and rolled on his side while the harness was being buckled around his middle. Then, on the back porch, he checked out the spots where the nefarious Oh Jay had left his scent. Next, he led the way down the back steps to a paved area where the last few leaves of autumn were waiting to be pawed, batted, chased, and chewed. While Koko was enjoying these simple pleasures, Qwilleran became aware of a familiar figure scrambling through the shrubs on the lot line.

"If you're looking for Oh Jay," he said to the attorney's son, "he's not here."

It appeared, however, that this was a social call. "It's gonna snow," Timmie said.

"So they say," Qwilleran replied, making no attempt to continue the conversation.

The boy looked critically at Koko. "Why is he so skinny?"

"He's not skinny. He's a Siamese."

"Oh." This was followed by a pause, then: "I can stand on my head."

"Good for you!"

There was another long pause as Timmie spread his arms wide and balanced on one leg. Finally he said, "You should marry the lady that lives in the back. Then you could live in one house, and she wouldn't have to take out the trash."

"Why don't you go and stand on your head?" Qwilleran asked.

"We're gonna move."

"What?"

"We're gonna move away from here."

"I sincerely hope you're planning to take Oh Jay with you."

"I'm gonna go to a new school and ride the school bus and have fun with the kids."

"Why do you want to leave a nice neighborhood like this?"

"My dad says some dumb fool bought the house."

"Excuse me," Qwilleran said. "I have to make a phone call." He hurried up the back steps, pulling a reluctant cat.

Ringing Junior at the office he said, "Have you heard the news? Another house on the boulevard has been sold. Pender Wilmot's. That makes two of them, side by side. What do you make of that?"

"Who bought it?" Junior demanded with suspicion. "Was it the realtor in Chicago?"

"My six-year-old informant wasn't specific."

"I hope this doesn't turn out to be anything detrimental to the neighborhood, like one of those cults or a front for something illegal."

"You don't need to worry about anything like that—not in Pickax," Qwilleran assured him, "but I admit it piques the curiosity . . . Well, get back to work. I'll see you tonight at the memorial service. Do you know why it's being held at the theatre instead of the Old Stone Church?"

"That's the way she wanted it, and Grandma never did anything in the ordinary way."

The K Theatre, converted from the former Klingenschoen mansion, shared the Park Circle with the public library, courthouse, and two churches. Shortly before eight o'clock on Thursday evening, more than a hundred residents of Moose County converged on the theatre, their expressions ranging from respectful to avidly curious. In dress they were less sweatery than usual, denoting the solemnity of the occasion.

When Qwilleran and Polly arrived in the lobby, they were greeted by two young members of the Theatre Club, who smiled guardedly and handed them programs. He said to Polly, "According to Junior, Euphonia planned this service down to the last detail, and I suspect the ushers were instructed to smile with sweetness and respect and not too much sadness."

After a glance at the program Polly said, "This is not a memorial service! It's a concert!"

In Memoriam

EUPHONIA ROFF GAGE

Piano prelude: Six Gnossiennes .... *Satie*
1. *Adagio* .... *Albinoni*
2. *Sonnet XXX* .... *Shakespeare*
3. *Pavane pour une Infante Défunte* .... *Ravel*
4. *Renouncement* .... *Meynell*
5. *En Sourdine (Verlaine)* .... *Fauré*
6. *Pas de Deux* .... *anonymous*
7. *Duet for Flutes* .... *Telemann*
8. *Non sum qualis eram bonae sub regno Cynarae* .... *Dowson*
9. *Adagio from Symphonie Concertante* .... *Spohr*
10. *Maestoso from Symphony No. 3* .... *Saint-Saëns*

Polly said in a voice unusually sharp, "Don't you think it's a trifle too precious? Number Five is a French art song. Number Eight . . . only Euphonia would use the Latin title for 'Cynara.' It's her last gasp of cultural snobbery. And what do you think of Number Three?"

"Try saying it fast three times," he said with a lack of reverence.

Polly threw him a disapproving glance. "You're being flip. I'm wondering if the reference to a dead princess means that she considered herself royalty."

Carol Lanspeak, a trustee of the theatre, hurried up to them. "I think you're in for some surprises tonight. Junior asked me to handle the staging because their baby is due momentarily. Larry's doing the readings, and we rehearsed the entire program to get the timing right. Euphonia left instructions for the stage set, lighting, programs, everything! Such a perfectionist!"

Qwilleran reached into his pocket for an envelope of snapshots. "One of her Florida neighbors sent these. You might like to see how she looked toward the end."

"Why, she looks wonderful!" Carol exclaimed after examining them. "Wouldn't you know she'd choose to go out while she was looking wonderful?"

"Do you recognize anyone else in the pictures?"

"No, I don't . . . Should I?"

"I thought some of them might be from Moose County. Snowbirds tend to flock together."

Carol and Polly conferred and agreed that they were all strangers. "But here comes Homer. Ask him," Carol suggested.

The aged Homer Tibbitt was entering with his brisk but awkward gait, accompanied by his attentive new wife. During his career as a teacher and principal he had shepherded several generations through the school system and claimed to know everyone in two counties.

He changed glasses to study the snapshots. "Sorry. I can't identify a soul except Euphonia."

"Let me see them," said Mrs. Tibbitt.

"You don't know anyone here," he said with impatience. "You never even met Euphonia . . . Rhoda's from Lockmaster," he explained to the others, as if she were from the Third World.

"Homer likes to put on his irascible-old-man act," his wife said sweetly.

"I believe it's time to go upstairs," Carol suggested. "Take the elevator, Homer."

Two matching stairways led to the auditorium entrance on the upper level, from which the amphitheatre seating sloped down to a dark stage. A pianist in the orchestra pit was playing the moody, mysterious prelude specified by the deceased.

"Who's that at the piano?" Qwilleran asked Polly.

"The new music director for the schools. I believe she taught in Lockmaster."

He admired anyone who could play the piano and found the pianist strikingly attractive. When the prelude ended, she moved to a seat in front of them, and her perfume made a strong statement. Polly wafted it away with her program.

A hush fell on the audience as the house lights slowly dimmed. There were a few dramatic seconds of total darkness before two glimmers of light appeared. One spotlighted a bouquet of purple and white flowers on a pedestal, stage right. The other, stage center, illuminated a thronelike chair on the seat of which was a wide-brimmed straw hat with a band of purple velvet. Flung across the high chairback was a filmy scarf in shades of lavender.

Qwilleran and Polly exchanged glances. He could read her mind: The pedestal! The throne! The royal purple!

The theatre had an excellent sound system, and from hidden speakers came the haunting music of Albinoni, the wistful yearning of the solo violin underscored by the heartbeat of the cello. The audience listened and stared, as if Euphonia herself might glide onto the stage. Other instruments joined in, and the volume swelled, then faded, leaving only the last searching notes of the violin.

The spotlights disappeared, and a beam of light focused on a lectern at stage left, where Larry Lanspeak stood waiting. His rich voice gripped the audience:

"When to the sessions of sweet silent thought
I summon up remembrance of things past . . ."

Qwilleran glanced questioningly at Polly, who was frowning as if unable to connect the woman she had known with the poem she was hearing. He wondered about it himself and listened for clues to Euphonia's past and possibly a clue to her suicide motive.

"Then can I drown an eye, unused to flow,
For precious friends hid in death's dateless night,
And weep afresh love's long since cancelled woe."

Again the spotlights flooded the throne and flowers as Ravel's slow dance painted its melancholy picture. Then came the poem *"I must not think of thee,"* followed by the French song "In Secret." Qwilleran deduced that Euphonia was mourning a lost lover, and it was not Grandpa Gage. The anonymous poem confirmed his theory:

"Two white butterflies
Kissing in mid-air,
Then darting apart
To flutter like lost petals,
Drifting together again
For a quivering moment in the sun,
Yet wandering away
In a white flurry of indecision,
Meeting once more
On the upsweep of a breeze,
Dancing a delirious pas de deux
Before parting forever,
One following the wind,
The other trembling with folded wings
On this cold rock."

After the "Duet for Flutes" Qwilleran's suspicions were reinforced by the poem *"I have been faithful to thee, Cynara, in my fashion."* He could hear sniffling in the audience, and even Polly was dabbing her eyes, a reaction that made him uncomfortable; he knew she was remembering her own past.

The program was building to its conclusion. A screen had been lowered at the rear of the stage, and when the "Adagio" for flute and harp began its flights of melody, the image of a dancer appeared, moving languidly across the screen, arching her back, fluttering her scarfs, twirling, twisting, sinking to her knees with bowed head, rising with head thrown back and arms flung wide. It was a joyous celebration. The dancer's white hair was twisted into a ballerina's topknot and tied with purple ribbon.

There had been gasps at first, but when the video ended, there was silence—and utter darkness. Then the stage burst into brilliant light as the crashing chords of the Organ Symphony stunned the audience. The majestic music rocked the auditorium in triumph—until one final prolonged chord stopped dead, leaving a desolate emptiness in the hall.

"Whew!" Qwilleran said as the house lights were turned up. Among the audience a gradual murmur arose as groups began to wander to the exit. In the lobby friends were meeting, asking questions, fumbling for appropriate comments.

Arch Riker said, "That was quite a blast-off!"

Carol Lanspeak informed everyone that the flower arrangement—dahlias, glads, lavender asters, orchids, and bella donna lilies—had been flown in from Chicago.

Susan Exbridge, the antique dealer, explained that the carved highback chair had been in the foyer of the Gage mansion and she had bought it from Euphonia for $2,000.

Lisa Compton wondered how Euphonia's knees could continue to function so well at eighty-eight.

Qwilleran and Polly were speaking with the Comptons when the pianist joined their group, and Lyle Compton introduced her as June Halliburton, the new music director from Lockmaster. "Now if they'll only send us their football coach," he said, "we'll be in good shape."

Her red hair was cut shorter and curlier than the accepted style in Moose County, and her perfume was a scent not sold at Lanspeak's Department Store. With playful hazel eyes fixed on Qwilleran's moustache, she said, "I enjoyed your historical show at Mooseland High School. How did you make your choice of music for the interludes?"

"Just some cassettes I happened to have in my meager collection," he replied.

"They worked beautifully! If I wanted to nitpick, though, I could object that 'Anitra's Dance' had not been written in 1869 when your imaginary radio station played it."

"Don't tell anyone," he said. "They'll never guess. Actually I doubt whether anyone has even noticed the music."

"I noticed it," said Polly crisply. "I thought the 'Francesca da Rimini' excerpts were perfect for the fire scene. I could visualize flames raging, winds howling, and buildings crashing."

Lyle said, "June is going to implement Hilary VanBrooks's theories about music education. You ought to write something about that in your column, Qwill."

"Okay, we'll talk," he said to her. "Where is your office located?"

"Why don't you come to my apartment in Indian Village where I have all my music?" she suggested engagingly.

Polly flushed, and Qwilleran could feel the heat waves coming from her direction. He said, "What we really need is to sit down at a desk and discuss the VanBrooks Method."

Lisa plunged in diplomatically. "Before I forget, Qwill, would you be willing to do 'The Big Burning' for the Senior Care Facility?"

"Sounds okay to me," he said gratefully. "When would you want it?"

"Before Thanksgiving."

"Call Hixie Rice to book it."

On the way out of the theatre he and Polly were intercepted by Junior Goodwinter. "What did you think of Grandma's send-off?"

"Thought-provoking, to say the least," Qwilleran replied.

"Want to hear something interesting? The attorney is questioning Grandma's will! He's talking about mental instability and undue influence."

"Does he plan to sue?"

"I don't know yet. It'll depend on the value of the estate, but it's a distinct possibility. She must have been worth millions around the time she liquidated everything."

On the way home Qwilleran and Polly were silent, for their own reasons. When she invited him to her apartment for dessert and coffee, he declined, saying he had work to do. It was the first time he had ever turned down such an invitation, and she regarded him with mild anxiety. She may have guessed he was about to call another woman.

Eleven

When Qwilleran returned from Euphonia's memorial extravaganza, he found the Siamese on the library sofa, curled into a round pillow of fur. One raised a sleepy head; the other twitched an ear irritably. "Excuse me for disturbing you," he said as he turned on the desk lamp. "I need to make a phone call."

They exchanged a few perfunctory licks, disengaged their entwined extremities, struggled to their feet, yawned widely, and stretched vertically and horizontally before leaving the room with purposeful step. He knew where they were going: to the kitchen to lap a tongueful of water and gaze hopefully at their empty plate.

He gave them a few crunchy morsels and prepared coffee for himself before placing his call to Florida. When a woman's voice answered, he said, "This is Dr. Clayton Robinson calling from Johns Hopkins." He changed his voice to sound like a thirteen-year-old changing his voice to sound like an M.D.

"Clayton!" she cried. "Does your mother know you're calling long distance? Hang up before you get in trouble!"

"April Fool!" he said hastily. "This is Jim Qwilleran phoning from Pickax. I hope I'm not calling you too late."

"Oh, what a relief!" said Clayton's grandmother, laughing at her gullibility. "No, it's not too late for me. The rest of the park thinks nine o'clock is midnight, but I stay up till all hours, reading and eating chocolate-covered cherries."

"What do you read?"

"Mostly crime and undercover stuff. I buy secondhand paperbacks at half price and then send them to Clayton. We like the same kind of books pretty much, although I could never get interested in science fiction."

"How's the weather down there?"

"Lovely! Have you had snow yet?"

"No, but they say the Big One is on the way. I want to thank you, Celia, for sending the snapshots. I took them to Mrs. Gage's memorial program tonight, and her friends remarked how well she looked. Shall I send you a copy of the program?"

"Oh, yes, please! And would it be too much trouble to send one for Mr. Crocus?"

"Not at all. Perhaps he'd also like one of her books as a keepsake. There's one here on correct breathing."

"He'd be overjoyed! That's very kind of you. He misses her a lot. I think there was something cooking between those two."

"Is Mr. Crocus the man with a magnificent head of white hair?"

"That's him. He plays the violin."

"You have some interesting-looking people in the park. Who's the couple standing with Mrs. Gage in front of a gigantic flowering shrub? They're wearing Pink Sunset T-shirts."

"They're new in the park—from Minnesota, I think. The bush is a hibiscus. Beautiful, isn't it? I never saw one so large."

"And who's the attractive woman at the wheel of the yellow convertible?"

"That's Betty, our manager. Isn't she glamorous? She sells cosmetics on the side. They're too expensive for me, but Mrs. Gage bought the works, and she really did look terrific."

Qwilleran said, "The car looks like the one she bought in Pickax before she left."

"That's right. She sold it to Betty—or maybe gave it to her. They were very chummy, like mother and daughter."

"Yow!" said Koko, who had ambled back into the library.

"I hear your cat."

"I like the picture of you in Mickey Mouse ears, Celia. Not everyone can wear them with so much panache."

She responded with a trill of pleasure. "I don't know what that means exactly, but it sounds good."

Qwilleran said, "I'm looking at a shot of your activity bus with the pink sunset painted on the side. There's a middle-aged man with his arm around Mrs. Gage, and they're both looking unusually happy."

"That's Claude, the owner of the park. He was very fond of her. He feels terrible about what she did. Everybody does."

"The Sunsetters impress me as one big happy family," he observed.

"Oh, sure. As long as you don't break the rules, everything's hunky-dory, but don't put pink plastic flamingoes on your lawn or all heck will break loose!"

"This Claude and Betty—are they the ones who used to take Mrs. Gage to the dog track?"

"Yes. She wanted me to drive her there, but the crowds are

humongous, you know, and not only that but I don't believe in gambling. I couldn't afford to take chances, for one thing. And then it hurts me to see those beautiful dogs being used that way. I've heard that they're killed after racing a few years."

Koko had been moving closer to the phone and was now breathing heavily into the mouthpiece. Qwilleran pushed him away. "Did Mrs. Gage enjoy gambling or just the excitement of the races?"

"Well, she seemed to get an awful big kick out of winning. Of course, people never tell you when they lose."

"Very true," he agreed. "By the way, she was a very wealthy woman. Did she give that impression?"

"She didn't talk big, but she was kind of high-toned, and her mobile home was a double-wide. I guessed she had plenty stashed away."

"Had she changed in any way since moving into the park? Was her mind still keen?"

"Oh, she was very sharp! She always knew what she wanted to do—and how to do it—and she did it! She sometimes said 'teapot' when she meant 'lamp shade,' but we all do that around here. I'm beginning to say 'left' when I mean 'right.' Clayton says it's something in the water in Florida," she said with a giggle.

Qwilleran cleared his throat, signifying an important question: "Were you aware that she drew up a new will after moving to the park?"

"Well, she never talked about anything like that—not to me, anyway—but I told her about this fellow—this lawyer—who does work for the Sunsetters for very reasonable fees. He did my will for only twenty-five dollars, and it was all tied up with red ribbon and red wax. Very professional! Of course, it was a simple will; I'm leaving everything to Clayton—not that I have much to leave."

"Yow!" said Koko.

"I hear my master's voice," Qwilleran said. "Good night, Celia. Thank you again for the snapshots, and give my regards to the thirteen-year-old doctor."

Her merry laughter was still pealing when he hung up. He arranged the snapshots in rows and studied them. Koko was purring loudly, and Qwilleran let him pass his nose over the glossy surfaces. Once again the long pink tongue flicked at two of the prints—the same two that had attracted him before. Qwilleran smoothed his moustache in deep thought; the cat never licked, sniffed, or scratched anything without a reason.

* * *

It snowed that night. There was a breathless stillness in the atmosphere as large, wet flakes fell gently, clinging to tree branches, evergreen shrubs, porch railings, and the lintels of hundreds of windows. Pickax, known as the City of Stone, was transformed into the City of Marshmallow Creme.

It was a good day to stay indoors and putter, Qwilleran decided after breakfasting on strong coffee and warmed-up rolls. He rummaged through the collection of Gage memorabilia that was accumulating in the desk drawer. The relics defined Grandpa Gage as a bon vivant, who smoked cigars, drank wine, collected women's garters, and liked the feel of money. There was a piece of Confederate money, and there were two large dollar bills of the kind issued before 1929. A pearl-handled buttonhook dated back to the days of high-button shoes. There was an old ivory pawn from a chess set that may have belonged to Euphonia's studious father-in-law. Koko's excavations were not entirely scientific; they included a small, dry wishbone and a racy postcard from Paris.

By afternoon the snow had stopped falling, and Qwilleran was tempted to drive out into the countryside and enjoy the fresh snow scene. He would take his camera. He would also check the church in Brrr where Hixie had scheduled the next performance of "The Big Burning." Phoning the number listed for the Brrr Community Church, he was assured that someone would meet him there. He dressed in heavy jacket, boots, and wool cap and was saying goodbye to the Siamese when Koko staged one of his eloquent demonstrations, jumping at the handle of the back door and muttering under his breath.

"Okay, this is your last ride of the season," Qwilleran told him. He started the car and ran the heater for a few minutes before carrying the cat coop out and placing it on the backseat.

The Moose County landscape—with its flat farmland, abandoned mine sites, and rows of utility poles—could be bleak in November, but today it was a picture in black and white. The plows were operating on the major highways, sending plumes of snow ten feet high. Even the town of Brrr, with its undistinguished architecture, looked like an enchanted village.

The church was a modest frame building with a cupola; it might have been a one-room schoolhouse except for the arched windows. As soon as Qwilleran pulled up to the curb, the front door opened and a woman came out to greet him, bundled up in a parka with the hood tied securely under her chin.

"Mr. Qwilleran, I'm Donna Sims. I was watching for you. Come in out of the cold, but don't expect to get warm. The furnace is out of order."

Qwilleran threw a blanket over the cat coop and followed the woman into the building. The vestibule was a small one, with a few steps leading up to the place of worship and a few steps leading down to a spick-and-span basement. Its concrete floor was freshly painted brick red, and its concrete block walls were painted white.

Ms. Sims apologized for the frigid temperature. "We're waiting for the furnace man. Emergencies like this are usually handled by a member of our congregation, but no one knows where he is. Maybe you heard about the potato farmer that disappeared. We're very much upset about it. He was such a wonderful help. When we decided to build a basement under this hundred-year-old church, he told us how to jack it up and do the job. He had all kinds of skills . . . So now we're waiting for a heating man from Mooseville."

"Don't apologize," Qwilleran said. "I'll cut this visit short because I have a cat in the car. What is that door?"

"That's the furnace room."

"Good! I'll use it for entrances and exits. Do you have anything in the way of a platform?"

"Not a regular platform, but one of our members manufactures industrial pallets—you know, those square wooden things—and we can borrow as many as necessary and stack them up. I think they're four by four feet."

"Are they sturdy? Are they solid?"

"Oh, yes, they're built to hold thousands of pounds."

"Eight of them should be enough, stacked two high in an eight-by-eight-foot square. How about electric outlets?"

"Two over here, and two over there. These tables are what we use for pot-luck suppers, but they fold up, and we can arrange the chairs in rows. Is there anything else you need?"

"A small table and chair on the platform and another table and chair for my engineer, down on the floor." He handed her a typewritten card. "This is how we like to be introduced. Will your pastor be doing the honors?"

"I'm the pastor," she said.

The chill of the basement had been worse than the cold snap outdoors, but the car interior was still comfortable. Qwilleran turned up the heat and said to Koko, "If it's all right with you, we'll go for a little ride along the shore, and see if the cabin's buttoned up for the winter." He had inherited a log cabin along with the rest of the Klingenschoen estate.

They headed along the lakeshore, where boarded-up cottages and beached boats huddled under a light blanket of snow. Then came a wooded stretch posted with red signs prohibiting hunting. At one point a large letter K was mounted on a post at the entrance to a narrow driveway, and this is where Qwilleran turned in. It was hardly more than an old wagon trail, meandering through the woods, up and down over brush-covered sand dunes. At the crest of one slight hill Koko created a disturbance in the backseat, throwing himself around in the carrier and yowling.

"Hold it, boy! We're just having a quick look," said Qwilleran, thinking the cat recognized the place where they had spent two summers. He stopped the car, however, and released the door of the coop.

Quivering with excitement, Koko darted to the rear window on the driver's side and pawed the glass.

"It's cold out there! You can't get out! You'd freeze your little tail off."

In a frenzy Koko dashed about the interior of the car as Qwilleran ducked and protested. "Hey! Cool it!" he said, but then he looked out the driver's window. Twisted trunks of wild cherry trees were silhouetted against the snow, and between them were animal tracks leading into the woods. Qwilleran jumped out, slammed the door, and followed the tracks.

A few yards into the woods there was a slight hollow, and what he found there sent him running back to the car, stumbling through the brush, slipping on wet snow. Without stopping to put Koko in the carrier, he backed down the winding trail to the highway. At the nearest gas station, on the outskirts of Mooseville, he called the sheriff.

Twelve

At eleven P.M. the WPKX newscast carried this item: "Acting on an anonymous tip, police today found the body of a Brrr Township man in the Klingenschoen woods east of Mooseville.

Gil Inchpot, fifty-two, a potato farmer, had been missing since October 24. Because of the condition of the body, decomposed and mutilated by wild animals, the medical examiner was unable to determine the cause of death. State forensic experts have been notified, according to the sheriff's department."

In phoning the tip to the police, Qwilleran had identified himself as a hunter trespassing on posted property and declining to give his name. He had altered his voice to sound like one of the locals who went "huntn" both in and out of "huntn" season. As the Klingenschoen heir and a well-known philanthropist, he had to fight to keep a low profile. Qwilleran preferred to be a newswriter, not a newsmaker.

As soon as he heard the broadcast, he called Gary Pratt at the Black Bear Café. "Have you heard the news?"

"Yeah, it's tough on Nancy," said the barkeeper. "She had to identify the body, and about all that was left was clothing. They didn't say anything about homicide on the air, but the thing of it is: If he'd been out hunting varmint and tripped on something in the woods, he'd be wearing a jacket and boots, wouldn't he? And what about a gun? He was wearing a plaid shirt and house slippers."

And no dentures, Qwilleran thought. "Is there anything we can do to help Nancy?"

"I don't know what it would be. She's a tough little lady, and I think she can take care of herself all right. When she talked to me on the phone, she didn't break down or anything like that—just said that her dogs need her and she can't afford to crack up."

As soon as the conversation ended, Arch Riker called. "Qwill, have you heard what happened? They found a body on your property."

Then Polly called. Next it was Junior with the same information. Qwilleran stopped answering the phone and went to bed. Twice he heard a distant ringing, followed by a much appreciated silence. In the morning he found the receiver off the phone. The cats, who slept on the library sofa, had been equally annoyed by the ringing phone and had taken matters into their own paws.

Qwilleran wrote Nancy a note of sympathy and mailed it at the same time he shipped a box of chocolate-covered cherries to Celia Robinson. Then, on Monday he attended Gil Inchpot's funeral at the Brrr Community Church, taking care to dress warmly. The furnace had been repaired, however, and the building was stiflingly hot. Gary Pratt was sitting alone in a rear pew, where an occasional blast of frigid air from the front door was a welcome relief. Qwilleran slipped in beside him.

Gary whispered, "Nancy's sitting down front with her ex. They'll be together again before long, I'm willing to bet."

Two days later, Qwilleran was back at the same church for the third time—to present "The Big Burning of 1869." It was snowing again, and he picked up Hixie Rice at the newspaper for the drive to Brrr. Large, wet snowflakes landed on the windshield.

"They're so beautiful, it's a shame to run the windshield wipers," she said.

"Beautiful, maybe, but this is the kind of snow that wrecks the power lines. I don't know what to expect at the church tonight. The first time I went there, the building was too cold; the second time, it was so hot we couldn't breathe."

Hixie was too happy to care about the temperature. She said, "Can you stand some good news? Arch is making me a vice president, in charge of advertising and promotion!"

"Congratulations! You deserve it."

"I have you to thank, Qwill, for steering me up to Pickax in the first place. You know, it's a funny thing. When I first met you Down Below, all I wanted was to find a husband. Now all I want is to be a vice president with a private office and a cute male secretary. I'll be sharing Wilfred with Arch. Wilfred isn't my idea of cute, but he's conscientious and reliable and computer-literate."

"You can't have everything," he philosophized. "But tell me something, Hixie: With your increased responsibilities, are you sure you want to go on pressing buttons and flipping switches for this show?"

"Are you kidding? I adore show biz!"

When they arrived at the church, he dropped her at the curb, telling her to check the stage while he unloaded the gear. By the time he opened the trunk, and set the suitcases on the sidewalk, Hixie came running out of the building.

"The furnace has conked out again! It's like a walk-in freezer! The audience is already there, and they're sitting in heavy jackets and wool hats and gloves. There's a little kerosene stove, but it doesn't do any good."

"The show must go on," he replied stoically. "If the audience can stand it, so can we. You keep your coat on, and I'll have the forest fire to keep me warm. It's surprising how much heat can be generated by concentrating on a role."

This was sheer bravado on Qwilleran's part. In portraying the studio announcer he was supposed to be working in 110-degree heat, and the act called for a short-sleeved summer shirt.

Hixie suggested, "Couldn't you cheat for once and wear a jacket?"

"And destroy the illusion? Better to contract pneumonia than to compromise one's art," he replied facetiously and a trifle grimly.

"Well, I'll visit you in the hospital," she said cheerfully.

There was a full house for the show, with everyone muffled to the eyebrows. Qwilleran stood in the furnace room, shivering as he waited for his entrance cue.

During the first act he steeled his jaw to keep his teeth from chattering as he said, "Railroad tracks are warped by the intense heat . . . Great blasts of hot air and cinders are smothering the city." The church basement was fogged by the frosty breath of the audience, while he went through the motions of mopping a sweating brow.

In the second act his frozen fingers fumbled with the script as he said, "The temperature is 110 degrees in the studio, and the window glass is still too hot to touch." It was not surprising that he completed the forty-five-minute script in forty minutes.

After the final words the audience clapped and cheered and stamped their feet. He suspected they were only trying to warm their extremities, but he bowed graciously and held out his hand to Hixie, who joined him on the stage. As they took their bows, Qwilleran could think only of a warm jacket and hot coffee, wishing fervently that the audience would sit on their hands. And then—during the fourth round of applause—the lights went out! Without warning the basement was plunged into the blackest darkness.

"Power's off!" the pastor's voice called out. "Everybody, stay right where you are. Don't try to move around until we can light some candles."

A man's voice said, "I've got a flashlight!" Its beams danced crazily around the walls and ceiling, and at that moment there was a cry, followed by the thud of a falling body and groans of pain. A dozen voices shrieked in alarm.

The flashlight beamed on the platform, where Qwilleran stood in a frozen state of puzzlement; Hixie was no longer beside him. She was writhing on the floor.

"Dr. Herbert! Dr. Herbert!" someone shouted.

"Here I am. Hand me that flashlight," said a man's gruff voice. Two battery-operated lanterns and some candles made small puddles of light as he kneeled at Hixie's side.

The audience babbled in shock. "What happened? . . . Did she fall off the stage? . . . It's lucky that Doc's here."

Qwilleran leaned over the doctor's shoulder. "How is she?"

"She can be moved. I'll drive her to the hospital." He jangled his keys. "Will someone bring my car around?"

While the others milled about anxiously, two men linked arms to form a chair lift and carry Hixie up the stairs.

"Hang in there," Qwilleran told her, squeezing her hand.

"*C'est la* rotten *vie,*" the new vice president said weakly.

He found his way to the furnace room for his flannel shirt and sweater and was packing the suitcases when Nancy Fincher walked up to the platform. "I'm very sorry about the accident," she said solemnly, "but Dr. Herbert will take good care of her. I feel bad about you, too. Your face looked frostbitten while you were talking, and at the end your lips were almost blue."

"I think I'll live," he said, "but I worry about my colleague. Let's go to the Black Bear for a hot drink. We can call the hospital from there."

They rode to the hotel in Qwilleran's car and found the café lighted by candles. Gary poured steaming cider heated on a small campstove and inquired, "What will Hixie's accident do to your show?"

Nancy spoke up, with more vigor than usual. "I could help out until she gets better. This is the second time I've seen the show, and I could learn the ropes if you'd tell me what to do."

"But what are your hours at the clinic? We have three shows scheduled back to back, and they're all matinees," Qwilleran pointed out.

"I could change my shift."

"The newspaper will reimburse you for your time, of course."

"They don't need to," she said. "I'd just like to do it. To tell the truth, Mr. Qwilleran, something like this would do me a lot of good. It'll take my mind off what's happened, you know."

He nodded sympathetically. "This is a painful time for you."

"Just having someone to talk to helps a lot. It was such a terrible thing!"

"Do you know if the police are getting anywhere with the investigation?"

"I don't know. They come to the house and ask questions but never tell me anything."

Qwilleran said gently, "You mentioned that your father had changed considerably after your mother died."

"Well, he was drinking more than before, and he stopped going to church on Sunday, although he still helped them when they needed repairs. And I told you about the way he was spending money on field equipment and drain tile. He said it was Mom's insurance, but she didn't have that kind of coverage. Another time he said he'd borrowed money from the bank, but everybody knows they aren't lending much to farmers these days."

"Did you tell the police about his spending spree?"

"No, I didn't," she said guiltily. "Do you think I should have?"

"They know it anyway. In a community like this it's no secret when someone starts making lavish expenditures." He looked at his watch. "We can call the hospital now." He used the bar telephone and reported to Nancy, "She's been transferred to the Pickax hospital. No information on her condition is available."

Qwilleran drove Nancy back to the church, where her truck was parked. "Our next booking is Saturday afternoon in downtown Pickax. We should have a rehearsal."

"Yes, I want to," she said eagerly. "I could stop by your house tomorrow when I drive to town for supplies."

Brrr was still blacked out when he drove away from the church, but Pickax had power. The old-fashioned street lamps on Goodwinter Boulevard glowed through a veil of gently falling snow. Hurrying into the house, he telephoned the Pickax hospital and learned that the patient had been admitted and was resting comfortably. No further information was available.

He immediately phoned Arch Riker at home in Indian Village. Without preliminaries he announced, "Your new vice president is in the hospital, and your star columnist is a candidate for an oxygen tent."

"What happened to her, for God's sake?"

"The power failed where we were giving our show, and she fell off the stage, probably because she was frozen stiff. The furnace was out of order. Fortunately there was a doctor in the house. He had her moved to Pickax. I don't know the nature or extent of the injury. The robot on the telephone isn't giving out any information."

"Our night desk will find out," Riker said. "I hate to sound crass, Qwill, but what will this do to our show schedule?"

"I have a substitute lined up. I told her you'd reimburse her, so be prepared to sign some checks, and don't be parsimonious."

"Who is it? Anyone I know?"

"Nancy Fincher, daughter of the potato farmer whose body was found last week."

Riker said, "I'll bet he was growing something besides potatoes."

"I don't know about that," Qwilleran said, "but it appears that he broke up his daughter's marriage to a deputy sheriff. How about that for a suggestive situation?"

"Don't waste your time sleuthing, Qwill. You always get off the track when you're playing detective."

Qwilleran ignored the advice. "And what were you doing tonight? Romancing Mildred?"

"We had dinner at Tipsy's and talked about her apartment in town and my condo here in the Village and her cottage at the beach. The apartment's gotta go, but we may build an addition to the cottage."

"Don't!" Qwilleran warned, speaking from experience.

"By the way, the Lanspeaks want us to have the wedding at their place on Purple Point, Christmas Eve."

"Excuse me a moment, Arch." He was sitting with his arms on the desk, and Koko was digging in the crook of his elbow. "What's your problem?" he asked the cat. "You're wearing out my sweater sleeve!"

Both cats liked to knead before settling down to sleep, but Koko was working industriously. At the sharp rebuke he jumped off the desk and went to the locked closet, where he rattled the door handle.

Turning back to the phone Qwilleran explained, "Koko wants me to pick the lock on the library closet."

"I wish you took orders from your editor-in-chief the way you take orders from that cat! Hang up! I'll call the night desk about Hixie's accident."

The next morning Qwilleran phoned the hospital and learned that the patient was receiving treatment; no further information was available. It was noon when he finally reached the patient herself.

"Hixie! How are you? We're all worried about you! What's the diagnosis?"

With her usual debonair flourish she replied, "Broken foot! But I've met this perfectly wonderful Dr. Herbert! He drove me to the Brrr hospital and stayed while they X-rayed and put on a soft cast. Then he drove me down here, where they have an orthopedic surgeon. Dr. Herbert is adorable, Qwill! He cares! He has a cabin cruiser! And he's not married!"

"You sound cheerful," Qwilleran said, "but how are you from the ankle down?"

"*C'est si bon!* And the food! I'm sitting here with a delectable bowl of seafood chowder on my lunch tray. They have a gourmet dietician who's *fantastique!* I expect a split of champagne on my dinner tray."

"Okay, I'll drop in to see you this afternoon. Now get back to your chowder while it's hot."

"Hot? I never said it was *hot!* This is a hospital, *mon ami!*"

When Qwilleran visited her a few hours later, he found her in a private room with soft pink walls, sitting in an arm chair with her foot elevated and encased in a bright pink cast.

"Chic, *n'est-ce pas?*" she said. "Casts now come in five decorator colors, and I thought the hot pink would coordinate with the walls."

"Never mind the color scheme. What did the surgeon say?"

"I have a displaced fracture of the metacarpus. Doesn't that sound exotic?"

"Do you have any pain?"

"Watch your language, Qwill. Four-letter words aren't allowed in the hospital. We don't feel *pain;* we don't *hurt;* we only experience discomfort. Fortunately I have a high discomfort threshold."

"How long will you be in a cast?"

"Six weeks, but when Dr. Herbert found out I live alone in a second-floor walk-up in Indian Village, he insisted that I stay with his mother in Pickax for a while. In a couple of weeks I can go into the office with a walker."

"I'll drive you," Qwilleran offered.

"But what about the show? Who'll be your engineer? Perhaps Arch will let you have Wilfred."

"I have someone prettier than Wilfred. Don't worry about it, Hixie. Meanwhile, is there anything you need?"

"No, thanks. Just keep your fingers crossed that I get out of the hospital before the Big Snow."

Qwilleran started to leave but remembered the snapshots in his pocket. "Did you ever meet Euphonia Gage?"

"No, but I saw her around town—in her eighties and walking like a young girl!"

"I have pictures of her taken in Florida, and some of her friends look familiar. You may recognize them."

"*Donnez-moi.* I'm good at remembering faces." Hixie studied the photos carefully. "I think I've seen a couple of these people before. Is it important?"

"It may be. I don't know," he admitted.

"Okay, leave them with me, and if I get a noodle, I'll call you."

From the hospital Qwilleran went to the Senior Care Facility to arrange the staging for the Sunday afternoon show. Lisa Compton, in charge of patient activities, showed him the all-purpose room with its rows of long tables.

"They take their meals here," she said, "but we remove the tables for a program like yours. We put the hearing-impaired in the front row and the mumblers in the back."

"What's behind that door?"

"The kitchen."

"Good! I can have a piece of pie between the acts." Everything, in fact, checked out: platform, electric outlets, two tables, two chairs.

"Cup of coffee?" Lisa asked.

"Thanks, but I've got to go home and rehearse a new partner for the show. Hixie has broken her foot."

"Oh, the poor dear! That can be so painful."

"She doesn't seem to have any discomfort," he said.

"But this is only the beginning. When the shock wears off, the nerve ends start to ache. Ask me! I've been there!"

"Let's not tell Hixie," he said. "I'll see you Sunday afternoon, Lisa."

When he arrived on Goodwinter Boulevard, Nancy's pickup—with its box top and eight barred windows—was already parked in the side drive. He ushered her directly downstairs to the ballroom, where the stage was set for rehearsal.

"I remember this room when I was a little girl," she said. "Mrs. Gage had dozens of little gold chairs around the walls. I loved those little chairs and always wished she'd give me one for Christmas instead of a book. I wonder what happened to them."

"Who knows?" he remarked, in a hurry to get down to business. He explained the code on the cuecard and the operation of the equipment. Then they rehearsed the timing and ended with a complete run-through.

"Perfect," Qwilleran said.

He packed the gear in preparation for the forthcoming performance and thanked his new engineer for coming to rehearse, but she showed no signs of leaving. "All of this is so exciting for me," she said. "And it's funny, Mr. Qwilleran—when I first met you I was tongue-tied because you were so important and so rich and everything, and I thought your moustache was—well—frightening, but now I feel very comfortable with you."

"Good," he said with an offhand inflection.

"It's because you *listen.* Most men don't listen to women when they talk—not really."

"I'm a journalist. Listening is what we do." His defenses were up. As a millionaire bachelor he had learned to dodge. Briskly he said, "Shall we wind up this session with a quick glass of cider in the library?"

She dropped with familiar ease into the scooped-out library sofa, displacing the Siamese, who walked stiffly from the room, and Qwilleran feared she was feeling too comfortable. Now that she had his therapeutic ear to talk into, she talked—and talked—about living in Alaska, potato farming, breeding dogs, working for a vet. Dinnertime approached, and he had had no real food since breakfast. Under other circumstances he might have invited such a guest out to dinner, but if the Klingenschoen heir were seen dining with a young woman half his age—the daughter of a murdered man whose body had been found on Klingenschoen property—the Pickax gossips would put two and two together and get the national debt.

The Siamese were still absent and unnaturally quiet, even though it was past their feeding time. Suddenly eight thundering paws galloped past the library door toward the entrance.

"What was that?" she asked.

"The cats are trying to remind me it's their dinnertime," he replied, looking at his watch.

"You should hear my dogs at feeding time! Go ahead and feed them if you want to." Nancy was obviously too comfortable to move.

The pelting paws rushed past again, like a herd of wild horses as they charged toward the kitchen. Next there was a frenzy of scuffling, thwacking, and snarling that brought Qwilleran and his guest to the scene in time for a shattering of glass.

"The coffee jar!" he shouted. Coffee beans and broken glass were everywhere, and the Siamese were on top of the refrigerator, looking down on the devastation with bemused detachment.

"I'll help you clean up," Nancy offered. "Don't cut yourself."

"No! No! Thanks, but . . . let me cope with this. I'll see you Saturday afternoon. You'll have to excuse me now."

As she drove away he swept up the mess, wondering whether they simply wanted their dinner or were trying to get rid of the doghandler. They always knew how to get what they wanted, and sometimes they merely wanted to be helpful.

While he was scrambling around the kitchen floor on his hands and knees, Hixie phoned and said excitedly, "I'm checking out of the hospital and moving in with Dr. Herbert's mother! He says she was born in Paris. I can brush up on my French!"

"Glad you're getting out before the Big Snow," he said. "Shall I mail these Florida snapshots back to you?"

"If it isn't too much trouble. Did anyone look familiar?"

"Well," said Hixie, "there's a man with upswept eyebrows—a middle-aged man. And there's a young woman in a yellow convertible—"

"They're the ones," he interrupted. "Who are they?"

"I'm not sure, but . . . do you remember the gate-crashers at the preview of our show? The woman was wearing an obvious wig."

"Thanks, Hixie. That's all I need to know. Enjoy your stay with Madame Herbert."

Qwilleran returned to the kitchen to finish cleaning up. The Siamese were still on the refrigerator. "What were Betty and Claude doing in Pickax?" he asked them. "And why did they attend the preview?"

Thirteen

Qwilleran was inclined to discount the tales of the Big Snow. For six winters he had heard about this local bugaboo, which was never as nasty as predicted. Yet, every year the residents of Moose County prepared for war: digging in, mobilizing snowplows and blowers, enlisting snowfighters, deploying troops of volunteers, disseminating propaganda, and stockpiling supplies. Every day a virtual convoy of trucks brought necessities from Down Below: food, drink, videos, batteries, and kerosene.

Everyone had some urgent task to finish or goal to achieve before the white bomb dropped: Hixie to get out of the hospital, Jody to get into the hospital and have her baby, Lori to finish Qwilleran's correspondence, and Nick to deliver it. Qwilleran's only important business was to do three shows: for a women's group on Saturday, for the Senior Care Facility on Sunday, and for a school on Monday.

Friday morning he was drinking coffee and conversing idly with the Siamese when, suddenly, Koko heard something! The cats were always hearing something. It might be a faucet dripping, or a truck on Main Street shifting gears, or a dog barking half a mile away.

This time Koko stretched his neck, swiveled his noble head, and slanted his ears toward the foyer. Qwilleran investigated. There was a moving van across the street, backing into Amanda Goodwinter's driveway. She was Junior's elder relative, a cantankerous businesswoman, and a perennial member of the city council.

Qwilleran hurried into boots and parka and climbed over the piles of snow that the sidewalk blowers had thrown into the street and the city plows had thrown back onto the sidewalk. A truck from the Bid-a-Bit Auction House had lowered its ramp, and Amanda herself was on the porch, directing the operation. She looked dowdier than ever in her army surplus jacket, Daniel Boone hat, and unfastened galoshes.

"Amanda! What's going on here?" Qwilleran hailed her as he plunged through the drifts.

"I'm getting out before the Big Snow! I'm selling everything! I'm moving to Indian Village!"

"But what will you do with your house?"

"It's sold! Good riddance! I always hated it!"

"Who bought it?"

"Some real estate vulture from Down Below!"

He joined her on the porch and teased her by saying, "You'll be sorry! Pickax is attracting investors. Land values will go up."

"Nothing'll go up on this godforsaken street until the property owners get off their hind ends and permit re-zoning . . . Stop! Stop!" she screamed at the movers, who were struggling with a hundred-year-old black walnut breakfront, twelve feet wide. "You're scratching the finish! Take the drawers out! Watch the glass doors!"

At the same moment a second moving van pulled up to the Wilmot house. Qwilleran shrugged, pulled up the hood of his parka, and trudged the length of the boulevard, counting for-sale signs. There were only four left, out of a recent seven. He enjoyed walking in snow and took the opportunity to hike downtown to the church where he would present "The Big Burning" the following afternoon.

The fellowship hall in the church basement was a large room paneled in pickled pine, with a highly waxed vinyl floor and a good solid platform. The custodian told Qwilleran he could use the men's restroom for exits and entrances. Seventy-five women were expected for lunch at noon, and they'd be ready for the show at one o'clock. Everything appeared to be well organized, and Qwilleran was impressed by the facilities.

As he arrived home, Nick Bamba was pulling into the driveway. "Come on in, Nick, and have a hot drink," he said hospitably.

"Not this time," Nick declined. "I have a dozen errands to do before the Big Snow." He handed over a folder. "Here's your correspondence from Lori, and I've brought my tool kit. I'll pick the lock in the library. Are you all ready for the Big Snow?"

"Polly has been nagging me about that," Qwilleran said, "but my vast experience convinces me that it's never as big as the kerosene dealers would have us believe."

"How long have you been here? Five years? The seventh year is always the really big one. Trust me!" Nick tackled the closet lock in professional fashion while dispensing advice. "You need a camp stove and kerosene heater in case of a long power outage . . . canned food, not frozen, in case you're snowbound . . . five-gallon jugs of water in case a water main busts . . . fresh batteries for your radio and flashlights."

"What do they do at the prison?" Qwilleran asked.

"We have generators. So does the hospital. Remember not to use your elevator after it starts to snow hard; you could be trapped in a blackout." Nick opened the closet door, collected his tools, and accepted Qwilleran's thanks, and on the way out he said, "If you're not concerned about yourself, Qwill, think about your cats."

Koko lost no time in entering the closet. It was filled with files in boxes and drawers, and a small safe stood open and empty. When Qwilleran left to go shopping for canned food, the cat was sitting in the safe like a potentate in a palanquin.

Throughout the weekend a storm watch was in effect, but Suitcase Productions presented all three scheduled shows to capacity audiences. By Monday afternoon Wetherby Goode announced a storm alert and said he was prepared for the worst; he had a sleeping bag in the studio as well as a package of fig newtons.

Monday evening Koko and Yum Yum began to behave abnormally, dashing about and butting furniture. They showed no interest in food or *Robinson Crusoe.* Eventually Qwilleran shut himself in his bedroom to escape the fracas, but he could still hear bursts of madcap activity. He himself slept fitfully.

Shortly after daybreak a peaceful calm settled on the house. Peering out the window, he witnessed a rare sight: the entire sky was the vivid color of polished copper. A weather bulletin on WPKX made note of the phenomenon and warned that it was the lull before the storm. Duck hunters and commercial fishermen were advised to stay on shore and resist the temptation to make one more haul before the end of the season.

By mid-morning large flakes of snow began to fall. Shortly after, the wind rose, and soon fifty-mile-an-hour gusts were creating blizzard conditions.

At noon the WPKX newscast announced: "A storm of unprecedented violence is blasting the county. Visibility is zero. Serious drifting is making roads impassable. All establishments are closed with the exception of emergency services. Even so, fire fighters, police, and medical personnel attempting to respond to calls are blinded by the whirling snow and are completely disoriented. State police have issued these directives: Stay indoors. Conserve water, food, and fuel. Observe safety precautions in using kerosene heaters and wood-burning stoves. In case of power failure, use flashlights or oil lanterns; avoid candles. Be prepared to switch radios to battery operation. And stay tuned for further advisories."

On Goodwinter Boulevard it was snowing in four directions: down, up, sideways and in circles. Strangely, the Siamese, having accomplished their advance warning, settled down to sleep peacefully.

At three o'clock WPKX reported: "Two duck hunters from Lockmaster left shore in a rented boat west of Mooseville early this morning and have not been seen since that time. Their boat was found bottom-up, blown high on the shore near Brrr . . . Distress calls from commercial fishing boats are being received, but the sheriff's helicopter is grounded in the blizzard, and rescue crews are unable to launch their boats in the mountainous waves. Thirty-five-foot waves are reported on the lake."

Then the power failed, and when Qwilleran tried to call Polly, the telephone was dead. The blizzard continued relentlessly, hour after hour, and he experienced the unnerving isolation of a house blanketed with snow. Without mechanical noises and without the sound of street traffic, the unnatural stillness left a muffled void that only amplified the howling of the wind, and a cold darkness settled on the rooms as snow drifted against the windows.

The blizzard lasted sixteen hours, during which Qwilleran found he could neither read nor write nor sleep. Then the wind subsided. The Big Snow was over, but it would take almost a week for the county to struggle back to normal. Broadcasting was limited to weather updates and police news on the half hour:

"The worst storm in the history of Moose County was the result of a freak atmospheric condition. Three low-pressure fronts—one coming from Alaska, one from the Rocky Mountains, and one from the Gulf of Mexico—met and clashed over this area. Winds of seventy miles an hour were recorded as thirty-two inches of snow fell in sixteen hours. Drifts of fifteen to thirty feet have buried buildings and walled up city streets and country roads, paralyzing the county."

For the next two days Qwilleran lived life without power, telephone, mail delivery, daily newspapers, or sociable pets. Koko and Yum Yum appeared to be in hibernation on the library sofa. His own intentions to catch up on his reading and write a month's supply of copy for the newspaper were reduced to a state of jittery boredom. Even when snowplows started rumbling and whooshing about the city streets, cars were still impounded in their garages and residents were imprisoned in their houses. The health department warned against overexertion in digging out.

On the morning of the fourth day Qwilleran was in the library, eating a stale doughnut and drinking instant coffee prepared with not-quite-boiling water, when the shrill and unexpected bell of the telephone startled him and catapulted the Siamese from their sofa. It was Polly's exultant voice: "Plug in your refrigerator!"

"How are you, Polly? I worried about you," he said.

"Bootsie and I weathered the storm, but I lacked the energy to do anything. I had planned to wash the kitchen walls, clean closets, and make Christmas gifts. How are you faring?"

"Strangely, I'm getting tired of canned soup and stale doughnuts."

"We'll be prisoners for a few days more," she predicted, "but fortunately we're in touch with the outside world."

Qwilleran immediately called the outside world, but all lines were busy. The gregarious, garrulous populace of Pickax seemed to be making up for lost time.

WPKX went on the air with more storm news, good and bad:

"The first baby born during the Big Snow is a seven-pound girl, Leslie Ann. The parents are Mr. and Mrs. Junior Goodwinter. Mother and child are snowbound at the Pickax hospital.

"In rural areas many persons are reported missing. It is presumed that they lost their way in the blizzard and have frozen to death. Homes have burned to the ground because help could not reach them. Much livestock is thought to be frozen in fields and barns. Bodies are still washing ashore from wrecked boats."

The sound of Polly's voice and the rumbling of the refrigerator restored Qwilleran's spark of life. He did some laundry, washed the accumulation of soup bowls in the kitchen sink, and eventually reached Junior to offer congratulations.

"Yeah, I got her to the hospital just before the storm broke and then had to rush home to take care of our little boy. I still haven't seen the baby," Junior said. "But hey, Qwill, let me tell you about the call I got from Down Below just before the phones went dead. It was some guy who deals in architectural fragments. He wanted to buy the light fixtures and fireplaces in Grandma's house!"

"You mean he wanted to strip this place?" Qwilleran asked in indignation.

"I told him to get lost. Boy, he had a lot of nerve! How do you suppose he found out what we've got?"

"I could make an educated guess. How valuable are the fixtures?"

"Susan Exbridge could tell you exactly. I only know that the chandeliers on the main floor are real silver, and the ones in the ballroom are solid brass and copper, imported from France before World War I . . . Anyway, I thought you'd be shocked, the way I was."

After five o'clock Qwilleran phoned Celia Robinson. "Good evening," he said in the ingratiating tone that had melted female defenses for years. "This is Jim Qwilleran."

"Oh! Thank you so much for the chocolate cherries!" she gushed. "They're my absolute favorite! But you didn't have to do it."

"It was my pleasure."

"I've been watching the weather on TV. Was it very bad up where you are?"

"Very bad. We've been snowbound for four days, with no meltdown in sight. Meanwhile, Celia, I'm working on my profile of Mrs. Gage and need to ask a few more questions. Do you mind?"

"You know I'm glad to help, Mr. Qwilleran—and not just because you sent me those lovely chocolates."

"All right. Going back to the morning when you found her body, what did you do?"

"I called the office, and they called the authorities. They came right away."

Casually he asked, "And how did Betty and Claude react?"

"Oh, they weren't here. They were out of town, and Pete was in charge. He's the assistant—very nice, very helpful."

"Did he appear shocked?"

"Well, not really. We've had quite a few deaths, you know, which you can understand in a place like this. Actually we have quite a turnover."

"Do Betty and Claude go out of town very often?"

"Well, they're from up north, and they go to see their families once in a while."

"Where up north?" he asked as if mildly curious.

"It could be Wisconsin. They talk about the Green Bay Packers and the Milwaukee Brewers. But I'm not sure. Want me to find out?"

"No, it's not important. But tell me: Did Mrs. Gage ever mention her mansion in Pickax? It was in her husband's family for generations."

"I know," said Celia. "She showed a video of it in the clubhouse—not that she wanted to show off, I'm sure, but we visited some historic homes down here, and she thought we'd like to see a hundred-year-old house up north. She had some wonderful things."

"Did Mr. Crusoe see the video?"

"Crocus," she corrected. "Yes, and he still talks about it. He comes over to my yard and wants to talk about her. Today he told me something confidential. I'm not supposed to mention it in the park until it's official, but I can tell you. You probably know already that she left a lot of money to the park to build a health club."

"How did he know about it?"

"She told him. They were very good friends, I guess. They liked the same things. We all thought it would be nice if they got married. That's why it's so sad."

"Yes," Qwilleran murmured, then asked, "Do you suppose Mr. Crocus would care to be interviewed for this profile?"

"I don't know. He's kind of shy, but I could ask him. Would you like me to break the ice, sort of?"

"Would you be good enough to do that?" he requested. "Your cooperation is much appreciated. And may I call you again soon?"

"You know you don't have to ask, Mr. Qwilleran. It's lots of fun answering your questions."

After the call he dropped into a lounge chair to think, and Yum Yum walked daintily into the library. "Hello, princess," he said. "Where have you been?"

Taking that as an invitation, she leaped lightly to his knee, turned around three times, and found a place to settle down.

He adjusted her weight slightly without discommoding her and asked, "What happened to your confrère?"

The muted answer came from the closet—a series of soft thumps that aroused Qwilleran's curiosity. He excused himself and went to investigate. Koko was batting a small object this way and that, apparently having fun. It was a small maroon velvet box.

Qwilleran intercepted it and immediately called Junior again. "Guess what Koko has just dredged up in one of the closets! A jeweler's box containing a man's gold ring, probably your grandfather's! It's the only valuable item he's found."

"What kind of ring?"

"A signet, with an intricate design on the crown. I'll turn it over to you as soon as they dig us out."

"Which can't be too soon for me," Junior said. "I'm getting cabin fever."

"I've been talking to Celia Robinson again. Did you know your grandmother had a video of the house when it was still furnished?"

"Sure. She had me film the interior before she broke it up. After she died, I found the tape among her effects and brought it home for the historical museum."

"Well, for your information, she showed the film at the Park of Pink Sunsets, so we can assume that the park management knew about the lavish appointments. Now I'm wondering if they came to see for themselves—with an ulterior motive. Listen to this, Junior: Betty and Claude were in this house when we previewed 'The Big Burning.' They wandered around the rooms with the rest of the crowd."

"How do you know?"

"I saw them. Hixie saw them. We both wondered who they were. Since then, we've identified them from snapshots that Celia sent us. Now you know and I know that nobody—*nobody*—ever stops in Pickax on the way to somewhere else. They come here for a purpose or not at all, and Betty and Claude don't strike me as being duck hunters. They must have known about the preview—and the exact date. Could your grandmother have told them? Did she know about it?"

"Jody wrote to her once a week and probably mentioned it," Junior said. "Grandma would be interested because the script was based on her father-in-law's memoirs, and she had a crush on him."

Qwilleran said, "Frankly, I've had doubts about the Pink Sunset operation ever since you told me they profiteer on the repurchase of mobile homes. Are they also in partnership with the guy who wanted to buy the light fixtures? We may have uncovered a story that's bigger than a profile of your eccentric grandmother."

"Wow! When it breaks," Junior said, "let's keep it exclusive with the *Moose County Something!*"

Fourteen

Gradually Moose County struggled out from under the snow, as armies of volunteers swarmed over the neighborhoods, tunneling through to buried buildings. The snowdrifts never diminished, only shifted from one location to another, with one more inch of snow falling every day. WPKX now aired the lighter side of the news:

"Sig Olsen, a farmer near Sawdust City, had his chicken coop wrecked by the storm, and a loose board sailed through his kitchen window. He didn't know it until morning, when he got up and found his whole flock roosting around the wood-burning stove."

Qwilleran finally reached Hixie by phone. "Your line's constantly busy," he complained.

"I'm working on logistics for the Christmas parade," she explained. "The *Something* is cosponsoring it with Lanspeak's Department Store."

"Are you comfortable where you're staying?"

"*Mais oui!* Madame Herbert is a *joli coeur!* Did you do the three shows I scheduled before the Big Snow? I thought the one at the Senior Care Facility might be amusing."

"Hilarious!" Qwilleran said dryly. "I played for fifty wheelchairs and two gurneys. They were attentive, but the assorted bodily noises in the audience were a new experience. After the show the attendants passed out bananas, and I circulated among the old-timers to hear their comments. They all handed me their banana peels."

"You're so adaptable, Qwill! *Je t'adore!*" she said.

He huffed into his moustache. "What are you planning for Thanksgiving?"

"Dr. Herbert is coming down from Brrr with some friends, and Madame is doing stuffed quail with apricot coulis. What about you?"

"Polly is roasting a turkey, and Arch and Mildred will join us."

When he hung up, both cats reported to the library, having heard the word "turkey."

"Sorry. False alarm," he said.

Koko, returning to work after the storm, was no longer collecting emery boards, teabags, pieces of saltwater taffy, and other domestic trivia. He was excavating the library closet and leaving a paper trail of postcards, newspaper clippings, envelopes with foreign stamps, and such. One was a yellowed clipping from the *Pickax Picayune,* the antiquated predecessor of the *Moose County Something.* It was a column headed "Marriages," and one of the listings attracted Qwilleran's attention:

> LENA FOOTE, DAUGHTER OF
> MR. AND MRS. ARNOLD FOOTE OF LOCKMASTER,
> TO GILBERT INCHPOT OF BRRR, OCT. 18.

The year 1961 had been inked in the margin. That date would be about right, Qwilleran figured, guessing at Nancy's age. Lena Foote was her mother and also Euphonia's longtime housekeeper. Apparently she was already employed in the Gage household before her marriage. What had Euphonia given the couple for a wedding present? A wooden nutcracker? He put the clipping in an envelope addressed to Nancy, adding thanks for her assistance with the three shows and mentioning that there might be more bookings after the holidays.

On the sixth day following the Big Snow Qwilleran was able to mail his letter. He also arranged to meet Junior for lunch at Lois's; he wanted to deliver the gold ring and two other items of interest that Koko had unearthed.

When it was time to leave for lunch, however, the jeweler's box was missing, and the desk drawer was ajar. "Drat those cats!" Qwilleran said aloud. He knew it was Yum Yum's fine Siamese paw that had opened the drawer, but he suspected it was Koko who assigned her the nefarious little task, like a feline Fagin. There was no time to search fifteen rooms and fifty closets; he hustled off to Lois's, where Junior was waiting in a booth.

The editor's first words were, "Did you remember to bring Grandpa's ring?"

"Dammit! I forgot it!" said Qwilleran, an expert at extemporaneous fibs.

"Today's special," Lois announced as she slapped two soiled menu cards on the table. "Bean soup and ham sandwich."

"Give us a minute to decide," Qwilleran said, "but you can bring us some coffee."

From an inner pocket of his jacket he produced a folded sheet of paper, ivory with age and turning brown at the creases. "Do you recognize this writing, Junior?"

"That's Grandma's!"

"It's the anonymous poem in her memorial program—the one about lovelorn butterflies."

Junior scanned the verses with the lightning speed of an experienced editor. "Do you suppose she wrote this?"

"Well, it wasn't Keats or Wordsworth. I think your sedate little grandmother had a passionate past."

"Could be. Jody always thought she had something to hide. How do women know these things?"

Lois returned with the coffee. "You guys decide what you want?"

"Not yet," said Junior. "Give us another couple of seconds."

Next, Qwilleran handed him an old envelope postmarked Lockmaster, 1929. The letter inside was addressed to "My dearest darling Cynara."

"Oh, God! Do I have to read it?" Junior whined. "Other people's love letters always sound so corny."

"Read it!" Qwilleran ordered.

Nov. 17, 1929

My dearest darling Cynara—

Last night I climbed to the roof of the horse barn—and looked across to where you live—thirty miles—but I can still feel you—taste you—smell your skin—fresh as violets—After sixteen months of heaven—it's hell to be without you—tossing and turning all night—dreaming of you—I want to climb to the top of the silo—and jump down on the rocks—but it would kill my mother—and hurt you—and you've suffered enough for my sake—And so—my own heart's darling—I'm going away—for good—and I beg you to forget me—I'm returning the ring—and thinking that maybe—some day—we'll meet in sweetness and in light—but for now—promise to forget—Goodbye—my Cynara—

The signature was simply "W." When Junior finished reading it, he said, "It turns my stomach."

"The content or the punctuation?" Qwilleran asked.

"How could Grandma fall for such rot?"

"She was young in 1929."

"In 1929 Grandpa was in prison. She couldn't face the scandal in Pickax, so she went to stay in Lockmaster for two years—on somebody's farm. It looks as if it turned out to be fun and games."

Qwilleran said, "This horse farmer was obviously the other butterfly in the poem. She put her memories in the closet and finally paraded them at her memorial bash: *Love's long since cancelled woes . . . I must not think of thee . . .* Wouldn't it be a poetic coincidence if her admirer in Florida turned out to be W? But if that were the case, why would she overdose?"

"Do you know anything about him?"

"Only that he has a magnificent head of white hair and plays the violin."

Lois advanced on their booth with hands on hips. "Are you young punks gonna order? Or do you want to pay rent for the booth?"

Both men ordered the special, and Junior said, "Grandpa got out of prison in time for the stock market crash, my mother used to say."

"That was the month before this letter was written."

"You're not putting Grandma's love life in your profile, are you, Qwill?"

"Why not?"

There was a thoughtful pause as family loyalty battled with professional principle. Then Junior said, "I guess you're right. Why not? The Gages are all dead. Where is Koko finding these choice items all of a sudden?"

Pompously Qwilleran said, "I cannot tell a lie. I picked the lock of the library closet. There are tons of papers in there. Also an empty safe. One thing Koko found was an announcement in the *Picayune* of Gil Inchpot's marriage to Euphonia's housekeeper. There was also a recipe for Lena's angel food cake with chocolate frosting that sounded delicious."

"I knew Lena," said Junior. "She was Grandma's day-help for years and years. After that, there was a series of live-in housekeepers who never stayed long. Grandma was hard to get along with in her old age."

"What about the Inchpot murder? Do the police have any suspects?"

"Haven't heard. The Big Snow brings everything to a crashing halt. Do you realize there are frozen bodies out there that won't be found until spring thaw?"

Their discussion was interrupted by the slam-bang delivery of two daily specials. They ate in silence until Junior inquired about Suitcase Productions.

"Several organizations want us after the holidays. We did three shows just before the Big Snow. The largest audience was in the basement of the Old Stone Church. Seventy-five women. Lunch at noon. Performance at one. I was supposed to use the men's restroom for exits and entrances, but there was a wedding upstairs, and the bridal party was using it as a dressing room. They said I'd have to use the women's restroom. After their lunch seventy-five women lined up to use the facilities, and it was two-thirty before we got the show on the boards. Then, just as I was describing the roaring of the wind and the crashing of burning buildings, there was a roar and a crash overhead! I thought the ceiling was caving in, but it was only the church organ upstairs, playing the wedding march full blast! I can project my voice, but it's not easy to compete with Mendelssohn on a five-hundred-pipe organ!"

Lois returned, brandishing the coffee server like a weapon. "Apple pie?" she demanded gruffly.

"I'm due back at the office," said the young editor.

"You go ahead. I'll get the check," Qwilleran told him. "And Lois, you can bring me some of your apple pie. I dreamed about it all the time I was snowbound."

"Liar!" she retorted, and she bustled away, smiling.

As soon as Nancy Fincher received Qwilleran's letter, she telephoned him. "Thanks for the clipping about my parents. It'll go in my scrapbook."

"Mrs. Gage must have had a high regard for your mother."

"Oh, yes, she relied on Mom a lot, and Mom loved Mrs. Gage. She didn't like Mr. Gage, though. When she went to work there as a young girl, he was too friendly, she told me."

"That's one way of putting it," Qwilleran said. "Why did she continue to work for them after her marriage?"

"Well, you see, Mom and Pop needed the money to get their farm started. Besides, she loved working in the big house. I took care of our farmhouse starting when I was nine years old—cooking and everything."

"Remarkable," Qwilleran murmured. "So your mother's maiden name was Foote. Did you keep in touch with your grandparents in Lockmaster?"

As before, Nancy was eager to talk. "No, it's funny, but I never saw them until they came to Mom's funeral."

"What was the reason for that?"

"I don't know. I had Grandma and Grandpa Inchpot right here in Brrr, and Mom never talked about her own parents. I thought Lockmaster was a foreign country."

"When they attended your mother's funeral, how did you react to them?"

"I didn't like them at all. They made me nervous, the way they stared at me. Pop said it was because they were surprised to see their granddaughter grown up. They were very old, of course."

Qwilleran asked, "Did it ever occur to you that your Lockmaster grandparents might have lent your father the money for his farm improvements after your mother died?"

"No way," she said. "They were only poor dirt farmers. Not everybody in Lockmaster is a rich horse breeder . . . Well, anyway, Mr. Qwilleran, I wanted to thank you and wish you a happy Thanksgiving. I'm spending it with Dan Fincher's relatives, and I'll take the kids for dogsled rides after dinner. What are you going to do?"

"Polly Duncan is roasting a turkey, and there'll be another couple, and we'll all eat too much."

"N-n-now!" shrieked Yum Yum.

It was a thankful foursome that gathered in Polly's apartment, thankful to be free after a week of confinement. The aroma of turkey was driving Bootsie to distraction, and the aroma of Mildred's mince pie, still warm from the oven, was having much the same effect on Qwilleran.

Arch Riker said, "The local pundits are saying that a Big Snow before Thanksgiving means mild weather before Christmas."

Mildred said, "I'd like to propose some ground rules for today's dinner. Anyone who mentions the Big Snow has to wash the dishes."

"What are we allowed to discuss?"

"For starters, Hixie Rice. How is she?"

"She came to the office once this week," Riker said. "Qwill drove her, and Wilfred met her at the curb with her desk chair and wheeled her into the building. She clomps around with a walker and something called a surgical boot."

"How is her substitute working out for the show, Qwill?"

"Not bad," he replied with an offhand shrug, careful not to praise too highly the petite young woman with soulful eyes.

Mildred said, "Your show has prompted a family history program in the schools. Kids are interviewing their grandparents and great-grandparents about the Depression, World War II, and Vietnam."

"Oh sure, we're sharpening their interest in history," Qwilleran said sourly as he drew a sheaf of papers from his sweater pocket. "At Black Creek School they had to write capsule reviews of the show. Would you like to hear a few of them?"

Riker said, "They'd be easier to take if I had a Scotch in my hand."

Drinks were poured, and then Qwilleran read the comments from sixth graders: "I liked the show because we got out of class . . . I liked the red light best . . . It was interesting but not so interesting that it was boring . . . My favorite part was where the guy got his arm burned off . . . It was better than sitting in English and learning . . . The man did most of the play. The woman should have more to do and not just sit there and push buttons."

"That's the spirit!" Mildred said.

He saved the rave review for the last: "It's neat how you came up with all that stuff. I would never know how to look it all up. Don't change it at all, no matter what. I'd like to see it go all over."

Riker said, "Sign that kid up! We could use a good drama critic."

Qwilleran omitted mentioning the spitball that sailed past his ear during the performance at Black Creek.

Polly carved the bird, pacifying Bootsie with some giblets, and the four sat down to the traditional feast. "Beautiful bird!" they all agreed. In deference to Mildred the bird was never identified; there had been a star-crossed turkey farmer in her painful past.

"Now let's discuss the wedding," Polly suggested. "What are the plans so far?"

The bride-to-be said, "It'll be at the Lanspeaks' house on Purple Point, and we're all invited to stay for the three-day weekend."

Riker said, "It's black tie, Qwill, so dust off your tux."

"Black tie!" Qwilleran echoed in dismay.

"Didn't you buy a formal outfit for that weekend in Lockmaster?"

"Yes, but I never had a chance to wear it, and do you know where it is now? My dinner jacket, cummerbund, expensive shirt, three-hundred-dollar evening pumps—they're all in a closet in my barn, behind twenty feet of snow, at the end of a half mile of unplowed driveway."

"You can rent an outfit," Riker said calmly, "but what will you do about your cats? I believe they're not invited."

Polly said, "My sister-in-law will come over twice a day to feed Koko and Yum Yum as well as Bootsie."

Everyone had seconds of the bird and the squash puree with cashews. Then the aromatic mince pie was consumed and praised, and coffee was poured, during which the telephone rang.

Polly answered and said, "It's for you, Qwill."

"Who knows I'm here?" he wondered aloud.

It was Hixie. "I hate to bother you, Qwill. Are you in the middle of dinner?"

"That's all right. We've finished."

"Carol Lanspeak just called. We have a problem."

"What kind of problem?"

"Larry was scheduled to play Santa in the parade on Saturday, and he's on the verge of pneumonia," Hixie said anxiously. "Carol and I wondered if you would substitute."

"You're not serious."

"I'm not only serious, I'm desperate! When Carol gave me the news, my foot started to throb again."

Scowling and huffing into his moustache, Qwilleran was alarmingly silent.

"Qwill, have you fainted? I know it's not your choice of role, but—"

"What would it entail?" he asked in a grouchy monotone.

"First of all, you'll have to try on Larry's Santa suit. It's in the costume department at the theatre."

"I suppose you know," he reminded her, "that Larry is three sizes smaller and three inches shorter than I am."

"But Carol says the suit is cut roomy—to accommodate the padding, you know—and Wally's mother could alter the length of sleeves and pants. We don't need to worry about the beard and wig; one size fits all."

"And what happens on Saturday?"

"You get into costume at the theatre, and Carol drives you to the Dimsdale Diner, where the parade units will assemble. The parade proceeds south on Pickax Road to Main Street, where the mayor gives you the official greeting."

"And what am I supposed to be doing?"

"Just wave at people and act jolly."

"I won't feel jolly," he grumbled, "but I'll try to make an adjustment . . . I'm doing this only for your foot, Hixie . . . *ma chérie,*" he added tartly.

When Qwilleran returned to the dinner table, the others regarded him with concern.

"I need another piece of pie," he said.

Later, when he returned from Polly's apartment with a generous serving of the bird, he was met by two excited Siamese.

"Ho ho ho!" he boomed with simulated jollity. They fled from the room.

"I beg your royal pardons," he apologized. "I was practicing. Would you entertain the concept of turkey for dinner?"

While they devoured the plateful of light meat and dark meat with studious concentration and enraptured tails, he collected the loot under the kitchen table: an inner sole, a silver toothpick in a leather sheath, a tortoiseshell napkin ring, and . . . the jeweler's box that they had pilfered from the desk drawer.

"You rascals!" he scolded affectionately. "Where did you have it hidden?"

In the library he examined the ring once more. It was now clear that the initials entwined on the crown were W and E. There was also an intimate inscription inside the band, with the initials ERG and WBK. Then Koko leaped to the desktop and showed unusual interest in the gold memento, touching it gingerly as if it might bite. Qwilleran tamped his moustache as he questioned the cat's reaction. Was he simply attracted to a small shiny object? Or did he detect hidden significance in the ring? If the latter, it would be something more topical than the illicit affair in Lockmaster, circa 1929. But what? Koko could sense more with his whiskers than most humans could construe with their brains. Unfortunately, he had an oblique way of communicating, and Qwilleran was not always smart enough to read him.

Ring . . . gold ring . . . horse farmer . . . E and W . . . wasn't ERG a unit of energy? It seemed nonsensical, and in years gone by Qwilleran would have scoffed at such speculation, but life with Kao K'o Kung had taught him to pay attention, even though he sometimes felt like a fool.

Fifteen

The day after Thanksgiving Qwilleran was still pondering the significance of the signet ring when he went downtown to the newspaper to hand in his copy. Before leaving the house he took a roll call, as he always did. Yum Yum with graceful tail was rubbing against his ankles, and he picked her up to whisper comforting sentiments in her twitching ear. Koko was in the library closet, sitting tall and solemn in the open safe like some mythic oracle with all the answers.

Qwilleran started out to walk downtown, but the footing was precarious; the daily snowfall was packing down and turning sidewalks into minor glaciers. He drove to the newspaper office.

Junior greeted him in high spirit. "Hixie tells me you're going to be our Santa Claus! You'll be terrific! And you'll have a good time!"

"I don't know about that, but I'll give it my best shot," he replied as he handed Junior the jeweler's box.

"My grandfather's ring!"

"Guess again! Look inside the band."

"Wow!" said Junior when he read the inscription. "So WBK is the horse farmer who wanted to jump off the silo!"

"It would be interesting to know if Euphonia's recent boyfriend in Florida spells his name with a K. I thought it was C-r-o-c-u-s. I'll have to check it out."

"I haven't told you the latest," said Junior. "In probating Grandma's estate we're having trouble finding enough assets to warrant contesting the will. The bank records show huge cash deposits at the time she liquidated everything. After that there were sizable withdrawals, as if she'd invested in securities, although she didn't play the stock market. She liked something safe. But we don't find any financial documents."

"Some old people are afraid of banks," Qwilleran said. "She may have hidden them. They may be in the library closet."

"Naw, she told me to burn everything in that closet."

"Or . . . you may not be aware of this, Junior, but Gil Inchpot spent heavily on farm improvements in the last two or three years, and no one knows where he got the money. Did Euphonia lend it to him on the strength of her affection for Lena?"

"Hey! That makes sense!" said Junior. "Some time back, Inchpot called me here at the office, asking for her address in Florida. He owed her some money and wanted to repay the loan."

"You gave him her address?"

"Sure. But if he paid her, what the devil happened to the dough! She couldn't have lost it all at the race track! Or could she?"

"When she decided to bequeath a health spa to the park, Junior, didn't she know her fortune was dwindling? Or did that happen after she wrote her new will?"

"Well, I don't know, but Wilmot hasn't given up yet. He has more possibilities to explore, but it takes time."

Qwilleran smoothed his moustache. "More and more I think the operation Down Below is shady—if not downright crepuscular. How about the lawyer who writes cheap wills? He could be in on it. How about the dealer who liquidated Euphonia's treasures? Does anyone know who he is or what he paid for the stuff? He could have robbed her blind!"

"Wow!" said Junior. "Maybe I should put a bug in Wilmot's ear."

"Not yet. Wait until I have more evidence." Qwilleran started to leave. "It just might be a well-organized crime ring!"

"Don't go, Qwill. This is getting good!"

"I have an appointment to try on my Santa Claus suit. We'll talk later."

En route to the theatre Qwilleran realized that his attitude toward the Christmas parade was mellowing. He could visualize himself riding in a sleigh behind a horse decked out in jingle bells. Sleighs were often seen on the unsalted streets of Pickax. The experience might make a good topic for his column.

At the K Theatre Carol Lanspeak and the seamstress were waiting for him, and Carol said, "We really appreciate your cooperation in the emergency, Qwill. Larry says he'll treat you to dinner at the Palomino Paddock, if he lives. Try on the pants first."

Qwilleran squeezed into the red breeches. "They're a good length for clam digging," he said.

Mrs. Toddwhistle, who worked on costumes for the Theatre Club, said, "I have some red fabric, and I can add about six inches to the length—also a stirrup to keep them down in your boots."

Carol looked critically at his yellow duck boots. "You should have black. What size do you wear? I'll bring a pair from the store."

The coat was roomy enough for two bed pillows under the belt, although snug through the shoulders and under the arms. The sleeves could be lengthened by adding more fake fur to the cuffs, the women assured him. They seemed to know what they were talking about . . . Everything would work out just fine! . . . No problem! . . . He would make a wonderful Santa!

With that matter settled he applied his attention to the situation in Florida and telephoned Celia Robinson without waiting for the discount rate. "Did you enjoy Thanksgiving, Celia?" he began.

"Oh, yes, it was very nice. About thirty of us went in the bus to a real nice restaurant. We had a reservation. It was buffet."

"Did Mr. Crocus go with you?"

"No, he didn't feel like it. He remembers last Thanksgiving when Mrs. Gage was with us and read a poem. She wrote it herself."

"I promised to send him a book of hers but got sidetracked because of the Big Snow. How does he spell his name?"

"I think it's C-r-o-c-u-s, like the flower."

"Are you sure? It could be K-r-o-k-u-s, you know. What's his first name?"

"Gerard. He has a shirt with GFC embroidered on the pocket. Mrs. Gage gave it to him, and he wears it all the time."

"Hmmm," Qwilleran murmured. Reluctantly he abandoned the long-lost-lover theory. Mr. Crocus was not WBK. "Did you ask him if he'd speak with me about Mrs. Gage?"

"Yes, I did, Mr. Qwilleran, but he said it wouldn't be in good taste to talk to the media about a dear departed friend. I don't feel that way. I'd like to see you write a beautiful article about her, and if there's anything more I can do—"

"You've been a great help, Celia, and—yes, there is more you can do. I believe I've uncovered something in the Park of Pink Sunsets that's a bigger story than Euphonia Gage."

"You don't mean it!" she said excitedly. "Is it something nice?"

Qwilleran cleared his throat and planned his approach before replying. "No, it isn't *nice,* as you say. I believe there's activity in your community that is highly unethical, if not illegal."

With sudden sharpness she said, "You reporters are always trying to dig up dirt and make trouble! This is a lovely place for retirees like me. Don't call me any more. I don't want to talk to you. You told me you were writing a nice article about Mrs. Gage! I don't want anything more to do with you!" And she slammed the receiver.

"Well! How do you like that?" Qwilleran asked the bookshelves.

"Yow!" said Koko from his reserved seat in the safe.

"Did I strike a raw nerve? Celia may be part of the ring—a simple, fun-loving grandmother, mixing with the other residents and singling out the likely victims. Now that she knows we suspect their game, what will she do?"

He thought of phoning Junior. He thought of by-passing Junior and calling Wilmot. Then he decided to wait and see.

The day of the parade was sunny but crisp, and Qwilleran wore his long underwear for the ride in an open sleigh. He assumed it would be a sleigh and not a convertible with the top down.

At the theatre, where he went to get into costume, he found the breeches lengthened and equipped with stirrups, which made them rather taut for comfort, but Carol said he would get used to the feeling. She strapped him into his two bed pillows and helped him into his coat. The sleeves had been extended with white fake fur from elbow to wrist.

"I look as if I had both arms in a cast," he complained. Trussed into the stuffed coat and taut breeches, he found it difficult to bend over. Carol had to pull on his boots.

"How is the fit?" she asked. "They run large to allow for thick socks."

"I feel as if I'm wearing snowshoes." He was hardly in a jolly mood. "Is this belly supposed to shake like a bowlful of jelly? It feels like a sack of cold oatmeal. Has Larry ever worn this getup?"

"Many times! At church and at the community Christmas party. He loves playing Santa!"

"Why does the old geezer have to look seventy-five pounds overweight? Even as a kid I doubted that he could come down a chimney. Now I question why the heart specialists don't get after him. Why aren't the health clubs coming forward?"

"Would you ruin a thousand-year-old image, Qwill? Come off your soapbox. It's all in fun." Carol powdered his moustache, reddened his cheeks, and adjusted the wig and beard before adding a red hat with a floppy pointed crown.

"I feel like an idiot!" he said. "I hope Polly won't be watching the parade from an upstairs window of the library."

They drove north in the Lanspeak van along Pickax Road, the sun glaring on the snowy roadbed and snowy landscape. Qwilleran had left his sunglasses at the theatre, and the scene was dazzling. Already the parade route was filling up with cars, vans, and pickups loaded with children.

"This is all very exciting," Carol said. "Pickax has never had a Christmas parade before. The welcoming ceremonies will be in front of the store, and when you arrive, Hixie's secretary will meet you and tell you what to do."

"Speaking of stores," Qwilleran said, "could you suggest a Christmas present for Polly? Jewelry, perhaps. She likes pearls, but she says she doesn't need any more."

"How about opals? I think she'd like opals, and there's a jeweler in Minneapolis who'll send some out on approval."

They were approaching the Dimsdale Diner, where vast open fields were covered with glaring snow. "It's incredibly bright today," he said, feeling as if his eyeballs were spinning.

"Yes, a perfect day for a parade," said Carol, who was wearing sunglasses.

"What kind of conveyance do you have for jolly old St. Nick with two arms in a cast?" he asked.

"Oh, didn't Hixie tell you?" she said, eager to break the news. "We've arranged for a dogsled with eight Siberian huskies!"

Parade units were gathering around the snowy intersection: floats, a brass band on a flatbed truck, a giant snowplow, a fire truck, a group of cross-country skiers, and a yelping dogteam.

"We meet unexpectedly," Qwilleran said to Nancy. He assumed it was Nancy; the glare was distorting his vision.

"No one told me you were going to be Santa," she said with delight. "I thought it was going to be Mr. Lanspeak. There's a bale of hay in the basket for you to sit on, and I covered it with a caribou skin. I think it'll work. We won't be going very fast. Where are your sunglasses?"

"I left them in town," Qwilleran said. "Santa with shades seemed inappropriate."

"Isn't this exciting? I've never been in a parade. I wish my mom could see me now—driving Santa Claus in a dogsled! She died before I even started dog-sledding. Today would have been her birthday . . . It looks as if they're getting ready to start."

The band struck up, the sheriff's car led the way, and the parade units fell into place, with the dogsled bringing up the rear—Nancy riding the runners, Qwilleran in the basket. She drove the team with one-syllable commands: "Up! . . . Go! . . . Way!"

All along the route the spectators were shouting to Santa, and Qwilleran waved first one arm and then the other at persons he could not clearly see. Both arms were becoming gradually numb as the tight armholes hampered his circulation. When they turned onto Main Street the crowds were larger and louder but just as blurred, and he was greatly relieved when they reached their destination.

Lanspeak's Department Store was built like a castle. An iron gate raised on heavy chains extended over the sidewalk, providing a marquee from which city officials could review the parade.

As the dogsled pulled up to the store, Nancy leaned over and said to Qwilleran, "I'll take the dogs behind the store until you've finished your speech."

"Speech! What speech?" he demanded indignantly.

"Mr. Qwilleran, sir," said a young man's voice coming out of the general blur.

"Wilfred? Get me out of this contraption! I can't see a thing!"

"They're waiting for you up there," said the secretary. "I'll hold the ladder."

Only then did Qwilleran become aware of a ladder leaning against the front edge of the marquee. "I can't bend my knees; my arms are numb; and I can't see! I'm not climbing up any damned ladder!"

"You've got to," said Wilfred in panic.

Hundreds of spectators were cheering, and the officials were looking over the edge of the marquee and shouting, "Come on up, Santa!" Qwilleran walked to the foot of the ladder with a stiff-legged gait, his knees splinted by the taut breeches. He looked up speculatively to the summit. "If I fall off this thing," he said threateningly to the nervous secretary, "both you and Hixie are fired!"

He managed to lift one foot to the first rung and grasp the siderails. Cheers! Then slowly he forced one knee after the other to bend, all the while maneuvering the long-toed boots and hoisting the two bed pillows ahead of him. More cheers! There was an occasional ripping sound—where, he was not sure—but the more the rips, the easier the climb. And the louder were the cheers. Gradually he felt his way to the top of the ladder, where helping hands reached out and hauled him onto the marquee.

There was a microphone, and the mayor said a few words of welcome, his speech slurred by the fortifying nips he had taken to keep warm. "And now . . . I give you . . . Santa Claus . . . in person!" he concluded.

Qwilleran was steered to the mike. "M-er-r-ry Christmas!" he bellowed. Then he turned away and said in a voice that went out over the speakers, "Get me outa here! How do I get down? I'm not going back down that stupid ladder!"

There were more cheers from the spectators.

The store had a second-floor window through which the city officials had arrived, and Qwilleran climbed through it. Wilfred was waiting for him in the second-floor lingerie department. He said, "The dogs are being brought around to the front door."

"To hell with the dogs! I'm through! Find someone to drive me back to the theatre!"

"But they're expecting you at the courthouse, Mr. Qwilleran."

"What for?"

"Lap-sitting."

"Lap-sitting? What the devil is that?"

"They built a gingerbread house for you in front of the courthouse, and the kids sit on your lap and have their pictures taken."

"Oh, no, they don't!" Qwilleran said fiercely. "I refuse flatly! Enough is enough!"

"Mr. Qwilleran, sir, you gotta!"

They rode down on the elevator, and even before they landed on the main floor they heard a voice on the public address system: "Paging Santa Claus! Paging Santa Claus!"

"Where's a phone?" he snapped . . . "Yes?" he yelled into the mouthpiece.

"Hey, Qwill! How did it go?" It was Junior's enthusiastic voice.

"Don't ask!"

"The city desk just had a strange phone call, Qwill: Celia Robinson in Florida, calling from a pay phone in a mall. She said she had to get in touch with you secretly. What's that all about? We never give out home phones, but she's calling back this afternoon to find out how to reach you. Extremely important, she says."

"Give her Polly's number," Qwilleran said, his voice calm for the first time in two hours. "Tell her to call around eight o'clock tonight."

"Whatever you say. Are you all through with your Santa stunt?"

"No," Qwilleran said in a matter-of-fact way. "I have to go to the courthouse for lap-sitting."

Sixteen

It was customary for Qwilleran and Polly to spend Saturday evening together, and this time the chief attraction was turkey leftovers, which she had prepared in a curry sauce with mushrooms, leeks and lentils. They could now call the bird a turkey.

"Do you think Mildred is still sensitive about her late husband?" Polly asked. "I hope not. She and Arch are very right for each other, and they should get on with their new life . . . Tell me about the parade, dear."

"I don't want to talk about it," he said in an even voice.

She knew better than to insist.

He said, "I'm expecting a phone call around eight o'clock, and I'd like to take it privately, if you don't mind."

"Of course I don't mind," she replied, although her lips tightened. He had not even told her who would be calling.

Exactly at eight o'clock the telephone rang, and he took the call in the bedroom with the door closed. Polly started the dishwasher.

The anguished voice of Celia Robinson blurted, "Oh, Mr. Qwilleran, I apologize for hanging up on you like that! What horrible things did you think of me? I didn't mean a word of what I said, but I was afraid somebody would be listening in. I'm making this call from a phone in a mall."

"Are you on a switchboard at the park? I thought the residents had private numbers."

"We do! We do! But Clayton thinks the whole park is bugged. I always thought he was kidding, but when you mentioned something illegal, I got worried. I thought it might be dangerous to talk to you. Is it true what you said? Are you an investigator?"

Experience warned him that she might be part of the ring, luring him to show his hand. Yet, a tremor in the roots of his moustache told him to risk the gamble. He had formulated a plan. He said, "I'm just a reporter with a suspicion that Junior's grandmother was a victim of fraud."

"Oh, dear! Are you going to expose it?"

"There's insufficient evidence at present, and that's where you can help. You thought highly of Mrs. Gage; are you willing to play a harmless trick on those who robbed her? I believe your grandson would approve."

"Can I tell Clayton about it? I write him every week."

"You're not to confide in him or Mr. Crocus or anyone else. Consider yourself an undercover agent. You'll be rewarded for your time and cooperation, of course. In Pickax we have an eleemosynary foundation that's committed to the pursuit of justice."

"I never heard of one of those," she said, "but I'm honored that you'd ask me to help. Do you think I can do it?"

"No doubt about it, provided you follow orders."

"What if it doesn't work? What if I get caught?"

Qwilleran said, "Whether it succeeds or fails, no one will suspect you of duplicity, and you'll be kept in chocolate-covered cherries for life."

Celia howled with delight. "What do I do first?"

"You'll receive your briefing along with a check to cover expenses. Where do you receive your mail?"

"It comes to the park office, and we pick it up there. It's a good excuse to go for a walk and chat with our neighbors. Sometimes we pick up each other's mail."

"That being the case," he said, "I'll send your orders to the post office in care of general delivery."

"Oh, goody!" Celia said as the elements of intrigue dawned upon her. "Is this a sting?"

"You might call it that. Now go home and say nothing. I'll put the wheels in motion, and you should receive your assignment in two days, unless we have another Big Snow."

"Thank you, Mr. Qwilleran! This gives me a real boot!"

He emerged from the bedroom patting his moustache with satisfaction. He even said a kind word to Bootsie, who was sitting outside the door, and he was very good company for the rest of the evening.

The next day, as he worked on Celia's briefing, he thought, This may be the dumbest thing I ever did in my life—sending $5,000 to a stranger who may be a double agent. And yet . . .

The document that went into the mail read as follows:

FOR YOUR EYES ONLY! Memorize, shred, and flush.

TO: Agent 0013½

FROM: Q

MISSION: Operation Greenback, Phase One

ASSIGNMENT: Your unmarried sister in Chicago has died, leaving you sole heir to a large house, valuable possessions, and financial assets. You wish to share your new fortune with your neighbors by giving a Christmas party in the clubhouse on December 11 or 12. Notify the management that you will spend as much as $5,000 on a caterer, florist, and live music. (A check for this amount, drawn on a Chicago bank, will arrive under separate cover.) Observe the management's reaction to the above and report to Q. Watch for further briefings in the mail.

Qwilleran had planned the tongue-in-cheek approach to relieve any apprehension Celia might have, and he could imagine her merry laughter upon reading the document. And if, he reflected grimly, she happened to be a double agent, her laughter would be even merrier. He still trusted the encouraging sensation on his upper lip, however, and he prepared a second secret document to go out in the mail the next day:

MISSION: Operation Greenback, Phase Two

ASSIGNMENT: Ask the management about the possibility of moving into a double-wide . . . Test them by saying that your sister wished you to adopt her cat, who has a trust fund of his own of $10,000 a year. Ask for a special permit to have an indoor cat who is quiet, and not destructive, and rich. Observe their reactions to the above and report to Q at HQ.

Qwilleran enclosed a card with his home phone number and instructions to call collect from a pay phone any evening between five and six o'clock. Then he waited. He wrote two columns for the *Moose County Something*. He signed a hundred Christmas cards for Lori Bamba to address. He looked at jewelry from Minneapolis and selected a lavaliere and earrings for Polly: fiery black opals rimmed with discreet diamonds. He read more of *Robinson Crusoe* to the cats.

One early evening, as he was beginning to doubt the wisdom of enlisting Celia, he was talking with Lori Bamba on the phone when Koko started biting the cord. "Excuse me, Lori," he said. "Koko wants me to hang up."

A moment later the phone rang, and a hushed voice said, "This is Double-Oh-Thirteen-and-a-half. Is it all right to talk?" Background noises assured him she was calling from the mall.

"By all means. I've been waiting for your report."

"Well! Let me tell you!" she said in her normal voice. "I've been having a ball! Everybody's excited about the party, and Betty and Claude are falling all over me! They used to treat me like a clown; now I get respect! They're giving me a special permit for the cat, and they're putting me at the top of the list for a double-wide!"

"You're a good operative, Celia."

"Shall I go ahead and get a cat?"

"Wait a minute! Not so fast! In the interest of realism, the cat should be shipped from Chicago."

"Clayton could bring it when he flies down for Christmas. I'd like a Burmese, but they're expensive. Maybe he could find one at an animal shelter."

Qwilleran said, "Cost is not the issue here, but let's not get ahead of the game. Wait for orders."

"I'm sorry. I'm just so excited! I feel as if I've really inherited my sister's fortune, and I don't even have a sister! What do I do next?"

"Keep checking the post office, and call whenever you have something to report."

"Isn't this *fun?*" she was squealing as he said goodnight.

Qwilleran had already plotted his next move. The following day he walked downtown to the store that had gold lettering on the window: EXBRIDGE & COBB, FINE ANTIQUES.

Susan Exbridge greeted him effusively. "Darling! You survived the Big Snow! Did you enjoy being snowbound?"

"It wasn't what John Greenleaf Whittier had led me to expect. The lucky bunch in his poem sat around a blazing fire, roasting apples and telling stories. I was alone with a kerosene stove and two cats, and all of us were bored stiff. How about you?"

"The people in my building in Indian Village played bridge for five days."

Wandering through the shop, Qwilleran lingered over a pair of brass candlesticks a foot high, with thick, twisted stems and chunky bases the size of a soup bowl. "I like candlesticks," he remarked.

"Most men do, and I refuse to guess why," she said. "These are Dutch baroque, but I found them in Stockholm."

"I'll take them," he said. "Do you know how or where Euphonia sold her belongings?"

"I know how . . . but not exactly where," said Susan. "I wanted her to work with some good dealers in New York and Philadelphia, but someone in Florida offered her a lump sum for everything, and she fell for it. People get lazy about liquidating and want to do it the easy way."

"How much did they offer? Do you know?"

"I have no idea, but we can assume that it was well under the going price."

He paid for his purchase and asked to borrow some magazines on antiques.

On the way home he stopped at the Bushland Studio. John Bushland had transferred his commercial photography studio from Lockmaster to Pickax, and Qwilleran asked if he had any interior photos of his previous house in Lockmaster.

"I've got a complete set. Want to see 'em?"

Qwilleran had visited the photographer's century-old house and remembered the foyer with its carved staircase, stained-glass windows, and converted gaslight fixtures. "I could use a copy of this shot," he said. "Also a close-up of the marble fireplace in the front parlor and the one with painted tiles in the dining room. Don't ask me why I want them, Bushy; it's too complicated. I need them, that's all."

"Sure," said the genial young man. "How quick?"

"A.S.A.P."

"Then take these prints. I'll make more for the file."

The magazines that Qwilleran carried home contained dealer ads for choice antiques at five-digit and six-digit prices that shocked his frugal psyche. Nevertheless, he made a list of items that would fit his scheme: Jacobean chair . . . carved and gilded divan from India . . . four-poster brass bed in Gothic style . . . spiral staircase from Irish country house . . . collection of botanical plates in porcelain, eighteenth century . . . Empire desk in mahogany and ormolu . . . and more. He omitted any reference to price.

He photocopied the list at the public library. One copy would go to Susan Exbridge for appraisal; the other, to Celia Robinson with another briefing:

> MISSION: Operation Greenback, Phase Three
> ASSIGNMENT: Your late sister was a collector of antiques and art objects, none of which you understand or even like. There are twelve rooms of such furnishings that you wish to sell with as little effort as possible. Ask the park management if they know how to go about it. Show them the enclosed list as a sampling of the items involved. Mention also that you must sell your sister's house. Show them the enclosed photos of the interior. Report their responses as usual.

December in Pickax was a month of crowded stores, sparkling decorations, holiday parties, school pageants, and carol singing, with a picturesque snowfall every day. In the "Qwill Pen" column the veteran newsman strove to write about these perennial subjects with a fresh approach, although his mind was on Operation Greenback. He was relieved when his agent made her second report:

"Oh, it was a wonderful party, Mr. Qwilleran! Everybody had a terrific time," she began. "All the Sunsetters congratulated me on my inheritance."

"Did Mr. Crocus attend?"

"Well, I had to coax him, but afterwards he said he had a good time. I don't know whether he meant it. He always says the polite thing."

"What do you know about his background?"

"Only that he was in some kind of wholesale business in Ohio. No one in his family ever visits him. Maybe that's why he enjoys Clayton's company. They play chess together."

Qwilleran asked, "And how did the management react to your questions?"

"They were very helpful. They have experience and a lot of connections, they said. They're going to show my list of furniture to a dealer, and he'll make an offer on the whole houseful."

"Did you show them the photographs of the house?"

"Yes, they were quite impressed and said there were things that should be removed before vandals get them. They know somebody who does that. He would pay for them, of course. And guess what! Betty and Claude invited me to the dog races! It looks as if I'm in solid! Things were going so good that I did something on my own. I hope I did right."

"What did you do?" Qwilleran asked sternly.

"I asked if my grandson could come for a whole week during the holidays, even though he's only thirteen. They said okay, but no singing dogs."

"I suppose you realize, Celia, that we're flirting with a security hazard. Clayton will want to know why the management is buttering you up and why the Sunsetters are raving about the big Christmas party you gave. You'll have to tell him the truth."

"He can be trusted, Mr. Qwilleran. He won't give me away. He'll be glad to see me putting one over on Betty and Claude."

"Hmmm . . . Let me think about this," Qwilleran said, cupping his moustache with his hand. "You say he plays chess with Mr. Crocus. Perhaps he could get the old gentleman to unburden himself about things that are troubling him. Is Clayton smart enough, mature enough, to handle this? Mr. Crocus knew about Mrs. Gage's bequest to the park; he might know other things that would shed light on the matter we're investigating."

"I'm sure Clayton could do it, Mr. Qwilleran. He's a very bright boy and much more on the ball than I am. He reads a lot, you know. Yes, I'm positive he could handle it. He's thirteen now."

"All right. It's worth a try," Qwilleran said. "Also, have Clayton bring a cat with him—full-grown, because this is supposed to be your sister's cherished pet. You'll receive a check from the Chicago bank to cover the purchase of the cat, air transportation, catfood, and a few holiday treats for you and Clayton."

"That's very nice of you," Celia said. "Now Clayton can have one of those five-dollar sundaes. Is there anything else I can do?"

"You should decide on a name for the cat and arrange to feed him or her in the manner to which a $10,000-a-year animal is accustomed."

"I've been thinking about a name. We don't know whether it will be a boy or a girl, but either way I think Windy would be a good name, since it's supposed to be from Chicago."

"Do you have a second choice?" Qwilleran asked. "Windy has other connotations when applied to an animal."

After discussing this weighty subject at length, they decided to call the cat Wrigley. Celia enjoyed a few laughs, and Qwilleran was in a good mood when he hung up.

The occasion seemed to call for a dish of ice cream, and while in the kitchen he picked up Koko's current collection: a petrified stick of chewing gum, a mildewed toothbrush, a card of tiny safety pins, and other items of more than usual interest to Qwilleran. One was a purple satin pincushion embroidered ERG and obviously homemade, possibly by a child. There was a business card from Breze Services on Sandpit Road, the nine-digit zip code indicating that it was of fairly recent date. A canceled check for $100—dated December 24, 1972—had been paid to Lena Inchpot; was that the housekeeper's Christmas bonus from Mrs. Gage, or a salary check? An unpaid traffic ticket issued by the sheriff department had been issued by D. Fincher.

Of greatest interest was a yellowed envelope inscribed "Lethe" in what Qwilleran now knew to be Euphonia's handwriting, which had an exaggerated up-stroke at the end of each word. It was another poem, he assumed, Lethe being the mythical river in Hades, said to induce forgetfulness. Forgetting and not forgetting had been much on Euphonia's mind, he thought. The envelope was sealed, and he used a kitchen knife to slit it. What he found was no poem, but an official paper, a birth certificate issued in Lockmaster County:

Date of birth: Nov. 27, 1928
Name of child: Lethe Gage
Sex: female *Color:* white
Name of mother: Euphonia Roff Gage
Name of father:

Qwilleran rushed to the telephone. "Brace yourself for some news, Junior!" he said when his young friend answered. "You've got an aunt you didn't know about!"

Junior listened to the reading of the certificate. "Can you beat that! That's when Grandpa was in prison! The father must have been the horse farmer."

"Here's the question," said Qwilleran. "Is Lethe still alive? Or is she the 'dead princess' in Euphonia's memorial program? If she's still around, wouldn't she have come forward for a slice of the inheritance?"

"She might be living somewhere else. She might not know Grandma's dead."

"Could be." Qwilleran thought of the foreign postcards and envelopes with foreign stamps that Koko had dragged out of the closet. "In any case, you should notify the attorney."

Seventeen

As Christmas approached, Qwilleran accepted invitations to holiday parties, but his mind was on Operation Greenback, and he made it a point to be home between five and six o'clock, the hour when Celia might call with another report. Increasing tremors in the roots of his moustache told him he was on the right track.

One evening at five-fifteen the telephone rang, and a hollow voice said, "This is Celia, Mr. Qwilleran."

"You sound different," he said.

"I'm calling from a different mall on the other side of town, and the phones are more private. I had a scare the last time I talked to you."

"What kind of scare?"

"Well, after I hung up, I saw Betty and Claude watching me. They were waiting in line outside a restaurant. I didn't know what to do. Should I make up some kind of explanation? Then I thought, What would Clayton do? He'd play it cool. So I walked over to them and said hello, and they invited me to have dinner with them, but I'd eaten already. Whew! I was worried for a while."

"You handled it very well," Qwilleran said. "Do you have anything to report on your last assignment?"

"Only that the furniture dealer down here will give me $100,000 for the things on the list you sent me, plus $50,000 for everything else in the house. Boy! What I could do with that much money! I'm beginning to wish I'd had a rich sister."

Qwilleran made no comment. The same list of antique furnishings had been appraised by Susan Exbridge at $900,000. He said, "Good job, Celia! That's the kind of information we need."

"Thank you, chief. Do you have another assignment for me?"

"Phase Four of Operation Greenback will be mailed tomorrow."

In mailing the briefing he included a Christmas bonus with instructions to buy something exciting for herself.

MISSION: Operation Greenback, Phase Four
ASSIGNMENT: Buy an expensive Christmas plant for the manager's office . . . Tell them you'll have a surplus of cash when you sell your sister's possessions; ask if they can recommend a safe investment . . . Inquire if it's possible to place bets on the dog races without going to the track, since you don't like crowds.

Although Qwilleran made generous Christmas gifts and ate more than his share of Christmas cookies, there was not a shred of holiday decoration in his cavernous, sparsely furnished living quarters.

"How can you stand this gloomy place?" Polly asked him.

One evening, on her way home from the library, she delivered a green wreath studded with holly berries and tiny white lights. "For your library," she said. "Just hang it up and plug it in."

The pinpoints of light only emphasized the somber effect of dark paneling, old books, and worn furniture, as they sat on the sofa sipping hot cider. The Siamese, sniffing Bootsie in absentia, applied wet noses to Polly's person, here and there.

"Out!" Qwilleran scolded, pointing to the door.

"They don't bother me," Polly protested.

"I expect them to have some manners to match their aristocratic facade . . . *Out!*"

They left the room but not immediately. First they thought about it, then scratched an ear and licked a paw, then thought about it some more, then sauntered out.

"Cats!" Qwilleran said, and Polly smiled with amusement.

They discussed cat-sitting arrangements for the Christmas weekend. Polly wanted to pick up a key for her sister-in-law. "Lynette lives only a block away, so she's happy to come twice a day. She loves cats and considers it a privilege."

Soon Koko returned, carrying in his jaws a small square paper packet, which he dropped at Qwilleran's feet.

Picking it up, Qwilleran read the label: "Dissolve contents of envelope in three pints of water and soak feet for fifteen minutes . . . Foot powder! Where did he find that?"

Polly, ordinarily given to small smiles, was overcome with mirth. "Perhaps he's telling you something, dear."

"This isn't funny! It could be poisonous! He could tear the paper and sprinkle the powder on the floor, then walk in it and lick his paws!" He dropped the packet in a desk drawer.

After Polly had gone on her way, Qwilleran had another look at the foot powder and read the precaution: "Poisonous if ingested. Keep away from children and pets." At the same time he realized how many of Koko's discoveries were associated with feet: corn plasters, a man's sock, a woman's slipper, shoelaces, toenail clippers, an inner sole, a buttonhook, a shoe-polishing cloth—even a man's spat! Either the cat had a foot fetish or he was trying to communicate. As for his occupation with Confederate currency, canceled checks, and the *safe,* was that related to the financial skulduggery that was becoming evident?

Qwilleran pounded his moustache as a sensation on his upper lip alerted him. He glanced at his watch. It was not too late to phone Homer Tibbitt. The nonagenarian lived in a retirement complex with his new wife, who was a mere octogenarian, and they were known to observe an early bedtime.

"Homer, this is Qwill," he said in a loud, clear voice. "I haven't seen you in the library lately. Aren't you doing any historical research?"

"Hell's bells!" the historian retorted. "She won't let me out of the house in winter! She hides my overshoes!" His voice was high and cracked, but his delivery was vigorous. "Never marry a younger woman, boy! If I drop a pencil, she thinks I've had a stroke. If I drop a shoe, she thinks I've broken a hip. She's driving me crazy! . . . What's on your mind?"

"Just this, Homer: You were in the Lockmaster school system for many years, and I wonder if you knew a family by the name of Foote."

"There are quite a few Footes in Lockmaster . . . or should I say Feete?" Homer added with a chuckle. "None of them left any footprints in the sands of time."

"You're in an arch mood tonight," Qwilleran said with a chuckle of his own. "The Foote I'm curious about is Lena Foote, who should have been a student between 1934 and 1946."

"Lena Foote, you say?" said the former principal. "She must have been a good girl. The only ones I remember are the troublemakers."

Another voice sounded in the background, and Homer turned away to say to his wife, "You don't remember that far back! You can't remember where you left your glasses ten minutes ago!" This was followed by muffled arguing and then, "Do you want to talk to him yourself? Here! Take the phone."

A woman who sounded pleasantly determined came on the line. "This is Rhoda Tibbitt, Mr. Qwilleran. I remember Lena Foote very well. I had her in high school English, and she showed unusual promise. Sad to say, she didn't finish."

"Do you know anything about her parents? Her father was Arnold Foote."

"Yes, indeed! I begged her parents to let her get her diploma, but they were poor farmers and needed the income. She went into domestic service at the age of fifteen, and that's the last I knew. Do you happen to know what happened to her?"

"Only that she died of cancer a few years ago, after a relatively short life as a farmwife, mother, and employed housekeeper," Qwilleran said. "Thank you for the information, Mrs. Tibbitt, and tell that ornery husband of yours that your memory is better than his."

"The testimonial is appreciated," she said, "and let me take this opportunity to wish you a very happy holiday."

Qwilleran was disappointed. He had learned nothing about Nancy's mother, and yet . . . Koko always had a motive for his actions—almost always. The more peculiar his behavior, the more likely it was to be important. Now there were all those references to feet!

On an impulse he called directory assistance and asked for the number of Arnold Foote in Lockmaster. There was no listing for that name. He pondered awhile. The public library was open until nine o'clock. He phoned and asked a clerk to look up Foote in the Lockmaster directory. There were fourteen listed, she said, with locations in various parts of the county.

"Give me the phone numbers of the first three," he asked.

He first tried calling Foote, Andrew. The woman who answered told him in no uncertain terms, "We don't know anything about that branch of the family. We've never had anything to do with them."

He phoned Foote, Charles. A man said, "Don't know. Long time since I saw Arnold at the farm co-op."

Finally there was Foote, Donald. "I heard he's in a nursing home but don't know for sure. His wife died, coupla years ago."

Before Qwilleran could plan his next move, he received an excited call from Celia Robinson. "I know it's after six o'clock," she said, "but I simply had to try to reach you!"

"What news?" he asked with intense interest.

"Your check! It's so generous of you! I've always wanted a three-wheel bike. A lot of ladies have them here and ride all over the park. Is that being too extravagant?"

"That's what Christmas presents are all about, and you're deserving," he assured her. "And how about your assignment?"

"I talked to Betty and Claude and wrote it all down," Celia said. "There's something called 'bearer bonds' that would be good for me, because my heirs could cash them easily if anything happened to me. Also there are some private boxes in the office safe, and I can have one for the bonds and any cash I don't want to put in the bank. If I win at the dog races, you see, there's a way of collecting without having to report it. They have an agent at the track."

"Beautiful!" Qwilleran murmured.

"Clayton flies in tomorrow, and I'll explain Operation Greenback in the car, driving in from the airport. I can hardly wait to see Wrigley!"

"Be sure to stress the need for secrecy," Qwilleran reminded her. "Tell Clayton we're investigating financial fraud, and the victim may have had fears or suspicions that she confided to Mr. Crocus."

"Don't worry. Clayton is a regular bloodhound. If we find out anything, is it okay to call you during the holidays?"

"Of course. Have a merry Christmas, Celia."

"Same to you, chief."

As soon as Qwilleran hung up, Koko walked across the desk and faced him eyeball to eyeball, delivering a trumpetlike "Yow-w-w!" that pained the aural and olfactory senses.

"What's your problem?" Qwilleran asked. In answer, the cat knocked a pen to the floor and bit the shade of the desklamp, then raced around the room—over the furniture, up on the bookshelves, into the closet and out again, all the while uttering a rumbling growl.

When Koko staged a catfit, it was a sure sign that Qwilleran was in the doghouse. "Oh-oh! I goofed!" he said, slapping his forehead. He had told Celia she could phone during the holidays; she would drive across town through dense traffic—just to call him—and he would be in Purple Point. He had been unforgivably thoughtless.

Koko had calmed down and was grooming the fur on his underside, and Qwilleran was faced with the problem of calling her on a phone that she insisted was bugged. He gave her an hour to drive back to the park before calling her mobile home. She was surprised to hear his voice.

In a tone of exaggerated jollity he said, "Just wanted to wish you a merry Christmas before *I leave town for the weekend*. I'll be gone *for three days.*"

"Oh," she said, unsure how to respond. "Where are you going, Mr. Qwilleran?"

"To a Christmas Eve wedding out of town. I won't be back home until *Monday evening.*"

"Oh . . . Who's getting married?"

"My boss."

"That's nice. Give him my congratulations."

"I'll do that."

"Will it be a big wedding?"

"No, just a small one. It's a second marriage for both of them. So . . . you and Clayton have a happy holiday, Celia."

"Same to you . . . uh . . . Mr. Qwilleran."

Hanging up the phone, he was sure she had got the message, and he complimented himself on handling it well. He turned to say to Koko, "Thank you, old boy, for drawing it to my attention." But Koko wasn't there. He was in the closet sitting in the safe.

On the morning of December 24 Qwilleran packed his rented formal wear for the wedding in Purple Point, all the while pondering the Euphonia Gage swindle. It was now clear to him what had happened to her money. Whether or not Clayton could coax anything out of Mr. Crocus, Qwilleran believed he had a good case to present to Pender Wilmot.

He called the attorney's office, and a machine informed him they would be closed until Monday. The Wilmots were now living in the fashionable suburb of West Middle Hummock, and he tried their residence. A childish voice answered, and he said, "May I speak to your father?"

"He isn't here. He went to a meeting. They have some lunch and sing a song and tell jokes. What do you want him for?"

"It's a business matter, Timmie."

"D'you want a divorce? Do you want to sue somebody?" the boy asked helpfully.

"Nothing like that," said Qwilleran, fascinated by the initiative of the embryo lawyer. "What else does he do besides divorces and lawsuits?"

"He writes wills. He wrote my will, and I signed it. I'm leaving my trains to my sister and all my wheels to my cousins and all my videos to the school."

"Well, have your father call me, Timmie, if he gets home before three o'clock. My name is Qwilleran."

"Wait till I get a pencil." There was a long wait before he returned to the line. "What's your name?"

"Qwilleran. I'll spell it for you. Q-w-i-l-l-e-r-a-n."

"Q?"

"That's right. Do you know how to make a Q? . . . Then W . . ."

"W?" asked Timmie.

"That's right. Q . . . W . . . I . . . Have you got that? Then double-L . . ."

"Another W?" Timmie asked.

A woman's voice interrupted. "Timmie, your lunch is ready . . . Hello? This is Mrs. Wilmot. May I help you?"

"This is Jim Qwilleran, and I'd like Pender to call me if he gets home before three. I was in the process of leaving a message with his law clerk."

"Pender is having lunch with the Boosters, and then they're delivering Christmas baskets, but we'll see you at the wedding tonight."

"Perfect! I'll speak with him there."

Eighteen

The marriage ceremony was scheduled early, so that family and friends of the couple might return home to observe their own Christmas Eve traditions. In mid-afternoon Qwilleran picked up Polly for the drive to Purple Point. It was a narrow peninsula curving into the lake to form a natural harbor on the northern shore of Moose County. Viewed across the bay at sunset it was a distinct shade of purple.

In the boom years of the nineteenth century Purple Point had been the center of fishing and shipbuilding industries, but all activity disappeared with the closing of the mines and the consequent economic collapse. Fire leveled the landscape, and hurricanes narrowed the peninsula to a mere spit of sand. Sport fishing revived the area in the 1920s as affluent families from Down Below built large summer residences, which they called fish camps.

By the time Qwilleran arrived in Moose County, these dwellings were called cottages but were actually year-round vacation homes lining both sides of the road that ran the length of the peninsula. There were few trees, and sweeping winds raised havoc with sand or snow according to season. The approach to the Point was across a low, flat, uninhabited expanse called the Flats, a wetland in summer and an arctic waste following the Big Snow. The county plows kept the road open, building high, snowy banks on both sides, while the individual cottages were walled in by their own snow blowers. It was a surreal landscape into which Qwilleran and Polly ventured on that Christmas Eve.

What the Lanspeaks called their cottage had a tall-case clock in the foyer, a baby grand piano in the living room, a quadrophonic sound system, and four bedrooms on the balcony. The only reminder of the original fish camp was the cobblestone fireplace. The bride and groom were already there, Riker assisting Larry in the preparation of an afternoon toddy, while Mildred raved about the tasteful decorations. There were banks of white poinsettias, garlands of greens, and a large Scotch pine trimmed with pearlescent ornaments, white velvet bows, and crystal icicles.

When the guests started to arrive, the wedding party was elsewhere, dressing. The first to pull into the driveway were Junior and Jody Goodwinter, car-pooling with Mildred's daughter, Sharon, and her husband, Roger MacGillivray. Qwilleran, looking down from the balcony, saw Lisa and Lyle Compton arriving with John Bushland (and his camera) and June Halliburton, who sat down at the piano and started playing pleasant music. Chopin nocturnes, Polly said. Among those from the neighboring cottages were Don Exbridge and his new wife and the Wilmot family, the bespectacled Timmie in his little long-pant suit and bow tie. Hixie Rice hobbled in with her surgical boot, walker, and attentive doctor. They brought the officiating pastor with them, Ms. Sims from the Brrr church, the Pickax clergymen having declined to leave their flocks on Christmas Eve.

At five o'clock the music faded away, the tall clock bonged five times, and Mildred's daughter lighted the row of candles on the mantel. An expectant hush fell over the assembled guests. Then the pianist began a sweetly lyrical melody. Schubert's Impromptu in G Flat, Polly said. Ms. Sims in robe and surplice took her place in front of the fireplace, and—as the tender notes developed into a strong crescendo—the groom and groomsman joined her. In dinner jacket and black tie the groom looked distinguished, and the best man looked especially handsome. There was a joyous burst of music, and all eyes turned upward as Polly walked downstairs from the balcony in her blue crepe and pearls. After a moment's suspense the tender melody was heard again, and Mildred—who had lost a few pounds—moved gracefully down the stairs in apricot velvet.

For the first time in his life Qwilleran performed his nuptial duty without dropping the ring. The only ripple of levity came when

Timmie Wilmot, standing in the front row, said, "Daddy, how is that lady gonna join those people together?"

After the ceremony there were champagne toasts and the cutting of the cake. Rightfully, the bride was the center of attention. Mildred—the good-hearted, generous, charitable supporter of worthy causes—was saying, "All the restaurants have been saving their pickle jars for us, and we now have a hundred of them at cash registers around the county, collecting loose change for spaying stray cats. I call them community cats because they don't belong to anyone but they belong to everyone."

Lisa said to Qwilleran, "Who's feeding Koko and Yum Yum?"

"Polly's sister-in-law."

Polly said, "Qwill's cats get food intended for humans, and I can't convince him it's the wrong thing to do."

"If you can convince Koko," he said, "I'll gladly go along. In his formative years Koko lived with a gourmet cook and developed a taste for lobster bisque and oysters Rockefeller. If I feed the female catfood while the male is dining on take-outs from the Old Stone Mill, I'll be accused of sex discrimination."

The groom said, "We want a couple of Abyssinians as soon as we're settled."

"It's my considered opinion," said Pender Wilmot, "that the world would be a better place if everyone had a cat."

Timmie spoke up. "Oh Jay weighs twenty pounds."

The pastor said, "Whenever I sneeze, my Whisker-Belle makes a sound as if she's blessing me."

"When I was a little girl taking piano lessons," June Halliburton put in, "our cat howled every time I hit a wrong note."

"Oh Jay has fleas," said the sociable Wilmot scion.

Qwilleran caught the attorney's eye, and the two men drifted into the library. Wilmot said, "This is the first wedding I've ever attended where the sole topic of conversation was cats."

"You could do worse," Qwilleran remarked.

"My wife says you called me."

"Yes, it's probably none of my business, but I've been researching a piece on Euphonia Gage, and a few facts about the Park of Pink Sunsets have aroused my suspicion."

"Their cavalier repurchase policy is enough to give one pause," Wilmot said.

"Right! That was the first clue. Then Junior told me about Euphonia's new will, cutting out her relatives. It was written for her by an in-house lawyer who charges surprisingly low fees."

Wilmot nodded soberly.

"There's more," said Qwilleran. "They have an associate who helps residents unload their valuables—and rips them off. One ostensibly wealthy woman was offered a lock-box in the office safe for financial documents and unreported cash. Who knows if they have extra keys to those boxes? Shall I continue?"

"By all means."

"The woman I mentioned has sent me snapshots that include the operators of the park, a couple who are chummily called Betty and Claude. Now here's a curious fact: On the weekend Euphonia died, Betty and Claude were in Pickax, attending the preview of 'The Big Burning.' Hixie Rice and I thought they were gate-crashers from Lockmaster, but they were evidently casing the place; shortly after, a dealer Down Below approached Junior about stripping the mansion of architectural features."

"Junior told me about that," said the attorney. "The dealer indicated that Mrs. Gage was negotiating a deal before she died."

"I could go on with this," Qwilleran said, "but we're supposed to be celebrating my boss's wedding."

"Let's live with this over the weekend and then get together downtown—" He was interrupted by hubbub outdoors. "Sounds like a pack of wolves out there!"

It was a pack of huskies. Nancy Fincher and her dogteam had arrived to transport the newlyweds to the honeymoon cottage that Don Exbridge was lending them. Arch and Mildred were changing clothes, Carol said. The guests bundled into their own wraps and went out on the porch to admire the dogs and the Christmas lights. It was dark, and every cottage on both sides of the road was outlined with strings of white lights.

"A magic village!" Polly said.

The bride and groom reappeared in togs suitable for an arctic expedition and were whisked away, huddled in the basket of the sled. With Nancy riding the runners, they sped down the avenue of snow through a confetti of tiny lights, while cottagers waved and cheered and threw poorly aimed snowballs.

Then the wedding guests departed for their own cottages or the mainland, and the two remaining couples had a light supper in front of the fireplace.

"Hixie arranged for the dog-sledding," Carol said. "Nancy will be here for the next two days, taking kids for rides."

"Adults, too," Larry added. "How about you, Qwill?"

"No, thanks."

The evening passed pleasantly. From speakers on the balcony

came recorded carols played on antique music boxes and great cathedral organs. At Qwilleran's request, Larry read a passage from Dickens's *Christmas Carol*—the description of the Cratchits' Christmas dinner. *"There never was such a goose!"* Then gifts were opened.

Polly was thrilled with the opals. She gave Qwilleran a twenty-seven-volume set of Shakespeare's plays and sonnets. They were leather-bound and old.

"Wait till my bibliocat sniffs these!" he said with detectable pride. He gave the Lanspeaks a pair of brass candlesticks, Dutch baroque.

The next morning began with wake-up music that Wagner had composed as a Christmas gift for his wife, and Carol prepared eggs Benedict for breakfast. It had snowed lightly, and Timmie Wilmot, with a broom over his shoulder, rang the doorbell.

"Sweep your porch?" he asked.

"All right, but be sure you do a good job," Larry admonished him. To the others he explained, "Timmie's parents want to develop his work ethic."

The snowy landscape was bright with winter sunshine, and the frozen bay was dotted with the small shanties of ice fishermen. All day the telephone jangled with holiday greetings from distant places, and the dogsled could be seen flying up and down the white canyon. After Christmas dinner—Cornish hen and plum pudding—Polly took a nap and Carol wrote thank-you notes, while Larry tinkered with his new model-building kit.

Later, they walked to an open house at the Exbridge cottage. Nancy Fincher was there, their guest for the weekend. "When are you going to run the article on dog-sledding?" she asked Qwilleran.

"As soon as the race dates are announced."

"Would you like to take a ride tomorrow?"

"I've had a ride!" he said testily.

"But the parade wasn't the real thing."

"It was real enough for me!" He remembered the discomfort of the costume and the horror of climbing the ladder while it ripped at the seams. He also remembered a conversation with Nancy. "What was the date of the parade?" he now asked her.

Her answer was prompt. "November 27."

"Are you sure?"

"I know, because it was my mother's birthday."

Qwilleran's impulse was to telephone Junior immediately, but other guests were demanding his attention. Conversation was animated until someone announced, "It's snowing, you guys! And the wind's rising! It looks like a blizzard's cooking!"

The guests said hasty farewells, and Larry guided his party home through the swirling flakes. Polly said, "I'm thankful we don't have to drive back to Pickax tonight. Crossing the Flats in a blizzard must be a horrendous experience!"

Back at the cottage Larry tuned in the weather forecast: "Snow ending by midnight. High winds continuing, gusting up to sixty miles an hour."

"If there's drifting on the Flats and the highway is buried, we'll be trapped," Carol said cheerfully, "but that's the excitement of weekending on the Point. You may have to stay longer than you intended . . . Dominoes, anyone?"

The wind howled around the cottage, making Polly nervous, and Carol sent her to bed with aspirin and earplugs. Soon she retired herself, leaving the two men sprawled in front of the fire.

Qwilleran said to Larry, "You manipulate that fireplace damper like a cellist playing Brahms."

"With this kind of wind, you have to know your stuff. Do you use the fireplaces where you're living?"

"With those old chimneys? Not a chance!"

Larry said, "I heard about Euphonia's will. Cutting off her own flesh and blood was bad enough, but throwing her fortune away at the racetrack was a crime! To be eighty-eight and suddenly broke must be tough to take. Is that why she ended it all?"

"I don't know," Qwilleran said. "They've had other suicides in the Park of Pink Sunsets."

"The name alone would drive me over the edge," Larry said. "How about a hot drink before we turn in?"

The morning after the blizzard the snowscape was smoothly sculptured by the wind, but the day was bright, and the air was so clear it was possible to hear the churchbells on the mainland.

During breakfast Larry tuned in WPKX, and Wetherby Goode said, "Well, folks, December has been mild, but last night's blizzard made up for lost time. The ice fishermen have lost their shanties. The entire westside of Pickax is blacked out. And the Purple Point Road is blockaded by ten-foot snow drifts. The plows won't be out till Monday morning, because the crews get double-time for Sundays, so you holiday-makers on the Point will have to go on drinking eggnog for another twenty-four hours. Today's forecast: mild temperatures, clear skies, variable winds—" The announcement was interrupted by the telephone.

Carol answered and said, "It's for you, Polly."

"Me?" she said in surprise and apprehension. Conversation at the breakfast table stopped as she talked in the next room. Returning, she looked grave as she said, "Qwill, I think you should take this call. It's Lynette. She's calling from your house."

He jumped up, threw his napkin on the chairseat, and hurried to the phone. "Yes, Lynette. What's the trouble?"

"I'm at your house, Mr. Qwilleran. I stopped to feed the cats on my way to church, but I can't find them! They usually come running for their food. I've searched all the rooms, but the power is off, you know, and it's hard to see inside the closets, even with a flashlight . . ."

He listened in silence, his mind hurtling from one dire possibility to another.

"But there's something else I should tell you, Mr. Qwilleran, although I don't know if it means anything. When I came over here early last evening, I drove to the carriage house first to feed Bootsie. It was dark, but I had a glimpse of a van parked behind the big house. I didn't remember seeing it before, and when I came downstairs a half hour later, it was gone. I didn't think much about it. Koko and Yum Yum gobbled their food and talked to me—"

"What kind of van?"

"Sort of a delivery van, I think, although I didn't pay that much attention—"

"I'm coming home," he interrupted. "I'll get there as fast as I can. I'll leave at once."

"Shall I wait here?"

"There's nothing more you can do. Go on to church. I'll be there in forty-five minutes." He returned to the table. "I've got to get out of here fast. Lynette can't find the cats, and she saw a strange vehicle in the yard. I won't stop to pack." He was headed for the stairs. "I'll just grab my parka and keys. Polly can drive home with you."

"Qwill!" Larry said sternly, following him to the stairway. "The road's closed! You can't get through! The highway is blocked by ten-foot drifts!"

"Could a snowmobile get through?"

"Nobody's got one. They're outlawed on the Point."

Qwilleran pounded his moustache with his fist. "Could a dogsled get through?"

"I'll call Nancy," Carol said. "She's staying with the Exbridges."

"Tell her to hurry!"

Polly said anxiously, "What can have happened, Qwill?"

"I don't know, but I have a hunch that something's seriously wrong!"

"Nancy's on her way," Carol reported. "Luckily she was harnessing her team when I called."

They were all on the porch when the dogsled and eight flying huskies arrived. Qwilleran was in his parka with the hood pulled up.

Larry asked, "Can your dogs get through ten-foot drifts, Nancy?"

"We won't use the highway. We'll cross the bay on the ice. It'll be shorter anyway."

"Is that safe?" Polly asked.

"Sure. I've been ice-fishing on the bay all my life."

Qwilleran asked, "Where do we touch land on the other side?"

"At the state park."

"Someone should meet me there and drive me to Pickax . . . Larry, try to reach Nick Bamba. Second choice, Roger. Third choice, the sheriff . . . How long will it take, Nancy?"

She estimated an hour at the outside. Carol gave them thermos bottles of hot tea and coffee.

"Stay close to shore!" Larry shouted as they took off down an easement to the bay.

Qwilleran was sitting low in the basket on caribou skins as they skimmed across the ice at racing speed. The high winds had left hillocks of snow and wrecked shanties, but Nancy guided the team between obstacles with gruff commands. The shoreline behind them receded quickly.

"Where are we going?" Qwilleran shouted, mindful of Larry's advice.

"Taking a shortcut. There's an island out there," she called back. "It's reached by an ice bridge."

Leaving the shore behind, they encountered a strong wind sweeping across the lake from Canada, and they were grateful for their hot drinks when they stopped at the island to rest the dogs.

When they started out again, the wind changed to offshore and was not quite as cutting. They sped along through a world of white: ice under the runners, wintery sky overhead, shoreline in the distance. But soon they began to slow down, and Qwilleran could feel the runners cutting into the ice. The dogs seemed to find it hard going.

"It's softer than it should be," Nancy shouted. "It rained one day last week." She turned the team farther out into the lake where the surface was firm, but they were traveling farther from their destination.

Then Qwilleran saw a crack in the ice between the sled and the shore. "Nancy! Are we drifting? Are we being blown farther out?"

"Hang in there! We'll get around it!"

She headed the team even farther out, and soon they were climbing a hill of snow. She stopped the dogs with a command. "From here you can see what's happening. The north wind pushed the loose ice into shore, but the offshore breeze is breaking it up. Stand up! You can see the ice bridge."

Qwilleran peered across the bay and saw only more slush and more cracks. God! he thought . . . What am I doing here? Who is this girl? What does she know?

"Okay, let's take off! . . . Up! . . . Go! . . . haw!"

He clenched his teeth and gripped the siderails as they zigzagged across the surface. Slowly the distant shore was coming closer. At last he could see the roof of the lodge at the state park . . . Then he could see a single car parked on the overlook . . . Then he could see a man waving. Nick Bamba!

"Am I glad to see you!" Qwilleran shouted. To Nancy he said, "Dammit, woman! You deserve a medal!"

She smiled. It was a remarkably sweet smile.

"Where are you going from here, Nancy? You're not going back across the bay, I hope."

"No, I'll take the dogs home. It's only a few miles inland. I hope you find your cats all right."

"What happened?" Nick wanted to know. "What's going on here?"

"Start driving, and I'll tell you," Qwilleran said. "Drive fast!"

On the road to Pickax he summed up the situation: the missing cats, the strange van parked behind the house, the cat-sitter's frantic call to Purple Point. "I've been doing an unofficial investigation of some unscrupulous individuals, and it caused me to worry," he said. "I had to get home, but the highway is blockaded. When Nancy proposed crossing the bay on the ice, I was apprehensive. When we got into slush and started drifting out on an ice floe, I thought it was the end!"

"You didn't need to worry," Nick said. "That girl has a terrific reputation. She's a musher's musher!"

"Have you heard anything more about her father's murder?"

"Only that the state detectives are sure it wasn't a local vendetta.

They think he was involved in something outside the county. The cause of death," he said, "was a gunshot to the head."

When they reached Goodwinter Boulevard, Nick parked in the street. "Let's not mess up any tire tracks in the driveway . . . The power's still out in Pickax, they said on the air, so take the flashlight that's under the seat. I've got a high-powered lantern in the trunk."

They walked to the side door under the porte cochere, where wind currents had swept the drive clear in one spot and piled up the snow in another.

Qwilleran said, "The tire tracks leading to the carriage house are Lynette's. They were made this morning after the blizzard. She saw the van in the rear last evening before the blizzard. If they broke into the house, it would be through the kitchen door." He was speaking in a controlled monotone that belied the anxiety he felt in the pit of his stomach.

"The van has been back again since last night," Nick said. "I'd guess it was here during the blizzard and left before the snow stopped."

Qwilleran unlocked the side door and automatically reached for a wall switch, but power had not been restored. The foyer with its dark paneling and dark parquet floor was like a cave except for one shaft of light slanting in from a circular window on the stair landing, and in the patch of warmth was a Siamese cat, huddled against the chill but otherwise unperturbed.

"Koko! My God! Where were you?" Qwilleran shouted. "Where's Yum Yum?"

"There she is!" said Nick, beaming the big lantern down the hall. She was in a hunched position with rump elevated and head low—her mousing stance—and she was watching the door of the elevator.

At the same time there was pounding in the walls and a distant cry of distress.

The two men looked at each other in a moment's perplexity.

"Someone's trapped in the elevator!" Qwilleran said in amazement.

Nick peered through the small pane of glass in the elevator door. "It's stuck between here and the basement."

There was more pounding and hysterical yelling, and Qwilleran rushed to the lower level. "Call the police!" he shouted up to Nick. "The phone's in the library!"

The beam of his flashlight exposed a ravaged ballroom. Electrical wires were hanging from the ceiling and protruding from the walls, and canvas murals, peeled from their backgrounds, were lying in rolls on the floor.

Nineteen

The thwarted burglary on Goodwinter Boulevard was the subject of a news bulletin on WPKX Sunday afternoon. It was a newscaster's dream: breaking and entering, vandalism, attempted theft, and four big names: the *Gage* mansion owned by Junior *Goodwinter* and occupied by James *Qwilleran,* the *Klingenschoen* heir.

After the broadcast, Junior was the first to call. "Hey, Qwill! Is there a lot of damage?"

"The ballroom's a wreck, but they didn't get around to anything on the main floor, thanks to the blackout. The light fixtures are still on the elevator. The murals are rolled up on the ballroom floor; I hope they can be salvaged."

"I'd better buzz over and take a look. Is the power back on?"

"It was restored while the police were here. I'll plug in the coffeemaker."

Minutes later, when Junior viewed the dangling wires and stripped walls, he said, "I can't believe this! Who did it? He wasn't named on the air, and our reporter couldn't get anything at police headquarters. The suspect won't be charged until tomorrow."

"Suspect! That's a laugh! He was caught red-handed when the cops arrived—trapped in the elevator with his loot. Brodie himself was here . . . Come into the kitchen." Qwilleran poured coffee and said, "It's my guess that he's the dealer who phoned you and wanted to buy the stuff. He's from Milwaukee."

Junior unwrapped a few slices of fruitcake. "What made him think he could help himself?"

"It wasn't his own idea—or so he swears. He had a partner, an electrician, who decamped with the van when the power failed. It was the dealer's van, and he was madder'n hell! He was glad to name his accomplice, thinking the guy had thrown a circuit breaker in order to steal the vehicle. He didn't know it was a general blackout."

"How do you know all this?"

"I talked to Brodie afterward. The state police are tracking the van. And listen, Junior: Anything I tell you is off the record. If you jump the gun and I lose my credibility with Andy, your name isn't Junior anymore; it's something else."

"Agreed," said the editor.

"That isn't good enough."

"Scout's honor! . . . So if the neighborhood hadn't blacked out, the rats would have gotten away with it. That's some coincidence!"

"And if I hadn't come home when I did," Qwilleran said, "the suspect, as he is charitably called, wouldn't be in jail."

"What brought you home, Qwill? I thought you were staying till Monday. And how did you get off the Point? The highway's still blocked."

"Regarding the latter question, read my column in Tuesday's paper. The other question . . ." He related the cat-sitter incident: the missing cats, the frantic phone call, the strange vehicle, the alarming possibilities. "But when I walked in, there they were! Both cats! Acting as if nothing had happened! Where were those two devils hiding when Lynette was looking for them, and *why* were they hiding? I'm convinced that Koko can sense evil, but did he know that their absence would bring me home in a hurry?. . . This is good fruitcake. Who made it?"

"Mildred . . . But how did the thieves know you wouldn't be home?"

"That part of the story gets complicated." Qwilleran smoothed his moustache, a familiar gesture. "With Celia Robinson's help, I've been collecting evidence about those con artists down there. She's been reporting to me from a mall, thinking her home phone is tapped. Just before Christmas I took a chance on calling her at home—about a small but urgent matter—and that's the only way those crooks could find out I'd be gone for the weekend. Her phone really was tapped, and they'd connect my name with the Gage mansion. Betty and Claude were here, you remember, for the preview of our show. They're no dummies! They're real professionals!"

Junior said, "Wait till Wilmot hears your story!"

"I discussed my suspicions with him at the wedding, but now that it's become police business, it puts a new face on the matter. There's some hard evidence."

"It'll make a hot story," the editor said, "especially with the cats involved."

"Leave the cats out of it," Qwilleran said sternly.

"Don't be crazy! That's the best part!"

"If you want a hot story, get this, Junior: Your aunt Lethe was born on the same day as your grandmother's housekeeper and in the same place. In a county as small as Lockmaster was in 1928, how many girl babies would be born on November 27? It's my contention that Euphonia paid a farm family to take Lethe and change her name to Lena Foote . . . That would make Nancy Fincher your cousin."

Junior gulped audibly. "That's a wild guess on your part."

"Okay. Send a reporter to Lockmaster to search the county records for a Lena Foote and a Lethe Gage born on the same day. I'll bet you a five-course dinner there's only one . . . unless . . . your esteemed grandmother bribed the county clerk to rig the books."

"That's a possibility," Junior admitted. "We all know how corrupt they are in Lockmaster."

"Don't you find it significant that Lena dropped out of school at the age of fifteen and entered the employ of the Gages—where she remained for more than forty years? Don't you think Nancy has your grandmother's genes? Euphonia was tiny, and so is she—"

"And I'm vertically challenged myself," Junior interrupted.

"Now you're getting it! Also, a deceptively young countenance is characteristic of all three of you. Nancy even has Euphonia's sweet smile. Sorry I can't say the same about you . . . More coffee?"

"No, thanks. I'll amble home and break the news to Jody that we have a pack of Siberian huskies for first-cousins-once-removed."

"And don't forget that the murdered potato farmer was your uncle-by-marriage," Qwilleran added.

Junior wandered out of the house in an apparent daze.

The Siamese were under the kitchen table, waiting for crumbs, and Qwilleran shared the last slice of fruitcake with them. They slobbered over it eagerly, being careful to spit out the nuts and fruits.

On Monday the snowbound Purple Pointers were able to return to town. An electrical contractor sent a crew to the Gage mansion to restore the ballroom fixtures. An installer from Amanda's design studio prepared to rehang the murals. Qwilleran wrote a column about his experience on the frozen bay, with paragraphs of praise for the musher's musher. And at five o'clock Celia Robinson called.

"Did you enjoy Christmas?" he asked.

"Yes, we had a good time," she said in a subdued manner that was unusual for her. "We splurged on dinner at a nice place, and Clayton had a real steak, not chopped."

"Did he bring Wrigley with him?"

"Yes, Wrigley's a nice cat. Black and white. But something odd is happening here, Mr. Qwilleran. Pete, the assistant manager, went to Wisconsin to spend Christmas with his parents, and he hasn't come back. Betty and Claude haven't been seen since yesterday noon. There's no one in charge of the office. Clayton and I went in and sorted the mail today, but everybody's upset."

"What is Claude's last name?"

"I think it's Sprott. Another thing, Mr. Qwilleran. I've decided to leave Florida. Too many old people! I'm only sixty-eight."

"Where would you go?" he asked.

"Someplace back in Illinois, where I can get a part-time job and be closer to my grandson."

"Excellent idea!"

"But I'm babbling about myself. How was your Christmas? That was a funny phone call I got from you, but I figured out why you did it. Was it a nice wedding?"

"Very fine."

"Did Santa bring you something exciting?"

"Some books, that's all, but that's better than a necktie. Was Clayton able to carry out his assignment?"

"Didn't you get his tape recording? We mailed it Friday afternoon. When I told him what you wanted, he went right out and bought a little tape recorder to wear under his cap. He wore it when he visited Mr. Crocus."

"Did you listen to the tape?"

"No, we wanted to get it into the mail before the holiday. I thought you'd have it today."

"Mail is always slow in reaching Moose County. Meanwhile, Celia, I have a question for you, if you can think back to the day you discovered Mrs. Gage's body. It was a Monday noon, you told me. She'd been dead sixteen hours, the doctor said, meaning she died Sunday evening. Did you see anyone go to her home on Sunday?"

"Oh dear! Let me think . . . You think someone might have given her disturbing news that made her take those pills?"

"Whatever."

"I can't recall right off the bat, but maybe Mr. Crocus will know. He's the kind that notices things."

"Well, give it some serious thought, and I'll watch the mail for Clayton's tape."

"And Mr. Qwilleran, I put something in the package for you personally. It isn't much. Just a little holiday goodie."

"That's very thoughtful of you, Celia. I'll keep in touch."

When Celia's package arrived on Tuesday, Qwilleran sank his teeth into a rich, nut-filled, chewy chocolate brownie, and he had a vision. He envisioned Celia transplanted to Pickax, baking meatloaf for the cats and brownies for himself, catering parties now and then, laughing a lot. Then he abandoned his fantasy and listened to Clayton's tape. What he heard prompted him to phone Pender Wilmot immediately.

"I'd like to hear it," the attorney said. "Would you like to bring it to my office tomorrow afternoon?"

"No. Now!" Qwilleran said firmly.

The law office in the new Klingenschoen Professional Building was unique in Pickax, where dark mahogany and red leather were the legal norm. Wilmot's office was paneled in light teakwood, with chrome-based chairs upholstered in slate blue and plum.

Qwilleran noticed a black iron lamp with saucer shade. "That looks like a Charles Rennie Mackintosh design," he said. "I saw his work in Glasgow last September. My mother was a Mackintosh."

"I have Scots blood myself," said the attorney. "My mother's ancestors came out in the 1745 Rising." He showed Qwilleran a framed etching of an ancestral castle. "Now, what is the new development you mentioned?"

"The attempted burglary," Qwilleran began, "confirms my theory about the Pink Sunset management, and news of the arrest has obviously reached them through their assistant. He's undoubtedly the electrician who removed the light fixtures and then stole the other fellow's van. All three of them have disappeared, according to my informant at the park. She has also sent me a taped conversation that warrants further investigation."

"Who made the tape?"

"Her grandson. He's friendly with an elderly resident who was a confidant of Mrs. Gage. The young man secreted a recording device under his cap when he went to see the old gentleman. I had a hunch that this Mr. Crocus might know something enlightening about her last days." Qwilleran started the tape. "The preliminary dialogue is irrelevant but interesting. He was probably testing the equipment."

As the tape unreeled, it produced the charming voice of a young woman and an adolescent baritone with falsetto overtones.

. . .

"Are you Betty? My grandma sent you this plant. She's Mrs. Robinson on Kumquat Court."

"A Christmas cactus! How sweet of her! And what is your name?"

"Clayton."

"Tell her thank-you, Clayton. We'll put it right here on the counter, where all the Sunsetters can enjoy it when they come in for their mail."

"Last year she gave a Christmas plant to the old lady next door, but she died."

"We say *elderly,* not *old,* Clayton."

"Okay. What was her name?"

"Mrs. Gage."

"What happened to her, anyway?"

"She passed away in her sleep."

"She looked healthy last Christmas."

"I'm afraid she accidentally took the wrong medication."

"How do you know?"

"The doctor said so. We really don't like to talk about these things, Clayton."

"Why not?"

"It's so sad, and at this time of year we try to be happy."

"Was it written up in the paper?"

"No, this is a large city, and they can't report everything."

"But my grandma says she was rich. They always write up rich people when they die, don't they?"

"Clayton, this is an interesting conversation, but you'll have to excuse me. I have work to do."

"Can I help?"

"No, thank you, but it's kind of you to offer."

"I could sort the mail."

"Not today. Just tell your grandmother that we appreciate the plant."

"I know computers."

"I'm sure you do, but there's really nothing—"

"You're a very pretty lady."

"Thank you, Clayton. Now please . . . just go away!"

Wilmot chuckled. "His ingenuous performance is ingenious. How old is he?"

"Thirteen."

After a few seconds of taped silence, the adolescent voice alternated with the husky, gasping voice of an elderly man.

. . .

"Hi, Mr. Crocus! Remember me?"

"Clayton! I hardly recognized you. . . . No beard this year."

"I shaved it off. How're you feeling, Mr. Crocus?"

"Moderately well."

"What are you doing? Just sitting in the sun?"

"That's all."

"Grandma sent you this plant. It's a Christmas cactus."

"Very kind of her."

"Where'll I put it?"

"Next to the door. Tell her thank-you."

"Okay if I sit down?"

"Yes . . . yes . . . please!"

"Been doing any chess lately?"

"No one plays chess here."

"Not even your grandkids?"

"My grandchildren never visit me. Might as well not have any."

"I don't have a grandpa. Why don't we work out a deal?"

(Slight chuckle.) "What terms do you propose?"

"We could play chess by mail, and I could tell you about school. I just made Junior Band."

"What instrument?"

"Trumpet. Do you still play the violin?"

"Not recently."

"Why not?"

"No desire. I've had a very great loss."

"That's too bad. What happened?"

"Mrs. Gage . . . passed away."

"She was a nice lady. Was she sick long?"

"Sad to say, it was . . . suicide."

"I knew somebody that did that. Depression, they said. Was she depressed?"

"She had her troubles."

"What kind of troubles?"

"One shouldn't talk about . . . a friend's personal affairs."

"Our counselor at school says it's good to talk about it when you lose a friend."

"I have no one who's . . . interested."

"I'm interested, if you're going to be my grandpa."

"You're a kind young person."

"Do you know what kind of troubles she had?"

(Pause.) "Someone was . . . taking her money . . . wrongfully."

"Did she report it to the police?"

"It was not . . . She didn't feel . . . that she could do that."

"Why not?"

"It was . . . extortion."

"How do you mean?"

"She was being . . . blackmailed."

"That's bad! What was it about? Do you know?"

"A family secret."

"Somebody committed a crime?"

"I don't know."

"Did she say who was blackmailing her?"

"Someone up north. That's all she'd say."

"How long did it go on?"

"A few years."

"I'd go to the police, if it was me."

"I told her to tell Claude."

"Why him?"

"She was leaving her money to the park, and . . . she was afraid . . . there wouldn't be any left."

"Is he Betty's husband?"

"Something like that."

"What did he say?"

"He told her not to worry."

"That's not much help."

"He said he could put a stop to it."

"What did she think about that?"

"She worried about it. In a few days . . . she was gone."

"Did she leave a suicide note?"

"Not even for me. That grieved me."

"You must have liked her a lot."

"She was a lovely lady. She liked music and art and poetry."

"I like music."

"But what kind? You young people—"

"Would you like a game of chess after supper, Mr. Crocus?"

"I would look forward to that with pleasure."

"I have to go somewhere with my grandma now. I'll see you after supper."

The attorney said, "So we know—or think we know—what happened to Mrs. Gage's money."

"We know more than that," Qwilleran said. "We know that she gave birth to a natural daughter in 1928 while her husband was in prison. In those days, and in a community like Pickax, that was an intolerable disgrace for a woman with her pride and pretensions. It's my contention that she gave her daughter—with certain stipulations and considerations—to a Lockmaster farm family, who raised her as Lena Foote. In her teens Lena went to work in the Gage household and remained there for the rest of her life. I'm guessing that Euphonia continued to pay hush money to the foster parents. Lena lost contact with them, but they came to her funeral a few years ago. Shortly afterward, Lena's widower began spending large sums of money for which there was no visible source. I say he's your blackmailer. The foster parents, being very old, may have passed on their secret to him—a kind of legacy for his daughter."

Wilmot had been listening intently to Qwilleran's fabric of fact and conjecture. "How did you acquire your information?"

"It's remarkable how many secrets you uncover when you work for a newspaper. When Mrs. Gage moved to Florida, the man I suspect of being the blackmailer obtained her address from her grandson, saying he owed her money which he wished to repay. He continued to hound her, until she confided in Claude Sprott. A few days later, Gil Inchpot was murdered, and the state detectives have neither a motive nor a suspect."

Wilmot was swiveling in his chair, a rapt listener. "Sprott had a vested interest in Mrs. Gage's estate, of course."

"What was left of it," Qwilleran added. "His sticky fingers had already been in the pie, one way and another."

"If he arranged for Inchpot's murder, who could have pulled the trigger?"

Qwilleran was ready for the question. "When you and I talked about it at the wedding, Pender, I told you that Sprott and his companion were in Pickax, incognito, for the preview of 'The Big Burning.' Now it occurs to me that they had flown up here not only to appraise the rare chandeliers. That was the weekend Inchpot disappeared. They probably rented a car at the airport and knocked on the door of his farmhouse, saying they were out of gas—after which they dropped his body in the woods and left his truck at the airport."

"Odd, isn't it, that they chose the Klingenschoen woods?"

"Not odd. Virtually unavoidable. Do you realize how many square miles of woodland belong to the Klingenschoen estate around Mooseville and Brrr? . . . And here's something else I've just learned," Qwilleran told the attorney. "As soon as their Milwaukee associate was arrested in my elevator and their Florida assistant was fugitive in a stolen vehicle, they skipped the Park of Pink Sunsets."

"We should see the prosecutor fast," Wilmot said. "Let's try to catch him before he goes to lunch."

Twenty

After a long session with the Moose County prosecutor, Qwilleran telephoned Celia Robinson. "I called to sing the praises of your chocolate brownies," he said. "I assume no one is listening to our conversation."

"Nobody ever came back," she said in a tone of bewilderment. "The police have been here, asking questions. Clayton and I have sort of taken charge of the office. We're trying to keep people calm, but the oldsters at the park get very upset."

"I also want to compliment your grandson on the tape. He's a smart young man."

"Yes, I'm proud of him."

"Have you been able to recall anything about the Sunday that Mrs. Gage died?"

"Well, Mr. Crocus and I put our heads together," she said, "and we remembered that the electricity went off around suppertime. There was no storm or anything, but every home on Kumquat Court lost power, and Pete came looking for a short circuit. He went to every home on the court."

"Including Mrs. Gage's?"

"Everybody's. We never found out what caused it. The power wasn't off for long, so it wasn't serious. That's the only thing we can remember."

"Good enough!" Qwilleran commended her.

"Is there anything else I can do for you, Mr. Qwilleran?"

"I may have an idea to discuss with you later on . . . Excuse me a moment. The doorbell's ringing."

"That's all right. I'll hang up. Happy New Year!"

It was Andrew Brodie at the door. "Come on in, chief," Qwilleran said. "Is this a social call, or did you come to talk shop?"

"Both. I'll take a nip of Scotch if you've got any. I'm on my way home." He followed Qwilleran into the kitchen. "A little water and no ice. What are you gonna drink?"

"Cider. Let's take our glasses into the library."

Brodie dropped into a large, old, underslung leather chair. "Feels like a hammock," he said.

"You'll sag, too, when you're that old."

"That's some Christmas tree you've got." The chief was looking at Polly's wreath.

"Have a good Christmas, Andy?"

"The usual. Did you get your lights fixed downstairs?"

"Good as new."

Something was on Brodie's mind. His staccato small talk was a kind of vamp-till-ready until he came to the point. "What's happening on Goodwinter Boulevard?" he asked. "A lot of property's changing hands."

"Is that good or bad?" Qwilleran asked.

"All depends. There's a rumor that the Klingenschoen money is behind it."

"Interesting, if true."

Brodie threw him a swift, fierce Scottish scowl. "In other words, you ain't talkin'."

"I've nothing to say."

"You had plenty to say to the prosecutor's office today. I hear they even sent out for roast beef sandwiches from Lois's."

"Your operatives don't miss a thing, Andy."

"I knew Inchpot," the chief said, "and I'd never figure him for a blackmailer."

"Perhaps he had professional advice," Qwilleran suggested slyly. "Extortion consultation and one-stop money-laundering would be the kind of services George Breze might offer. His business card was found in Euphonia's files. Was he an intermediary?"

Brodie brushed the jest aside. "He serviced her Mercedes . . . How come you came up with all those clues in the Inchpot case when the state bureau was stymied? Did your psychic cat work on it?" He had learned about Koko's unique capabilities from a city detective Down Below.

"Well, I'll tell you this: Koko and his sidekick collaborated to catch the thief in the elevator. I don't know how many hours he'd been trapped in pitch darkness, but claustrophobia had made him a screaming maniac by the time Nick Bamba and I walked in . . . Freshen your drink?"

"A wee drop."

Qwilleran brought in the bottle and a jug of water. "Help yourself."

"By this time I thought Koko would come up with a clue to Euphonia's suicide."

"Well, let me tell you something that's just occurred to me, Andy. I think she was not the first victim of fraud at the mobile home park, and I know for a fact she was not the first suicide. I have a hunch . . ." Qwilleran combed his moustache with his fingertips. "I have a hunch they were all murders. The management profited by a quick turnover. Rob 'em and rub 'em out!"

"You didn't tell that to the prosecutor!"

"I had nothing to support my suspicions when I was at the courthouse, but a phone call from Florida filled in some blanks."

"You know," said the chief, "I never thought that feisty woman would cash in like they said she did. Overdose, they said."

"It could have been a drop of poison in her Dubonnet. She always had to have her apéritif before dinner, I'm told. The medical examiner who wrote it off as suicide could have been one of those overworked civil servants you hear about, or he could be another useful link in the crime ring. At any rate, I'm going back to the courthouse tomorrow." The telephone jangled, and he let it ring.

"Answer it!" Brodie snapped, tossing off his drink. "I'll let myself out."

It was Junior on the line, getting straight to the point with his usual impetuosity. "Hey, Qwill! I just heard a terrific rumor! They say we're getting a community college in Pickax! And Goodwinter Boulevard is gonna be the campus! How d'you like that? All those white elephants are made to order for administration offices, classrooms, dorms—I hope it's true!"

"I don't see why it shouldn't be true," Qwilleran said calmly. "Lockmaster has its College of Animal Husbandry. Pickax could have an Institute of Rumor Technology, with courses in Conspiracy Theory, Advanced Gossip, and Media Leak."

"Very funny," Junior said sourly. "I'll call Lyle Compton. He'll know what's happening."

Qwilleran lost no time in phoning Polly. "Have you heard the rumors about Goodwinter Boulevard?"

"No, I haven't. What are they saying?" she asked anxiously.

"The police have heard one rumor, and the newspaper has heard another," he said, "and they're both true. I merely want you to be assured, Polly, that your carriage house won't be affected."

"Are you involved, Qwill? Aren't you going to tell me what the rumors are?"

"No. At the rate gossip travels in Pickax, you'll find out soon enough."

"You're cruel! I'm going to phone my sister-in-law."

Within hours, Betty and Claude were picked up in Texas near the Mexican border. Pete was arrested at an airport in Kentucky, having abandoned the stolen van. All three suspects would be arraigned on murder charges.

For Qwilleran the case was closed, and he entertained himself with speculations: If he had not rented the Gage mansion for the winter, Koko would not have discovered the historically important scrap of paper that led to "The Big Burning of 1869," and if the cat had not become a closet archaeologist, the mysterious deaths of Euphonia Gage and Gil Inchpot might have gone unsolved, and if Oh Jay had not infuriated Qwilleran by spraying the back door, Pickax would not be getting a community college. Would it be named after the Goodwinters, who founded the city? Or the eleemosynary foundation that was funding it? Or the orange cat with fleas and bad breath?

They were fanciful thoughts, but Qwilleran was feeling heady from too much caffeine. It was shortly before New Year's. He plugged in the lighted Christmas wreath in the dingy library and relaxed in the hammock-contoured lounge chair with yet another cup of coffee. With refurbishing, he reflected, the library would make an impressive office for the president of the college. Yum Yum was lounging on his lap, her chin resting heavily on his right hand, forcing him to lift his coffee cup with his left. Koko was sitting on *Robinson Crusoe* in the warm glow of a table lamp. It was a strange coincidence that the cat had chosen that title for their winter reading; it would be even stranger if Celia Robinson were to move to Pickax and become a purveyor of meatloaf to their royal highnesses.

The Robinson Connection was not the only coincidence that aroused Qwilleran's wonder. There were three desk drawers filled with pipe cleaners, used emery boards, half-empty matchbooks, pencil stubs, and other junk destined for the trashcan. Yet, among them were articles clearly associated with the recent investigation: the chess piece, for example . . . someone's denture . . . the 1928 birth certificate . . . a great deal of *purple* . . . and many items related to financial affairs. And then there was the safe! All these were obvious. It required a great leap of imagination, however, to link shoelaces and corn plasters with the Foote family. Nevertheless, Qwilleran had learned to give his imagination free rein when Koko telegraphed his messages. After all, it was a gold signet *ring* that finally suggested a ring of criminals in the Pink Sunset case. Was it all happenstance? he wondered.

"YOW!" said the cat at his elbow—a piercing utterance with negative significance.

If Qwilleran had any further doubts about Koko's role in the investigation, they were dispelled by the cat's subsequent behavior: He never sat in the safe again . . . He lost interest in *Robinson Crusoe* . . . He completely ignored the fifty closets.

The case was closed, he seemed to be indicating. Or was it only feline fickleness?

Cats! Qwilleran thought; I'll never understand them.

For the remainder of the winter Koko was content to watch falling snowflakes from the window of the library, meditate on top of heat registers, chase Yum Yum up and down the stairs, and frequently bite her neck. She loved it!

The Cat Who Came to Breakfast

One

It was a weekend in June—glorious weather for boating. A small cabin cruiser with *Double-Six* freshly painted on the sternboard chugged across the lake at a cautious speed. Stowed on the aft deck were suitcases, cartons, a turkey roaster without handles, and a small wire-mesh cage with a jacket thrown over the top.

"They're quiet!" the pilot yelled above the motor noise.

The passenger, a man with a large moustache, shouted back, "They like the vibration!"

"Yeah. They can smell the lake, too!"

"How long does it take to cross?"

"The ferry makes it in thirty minutes! I'm going slow so they don't get seasick!"

The passenger lifted a sleeve of the jacket for a surreptitious peek. "They seem to be okay!"

Pointing across the water to a thin black line on the horizon, the pilot announced loudly. "That's our destination! . . . Breakfast Island, ahoy!"

"YOW!" came a piercing baritone from the cage.

"That's Koko!" the passenger yelled. "He knows what 'breakfast' means!"

"N-n-NOW!" came a shrill soprano echo.

"That's Yum Yum! They're both hungry!"

The cabin cruiser picked up speed. For all of them it was a voyage to another world.

Breakfast Island, several miles from the Moose County mainland, was not on the navigation chart. The pear-shaped blip of land—

broad at the south end and elongated at the northern tip—had been named Pear Island by nineteenth-century cartographers. Less printable names were invented by lake captains who lost ships and cargo on the treacherous rocks at the stem end of the pear.

The southern shore was more hospitable. For many years, fishermen from the mainland, rowing out at dawn to try their luck, would beach their dinghies on the sand and fry up some of their catch for breakfast. No one knew exactly when or how Breakfast Island earned its affectionate nickname, but it was a long time before the economic blessing known as tourism.

Moose County itself, 400 miles north of everywhere, had recently been discovered as a vacation paradise; its popularity was developing gradually by word of mouth. Breakfast Island, on the other hand, blossomed suddenly—the result of a seed planted by a real-estate entrepreneur, nurtured by a financial institution, and watered by the careful hand of national publicity.

Two days before the voyage of the *Double-Six,* the flowering of Breakfast Island was the subject of debate on the mainland, where two couples were having dinner at the Old Stone Mill.

"Let's drink a toast to the new Pear Island resort," said Arch Riker, publisher of the local newspaper. "Best thing that ever happened to Moose County!"

"I can hardly wait to see it," said Polly Duncan, head of the Pickax Public Library.

Mildred Riker suggested, "Let's all four of us go over for a weekend and stay at a bed-and-breakfast!"

The fourth member of the party sat in moody silence, tamping his luxuriant moustache.

"How about it, Qwill?" asked Riker. "Will you drink to that?"

"No!" said Jim Qwilleran. "I don't like what they've done to Breakfast Island; I see no reason for changing its name; and I have no desire to go there!"

"Well!" said Polly in surprise.

"Really!" said Mildred in protest.

The two men were old friends—journalists from "Down Below," as Moose County natives called the population centers of the United States. Now Riker was realizing his dream of publishing a country newspaper, and Qwilleran, having inherited money, was living a comfortable bachelor life in Pickax City (population 3,000) and writing a column for the *Moose County Something*. Despite the droop of his pepper-and-salt moustache and the melancholy look in his heavy-lidded eyes, he had found middle-aged contentment here.

He walked and biked and filled his lungs with country air. He met new people and confronted new challenges. He had a fulfilling friendship with Polly Duncan. He lived in a spectacular converted apple barn. And he shared the routine of everyday living with two Siamese cats.

"Let me tell you," he went on to his dinner partners, "why I'm opposed to the Pear Island resort. When I first came up here from Down Below, some boaters took me out to the island, and we tied up at an old wooden pier. The silence was absolute, except for the scream of a gull or the splash of a fish jumping out of the water. God! It was peaceful! No cars, no paved roads, no telephone poles, no people, and only a few nondescript shacks on the edge of the forest!" He paused and noted the effect he was having on his listeners. "What is on that lonely shore now? A three-story hotel, a marina with fifty boat slips, a pizza parlor, a T-shirt studio, and *two fudge shops!*"

"How do you know?" Riker challenged him. "You haven't even been over there to see the resort, let alone count the fudge shops."

"I read the publicity releases. That was enough to turn me off."

"If you had attended the press preview, you'd have a proper perspective." Riker had the ruddy face and paunchy figure of an editor who had attended too many press previews.

"If I ate their free lunch," Qwilleran shot back, "they'd expect all kinds of puffery in my column . . . No, it was enough, Arch, that you gave them the lead story on page one, three pictures inside, and an editorial!"

The publisher's new wife, Mildred, spoke up. "Qwill, I went to the preview with Arch and thought XYZ Enterprises did a very tasteful job with the hotel. It's rustic and blends in nicely. There's a shopping strip on either side of the hotel—also rustic—and the signage is standardized and not at all junky." This was high praise coming from someone who taught art in the public schools. "I must admit, though, that you can smell fudge all over the island."

"And horses," said her husband. "It's a heady combination, let me tell you! Since motor vehicles are prohibited, visitors hire carriages or hail horse cabs or rent bicycles or walk."

"Can you picture the traffic jam when that little island is cluttered with hordes of bicycles and strollers and sightseeing carriages?" Qwilleran asked with a hint of belligerence.

Polly Duncan laid a hand softly on his arm. "Qwill, dear, should we attribute your negative attitude to guilt? If so, banish the thought!"

Qwilleran winced. There was some painful truth in her well-intended statement. It was his own money that had financed, to a great degree, the development of the island. Having inherited the enormous Klingenschoen fortune based in Moose County, he had established the Klingenschoen Foundation to distribute mega-millions for the betterment of the community, thus relieving himself of responsibility. A host of changes had resulted, some of which he questioned. Nevertheless, he adhered to his policy of hands-off.

Polly continued, with sincere enthusiasm. "Think how much the K Foundation has done for the schools, health care, and literacy! If it weren't for Klingenschoen backing, we wouldn't have a good newspaper and plans for a community college!"

Riker said, "The Pear Island Hotel alone will provide three hundred jobs, many of them much-needed summer work for young people. We pointed that out on our editorial page. Also, the influx of tourists will pour millions into the local economy over a period of time. At the press preview, I met the editor of the *Lockmaster Ledger,* and he told me that Lockmaster County is green with envy. They say we have an offshore goldmine. One has to admire XYZ for undertaking such a herculean project. Everything had to be shipped over on barges: building materials, heavy equipment, furniture! Talk about giving yourself a few problems!"

The man with a prominent moustache huffed into it with annoyance.

"Why fight it, Qwill? Isn't the K Foundation a philanthropic institution? Isn't it mandated to do what's best for the community?"

Qwilleran shifted uncomfortably in his chair. "I've kept my nose out of the operation because I know nothing about business and finance—and care even less—but if I had offered more input, the directors might have balanced economic improvement with environmental foresight. More and more I'm concerned about the future of our planet."

"Well, you have a point there," Riker admitted. "Let's drink to environmental conscience!" he said jovially, waving his empty glass at a tall serving person, who was hovering nearby. Derek Cuttlebrink was obviously listening to their conversation. "Another Scotch, Derek."

"No more for me," said Mildred.

Polly was still sipping her first glass of sherry.

Qwilleran shook his head, having downed two glasses of a local mineral water.

Everyone was ready to order, and Riker inquired if there were any specials.

"Chicken Florentine," said the server, making a disagreeable face.

The four diners glanced at each other, and Mildred said, "Oh, no!"

They consulted the menu, and the eventual choice was trout for Mildred, sweetbreads for Polly, and rack of lamb for the two men. Then Qwilleran returned to the subject: "Why did they change it to Pear Island? I say that Breakfast Island has a friendly and appetizing connotation."

"It won't do any good to complain," Riker told him. "XYZ Enterprises has spent a fortune on wining and dining travel editors, and every travel page in the country has hailed the discovery of Pear Island. Anyway, that's what it's called on the map, and it happens to be pear-shaped. Furthermore, surveys indicate that a sophisticated market Down Below finds 'Pear Island' more appealing than 'Breakfast Island,' according to Don Exbridge." He referred to the X in XYZ Enterprises.

"They like the pear's erotic shape," Qwilleran grumbled. "As a fruit it's either underripe or overripe, mealy or gritty, with a choice of mild flavor or no flavor."

Mildred protested. "I insist there's nothing to equal a beautiful russet-colored Bosc with a wedge of Roquefort!"

"Of course! A pear needs all the help it can get. It's delicious with chocolate sauce or fresh raspberries. What isn't?"

"Qwill's on his soapbox again," Riker observed.

"I agree with him on the name of the island," said Polly. "I think 'Breakfast Island' has a certain quaint charm. Names of islands on the map usually reflect a bureaucratic lack of imagination."

"Enough about pears!" Riker said, rolling his eyes in exasperation. "Let's eat."

Mildred asked Qwilleran, "Don't you have friends who've opened a bed-and-breakfast on the island?"

"I do indeed, and it disturbs me. Nick and Lori Bamba were about to convert one of the old fishing lodges there. Then the Pear Island resort hoopla started, and they got sucked into the general promotional scheme. They would have preferred leaving the island in its natural state as much as possible."

"Here comes the food," Arch Riker said with a sigh of relief.

Qwilleran turned to the young man who was serving the entrées. "How come you're waiting on tables, Derek? I thought you'd been promoted to assistant chef."

"Yeah . . . well . . . I was in charge of French fries and garlic toast, but I can make more money out on the floor, what with tips, you know. Mr. Exbridge—he's one of the owners here—said he might give me a summer job at his new hotel. You can have a lot of fun, working at a resort. I'd like to be captain in the hotel dining room, where they slip you a ten for giving them a good table."

"As captain you'd be outstanding," Qwilleran said. Derek Cuttlebrink was six-feet-eight and still growing.

Polly asked him, "Now that Pickax is getting a community college, do you think you might further your education?"

"If they're gonna teach ecology, maybe I will. I've met this girl, you know, and she's into ecology pretty heavy."

Qwilleran asked, "Is she the girl who owns the blue nylon tent?"

"Yeah, we went camping last summer. I learned a lot . . . Anything else you guys want here?"

When Derek had ambled away, Riker muttered, "When will his consumption of French fries and hot dogs start nourishing his brain instead of his arms and legs?"

"Give him a break. He's smarter than you think," Qwilleran replied.

The meal was untainted by any further argument about Breakfast Island. The Rikers described the new addition to their beach house on the sand dune near Mooseville. Polly announced that her old college roommate had invited her to visit Oregon. Qwilleran, when pressed, said he might do some free-lance writing during the summer.

In pleased surprise, Polly asked, "Do you have something important in mind, dear?" As a librarian, she entertained a perennial hope that Qwilleran would write a literary masterpiece. Although the two of them had a warm and understanding relationship, this particular aspiration was hers, not his. Whenever she launched her favorite theme, he found a way to tease her.

"Yes . . . I'm thinking . . . of a project," he said soberly. "I may undertake to write . . . cat opera for TV. How's this for a scenario? . . . In the first episode we've left Fluffy and Ting Foy hissing at each other, after an unidentified male has approached her and caused Ting Foy to make a big tail. Today's episode starts with a long shot of Fluffy and Ting Foy at their feeding station, gobbling their food amicably. We zoom in on the empty plate and the wash-up ritual, frontal exposures only. Then . . . close-up of a cuckoo clock. (Sound of cuckooing.) Ting Foy leaves the scene. (Sound of scratching in litter box.) Cut to female, sitting on her brisket, meditating. She turns her head. She hears something! She reacts anxiously. Has her mysterious lover returned? Will Ting Foy come back from the litter box? Why is he taking so long? What will happen when the two males meet? . . . Tune in tomorrow, same time."

Riker guffawed. "This has great sponsorship potential, Qwill: catfood, cat litter, flea collars . . ."

Mildred giggled, and Polly smiled indulgently. "Very amusing, Qwill dear, but I wish you'd apply your talents to belles lettres."

"I know my limitations," he said. "I'm a hack journalist, but a *good* hack journalist: nosy, aggressive, suspicious, cynical—"

"Please, Qwill!" Polly remonstrated. "We appreciate a little nonsense, but let's not be totally absurd."

Across the table the newlyweds gazed at each other in middle-aged bliss. They were old enough to have grandchildren but young enough to hold hands under the tablecloth. Both had survived marital upheavals, but now the easygoing publisher had married the warm-hearted Mildred Hanstable, who taught art and homemaking skills in the public schools. She also wrote the food column for the *Moose County Something*. She was noticeably overweight, but so was her bridegroom.

For this occasion Mildred had baked a chocolate cake, and she suggested having dessert and coffee at their beach house. The new addition had doubled the size of the little yellow cottage, and an enlarged deck overlooked the lake. Somewhere out there was Breakfast and/or Pear Island.

The interior of the beach house had undergone some changes, too, since their marriage. The handmade quilts that previously muffled the walls and furniture had been removed, and the interior was light and airy with splashes of bright yellow. The focal point was a Japanese screen from the VanBrook estate, a wedding gift from Qwilleran.

Riker said, "It's hard to find a builder for a small job, but Don Exbridge sent one of his crackerjack construction crews, and they built our new wing in a jiffy. Charged only for labor and materials."

A black-and-white cat with rakish markings walked inquisitively into their midst and was introduced as Toulouse. He went directly to Qwilleran and had his ears scratched.

"We wanted a purebred," said Mildred, "but Toulouse came to our door one day and just moved in."

"His coloring is perfect with all the yellow in the house," Polly remarked.

"Do you think I've used too much? It's my favorite color, and I tend to overdo it."

"Not at all. It makes a very spirited and happy ambiance. It reflects your new lifestyle."

Riker said, "Toulouse is a nice cat, but he has one bad habit. He pounces on the kitchen counter when Mildred is cooking and steals a shrimp or a pork chop, right from under her nose. When I lived Down Below, we had a cat who was a counter-pouncer, and we cured his habit with a spray bottle of water. We had a damp pet for a couple of weeks (that's spelled d-a-m-p), but he got the message and was a model of propriety for the rest of his life—except when we weren't looking."

The evening ended earlier than usual, because Polly was working the next day. No one else had any Saturday commitments. Riker, following his recent marriage, no longer spent seven days a week at the office, and Qwilleran's life was unstructured, except for feeding and brushing the Siamese and servicing their commode. "My self-image," he liked to say, "was formerly that of a journalist; now I perceive myself as handservant to a pair of cats—also tailservant."

He and Polly drove back to Pickax, where she had an apartment on Goodwinter Boulevard, not far from his converted apple barn. As soon as they pulled away from the beach house he popped the question: "What's all this about going to Oregon? You never told me."

"I'm sorry, dear. My old roommate phoned just before you picked me up, and the invitation was so unexpected, I hardly knew how to decide. But I have two weeks more of vacation time, and I've never seen Oregon. They say it's a beautiful state."

"Hmmm," Qwilleran murmured as he considered all the aspects of this sudden decision. Once she had gone to England alone and had become quite ill. Once she had gone to Lockmaster for a weekend and had met another man. At length he asked, "Shall I feed Bootsie while you're away?"

"That's kind of you to offer, Qwill, but he really needs a live-in companion for that length of time. My sister-in-law will be happy to move in. When I return, we should think seriously about spending a weekend on the island at an interesting bed-and-breakfast."

"A weekend of inhaling fudge fumes could be hazardous to our health," he objected. "It would be safer to fly down to Minneapolis with the Rikers. You and Mildred could go shopping, and Arch and I could see a ballgame." He stroked his moustache in indecision, wondering how much to tell her. He had an uneasiness about the present situation that was rooted in the old days, when he and Riker worked for large newspapers Down Below. They kept a punctilious distance from advertisers, lobbyists, and politicians as a matter of policy. Now, Riker was getting too chummy with Don Exbridge. XYZ Enterprises was a heavy advertiser in the *Moose County Something;* Exbridge had lent the Rikers a cottage for their honeymoon; and he had expedited the building of an addition to their beach house.

To Qwilleran it looked bad. And yet, he tried to tell himself, this was a small town, and everything was different. There were fewer people, and they were constantly thrown together at churches, fraternal lodges, business organizations, and country clubs. They were all on first-name terms and mutually supportive. And there were times when they covered up for each other. He had met Don Exbridge socially and at the Pickax Boosters Club and found him a hearty, likable man, ever ready with a handshake and a compliment. His cheerful face always looked scrubbed and polished; so did the top of his head, having only a fringe of brown hair over his ears. Exbridge was the idea man for the XYZ firm, and he said his cranium could sprout either ideas or hair but not both.

Polly said, "You're quiet tonight. Did you have a good time? You look wonderful—ten years younger than your age." Under his blazer he was wearing her birthday gift—a boldly striped shirt with white collar and a patterned tie.

"Thanks. You're looking pretty spiffy yourself. I'm glad to see you wearing bright colors. I assume it means you're happy."

"You know I'm happy, dear—happier than I've ever been in my life! . . . What did you think of Mildred's decorating?"

"I'm glad she got rid of all those quilts. The yellow's okay, I guess."

They turned into Goodwinter Boulevard, an avenue of old stone mansions that would soon be the campus of the new community college. The Klingenschoen Foundation had bought the property and donated it to the city. Currently there was some debate as to whether the institution should be named after the Goodwinters, who had founded the city, or after the original Klingenschoen, who was a rascally old saloonkeeper. Polly's apartment occupied a carriage house behind one of the mansions—within walking distance of the public library—and she was assured of a leasehold.

"Things will get lively here when the college opens," Qwilleran reminded her.

"That's all right. I like having young people around," she said, adding slyly, "Would you like to come upstairs and say goodnight to Bootsie?"

Afterward, driving home to his barn, Qwilleran considered the hazards of letting Polly out of his sight for two weeks. She was a perfect companion for him, being a loving, attractive, intelligent woman of his own age, with a gentle voice that never ceased to thrill him.

Anything could happen in Oregon, he told himself as he turned on the car radio. After the usual Friday night rundown on the soccer game between Moose County and Lockmaster, the WPKX announcer said:

"Another serious incident has occurred at the Pear Island Hotel, the second in less than a week. An adult male was found drowned in the hotel pool at eleven-fifteen this evening. The name of the victim is being withheld, but police say he was not a resident of Moose County. This incident follows on the heels of the food poisoning that caused fifteen hotel guests to become ill, three of them critically. Authorities have given the cause as contaminated chicken."

As soon as Qwilleran reached the barn, he telephoned Riker. "Did you hear the midnight news?"

"Damn shame!" said the publisher. "The island's been getting so much national coverage that the media will pounce on these accidents with perverse glee! What concerns me is the effect the bad publicity will have on the hotel and other businesses. They've gambled a helluva lot of money on these projects."

"Do you really think the incidents are accidents?" Qwilleran asked pointedly.

"Here we go again! With your mind-set, everything's foul play," Riker retorted. "Wait a minute. Mildred's trying to tell me something." After a pause he came back on the line. "She wishes you'd reconsider the idea of a weekend on the island—the four of us—when Polly returns from vacation. She thinks it would be fun."

"Well . . . you know, Arch . . . I don't go for resorts or cruises or anything like that."

"I know. You like working vacations. Well, sleep on the idea anyway. It would please the girls . . . and since you're such a workaholic, how about writing three columns a week instead of two during the summer? Staff members will be taking vacations, and we'll be short-handed."

"Steer them away from Pear Island resort," Qwilleran said. "I have a hunch the ancient gods of the island are frowning."

Two

The morning after the drowning in the hotel pool, Qwilleran was roused from sleep at an early hour by the ringing of the telephone. After a glance at his watch, he answered gruffly.

"Sorry to call so early," said a familiar voice, "but I need to see you about something."

"Where are you?"

"In Mooseville, but I can be in Pickax in half an hour."

"Come on down," Qwilleran said curtly. Then, grumbling to himself, he pressed the button on the computerized coffeemaker, threw on some clothes, and ran a wet comb through his hair. There was no sound from the loft, where the Siamese had their private quarters, so he decided to let sleeping cats lie. His mind was on Nick Bamba, who had phoned so urgently.

In Qwilleran's book, Nick and Lori were an admirable young couple. She had been postmaster in Mooseville until she retired to raise a family. Nick was head engineer at the state prison. It had been their dream to own and operate a bed-and-breakfast, in the hope that he could quit his well-paying but demoralizing job. Thanks to a low-interest loan from the Klingenschoen Foundation, they had bought an old fishing lodge on Breakfast Island. Before they could open their inn, however, they found themselves involved in the wholesale commercialization of the primitive island.

As Qwilleran understood its history, the island had been populated for generations by the descendents of shipwrecked sailors and travelers. According to popular legend, some of the early castaways on this deserted shore turned to piracy in order to survive, luring other ships onto the rocks to be looted. That was only hearsay, however; historians had found no proof. One fact was known: Subsequent generations lived in privation, hauling nets in summer and living on salt-dried fish and wild rabbits in winter, eked out by goat's milk and whatever would grow in the rocky, sandy terrain. Through the years, many islanders had moved to the mainland, but those who remained were independent and fiercely proud of their heritage. This much Qwilleran had learned from Homer Tibbitt, the Moose County historian.

In the 1920s, according to Tibbitt, affluent families from Down Below discovered the island. Railroad czars, mercantile kings, beer barons, and meat-packing tycoons were attracted by the sport fishing, healthful atmosphere, and utter seclusion. They built fishing lodges on the west beach—rustic pavilions large enough to accommodate their families, guests, and servants. Native islanders did the menial work for them, and for a while local goat cheese was all the rage at parties on the west beach. Then came the 1929 Stock Market Crash, and suddenly there were no more yachts moored offshore, no gin and badminton parties on the terraces. Not until after World War II did descendents of the czars and tycoons return to the family lodges to escape allergies and the stress of high-tech life Down Below.

Meanwhile, the islanders clung to their simple pioneer lifestyle. Once, when Qwilleran had visited the south end of the island with boating friends, it appeared deserted except for two gaunt old men who materialized out of the woods and stared at them with brooding hostility. That was several years before XYZ Enterprises moved in with their planners and promoters.

Nick Bamba's pickup truck pulled into the barnyard exactly on schedule, and a young man with a boat captain's cap on his curly black hair walked into the barn. With his flashing black eyes roving about the interior, he said what he always said: "Man! What a B-and-B you could make out of this baby!"

It was an octagonal apple barn, well over a hundred years old, with fieldstone foundation, shingled siding, and windows of various shapes and sizes. The interior was open to the roof, four stories overhead, and a ramp spiraled around the walls, connecting the rooms on three upper levels. On the main floor a large white fireplace cube in dead center divided the open space into areas for lounging, dining, and food preparation. In Qwilleran's case this meant opening cans, thawing frozen dinners, and pressing the button on the coffeemaker.

He poured mugs of coffee and ushered his guest into the lounge. Ordinarily Nick radiated vitality; today he looked tired, overworked, and dispirited. To open the conversation on a comfortable note Qwilleran asked him, "Is your entire family on the island?"

The young man recited in a monotone: "Jason is staying with my mother in Mooseville until school's out. I take him to the island for weekends. The two young ones are with Lori at the inn. So are the cats. We have five now, one pregnant. The island is overrun with feral cats, so ours don't go out, but they have the run of the inn. We also have a rent-a-cat service for guests who'd like a cat in their room overnight—just a gimmick—no extra charge."

"Can Lori manage the inn and take care of two youngsters?"

"She employs island women to help."

"I hope you're charging enough to make your venture worthwhile."

"Well, Don Exbridge advised us on rates. We're not cheap, but we're competitive."

"How many rooms?"

"Seven rooms, two suites, and five housekeeping cottages."

Nick's terse replies reflected his nervousness, so Qwilleran said, "You wanted to see me about something urgent."

"Did you hear about the drowning last night?"

"Only briefly, on the air. What were the circumstances? Do you know?"

"He'd been drinking in the hotel bar. They'll have to lock the pool gates after a certain hour or provide better security. But the worst thing was the food poisoning! Contaminated chicken brought in from the mainland! All food has to come by boat."

"Did the first incident affect business?" Qwilleran asked.

"Sure did! Sunday papers around the country had carried all kinds of publicity, so it was hot news when fifteen guests were struck down. Rotten timing! The hotel had wholesale cancellations right away. We had a honeymoon couple booked for the bridal suite in July, and they canceled."

"Sorry to hear that."

Nick lapsed into rueful silence while Qwilleran refilled the mugs. Then he said, "We had a bummer ourselves last Tuesday."

"What happened? I didn't hear about it."

"One of our front steps caved in, and a guest fell and broke a rib. An old man. He was airlifted to the hospital on the mainland. It wasn't a big enough disaster to make the headlines, but I worry just the same."

"Are you afraid of being sued? Who was the victim?"

"A retired clergyman from Indiana. We're not worried about a lawsuit. He's not the type who'd take advantage of our insurance company. We're paying his medical expenses and giving him free rent, but . . . Qwill, there was nothing wrong with those steps! I swear! The building was thoroughly inspected before they gave us a license!"

Qwilleran patted his moustache in self-congratulation; it was just as he had guessed. "Are you suggesting sabotage, Nick?"

"Well, you know how my mind works, after eight years of working at the prison. I can't help suspecting dirty tricks. Three incidents right after the grand opening of the resort! It looks fishy to me! How about you?"

Qwilleran was inclined to agree. A tingling on his upper lip, which was the source of all his hunches, suggested an organized plot to embarrass, discredit, and possibly ruin the Pear Island resort. "Do you have any clues?" he asked.

"Well, this may sound crazy, and I wouldn't tell anyone but you." Nick leaned forward in his chair. "The island is getting a bunch of day-trippers from Lockmaster—dudes swaggering up and down the waterfront in high-heeled boots. They wear Lockmaster T-shirts and baseball caps with six-inch bills and raunchy slogans. They're just looking for trouble."

The enmity between Moose County and the relatively rich county to the south was well known. Violence often broke out at soccer games. Troublemakers periodically invented rumors of border incidents and then took vigilante revenge. Even mature citizens of Lockmaster took pleasure in vaunting their superiority, boasting about their rich horse farms, good schools, winning athletic teams, and fine restaurants. That was before Qwilleran's fluke inheritance. After that, the Klingenschoen millions began improving the quality of life in Moose County. Besides building a better airport and giving the high school an Olympic-size swimming pool, Klingenschoen money was luring the best teachers, physicians, barbers, and TV repairmen from Lockmaster. And now . . . Moose County had the Pear Island resort—an economic plum pudding, sauced with the sweet taste of national publicity.

Nick went on with his story: "Last Sunday three of these goons were actually sitting on our porch swings at the inn, smoking God-knows-what. I pointed to the No Smoking sign and asked if they were taught to read in Lockmaster. They gave me the finger and went on puffing, so I called Island Security. The county doesn't supply much police protection—Don Exbridge is lobbying for more—so we hire our own weekend security guys. They're uniformed like Canadian Mounties and look pretty impressive when they ride up on horses. So the hoods took off without any more trouble, but . . . it makes me wonder, you know?"

"Have you mentioned your suspicions to Exbridge?"

"Well, he's not on the island weekends, and I can't be there during the week. Besides, I'd feel stupid talking to him when I don't have anything but a gut feeling. What I wish, Qwill, is that you'd go to the island and snoop around. You're good at that kind of thing. You might come up with some evidence, or at least a clue. You could stay in one of our cottages. Bring the cats."

Qwilleran had an unbridled curiosity and a natural urge to find answers to questions. Also, he had spent years as a crime reporter Down Below. "Hmmm," he mused, tempted by the prospect of snooping.

Nick said, "It's really nice on the island, and you'd like the food. Lori's breakfasts are super; everybody says so. And the hotel has a chef from New Orleans."

"New Orleans?" Qwilleran repeated with growing interest. Food often figured in his decision making. "If I were to go over there, when would you suggest—?"

"Soon as possible. I have to bring Jason back here tomorrow afternoon, and I could ferry you to the island after that. I have my own boat now. If you meet me at the dock in Mooseville around four o'clock, we'll reach the island in plenty of time for you to get settled and go to the hotel for a good dinner."

"But no chicken!" Qwilleran quipped.

When Nick said goodbye and jumped into his pickup, there was more buoyancy in his attitude than when he arrived. It was still early, but Qwilleran climbed the ramp to release the Siamese from their loft apartment. Surprised at the early reveille, they staggered out of the room, yawning and stretching and looking glassy-eyed.

"Breakfast!" he announced, and they hightailed it into the kitchen, bumping into each other in their eagerness. "What would you two carnivores like to eat this morning? I can offer you a succulent rack of lamb from the famous kitchen of the Old Stone Mill, minced by hand and finished with a delicate sauce of meat juices." He liked to talk to them in a declamatory voice when he was in a good mood, and the louder his voice, the more excited they became, prancing in circles and figure eights and yowling with ever-increasing volume. The noise stopped abruptly when he placed the plate on the floor, and they attacked it with quivering intensity.

They were seal-point Siamese with blue eyes, sleek bodies, and light fawn fur shading into dark brown. Yum Yum was a dainty minx with a piquant expression and winning ways. Koko, whose real name was Kao K'o Kung, was the noble male with imperial manner and inscrutable gaze. He was the quintessential Siamese—with some additional talents that were not in the breeders' manual.

Qwilleran watched them devour their breakfast, while pondering his next step: how to break the news to Arch Riker without losing face. After blasting the Pear Island resort all evening, he was now joining the enemy for two weeks, that being the length of Polly's vacation.

He waited until eight o'clock and then telephoned the Rikers' beach house. "Great party last night, Arch! Did I make myself a bore?"

"What do you mean?"

"My tirade against the Pear Island resort must have been somewhat tiresome. Anyway, I'd like to make amends."

"Uh-oh! What's the catch?" asked the man who had known Qwilleran since kindergarten. Their friendship had survived almost half a century of confiding, bantering, arguing, leg-pulling, rib-poking, and caring. "I suspect you have devious intentions."

"Well, to tell the truth, Arch, I'm still ticked off about the commercial rape of Breakfast Island, but—without playing politics—I'm willing to go there for a couple of weeks and write about island history, customs, and legends. I'd call it 'The Other Side of the Island.' How does it sound?"

"I'll tell you how it sounds, you dirty rat! It sounds as if Polly is going out of town for two weeks, and you're desperate for something to occupy your time! I can always read your hand; I've known you too long to fall for a fast shuffle."

"Will you okay my expense account?" Qwilleran asked to taunt him.

There was a moment of silence on the line. Riker was editor and publisher of the *Moose County Something,* but the Klingenschoen Foundation owned it. "Okay, go ahead," Riker said. "But it had better be good."

"I'll be staying at the Bambas' B-and-B. I don't know the phone number, but they call it the Domino Inn."

After that hurdle was cleared, the rest was easy. Qwilleran called his janitor, Mr. O'Dell, who said, "Faith an' you'll not catch me settin' foot on that island no more! What they're doin' is ag'in Auld Mither Nature, it is. Nothin' good'll come of it, I'm thinkin'."

Qwilleran also gave instructions to his secretarial service to forward mail in care of General Delivery at Pear Island—but only letters postmarked Oregon.

Finally, he phoned Andrew Brodie at home on Saturday evening. Brodie was chief of police in Pickax—a towering, swaggering Scot who played the bagpipe at weddings and funerals. When Mrs. Brodie answered, the inevitable television audio could be heard blatting in the background, and the chief came on the line with the gruffness of a televiewer whose program has been interrupted.

Amiably, Qwilleran opened with, "Sorry to snatch you away from your favorite cop series."

"Are you kidding? I'm watching a nature program. Terrible what's happening to the rain forest! Last week it was black bears, and before that, oil spills! What's on your mind? Want me to pipe at your wedding to Polly? For you two I'll do it for free."

"Polly's going to Oregon and may never return, and I'm going to so-called Pear Island and may never return. They say the fudge fumes are potentially lethal."

"What d'you want to go there for? You won't like what they've done to our Breakfast Island," Brodie predicted.

"Mainly I'm going to write about island life for the 'Qwill Pen' column," Qwilleran explained glibly, "but I might do a little amateur sleuthing on the side. They've had some incidents that raise questions—three in a little over a week."

"I only heard about two—the food poisoning and the drowning. The island is the sheriff's jurisdiction, and he's welcome to it. He'll have his hands full this summer, mark my word. All those tourists from Down Below—no good! No good!"

"How come we never hear any results of the sheriff's investigations, Andy?"

"If it's a big case, he calls in the troopers. If it isn't . . . well . . . no comment. Are you taking your smart cat with you? He'll show the sheriff's department a thing or two."

"I'm taking both cats. My barn will be unoccupied for two weeks, but Mr. O'Dell has the key and will check it regularly."

"We'll keep an eye on it, too," said the chief.

Brodie was one of the few persons who knew about Koko's investigative abilities. All cats are inquisitive; all cats are endowed with six senses, but Kao K'o Kung had more than the usual feline quota. His unique sensory perception told him when something was wrong. In many cases he knew what had happened, and in some cases he knew what was going to happen. The black nose quivered, the brown ears twitched, the blue eyes stared into space, and the whiskers curled when Koko was getting vibrations.

It was the whisker factor that tuned into the unknowable, Qwilleran had decided. In fact, his own moustache bristled and his upper lip tingled when he suspected malfeasance. These hunches, coupled with his innate curiosity, often led Qwilleran into situations that were none of his business. The fate of Breakfast Island was none of his business, yet he felt irresistibly drawn to the island, and he patted his moustache frequently.

Qwilleran's usual Saturday night dinnerdate with Polly was canceled, because she had to pack for her trip, but he drove her to the airport Sunday morning, without mentioning his own forthcoming excursion; he wanted to avoid explaining. "I'll miss you," he said, a declaration that was true and required no dissembling. "I suppose you're taking your binoculars and birdbook."

"They were the first things I packed," she said joyously. "It would be a thrill to add some Pacific species to my lifelist. I'd love to see a puffin bird. My college roommate lives on the shore and is quite knowledgeable about waterfowl."

"Is she—or he—also a librarian?"

Polly patted his knee affectionately. "There were no coed dormitories when I went to the university, dear. She's a residential architect, and I'm going to show her the snapshots of your barn renovation. She'll be greatly impressed. And what will you do while I'm away? Perhaps I shouldn't ask," she said coyly.

"I'll think of something," he said, "but life will be dull and devoid of pleasure and excitement."

"Oh, Qwill! Am I supposed to cry? Or laugh?"

After Polly had boarded the shuttle plane to Minneapolis, he went home to pack his own luggage. It was June, and the temperature was ideal in Moose County, but an island in the middle of the lake could have unpredictable weather. He packed sweaters and a light jacket as well as shorts and sandals. Not knowing how formal the hotel dining room might be, he packed good shirts and a summer blazer as well as knockabout clothing. He packed his typewriter, radio, tape recorder, and a couple of books from his secondhand collection of classics: Thoreau's *Walden* and Anatole France's *Penguin Island.* They seemed appropriate.

The Siamese watched with concern as a bag of cat litter and some canned delicacies went into a carton. Then the cagelike carrier was brought from the broom closet, and Yum Yum took flight. Qwilleran made a grab for her, but she slithered out of his grasp and escaped between his legs. The chase led up the ramp and across the balconies until he trapped her in the guestroom shower. "Come on, sweetheart," he said, lifting her gently, and she went limp.

Back on the main floor he put her in the carrier and announced, "All aboard for Breakfast Island!"

"Yow!" said Koko, and he jumped into the carrier. That was unusual. Ordinarily he disliked a change of address. Qwilleran thought, Does he know there's sabotage on the island? Or does he recognize the word 'breakfast'?

With the luggage stowed in the trunk of his sedan, and with the cat carrier on the backseat, Qwilleran drove north to Mooseville—past landmarks that had figured prominently in his recent life: the Dimsdale Diner, Ittibittiwassee Road, the turkey farm (under new management), the extensive grounds of the federal prison, and the significant letter K on a post.

Nick Bamba was waiting for him at the municipal pier, where a boat named *Double-Six* was bobbing lazily in the dock, but the young man's glum expression caused Qwilleran to ask, "Is everything all right?"

"Another incident!" Nick said. "Just this afternoon! A cabin cruiser blew up at the Pear Island marina. Owner killed."

"Any idea what caused it?"

"Well, he'd just bought this boat—a neat craft only three years old—and filled up at the marina gas pump. The manager thinks he didn't blow out the fumes before starting the engine."

"Inexperienced boater?" Qwilleran asked.

"Looks like it. When I bought this boat, I took a course in marine safety, but the majority of boaters don't bother. It's a bad mistake."

"Who owns the marina?"

"XYZ owns everything on the south beach. There was some damage to the pier and nearby craft, but luckily most boaters were out in the lake, fishing. What depresses me, Qwill, is that the guy was a family man. He came over on the ferry to close the deal on the boat. He paid cash for it and was going back to the mainland to pick up his wife and kids."

"A sad situation," Qwilleran said.

"What makes me sick," Nick said, "is the thought that . . . maybe it wasn't an accident!"

Three

As they stowed the luggage and the cat carrier on the deck of the *Double-Six,* Nick Bamba said, "It's great of you to do this, Qwill. How long can you stay?"

"A couple of weeks. Officially I'll be researching fresh material for the 'Qwill Pen' column."

"You're our guest, you know. Stay as long as you want."

"I appreciate the invitation, but let the newspaper foot the bill. It'll look better, and they can afford it."

As the pilot carried aboard the turkey roaster that had no handles, he said, "What's this for? Are you gonna do some serious cooking? I know the cats are crazy about turkey, but the cottage has all the pots and pans you'll need—or you can borrow from Lori's kitchen."

"That's the cats' commode," Qwilleran said in an offhand way.

"Well, I've gotta say I've never seen one like it, and I've seen a lot of cat potties."

"It's practical."

"I hope Koko and Yum Yum are good sailors."

"They've never had a boat ride, as I recall," said Qwilleran. "I'll throw my jacket over their coop in case there's too much breeze or spray from the wake. The water looks fairly choppy. I hope it won't be a bumpy ride. I don't worry about Koko, but the little one has a delicate stomach."

There was no need to worry about either of them. For the rest of the journey the Siamese were beguiled by the pleasures of the nose, raising their heads like beached seals and sniffing eagerly. During the voyage they registered the assorted smells of lake air, marine life, aquatic weeds, seagulls, and petroleum fumes. Arriving at the island they detected pails of bait, crates of fish, horses, fudge, and newness everywhere: new piers, new hotel, new shops selling new merchandise, new black-top paving, and new bicycles. Also assaulting their inquiring noses was a heady bouquet emanating from the milling mass of tourists—young and old, teen and preteen, washed and unwashed, healthy and unhealthy, tipsy and sober. Perhaps Koko's personal radar picked up friendly and unfriendly, as well, or even innocent and guilty.

As for Qwilleran, he found the island disturbingly different from the primitive scene he remembered. He had seen the photographs in the newspaper, but experiencing the altered environment was entirely unreal. The lakefront was fringed with the masts of sailboats and the superstructures of deepwater trolling vessels. A ferryboat, halfway between a tug and a barge, was unloading vacationers with luggage, and another was returning to the mainland carrying day-trippers with sunburn. Overlooking the marina was the rustic facade of the new Pear Island Hotel, artfully stained to look fifty years old. It was three stories high and a city-block long, with a porch running the entire length. Much had been said in the national publicity about the long porch and its fifty rocking chairs. Behind the hotel, making a dark-green backdrop, were tall firs and giant oaks that had been there before the first castaways were stranded on the shore.

Qwilleran thought, This is the forest primeval, and the pines and the hemlocks are murmuring "Ye gods! Wha' happened?"

The hotel was flanked by rows of rustic storefronts, each with a hitching post. Window-shoppers strolled along wooden sidewalks called "the boardwalk" in the publicity releases.

Nick said, "This is what the XYZ people call downtown."

"It resembles a movie set," Qwilleran remarked. "At least they had the good taste not to paint yellow lines on the black-top."

"Right! Don Exbridge wants to keep everything as natural as possible. The only motor vehicles permitted are police, ambulance, and fire, and they can't use sirens because of the horses. They use beepers."

There was indeed a unique hush along the waterfront, resulting from the absence of combustion engines—just a murmur of voices, the clop-clop of hooves, and the screams of seagulls and excited youngsters.

Nick hailed a horse-drawn conveyance, loaded the luggage, and said "Domino Inn" to the old man hunched sullenly over the reins. Without answering, he shook the reins, and the horse moved forward.

"What prompted the name of your inn?" Qwilleran asked.

"Well, it was a private lodge in the Twenties, and the family that owned it was nuts about dominoes. We bought it completely furnished, including a couple-dozen sets of dominoes. My name is really Dominic, you know, so Lori thought we were destined to own the place and call it the Domino Inn. It's different, anyway."

The downtown pavement and boardwalk ended, and the road became a dusty mix of sand, gravel, and weeds. "This is called West Beach Road," Nick went on. "It should be sprayed with oil, but the county is tight-fisted. They're getting all the new tax money, but they don't want to supply any services." He waved to a mounted security officer in red coat and stiff-brimmed hat. "We get spectacular sunsets on the west beach. Farther up the road is the exclusive Grand Island Club, where the rich folks have always had their clubhouse, private marina, and big summer estates. Where we are, the lodges are outside the Golden Curtain, as it's called, and they've been rezoned commercial. There are three B-and-Bs. We get a nice class of people at our inn—quiet—very friendly. Do you play dominoes?"

"No!" Qwilleran replied promptly and with resolve.

"I know you like exercise. We have a sandy beach for walking, or you can rent a bike and pedal up to Lighthouse Point. It's all uphill, but is it great coasting down! Try it! There's also a nature trail through the woods. If you like hunting for agates, go to the public beach on the other side of the island. It's all pebbles, no sand."

"Can you keep the public off this beach? I thought the law had been changed in this state."

"The public-access ordinance applies only to new owners like us," Nick explained. "Members of the Grand Island Club come under a grandfather clause, or so they say. I don't know how legal it is, but they get away with it."

"Where do the natives live?"

"In Piratetown, back in the woods, very isolated. Tourists are discouraged from going there."

There were fewer vehicles, cyclists, and joggers on West Beach Road than Qwilleran expected, leading him to ask, "How's business?"

"Well, it started off with a bang, but it's slowing down. Lori says people are busy with weddings and graduations in June. It'll pick up in July. We hope. We don't know, yet, how harmful the negative publicity is going to be."

They passed six hikers with oversize backpacks, trudging single-file on their way to the ferry, and Nick said they had been hang gliding on the sand dune near the lighthouse.

The Siamese had been quiet in their carrier, which was on the floor of the wagon, close by Qwilleran's feet, but now there was a rumble of discontent. Before he could give them any soothing reassurances, a two-wheeled horse cab passed them, headed for downtown, and the passenger—a woman in a floppy-brimmed sunhat—waved and gave him a roguish smile. Taken by surprise, he only nodded in her direction.

"Who was that woman?" he asked Nick, although he thought he recognized the white makeup and red hair.

"Who? Where? I didn't notice. I was looking at the backpackers. They've got some healthy-looking girls in that group. I'm not good at names and faces, anyway. Lori says I've got to work on that if I'm gonna be an innkeeper. In my job, people are just numbers."

Qwilleran was hardly listening to the rambling discourse. The redhead was one person whom he actively disliked, and Polly shared his sentiments. Fortunately she was going in the opposite direction, and there was luggage piled in the cab. He allowed himself to wonder what she had been doing at Pear Island; it was hardly her kind of resort. Perhaps she had been a guest behind the Golden Curtain; that was more likely.

They had been ascending gradually after leaving downtown, and now the beach was below them, reached by steps, and the woods loomed on the other side. The road curved in and out along the natural shoreline, and when the wagon rounded a bend and stopped, Qwilleran let out a yelp. "Is that yours, Nick? I don't believe it! Why didn't you tell me?"

"Wanted to surprise you. It's the only one on the island—maybe the only one in the world!"

Domino Inn was a large ungainly building with small windows, completely sided with a patchwork of white birchbark. Qwilleran thought, Why would anyone strip a whole forest of white birches to produce such an eyesore? How could they get away with it? He answered his own question: Because no one cared, back in the Twenties. Then he asked himself, Why would they buy such a thing? Why would the K Foundation finance it?

Misconstruing his silence for awe, Nick said proudly, "I thought you'd be impressed. It was written up in most of the out-of-state publicity."

To Qwilleran it looked vaguely illegal. It looked like a firetrap. It could be, or should be, riddled with termites. Mentally he renamed it the Little Inn of Horrors.

The wagon turned into the driveway and stopped at a flight of wooden steps that led up to a long porch. There were no rocking chairs, but there were porch swings hanging from chains. Immediately the front door flew open, and Lori came bounding down the steps to give Qwilleran a welcoming hug. His former secretary was now an innkeeper and mother of three, but she still wore her long golden hair in girlish braids tied with blue ribbons.

"I could barely wait for you to see it!" she cried with excitement. "Wait till you see the inside! Come on in!"

"If you don't mind," he said, "I'd like to unload the cats first. They might express their emotions in some unacceptable way, if they don't de-coop soon. I'll feed them and then come in to register."

"Do you need catfood? Do you need litter?"

"No, thank you. We're well equipped."

Nick instructed the driver to continue around to the rear and then down the lane to the fourth cottage. The sandy lane was marked with a rustic street sign: PIP COURT. It reminded Qwilleran of a poultry disease and other illnesses, and he inquired about it. The spots on dominoes are called pips, he was told.

The five cottages, hardly larger than garages, were stained a somber brown, and the door of each was painted black with white pips. The fourth cottage was identified with a double-two.

"Yours is called 'Four Pips,' and it's deeper in the woods than the first three. The cats can watch birds and rabbits from the screened porch in back. Here's the key. You go in, and I'll offload everything."

The doorstep was hardly large enough to accommodate a size-twelve shoe, and when Qwilleran unlocked the giant domino, he stepped into the smallest living quarters he had experienced since an army tent. He was a big man, accustomed to living in a four-story barn, and here he was faced with a tiny sitting room, snug bedroom, mini-kitchen, and pocket-size bathroom. True, there was a screened porch, but it was minuscule and rather like a cage. How could he exist in these cramped quarters for two weeks with a pair of active animals?

There was more. Someone had painted the walls white and dressed them up with travel posters. Then someone had gone berserk and camouflaged furniture, bed, and windows with countless yards of fabric in a splashy pattern of giant roses, irises, and ferns.

"How do you like everything?" Nick asked as he looked for places to put the luggage. "Not much extra floor space," he admitted, "and the place gets a little musty when it's closed up." He rushed around opening windows. The kitchenette was new, he said, and the plumbing was new, although it took a while for the water to run hot. The cottages had originally been built for servants.

"Did I hear a gunshot?" Qwilleran asked.

"Just rabbit hunters in the woods. From Piratetown . . . If there's anything else you want, just whistle."

Qwilleran switched on two lamps and mentioned that he could use a higher wattage for reading.

"Will do. And now I've got to take Jason back to the mainland. I'll see you next weekend . . . G'bye, kids," he said to the occupants of the portable cage.

They emerged from the carrier with wary whiskers, their bodies close to the floor and their tails drooping. They sniffed the green indoor-outdoor carpeting. They sniffed the slipcovers critically and backed away. Qwilleran sniffed, too; "musty" was not quite the word for the pervading aroma. He thought it might be the dye in the gaudy slipcovers. They really belonged in the grand ballroom of a hotel in South America, he thought.

Before unpacking, he stripped the rooms of the homey touches that Lori had supplied and put them in drawers: doilies, dried flowers, figurines, and other knickknacks. The Siamese watched him until a knock on the door sent them scuttling under the bed. A small boy stood on the doorstep, holding out a brown paper bag.

"Thank you," Qwilleran said. "Are these my light bulbs?"

The messenger made a long speech that was unintelligible to a middle-aged, childless bachelor. Nevertheless, he made an effort to be sociable. "What's your name, son?"

The boy said something in an alien tongue and then ran back to the inn. In closing the door Qwilleran saw a notice nailed to an inside panel, along with a large No Smoking sign:

WELCOME TO DOMINO INN
For your pleasure, convenience, and
safety we provide the following:

At the Inn
Breakfast in the sunroom, 7 to 10 A.M.
Games, puzzles, books, magazines, and newspapers
in the Domino Lounge
Public telephone on the balcony landing
Television in the playroom
Fruit basket in the lounge. Help yourself

In Your Cottage
Set of dominoes
Two flashlights
Oil lamps and matches

Umbrella
Mosquito spray
Fire extinguisher
Ear plugs

The notice was signed by the innkeepers, Nick and Lori Bamba, with an exhortation to "have a nice stay."

Sure, Qwilleran thought, cynically anticipating rain, mosquitoes, forest fires, power outages, stray bullets from the woods, and whatever required ear plugs—all this in a rustic strait-jacket with slipcovers like horticultural nightmares. He located the emergency items listed on the door. Then he found the dominoes in a box covered with faded maroon velvet and put them in a desk drawer, out of sight. The drawers were hard to open, possibly because of island dampness; Yum Yum, who had the instincts of a safecracker and a shoplifter, would be frustrated. When she was frustrated, she screamed like a cockatoo; the ear plugs might be useful, after all. Koko was already eying a wall calendar with malice; it had a large photograph of a basset hound and a tear-off page for each month. It was a giveaway from a maker of dogfood.

Before dressing for dinner or even feeding the cats, Qwilleran went to the inn to register. On the way he noted that the five cottages were about fifty feet apart. Five Pips had the window shades drawn. Beyond it, at the end of Pip Court, was the start of a woodland trail that looked inviting. In the front window of Three Pips he could see an elderly couple playing a table game. A pair of state-of-the-art bicycles with helmets hanging from the handlebars were parked in front of Two Pips. One Pip appeared to be empty. At the head of the lane, a large cast-iron farm bell was mounted on a post with a dangling rope and a sign: FOR EMERGENCY ONLY. Three stray cats were scrounging around trash cans at the back door of the inn.

And then Qwilleran mounted the front steps of the inn, entered the lobby, and gazed upward in amazement. The Domino Lounge had a skylight about thirty feet overhead and balcony rooms on all four sides, and the entire structure was supported by four enormous tree trunks. They were almost a yard in diameter. The bark on these monoliths was intact, and the stubby ends of sawed-off branches protruded at intervals.

There were no guests in evidence at that hour, but the same boy who had delivered the light bulbs was sitting on the floor and playing with building blocks of architectural complexity. As soon as he caught sight of the man with a large moustache, he scrambled to his feet and ran to the door marked OFFICE.

A moment later, Lori came hurrying into the lounge. "What do you think of it, Qwill? How do you like it?" She waved both arms at the gigantic tree trunks.

"Words fail me," he said truthfully. "Are you sure they're not cast concrete?"

"They're the real thing—one of the wonders of the world, I think. And I hope you're impressed by the slipcovers." All the furniture in the lounge was covered in the same overscale pattern of roses and irises, but with the three-foot tree trunks, they looked good. "I made them all myself. It took six months. I bought an entire factory closeout for practically nothing."

They were glad to get rid of it, Qwilleran thought.

The boy who had summoned his mother was back again, and he said something to Qwilleran in the same mystifying language.

Lori came to the rescue. "Mitchell wants you to know he saw a flying saucer over the lake last week."

"Good for you, son!"

"Mitchell is four years old, and he's in charge of deliveries and communications. He's very enthusiastic about his job," she said. They went into the office to register. "I hope you like your cottage, Qwill. We also have a bridal suite upstairs, in case you and Polly ever make up your minds."

"We've made up our minds. Polly and I are happily unmarried until death do us part," he said gruffly. Then, pleasantly, he asked, "Who painted the cottage doors like dominoes?"

She raised her right hand. "Guilty! They needed refinishing, so I thought it would be fun to paint them black with white pips. Nick thought I was crazy, but Don Exbridge is pushing the fun ethic. What do you think, Qwill?"

"I think it's crazy . . . and fun. And what is the purpose of the big bell?"

"Oh, that! That's to alert everyone in case of fire. There's a volunteer fire department—Nick's on call weekends—but so far, there's been no alarm—knock on wood."

"Nick mentioned that one of your elderly guests took a tumble on the front steps."

Lori nodded contritely. "I feel terrible about that! Mr. Harding in Three Pips. He was vicar of a small church in Indiana before he retired. He and Mrs. Harding are such a sweet couple. He's back from the hospital now and insists he'll heal faster here than Down Below."

"Who repaired the step?" Qwilleran asked.

"Well, that was last Tuesday. Nick wasn't here, so I had to find an islander to fix it—an old man. He looked a hundred years old, but he did a good job and didn't charge too much."

"Did he say what had happened to the step?"

"They're not very communicative—these islanders—but he said the nails were rusty. He reinforced the whole flight with new nails and braces of some kind."

"And yet, the county inspector okayed the building before you opened for business," Qwilleran said.

"That's right. It makes you wonder how good the inspection was. The county commissioners, you know, were pushing to get the resort open by mid-May, because they wanted those tax dollars. I'll bet they told the inspectors not to be too fussy."

Qwilleran glanced at his watch. "Do I need a reservation for dinner at the hotel? Should I wear a coat and tie?"

"Heavens, no! Everything's informal, but I'll call the hotel and tell them you're coming. They'll put out the red carpet for the popular columnist from the *Moose County Something.*"

"No! Not that!" he protested. "I'm keeping a low profile during this visit."

"Okay. Shall I call a horse cab?"

"I think not. I'd like to walk. But thanks just the same."

"Walk on the edge of the road," Lori advised. "The horses, you know."

On the way back to the cottage to feed the cats and change into a fresh club shirt, Qwilleran met the elderly couple from Three Pips. "Don't miss the sunset tonight," said the man, who wore a black French beret at a jaunty angle. "We always order a special performance for a new guest."

Qwilleran could see the Siamese on the back porch, and he walked around to talk to them through the screen. "Are you fellow travelers ready for a can of boned chicken imported from Pickax?"

There were two chairs on the porch, one more comfortable than the other, and with catly instinct they had chosen the better of the two. They were sitting there calmly—too calmly. It meant that one or both had committed some small misdemeanor of which they were proud. He knew them so well!

Unlocking the front door, he walked into the scene of the crime. The desktop was littered with scraps of paper, and other bits were strewn about the floor. One said: Tuesday. Others were blank squares with numbers in the upper left-hand corner. Someone had attacked the wall calendar hanging above the desk. The glossy, full-color photo of a basset hound and the name of the dogfood manufacturer were still intact, but the month of June had been ripped off piece by piece, or day by day. It was now July in Four Pips.

"Which one of you incorrigible miscreants vandalized this calendar?" he shouted toward the porch. They paid no attention, being occupied with woodland sights and sounds.

He knew the culprit; Koko was the paper shredder in the family, but only when he had a reason. Did he think he could accelerate the passage of time by canceling the month of June? Did he want to get out of this Domino Dump and go home? "Clever thinking," Qwilleran called out to him, "but unfortunately it doesn't work that way."

Four

Days were long in June and even longer in the north country. The sun was still high in the sky as Qwilleran walked downtown for his first dinner at the Pear Island Hotel. On the way, he passed the row of rustic shops on the boardwalk. Their standardized signs were computer-carved from weathered wood. A single generic label identified each establishment: SOUVENIRS, TEA ROOM, ANTIQUES, PIZZA, T-SHIRTS and, of course, FUDGE. He saw something in the window of the antique shop that he liked, but the door was locked, even though the sign in the window said Open. The T-shirt studio offered tie-dyes in garish colors, sweats and tees with slogans printed to order, and the official resort T-shirt with a large blushing pear, the size of a watermelon. Boaters, teens, retirees, couples walking hand in hand, and parents with their broods wandered aimlessly up and down the boardwalk or stood in line at the fudge shop. On the hotel porch they rocked in the fifty rocking chairs, and a few were eating take-outs from the pizza parlor.

The hotel lobby burst upon the senses as a celebration of piracy. A mural depicted swashbuckling pirates with chests of gold. Banners hanging from the ceiling had the skull-and-crossbones on a field of black. The reservation clerks wore striped shirts, red head bandanas, and a gold hoop in one ear. Qwilleran consulted the directory. There was a bar named the Buccaneer Den. The two dining areas were the Corsair Room and Smugglers' Cove. Glass doors led to the Pirates' Hole, a large swimming pool rimmed with sun lounges and umbrella tables. Youngsters splashed and squealed at the shallow end of the pool, while adults sipped drinks around the rim. The latter kept the barhops busy—young men and women wearing black T-shirts with the pirate insigne.

Qwilleran ambled into the Buccaneer Den and sat at the bar. Spotlighted on the backbar was a chest of gold coins and the words of a sea chantey: *Fifteen men on a dead man's chest! Yo ho ho and a bottle of rum!* He was comfortable on a bar stool. Before circumstances had changed his habits and hobbies, he had leaned on press club bars all around the country and had developed a barfly's savoir faire that was instantly recognized by the professionals pouring drinks. There were three of them behind the bar in the Buccaneer Den, all wearing the skull-and-crossbones.

He signaled the one who appeared to be in charge and asked, "Is it against the law to order a Bloody Mary without any booze?"

"How hot?" asked the man with expressionless face and voice. He reached for a glass.

"Three-alarm fire." Qwilleran counted the dashes of hot sauce going into the tomato juice, took a critical sip, and nodded his approval. The bartender leaned against the backbar with arms folded, and that was Qwilleran's cue to say, "You run a smooth operation here."

"Keeps us stepping, all right. We service two dining rooms and the pool, as well as this bar and lounge. We've got twenty-five stools here, and on Friday and Saturday night they're double-parked." He had the eyes of a supervisor, roving around the room as he talked.

"I know what it takes," Qwilleran said sympathetically. "I've tended bar myself." He was referring to a Saturday night gig during senior year in college. "Are you from Washington? I seem to remember you at the Mayflower."

"Nope. Wasn't me,"

"The Shoreham! That's where I've seen you."

The man shook his head. "Chicago. I worked the Loop for eighteen years. Poured enough booze to flood Commiskey Park."

"You get a different class of customer at a place like this."

"You tellin' me? Big crowds, small tabs, smaller tips." He looked hastily up and down the bar before saying, "The cola crowd—they're the worst! Order a soft drink, spike it with their own flask, and fill up on free peanuts." His busy eyes spotted an empty glass, and he signaled to a barhop.

Qwilleran asked, "What's the Pirate Gold drink that you're pushing?"

"All fresh, all natural. Fruit juice with two kinds of rum and a secret ingredient. The health nuts go for it."

Qwilleran gulped the rest of his tomato juice and slid off the stool. "Thanks. What's your name?"

"Bert."

"You mix a helluva good drink, Bert. Wish I'd known you when I was on the hard stuff. I'll be back." He left a tip large enough to be remembered.

In the lobby, a fierce character in pirate garb presided at a reservation desk. Qwilleran asked him, "Do you have a no-smoking section?"

"There's no smoking anywhere in the hotel, sir—orders of the fire department."

"Good! Do you have a no-kids section?" The lobby was teeming with vacationing small-fry, whooping and jumping with excitement.

"Yes, sir! The captain in the Corsair Room will seat you."

At that moment a friendly voice boomed across the lobby. "Qwill, you dirty P.O.B.! What are you doing here?" A young man grabbed his arm. Dwight Somers was employed as director of community services for XYZ Enterprises. They had met on a trip to Scotland and had developed an instant camaraderie. Jovially Dwight called Qwilleran a print-oriented bum and was called, in turn, a Ph.D., or doctor of publicity hackery.

"If the piracy doesn't extend to the prices," Qwilleran said, "I intend to take my life in my hands and have dinner here. Want to join me?"

It was quiet in the Corsair Room. The tables, most of them unoccupied, gleamed with white tablecloths, wine glasses, and flowers in crystal vases. "We're making some changes," Dwight said. "This class act intimidates your average tourist. We're down-scaling to vinyl tablecovers and ketchup bottles. Only tank tops will be a no-no. If you look around, you'll see we're the only dudes in club shirts."

A server in the official black-and-bones T-shirt took their order for drinks, and Qwilleran remarked to his dinner partner, "Don't you think you're working the pirate theme overtime?"

The XYZ publicity man shrugged apologetically. "The kids like it, and Don Exbridge says it's a historical reference. The island was a base of operations for lake pirates at one time. They lured ships onto the rocks so they could loot their cargo."

"You should change the name of this place to the Blackbeard Hotel. I hear one of your guests walked the plank last week. And that sea chantey on the backbar is right on target, with fifteen guests poisoned and one guest dead. Who was the guy? Do you know?"

"Just some lush from Down Below, looking for girls, or whatever."

"I'd question the secret ingredient in your Pirate Gold," Qwilleran advised.

The drinks came to the table, and Dwight said, "Where've you been? Don asked me why you didn't attend the press preview."

"I prefer to sneak around incognito and dig up my own stories. I'll be here a couple of weeks."

"Where are you staying? I know you're not on the hotel register, unless you're using an alias. I check daily arrivals."

"I'm at the Domino Inn."

"How come? There's a posh bed-and-breakfast on the west beach—called the Island Experience. It's run by two widows. Expensive, of course, but a lot better than where you're staying."

"Well, you see, I had to bring my cats," Qwilleran explained. "The Bambas are letting me have a catproof cottage."

"That makes sense, but isn't the Domino Inn the most godawful dump you ever saw? Still, it gets mentioned in all the national publicity, so maybe the Bambas knew what they were doing . . . I'm hungry. What are you going to eat?"

"Not chicken! Where has the hotel been getting its poultry?"

"From a chicken factory in Lockmaster. It's being investigated by the board of health. The hotel is absolved of blame. Don Exbridge has been in Pickax, smoothing things over. In the matter of the drowning, our head bartender is being fined for serving the guy too much liquor."

Qwilleran nodded and thought, The hotel pays his fine, and Exbridge gives him a bonus for keeping quiet. The menu featured Creole and Cajun specialties, and he ordered a gumbo described as "an incredibly delicious mélange of shrimp, turkey, rice, okra, and the essence of young sassafras leaves." "Turkey" was inked in where a previous ingredient had been inked out.

"You'll like it," said the enthusiastic waitress. "Everyone in the kitchen is giving it raves!" The waitstaff consisted of college men and women, who breezed around the dining room in a festive mood—all smiles, quips, and fast service.

Dwight, who had ordered a steak, said, "Okra! How can you eat that mucilaginous goo?"

"Are you aware that gumbo is the African word for okra?" Qwilleran asked with the lifted eyebrows of a connoisseur.

"By any other name it's still slimy." The two men concentrated on chomping their salads for a while, and then Dwight said, "How do you like the generic signs on the strip mall? There's a big turnover in resort businesses, and if Luigi's pizza parlor doesn't make a profit this summer, he can be replaced by Giuseppe next summer."

"Sounds like Exbridge's idea."

"Yeah, he comes up with some good ones, and others not so good—like his helicopter stunt. There's a landing pad behind the rescue station, and Don wants to rent a chopper and offer sightseeing trips over the island."

"If he does that," Qwilleran said with a threatening scowl, "the islanders will shoot it down with their rabbit guns; the private club will take him to court; and I'll personally crucify XYZ in my column! I don't care how much advertising revenue they pour into our coffers."

"I don't like it either," said Dwight, "but my boss is a hard guy to reason with, and now he's in a bad mood because of the boat explosion and the pickets that were parading in front of the hotel this weekend."

"Who were they?"

"Just kids from the mainland, protesting the name change from Breakfast Island, but it ruined the view for guests sitting in the porch rockers, and the chanting drowned out the seagulls and frightened the horses."

Qwilleran said, "Downtown isn't the only target. Did you hear about the accident at the Domino Inn?"

Dwight snapped to attention. "What kind of accident?" He listened to Qwilleran's description of the broken step and the injury to the elderly guest. "If you ask me, Qwill, that whole building will collapse one day like the One Hoss Shay."

"Does the island have a voice on the board of commissioners? Or is it a case of exploitation without representation?"

"Well, there's a so-called Island Commissioner, but he lives in Pickax and has never been to the island. He gets seasick on the lake. He's very cooperative, though, and Don has a good rapport with him."

The waitress interrupted with the entrées and a flutter of bonhomie: "The gumbo looks so good, and the cornbread is right out of the oven! . . . And look at this steak! Yum! Yum!"

When she was out of earshot, Qwilleran asked Dwight, "Do you write her script? Or is she a graduate of the Exbridge Charm School?"

After a few moments of serious eating, Dwight said, "The initial response to the resort has been largely motivated by curiosity, we can assume, so my job is to keep interest alive—bike races, kite-flying contests, prizes for the biggest fish, and all that hoopla, but we also need some indoor programs for the rocking chair crowd—and for rainy days, heaven forbid! The conservation guys will show videos on wildlife and boat safety. How would you like to give a talk on our trip to Scotland?"

"I wouldn't. Get Lyle Compton. He tells hair-raising tales about Scottish history."

"Good idea!" Dwight scribbled in a pocket notebook. "Any more suggestions? We can offer an overnight and dinner for two, plus a small honorarium."

"How about Fran Brodie? She gives a talk on interior design that's entertaining as well as informative, and she's attractive."

Dwight made another note. "That'll be something for the wives while their husbands are out fishing."

"Or vice versa."

"You're really clicking tonight, Qwill. Does okra stimulate the brain cells? It might be worth the yucky experience."

"Then there's Mildred Hanstable Riker," Qwilleran suggested. "She gives talks about cats and shows a video."

"Scratch that one. My boss hates cats. There are wild ones hanging around the hotel all the time."

For dessert Qwilleran ordered sweet potato pecan pie, which the waitress delivered with a rah-rah flourish, and he asked Dwight, "Where do you get these cheerleaders to wait on tables? When I was in college, I didn't have half that much bounce. Does your boss put steroids in their gumbo?"

"Aren't they great kids? We're planning to use them for a Saturday night cabaret show. All they have to do is sing loud and kick high. Vacation audiences aren't too critical of the entertainment at a resort. You said you used to write stuff for college revues. Would you like to write a skit for us?"

Qwilleran said he could write a song parody, such as, *Fudge, your magic smell is everywhere.* "But Riker wants me to bear down on writing more copy for the paper."

"I see . . . Well, you're welcome to use the hotel fax machine for filing your copy, Qwill."

"Thanks. I'll remember that."

Then Dwight made a startling announcement. "Don has hired Dr. Halliburton as our summer director of music and entertainment."

"Dr. who?"

"June Halliburton, head of music for the Moose County schools."

"Yes, I know," Qwilleran said impatiently. "I didn't realize she had a doctorate."

"Oh, sure! She has lots of degrees and lots of talent, as well as sexy good looks. She'll be here all summer after school's out. Right now she's spending only weekends and getting the feel of the resort."

Qwilleran cleared his throat. "I believe I saw her driving to the ferry today, when I was arriving."

"Then you know her! That's great! You'll be neighbors, in case you want to collaborate on something for the cabaret. She'll be staying at the Domino Inn."

Qwilleran huffed into his moustache. "Why not the hotel?"

"She wants housekeeping facilities and a studio; we're sending a small piano to her cottage. But I think the real reason is that she likes her cigarettes, and Don has outlawed smoking anywhere on the hotel grounds."

On this sour musical note the dinner ended. Leaving the hotel, Qwilleran was in a bad humor, contemplating two weeks in confined space plus a next-door neighbor he actively disliked. There was nothing to improve his mood when he explored the strip mall on the far side of the hotel: VIDEO, DELI, CRAFTS, POST OFFICE, FUDGE again, and GENERAL. The general store sold chiefly fishing tackle, beach balls, and paperback romances. He turned around and headed for home—or what he was to consider home for the next two painful weeks.

At the antique shop he had another look at the display window. There it was—something he had always wanted—the classic pair of theater masks called Tragedy and Comedy. They had a mellow gilded finish and could be, he thought, ceramic, metal, or carved wood. Also in the window were pieces of glass, china, brass, and copper, plus a tasteful sign on a small easel:

ANTIQUES BY NOISETTE
PARIS . . . PALM BEACH

The sign piqued his curiosity. Why would a dealer with Paris and Palm Beach credentials choose Pear Island as a summer venue?

There were other signs that interested him. The one in the window that had said Open when the shop was closed had now been turned around to read Closed when the shop was open. Taped on the glass panel of the door was another piece of information:

No Children Allowable If Not in Chargement of an Adult

There were no customers in the store, and he could understand why. Noisette sold only antiques—no postcards, fudge, or T-shirts. He sauntered into the shop in slow motion to disguise his eagerness about the masks; that was the first rule of standard antiquing procedure, he had been told. First he examined the bottom of a plate and held a piece of crystal to the light as if he knew what he was doing.

From the corner of his eye he saw a woman sitting at a desk and reading a French magazine. She was hardly the friendly, folksy dealer one would expect on an island 400 miles north of everywhere. She had the effortless chic that he associated with Parisian women: dark hair brushed back to emphasize a handsomely boned face; lustrous eyes of an unusual brown; tiny diamond earrings.

"Good evening," he said in the mellifluous voice he reserved for women he wanted to impress.

"Oh! Pardon!" she said. "I did not see you enter." Her precise speech said "Paris," and when she stood up and came forward, her jade silk shirt and perfectly cut white trousers said "Florida."

"You have some interesting things here," he said, mentally comparing them with the plastic pears and bawdy bumper stickers in the shop next door.

"Ah! What is it that you collect?"

"Nothing in particular. I walked past earlier and your door was locked."

"I was taking some sustainment, I regret." She walked to a locked vitrine that had small figures behind glass. "Are you interested in pre-Columbian? I take them out of the case."

"No, thanks. Don't bother. I'm just looking." He did some more aimless wandering before saying, "Those masks in the window—what are they made of?"

"They are fabrications of leather, a very old Venetian craft, requiring great precisement. I have them from the collection of a famous French film actor, but I have not the liberty to use his name, I regret."

"Hmmm," said Qwilleran without any overt enthusiasm. He then picked up an ordinary-looking piece of green glass. "And what is this?"

"It is what one calls Depression glass."

The rectangular tray of green glass was stirring vague memories.

His mother used to have one on her dresser when he was young. She would say, "Jamesy, please bring my reading glasses from the pin tray on my bureau—that's a good boy." He had never seen any pins on the pin tray, but he definitely remembered the pattern pressed into the glass.

"How much are you asking for this?" he asked.

"Twenty-five dollars. I have a luncheon set in the same pattern—sixteen pieces—and I make you a very good price if you take the entirement."

"And how much are you asking for the masks?"

"Three hundred. Are you a theater activist?"

"I'm a journalist, but I have an interest in drama. I'm here to write some features about the island. How's business?"

"Many persons come in for browsement, but it is too early. The connoisseurs, they are not yet arrived."

With studied nonchalance Qwilleran suggested, "You might let me have a closer look at the masks."

She brought Comedy from the window display, and he was surprised to find it lightweight (when it looked heavy) and soft to the touch (when it looked hard). He avoided making any comment or altering his expression.

"If you really like them," the dealer said, "I make you a little reducement."

"Well . . . let me think about it. May I ask what brought you to the island?"

"Ah, yes. I have a shop in Florida. My customers fly north in the summer, so I fly north."

"Makes good sense," he said agreeably. After a measured moment he asked, "What is the very best you can do on the masks?"

"For you, two seventy-five, because I think you appreciate."

He hesitated. "What will you take for the piece of green glass?"

"Fifteen."

He hesitated.

Then Noisette said, "If you take the masks, I give you the piece of glass."

"That's a tempting offer," he said.

"Then in probability you will come back and take the luncheon set."

"Well . . ." he said reluctantly. "Will you take a personal check?"

"With the producement of a driver's license."

"To whom do I make the check payable?"

"Antiques by Noisette."

"Are you Noisette?"

"That is my name." She wrapped the masks and the tray in tissue and put them in an elegant, glossy paper totebag.

As he was leaving, he remarked, "You and your shop would make an interesting feature for my newspaper—the *Moose County Something* on the mainland. Might we arrange an interview?"

"Ah! I regret I do not like personal publicity. But thank you, with apologies."

"That's perfectly all right. I understand. Do you have a business card?"

"But no. I have ordered some cards, and they have not yet arrived. How to explain the delayment, I do not know."

As Qwilleran walked up West Beach Road with his totebag he frequently touched his moustache; his curiosity about Noisette was turning into suspicion. Any individual in the business world who declined free publicity in his column was suspect. Her stock was scant; customers were few, if any; she was out of place on Pear Island, where a flea market would be more appropriate; her prices seemed high, although . . . what did he know about prices? He knew what he liked, that was all, and he liked those masks.

On West Beach Road the sky was gearing up for a spectacular sunset. Even the Domino Inn looked less objectionable in the rosy glow, and all the porch swings were occupied by swingers waiting for the color show. The wooden two-seaters squeaked on their chains, musically but out of tune. As Qwilleran crossed the porch on the way to see Lori, two white-haired women smiled at him sweetly, and the Hardings waved.

"How was your dinner?" Lori asked.

"Excellent! I had shrimp gumbo, and I stopped in the antique shop and bought you a pencil tray for your desk—Depression glass, circa 1930."

"Oh, thank you! My grandmother used to collect this!"

"I also bought a couple of masks I'd like to hang on my sitting room wall, if it's permissible."

"Sure," she said. "Two more holes in those old walls won't hurt. I'll give you a hammer and some nails. How do the cats like the cottage?"

"I believe they're victims of culture shock." Gallantly he refrained from mentioning the slipcovers that discomforted all three of them with their pattern if not their odor.

"Cats sense when they are surrounded by water," Lori said with assurance. "But in three days they can get used to anything."

Qwilleran said, "Koko has vandalized your wall calendar, but I'll buy you a new one and take it out of his allowance. He tore off the month of June, and now . . ." He stopped abruptly as the roots of his moustache tingled. "By the way, who are my next-door neighbors on Pip Court?"

"In Three Pips we have Mr. and Mrs. Harding, a darling elderly couple. Five Pips is rented for the season to June Halliburton from the mainland. I'm sure you know her."

"I do indeed," he said crisply. "Did anyone occupy Four Pips before we arrived?"

"As a matter of fact, she used it the first two weekends but asked to move to the end of the row. She was afraid her music would disturb the Hardings. It was very thoughtful of her . . . Are you going to watch the sunset from the porch, Qwill?"

"I have something to do first," he said as he hurried from the office.

Five

When Qwilleran returned from dinner at the hotel, the Siamese were still boycotting the slipcovers. Instead of lounging on seat cushions or bed, they crouched in awkward positions on the desk, kitchen counter, dresser, or snack table.

"Okay, you guys!" he ordered. "Clear out! We're trying an experiment." He chased them onto the porch while he stripped the premises of slipcovers, draperies, and bedcover. He also opened all the windows to dispel the haunting memory of June Halliburton, which blended her musky perfume with stale cigarette smoke. Did the Bambas know she was an inveterate smoker? Probably not. He stuffed the offending slipcovers into the bedroom closet temporarily.

What remained—when the roses and irises were gone—was as grim as the previous decor was flashy: roller blinds on the windows, a no-color blanket on the bed, and well-worn leatherette upholstery on sofa and chairs. He felt guilty about leaving the Siamese cooped up in this stark environment.

"How about a read?" he asked them. He stretched out in a lounge chair that was comfortable except for one broken spring in the seat. Yum Yum piled into his lap, and Koko perched on the arm of the chair as he read to them from *Walden.* He read about the wild mice around Walden Pond, the battle of the ants, and the cat who grew wings every winter. Soon his soothing voice put them to sleep, their furry bellies heaving in a gentle rhythm.

It was their first night on the island, and it was deadly quiet. Even in rural Moose County one could hear the hum of tires on a distant highway. On the island there was breathless silence. The wind was calm; there was no rustling of leaves in the nearby woods; the lake lapped the shore without even a whisper.

Suddenly—at the blackest hour of the night—Qwilleran was frightened out of slumber by a frenzy of demonic screams and howls. He sat up, not knowing where he was. As he groped for a bedside table, he regained his senses. The cats! Where were they? He stumbled out of the bedroom, found a light switch, and discovered the Siamese awake and ready for battle—arching their backs, bushing their tails, snarling and growling at the threat outside.

He rushed to the porch with a flashlight and turned it on a whirlwind of savage creatures uttering unearthly screeches. He ran back to the kitchen, filled a cookpot with water, and threw it out the back door. There was a burst of profanity, and then the demons disappeared into the night. The Siamese were unnerved, and he left the bedroom door open, spending the rest of the night as a human sandwich between two warm bodies.

While dressing for breakfast the next morning, he thought, Dammit! Why should we stay here? I'll make some excuse. We'll go back on the ferry.

"Ik ik ik" came a rasping retort from the next room, as if Koko knew what Qwilleran was thinking.

"Is that vote an aye or a nay, young man?"

"Ik ik ik!" The connotation was definitely negative.

"Well, if you can stand it, I can stand it, I suppose." Avoiding the closet, with its aromatic bundle of slipcovers and whatnot, Qwilleran dressed in shorts and a tee from the dresser drawer and went to the inn for breakfast, carrying a hammer. He had hung the two gilded masks over the sofa, between two travel posters, and their elegance made the sturdy, practical furnishings look even bleaker by comparison.

In the sunroom he nodded courteously to a few other guests and took a small table in a corner, where he found a card in Lori's handwriting:

GOOD MORNING
Monday, June 9
Pecan Pancakes With Maple Syrup
and Turkey-apple Sausages
or
Tarragon-chive Omelette
With Sautéed Chicken Livers
Help yourself to fruit juices, muffins, biscuits,
homemade preserves, and coffee or milk

"These pancakes are delicious," Qwilleran said to the plain-faced waitress, who shuffled about the sunroom. "Did Mrs. Bamba make these herself?"

"Ay-uh," she said without change of expression.

When the serving hours ended, he stopped drinking coffee and went to the office, where he found Lori slumped in a chair, looking frazzled. "That was a sumptuous breakfast," he said. "My compliments to the chef."

"Today I had to do it all myself," she replied wearily. "My cook didn't show up, and the waitress was late. Two of the guests volunteered to wait on tables until she came. I believe in hiring island women, but they can be annoyingly casual. Perhaps that's why the hotel hires college kids. Anyway, I'm glad you liked your first breakfast. Did you have the pancakes or the omelette?"

"To be perfectly honest, I had both."

Lori shrieked with delight. "Did you sleep well? Did you find the bed comfortable?"

"Everything was fine except for the catfight outside our back door."

"Oh, dear! I'm sorry. Did it disturb you? It only happens when strays from the other inns come over in our territory. We have three nice strays that we take care of: Billy, Spots, and Susie. They were here before we were, so we adopted them. You'll notice a lot of feral cats around the island."

Qwilleran asked, "What do the islanders think about the resort's invasion of their privacy?"

"The old-timers are dead-set against it, but they can use the jobs. My cook is an older woman. Mr. Beadle, who fixed our steps, is a great-grandfather; he's grumpy but willing to work. And the old men who drive the cabs are as grumpy as their horses. The young islanders are glad to get jobs, of course; they're not exactly grumpy, but they sure don't have any personality. They're good workers—when and if they report—but I wish they'd take their commitments more seriously."

"I'd like to talk with some of them about life on the island before the resort opened. Would they cooperate?"

"Well, they're inclined to be shy and suspicious of strangers, but there's one woman who'd have a wider perspective. She grew up here, attended high school on the mainland, and worked in restaurants over there. Now she's back on the island, operating a café for tourists—with financial aid from the K Foundation, of course. You probably know about Harriet's Family Café."

"The K Foundation never tells me anything about anything," he said. "Where is she located?"

"Up the beach a little way, in one of the old lodges. She serves lunch and dinner—plain food at moderate prices. Most of our guests go there. She also rents out the upper floors as dorm rooms for the summer help at the hotel. It's a neat arrangement. Don Exbridge masterminded this whole project, and he thought of everything."

"What is Harriet's last name?"

"Beadle. The island is full of Beadles. It was her grandfather who fixed our steps. She got him for me when I was desperate. Harriet's a nice person. She's even a volunteer firefighter!"

Before leaving the inn, Qwilleran was introduced to the Bamba brood. Shoo-Shoo, Sheba, Trish, Natasha, and Sherman were the resident cats.

"Didn't you have a Pushkin?" Qwilleran asked.

"Pushkin passed away. Old age. Sherman is pregnant."

Then there were the children. The eldest, Jason, was in first grade on the mainland; a photo of him showed a lively six-year-old with his mother's blond hair. The talkative Mitchell, age four, had his father's dark coloring and serious mien, and he spoke so earnestly that Qwilleran tried his best to understand him.

"He wants to know," his mother translated, "if you'll play dominoes with him."

"I don't know how," Qwilleran said. Actually, he had played dominoes with his mother while growing up as the only child in a single-parent household. The game had been his boyhood bête noir, along with practicing the piano and drying the dishes.

"Mitchell says he'll teach you how to play," Lori said. "And this is Lovey, our youngest. She's very smart, and we think she'll be president of the United States some day . . . Lovey, tell Mr. Qwilleran how old you are."

"Two in April," said the tot in a clear voice. She was a beautiful little girl, with a winning smile.

"That was last year, Lovey," her mother corrected her. "Now you're three in April."

"I'll tell you one thing," Qwilleran said, "you'd better change her name, or she'll never get past the New Hampshire primary. The media will have a picnic with a name like Lovey." Then he asked Lori if she had a place to store the slipcovers from Four Pips, as he seemed to be allergic to the dye. "I tried stripping the rooms last night," he said, "and haven't had any bronchitis or asthma today."

"I never knew you had allergies, Qwill! That's too bad! The housekeeper will get them out of your way as soon as possible."

"They're all in the bedroom closet," he said. "Tell her not to let the cats out."

At the bike rack downtown Qwilleran rented an all-terrain bicycle for his first island adventure, a trip to Lighthouse Point. West Beach Road was uphill all the way. As he passed the Domino Inn, guests waved to him from the porch, and Mitchell chased him like a friendly, barking dog. Next came three other B-and-Bs, Harriet's Family Café, and a unique service operation called Vacation Helpers. According to the sign in front of the converted lodge, they would "sit with the baby, wash your shirt, bake a birthday cake, sew a button on, cater a picnic, address your postcards, mail your fudge, clean your fish."

Qwilleran stopped to read it and thought it a good idea. The upper floors were apparently dormitories for hotel employees, because a group of them were leaving for work, wearing the skull-and-crossbones. One of them waved to him—the waitress from the night before.

At that point the commercial aspect of the beach road ended, and a forbidding sense of privacy began. First there was the exclusive Grand Island Club with tennis courts, a long row of stables, and a private marina, docking small yachts and tall-masted sailboats. Beyond were the summer estates, with large, rustic lodges set well back behind broad lawns. On the other side of the road, flights of wooden steps led down to private beaches with white sand. There were no bathers; the lake was notoriously cold, even in summer, and the lodge owners would undoubtedly have heated swimming pools.

Driveways were marked with discreet, rustic signs identifying the estates as RED OAKS or WHITE SANDS or CEDAR GABLES. The last and largest was THE PINES, protected by a high iron fence similar to that in front of Buckingham Palace.

How, Qwilleran wondered, were these elite vacationers reacting to the increased traffic on the beach road? On weekends there would be a continual parade of cyclists pedaling to the lighthouse. Carriageloads of gawking sightseers would stop in front of the grandest lodges to take pictures and listen to the guides spieling about family scandals.

By the same token, how would the reclusive islanders react to the noisy strangers, the aroma of fudge polluting their lake-washed air, and brash cityfolk wearing clown colors and trespassing on their sacred privacy? Would these rugged natives resent the intrusion strongly enough to retaliate? They might be an underground army of little Davids aiming slingshots at a well-capitalized Goliath who was getting a tax break.

After The Pines, the lush woods dwindled to stunted, windswept vegetation atop a mountain of sand. Beyond could be seen the lighthouse, a pristine white against a blue sky. For the last few hundred yards the road was steep, but Qwilleran bore down on the pedals resolutely. He was breathing hard when he reached the summit, but he was in better shape than he had realized.

Lighthouse Point was a desolate promontory overlooking an endless expanse of water to the north, east, and west. The tower itself was dazzlingly white in the strong sunlight, and adjacent buildings were equally well maintained. There was no sign of life, however. Such romantic figures as the lighthousekeeper and the lighthousekeeper's daughter had been made obsolete by automation. A high, steel fence surrounded the complex. Inside the fence, but visible to visitors, a bronze plaque was a reminder of the old days:

IN MEMORY OF THREE LOYAL LIGHTKEEPERS
WHO SAVED HUNDREDS OF LIVES BY
KEEPING THE BEACON BURNING BUT
LOST THEIR OWN IN THE LINE OF DUTY

There followed the names of the three men—typical north-country names that could be found in the old cemeteries of Moose County: Trevelyan . . . Schmidt . . . Mayfus. Yet, for some reason they were considered heroes. Qwilleran asked himself: What did they do to earn this recognition? Were there three isolated incidents over a period of years? Or were they swept off the rock in a storm? Why is none of this in the county history? He made a mental note to discuss the oversight with Homer Tibbitt.

On the public side of the fence the ground was a plateau of stones and weeds that showed evidence of unauthorized picnicking. There were no picnic tables or rubbish containers provided. Empty bottles were scattered about the site of a campfire, and food wrappers had blown against the fence and over the edge of the cliff. Down below were the treacherous rocks, where old wooden sailing ships had been dashed to pieces in the days before the lighthouse was built.

Moose County, in its nineteenth-century boom years, had been the richest in the state. Every month hundreds of vessels passed the island, transporting lumber, ore, gold coins, and rum, according to Mr. Tibbitt. Hundreds of wrecks now lay submerged and half buried in sand under those deep waters.

Today the lake could only gurgle and splash among the boulders, but the wind was chill on top of the cliff, and Qwilleran soon coasted back down the hill. He gripped the handlebars and clenched his jaw in concentration as the bike loped recklessly over rocks and ruts. Two young athletes in helmets and stretch pants were pedaling their thirty-speed bikes easily up the slope that had caused him so much effort. They even had breath enough to shout "Hi, neighbor! Nice goin' " as they passed.

After returning his own bike to the rental rack, he bought a supply of snacks and beverages at the deli—for himself and possible visitors. There were two large shopping bags, and he hailed a horse cab to carry them home. Without even greeting the Siamese, he checked the bedroom closet. The slipcovers had been removed, as Lori had promised, but the same odor rushed out to meet his offended nose; it had permeated his clothing.

"That woman!" Qwilleran bellowed. "May her piano always be out of tune!" Without a word to the bewildered cats, he stuffed his belongings into the two shopping bags and hiked up the beach road to Vacation Helpers.

The enterprise occupied the main floor of the former fishing lodge. In one large, open space there were work tables and such equipment as washer, dryer, ironing board, sewing machine, word processor, and child's playpen.

When Qwilleran dumped the contents of his shopping bags on one of the tables, the young woman in charge sniffed and said, "Mmm! Someone lovely has been hanging around you!"

"That's what *you* think," he said grouchily. "How fast can you do this stuff? I need some of it to wear to dinner."

"One shirt is silk, and it'll need special care, but most of it's wash-and-wear. I can have everything ready by . . . six o'clock?"

"Make it five-thirty. I'll pick it up." Without any of his usual pleasantries he started for the door.

"Sir! Shall I give your bundle to anyone with a big moustache?" she asked playfully. "Or do you want to leave your name?"

"Sorry," he said. "I had something on my mind. The name's Qwilleran. That's spelled with a QW."

"I'm Shelley, and my partners are Mary and Midge."

"How's business?" he asked, noticing that none of the roomful of equipment was in use.

"We're just getting organized. The rush won't start till July. Our picnic lunches are the most popular so far. Want to try one?"

He was going out to dinner, but it appeared that they needed the business, so he paid his money and took home a box that proved to contain a meatloaf sandwich, coleslaw, cookies, and . . . a pear! He put it in the refrigerator and dropped into his lounge chair. Oops! He had forgotten the broken spring. He seated himself again, this time with circumspection.

Then: What are those cats doing? he asked himself.

Koko was on the porch, trying to catch mosquitoes on the screen, the problem being that they were all on the outside.

"And you're supposed to be a smart cat," Qwilleran said.

Yum Yum was in the tiny kitchen area, fussing. When Yum Yum fussed, she could work industriously and stubbornly for an hour without any apparent purpose and without results. In Qwilleran's present mood he found the unexplained noises nerve-wracking—the bumping, clicking, thudding, and skittering.

"What on God's green earth are you doing?" he finally said in exasperation.

She had found a rusty nail in a crevice and, having worked and worked and worked to get it out, she pushed it back into another crevice.

"Cats!" he said, throwing up his hands.

Nevertheless, the rusty nail brought to mind the front steps of the

Domino Inn. The aged carpenter blamed the collapse of the steps on rusty nails. Lori blamed a careless inspection. Nick wanted to blame the troublemakers from Lockmaster. Qwilleran favored the David-and-Goliath theory. Meanwhile, it was advisable to return to the Buccaneer Den while the bartender still remembered him and his magnanimous tip.

The bartender's craggy face—hardened after eighteen years in Chicago's Loop—brightened when Qwilleran slid onto a bar stool. "Have a good day?" he asked jovially as he toweled the bartop.

"Not bad. Has the bar been busy?"

"Typical Monday." Bert waggled a double old-fashioned glass. "Same?"

"Make it a four-alarm this time. Gotta rev up for one of those Cajun specials in the Corsair Room."

"Yep, pretty good cook we've got. I send a Sazerac to the kitchen several times a day." He placed the blood-red glassful on the bar and waited for Qwilleran's approval. "How long y'here for?"

"Coupla weeks."

"Staying in the hotel?"

"No. At the Domino Inn. Friend of mine owns it."

"Sure, I know him. Short fella, curly black hair. Nice guy. Family man."

"What do you think of his inn?"

"Sensational!" said Bert. "That treebark siding has acid in it that keeps insects out. That's why it's lasted. Besides that, it looks terrific!"

"Have you been to the lighthouse?" Qwilleran asked.

"Sure. A bunch of us went up there in a wagon before the hotel opened. Mr. Exbridge arranged it. He's a good boss. Very human. Owns a third of XYZ, but you'd never know it from his attitude. Pleasure to work for him."

"I've heard he's a good guy. Too bad about the food poisoning and the drowning. Were they accidents? Or did someone have it in for XYZ?"

Bert paused before answering. "Accidents." Then he became suddenly busy with bottles and glasses.

Qwilleran persisted. "The guy that drowned—do you remember serving him?"

"Nope."

"Was he drinking in the lounge or by the pool?"

The bartender shrugged.

"Do any of the poolside waiters remember him?"

Bert shook his head. He was looking nervously up and down the bar.

"Was he a boater or a guest at the hotel? It would be interesting to know who was drinking with him."

Bert moved away and went into a huddle with his two assistants, who turned and looked anxiously at the customer with a sizable moustache. Then all three of them stayed at the far end of the bar.

So Exbridge had imposed the gag rule. Qwilleran had guessed as much when having dinner with Dwight Somers. Finishing his drink, he went to the Corsair Room for jambalaya, a savory blend of shrimp, ham, and sausage. He had been on the island twenty-four hours, although it seemed like a week. There was something about an island that distorted time. There was also something about jambalaya that made one heady.

He hailed a cab for the ride home—a spidery vehicle with a small body slung between two large spoked wheels that looked astonishingly delicate. He climbed in beside the lumpish old man holding the reins and said, "Do you know the Domino Inn on the west beach?"

"Ay-uh," said the cabbie. He was wearing the shapeless, colorless clothes of the islanders. "Giddap." The gig moved slowly behind a plodding horse with a swayback.

"Nice horse," Qwilleran said amiably.

"Ay-uh."

"What's his name?"

"Bob."

"How old is he?"

"Pretty old."

"Does he belong to you?"

"Ay-uh."

"Where do you keep him?"

"Yonder."

"How do you like this weather?" Qwilleran wished he had brought his tape recorder.

"Pretty fair."

"Is business good?"

"Pretty much."

"Have you always lived on the island?"

"Ay-uh."

"Do you get a lot of snow in winter?"

"Enough."

"Where is Piratetown?"

"Ain't none."

Eventually the cab reached the Domino Inn, and Qwilleran paid his fare plus a sizable tip. "What's your name?" he asked.

"John."

"Thanks, John. See you around."

The old man shook the reins, and the horse moved on.

Six

It was sunset time. Guests filled the porch swings as Qwilleran walked up the front steps of the inn.

"Beautiful evening," said the man who wore a French beret indoors and out. He spoke with a pleasant voice and a warmly benign expression on his wrinkled face.

"Yes, indeed," Qwilleran replied with a special brand of courtesy that he reserved for his elders.

"I'm Arledge Harding, and this is my wife, Dorothy."

"My pleasure. My name is Qwilleran—Jim Qwilleran."

The retired vicar moved with a physical stiffness that added to his dignity. "We're quite familiar with your name, Mr. Qwilleran, being privileged to read your column in the Moose County newspaper. It's most refreshing! You write extremely well."

"Thank you. I was sorry to hear about your accident. Which was the faulty step?"

"The third from the top, alas."

"Were you walking down or coming up?"

"He was going down," said Mrs. Harding. "Fortunately he had hold of the railing. I always remind him to grip the handrail. It's strange, though. Arledge weighs like a feather, and that husky young man who rides a bicycle runs up and down the steps all the time—"

"But in the middle, my dear. I stepped on the end of the step, and the other end flew up in a seesaw effect. The carpenter blamed it on rusty nails, and I do believe the nails in this building are even older than I am."

His wife squirmed to get out of the wooden swing. "Do sit here, Mr. Qwilleran."

"Don't let me disturb you," he protested.

"Not at all. I have things to do indoors, and I'll leave my husband in your good hands . . . Arledge, come inside if you feel the slightest chill."

When she had bustled away, Qwilleran said, "A charming lady. I didn't mean to chase her away."

"Have no compunction. My dear wife will be glad of a moment's respite. Since my accident she feels an uxorial obligation to attend me twenty-four hours a day—and this for a single fractured rib. I tremble to think of her ceaseless attention if I were to break a leg. Such is the price of marital devotion. Are you married, Mr. Qwilleran?"

"Not any more, and not likely to try it again," said Qwilleran, taking the vacant seat in the creaking swing. "I understand you have visited the island in the past."

"Yes, Mrs. Harding and I are fond of islands, which is not to imply that we're insular in our thinking—just a little odd. Individuals who are attracted to islands, I have observed, are all a little odd, and if they spend enough of their lives completely surrounded by water, they become completely odd."

"I daresay you've noted many changes here."

"Quite! We were frequently guests of an Indianapolis family by the name of Ritchie—in the decades B.C. Before commercialization, I might add. The Ritchies would have deplored the current development. They were a mercantile family, good to their friends and employees and generous to the church, rest their souls."

Qwilleran said, "The name of Ritchie is connected with the Mackintosh clan. My mother was a Mackintosh."

"I recognized a certain sly Scottish wit in your writing, Mr. Qwilleran. I mentioned it to Mrs. Harding, and she agreed with me."

"What was this island like in the years B.C.?

Mr. Harding paused to reflect. "Quiet . . . in tune with nature . . . and eminently restorative."

"Did the Ritchies have the lodge behind the high iron fence?"

"Gracious me! No!" the vicar exclaimed. "They were not at all pretentious, and they found delight in poking fun at those who were."

"Then who is the owner of The Pines? It looks like quite a compound."

"It belongs to the Appelhardts, who founded the private club and were the first to build in the 1920s. The Ritchies called them the royal family and their estate, Buckingham Palace . . . What brings you to the island, Mr. Qwilleran?"

"A working vacation. I'm staying in one of the cottages because my cats are with me, a pair of Siamese."

"Indeed! We once had a Siamese in the vicarage. His name was Holy Terror."

Mrs. Harding suddenly appeared. "A breeze has sprung up, and I'm afraid it's too chilly for you, Arledge."

"Yes, a storm is brewing. I feel it in my bones, and one bone in particular." The three of them went into the lounge and found comfortable seating in an alcove, whereupon the vicar asked his wife, "Should I tell Mr. Qwilleran the story about Holy Terror and the bishop?"

"Do you think it would be entirely suitable, Arledge?"

"The bishop has been entertaining the civilized world with the story for twenty years."

"Well . . . you wouldn't put it in the paper, would you, Mr. Qwilleran?"

"Of course not. I never mention cats and clergymen in the same column."

"Very well, then," she agreed and sat nervously clutching her handbag as her husband proceeded:

"It was a very special occasion," Mr. Harding said with a twinkle in his left eye. "The bishop was coming to luncheon at the vicarage, and we discovered that he enjoyed a Bloody Mary at that time of day. This required much planning and research, I assure you. After consulting all available experts, we settled upon the perfect recipe and took pains to assemble the correct ingredients. On the appointed day our distinguished guest arrived and was duly welcomed, and then I repaired to the kitchen to mix the concoction myself. As I carried the tray into the living room, Holy Terror went into one of his Siamese tizzies, flying up and down stairs and around the house at great speed until he swooped over my shoulder and landed in the tray. Glasses catapulted into space, and the Bloody Mary flew in all directions, spraying tomato juice over the walls, furniture, carpet, ceiling, and the august person of the bishop."

The gentle Mr. Harding rocked back and forth with unholy mirth until his wife said, "Do try to control yourself, Arledge. You're putting a strain on your rib." Then she turned to Qwilleran and asked the inevitable question: "Do you play dominoes?"

"I'm afraid I have to say no, and I suppose I should go home and see what profane terrors my two companions have devised."

Gasping a little, Mr. Harding said, "I would deem it . . . a privilege and a pleasure . . . to introduce you to a game that promotes tranquility."

Sooner or later, Qwilleran knew, he would have to play dominoes with *someone,* and he could use a little tranquility after the events of the day. He followed the Hardings to a card table under a bridge lamp. When the old man was properly seated, his wife excused herself, saying the best game was two-handed.

The vicar opened a box of dominoes and explained that there were twenty-eight pieces in the set, having pips similar to the spots on dice. "Why the one game is considered nice and the other is considered naughty, I am unable to fathom, especially since the naughty game is so often played on one's knees with certain prayerful exhortations. Or so I am told," he added with a twinkle in his good eye. "You might address that weighty question in your column some day. As a clue, let me mention that a domino was originally a hood worn by a canon in a cathedral."

The two men began matching pips in geometric formations, and Qwilleran began thinking longingly about a chocolate sundae, a symptom of boredom in his case. When the game ended, and the Hardings retired to their cottage, he found Lori and asked if Harriet's Family Café would be open at that hour.

"She'll be open, but she may not be serving the regular menu. If you're starving, though, she'll scramble some eggs for you."

"All I want is some ice cream."

Before walking to the restaurant, Qwilleran picked up his tape recorder and a flashlight at the cottage, moving quietly to avoid waking the Siamese. They were sleeping blissfully in the bowl-shaped leatherette cushion of the lounge chair. Groggy heads raised indifferently, with eyes open to slits, and then fell heavily back to sleep.

The café occupied one of the more modest lodges, built when the west beach was being invaded by the *lower* upperclass and even the upper *middleclass.* Whatever residential refinements had been there were now superseded by a bleak practicality: fluorescent lights that made it easy to clean the floor; dark, varnished paneling that would not show grease spots; tables with stainproof, plastic tops and kickproof, metal legs. It had been a busy evening, judging by the number of highchairs scattered among the tables. The last customer stood at the cash register, counting his change, and the cashier was clearing tables and sweeping up jettisoned food.

"Sorry to bother you," Qwilleran said. "Am I too late for an ice cream sundae?"

"You can sit down," she said in a flat voice. "What kind?"

"Can you rustle up some chocolate ice cream with chocolate sauce?"

She left the dining room and returned, saying, "Vanilla is all."

"That'll do, if you have chocolate sauce." He sat at a table near the kitchen to save the weary employee a long trek. To his surprise, another woman burst through the kitchen door, carrying his sundae. She was a husky woman of about forty, wearing a chef's hat (unstarched) and a large canvas apron (streaked with tomato sauce). She had the lean face and stony expression typical of island women, and she walked with a lumbering gait.

Plunking the dish down in front of the customer, she said, "I know you—from Pickax. You came into the Old Stone Mill to eat. I worked in the kitchen. Derek would come back and say, 'He's here with his girlfriend.' Or he'd say, 'He's here with a strange woman, much younger.' Then we'd peek through the kitchen door, and we'd put an extra slice of pork or turkey on your plate. We always had a doggie bag ready for you . . . Eat your ice cream before it melts."

"Thank you," he said, plunging his spoon into the puddle of chocolate sauce.

"How come you didn't ask for hot fudge? I can cook some up if you want. I know you like it."

"This is fine," he said, "and it's late, and you must be tired."

"I'm not tired. When you have your own business, you don't get tired. Funny, isn't it?"

"You must be Harriet Beadle. I'm staying at the Domino Inn, and Lori told me you helped her find a carpenter when she was in trouble."

"Lori's nice. I like her . . . Want some coffee?"

"I'll take a cup, if you'll have one with me."

Harriet sent her helper home, saying she'd finish the cleanup herself. Then she brought two cups of coffee and sat down, having removed her soiled apron and limp headgear. Her straight, colorless hair had been cut in the kitchen, Qwilleran guessed, with poultry shears and a mixing bowl. "I know you like it strong," she said. "This is island coffee. We don't make it like this for customers."

He could understand why; he winced at the first sip. "What brought you back to the island?"

"There's something about the island—always makes you want to come back. I always wanted to run my own restaurant and do all the cooking. Then Mr. Exbridge told me about this and told me how to go about it—borrow the money, buy secondhand kitchen equipment, and all that. He's a nice man. I s'pose you know him. What are you doing here? Writing for the paper?"

"If I can find anything to write about. Perhaps you could tell me something about island life."

"You bet I could!"

He placed his recorder on the table. "I'd like to tape our conversation. Don't pay any attention to it. Just talk."

"What about?"

"Breakfast Island when you were growing up."

"It was hard. No electricity. No bathrooms. No clocks. No phones. No money. We don't call it Breakfast Island over here. It's Providence Island."

"Who gave it that name?"

"The first settlers. A divine providence cast 'em up on the beach after their ship was wrecked."

"You say you had no money. How did you live?"

"On fish. Wild rabbit. Goat's milk." She said it proudly.

"What about necessities like shoes and flour and ammunition for hunting rabbits?"

"They used traps, back then. Other things they needed, they got by trading on the mainland. They traded fish, mostly, and stuff that washed up on the beach. My pa built a boat with wood that washed up."

"Is he still living?" Qwilleran asked, thinking he might be one of the unsociable cab drivers.

"He drowned, trying to haul his nets before a storm." She said it without emotion.

"And your mother?"

"Ma's still here. Still using oil lamps. Never left the island—not even for a day. She'd just as soon go to the moon."

"But surely electricity is now available to islanders. The resort has it. The summer estates have had it a long time."

"Ay-uh, but a lot of people here can't afford it. A lot of 'em still make their own medicines from wild plants. My ma remembers when there was no school. Now we have a one-room schoolhouse. I went through eight grades there—everybody in one room with one teacher." She said it boastfully.

"How did you arrange to go to high school?"

"Stayed with a family on the mainland."

"Did you have any trouble adapting to a different kind of school?"

"Ay-uh. Sure did. It was hard. I was ahead of the mainland kids in some things, the teachers said, but islanders were supposed to be dumb, and we got called all kinds of names."

"How did you feel about that?" Qwilleran asked sympathetically.

"Made me mad! Had to beat up on 'em a coupla times." Harriet clenched a capable fist

He regarded this Amazon with astonishment and grudging admiration. "You must be very strong."

"Gotta be strong to live here."

"Where do the islanders live? I don't see any houses."

"In Providence Village, back in the woods."

"Is that what the mainlanders call Piratetown?"

"Ay-uh. Makes me mad!" The clenched fist hit the tabletop and made the dishes dance.

"How do your people feel about the new resort?"

"They're afraid. They think they'll be chased off the island, like they were chased off the west beach when the rich folks came."

"What do they think about the tourists?"

"They don't like 'em. Some of the tourists are cocky . . . rowdy . . . half-naked. Last coupla weekends, a bunch of 'em camped near the lighthouse and flew kites big enough to ride in."

"Hang gliders," Qwilleran said, nodding. "Was that considered objectionable?"

"Well . . . they sat around with *no clothes on,* drinking beer and playing the radio loud."

"How do you know?"

"Some rabbit hunters saw 'em . . . Want more coffee?"

For the first time in his life Qwilleran declined a second cup; he could feel drums beating in his head. "What's your personal opinion of the Pear Island Hotel?" he asked her.

"Too much stuff about pirates. Makes me mad!"

"Are you saying that there were no pirates in the history of the island? Maybe they were here before your ancestors came."

Harriet looked fierce and banged the table. "It's all lies! Made-up lies!"

He thought it a good idea to change the subject. "There's a plaque at the lighthouse, honoring three lightkeepers. Do you know what happened to them?"

"Nobody knows," she said mysteriously. "I could tell you the story if you want to hear it."

The drums stopped beating in Qwilleran's head, and he snapped to attention. "I'd like to hear it, but you've had a long hard day. You probably want to go home."

"I don't go home. I have a bed upstairs."

"Then let me take you to lunch on your day off. We'll eat in the Corsair Room."

"I don't take a day off. I work seven days a week. Wait'll I get another cup of coffee. Sure you don't want some?"

Qwilleran had a feeling that he had just found buried treasure. The lighthouse mystery had never been mentioned by Homer Tibbitt.

Harriet returned. "My grampa told this story over and over again, so I practically know it by heart. My great-grampa was mixed up in it."

"Is that so? Was he a lightkeeper himself?"

"No, the guv'ment never hired islanders. That made 'em mad! It was like saying they were too dumb, or couldn't be trusted. The guv'ment hired three men from the mainland to live on the rock and keep the light burning. It was an oil lamp in those days, you know. Every so often a guv'ment boat delivered oil for the beacon and food for the keepers, and it was all hauled up the cliff by rope. There were some zigzag steps chiseled in the side of the cliff—you can see 'em from the lake—but they were slippery and dangerous. Still are! When the guv'ment boat brought a relief man, he was hauled up like the groceries, by rope."

"How did your great-grandfather become involved, Harriet?"

"Well, he was kind of a leader, because he could read and write."

"Was that unusual?"

"Ay-uh. They didn't have a school. The settlers were kind of a forgotten colony—not only forgotten but *looked down on.*"

"Where did your great-grandfather get his learning, then?"

"His pa taught him. His pa was kind of a preacher, but that's another whole story."

Qwilleran said impatiently, "Don't keep me in suspense, Harriet. What happened?"

"Well, one dark night my great-grampa woke up suddenly and didn't know why. It was like a message from the Lord. Wake up! Wake up! He got out of bed and looked around outside, and he saw that the beacon wasn't burning. That was bad! He put on his boots and took a lantern and went to the lighthouse, to see what was wrong. It was about a mile off. When he got there, there weren't any men around, and then he shouted—no answers! The fence gate was locked, so he climbed over. The door on the keepers' cottage was standing open, but there was nobody there. He thought of trying to light the beacon himself, but the door to the tower was locked. He didn't know what to do."

"There was no wireless at that time?" Qwilleran asked.

"No wireless—no radio—no telephone. That was a long time ago, Mr. Q. So . . . my great-grampa went home. Passing ships must've reported the beacon being out, because . . . pretty soon the island was swarming with constables and soldiers, arresting people, searching houses, and even digging up backyard graves. They didn't have regular cemeteries then."

"Did they think the islanders had murdered the men? What would be the motive?"

"The guv'ment thought the islanders really wanted ships to be wrecked so they could rob them. They believed the old lie about pirate blood. That was a hundred years ago, and people still believe it! Makes me boiling mad!"

"Old legends never die," Qwilleran said. (They only get made into movies, he thought.) "Were the bodies ever found?"

"Never. The police suspected my great-grampa and took him to the mainland for questioning."

"Why? Because he climbed over the fence?"

"Because he could read and write. They thought he was dangerous."

"Incredible! Are you sure this story is true, Harriet?"

She nodded soberly. "He kept a diary and wrote everything down. My ma has it hidden away."

Qwilleran said, "I'd give a lot to see that diary!" He was thinking, What a story this will make! . . . Homer Tibbitt, eat your heart out!

"Ma won't show the diary *to anybody,*" Harriet said. "She's afraid it'll be stolen."

"Haven't you ever seen it?"

"Only once, when I was in seventh grade. I had to be in a program for Heritage Day, so my ma let me see it. It had some weird things."

"Like what?" he asked.

"I remember one page, because I had to memorize it for the program. *August 7. Fine day. Lake calm. Light wind from southeast. Hauled nets all day. Mary died in childbirth. Baby is fine, thank the*

Lord . . . August 8. Cool. Some clouds. Wind shifting to northeast. Three rabbits in traps. Buried Mary after supper. Baby colicky. A few days after, the light burned out," Harriet concluded, "and the soldiers dug up the grave."

"Ghastly!" Qwilleran said. "How could your great-grandfather write about such things without emotion?"

"Islanders don't cry. They just do what they have to do," said Harriet, "and it doesn't matter how hard it is."

Qwilleran thought, They never laugh either. He asked her, "Had the islanders been on friendly terms with the lightkeepers?"

"Ay-uh. They celebrated feast days together, and Grampa took them fresh fish sometimes. They'd give him some hardtack. The islanders couldn't go inside the fence, but the keepers could come out."

"Were there any changes in the system after the disappearance?"

"Well, the guv'ment kept on sending three men from the mainland to do the job, but they had big dogs."

"Congratulations, Harriet. You report the facts as if you were actually there."

"I've heard it so many times," she said modestly.

"It'll make a sensational piece for the 'Qwill Pen' column. Is it okay to quote you?"

Her pleasure at being complimented turned to sudden alarm. "Which do you mean? Not the lighthouse story!"

"Especially the lighthouse mystery," he corrected her. "This is the first I've heard of such an incident, and I've read a lot of county history."

Harriet put her hands to her face in chagrin. "No! No! You can't write anything about that! I just told you because I thought you'd be personally interested. I didn't know . . ."

Why, Qwilleran wondered, do people give journalists sensational information or personal secrets that they don't want published? And why are they so surprised when it appears in print? What would happen if I ran this story anyway? *Historical data obtained from an anonymous source* . . . And then he thought, The lighthouse story might be a hoax. Does she know it's not true? It might be a family fiction invented to go with the ambiguous bronze plaque in the lighthouse compound. As for the diary, that's probably a myth, too. To Harriet he said, "Give me one good reason why I shouldn't publish the lighthouse story. Your reason will be confidential."

"It'll make trouble. It'll make trouble in the village." She moistened her lips anxiously.

"What kind of trouble?"

"Don't you know what happened Memorial weekend? I think Mr. Exbridge stopped it from getting in the paper. Some men from the mainland—from Lockmaster—came to the village with shovels and started digging for buried pirate treasure. They dug big holes in front of Ma's house and near the school. They had a map that they'd bought for fifty dollars from some man in a bar."

Qwilleran suppressed an urge to chuckle. "How did the villagers get rid of them?"

"Some rabbit hunters chased them out. The diggers complained to the sheriff's deputy about harassment, but he laughed and told them to go home and say nothing about it, or they'd look like fools. He reported it to Mr. Exbridge, though, and Mr. Exbridge said he'd done right."

Qwilleran said, "I'm sure it was annoying to the villagers, but I don't blame the deputy for laughing. The question is: What does this have to do with my running the lighthouse mystery?"

"Don't you see?" she said angrily. "Someone would sell maps, and the men would be back, digging for bones!"

Seven

On the way home from Harriet's Family Café, Qwilleran's mind was busy filming mental images: Harriet built like a Mack truck, working like a Trojan, and apparently happy as a lark . . . Harriet in her drooping chef's hat . . . Young Harriet piling into a bunch of kids with her fists flying. Was she honest? Were any of the islanders honest? They never cry, she had said; they do what they have to do. Were they capable of committing the perfect crime a hundred years ago? Generations of hardship would make them crafty. They could lure the lightkeepers to their deaths under the pretext of friendship. (A few cups of island coffee would do it!) But what was their motive? And where were the bodies?

Mist was rising from the lake and shrouding the dark beach road. Darting lights in the distance, like a swarm of fireflies, were the flashlights of hotel employees returning to their dormitories. Yelling, laughing, singing, they were a different breed from the shy, tongue-tied, sober-faced islanders.

A storm was on its way, no doubt about it. Mr. Harding could feel it in his bones; Koko and Yum Yum could feel it in their fur. As soon as Qwilleran, arriving at the cottage, slid cautiously into his lounge chair, both cats clomped to his side, looking heavy; then they landed in his lap like two sacks of cement. Even Koko, not normally a lap sitter, felt the need for propinquity. As barometers, the Siamese could predict "too wet" and "too windy." A heavy cat meant a muggy downpour; a crazy cat meant an approaching hurricane.

Now they sank ponderously into his lap, and he sank into the seat cushion with his feet up and his head back, thinking great thoughts: What would Lori serve for breakfast on Tuesday? When would he hear from Polly? Who won the ballgame in Minneapolis? . . . From there he progressed to deeper speculation: Why was the classy Noisette doing business in this backwoods resort? More to the point, what kind of business was she doing? Was the boat explosion really an accident? Who had been drinking with the hotel guest found floating in the pool? How could contaminated chicken sneak past the nose of a good chef? Wouldn't it smell? Where could one find an informant—an insider—who could ask gossipy questions without being suspected?

Before he could think of answers, he dozed off and slept soundly until shocked awake by a terrifying roar, as if a locomotive were crashing through the house! It was followed by a hollow silence. Had it been an audio dream? The cats had heard it, too. Both were on top of the wallcabinet in the kitchenette. Then the empty silence was broken by another bellowing blast. It was the Breakfast Island foghorn on Lighthouse Point. It could be heard thirty miles out in the lake, and on Pip Court it sounded as if it were in the backyard. Now Qwilleran understood the ear plugs on the emergency list. The Siamese came down from their perch and slept peacefully throughout the booming night. Lori, in her infinite wisdom about cats, explained to Qwilleran the next day that they associated the regular bleating of the horn with their mother's heartbeat when they were in the womb.

Reporting for breakfast, he appreciated the green-and-white golf umbrella that came with the cottage. Two others were dripping on the front porch of the inn, and his neighbors from Pip Court were seated at a large, round table.

"Please honor us with your company," said Mr. Harding, his dignified stiffness aggravated by the dampness. He introduced the other couple as the newlyweds in Two Pips.

"We're checking out today," they said. "We have to bike back to Ohio before the weekend."

"In this weather?" Qwilleran questioned.

"We have raingear. No problem."

"Can you tell me anything about the nature trail at the end of the lane"

"Super!" said the young woman. "It goes all the way to the sand dune, and there's a hidden pond with a beaver dam and all kinds of wildflowers."

"It's really a swamp with all kinds of mosquitoes," said the young man, a realist.

"Is the trail well marked?" Qwilleran asked. "Last year I lost my way on a mountain and would still be wandering in circles if it weren't for a rescue dog."

"Stay on the main path; you can't go wrong. Just be alert for snakes, wood ticks, and bush shooters. The rabbit hunters shoot at anything that moves, so wear bright colors." The bikers stood up. "We've got to catch the ten o'clock ferry. Have a nice day, you guys." This was said with a humorous nod at the rain-drenched windows.

"Deck thyself in gladness," Mr. Harding said with ecclesiastical pomp and a twinkle in his good eye.

"Charming young people," Mrs. Harding muttered when they had loped with athletic grace from the breakfast room. "There should be more like them on Pear Island."

Qwilleran said, "Are you aware that this island has three names? It's Pear Island on the map, Breakfast Island to mainlanders, and Providence Island to the natives."

"There is yet another name," said the vicar. "When the millionaires built their stately mansions—for their souls and their social prestige, we presume—they considered 'Pear Island' incompatible with their delusions of grandeur, so they renamed it. Perhaps you've seen the sign: GRAND ISLAND CLUB."

Qwilleran ate slowly and prolonged his first breakfast, hoping the elderly couple would leave and allow him to order a second breakfast without embarrassment.

They lingered, however. "Good day for a friendly game of dominoes, if you feel so inclined," the vicar said.

"Unfortunately I have a deadline to meet," Qwilleran replied, and he excused himself from the table, having had the souffléed ham and eggs with fresh pineapple, but not the waffles with ricotta cheese and strawberries. He felt deprived.

On the way out he was selecting a couple of apples from the communal fruit basket when a sweet voice at his elbow said, "You should take a banana." She was one of the two white-haired women who always smiled at him in unison when he crossed the porch or entered the lounge.

"An apple a day keeps the rain away," he said.

"But bananas, you know, are an excellent source of potassium."

"The banana," he declaimed facetiously, "was invented as a base for three scoops of ice cream, three sundae toppings, two dollops of whipped cream, a sprinkling of nuts, and a maraschino cherry. Other uses are marginal."

"Oh, Mr. Qwilleran," she said with a delighted smile, "you sound just like your column! We've been reading it in the local paper. You should be syndicated. It's so trenchant!"

"Thank you," he said with a gracious bow. He liked compliments on his writing.

"I'm Edna Moseley, and I'm here with my sister Edith. We're retired teachers."

"A pleasure to meet you. I hope you're enjoying your stay. Let's hope the weather clears shortly." Taking two apples and a banana, he edged away. She and her sister were domino players, as were the Hardings. He had classified most of the guests. The newlyweds had been jigsaw puzzlers. Two older men played chess; probably retired teachers. A young couple with a well-behaved child played Scrabble.

Then there was an attractive young woman who read magazines or talked to two men who were traveling together. None of them looked like a vacationer or showed any interest in dominoes, puzzles, sunsets, or the fruit basket. Qwilleran suspected they were a detective team from the state police. All three left the next day.

Back at Four Pips Qwilleran tried to write a trenchant column, but the pelting rain and fretting Siamese disturbed him. He empathized with the cats. They had no room to practice their fifty-meter dash or their hurdles or broad jumps. For a while he amused Yum Yum by flipping a belt around for her to chase and grab. Floor space was limited, however. The sport entertained her briefly; Koko, not at all. He watched the performance as if they were both numbskulls. Koko preferred pastimes that challenged his sentience. It was that understanding that gave Qwilleran his next idea—one that would prove more significant than he expected.

"Okay, old boy, how about a friendly game of dominoes?" he proposed. He remembered Koko's interest in Scrabble and his fascination with a dictionary game they had invented Down Below. "Cats," he had written in his column, "are ingenious inventors of pastimes. Even a kitten with a ball of yarn can play an exciting game of solitaire with original rules." That column had brought him a bushel basket full of fan mail.

On that rainy day in June he and Koko collaborated on a new version of dominoes, predicated ostensibly on blind chance. First, the contents of the maroon velvet box were emptied onto the small oak table in the front window, where they were spread at random, facedown. Then Qwilleran pulled up two oak chairs facing each other. Koko enjoyed moving any small object around with his paw, whether bottlecap or wristwatch, and there were twenty-eight small objects. He stood on his hind legs on the chair, placed his forepaws on the table, and studied the black rectangles with eyes that were wide, intensely blue, and concentrated. A faltering paw reached out, touching first one domino and then another until, with a swift movement, he knocked one off the table.

"Interesting," said Qwilleran as he picked it up and found it to be 6-6. The name painted on Nick's boat was *Double-Six,* and it happened to be the highest scoring piece in the set. "That was only a test. Now we start to play." He found paper and pen for scoring and shuffled the dominoes facedown. "Your draw."

Koko looked down at the jumbled mass in his studious way, then swiped one off the table. It was 6-6 again.

"Amazing!" Qwilleran said. "That's twelve points for you. You're entitled to four draws, then it's my turn. It's not necessary or desirable to knock everything on the floor. Just *draw,* like this."

Nevertheless, Koko enjoyed shoving a small object from a high place, peering over the edge to see it land. His second draw was also high-scoring, 5-6, but the next to land on the floor were 2-3 and 0-1, reassuring Qwilleran that it was the luck of the draw. When all the pieces had been drawn, the fourteen on the floor totaled 90 pips; Qwilleran's score was 78. The game proved only one thing: Cats like to knock things down.

The game had been stimulating enough to satisfy Koko's needs, and he joined Yum Yum in her leatherette nest, while Qwilleran set up his typewriter on the oak table. The thousand words he wrote for his "Qwill Pen" column were about the island with four names and four cultures: the natives, who had lived on Providence Island for generations; the mainlanders who knew Breakfast Island as a haunt for fishermen; the summer residents from Down Below, pursuing their affluent lifestyle on Grand Island; and now the tourists, bent on having a good time on Pear Island, as it was named on the map. He called the demographic situation "a heady mix on a few square miles of floating real estate."

When he finished his column, it was still raining, and he rode downtown in a horse cab to fax his copy. In the hotel lobby, bored tourists were milling aimlessly, or they were slumped in lobby chairs, reading comic books. From adjacent rooms came electronic sounds mingling in jarring dissonance: television, video games, and bar music.

Qwilleran spotted a conservation officer in a Boat Patrol uniform, and he asked him. "Shouldn't you be out on the lake, protecting the fish from the fishermen?"

The officer acknowledged the quip with a dour grimace. "In this weather, who's crazy enough to be out fishing? I'm showing educational videos in the TV room."

"Has the influx of boaters increased your work?"

"You can bet it has! We chug around the lake counting poles and writing up violations. The law allows two poles per licensed fisherman, you know. Coupla days ago we saw a sport-fishing craft with eight poles and only three men visible on deck. We stopped them and asked to see their fishing licenses. When they could show us only two, they explained that the third guy wasn't fishing; he just came along for the ride. That was a big laugh. Now they had eight poles and only two fishermen! But that wasn't the end of it. We did a safety check, and their fire extinguisher wasn't charged! We sent 'em back to shore to get it recharged and face a hefty fine for illegal lines."

"How about the sport divers?" Qwilleran asked. "Are they giving you any trouble?"

"They're the sheriff's responsibility. He has divers and patrol boats that keep tabs on them. Divers aren't supposed to take artifacts from wrecks, but they're crazy about those brass portholes!"

Qwilleran asked, "Do you know what caused the explosion at the marina last weekend?"

"Sure. The usual. Carelessness and ignorance. Landlubbers know they have to take a road test and written exam to drive a car, but they buy a $25,000 boat and think it's just a toy." He looked at his watch. "Gotta grab something to eat, then do another video for this captive audience. When it rains, they're so bored, they'll watch anything!"

While Qwilleran was waiting for the dining room to open, he looked at the Tuesday edition of the *Moose County Something*. On the editorial page there were several letters from readers regarding Pear Island.

To the Editor:

My family and I just spent a wonderful weekend at Pear Island. We are so fortunate to have such an exciting playground, just a short ferry ride away. We rode bikes, swam in the hotel pool, and hunted for agates on the beach. It was super fun!

—Cassie Murdoch
Pickax

Qwilleran assumed that Cassie was Exbridge's secretary or sister or mother-in-law.

To the Editor:

Pear Island is okay for people who have money to spend, but what it needs is a campground for tents and cookouts. I'd like to see a tent city where you could meet people. All they'd have to do is cut down some trees in the center of the island.

—Joe Ormaster
North Kennebeck

Qwilleran thought, No one's going to love you, Joe. Not XYZ. Not the environmentalists. Not the islanders.

To the Editor:

I took my elderly mother to Pear Island for the day, and she was shocked by some of the distasteful slogans on shirts and caps worn by some of the other visitors. Also, the restrooms are too far from the ferry dock, and the smell of fudge everywhere made her sick, but we had a good time. She enjoyed the ferry ride, although all the benches were taken, and no one offered her a seat. She is 84.

—Mrs. Alfred Melcher
Mooseville

To the Editor:

My husband and I had a lovely time on Pear Island. But why do they allow those people to march back and forth in front of the hotel, carrying signs and yelling? It spoils the happy vacation mood for the rest of us who pay good money to sit in the rocking chairs and enjoy the view.

—Mrs. Graham MacWhattie
Toronto, Canada

When it was time for the dining room to open, Qwilleran reported to the reservation desk in the lobby. To his surprise, the new captain was seven feet tall, if one included the black pirate tricorne. "Derek! Glad to see you got the job!" Qwilleran greeted him.

"How d'you like my costume?" Derek asked. "I think I should have one gold earring." As a member of the Pickax Theater Club, Derek liked roles that required spectacular costumes.

"You're perfect. Don't change a thing."

"Are you staying at the hotel?"

"No, I merely came for dinner. I'm lodging at the Domino Inn."

"I get a room at the Vacation Helpers, rent paid. That's one of the perks. The job only pays minimum wage, but it'll look good on a resumé, and I get to meet a lot of girls," Derek said.

In a lower voice Qwilleran asked, "Would you be interested in doing some undercover work for an investigative reporter—as a side job?"

"Who? You?"

"I'm the go-between."

"Any risks? How much does it pay?"

A line was beginning to form behind Qwilleran, and he said loudly, "I'd like a table for one in the Corsair Room." In a conspiratorial whisper he added, "Stop at Domino Inn on your way home tonight. We'll talk."

Qwilleran hurried through dinner and was ordering a horse cab for the ride home when Dwight Somers hailed him. "Are you here for dinner, Qwill?"

"Just finished."

"Come into the lounge and have a drink."

"I can stand another cup of coffee and some dessert."

They sat in a booth to assure conversational privacy, and Dwight said, "Just got some good news. Don Exbridge has been in Pickax lobbying to get the island sprayed for mosquitoes, and the county's going to do it."

"That's good news for tourists," Qwilleran said, "but the ecologists will hit the ozone layer."

"By the way, Qwill, we don't call them tourists any more; it has a negative connotation. They're *vacationers,* by decree from the boss. He's also twisting some political arms to get the beach road paved all around the island, with a strip for bikers and joggers."

"I hate to be a wet blanket, Dwight, but the summer people will fight it to the last drop of their blue blood. The natives won't be so hot for it, either."

"The natives are against any kind of progress. They almost rioted when the post office was moved downtown. It had been in some woman's kitchen in Piratetown for years."

"We don't call it Piratetown any more, Dwight; it has a negative connotation. It's Providence Village."

Dwight ordered a burger and beer. Their booth was within sight of the bar, and Qwilleran noticed the head bartender eying him strangely as he talked with the hotel's publicity chief. "What do you think of this rain?" Dwight asked. "It wasn't predicted."

"The ancient gods of the island are not only frowning, they're weeping. Maybe your boss is lobbying the wrong hierarchy. In less than two weeks you've had two deaths, one broken rib, a wrecked boat, fifteen stomach aches, and unscheduled rain. Someone is trying to tell you something."

"Well, those are the bugs you have to expect in new operations. Did you see the letters to the editor today? We're batting about .200."

"What kind of response are the merchants getting? I never see any customers in the antique shop."

"Her stuff is too good for this place. A flea market would be more in line."

"Why would someone like Noisette choose to come here? Or did Exbridge party in Palm Beach last winter and invite her?"

"Don't ask *me.*"

"Not only are her prices high, but she has a very limited inventory. I recall a similar instance Down Below; it was a front for something else. Maybe that's the situation here."

"Please! Not that!" Dwight pleaded. "We've got problems enough! The latest is bird droppings. The—uh—vacationers sit on the porch and throw bread to the seagulls. Then the stray cats come around for the crumbs. The birds make a mess. The cats fight . . . Honestly and confidentially, Qwill, how do you size up this whole project?"

"I think you've got a tiger by the tail. A resort should be a happy place. XYZ has created a rat's nest of conflict, culture clash, and—if you'll pardon my frank opinion—sabotage."

"You're not serious," Dwight said.

"I'm serious. It's easy to second-guess, of course, but it now becomes clear to me that XYZ should have done a feasibility study before launching this project. They might have discovered that the pirate legend has no historical verification and that the islanders resent the implication. It's my belief that the hotel's celebration of the pirate myth is creating hostility."

"It's all in fun. It's just fantasy."

"The islanders have no sense of humor. Neither would you, if you lived in Providence Village."

"But what harm can it do?"

"Do you realize a con artist was selling Pear Island treasure-hunting maps for fifty dollars in bars on the mainland? Dunderheads are coming over on the ferry with shovels."

"That's a cheap racket."

"Your promotional theme is responsible. Why not taper off a little?"

Dwight said, "XYZ has invested a bundle in the pirate gimmick."

"My heart bleeds for XYZ," Qwilleran said.

"Well, shed a few drops for me, too. Don's a great boss as long as things are going right, but when something backfires, he goes berserk, and I get hell!"

With a surge of sympathy for his friend, Qwilleran said, "Are you still looking for material for your cabaret? I have an idea for a humorous skit, although it might not appeal to your literal-minded boss."

"Write it anyway," Dwight said. "Write it!"

As Qwilleran rode home to domino headquarters in a cab, he congratulated himself on lining up Derek Cuttlebrink as an undercover agent. There were those who thought the young man scatterbrained, but Qwilleran was confident that he had promise. Inside that lanky, goofy kid there was a short, serious young man trying to find himself.

Derek had muttered a cryptic "Ten-fifteen" as Qwilleran passed the reservation desk on the way out. Shortly before that hour Qwilleran took the green-and-white golf umbrella and walked to the wet and deserted porch to meet him. The wooden swings were covered with plastic, and the chairs were leaning against the back wall. Soon a babble of young voices could be heard coming up the beach road. When the troupe reached the Domino Inn, the tallest one peeled off and approached the porch steps, flapping his arms with a surplus of youthful energy. In his yellow slicker, nor'easter rainhat, and muddy boots, Derek looked like a scarecrow.

Qwilleran raised his hand for silence and put an index finger to his lips. "Say nothing," he whispered. "Follow me. This meeting is confidential." He led the way to the dark end of the porch. "Sorry it's too wet to sit down."

"I never sit down," Derek said. "What's it all about?"

"I'll make this brief. Some suspicious incidents have occurred on the island. No doubt you know about the food poisoning."

"Yeah, they crack a lot of chicken jokes in the kitchen."

"Good! I want you to listen to the scuttlebutt and report to me what you hear." He knew that would come naturally for Derek. As a native of Moose County, he had been weaned on gossip. "Another incident was a drowning in the hotel pool. The victim was a guest who had been drinking on the premises. Employees have obviously been instructed not to talk to outsiders, but we can be sure they gossip among themselves. As a newcomer to the staff, you can show a healthy curiosity about the case. Right?"

"Check!" said Derek.

"What was he drinking? Pirate's Gold? How much did he consume? Did he drink in the bar or on the edge of the pool? Who found the body? Was he dressed for a swim or fully clothed? Did anyone see him dive in or fall in?"

"Maybe he was pushed."

"You're getting the idea, Derek," said Qwilleran as he patted his moustache. "I have a hunch there's more to the story than anyone wants to admit. Who was the guy? Why was he there? Was he a registered guest or a drop-in? Was he drinking alone? If not, who was with him? Male or female? One or more companions? I've heard that he was hunting."

"Yeah," said Derek, "it's kind of a singles bar. If we're caught hanging out there, we get fired . . . What about the food poisoning?"

"It would be interesting to know who was working in the kitchen that night. Islanders or mainlanders? What was their background? How did they get their jobs? Was anyone fired after the poisoning? Was anyone fired shortly *before the poisoning?*"

"Yeah, that's a good question."

"You're a good actor, Derek. You can carry this off without blowing your cover, and you make friends easily; people will talk to you. If they know anything, they'll be only too glad to spill it in a safe ear. What hours do you work?"

"Split shift, lunch and dinner. It's a good deal—gives me time to play volleyball, ride a bike, meet girls. How do you want me to report?"

"I'll be in for dinner frequently. Slip me a note."

"Check!"

Eight

It rained again on Wednesday. One day of rain at a resort is an adventure, of sorts. Two successive days of rain are a bore. The Siamese were bored and still heavy from the hundred percent humidity. Qwilleran was equally bored and felt heavy mentally and physically.

First he gave the cats their breakfast and their daily grooming. Waving the walnut-handled brush that Polly had given them for Christmas, he announced, "Brush! Brush! Who wants to go first?" Koko always went first, despite efforts to introduce him to precepts of chivalry. Both of them had their ideas about the grooming process. Koko liked to be brushed while walking away, forcing his human valet to follow on his knees. Yum Yum missed the point entirely; she fought the brush, grabbing it, biting the bristles, and kicking the handle. The daily ritual was a farce, but it was an expected prelude to their morning nap.

Qwilleran reported to the inn for his own breakfast with *Penguin Island* in one pocket of his waterproof jacket; in another pocket he had the pear from his box lunch of the day before. The walk up the lane was surprisingly unmuddy; the sandy island drained like a sieve. Parking his green-and-white umbrella on the porch, he went directly to the sunless sunroom. There were no other guests, and he was able to order both breakfasts without embarrassment: eggs Benedict with Hollandaise sauce and johnnycakes with sausages and apple sauce. On the way out he avoided the domino players but stopped at the fruit basket, where he exchanged his pear for two apples, one red and one green. So far, so good.

At Four Pips the boredom descended more heavily with every bucket of rain. He tried to read; he paced the floor; he ate an apple; he took a nap; he made a cup of instant coffee; he tried to write something trenchant. All his typewriter could produce was "The rain in the lane goes mainly to the brain." It was still only one o'clock, and out of sheer boredom he ate his box lunch from the Vacation Helpers. It was not bad for day-old food. The meatloaf, in fact, was very well flavored. When the Siamese finally struggled out of their somnolence, he offered them a morsel, but they were not interested.

"Good! All the more for me!" he said. "How about a stimulating game of dominoes?"

They recognized the maroon velvet box and took their places: Yum Yum crouching on the table as referee; Koko standing on the chair, ready to push dominoes onto the floor.

In the interest of scientific research and the hope that it might make a trenchant subject for his column, Qwilleran was keeping a daily record of Koko's selections. Strangely, one of his draws duplicated the first one of the day before, although in a different order: 5-6, 0-1, 6-6, 2-3.

Also, the cat won again. Did he sense that certain black rectangles had more white pips than others? If so, what did he know—or care—about winning? Was he trying to convey a message? Double-six! Double-five! There was usually a message in his madness. Or was he making a contribution to parapsychology? In some ways, Qwilleran was convinced, Koko knew more than he did.

When the game was over and Qwilleran was boxing the dominoes, he felt a pang of loneliness. There was no one with whom he could discuss these abstruse theories seriously. Polly listened politely; Riker kidded him; even the police chief talked about Koko's proven exploits with tongue in cheek. Perhaps one had to be a trifle odd to believe in the cat's ESP. Perhaps the Hardings—

His ruminations were interrupted by an urgent hammering on the door. Opening it, he found himself looking down on an open umbrella, from under which a small hand extended, holding a note.

"Thank you," Qwilleran said. "Are you Mitchell, vice president in charge of communications?"

The messenger jabbered something and ran back to the inn.

The note was a message from Lori: "Arch Riker phoned. Call him at the office. Urgent."

Qwilleran huffed into his moustache. What could be so urgent? He had faxed his copy yesterday, and it was already past the Wednesday deadline. Furthermore, it was still raining hard. He would have to change his shoes and put on his waterproof jacket . . . Then it occurred to him that the apple barn might have been damaged by the storm. There had been flashes of lightning over the mainland. He pulled on his duck boots and grabbed his umbrella.

Most of the guests were in the lounge, playing dominoes or

snoozing in their chairs; even Koko and Yum Yum went to sleep after a domino session. Qwilleran strode purposefully up the stairs to the phone booth on the landing and called the newspaper office, collect.

An annoyingly cheerful voice came on the line. "How're things on the island with four names?"

"Wet!" Qwilleran answered curtly. "What's on your mind, Arch?"

"I like your column in today's paper. No one but you can write a thousand words about nothing and make it sound interesting."

"Some of my readers consider my stuff trenchant and not just interesting."

"So be it. When can we expect your next copy?"

"Is that all you called about? I risked drowning to get to this blasted phone! . . . But to answer your question: I've talked to an island woman who dismisses the pirate myth completely."

"Soft-pedal that aspect," the editor advised. "It's the main theme of the hotel."

"I know Don Exbridge has invested his life savings in black T-shirts, but the natives object. I don't see why we should support a commercial gimmick and reinforce a spurious legend because of an advertiser's ignorant whim."

"Cool it, Qwill. Isn't the native community called Piratetown?"

"Only by ignorant outsiders. Officially it's Providence Village, and trespassers are not welcome. In fact, I suspect a covert hostility that may explain the so-called accidents. The boat explosion was the fourth, and the people in charge of the waterfront are doing a lot of fast talking, so no one will get the idea it was a bomb. I'll tell you more when I see you."

"Which is why I called, Qwill," said the editor. "Mildred and I want to spend a weekend at a bed-and-breakfast before the resort gets crowded—this weekend, if it isn't too short a notice. The weather's due to clear up tomorrow and stay nice for a while. Would you make a reservation for us? Mildred wants you to pick out a B-and-B with a little class."

That eliminates the Domino Inn, Qwilleran thought. "Do you trust my judgment?"

"No, but Mildred apparently does. We plan to arrive late Friday, and we hope you'll have dinner with us Saturday night."

"I'll see what I can find. I'll call you tomorrow."

"Great! How are the mosquitoes?"

"Not too bad if you stay out of the woods. In the tourist area, they're automatically gassed by the fudge fumes."

Qwilleran walked slowly downstairs from the phone booth, regretting that he had mentioned the pirate controversy prematurely. Harriet may have been lying. She might not know the real truth about her heritage. The island might very well have been a pirate stronghold in prehistoric times. (Prehistoric in Moose County was anything before the War of 1812.) There was a hotel owner on the mainland who boasted of his pirate ancestry; why were the islanders so sensitive about the possibility?

He was intercepted at the foot of the stairs by Lori. "Is everything all right, Qwill?"

"Just a misplaced comma in my copy," he said archly. He opened his mouth to mention the Rikers' impending visit but closed it again; he could hardly ask the owner of the Domino Inn to recommend a B-and-B with more class!

Later, he remembered seeing a bed-and-breakfast brochure near the cash register at Harriet's café. He went there for dinner and ordered vegetable soup, two hot dogs with everything, and apple pie with ice cream. He could hear Harriet shouting orders in the kitchen like a drill sergeant. While eating, he read the advertising blurbs in the brochure: The Domino Inn was described as "Absolutely unique, with hearty, delicious breakfasts lovingly prepared. Newly redecorated with original 1920s furniture." The Seagull Inn featured brass beds and a billiard room. The B-and-B called Yesteryear-by-the-Lake had a cobblestone fireplace and a collection of toy trains. None of these would thrill the Rikers.

Then he read about the Island Experience: "Charming ambiance and gracious hospitality, with antique furnishings and gourmet breakfasts! Canopied beds have eyelet-embroidered bedlinens and handmade quilts. Complimentary champagne in the gazebo every afternoon."

Mildred would swoon over such amenities. Arch would prefer complimentary Scotch in the gazebo but would appreciate the antiques; he and his first wife Down Below had been experienced collectors. It was the bottom line that interested Qwilleran personally: *Innkeepers Carla Helmuth and Trudy Feathering are former members of the Grand Island Club.* With no motive other than curiosity about the private estates, he determined to check out the Island Experience the next day, rain or shine. He went home and trimmed his moustache.

The sun was shining Thursday morning. Before going to breakfast, Qwilleran laid out his clothing for the visit with the former members of the Grand Island Club: a brushed silk shirt that Polly had given him for Sweetest Day, his new khaki twill trousers, and his British tan loafers.

The Hardings were leaving the breakfast room as he arrived. "Lovely day for the nature trail!" Mrs. Harding told him. "The wildflowers will be at their best, but don't forget the mosquito repellent. Spray and pray, as Arledge says."

"With emphasis on the latter," said her husband. "After a heavy rain, their buzzing sounds like a pondful of bullfrogs."

"By the way," Qwilleran asked them, "when you used to visit the Ritchies, did you meet any clubmembers named Feathering or Helmuth?"

The couple searched each other's eyes for answers, then admitted that the names were only vaguely familiar. "We didn't know any of the clubmembers well. The Ritchies were not what you would call clubby."

"It's not important," he said. "I merely heard that their widows were running a bed-and-breakfast here."

"How interesting," murmured Mrs. Harding, although it was clear that she was not interested at all.

After smoked salmon and scrambled eggs, followed by ham-and-potato cakes with chutney, Qwilleran returned to Four Pips to dress for his visit with the widows. As he unlocked the door he heard sounds of commotion; when he walked in, he saw a scene of disaster: table lamp on the floor, chair knocked over, desk papers scattered. He stepped on something; it was a domino. He kicked something; it was his green apple. Koko was circling the room wildly, jumping over furniture, ricocheting off the walls, and yowling with pain—or glee. He was having a catfit.

"Stop! Stop!" Qwilleran yelled.

Koko made a few more turns about the room before stopping and licking his battered body. Yum Yum came crawling out from under the sofa.

"You ruffian! What's the matter with you?" Qwilleran scolded. Patiently he put the room in order. Nothing was broken. The lamp shade had flown off, and the harp was bent, but there was no harm done. The dominoes scattered about the floor were found; only the cover of the maroon velvet box was missing. It would show up somewhere. He put the dominoes in a desk drawer. Then he went into the bedroom to change clothes.

First he noticed a sock on the floor. Next he saw his trousers crumpled on the floor behind the bedside table. And where was his silk shirt? Hunting for it on hands and knees, he found it wadded up under the dresser.

"You fiend!" Qwilleran exploded. "I just had this washed and pressed! I can't wear any of this now."

Koko stood in the doorway, looking impudent—with legs splayed, tail stiffly curled, and ears pointed in two directions.

Qwilleran sat down abruptly on the bed. Could it be that Koko did not want him to visit the Island Experience? The cat knew nothing about the inn, or the women who ran it, or the reason for going there! Or did he? Something was going on in that little cat brain!

Qwilleran shrugged in resignation. No one would believe that a man of his size, intelligence, education, and *wealth* could be tyrannized by a ten-pound animal. Now he had lost the wherewithal and the incentive to visit the Island Experience.

He brought a bottle of club soda from the refrigerator and took it to the porch to drink while he simmered down. It was calm on the porch. The woods were beautiful after the rain. He saw some yellow flowers outside the screens that had not been there before. When a rabbit hopped out of the underbrush and came close to the porch, Qwilleran remained quiet and motionless. And then he witnessed the incredible. The Siamese came out of the house and ambled toward the rabbit. There was no stealth, no stalking, no hostile posturing. They looked at the visitor, and the rabbit looked at them with his nose twitching. Then he hopped away.

Qwilleran finished his drink and then changed clothes. He put on some lightweight jeans, a long-sleeved T-shirt, and his yellow baseball cap. "I'll be back after a while," he told the Siamese. He found the mosquito repellent and headed for the nature trail.

There was a wagon in front of Five Pips, delivering a small barroom piano. Lori had unlocked the door for the deliverymen, but the window shades were still drawn. "Hi, Qwill!" she said. "The hotel is lending her a piano. Isn't that nice? She'll be here starting this weekend."

"Have you ever taken the nature trail?" he asked.

"I haven't had time, but I hear it's lovely."

The approach to the trail was mysteriously inviting. The path was thick with pine needles and spongy after the rain. On either side there were tall, straight pines with lofty branches admitting shafts of sunlight, while oaks and graceful birches dappled the path with shade. At intervals, small paths led into the underbrush on the left, each marked by a name painted on a shingle or small boulder: SEAGULL INN . . . ISLAND EXPERIENCE. Farther along there was a larger marker: GRAND ISLAND CLUB—PRIVATE, followed by the elegantly simple names of summer estates like SEVEN OAKS and THE BIRCHES. Narrower trails, darkly forbidding, led into dense woods on the right; an occasional sign said KEEP OUT . . . or simply DOGS.

Qwilleran never attempted to identify flora and fauna. Through painful experience he knew poison ivy when he saw it, and he knew which small animals had long ears and which had bushy tails. Otherwise he was botanically and zoologically illiterate. He merely enjoyed being alone in the forest with his thoughts. No one else was abroad after the recent deluge. He was in a small, green, private world of sights and sounds, plus the occasional prick of a proboscis on the back of his neck. The trail went on and on. He climbed over hillocks and trotted down into bosky gullies. At one time he asked himself, Will I be able to write a thousand words about this?

Eventually the fresh, verdant aroma mingled with another—the dark muskiness of marshland. Once more he misted his clothing with mosquito spray. When he passed a boulder marked THE PINES, he knew he would soon reach the sand dune and the end of the trail. He would round one more bend and then turn back.

As he skirted a large shrub, however, he caught a glimpse of an apparition on the path ahead. He stepped back out of sight to assess the situation, then cautiously peered through the shrub's branches. It was a woman on the path ahead . . . with fluttering garments of pale green . . . and long, lank hair like a mermaid. In a flash of nonthink he imagined a lacustrine creature washed ashore in the recent rain. The notion soon vanished. This woman was real, and she was apparently studying the low-growing plant life. He found himself thinking, Watch out for poison ivy, lady! She would stoop to touch a leaf, rise to write in a book, then turn to the other side of the trail to examine another specimen. It was odd garb for a botanist, Qwilleran thought; when Polly went birding, she wore hiking boots and jeans. This woman's movements were graceful, and her apparel added to the enchantment. He felt like a mythic satyr spying on a woodland nymph.

A sudden scream brought him back to reality. She had been reaching into the ground cover when she shrieked and recoiled in horror!

Without thinking, he rushed forward, shouting inanely, "Hello! Hello!"

"Ricky! Ricky!" she screamed in panic.

"What's the trouble?" he called out as he ran toward her.

"A snake!" she cried hysterically. "I'm bitten! I think it was a cottonmouth! . . . Ricky! Ricky!"

"Where is he?"

She pointed vaguely with her left hand, dropping her book. "At home," she groaned between sobs.

"I'll help you. Where d'you live?"

"The Pines." Then she cried in a weaker voice, "Ricky! Ricky!"

"Take it easy! I'll get you there." Scooping her up in his arms, he started backtracking toward the boulder that marked the right path, keeping his pace fast but smooth. She was surprisingly lightweight; the voluminous garments covered an emaciated frame. She clutched her right wrist, which was swelling rapidly. "Let your arm hang down," he ordered.

"The pain!" she moaned. "My whole arm!"

He broke into a gliding trot. "You'll be okay . . . I'll get you home." They had reached the boulder and turned down the private path. "Won't be long now," he managed to say between heavy breathing. "We'll get a doctor."

"Ricky's a doctor . . . I feel sick!" Then she fell ominously silent, her thin face pale. The path was ending. He could see green grass ahead. Two men were standing on the grass.

"Ricky!" Qwilleran shouted with almost his last breath.

Startled, they looked up. One ran forward. "Elizabeth! What happened?"

"Snake bite," Qwilleran gasped.

"I'll take her!" The man named Ricky gathered her up and ran to a golf cart nearby. As the cart headed toward a clump of buildings in the distance, he was talking on a portable phone.

The other man calmly finished a maneuver with a croquet mallet. "Bonkers!" he announced with satisfaction. Turning to Qwilleran, he said, "I suppose I should thank you for rescuing my baby sister. She's been warned to stay out of the woods . . . I'm Jack Appelhardt. And you're . . . ?"

"Jim Qwilleran. Staying at the Domino Inn. I happened to be—"

"What?" the man interrupted with an unpleasant smile. "Does anyone actually stay at that place?" His remark was meant to be jocular.

Qwilleran was not amused. Gruffly he replied, "Hope she'll be all right." He turned away and walked up the access path as briskly as his lungs would permit. He could hear a motorized vehicle beeping in the languid atmosphere. It grew louder, then stopped. He could visualize the rescue squad running with a stretcher, loading the victim into the ambulance, radioing for the helicopter. "Ricky" would accompany the patient; it helped to have a doctor in the house. This was one island incident that Qwilleran could not attribute to foul play.

Reaching the main trail, he sat on the boulder to catch his breath before starting home. Then a prick on the back of his neck made him realize he had lost his mosquito spray. He returned to the scene of the rescue and retrieved not only the spray can but a silver pen and a leatherbound book stamped in gold: "E. C. Appelhardt." It contained lists of botanical names, along with dates and places. The latest entry was: *Dionaea muscipula (Venus's flytrap).*

He returned home with the lost articles and a potpourri of thoughts: Strange woman . . . so thin . . . how old? . . . Could be young . . . face full of pain . . . why so thin? . . . who was the doctor? . . . strange brother . . . very strange woman . . . unusual clothing . . . hair like a mermaid . . .

As he reached the end of the trail and turned into Pip Court, he remembered the last-minute catfit that had raised havoc with a silk shirt and a good pair of pants. Otherwise, he would have been having refreshments in a gazebo with two widows instead of risking a heart attack to rescue a not-so-fair damsel in distress . . . And then he thought, Was the cat's tantrum just a coincidence? Or what?

He could never be sure whether Koko's catfits were the result of a stitch in the side, a twitch in a nerve end, or an itch in the tail. Sometimes the cat had an ulterior motive. Sometimes he was trying to communicate.

Nine

When Qwilleran arrived at Four Pips following the episode on the nature trail, the Siamese were playing a cozy domestic scene in the lounge chair, which they had commandeered as their own. Koko was biting Yum Yum's neck, and she was slobbering in his ear.

"Disgusting!" Qwilleran said to them.

He stripped off his clothes and took a shower. Despite the arduous detour through the woods, he still had to check the Island Experience and make a reservation for the Rikers. He took a rest and revived himself with some packaged snacks before dressing in his second-best shirt and pants. His crumpled duds he stuffed into a plastic bag for another trip to the Vacation Helpers.

On the way he could not resist stopping at the inn to report his adventure to the Hardings. They were sitting in their favorite swing, close to the front door, where they could see everyone coming and going.

"I've just met some members of the royal family," he told them as he walked up the steps.

"The Appelhardts?" the vicar said in surprise. "Dare one inquire how that came about?"

Qwilleran related the story without mentioning his aerobic feat with an armful of hysterical botanist. "She said she lived at The Pines, and I helped her get home. Two men were playing croquet, and one of them happened to be a doctor. He took her away in a golf cart, and I would guess she was airlifted to the mainland."

"Well, well, well!" Mrs. Harding exclaimed.

"Three holes in the ground," her husband said mockingly.

"Oh, Arledge!" She slapped his wrist. "He always says that," she complained to Qwilleran fussily.

The vicar said, "We haven't seen the royal family since the Ritchies disposed of their property. As their house guests we were invited to garden parties at The Pines. The matriarch of the Appelhardts always presided like the dowager queen mother."

"The refreshments were sumptuous," Mrs. Harding recalled, "and there were peacocks strutting around the garden, spreading their tails and making horrendous noises when one least expected it."

"Alas, the Ritchies are gone, and the royal family is still with us," the vicar said in a grieving tone. "If you are interested in a little authentic history, Mr. Qwilleran—"

"I'm very interested!" He pulled up a chair.

"In the 1920s, the Appelhardts bought the western half of the island from the government and displaced the islanders, who had been tolerated as squatters. They established the Grand Island Club for millionaires who enjoy nature—if not too uncomfortably natural. According to widespread belief, they bought the land for ten dollars an acre and sold it to club members for ten dollars a square foot. I suspect it is now worth ten dollars a square inch." He finished with a chuckle that developed into a coughing spell.

Mrs. Harding rummaged in her handbag. "Here, Arledge, take this lozenge, and do be careful!"

Qwilleran said, "I had only a brief glimpse of their estate from the rear, but it seems extensive."

"Oh, yes!" she said. "Besides the main lodge there are smaller lodges for the married sons, cottages for the help, stables for the horses, a large swimming pool with pool house, tennis courts—"

"My dear, you sound like a real-estate agent," her husband chided.

She gave him a reproving glance and continued. "The married sons are professional men. The young woman you met is their only daughter. She never married. There's also a very handsome son—married several times, I believe. He appears to have no serious calling."

"The prodigal son," Mr. Harding explained. "Inevitable in every family of means."

His wife said, "The Moseley sisters will want to hear about this, Mr. Qwilleran. The daughter was a student at the school where they taught. I'm sure you've met Edith and Edna, haven't you?"

"I met one of them at the fruit basket, but I don't know whether it was Edna or Edith. She was promoting bananas as a source of something-or-other."

"That was Edna. She's the taller of the two and wears glasses."

"It's Edith who wears glasses," her husband corrected her. "Edna wears corrective shoes and speaks with a soft voice. Edith taught dramatic arts and always projects from the diaphragm. Edna taught science, I believe. She's the prettier of the two—"

"Well, you must excuse me," Qwilleran said as Mr. Harding paused for breath. "I have an important errand to do. We'll continue this later."

His next stop was the Vacation Helpers service center, where he dropped off his clothes to be pressed. Shelley greeted the silk shirt like an old friend. "You're really hard on your clothes," she said.

"Don't blame me. My roommate flew off the handle."

"Do you let her get away with that?"

"My roommate is a male with four legs and a tail and sharp teeth," he explained.

"Oh, don't tell me! Let me guess! You have a German shepherd. . . . No? A Weimaraner?"

"You're not even warm. I'll give you a clue. He has a dark mask."

"A Boxer!"

"No. I'll tell you what," Qwilleran said. "I'll pick up my pressing in an hour or so, and you think about it in the meantime."

The Island Experience was the last in the row of commercial establishments on West Beach Road, and it was the most imposing. The rustic lodge was landscaped with taste and money. Instead of the traditional porch, a contemporary deck spanned the front elevation, overlooking the lake. There were tubs of salmon-pink geraniums to match the salmon-pink umbrella tables, but there were no guests in the salmon-pink canvas chairs.

Qwilleran assumed they were all in the gazebo, drinking the complimentary champagne. He rang the bell.

The woman who greeted him was a handsome, well-dressed, mature woman with a sparkling smile. "Welcome to Island Experience! I'm Carla, your merry innkeeper."

"I'm Jim Qwilleran, a bad-humored traveler from the mainland."

"Trudy!" she called over her shoulder. "Guess who just walked in! The Qwill Pen himself!"

Another woman with designer-style appearance and personality came briskly into the foyer, smiling and extending both hands in welcome. "We've been reading your column in the little newspaper here, and it's enchanting! We remember your by-line from Chicago, too. Are you looking for a place to stay? Be our guest!"

"To tell the truth, I've been on the island since Sunday," he said. "I'm traveling with pets, so I'm obliged to stay in one of the cottages at Domino Inn."

"Why don't you stay here and let the animals have the cottage? The Vacation Helpers will feed them and walk them for you."

"It's not so simple as that," he objected. "I appreciate the suggestion, but my purpose here at the moment is to find lodgings for a couple of friends. Arch Riker and his wife—he's publisher of the 'little newspaper'—want to spend this weekend on the island. I believe they'd enjoy your inn."

While standing in the foyer he had scanned the adjoining rooms and had noted the impressive antiques and impressive decor and also the lack of guests. Someone was hovering in the living room, but she wore a salmon-pink uniform and was dusting the bric-a-brac.

"Let us show you around," Carla offered. "It took nerve to paint the plank paneling white, but I think it enhances our country antiques, don't you?"

There were loungy sofas in the living room, foils for the expensively severe tables, desks and cupboards. In the dining room Windsor chairs surrounded a long trestle table; its pedigree was palpable even to Qwilleran. Upstairs, only one door was closed; open doors revealed perfectly appointed bedrooms and sitting rooms that seemed to be waiting for a magazine photographer.

"Do you think your friends would like a suite?" Trudy asked as she handed him a card listing the rates.

There were four bedrooms and two suites. The Garden Suite was twice the price of a bedroom, and the English Suite was the most expensive of all, having a Jacobean canopy bed with twisted posts.

"I think Mr. and Mrs. Riker would like the English Suite," he said, chuckling inwardly at the thought of his friend's indignation. Arch could afford it, but he always played the tightwad. Furthermore, he had been goading Qwilleran for his Scottish thrift for four decades. It was time for sweet revenge.

"We put fresh flowers in the English Suite," one of the women said. "Do you happen to know what the lady likes?"

"Yellow."

"Perfect! Yellow looks lovely with the dark oak. We'll phone the mainland and have them shipped over by ferry."

With the arrangements completed, Qwilleran was invited to have champagne in the gazebo. "Make mine a soft drink, and I'll accept with pleasure," he said.

The gazebo was screened, not only against mosquitoes but against wandering cats. Several healthy specimens, two of them pregnant, were prowling about the backyard, waiting for the hors d'oeuvres.

"Everyone feeds them," Trudy said. "The island is really overcatted."

They sat in white wicker chairs while a timorous young island woman in salmon pink brought the champagne bucket, glasses, and a flavored mineral water for Qwilleran. He proposed a toast to the two merry innkeepers and then asked the standard question: What had brought them to the island? The women looked at each other briefly for cues and then began an overlapping dialogue:

Carla: "Both our families have been members of the Grand Island Club since it began, so we've been summer neighbors all our lives, until—"

Trudy: "Our husbands died, and our children thought the Caymans were more exciting, so—"

Carla: "We sold our memberships and—"

Trudy: "Started traveling together, buying antiques and staying at country inns."

Carla: "We collected so much stuff, we had two options—"

Trudy: "To open an antique shop or start a bed-and-breakfast, so—"

Carla: "We decided we'd like an inn, because we love meeting people and playing the host."

Trudy: "And then we heard about the Pear Island opportunity. Imagine our surprise when—"

Carla: "We realized it was our own Grand Island with a different name."

Trudy: "Actually, we're delighted, because—"

Carla: "There's something about this island that gets into the blood."

As they stopped for breath, Qwilleran blinked his eyes and shook his head. Seated between them, he was turning rapidly from side to side to keep up with their dizzying recital. "May I change my seat in order to see both of you lovely ladies?" he asked. It was no exaggeration; he wondered how many hairdressers, masseuses, dressmakers, cosmetic surgeons, orthodontists, and voice coaches had labored to produce these perfect womanworks. Their well-modulated voices assumed a higher pitch, however, with each pouring from the bottle.

A tray of canapés was brought to the gazebo by the painfully awkward server, who was trying hard to do everything right. When she had gone, Qwilleran asked, "Do you staff your inn with islanders?"

"We debated that. Don Exbridge wanted us to hire students from the mainland, but our families always hired islanders, and we felt comfortable with them. They're part of the island experience, you know."

Another chilled bottle of champagne arrived, and another bottle of kiwi-flavored mineral water, and Qwilleran said, "You mentioned that you sold your *memberships*. Not your real estate?"

The women exchanged a glance that said, Shall we tell him? Then they succumbed to his sincere gaze and sympathetic manner. They were relaxing. They were eager to talk.

"Well," Trudy began, "when we decided to sell our property—which our families had held since the 1920s—we learned we had to sell it back to the club *at their price*, which was much less than market value. It was in the original contract. Nothing we could do about it."

Carla interrupted with belligerence, "If my husband had been alive, he'd have found a loophole, believe me!"

"The Grand Island Club is controlled by the Appelhardt family, who founded it, and Mrs. Appelhardt, the mother, is a hard woman," Trudy said.

Carla again: "I call her a Harpy! I always felt sorry for her kids. They grew up with our kids. None of them turned out the way she intended."

Trudy: "Poetic justice! She wanted the eldest to be a lawyer. He got through law school but could never pass the bar exam."

Carla: "The next was supposed to be a heart surgeon. And what is he? A perfectly wonderful vet! He always loved animals."

Trudy: "And what about the girl? She's a real flake!"

Carla: "And the youngest boy! She's bailed him out of three marriages already."

Trudy: "It would be funny if it wasn't so sad."

Carla: "Why does he bother to get married?"

Trudy: "He's just an easy mark who can't say no."

When the merry innkeepers signaled for a third bottle of champagne, Qwilleran stood up, thanked them for their hospitality, and explained that he had another appointment. Leaving them happily relaxed in the wicker chairs, he walked down West Beach Road, marveling at the intrigue behind the Golden Curtain. He picked up his pressed garments, then stopped at the Domino Inn to phone Riker's office. He left the information about the reservation with the secretary.

"He's here. Want to talk to him?" asked Wilfred.

"Haven't time. Late for an appointment." Qwilleran knew that his friend's first question would be "How much?"

On the way out of the building he was stopped by the Moseley sisters. "You're a hero!" they said. "The Hardings told us about the rescue."

"Just happened to be in the right place at the right time."

"We knew Elizabeth very well," said the one with glasses. "She was a student at our school in Connecticut. When we read about Pear Island resort in the Boston papers and made our reservation, we had no idea we were coming to her beloved Grand Island."

"Have you seen her since you've been here?"

"Oh, no! We wouldn't think of intruding," said the pretty one with a soft voice. "Is she looking well?"

"In the throes of a snake bite one is never at one's best."

"Very true." They nodded, smiling at his arch observation.

"But to answer your question seriously, she seems to be unhealthily thin."

One sister murmured to the other, "She's having problems again. She's not eating. Too bad she can't get away from that environment."

A profile of the rich little mermaid was forming in Qwilleran's mind. "Was she a good student?"

"Oh, yes," said Edith. "All her life she'd had private tutors and was a prodigious reader, but she was a nervous wreck when she came to us. We all worked hard to improve her diet and elevate her spirit and draw her into campus life."

"We succeeded to a degree, and she should have gone on to college, but . . . it didn't happen. The reason was never explained. We corresponded for a while, but gradually she slipped away into her small world. Poor Elizabeth!"

Qwilleran concealed his personal curiosity by inquiring, "And now that you've seen her beloved island, what do you think of it?"

"It's not the idyllic spot we expected," said Edna ruefully. "The Bambas are a lovely family, but we doubt that we'll stay our full two weeks."

"The island isn't even pear-shaped," Edith said. "We've taken carriage rides on both beaches, and it's an isosceles triangle!"

Edna said, "You should put that in your column, Mr. Qwilleran."

As he ambled back to Four Pips, he was painting a mental picture of the royal family, brushstroke by brushstroke: the daughter who wouldn't eat . . . the son who couldn't stop marrying . . . the law graduate who couldn't (or wouldn't) pass the bar exam . . . the doctor who preferred to treat animals . . . the autocratic mother who was said to be a Harpy.

Upon arriving home he immediately wrote a brief note to Mrs. Appelhardt: "Found these on the nature trail. Hope your daughter recovers swiftly." He signed it "J. Qwilleran." Then he set out for the Vacation Helpers once more, carrying the botany book and the silver pencil.

Shelley was at the counter. "Back again?" she said in surprise. "Was the pressing okay?"

"No complaint," he said, "except for the scorch marks on the back of the shirt."

Her look of horror melted quickly to a smile. "Oh, you're a male chauvinist comic! What can we do for you now?"

"Could you wrap these two articles and deliver them to an address on West Beach Road? Tomorrow will do."

"We'll be happy to. I have a nice box and some seagull giftwrap."

"This is not a gift," he said. "On the other hand, I don't want it to look like a homemade bomb. Here's the note to go with it, and here's the address." He looked over her shoulder to the rear of the room. "Is your cat supposed to be scratching himself in the baby's playpen?"

"No! No! Out! Out!" she screamed, chasing him and slamming a door. "Somebody left the door open. That's Hannibal, one of our resident strays."

"A 'resident stray' sounds like an oxymoron," he said.

"Hannibal is foxy, but he's no moron," she quipped. "He knows a good place to eat. How did you like your box lunch?"

"The meatloaf was excellent. Could you deliver a whole one to me, say, every other day? I'd pay in advance."

"Absolutely!" said Shelley. "We'll start tomorrow. Midge makes four-pounders for sandwiches and two-pounders for snacks."

"Two-pounders will be ample."

"Is it for your roommate?" she asked, looking him steadily in the eye. "Your roommate is a raccoon, isn't he?"

Shelley looked so triumphant, so pleased with herself, that he said mildly, "How did you guess?"

Ten

On Friday morning Qwilleran opened a can of lobster for the cats' breakfast. "This is the last junk food you're going to get for a while. For the rest of our stay here, you'll have homemade meatloaf, delivered fresh, every other day, by bicycle. That's the good news. The bad news is that you are now raccoons."

Through long association with this pair of connoisseurs, he knew their favorites: freshly roasted turkey, homemade meatloaf, and canned red salmon, top grade. Nevertheless, they gobbled the lobster with rapturous slurping, waving of tails, and clicking of fangs on the plate. Yum Yum looked up after each swallow to confirm that Qwilleran was still there. Afterward, she jumped onto his lap while he drank his coffee, stroked her fur, and paid her extravagant compliments. He called it their après-breakfast schmooz.

Their dinner was served earlier than usual that evening, because Qwilleran wanted to check the post office before it closed. He cubed the meatloaf precisely—five-sixteenths of an inch, he estimated. "Don't say I never do anything for you," he said to the waiting cats. They were quieter than usual, and they were sitting a little farther away. After placing a generous plateful on the floor, he stepped back to enjoy their ecstasy. They approached it stealthily and backed away. He sampled a cube himself. There was nothing wrong with it; in fact, it might be described as . . . *tasty.* "Try it! You'll like it!" They walked away with heads lowered and tails drooping.

"Well, I'm not going to stand here and do catfood commercials for you brats!" He left the plate on the floor and dressed for his trip downtown.

The resort area was gearing up for what everyone hoped would be a busy weekend, although the atmosphere was more wishful than confident. Horse cabs lined up at the ferry dock. Cargo was being offloaded for the deli and general store—mostly beer. In an extra bid for business, the T-shirt studio was hanging choice designs on clotheslines strung across the front of the shop.

In the same spirit of hopeful doubt, Qwilleran checked the post office, but there was no news from Oregon. He assumed Polly was having a rollicking vacation—looking for puffin birds, giggling with her college roommate, and talking about *him.*

For a while he watched vacationers disembarking with bevies of children, their shouts punctuating the waterfront hush: "Junior, don't hang over the railing! . . . Mom, did you bring my rollerblades? . . . Lookit all the horses! What are they for? . . . Hey, Dad, could this island sink?"

Among the arrivals were six backpackers. The size of their gear suggested they were the crew who had been camping at the lighthouse on weekends and hang gliding on the dune. They were attractive young people, Qwilleran thought: the women, healthy; the men, athletic; and all exposed skin, enviably suntanned. Also arriving, with luggage to be loaded into a carriage, was Dr. June Halliburton with a limp-brimmed sunhat shading her white skin and red hair.

In the hotel lobby Qwilleran picked up a copy of Friday's *Moose County Something* and was surprised to find the following item on page one:

SNAKE-BITE VICTIM
AIRLIFTED FROM ISLAND

The sheriff's helicopter evacuated a victim of snake bite from Pear Island to the Pickax General Hospital Thursday. Elizabeth C. Appelhardt, 23, a summer resident of the Grand

Island Club, was in good condition today after treatment, according to a hospital spokesperson. This is the third medical emergency handled by the sheriff's airborne division this month.

Only the sheriff would like the coverage, Qwilleran mused; he was always campaigning for re-election or lobbying for more funds to buy rescue equipment. The queen mother would dislike the publicity because it invaded her family's Olympian privacy. The victim would take umbrage at the mention of her age. Don Exbridge would explode because the report made the island sound hazardous to one's health.

There was already a commotion erupting in the manager's office, and Qwilleran caught sight of a bald head and waving arms as Exbridge shouted, "Get those damned T-shirts off the front of the store! What do they think this is? A Persian bazaar?"

As soon as the dining room opened, Qwilleran presented himself at the reservation desk.

"Hi, Mr. Q! You're early," said Derek Cuttlebrink, resplendent in pirate's tricorne and one gold earring. "Are you all alone tonight?"

"No, I've brought my friend, Anatole France." He held up his copy of *Penguin Island.* "I'd like a quiet table where I can read—also a reservation for tomorrow night at eight o'clock—three persons." In a lower voice he asked, "Any luck with your assignment?"

Derek nodded importantly. "Gotta contact," he mumbled while appearing to study his reservation chart. "How about Sunday night? I'm off early."

"Come to the fourth cottage behind the inn."

Over shrimp bisque and Cajun pork chops Qwilleran finished reading his book and was leaving the dining room when another blowup occurred in the manager's office. There was a torrent of invective, and Dwight Somers came rushing out. He caught sight of Qwilleran. "I need a drink! Come into the bar."

He led the way to a secluded booth and ordered a double martini. "That guy's a madman when things don't go the way he planned. And don't try to reason with him, or you'll get your head lopped off. If I'm still here by the Fourth of July, I'll be surprised. Either I'll be fired, or I'll be in jail for murder."

"What's happened now?" Qwilleran asked sympathetically.

"It's a funny thing, Qwill. The chicken incident didn't faze him because he could use his clout to squash the implications, but little things drive him bananas—like the pickets last weekend, and the critical letters to the editor, and the snake-bite item in today's paper. He says, 'Who cares if some snooty rich kid gets bitten by a snake?' He says it's not important news. He says it only tarnishes the image of the resort, which is a boon to the community. When the paper reported the county's decision to spray for mosquitoes by plane, he got all kinds of flak, and he blamed you guys for playing it up on page one."

"Are we running a newspaper or a publicity agency?" Qwilleran asked.

"He's not dumb; he knows he can't dictate to the press," said Dwight, "but he has these insane tantrums! If I play Devil's advocate, in the interest of public relations, I get dumped on. Wait'll you hear his latest brainstorm!" He gulped the rest of his drink and waved his glass at the waiter.

Qwilleran advised him to order some food, too. "I'll have coffee and a piece of pie . . . Okay, what's his latest noodle?"

"Well, he's afraid we're getting too many families with five kids and a picnic basket, instead of the sophisticated crowd he intended. So he wants to offer a Midsummer Night's Dream weekend package—everything first class and limited to thirty persons, adults only. It includes transportation from the mainland by private boat; flowers and champagne in the rooms; breakfast in bed; and a supper-dance on Midsummer's Eve."

"Sounds okay," Qwilleran said.

"He wants it outdoors, with white tablecloths, fresh flowers on the tables, three wine glasses at every place, hurricane candles, strolling musicians, and waiters in white coats with black bow-ties. No pirate shirts! That would be okay around the pool; if it rained, we could set up indoors. But here's the fly in the soup: He wants it at the lighthouse!" Dwight took a swig of his second double martini.

"Can you imagine the logistics?" he went on. "First you need a fleet of wagons to transport tables, chairs, portable dance floor, table settings, food warmers, chilled wine, and portable johns. There are no facilities up there. Then you need a fleet of carriages to transport the guests. The ground behind the lighthouse is uneven, and how do you keep the tables and chairs from wobbling? The wind is capable of whipping the tablecloths around, blowing the napkins away, putting out the candles, breaking the glass chimneys, and even blowing the food off the plates! And suppose it starts to rain!"

"Hasn't Don ever been to Lighthouse Point?"

"Of course he has, but he never lets reality and common sense get in the way of a fanciful idea."

Qwilleran said, "I see a great scenario for a comedy skit. You have all the guests on the rock, getting happily plastered, and it starts to rain. No shelter. No carriages; they've returned to the stables. Everyone's drenched. The steaks are swimming on the plates. Thunder is crashing; lightning is flashing. Then the fog horn starts blatting, fifty feet from everyone's eardrums. The guests riot. Two of them take refuge inside the portable potties and refuse to come out. I think it has infinite possibilities for laughs."

"Not funny," said Dwight, but he laughed just the same and applied himself to his steak. Finally he said to Qwilleran, "And what have you been doing all week?"

"Not much. I rescued a mermaid from certain death, that's all." He described the incident with more detail than he had wasted on other listeners.

"It figures," Dwight said with envy. "The guy who has an indecent fortune of his own is the lucky one who rescues an heiress. What's she like?"

"She has the svelte figure of a rainbow trout, the hair of a mermaid, and flowing garments that probably hide a tail. Want me to line her up for you? In case you get fired, it would be useful to have an heiress on the string."

"No, thanks. Finders keepers," said Dwight. "What do you hear from Polly?"

"She hasn't even sent a postcard, but I bet she phones Pickax every night and talks to Bootsie."

"I'm envious of your relationship with Polly, Qwill. You're comfortable friends, and you keep your independence. I've been in Moose County almost a year without any luck. I've bought dinner for every unattached female within fifty miles, except Amanda Goodwinter, and I may get around to her yet. So far, no one has passed the litmus test. Hixie Rice is my type, if you want to know, but she's tied up with that doctor."

"It won't last long," Qwilleran reassured him. "No one ever lasts long with Hixie, and that would go for you, too."

Dwight said sheepishly, "I even took June Halliburton to dinner at the Palomino Paddock and spent half a week's salary. It was a bust!"

"What happened?" Qwilleran asked, although he could guess.

"You know how she is! She has looks, talent, and credentials, but she says the damnedest things! We were drinking seventy-dollar champagne, and she looked at me with those suggestive eyes and said, 'You're a handsome, intelligent man, Dwight, with a wonderful personality. Why don't you shave off that scruffy beard and invest in a good toupee?' That's typical of that woman. She pursues guys as if she likes them, and then stomps on 'em. How well do you know her?"

"Well enough to know I don't want to know her any better."

"I think of her as a predatory misanthrope."

"That'll do until a stronger word comes along," Qwilleran said. "At the Rikers' wedding she was coming on to every man at the reception, including the bridegroom. Polly can't stand her. When they meet, you could light a cigarette from the sparks."

"Did you ever write June up in your column?"

"Almost. I intended to interview her about music in the schools, but she wanted to make it a social occasion at her apartment. When I insisted on an office appointment, she proved impossible to interview. It was verbal football. She called the plays, carried the ball, straight-armed questions, and made end runs around the subject. The way it ended, she scored all the points, but I won the game. I never wrote the column."

"You media types always get the last word. I'm in the wrong business."

Qwilleran said, "Another time, I invited the Comptons over for a drink after the theater, and they brought June. She didn't stay long. She said the circular building and diagonal ramps gave her a headache. Actually it was Koko giving her the whammy. When he stares at someone's forehead, it's like a gimlet boring into the brain."

"What was his problem?" Dwight asked.

"Apparently he didn't like her scent."

"Starting this weekend, she'll be here for the whole summer."

"I know," Qwilleran said. "I saw her getting off the ferry with a lot of luggage—and an eye for the mounted security men in red coats. Was she another of Exbridge's bright ideas?"

"No, she approached him with the proposition."

"What is she doing in this remote part of the country anyway? With all her talents she belongs in a major city Down Below. I'll have to ask Lyle Compton how she landed in Moose County. He's the one who hired her."

"Lyle will be here Sunday night, doing his talk on Scotland. Do you have any big plans for the weekend?"

"Just dining with Arch and Mildred tomorrow night," Qwilleran said, "and avoiding my musical neighbor."

As Qwilleran walked back to the Domino Inn, he had to stand aside for emergency vehicles speeding up the beach road. He could imagine that a member of the Grand Island Club had a heart attack, or a carriageful of tourists overturned, or the kid who was leaning over the ferry railing fell over the cliff at the lighthouse. By the time he reached the inn, the vehicles were speeding back downtown, and the sheriff's helicopter could be heard.

The guests sitting in porch swings were all agog when Qwilleran walked up the driveway. Someone called out, "Mitchell, he came back!" The four-year-old rushed indoors and rushed out again to hand him an envelope with an important crest on the flap.

Mrs. Harding said, "It was delivered by a man in green livery, driving a very handsome buggy with a beautiful horse!"

At Four Pips the Siamese were allowed to sniff the envelope, and their noses registered excitement. The note read:

Dear Mr. Qwilleran,

Please honor us by having tea at The Pines Sunday afternoon. We wish to thank you in person for coming to the rescue of our daughter Elizabeth after her unfortunate mishap. She is out of danger, we are glad to say, and returns to the island tomorrow. It will be our pleasure to send a carriage for you at four o'clock Sunday.

It was signed "Rowena Appelhardt." She was the queen mother, Qwilleran guessed, and this was to be a command appearance at Buckingham Palace. At least, he would see the peacocks, and Mrs. Harding said the refreshments were commendable.

The Siamese were prowling and yowling and looking lean and hungry. He checked their feeding station. The plate was empty, but the cubes of meatloaf had merely been scattered about the floor of the kitchenette. They looked dry and unappetizing.

"Shame on you!" he said. "There are homeless cats that would kill for a taste of this meatloaf! And it behooves you to get used to it, because we have another eight pounds coming."

He shoveled up the rejected delicacy and took it up the lane to the old glazed birdbath that served as a feeding station for the wild cats. Before he could even empty his bowl, three of them came from nowhere to fight for their share. Then he saw Nick Bamba, home for the weekend and hammering nails into a wooden contraption.

"What are you doing?" Qwilleran asked.

"Building a rack to keep the trash barrels off the ground. It's neater, and the strays can sleep underneath. Lori's idea."

"You never quit, do you, Nick?"

"Compared to my job at the prison, this is R-and-R. Did you have a good week? Did you find out anything?"

"So far I've been feeling my way and making contacts. Stop in tomorrow, and we'll talk."

Qwilleran went into the lounge for an apple and found that the basket was filled with pears! While there he heard a radio newscast coming from an alcove, where a family of three were playing dominoes. He walked over and said, "Mind if I listen? I'm interested in tomorrow's weather."

"You've just missed it," said the father. He turned to his son. "Do you remember what they said about the weather, Brad?"

The boy was about ten years old and looked too intelligent for his age; he wore a T-shirt printed with the words: Ask Me. He said, "Moderately high winds subsiding at midnight. Waves three to four feet. Tomorrow sunny and warm with light winds from the southeast, veering to southwest by afternoon. High tomorrow: seventy-five. Low—"

"Hush," his father said, holding up a hand and inclining his head toward the radio. The announcer was saying:

". . . police bulletin from Pear Island, where a shooting claimed the life of a vacationer this evening. The victim, an adult male, was hang gliding on the sand dune at the north end of the island when his companions heard a gunshot and the kite fell into the shallow water of the lake. Suffering from hypothermia as well as loss of blood, he was given emergency aid at the scene by the volunteer rescue squad before being airlifted by sheriff's helicopter to the mainland. He was pronounced dead on arrival at the Pickax General Hospital. Gunfire, not unusual on the island, had been noted throughout the day and evening. The fatal bullet is thought to be a stray shot fired by a varmint hunter, according to the sheriff's department. The victim's name has not been released at this time, but police say he was not a resident of Moose County."

"Nobody told us about gunfire on the island!" said the mother. "I hate guns!"

As Qwilleran walked back to Four Pips, he thought, Another incident! . . . Nick will spend a sleepless night, worrying about the future of the inn . . . The woman who hates guns will convince her husband to cut their visit short . . . The Moseley sisters will be glad they're canceling . . . The two men who look like detectives, having left, will come back.

He counted on his fingers: One, food poisoning. Two, drowning. Three, bad fall. Four, explosion. Five, shooting . . . He was impressed by the diversity of the mishaps. There was no pattern, except that they all targeted tourists at regularly spaced intervals. Qwilleran pictured a consortium of saboteurs, each performing his own specialty. The islanders were crafty, skilled, and knowledgeable as a result of the hard life they lived. What mystified him was Koko's lack of interest and cooperation. In the past he had sensed the presence of crime and sniffed for clues. Perhaps the island atmosphere dulled his senses. True, he had staged a catfit that caused Qwilleran to be the right person in the right place at the right time, but that had nothing to do with the five suspicious incidents.

At Four Pips the Siamese continued to look at Qwilleran reproachfully and hungrily, and it required great fortitude to hold out against their wiles. He would give them their crunchy bedtime snack, but that was all; for breakfast he would serve meatloaf again on a take-it-or-leave-it basis.

After dark the three of them liked to sit on the screened porch, listening to mysterious sounds in the trees and underbrush, but tonight there was competition from Five Pips: piano playing, voices, recorded music, laughter. Qwilleran sorted out the voices: two of them, one female, one male. Later, the music stopped and the voices were muffled. He went indoors, read for a while, gave the cats their treat, and then retired.

He fell asleep easily and had one of his fanciful dreams: The natives living on Pear Island were penguins, and the tourists were puffin birds. A great bald eagle appeared and attempted to tow the island to the mainland, but he was shot down by a rabbit hunter, and the island sank to the bottom of the lake.

"Whew!" Qwilleran gasped, waking and sitting up in bed. He could hear happy voices next door, saying good night. The male guest was leaving with a flashlight, and Qwilleran hoped it would illuminate the man's face when he passed Four Pips—not that it was any of Qwilleran's business, but he was observant by nature and by profession. His curiosity was aroused, however, when the visitor left by way of the nature trail.

Eleven

Qwilleran may not have known it, but he was losing the Battle of the Meatloaf. Two hungry and indignant cats started yowling outside his bedroom door at six A.M. Saturday. He endured it for almost an hour and then—in bare feet and pajama bottoms—went to the kitchen to prepare another plate of meatloaf for the ungrateful wretches. They were quiet as he cut the food, mincing it this time instead of cubing it. They were quiet when he placed the plate on the floor. They looked at it in disbelief, as if to say, What is this stuff? . . . Are we supposed to eat this dog dinner? Just as they were shaking their paws exquisitely and walking away from the plate, there was a knock on the front door.

Qwilleran's watch said seven-fifteen. It must be Mitchell—who else? He might be bringing a message from the Rikers. Perhaps they had not arrived last night. Perhaps some emergency had arisen. He pulled the door open with anxiety.

To his embarrassment it was June Halliburton, fully clothed and squinting through the smoke of a cigarette that she held gracefully in one hand. She appraised his rumpled pajama bottoms and uncombed hair and grinned impishly. "Want to go to breakfast with me? Come as you are."

"Sorry," he said. "I won't be ready for food for another couple of hours. Go along without me. They serve an excellent breakfast."

"I'm aware of that," she said loftily. "I spent two weekends in this cottage, keeping your bed warm for you. Did anyone tell you I'm handling the entertainment for the hotel? While you're sitting around doing nothing, you might try writing some material for me. I can't guarantee I'll use it, but it should be good practice for you." These typically shabby remarks were made with the insolent smile that was her trademark.

Qwilleran had been writing college revues when she was still sucking teething rings. Before he could think of a retort within the bounds of civility, Koko came up behind and swooped to his shoulder, teetering there as if ready to spring and fixing the intruder with his laser stare.

"Well," she said, "come over to Five Pips for a drink, or some music, or anything—anytime." She flicked her cigarette, tossed her glistening red hair, and sauntered away.

Koko jumped to the floor, and Qwilleran said, "Thanks. You're a good egg! Tell you what I'm gonna do. I'll chop some smoked oysters and add them to the meatloaf."

Both cats went to work on the exotic hash and extracted the oyster while avoiding the meatloaf.

"Cats!" Qwilleran said. "You can't win!"

For his own breakfast he had ham biscuits with cheese sauce and then codfish cakes with scrambled eggs. It was late, and only one other table was taken. The family who had checked into Two Pips had an infant in a highchair and a tot who was attracted to Qwilleran's moustache. When he inadvertently made eye contact, she squirmed out of her chair and toddled to his table, offering him a piece of toast, partly masticated.

"Sandra, don't bother the man," her father said.

"She's very friendly," her mother explained.

Qwilleran groaned inwardly. He felt besieged by finicky cats, pushy piano players, and now gregarious youngsters. When he returned to Four Pips, the piano player was doing scales and finger exercises, a monotonous recital that made it difficult to concentrate on reading or writing. Eventually there was a pause. It felt good when she stopped! Then there was a knock on the front door. Irritably he yanked it open.

"Morning, Qwill," said Nick Bamba. He had two of his children by the hand. "Lovey wants to see your kitties, and this is Jason, who just graduated from first grade. He's our vice president in charge of waste baskets and litter boxes."

"We learned about Indians and squabs and cabooses," said the blond boy. "They lived in wigs with a hole for the smoke."

Qwilleran said, "And how is the future Madame President this morning?"

"Two in April," she said and lunged after Yum Yum, who slithered under the sofa. Koko looked on with haughty disapproval.

"The kitties are bashful," her father said, "but you've seen them now, and you can go home . . . Jason, take your sister back. Mr. Qwilleran and I have business to discuss."

"Okefenokee!" said Jason. He grabbed his sister's hand, and the two of them trudged up the lane, Lovey gazing back longingly.

Nick handed Qwilleran a plastic sack. "Here's some pears, Qwill. I bought a bushel on sale, but they have to be eaten right away."

"Thanks. Shall we sit on the porch?"

"Better sit indoors. The air is still this morning, and voices carry. Have you been downtown yet? The pickets came over on the first ferry, and they're marching again. They don't want the mosquitoes sprayed."

"What do you think about the hang-glider shooting?" Qwilleran asked.

"The sheriff blames a stray shot from a hunting gun. I say the sheriff is full of it! . . . So what's with you, Qwill?"

"I've lined up an undercover agent who can work from the inside. It's my contention that there's covert hostility among the natives. They don't come out punching, but they've infiltrated the resort as kitchen helpers, hack drivers, servants, busboys, dockworkers, handymen, and plenty we don't know about. They're silent. They're shadowy. I'm convinced your front steps were okay until one of these silent, shadowy islanders tampered with them—perhaps pulled a few nails under cover of darkness. Unfortunately I have no evidence . . . Is there any more news about the poultry farm in Lockmaster?"

"That investigation fizzled out," said Nick. "Nobody died. Everybody wants to forget it. Food poisoning is something that just happens."

"How will Exbridge react to the shooting last night?"

"This is not for publication, Qwill, but he's lobbying to get hunting banned on the island. The sound of gunfire makes tourists nervous, he says, especially those from big cities."

Qwilleran said, "The pickets will have a grand old time with that issue! Rabbit is a staple of the islanders' diet, and a mainstay of their economy."

"Want to hear something else, off the record? Don wants the county to pave the beach roads and cut through the sand dune to make it a ring road."

"The environmentalists are hypersensitive about sand dunes, you know, and the summer people will fight the paving project to the last drop of their blue blood. How do you and Lori feel about all these changes?"

"Well, it isn't the dream we had—not by a long shot—but now we're in it with both feet and every dollar we have, plus some we don't have."

"Nick, I hate to be a pessimist, but I bet Exbridge will want a golf course next. Then the ordinance against motor vehicles will be rescinded. There'll be RVs, motorcycles, bumper-to-bumper traffic and a gas station on Lighthouse Point. Emissions will kill the wildlife and defoliate the woods, and Piratetown will go condo. The island will be so honeycombed with wells and septic tanks that it'll sink like a sieve to the bottom of the lake."

"Qwill, I hope you're not gonna write anything crazy like that for your column. This was all confidential, you know." Nick stood up. "I've gotta go and do my chores . . . G'bye, kids," he said to the Siamese.

Qwilleran walked with him up the lane. The strays were hanging around the trash cans as usual. "They're all over," Nick said. "They're around restaurants, picnic tables, docks—wherever there's food. Exbridge wants the board of health to exterminate them."

"If he proposes that, he'll have another American Revolution on his hands."

"For God's sake, don't mention it!"

Qwilleran looked up sharply. "What's all that noise?"

"They're picnickers and day-trippers," Nick said. "They're supposed to use the public beach on the other side of the island, but they like our sand. You can't blame them."

Qwilleran left him and ambled across the road to the beach, where children were screaming and throwing sand and having a wonderful time; young adults were rocking to boom boxes; and volleyball players were yelling good-natured threats and insults. The scene gave him an idea for a satire on tourism, and he went back to Four Pips to set up his typewriter on the snack table. What he had in mind was a skit spoofing package weekends. It would require a cast of two: a tourist couple in shorts, sandals, and Pear Island T-shirts. The scene would be the hotel porch with rocking chairs. The tourists would be rocking, eating a box lunch, and reading aloud from an advertising flyer.

FANTASTIC FUN-FILLED WEEKEND
ON WONDERFUL PEAR ISLAND
ONLY $149.50
(Children under 12, 15% extra)

Friday Afternoon . . . You are met at the jetport by our friendly guide, who will give you a pear-shaped luggage tag (one per person) and a discount coupon for a T-shirt. Depart promptly for enchanting Moose County aboard a deluxe single-engine prop aircraft with seat belts and headrests. Peanuts will be served in flight, with only one scheduled stop for refueling, repairs, and use of facilities. Arrive at Moose County airport and proceed in the comfort of a converted school bus to an all-night restaurant famous for pirogi and boiled cabbage. After a delicious repast, continue to the historic Hotel Booze in the unspoiled lakeside town of Brrr, where you will spend your first exciting night.

Saturday . . . After a complimentary breakfast (choice of biscuit or muffin), you depart on a delightfully quaint coal-burning ferry for the voyage to the island. (Life preservers provided, but passengers are advised to use facilities before leaving hotel.) Enjoy the rare thrill of feeding the seagulls that follow the boat. (Bird bread not included.) Folding chairs available for passengers over 75. (Birth certificate required.)

On arrival at fabulous Pear Island, transfer to the spectacular Pear Island Hotel to register and receive your generous sample of mosquito spray. Your first day is entirely free—for walking around, splashing in the hotel pool, and rocking in the hotel's fifty rocking chairs. Watch the ferries unload; write postcards; shop for T-shirts; buy fudge; and thoroughly enjoy yourself. Feeling adventurous? Walk to the Riviera-type stone beach to hunt for agates. (Not included in the package: carriage rides, bike rentals, fishing parties, or lunch.)

Your exciting, fun-filled evening begins with a memorable dinner featuring the hotel's Very Special Chicken and a choice of sinfully delicious desserts: pears Romano, pears Chantilly, or pears Escoffier. Live entertainment follows, headlining the celebrated "Maestro of Moose County" and his accordion. When you retire after your full day of fun, you will find an individually wrapped square of fudge on your pillow. Sweet dreams!

Sunday . . . The excitement begins with a sumptuous breakfast buffet offering 85 items. (Choose any four.) Then it's "all aboard" a specially prepared hay wagon for a ride to Lighthouse Point via the exclusive West Beach Road. See the summer homes of the rich and famous! Photograph the picturesque lighthouse! See where hundreds of ships sank and thousands of persons drowned! Thrill to the sound of gunfire in the woods! After lunch (not included), you board the ferry and bid a reluctant farewell to magical Pear Island, an experience you will never forget . . . And only $149.50, based on triple occupancy! Price includes a short-term life insurance policy *plus* a free cat for each and every visitor to take home. Choice of colors. (Black-and-whites temporarily out of stock.)

Writing the skit put Qwilleran in a good mood for an evening with the Rikers, and shortly before eight o'clock he called for a carriage and picked them up at their bed-and-breakfast.

"How do you like the Island Experience?" he asked.

"It's a dream!" Mildred exclaimed. "The innkeepers are positively charming!"

"But their rates are atrocious!" Arch said. "Do you know what we're paying for that suite you reserved? There's only one other guest registered; that should tell you something."

"But the decor is exquisite," Mildred insisted, "and there's a lovely arrangement of fresh flowers in our suite. Pink carnations and snapdragons."

"Frankly, I think those two women are just going through the motions of innkeeping," her husband said. "They take the inn as a loss for tax purposes, while they spend the summer getting sloshed in the gazebo."

"Yes, they do seem to imbibe quite a bit," said Mildred, who was on the wagon. "Oh! Isn't that a hideous building!" she added as the carriage passed the Domino Inn.

"But it's popular," Qwilleran said.

"Because the prices are right; that's why," Riker snapped.

At the hotel they pushed through a phalanx of pickets, tourists, and stray cats. Mildred said it was a mess. In the lobby she said the black flags were too somber. Then she caught sight of Derek Cuttlebrink at the reservation desk. She had taught him in high school and had applauded him in Pickax theater productions. "Derek! What are you doing here?" she cried.

"I'm playing Captain Hook this week. Next week, King Kong." With a flourish he assigned them to a choice booth in the Corsair Room. Unobtrusively he slipped a scrap of paper to Qwilleran, who dropped it in his pocket.

The three old friends had much to talk about after being apart for a whole week: the shooting on the sand dune, the mosquito controversy, and ordinary newspaper shoptalk. Then Riker asked Qwilleran, "Do you consider this boondoggle of yours worthwhile? You're not jamming the fax machine with copy."

"Did you come over here to check up on your hired help?" Qwilleran retorted.

"The paper is paying for your junket, don't forget."

"Well," Qwilleran began cagily, since Riker was not aware of his real mission, "I have a lot of notes and tapes, but I need time to organize them. I've discovered, for example, that Pear Island is not pear-shaped. It may have been pear-shaped when it was surveyed a couple of centuries ago, but erosion has changed it to an isosceles triangle."

"That's a world-shaking discovery," the publisher said dryly. "Let's see you write a thousand words on that profound subject. Do you recommend changing the name again? It'll sound like a Greek island."

The entrées were served. Qwilleran had recommended the Cajun menu, and all three had ordered pork chops étouffée.

"Why, these are nothing but smothered pork chops, highly seasoned," Riker said. "Mildred fixes these all the time. How much are they paying this New Orleans chef?"

When they settled down to serious eating, Qwilleran told them the story behind the story of the snake-bite incident, with hitherto unrevealed descriptions, reactions, apprehensions, and conclusions. "First aid was the only merit badge I ever earned in scouting, and it finally paid off," he said.

Mildred was thrilled. Even Riker was impressed and wanted to know why the facts had been withheld from the newspaper. "It would have made a great feature: everybody's favorite columnist rescuing an heiress."

"There may be more to the story. They're an unusual family, and I'm invited to tea tomorrow afternoon."

"Speaking of tea," Mildred said, "have you been to the tea room? They serve real tea in fat English teapots with thin porcelain cups and all the shortbread you can eat."

Her husband said, "Qwill and I had enough shortbread in Scotland to last a lifetime. It hardly strikes me as tourist fare in this country. They certainly weren't doing any business when we were there."

"Did you go into the antique shop?" Qwilleran asked.

"Yes, and we recognized the woman who runs it," said Mildred. "She's staying at the Island Experience. We saw her in the breakfast room this morning, but she was rather aloof."

"No wonder the prices in her shop are so high," Riker said. "She has to pay for that suite with fresh flowers and champagne. Moreover, her inventory is questionable. She has some reproductions of Depression glass that she represents as the real thing. There's a lot of fraud these days in scrimshaw and netsuke and pre-Columbian figures. Is she uninformed or deliberately falsifying?"

"How would Exbridge react to this information?" Qwilleran asked. "He seems to run a tight ship."

"Well, I'm not going to be the one to tell him. He's been hard to get along with lately. Thinks he can tell us how to run the paper."

Over dessert—the inevitable pecan pie—Mildred asked about the Siamese.

"Koko is learning to play dominoes," Qwilleran said, "and he beats me every time."

"That shouldn't be hard to do," Riker said gleefully.

"What do you think of the feral cats on the island?"

Mildred was an activist in humanitarian causes, and she said vehemently, "There are too many! Overpopulation is inhumane. To maintain a healthy cat colony in an area like this, they should be trapped, neutered, and released—the way we're doing on the mainland."

Riker said, "Our editorials finally convinced the bureaucrats it's not only humane but cheaper in the long run than wholesale killing."

Qwilleran, who liked to stir things up, made a sly suggestion. "Why don't you send a reporter over here to discuss feral cats with vacationers, businesspeople, and the chief honcho himself? You could get some good photos."

"Don't assign my son-in-law," said Mildred. "Roger will break out in a rash even before the ferry docks."

After dinner, riding up the beach road in a carriage, Qwilleran announced that he was staying at the "hideous" inn to save the newspaper money. Then he had the driver wait a few minutes while he showed the Rikers the four tree trunks in the lounge and the cottage on Pip Court.

"Don't you get claustrophobia?" Riker asked.

The Siamese and Mildred indulged in a display of mutual affection (she had been their cat sitter once for two weeks) and then she said excitedly, "Where did you get those?" She pointed to the gilded leather masks.

"They were a birthday present," Qwilleran said, thinking it better not to tell the truth. "Do you know anything about that kind of work? They're leather."

"Yes, I know," she said. "It's an old Venetian craft that's been revived by a young artist down south. She does excellent work."

Then the Rikers drove back to their B-and-B. Everyone had enjoyed the evening: the usual joshing, frank talk, and exchange of news. To Qwilleran the news about Noisette confirmed his suspicion that she was an impostor. Why was she on the island? He sat on the porch and listened to June Halliburton playing jazz. She had a male visitor again. The voice sounded younger.

The Siamese sat with him; they were friends again. Before going to dinner he had bitten the bullet and given them a can of red salmon. The partying next door was still going on when he retired. It was not until he emptied his pockets that he remembered the scrap of paper from Derek. It was a one-word message: Gumbo. Later, after his lights were out, he heard good nights being said next door, and the beam of a flashlight preceded the departing guest—not to the nature trail but up Pip Court. The tall, lanky scarecrow of a figure was that of Derek Cuttlebrink.

Twelve

The arrival of two more pounds of meatloaf on Sunday morning steeled Qwilleran's determination, and the standoff between man and cats resumed. "Take it or leave it," he said. They left it.

Sunday was the turning point, however, in Qwilleran's floundering mission. He took tea with the Appelhardts; his undercover agent made his first report; Lyle Compton presented his program on Scotland at the hotel; and Yum Yum found something among the sofa cushions.

While Qwilleran was dressing for breakfast, he heard the musical murmuring that meant Yum Yum was digging a rusty nail out of a crevice, or trying to open a desk drawer, or retrieving a lost toy. She was on the seat of the sofa, thrusting first one paw and then the other behind a cushion. As the mumblings and fumblings became frantic, he went to her aid. As soon as he removed the seat cushion, she pounced on a half-crumpled piece of paper and carried it to the porch in her jaws, to be batted around for a few seconds and then forgotten.

It looked like a piece of music manuscript paper, and he picked it up.

"N-n-now!" she wailed, seeing her prize confiscated.

"N-n-no!" He retorted.

Offended by the mockery, Yum Yum went into a corner and sat with her back toward him.

"Sorry, sweetheart. I won't say that again," he apologized.

She ignored him.

Smoothing the scrap of paper, he found a phone number. The first three digits identified it as a local number—not the cab stand and not the hotel, both of which he would recognize. The style of the numerals had an affectation that he would associate with June Halliburton, and the type of paper confirmed his guess. Obviously she had dropped it while occupying the cottage. Then the question arose: Whom would she be phoning on the island? It was none of his business, but, still, it would be interesting to know. He could call the number and then hang up—or ask to speak to Ronald Frobnitz.

The first time he tried it—when he went to the inn for breakfast—the line was busy. After corned beef hash with a poached egg, plus hominy grits with sausage gravy (Lori was running out of ideas, he thought), he called the number again. It rang several times, and then a gruff voice answered: "The Pines gatehouse."

"Sorry. Wrong number," he said. Why June would be phoning the Appelhardt gatehouse was a question even more puzzling than why she would be making an island call at all. There was a possibility, of course, that he had punched the wrong digits. He tried again and heard the same voice saying, "The Pines gatehouse." This time he hung up without apology.

Qwilleran spent some time that day in deciding what to wear to tea. The role he was playing was not that of an inquiring reporter, nor Sherlock Holmes in disguise, nor a commoner being patronized by the royal family. He was playing a hero who had saved the life (probably) of an only daughter. Furthermore, while Elizabeth was an heiress, he himself was the Klingenschoen heir, and the K Foundation was capable of buying The Pines and the entire Grand Island Club and restoring it to a wildlife refuge. The idea appealed to him. He would not wear his silk shirt nor even his blue chambray that screamed "designer shirt"—another gift from Polly. No, he would wear his madras plaid that looked as if it had been washed in the Ganges for twenty years and beaten with stones to a muddy elegance.

In this shirt and some British-looking, almost-white, linen pants, he went out to meet the carriage that was picking him up at four o'clock. The conveyance that pulled up to the carriage block in front of the inn caused a murmur of admiration among the guests on the porch. A glossy-coated horse, quite unlike the nags pulling cabs-for-hire, was harnessed to a handsome buggy of varnished wood and leather.

The driver in green livery with an apple logo stepped down and said, "Mr. Qwillum, sir?" He pointed to the passenger seat on the left, then sprang nimbly into the seat behind the reins. He was a young version of the gaunt old islanders who drove the hacks.

As the carriage started up West Beach Road, Qwilleran remarked that it was a nice day.

"Ay-uh," said the driver.

"What's your name?"

"Henry."

"Nice horse."

"Ay-uh."

"What's his name?"

"Skip."

"Do you think we'll have any rain?" It was a brilliant day, with not a cloud in the sky.

"Might."

At The Pines, the carriage rolled through an open gate and past a gatehouse of considerable size, then to the rear of the main lodge. It stopped at a carriage block on the edge of a stone-paved courtyard. Beyond were acres of flawless lawn, a swimming pool with a high-dive board, and a croquet green, where white-clad youths were screaming epithets and swinging mallets at each other. In the foreground was a grassy terrace with verdigris iron furniture and a scattering of adults in the same croquet white. They looked clinical, compared to Qwilleran's mellow nonwhiteness.

One of the men came forward toward him. "Mr. Qwilleran? I'm Elizabeth's brother, Richard. We met last Thursday for about three seconds. We're grateful for your help in the emergency."

"I'm grateful there was a doctor in the house," Qwilleran replied pleasantly. "How is the patient?"

"Right over there, waiting to thank you personally." He waved a hand toward a chaise longue, where a young woman reclined. She wore a flowing garment of some rusty hue, and long, dark hair cascaded over her shoulders. She was looking eagerly in their direction.

The two men started toward her but were intercepted by an older woman—buxom, regally handsome, and dramatically poised like an opera diva on stage. Gliding forward with outstretched hand, she said in a powerful contralto, "Mr. Qwilleran, I'm Rowena Appelhardt. Welcome to The Pines."

"My pleasure," he murmured courteously but cooly. As a journalist Down Below and abroad, he had been everywhere and seen everything, and he was not awed by the vastness of the estate.

Rather, it seemed to be the Appelhardts who were awed. Had they made a quick background check and discovered his Klingenschoen connection and bachelor status? He became warily reserved.

The matriarch introduced the family: Richard was genuinely cordial; William smiled continually and was eager to talk; their wives sparkled with friendliness. Qwilleran suspected the queen mother had briefed them. She herself was an effusive hostess. Only Jack hung back, his face handsome in a bored and dissipated way. Finally there was the undernourished, unmarried daughter. She made a move to rise from her chaise.

"Stay where you are, Elizabeth," her mother admonished. "You must avoid exertion."

"Mother—" Richard began, but she stopped him with a glance.

Soulfully, the patient said, "I'm so grateful to you, Mr. Qwilleran." She extended her left hand; her right wrist was bandaged. "What would have happened to me if you hadn't been there?"

She had that loving look that women are said to bestow on their rescuers, and he kept his tone brusquely impersonal. "Fortunate coincidence, Ms. Appelhardt," he said.

"It was karma. And please call me Elizabeth. I don't remember what happened after that frightening moment."

"You were only minutes away from home; your brother was waiting with the golf cart; and you were choppered off the island by the Moose County sheriff."

"I love your shirt," she said, scoring several points.

Tea was served, and the conversation became general. The servers were two young men in green seersucker coats—island types but meticulously trained. There was tea with milk or lemon, and there was pound cake. This was no garden party with peacocks and memorable refreshments; this was a simple family tea with seven adult Appelhardts, while the younger members of the family squabbled on the croquet court.

"Richard," came the deep voice of authority, "must my grandchildren behave like savages while we are having tea with a distinguished visitor?"

Her son sent one of the seersucker coats to the croquet green, and the fracas ended abruptly.

"Do you play croquet, Mr. Qwilleran?" she asked.

Mallets, wire wickets, and wooden balls interested him as much as dominoes. "No, but I'm curious about the game. What is the major attraction?"

"Bonking," said Jack, entering the conversation for the first time.

"It's more than a matter of knocking a ball through a wicket. You hit your ball so that it sends your opponent's ball off the field. That's bonking. It takes practice. You can also bop your ball over your opponent's ball, blocking his path to the wicket."

"Jack is a sadistic bonker," said William's wife as if it were a compliment.

"It's changed from a harmless pastime to a strategic sport," William said. "It requires deliberation, like chess, but you're limited to forty-five seconds to make a shot."

Richard talked fondly about his Jack Russells, three well-behaved dogs who mingled with the family and never barked, jumped, or sniffed.

Mrs. Appelhardt asked prying questions, skillfully disguised, about Qwilleran's career, lifestyle, and hobbies, which he answered with equally skillful evasion.

Elizabeth was quiet but looked at him all the time.

Then William said, "How did you like that carriage we sent for you? My hobby is restoring antique vehicles."

"It's a beauty!" Qwilleran said in all honesty.

"It's Elizabeth's favorite—a physician's phaeton, so-called because of the hood design. It's deeper and has side panels, the idea being that physicians had to call on patients in all kinds of weather. In fact, this type of vehicle became the badge of the profession, along with the little black leather bag."

"How many carriages have you restored?"

"About two dozen. Most are at our farm in Illinois. There are five here. Would you like to see them?" To his mother, William said, "Do you mind if I show Mr. Qwilleran the carriage barn?"

"Don't keep him away from us too long!" she cautioned with a coy smile. The corners of her mouth turned down when she smiled, making emotion ambiguous.

He was glad to get away from the chatter of the tea table. "This will be highly educational," he said to the eldest brother. "I don't know anything about America's wheels prior to Henry Ford."

"Wheels built the country," William said. "There were carriage makers everywhere, always improving and innovating. In the early 1900s, there were dozens of models shown in the Sears Roebuck catalogue."

"How do you bring them to the island?"

"Disassembled—on my boat. To restore a vehicle you have to take it apart completely in order to strip and sand the wood parts. It takes hours of sanding to make a finish that looks like glass."

The physician's phaeton stood in the courtyard with empty shafts resting on the pavement. Two other four-wheelers were inside the barn, one of them enameled in glossy yellow with black striping and a fringed canopy.

"We use the surrey to drive to the club for lunch or dinner," William said. "The red wagon is for a pack of kids. I personally like the two-wheeled carts—light and easy to drive and safe. You can make a sudden turn without upsetting. If you ever turned over in a carriage with a frightened horse fighting to get free, you'd know why I stress the safety factor. Here . . . sit in this one."

Qwilleran climbed into a bright green dogcart with carriage lanterns and seats perched high over a box intended for hunting dogs.

"Do you think you might get interested in driving?" William asked. "There's a driving club in Lockmaster—and driving competitions. Are you anywhere near Lockmaster?"

"Yes. Good horse country. I'd like to sit down with you and a tape recorder some day and do an interview," Qwilleran said. "This is good material for my newspaper."

William hesitated. "I'd like that, but . . . it's like this: Mother is adamant about avoiding publicity. I wish we could, but no way!"

"How did you learn this craft?"

"Believe it or not, our steward was my mentor, beginning when I was a kid. He's an islander and a rustic Renaissance man—no formal education, but he can do anything. He taught us kids how to drive, sail, fish, hunt—"

"I'm doing a series on islanders for my column," Qwilleran said, "and he sounds like a good character study."

"I'm afraid Mother would never okay it. Other families would try to get him away from us. Sorry to have to say that."

They started walking back to the terrace, and Qwilleran asked him how much time he spent on the island. "I personally? No more than I have to. There's a limit to the amount of croquet a sane person can play, as someone once said."

"Dorothy Parker, but not in those exact words. How do you feel about the new resort development?"

"It's inevitable, if you want my personal opinion. That's the way our country is going. Mother is vastly unhappy, of course. She wants the islanders to file a class-action suit against the resort, and she'll cover the legal fees, but it's a lost cause, and attorneys avoid lost causes. The courts have ruled again and again that the owner of property can use it in any way that's not illegal."

As they returned to the terrace, he said to Qwilleran, "Talking to you has been a distinct pleasure. If you ever get down to the Chicago area, I'd like to show you the vehicles on my farm." They both looked up in surprise; Elizabeth had dared to rise from her chaise and was approaching them.

She said, "I forgot to thank you, Mr. Qwilleran, for finding the things I lost on the trail."

"I couldn't help noticing the entries in your book. You must be a botanist."

"Just an amateur. I'm fascinated by plant life. Would you like to see the herb garden I've planted?"

Qwilleran appreciated herbs in omelettes, but that was as far as his interest extended. Nevertheless, he acquiesced, and she asked her mother for permission to take him away from the party.

The queen mother said, "Promise not to tire yourself, Elizabeth."

On the way to the herb garden near the kitchen door, Qwilleran might be said to amble while the amateur botanist wafted in her long flowing robe. "Herbs thrive in the island sun and air," she said.

He stared blankly at two wooden tubs, a stone planter, and some large, clay pots, holding plants of various sizes, shapes, and colors. Finally he ventured, "What are they?"

She pointed out sage, rosemary, sweet basil, mint, lemon balm, chives, dill, and more, explaining, "There's something mysterious about herbs. For centuries they've been used for healing, and when they're used in food, something lovely happens to your senses."

He asked about the tea they had been drinking. To him it tasted and smelled like a product of the stables. It was Lapsang souchong, she said.

"Do you grow catnip?" he asked. "I have two Siamese cats."

"I adore Siamese!" she cried. "I've always wanted one, but Mother . . ." Suddenly she appeared weary, and he suggested sitting on a stone bench near the herbs, which were aromatic in their way.

He asked, "Where do you live when you're not on the island?"

"Mother likes to spend autumn at our farm, the holidays in the city, and winters in Palm Beach."

"Have you always lived with your mother?"

"Except when I was away at school."

They sat in silence for a few moments, but her eyes wandered, and her thoughts were almost audible. She had an intelligent face, delicate but wide-browed.

Speaking like a kindly uncle, he said, "Did you ever think you'd like a place of your own?"

"Oh, Mother would not approve, and I doubt whether I'd have the courage to break away or the strength to face responsibility. My two older brothers have suggested it, but . . ."

"Do you have money of your own?"

"A trust fund from my father—quite a good one. Mother is trustee, but it's mine, legally."

"Have you ever contemplated a career?"

"Mother says I'm not cut out for anything requiring sustained commitment. She says I'm a dilettante."

"You do have a college degree, don't you?"

She shook her head sheepishly. He felt she was going to say, Mother didn't think it was necessary, or Mother didn't think I could stand the pressure, or Mother-this or Mother-that. To spare her the embarrassment he stood up and said, "Time for me to go home and feed the cats."

They returned to the terrace, and Qwilleran thanked Mrs. Appelhardt for a pleasant afternoon; he commented that she had an interesting family. She mentioned that tea was always poured at four o'clock, and he was always welcome.

Unexpectedly Elizabeth spoke up. "I'll drive you home, Mr. Qwilleran, and we'll take some fresh herbs for the cook at your inn."

"Henry will drive our guest home," her mother corrected her.

Flinging the hair away from her face, the young woman raised her voice bravely. "Mother, I wish to drive Mr. Qwilleran myself. He has two Siamese cats that I'd like to see."

Other members of the clan listened in hushed wonder.

"Elizabeth, you're not quite yourself," Mrs. Appelhardt said forcefully, "and certainly in no condition to drive. We prefer not to take chances. You're so sensitive to medication . . . Richard, don't you agree?"

Before the elder brother could reply, Jack raised his voice. "For God's sake, Mother, let her do what she wants—for once in her life! If the buggy turns over and she breaks her neck, so be it! It's karma! That's what she's always telling us."

Qwilleran, a reluctant witness to this embarrassing moment in family history, walked over to the daughters-in-law and asked if they had heard about the unsolved lighthouse mystery. Fortunately they had not, so he recounted the story in detail, with a few embellishments of his own. By the time his listeners had speculated on the fate of the lightkeepers, Elizabeth reappeared in culottes, boots, straw sailor hat, and tailored shirt. "The groom is bringing the phaeton around," she said in a voice that trembled slightly.

Thirteen

The groom handed Elizabeth into the driver's seat, and one of the seersucker coats came running with a bouquet of herbs. She sat straight and square, with elbows close to her body and reins between the fingers of her left hand. Her right hand held the whip. She was in perfect control as they drove away from the lodge.

Qwilleran thought, All we need for this climactic scene is some melodramatic background music with full orchestra, as we drive away into the sunset. And what a cast of characters! Autocratic mother, timid daughter, two obedient sons, plus one who's sufficiently cavalier to deliver the defiant punch line.

Seated alongside the frail driver, he said, "Are you sure your injured wrist can handle that whip?"

"It's only a symbol," she replied. "Skip responds to the reins and the driver's voice. Our steward happens to be a wonderful trainer." They had stopped at the gate before turning into the procession of Sunday sightseers. "Walk on, Skip!" Nodding his head as if acknowledging the request, the horse moved forward into a left turn.

"Mother says you write for a newspaper. Which one?" Elizabeth asked.

"The *Moose County Something* on the mainland."

"Is that really its name? I don't read newspapers. They're too upsetting. What do you write?"

"A column about this and that . . . If I may ask, where were the peacocks today? It was my understanding that you have peacocks."

"Mother sold them to a zoo after Father died. Their screams made her nervous. Actually they were Father's pets. She sold his telescopes and astronomy books, too. That was his hobby. Did you ever see a UFO? Father said they hang over large bodies of water. If he spotted one, he'd wake us up in the middle of the night, and we'd all go out on the roof with binoculars—except Mother and Jack. She said it was foolish; Jack said it was boring. Jack is easily bored."

Elizabeth was more talkative than Qwilleran had expected. As she rambled on, he silently classified the family he had just met. Jack and his mother had the same assertive manner, good looks, and inverted smile. It was a safe bet that he was her favorite. He caused her trouble with his marrying addiction, but she kept on bailing him out. The three other siblings probably favored their male parent. They had wide brows, delicate features, and a gentler personality.

Elizabeth was still talking about her father. "He taught me proper driving form when I was quite little. It's more fun than driving a car." She identified two private vehicles returning from the Grand Island Club: a Brewster and a spider phaeton, both restored by William. When they reached the commercial strip, she expressed surprise and sadness at the conversion of private lodges.

Qwilleran said, "You probably remember the birchbark lodge. It's now the Domino Inn, and I'm staying in a cottage at the rear. It's small and quite confining, but I tell the cats to be patient; it's better than a tent."

"Do you really talk to them like that?"

"All the time. The more you talk to cats, the smarter they become, but it has to be intelligent conversation."

In front of Four Pips, Qwilleran handed her down from the driver's seat. "I hear lovely music! A flute with harp!" Her face was suddenly radiant.

"My next-door neighbor is a musician, and if she isn't playing the piano, she's playing recorded music."

"I wanted so badly to play the flute. I had visions of piping on the nature trail and luring small animals out of the woods. But my mother insisted on piano lessons. I wasn't very—" She stopped and squealed with delight as she saw two pairs of blue eyes watching from the front window. Koko and Yum Yum were sitting tall on the domino table with ears alert and eyes popping at the sight of a large beast outside their cottage. Indoors, Elizabeth extended her left hand to them, and they sniffed the fingers that had held the reins.

Qwilleran made the introductions, mentioning that Koko was unusually smart; his latest interest was dominoes.

"He feels the power of numbers," Elizabeth said seriously. "Cats are tuned into mystic elements, and there's magic in numbers. Pythagoras discovered that thousands of years ago. Do you know anything about numerology? I've made an informal study of it. If you write down your full name for me, I'll tell you something about yourself. I don't do fortune-telling—just character delineation. Write down the cats' names, too, in block letters."

Qwilleran thought, Wait till Mildred hears about this! Riker's new wife was involved in tarot cards and other occult sciences. Soberly he did what Elizabeth requested:

JAMES MACKINTOSH QWILLERAN
KAO K'O KUNG a.k.a. KOKO
YUM YUM, formerly called FREYA

"Notice," he pointed out, "that my name is spelled with a QW."

"That's important," she said. "Each letter has a corresponding number. I'll take them home and work on them. And now I must drive back to The Pines, or Mother will fret. Your little friends are so beautiful. I hope we'll meet again."

"Yow!" came a stentorian voice from the desk.

"He's thanking you for the compliment," Qwilleran explained.

Koko had something else in mind, however. As soon as he had their attention, he nosed the maroon velvet box across the desk until it fell to the floor.

Qwilleran picked it up. "He has a parlor trick he performs. If I place the dominoes facedown on the table, he can make a blind draw and come up with high-scoring pieces, like double-six and double-five. You sit down and watch quietly." He spread the entire set on the table and encouraged Koko to draw.

The four dominoes that landed on the floor were not high-scoring pieces; they were 0-1, 1-2, 1-4, and 3-4. Elizabeth laughed merrily. It was the first time Qwilleran had heard her laugh. "Do you think cats have a sense of humor?" she asked.

"I think Koko gets a kick out of making me look like a fool."

She was toying with the four dominoes Koko had selected. "He's smarter than you think," she said. "If you add the spots on each one, you get one, three, five and seven. If you match them with the letters of the alphabet, you get A, C, E and G. And if you shuffle them, you get *Cage*. That's my middle name."

Qwilleran felt goosebumps on the back of his neck. It had to be pure coincidence, he thought. And yet he said, "I'd like to hear more about numerology. Would you have lunch with me at the hotel some day this week?"

"I'd be delighted!" she said, and her eyes sparkled.

He thought, There's nothing wrong with this girl that can't be cured by a reduction in motherpower and a few chocolate malts.

On the way out, Elizabeth caught sight of the gilded leather masks over the sofa. "Your theater masks are stunning!" she said and then she giggled. "One looks like my brother William, and one looks like Jack."

After the phaeton had rolled away from Four Pips, Qwilleran remembered an episode in his early school years. His teacher, Miss Heath, had a toothy and ambiguous smile that could mean either good news or bad news. Being a domino player at home, although a reluctant one, his private name for her was Miss Double-six. The class was seated alphabetically, and James Qwilleran was assigned to sit in front of a fat kid named Archibald Riker. In dull moments they amused each other by exchanging notes in secret code. It was nothing that would stump a cryptographer—or even Miss Double-six if she had caught them; the letters of the alphabet were numbered 1 to 26. One day, while her back was turned, Qwilleran tossed a wad of paper over his shoulder: 13-9-19-19 8-5-1-20-8 8-1-19 2-9-7 20-5-5-20-8. Arch decoded it and laughed so hard that he choked and was sent into the hall for a drink of water. Forty years later, he still quaked with internal laughter whenever he saw someone with prominent dentition.

And now, after all those years, Qwilleran had a cat who was interested in double-six—most of the time. That was the name of Nick's boat; did it mean that Koko wanted to go home? Or did the twelve pips signify the letter L? And if so, what did the letter L have to do with anything? Kao K'o Kung had some obscure ways of communicating. Often it was merely a matter of nudging Qwilleran's thought processes. In this case, nothing clicked.

The morning plate of meatloaf was still untouched, and Qwilleran's determination to win the argument struggled with his humane instincts—and lost. Just because he had been impulsive enough to pay for ten pounds of meatloaf up front, he could not let them starve. He opened a can of boned chicken. The breakfast that the Siamese had ignored was carried to the trash cans for the strays.

Nick was there, working on the foundation of the building. "Mildew's a problem," he explained. "I'm taking a week of my vacation and trying to catch up on the maintenance . . . Say, Qwill, does the music from Five Pips bother you?"

"It's a little mind-numbing when she practices technique, but I've learned to wear ear plugs for catfights, fog horns, and finger exercises."

"I had to speak to her about smoking this afternoon," said the hard-working innkeeper. "I was repairing one of her porch screens and saw a saucerful of butts. She thinks she's a privileged character because Exbridge pays her rent . . . How about you? Is everything okay?"

"So far, so good. Tonight I meet with my undercover man. Right now I'm on my way downtown for something to eat."

At the hotel he waited for the Comptons to come out of the small auditorium where Lyle had delivered his lecture on "Bloody Scotland." The superintendent of schools had a perverse sense of humor that Qwilleran enjoyed, and Lisa's agreeable disposition was a foil for her husband's orneriness.

She said, "We had a good crowd, with lots of young people. They like blood, and Lyle always pours it on: the massacre at Glen Coe, the atrocities of the Highland Clearances, and the slaughter at the Battle of Culloden."

They took a booth in the Buccaneer Den and ordered burgers, and Qwilleran said, "You talk about the farmers being cleared out of the Scottish Highlands and replaced by corporate flocks of sheep. It wouldn't surprise me if the natives were driven from Breakfast Island and replaced by something like corporate oil wells."

The cynical jest appealed to Lyle. "That would be a juicy rumor to start on the mainland! All I'd have to do is whisper confidentially to my next-door neighbor that XYZ has struck oil behind the swimming pool, and in two days it would be all over Moose County, and Don Exbridge would be denying it in the headlines. Of course, no one would believe him!"

"It would be just like you to do it, too," said his wife, "and that's really sick!"

"I'll tell you what's sick, sweetheart. It's sick what XYZ did with the new elementary school building. It's lousy construction! They keep patching it up, but what we really need is one good tornado, so we can start again from scratch—with a different builder."

Lisa said, "Be careful what you wish for; you may get your wish! The weatherman says there's a peculiar front headed this way." Then the food was served, and she said, "It's so dark in here, I can't tell whether this is a burger or chocolate cake."

"That's because people patronize bars for illicit trysts, graft payoffs, and subversive plotting," her husband informed her. "Nice people like you should eat in the coffee shop."

After a while, Qwilleran asked him if he remembered a student named Harriet Beadle, an islander who attended high school on the mainland.

"No, but we've had a pack of Beadles from the island. Another common name is Kale. Another is Lawson. They're all descended from survivors of the same shipwreck, supposedly. They work hard to get good grades, and some even earn scholarships. Those one-room schools aren't all bad."

"How do the other students treat them?"

"They taunt them about their so-called pirate ancestry, and there are some bloody fights. And who knows whether it's true or not? But I'll tell you one thing for sure: The islanders know more about ecology than we do. They grow up with a respect for the earth and the elements."

Over coffee Lisa asked about Polly.

"She's in Oregon, visiting an old college chum."

"Great country out there!" said Lyle. "Let's hope she doesn't decide to stay. She's a great librarian."

"Everybody loves her," said Lisa.

"Nobody loves a school superintendent. I'm on everybody's hit list—board of ed, taxpayers, and parents."

Qwilleran asked him, "Do you know that one of your department heads has a summer job over here?"

"Wish she'd stay on the island permanently," he grumbled. "June is an independent so-and-so."

Lisa said, "She's certainly not popular with the wives of Moose County. She thinks she's God's gift to husbands—mine included, and Lyle is no Robert Redford."

"Why," Qwilleran asked, "does an educator with her credentials choose a rural county like ours?"

"Horses! She likes to ride. That's how she landed in Lockmaster after a divorce Down Below. Then we offered her a good contract, and now we're stuck with her. But she's good! She sailed through school on scholarships and did a concert tour before coming to us." The check came to the table, and when Qwilleran reached for it, Lyle said, "Drop it! The hotel's paying for this one."

The Comptons were staying for a nightcap, but Qwilleran groped his way out of the murky bar, bumping into tables and kicking chair legs. In passing the corner booth he squinted into the gloom and saw a man and a woman leaning amorously toward each other. Their faces were in shadow, but he heard the woman say, "Shall we have a replenishment?"

Before riding home in a cab, Qwilleran picked up some beer for Derek Cuttlebrink, as well as crackers and pickles to go with the meatloaf. On the way he pondered several of Lyle Compton's remarks, chiefly his hint that Polly might decide to relocate in Oregon. It was a possibility that had never crossed his mind. It made him vaguely uneasy.

At Four Pips he was met by a highly disturbed cat. Koko was yowling in two-part harmony and running back and forth between sitting room and porch. A casual inspection showed nothing amiss, but after refrigerating the beer Qwilleran investigated with deepening concern. The cat was jumping up and pawing the porch screen as he did when batting down an insect. This time there were no insects—only small holes in the screen. Alarmed, Qwilleran hurried to the inn and confronted Nick in the office.

"Someone's been taking pot shots at the cats!" he said with indignation.

Nick looked up from the bookkeeping. "I can't believe it! How do you know?"

Qwilleran described Koko's behavior and his discovery of the holes. "There's growing hostility among the islanders, I'm convinced, and someone may have connected me with the financial backers of the resort. Someone may be using this method of harassment!"

"Did you look for spent shot on the porch?"

"There was nothing that I could find, but the porch is shaded at this hour."

"Which screens had the holes?"

"Both side panels, east and west."

"Birds!" Nick said. "Bird beaks! They try to fly through the porch, not realizing it's screened. All the cottages have holes in the porch screens."

Qwilleran huffed into his moustache. "Well . . . sorry to bother you, Nick. Now all I have to do is explain it to Koko."

Back at Four Pips he prepared for Derek's visit. He opened a can of mixed nuts and dumped them into a soup bowl, filled another bowl with dill pickle chips, and arranged a platter of crackers and meatloaf slices.

When the young man arrived, the Siamese gave him the royal welcome, prancing with lofty tails curled like question marks. "They like me," he said. "I'm getting a standing ovation."

"Before you congratulate yourself," Qwilleran parried, "bear in mind that these opportunists have an instinctive affinity for dairy farmers, fishermen, butchers, and restaurant employees. I leave it to you to figure out."

Derek's height made the ceilings look lower than ever. He walked around, looking at the travel posters. Then he pointed to the tragedy and comedy masks. "I'll bet those didn't come with the cottage. Where'd you get them?"

"In Venice—from a small antique shop near the Accademia delle Belle Arti" was the casual reply. "How about a beer? Sit down and help yourself to the food. What time did you have dinner?"

"They feed us just before we start the dinner shift, at five o'clock."

"Then you must be hungry. Dig in. The meatloaf is homemade." Then craftily he asked his guest, "Did you have any trouble finding this place?"

"No. I was down here last night," Derek said with youthful candor. "Dr. Halliburton wanted me to audition."

"Did you read a script? Or sing?"

"We just rapped. She wanted to know what acting I'd done, and how I felt about theater, and what kind of role I liked to play. I told her what I'd done in *Macbeth*. We just drank beer and listened to jazz and had a good time. She's very friendly. I was surprised. She may get me the job of assistant entertainment director. That would pay more money than I'm getting now."

Uh-huh, Qwilleran thought. "So explain the note you handed me last night, Derek. What's all this about gumbo?"

"Yeah . . . well . . . I met this girl where I'm rooming, and she kinda likes me. Her name is Merrio. How's that for a name? She's a waitress in the Corsair Room, but she was hired for the kitchen in the beginning. Then Mr. Ex decided she had a good personality for meeting the public, so now she's out on the floor, serving."

"Did the switch—or promotion, whatever it was—occur after the poisoning incident?"

"I guess so, because she was still on salads when it happened."

"Where does gumbo fit into the picture?"

"That's the interesting part," Derek said. "They had several chicken specials that night, but the only people that got sick were the ones that ordered chicken gumbo. The shrimp gumbo—no trouble!"

Qwilleran thought, So it wasn't necessarily contaminated chicken from Lockmaster. It could have been the fault of the hotel kitchen. "Who was working that night?" he asked.

"Well, besides the chef and sous chef, they had some college kids from restaurant schools and some islanders for the support staff—that's what they call the unskilled jobs."

"Who was responsible for the gumbo? Was it a single individual, or were others involved? And was it *freshly made that day?* If so, was it the usual recipe? Did anything unusual happen in the kitchen that night? Had anyone been fired?"

"I'll have to get back to Merrio," Derek said.

Qwilleran said, "It might stimulate her memory if you showed her a good time and spent a little money. You have an expense account, of course."

Derek liked that idea.

"Okay. Now, what about the guy that drowned. Any luck? Have you found a source?"

"Yeah. One of the barhops—his name is Kirk—rooms at our place, and he remembers serving them."

"Them?"

"The guy was drinking with some woman. They were sitting by the pool."

"What were they drinking?"

"Wine. He remembers that, because most people want beer or Pirate's Gold or a straight shot."

"Did they seem like friends? Or was it a pickup?"

"Oh, they knew each other all right. They were arguing. The guy was pretty upset."

"Was he a hotel guest or a drop-in? And what about her?"

"Kirk didn't know her, but the guy was registered, and the drinks were charged to his room. They had a few rounds, and then Kirk took his break. When he got back, the pool lights were off, and the busboy was cleaning up the rim. He's the one that saw something floating. He rushed into the bar; the head barman called security; the police came, and the rescue squad; and that was it!"

"Did the police investigate?" Qwilleran asked.

"They hung around for a while, asking questions, but the boss told everybody not to talk to outsiders—or even discuss it with other employees—or they'd lose their jobs. When I talked to Kirk, we went down on the beach for privacy. He was glad to get it off his chest. He'd been thinking about it a lot. Because of the secrecy thing, he was suspicious, you know."

"What did he remember about the couple who were drinking?"

"Only that they were sharp-looking—young, but not too young—and they were speaking a foreign language."

"That's a big help," Qwilleran said. "The last time I counted, there were five thousand foreign languages."

Derek had another beer and finished the meatloaf before leaving with some extra money in his pocket. As they stepped out of the cottage, music was coming from Five Pips, and voices could be heard, a male and a female.

"Sounds like another audition," Qwilleran said.

Derek galumphed up the lane, wielding his flashlight and swinging a sack of pears for his fellow roomers.

Qwilleran went back indoors and immediately stepped on something small and hard. At the same time he caught Koko with his paw in the nutbowl.

"No!" he yelled. "Bad cat!" he scolded as he gathered up the nuts scattered on the floor. It was no great loss; they were all hazelnuts, and he considered them a waste of chewing time. The walnuts, pecans, almonds, and cashews were untouched.

"Smart cat!" Qwilleran said, changing his tone. Koko sat up like a kangaroo and laundered a spot on his underside.

Fourteen

When Qwilleran went to breakfast Monday morning, he first detoured into the office. Lori, of course, was busy in the kitchen, and Nick could be heard hammering nails somewhere, but Jason and Lovey were playing with toy telephones. The two youngsters sat on the floor, three feet apart, holding pink, plastic instruments to their ears.

The three-year-old said, "Are you there?"

"You're supposed to wait till the phone rings and I say hello," her brother said.

"Who's this?"

"We're not connected! You didn't dial!"

"How are you?"

"That's not right, Lovey," the exasperated six-year-old shouted.

"You look very nice today," she said sweetly into the mouthpiece.

Qwilleran interrupted. "Excuse me, Jason. Would you find your father for me?"

"Okefenokee!" The boy scrambled to his feet and disappeared into the family quarters.

Nick soon walked in, wearing his carpenter's apron. "Hi, Qwill! What's up?"

"I've received a report that's somewhat revealing."

"You did? Sit down . . . Jason, take your sister into the other room."

"Okefenokee!"

"Thanks, Nick, but I'm staying only a minute. I want to get into the breakfast room before it closes. Here's what I heard last night:

The guests who were poisoned were *not* eating Cajun chicken, or chicken étouffée, or chicken Creole. They had all ordered chicken gumbo! It seems to me that an extra ingredient went into the pot, accidentally or on purpose."

"You think Don deliberately twisted the truth when he blamed the poultry farm?"

"Or the kitchen didn't give him the true facts. It may be that chef—Jean-Pierre Pamplemousse, or whatever his name is—didn't want his reputation besmirched. So that's where we stand at the moment." Qwilleran started toward the door but turned back. "Do you know anything about the woman called Noisette, who runs the antique shop?"

"No. She hasn't attended any of Don's business meetings or get-togethers."

"One more question: What happened to the Hardings? I haven't seen them for the last day or so."

"The old gentleman caught cold," Nick said, "and they wanted to get off the island, so I ferried them across yesterday and put them on a plane."

Too bad, Qwilleran thought. They would have enjoyed hearing about the visit to Buckingham Palace, the eccentricities of the royal family, William's antique carriages, and the fate of the peacocks. The vicar would have had his own sly comments to make, and his wife would have rebuked him gently.

For breakfast he had pecan pancakes with homemade sausage patties, followed by brioches filled with creamed chipped beef. The sausages were particularly good, and he attributed their distinctive flavor to fresh herbs from Elizabeth's garden.

There were things Qwilleran wanted to do that day. He wanted to visit the antique shop once again, have a few words with Dwight Somers, and check the post office for a postcard from Oregon—all errands that were better done in the afternoon. Before leaving the inn, therefore, he picked up a couple of their Sunday papers from Down Below—to read in the privacy of his screened porch.

It was warm and humid on the porch, and the Siamese had found a cool patch on the concrete slab: Yum Yum lounging like an off-duty sphinx with forelegs fully extended and paws attractively crossed; Koko with hind quarters sitting down and front quarters standing up. His elongated Siamese body made him look like two different cats with a single spine, and the thinking end of the cat was now alert and waiting for something to happen. Suddenly ears pricked, whiskers curled, and nose sniffed. A few moments later

Qwilleran caught a whiff of smoke and turned to see June Halliburton approaching through the weeds.

"Don't invite me in. I'm just enjoying a legal smoke," she said, holding a cigarette gracefully in one hand and a saucer in the other. As usual, a limp Panama drooped over her red hair and white complexion. "The esteemed management will have me shot if I smoke indoors or drop live ashes outdoors."

"I agree with the esteemed management," Qwilleran said. "Today's too warm for anything as uncomfortable as a forest fire."

Peering through the screen at the three of them, she said with an arch smile, "What a touching domestic scene! I suppose the demographers have you classified as an untraditional family: one man, two cats."

"One man, two *animal companions,*" he corrected her.

"And how do you like your cottage?"

"The roof doesn't leak, and the refrigerator works," he said. "What more can one ask?"

"My refrigerator is full of ice cubes, so join me for a drink, any time."

"Yow!" said Koko impatiently, his nose twitching.

"No one invited *you,*" she said. Stubbing her cigarette in the saucer, she walked away at a languid pace, and Koko shook himself so vigorously that the flapping of his ears sounded like a rattlesnake. Then he ran indoors and yowled over the domino box.

"Okay," Qwilleran agreed, "but this is a whole new ballgame. We don't add scores any more; we spell words."

Koko watched with near-sighted fascination as the dominoes were randomly scattered over the tabletop. Instead of standing on the chair with forepaws on the table, however, he elected to sit on the dominoes like a hen hatching eggs.

"What's that all about?" Qwilleran demanded. "Are you getting a gut feeling?"

The cat seemed to know what he was doing. Suddenly he rose and, with a grunt, pushed several pieces onto the floor. Quickly and with high anticipation Qwilleran retrieved them: 0-2, 1-3, 3-4, 2-6, and 5-6. By adding the pips on each piece he got 2, 4, 7, 8, and 11, which corresponded to B, D, G, H, and K in the alphabet.

"That won't fly," Qwilleran said in disappointment. "We need *vowels,* the way we did when we played Scrabble." He asked himself, What does a cat know about vowels? And yet . . . Koko could read his mind without understanding his speech.

Either Koko understood, or the next draw was a phenomenal coincidence. It produced 0-1, 0-5, 1-4, 2-3, 4-5, and 3-6, all of which corresponded to the vowels, A, E and I.

Qwilleran groaned and pounded his forehead with his fists. It was beyond comprehension, but luckily he had learned to take Koko's actions on faith, and he continued the game. Who would believe, he asked himself, that a grown man in his right mind would participate in such a farce? He took the precaution of drawing the window blind.

After that, Koko's efforts were more to the point. Sometimes he swept pieces off the table with a swift flick of his tail, and from the seven or eight designated dominoes Qwilleran was able to spell words like *field, beach, baffle* and *lake.* (It could also be *leak.)* Unfortunately, the operation was limited to the first twelve letters of the alphabet. Nevertheless, he liked the challenge and kept a record: *fable, dice, chalk, chick, cackle.* Koko pushed dominoes off the table; Qwilleran translated them into words; Yum Yum sat on her brisket and kibitzed.

Eventually the cats lost interest, having a short attention span, and Qwilleran decided it was time to walk downtown. His first stop was the antique shop. Noisette was sitting at her desk, looking stunning, and reading another magazine, or perhaps the same one.

"Good afternoon, mademoiselle," he said pleasantly.

She looked up with a smile of recognition, and he realized that her lustrous brown eyes were a rich shade of hazel. "Ah, you have returned! What is it that interests you today?" she asked.

"The green glass luncheon set," he said. "It would be a good gift for my sister in Florida, but I don't know about the color."

"Green glass can be used with pink, yellow, or white napery," she said. "It gives the most enjoyment of color."

"I see . . . My sister lives near Palm Beach. She'd enjoy your kind of shop. Are you on Worth Avenue?"

Noisette shrugged apologetically. "At the moment I regret I do not know my address. I am moving due to the expirement of my lease."

Qwilleran mumbled something about the luncheon set and his sister and edged out of the shop. He was convinced that this was the woman he had seen, and heard, in the Buccaneer Den. A ripple of sensation in the roots of his moustache told him that she was also the woman drinking with the man who drowned.

Qwilleran's next stop was the post office. He was sure that Polly would have mailed a postcard the day after she arrived. Then, he figured cynically, it would go from her friend's country address to the General Mail Facility in Portland and then across the country to the General Mail Facility in Minneapolis, from which it would be delivered to Pickax and forwarded by his secretarial service to the island, via the General Mail Facility in Milwaukee, which would have no "Breakfast Island" in the computer, so Polly's postcard would go to the dead letter office in Chicago. At least, he thought that was the way it worked. Only one thing was certain: It had not arrived at Pear Island.

At the hotel he found Dwight Somers in his office and asked to have a few private words. They sauntered out to the farthest rim of the pool.

"Something on your mind?" Dwight asked.

"I'd like to ask a favor," Qwilleran said. "I need to know the last name of Noisette, who runs the antique shop. She must have signed a lease or other contract with the hotel. Would it be in the hotel files?"

"Probably, but I wouldn't have access to them."

"You could wangle your way into the vault."

"Is it that important? Okay, I'll give it a try."

"Do that, and I'll owe you one," Qwilleran said. "By the way, I'm bringing the mermaid to lunch at the Corsair Room tomorrow, in case you want to size her up."

Dwight asked, "How are you getting along with your next-door neighbor?"

"I avoid her, but I found out why she's working 400 miles north of everywhere. She came up to Lockmaster because it's horse country, and she's fond of riding."

"Are you sure?" Dwight asked. "When we had dinner at the Palomino Paddock, surrounded by bales of hay, saddles, and photos of famous horses, she never once said anything about riding, and that pale face doesn't belong on an outdoorswoman."

"Something's wrong somewhere," Qwilleran acknowledged. "How's your boss's disposition lately?"

"He's hot under the collar today. A photojournalist from your paper has been over here, questioning hotel guests about how they feel about feral cats on the island. Don had him thrown out and refused to speak for publication."

On the way out of the hotel Qwilleran saw a towering figure occupying one of the rocking chairs on the porch and rocking vigorously. He had to look twice; he had never seen the Pickax police chief dressed in anything but the official uniform or full Scottish kit. He dropped into a rocker next to Brodie and said, "Andy! What are you doing here?"

"It's my day off, and we came over for the ferry ride—the wife and me. I'm cooling my heels while she's off buying T-shirts for the grandkids."

"What does she think of the resort?"

"Same as we all think: too expensive and too built up!" Brodie said. "Nobody on the mainland likes what they've done to our Breakfast Island. We used to bring our three girls over here for picnics when they were growing up. It was a wild and lonely beach then."

"Did the islanders object?"

"Naw, we didn't bother them. We weren't rowdy, and we didn't spoil anything."

As they talked, Qwilleran noticed listening ears in the nearby rocking chairs. "Let's walk down to the docks, Andy," he suggested.

One of the piers, damaged by the boat explosion, was closed for repairs. They walked to the end of the longest pier and looked back at the flat-roofed hotel, the strip malls on either side, and the dense forest beyond. The ancient evergreens were so tall, they dwarfed the man-made structures.

Brodie said, "What's going to happen to that flat roof when they get tons of snow this winter? You know why they made it flat, don't you? Exbridge wanted to be able to land a helicopter on top of the hotel, but he found out they'd have to have special roof construction, and his partners at XYZ didn't want to pay for it. So now there's a pad behind the rescue headquarters, for when they have to chopper out an emergency case. They've had quite a few of those lately. I'll tell you one thing: I wouldn't want to be in that hotel during a bad wind storm. See all those tall trees? You can bet that their roots are drying out because of the drain on available ground water. It takes a lot of water to service the hotel, twelve stores, a big swimming pool, and all those food operations. A tall tree with a dry root system is a pushover in a big blow. No, sir! I wouldn't want to be here. How about you, Qwill?"

"Ditto."

Brodie said, "There was another incident this weekend—the shooting. That was a strange one, if you ask me."

"That makes five incidents," Qwilleran said, "and they have five logical explanations."

"Have you come up with any theories?"

"Nothing conclusive, but I have some leads and a couple of good contacts. You could do me a favor when you get home, Andy. Get me the name and hometown of the hotel guest who drowned. They're hushing it up over here."

Andy said, "If you find any evidence, don't waste time talking to the sheriff's department. Go right to the prosecutor. The sheriff has no background in crime fighting; he's a good administrator, that's all, and if you ask me, it was XYZ backing that got him elected. How much longer will you be here?"

"Another week."

"How's Polly enjoying her vacation? Where did you say she was going?"

"Oregon. She's having a good time."

"When are you two gonna—"

"We're not *gonna,* Andy, so don't plan on doing any bagpiping for us unless we kick the bucket."

"Let's mosey back to the hotel," the chief said. "The wife will be looking for me, now that she's spent all my money. Also, we have to watch the ferry schedule; they've cut back the number of crossings. They're not getting the crowds they expected. Look! Half the rocking chairs are empty. There's a rumor that the hotel may fold. Did you hear that?"

"I'm not up on my rumorology," Qwilleran said with mock apology.

"There's also a rumor that the hotel was planned to fail. Don't ask me how that works. I don't understand financial shenanigans. They say XYZ is too successful to be healthy, whatever that means."

Leaving Brodie, Qwilleran started to walk home and found himself face to face with the Moseley sisters on the boardwalk. They had just stepped out of a horse cab and were headed for the tea room.

"Oh, Mr. Qwilleran! We were just talking about you. Have you any news about our dear Elizabeth?"

"She's fine. She's back on the island. I visited her family yesterday."

"You must tell us about her. Will you join us for tea? We're leaving tomorrow." They were pleasant women, and they looked at him eagerly.

"I'd be happy to," he said, although he usually avoided tea rooms. This one was bright with posters of Scottish castles and displays of ornamental teapots. A cheery, pink-cheeked woman in a tartan apron brought a platter of shortbread and offered a choice of five teas. The Moseleys recommended a tisane, blending leaves, roots, flowers, and grasses.

Qwilleran gave them an update on their former student, and they described their vacation week. They had enjoyed the people at the inn, the sunsets, the carriage rides, and the lectures at the hotel.

"A conservation officer told us that this island was completely submerged thousands of years ago, except for the promontory where the lighthouse stands," said the one who had taught science. "Now all that's left of the wetland is the peat bog in the center of the island. I do hope they won't spray for mosquitoes. Insects, birds, frogs, snakes, turtles and all of those creatures work together to preserve the bog, which in turn preserves the quality of air and water."

"A peat bog," said the other sister, "is a mysterious miracle of nature. Did you know that a human body can sink in a bog and be perfectly preserved forever?"

Altogether, the conversation was better than the tea, although Qwilleran drank three cups of the stuff—not because he liked it, but because it was there. Later, while walking home, he formulated a new theory about the missing lightkeepers. First he thought they had been drugged with island coffee and dropped into the bog. Yet, that would require a motive on the part of the islanders, and motive was the missing piece in the puzzle.

Next, he decided that the lightkeepers had wandered into the bog themselves—but why all three of them? And what were they doing in the woods?

Stimulated by the tea blended of leaves, roots, flowers, and grasses, Qwilleran composed a scenario: The islanders had entertained the lightkeepers with tall tales about chests of pirate gold, buried in the marsh long before the Beadles, Kales, and Lawsons washed up on the shore. The lightkeepers believed the stories. Perhaps they were bored; perhaps they were greedy; perhaps they had been drinking too much ale. Whatever the reason, the head lightkeeper sent an assistant to reconnoitre on one moonlit night. The fellow went out with a lantern and shovel and failed to return. The second assistant was dispatched to look for him. And finally the lightkeeper himself went in search of the other two, with the result that Trevelyan, Schmidt, and Mayfus are honored by a bronze plaque on Lighthouse Point.

* * *

That evening, the crew in Four Pips played dominoes again, and the highlight occurred when Koko made one grand swipe with his tail, knocking a dozen pieces on the floor and enabling Qwilleran to spell *hijacked.* Otherwise, the words were ordinary: *jailed, ideal, field* (again), *lake* (again), *deface, flea* (which could also be *leaf), lice, bike,* and *feed.* Then, just as Qwilleran was getting bored, he was able to spell *Beadle,* and that gave him an idea. He walked up the road to Harriet's café to get a chocolate sundae and try out his lightkeeper scenario.

It was late, and there were no customers. "Just a chocolate sundae," he said to the island woman who was waitress, cashier, and busgirl.

As soon as his order was placed in the kitchen, Harriet came through the swinging doors. "I knew it was you, Mr. Q. Would you rather have hot fudge? I know you like it, and I can boil some up, if you don't mind waiting a bit."

"I appreciate that," he said, "but you look tired. Just sit down with me and have a cup of coffee."

Her plain face looked drawn, and her shoulders drooped. "Yes, I'm beat tonight . . . Hettie, dish up a chocolate sundae and bring us two cups of coffee. Then go home. I'll clean up. Thanks for staying late."

Qwilleran said, "Your long hours are getting you down. Why don't you take some time off once in a while?"

"It's not that so much," she said as she dropped into a chair. "I'm discouraged about business. All those accidents are scaring people away, and the radio is saying it'll be a bad summer—rain, high winds, and low temperatures. The B-and-Bs aren't getting reservations for the holiday weekend—not what they expected, anyway. And the hotel is cutting down on help. Some of my roomers upstairs have been laid off, and they're going back to the mainland. And then . . ." She stopped and heaved a long tired sigh. "Yesterday I heard something that upset me."

"Is it something you can tell me?" he asked.

"I don't know. It's something I heard when I visited my ma yesterday. I just don't know what to do. I always thought islanders were good people who wouldn't hurt a soul, but now . . ." She shook her head in despair.

"It might help you to talk about it," he said, mixing genuine sympathy with rampant curiosity.

"Maybe you're right. Will you promise not to say anything?"

"If that's what you want me to do."

"Well . . . one of our people was involved in the accidents."

"Do you know who it is?"

She nodded.

"Those are serious crimes, Harriet. This person must be stopped."

"But how can I squeal, Mr. Q?" she said in desperation. "We've always stuck together, here on the island, but I'm getting to feel more like a mainlander. I lived there so long."

"It's not a case of islander against mainlander," he said. "It's a matter of right and wrong. You're a good person, Harriet. Don't wait until someone else is killed or injured. If that happens, you'll never forgive yourself. You'll feel guilty for the rest of your life."

"I wish I hadn't come back to the island," she moaned. "Then I wouldn't be faced with this terrible decision."

"That's understandable, but it doesn't solve any problems. You're here now, and you're involved, and it's your duty to come forward."

"My ma thinks I should keep my mouth shut. She's afraid something will happen to me."

"You won't be at any risk. I've been doing some snooping myself, and if you tell me what you know, I'll be the one to blow the whistle. No one will be the wiser."

"I've got to think about it," she said, wringing her hands.

Qwilleran's moustache bristled, as it did at moments of suspicion or revelation. This was a breakthrough waiting to break through, and it was a delicate situation. These islanders required special handling. He had to be at his sympathetic best.

"More coffee?" she asked.

"No, thanks," he said. Already the drums were beating in his head. There was no telling what wild-growing leaf, root, flower, or grass the islanders put in their coffee. "I think you should call it a day and get some rest. In the morning you'll be thinking clearly, and you'll make the right decision."

"Yes," she agreed with a sigh of relief. "I just have to clean up a bit, and then I'll go upstairs."

"What has to be done?"

"I always sweep the floor, straighten the chairs, and tidy up the kitchen."

"I'll help you," he said. "Where's the broom?" Gripped by the immediacy of the situation, Qwilleran forgot to mention his peat bog theory.

Fifteen

Qwilleran greeted Tuesday with the feeling that it would be momentous, and so it proved to be, although not in the way he expected. As he envisioned the day's prospects, Harriet would agree to tell all; the post office would have a postcard for him; and Koko would unearth a blockbuster of a clue. To start with, breakfast was auspicious: French toast with apple butter and bacon strips, then a poached egg on corned beef hash. Afterward, the Siamese were in the mood for dominoes: Koko as player, Yum Yum as devoted spectator.

Koko started conservatively, flooring only four or five dominoes with each swish of the tail, thus limiting the play to short words: *lie, die, bad, egg, cad* . . . or *gaff, jail, lice, dead.*

The connotation was generally negative, and it caused Qwilleran to wonder. He said, "Loosen up, old boy. Put more swish in your tail."

After that, words of special relevance cropped up: *bleak,* as in Four Pips; *bald,* like Exbridge; and *fake,* like the antique shop. Certain pairs were linked in tandem: *black* followed by *flag,* and *head* followed by *ache.* If Koko really knew what he was doing, the last one meant he'd had enough!

Qwilleran gave them a treat before leaving for his lunch date with the Appelhardt heiress. Arriving at The Pines in a hired cab, he found her waiting on the porch of the main lodge, and when he handed her into the carriage, he realized she was trembling, as she was on Sunday after defying her mother. He assumed they had exchanged words. Mrs. Appelhardt had been an effusive hostess before her daughter showed signs of rebellion. No doubt he was now considered a bad influence; beware of journalists!

As they drove away from The Pines, he said to Elizabeth, "That color is very attractive on you."

"Thank you," she said. "I like all shades of violet, but Mother thinks it's less than respectable—whatever that means."

"I've noticed that women of spirit and individuality are drawn to purple," he replied, thinking of Euphonia Gage, who had been one of Pickax City's most original and independent citizens.

Elizabeth was wearing a lavender dress belted with braided rope, and her mermaid hair was rolled up under a tropical straw hat that looked as if it had been drenched with rain and stomped by a horse. "This hat belonged to my father," she said proudly. "He called it his Gauguin hat."

"You have interesting taste in clothing," he said. "Those long robes you wear . . ." He ran out of words. What could he say about them?

"Do you like them? They're from India and Africa and Java—handwoven cotton and batik-dyed. I love exotic fabrics. Mother says I look like a freak, but it's the only way I have to express myself."

They were approaching the Domino Inn, and he remarked, "Two of the guests here read about your accident in the paper and mentioned that you'd been a student of theirs—Edith and Edna Moseley."

"How wonderful! I want to see them."

"Unfortunately, they left this morning to return home—Boston, I believe."

"Why didn't they let me know they were here?" she said. "When Mother enrolled me in the academy, I was in a very bad state psychologically, and they were so kind! You're a very kind person, too, Mr. Qwilleran. Am I right in thinking you're not married?"

"I'm not married at the moment . . . but I'm committed," he added quickly.

"What is she like?" Elizabeth asked eagerly.

"She's intelligent and comfortable to be with and nice-looking, and she has a melodious voice. She's head of the public library in Pickax City . . ."

"I'd love to be a librarian," she said wistfully, "but I don't have the formal education. Mother convinced me I didn't have the temperament or the stamina for college."

They reached the downtown area, and she was appalled. "How could they desecrate this lovely island? Those dreadful shops! Those vulgar rocking chairs!"

To alleviate her horror he said lightly, "I have a vision of all fifty rockers occupied and rocking in unison like a chorus line and creating electromagnetic waves that would bring the entire resort tumbling down."

She relaxed and laughed a little.

"The worst is yet to come," he went on. "The lobby is hung with black pirate flags, and we're lunching in the Corsair Room, the entrance to which is guarded by a swash-buckling pirate."

At the reservation desk Derek looked at Elizabeth, and then at Qwilleran questioningly, and then back at the woman in the unusual hat. "Hi, Mr. Q! Do you want your usual corner booth?" he asked, adding under his breath, "Hey! Wow!"

When they were seated, Elizabeth said, "That person in the lobby is *so tall!*"

"That's Derek Cuttlebrink, a well-known figure in Pickax and an actor in the Theater Club . . . Would you have a cocktail, Ms. Appelhardt? Or an apéritif?"

"Please call me Elizabeth," she said.

"Only if you'll call me Qwill."

After a moment's hesitation she asked for a chardonnay spritzer, and he said he would have the same thing without the wine.

"And now I'm dying to know something about your name—James Mackintosh Qwilleran with a QW. Was that your name at birth?"

"As a matter of fact . . . no. Before I was born, my mother was reading Spenser's *Faerie Queene,* and she named me Merlin James. When I was in high school, you can imagine how my peers heckled a first baseman named Merlin! So I changed it when I went to college. My mother was a Mackintosh."

"That makes a big difference," she said. "When I charted 'James Mackintosh Qwilleran,' I knew something was wrong. First I have to explain how numerology works. Every letter of the alphabet has a corresponding number, beginning with *one* for the letter A. When you reach *ten*—for J—you drop the zero and start again with *one.* To chart a name, you give each letter its numeral equivalent, total them, and reduce the total to a single digit. Is that clear?"

"I think so," he murmured, although his mind was wandering back forty years to Miss Heath—she of the toothy smile.

"When I charted the name you gave me, the final digit was *two,* and instinct told me you were not a *two type!* I had a feeling that you are a *five!* . . . So now, if you'll give me a moment, I'll chart your birth name." As she scribbled in a notebook, she mumbled to herself, "Merlin reduces to *eight* . . . add *three* for James and *three* for Qwilleran . . . for a total of *fourteen* . . . which reduces to *five*. . . . I knew it! You're a *five!*" she cried in triumph.

"Is that good or bad?"

Excitedly she said, "It means you like freedom, adventure, and change. You've probably traveled extensively, because you're adaptable and have a lively curiosity about new places and new people. And you have ingenuity, which must be useful in your work."

"In all modesty," Qwilleran said, "I must say you've got it right. But how did you know the previous number was wrong? You don't know me that well."

"It's your aura," she said seriously. "You have the aura of a *five.*"

"And what is your digit?"

"I'm a *seven,* which happens to be the same as your male cat. In charting them I came upon an astounding fact. Kao K'o Kung adds up to *seven,* and so does Koko. In the case of Yum Yum and Freya, each name comes out to the same digit: *one.* That means she's patient and independent, with strong willpower. Koko is aristocratic, scientific, and mentally keen, but rather secretive."

"Remarkable!" Qwilleran said. Pensively he devoured a bowl of gumbo, while his guest nibbled half a chicken sandwich without mayonnaise. Gradually he led her into a discussion of cooking herbs, then medicinal herbs, and then toxic herbs.

"The islanders would probably know about poisonous plants," she said. "They make their own folk medicines. Have you ever been to the Dark Village?"

"Is that what the natives call Providence Village?"

"Yes, and it's a fascinating place. My father used to drive us through the village. If you'd like to rent a carriage after lunch, I could drive."

"Is it true they resent strangers?"

"Ordinarily, but we were always quiet and respectful of their privacy. The islanders liked my father. He'd talk to the fishermen on the beach and buy some of their catch."

She lapsed into a thoughtful silence and he left her alone with her memories for a while. Suddenly she said, "Qwill, would you call me Liz? No one but my father ever called me that. He was my best friend and the only one who ever really listened to me."

"I'd be honored . . . Liz," he said. "How long has your father been gone?"

"Six years, and I still feel lonely. I have no rapport with my mother. William and Ricky are good brothers, but they have their own families and their own life."

"What about Jack?"

"We don't get along," she said sharply. "When we were growing up, he used to torment me—paint moustaches on my dolls and glue the pages of my favorite books together."

"Did your parents let him get away with that?"

"Mother excused him, saying he was naturally playful and didn't mean any harm, and Father—well . . . Father never tried to argue with her. You see, Qwill, Jack was such a beautiful boy that he could get away with anything! He's lost his looks now, from too much partying."

"Does Jack have a profession?"

"Marriage!" she said acidly. "He's been divorced three times, and he's only twenty-six. Mother says she doesn't care how many women he has, but why does he have to marry them all? It's like an addiction. Did you ever hear of such a thing? It's not a subject the family likes to discuss, but I'm sure he's married again and wants to get out of it. Whenever Jack spends a few weeks at home, he has an ulterior motive. He's been married to a rock singer, a figure-skater (she was nice), and an Italian actress."

"Some day he'll marry a librarian and live happily ever after," Qwilleran said.

Liz laughed a little. "I'm doing all the talking, Qwill. Tell me about you. Where do you live?"

"I live in a converted apple barn in Pickax City, population 3,000. I used to write for large metropolitan dailies, but now a friend of mine publishes the small local newspaper. I write for it and get involved, somewhat, with small-town life."

"You seem happy," Liz said with a touch of envy.

"I've achieved contentment, I think. I have friends, and I'm writing a book."

"I'm not happy," she said with bitterness. "You were right when you said I need a place of my own. When I'm at home, I lose all my spirit and ambition and appetite."

"How do you account for that?" he asked gently, although he was eager for particulars. Some day he would actually write that book, and he was always scrounging for material.

"Mother wants to direct my life, choose my friends, and make my decisions. After a while one just . . . *gives up!* . . . There! That's all I'm going to say about it."

"Let's visit the Dark Village," Qwilleran said.

He rented a two-wheeled cart, and they headed toward the east beach with Liz at the reins. It was an expanse of pebbles with picnic tables and rubbish containers at intervals. A few tourists were sunning on beach towels or hunting for agates or sharing picnic lunches with stray cats. Qwilleran said, "I've seen feral cats everywhere except at The Pines."

"No," she said sadly. "They know they're not wanted."

After a while a rutted road forked to the left and plunged into the woods. The hush was almost oppressive.

"The Dark Village," Liz whispered. "Can't you feel its spell?"

Ancient trees spread a dense canopy of branches over the road. There were windswept cedars twisted into grotesque shapes and gnarled oaks with trunks five feet in diameter, crusted with lichens. As the horse plodded through the ruts, the wheels of the rented gig creaked noticeably; otherwise, there was a lonely silence. A ramshackle hut or collapsed roof might be seen in the woods, but there was no sign of humanity. Deeper and deeper into the forest the road followed a tortuous path between the arboreal giants. Qwilleran had to remind himself to take a deep breath occasionally.

Farther on, scattered habitations began to appear—pathetic shelters nailed together from fragments of wrecked ships or structures swept away from some distant shore long ago. Some of them had small yards fenced off with misshapen pickets of driftwood, enclosing two or three crude tombstones. Yet, there was evidence of the living as well as the dead. A few pieces of clothing hung forlornly on a clothesline; an old dog slept on a doorstep; hens pecked in the road, and a goat nibbled weeds in a front yard. Once, a wild cat dashed across the road, dodging the horse's hooves. Some children, playing in a yard, rushed out of sight when the cart approached. Occasionally there was a glimpse of movement in a window, as someone peered out at the strangers. Somewhere a rooster crowed.

At one point the road widened slightly, and there was a small but well-built schoolhouse with outhouses for boys and girls; the siding was government-issue aluminum. Nearby, a weatherbeaten structure looked like the ghost of an old general store; two gaunt old men sat on a bench in front and glared at the cart as it trundled past. One other building made a brave showing with white paint but only on the front; there was a cross above the door.

After that, there were fewer dwellings and more open spaces with more patches of sunlight, until the road came to an end at the mountainous sand dune. Here the road forked right to the pebble beach and left into a tangle of weeds and underbrush.

Liz told the horse to whoa. "It was a hard pull through those ruts. Let him rest awhile."

Now what? Qwilleran thought; there seemed to be more on her mind than the welfare of the old nag. She was preoccupied. He said, "This has been a spellbinding experience. It's hard to believe that people live like this. What is that overgrown road to the left?"

"It used to be the villagers' shortcut to the west beach. It was closed when the Grand Island Club originated."

He was searching for a topic that would focus her attention. "That must be the sand dune where the fellow was shot last weekend." Then he told himself, This woman doesn't even read newspapers; she may not know about the shooting.

Liz turned to him abruptly. "Qwill, I think my guardian angel sent me that snake, so I could meet you."

"That's a charming compliment," he said stiffly, "but you paid a high price for a dubious benefit." He hoped this avowal would not lead to embarrassment.

Speaking earnestly, she said, "Ever since my father died, I've had no one to confide in."

"Is something troubling you?" he asked cautiously.

"I had a horrible experience right here on this spot a few years ago, and I've never been able to tell anyone."

"How old were you?"

"Sixteen."

Qwilleran's curiosity went into high gear, but he said in an offhand way, "If it will help you to talk about it, I'll be willing to listen."

She pondered a few minutes, looking tragic in her father's old hat. "Well, I was spending the summer here with my mother. Father had just died, and I felt so alone! Then my brother Jack came up for a few weeks. Mother had just paid a big settlement to get rid of his first wife, and now he had married again. Mother was upset, but Jack was her pet and could wheedle her into anything." Her mind wandered off into realms of family intrigue.

Qwilleran nudged it back on track. "So he came up to The Pines for a few weeks."

"He was doing penance. He was being sweet to Mother and even to me. We played croquet and went sailing, and one day he took me for a drive through the Dark Village, just as Father had done. We took my favorite carriage and favorite horse and a basket lunch to eat on the south beach. I was so happy! I thought I had finally found a big brother who would be my confidant."

The rented horse snorted and stamped his hooves, but Liz was consumed by her memories.

"We drove through the Dark Village and when we came to this fork in the road, he turned left into the weeds. I said, 'Where are you going? This road is closed!' His mouth turned down with a nasty expression, and I can't tell you what he said! I can't tell you what he tried to do! I jumped out of the carriage and ran screaming to the beach road. There were some fishermen beaching their boats, and I told them I was from The Pines. I said my brother had played a trick and driven away without me. They remembered my father and took me home in their boat. It was full of wet, slippery, flopping fish, but I didn't care. I was grateful."

"What did you tell your mother?" Qwilleran asked.

"I couldn't tell her what happened. She wouldn't have believed me. I told her my mind suddenly went blank. Jack told her I went crazy. Ricky said I was grieving for Father, and the ride through the Dark Village triggered a seizure. I had to have a nurse companion all summer, and Mother sent Jack to Europe while she paid off his second wife. That turned out to be poetic justice, because he met an actress in Italy and married again."

There was a distant rumble on the horizon, and Qwilleran asked, "Is that thunder? Or is Canada being attacked by missiles?"

"It's a long way off," Liz said. "Sometimes we hear distant thunder for two days and nights before the storm reaches us. It's rather exciting."

"Nevertheless, we should take this tired nag back to the stable for his afternoon nap," Qwilleran said.

Downtown he checked the post office—there was no mail from Polly—and hailed a cab to take Liz home.

"I feel as if a great weight has been lifted from my mind and my heart," she said. "Would you be my guest for lunch at the clubhouse some day?"

He agreed, hoping the invitation would be delayed until he was safely back in Pickax. He had done his good deed—two of them, in fact. He had listened sympathetically and allowed himself to be adopted as a godfather of sorts. From a practical point of view, meeting the royal family had been unproductive, supplying no material for his column and no leads in his investigation. Furthermore, if and when he ever wrote his book, it would not be about people like the Appelhardts . . . What prompted this asocial thinking was an immediate concern of his own, prompted by Lyle Compton's casual remark that Polly might decide to stay in Oregon. Qwilleran's uneasiness increased as each day passed without a postcard.

Sixteen

After dropping his lunch date at The Pines, Qwilleran went into the lounge at the Domino Inn to borrow some newspapers. There were few guests in evidence, but that was understandable; it was a weekday, and weather predictions for the next five days were iffy. Thunder still rumbled sporadically. It was not coming any closer; it was simply a warning of something that might never happen.

At the fruit basket he was glad to see that the pears had been replaced by apples. He was helping himself to one red and one green when the vice president in charge of communications and deliveries dashed up to him with two slips of paper, a foil-wrapped package the size of a brick, and an excited announcement in the language that Qwilleran was beginning vaguely to understand. As far as he could construe, either Sherman had had kittens, or Sheba was afraid of thunder, or Shoo Shoo had thrown up a hairball. He nodded and thanked Mitchell and then read his two telephone messages:

TO: Mr. Q
FROM: Andrew Brodie
REC'D: Tuesday 1:15 P.M.
MESSAGE: George Dulac. Lake Worth FL

To Qwilleran the name sounded Slavic. This was the ill-fated hotel guest who had conversed with a woman in a foreign language. The other message was from Dwight Somers: "Leaving the island. Information you want is in the mail." From these few words Qwilleran deduced that the public-relations man had been fired, possibly for snooping in the hotel's confidential records. If that were the case, Qwilleran rationalized, his friend was better off; he was too good for XYZ; he deserved more civilized working conditions; he could start his own agency.

When Qwilleran returned to Four Pips, he found two restless

cats. They could hear the far-off thunder, and they knew instinctively what was in store. They might, in fact, know more than the weather forecasters. Koko was prowling and looking for ways to get into trouble. Yum Yum was murmuring to herself as she tried to open a desk drawer. When Qwilleran opened it to show her that it was empty, that was even more frustrating to her feline sensibility. He tried reading to the Siamese from the editorial page of the *Moose County Something,* but they were bored. So was he. All three of them were at sixes and sevens.

Polly was on his mind, along with the reasons why she would decide to move to Oregon: Her old school chum pressured her into relocating; the opportunities for birding were irresistible; a suburban library needed a librarian with Polly's expertise and made her a good offer; she had reached the restless age and was ready for a new challenge. Although he tried to be understanding, Qwilleran found it difficult to imagine life without Polly. True, he had many friends, and two animal companions, and an enviable place to live, and a column to write for the newspaper, and a host of devoted readers, and money to spend. Yet, Polly filled a long-felt need in his life.

"Enough of this sentimentality!" he said to the Siamese, and he made a meatloaf sandwich. They muddled through the evening, hearing sounds of yet another audition at Five Pips. The atmosphere was calm, and the unceasing thunder seemed to be coming from several directions. Shortly before midnight he gave the cats their bedtime treat and retired, taking care to close the bedroom door. When the weather was threatening, they liked to crowd into his bed. He thought he would have trouble sleeping, but . . .

Qwilleran was sound asleep when the disturbance started outside his door—first the yowling, then the urgent scratching on the door panels. He sat up in bed and checked the hour; it was almost two o'clock. Then he smelled smoke. It was not tobacco this time; it was something burning. He checked his own kitchen burners hastily and then stepped outside with a flashlight.

Black smoke was issuing from the cottage next door. Without a second's hesitation he ran to Five Pips and pounded on the door, shouting "June! June! Fire!" The door was locked. He tried to kick it in, but he was wearing only light slippers. He lunged at it, but it held fast. He smashed the front window with his flashlight and then ran up the lane to ring the firebell. He clanged it again and again. Lights appeared instantly in certain windows of the inn, and Nick's voice shouted. "Where is it?"

"The last cottage!"

"Get out! Get everybody out!"

Qwilleran ran back to pull on some clothes—he was still in pajama bottoms and slippers—and stuff the cats into their carrier. He could hear a motor vehicle in the distance and the emergency beep—beep—beep. As soon as he emerged, lugging the carrier, Nick was running down the lane in full firefighting gear.

"Get everybody to the inn!" he yelled.

Now the motors of heavy vehicles could be heard on the still night air. The family in the first cottage—parents and two children—stood outside, confused and frightened.

"Go to the inn!" Qwilleran shouted. "Keep out of the way! The fire trucks are coming!" Already the police car was rounding the building.

In the lounge, where guests were standing around in nightclothes and robes, the Bamba cats hissed and growled at the sight of the caged Siamese invading their territory.

"Take them upstairs and shut them up in any vacant room," Lori said to Qwilleran. She was moving among the guests and saying, "Everything's under control . . . Don't be alarmed . . . The fire trucks are on the way . . . We've got plenty of water in the lake . . . There's no wind tonight, so it won't spread."

From the upstairs window Qwilleran saw the police car floodlighting the burning building. Black smoke billowed from the windows. Then the tanker and pumper arrived, and a line was run down to the lake. Soon his own cottage was being hosed down with torrents of water. An ambulance lumbered onto the scene, and a stretcher was rushed to the end of the lane. When another firefighter came running, helmet in hand, he recognized Harriet Beadle; she went to work as a backup on the hose.

The Siamese, sensing the tension of the emergency, were solemnly quiet when he released them from the carrier and left them alone.

Downstairs Lori said, "I'm fixing coffee for the firefighters. Does anyone want to help make sandwiches?"

"I can do that," Qwilleran offered. While she cut lunchmeat and separated cheese slices, he spread mayonnaise on bread. "I saw her being loaded into the ambulance," he said gruffly.

"We were afraid she'd get us into trouble," Lori said in a quiet voice. "She was so self-willed."

"Today she was walking around the yard with a lighted cigarette and an ashtray, and she told me she was observing house rules. I assumed she had reformed, but she had company tonight, and they may have been careless."

Lori looked out the window. "I don't see flames. They must have contained the fire. Thank God there's no wind. You won't be able to use your cottage, Qwill. We'll make up a suite, and you can spend the rest of the week upstairs . . . Listen! I hear the chopper. They're taking her to the mainland."

The other guests were sent back to bed, but Qwilleran stayed and helped serve coffee and sandwiches to the sooty-faced volunteers, who reported to the inn in shifts to take a breather. Some would stay on duty all night, watching for hot spots. He talked to the chief and then phoned the night desk of the *Moose County Something*.

"Reporting fire at Pear Island resort. Discovered at one-fifty-five A.M. Confined to one cottage at Domino Inn on West Beach Road. Occupant removed by volunteer rescue squad and airlifted to mainland. Check Pickax hospital for condition. Adult female. Check sheriff for release of name. Got it? . . . Ten volunteer firefighters, one tanker, and one pumper responded. No injuries. Water pumped from lake. Calm atmosphere averted forest fire and damage to other buildings. Probable cause of fire: smoking in bed, according to fire chief. Got it? . . . Okay, now listen here: If the victim dies, police will withhold her name temporarily, but I can tell you that she was Dr. June Halliburton, head of music for Moose County schools. Check Lyle Compton for bio. She was also summer director of entertainment for the Pear Island Hotel. Check Don Exbridge of XYZ Enterprises for comments . . . Okay?"

As he hung up, Qwilleran said to himself, Lyle will be shocked! So will Dwight. So will the Rikers. And there goes Derek's job as assistant director—if such a job ever existed.

Lori was finally persuaded to get some rest, but Qwilleran was still manning the coffeemaker at six A.M., when the news was broadcast by WPKX:

"A fire in a cottage on Pear Island claimed the life of one person early this morning. Volunteer firefighters responded to the alarm and were able to contain the blaze that originated in a smoldering mattress. Cause of death was asphyxiation resulting from smoke inhalation. The victim, an adult female from the Pickax area, was airlifted from the island by sheriff's helicopter but was dead on arrival at Pickax General Hospital. The name is withheld pending notification of relatives."

After a few hours of sleep Qwilleran was roused by the yowling of two Siamese, who wanted their breakfast, fire or no fire. He ventured down the lane and salvaged a can of red salmon from Four

Pips. The family in Two Pips was packing up and leaving, and most of the guests in the inn were checking out. They said the continuous thunder made them nervous. According to weather reports, the storm would reach Moose County and environs in twenty-four hours.

A pale and weary Lori was serving scrambled eggs and toast, that was all, and when Qwilleran inquired about Nick, she said, "He took the kids and cats to the mainland at eight o'clock this morning. He's dropping them at his mother's house—nine cats, including the new kittens. Then he'll come right back. There's a lot of cleanup to do, as well as securing everything against the storm. High winds and thunderstorms are predicted. That means shuttering windows and removing anything that could blow away."

"I'll help, if someone will tell me what to do."

"First, you might bring all your belongings from Four Pips," she said. "And now that our cats have gone, yours can have the run of the inn."

"But not until I can supervise them," Qwilleran stipulated.

There was no fire damage at Four Pips, but the acrid smell of smoke and a mustiness from the drenching of the roof had permeated everything, including his clothing. Once more he bundled shirts, pants, and socks into pillow cases and carried them to the Vacation Helpers.

Wordlessly he tossed the bundles on the reception table.

"Oh, no! Not again!" said Shelley.

"How fast can you have it ready?"

"Two hours. Is it smoke damage? I heard about the fire. Too bad about the woman who died. Did you know her? Was she young?" In a high state of excitement induced by the approaching storm, Shelley talked nonstop, asking questions without waiting for answers. "Did you hear the storm warning on the radio? Did you see the ladders out in front? Some of our roomers are shuttering the windows. Mr. Ex wants all hotel employees to leave the island, but some of us are going to ride it out. We'll have plenty of beer and meatloaf sandwiches, and we'll have a ball! They predict gale winds or worse, but this building is good and solid. If there's high water, it'll be bad for the hotel. We're on a higher elevation, so I don't worry, do you? Have you ever gone through a hurricane?"

On the way out, Qwilleran encountered Derek Cuttlebrink, leaving with a duffelbag, and he asked the young man, "Are you one of the rats deserting a sinking ship?"

"Yeah . . . well . . . I'm laid off—for how long, I don't know—so

I might as well go home and see my girl. How d'you like this thunder? It hasn't stopped since yesterday noon. It spooks me!"

"The ancient gods of the island are having a bowling tournament," Qwilleran said, adding in a lower voice, "Did Merrio come up with any more information? Let's walk down to the beach."

They sat on the steps leading down to the abandoned beach, and Derek said, "I don't know if this has anything to do with the Chicken Stink or not. That's what they call the food poisoning behind the chef's back," he explained with a grin. "But here goes: The hotel doesn't buy all its food from the mainland. Some of the islanders bring the chef fresh fish, goat cheese, and rabbit, but no chicken."

"Do they simply walk into the kitchen and peddle their goods?"

"They used to, but now the back door is kept locked, and vendors have to be on the chef's list. But when the hotel first opened, Merrio remembers a man who used to bring fresh herbs to sell. The chef was glad to get them. He's French, you know, and they always make a big thing of fresh herbs. Fresh or dry, I don't see that it makes any difference."

A connection flashed across Qwilleran's mind: Does the chef know Noisette? Are they a couple? Is that why she's here? Is that why she has a suite at a secluded inn? Is the chef paying for it? Was it the chef drinking with her in the Buccaneer Den on Sunday night?

"So how'm I doin'?" Derek asked.

"Mission accomplished. Next assignment: *Kamchatka.*" He handed Derek some folded bills. "Now you'd better get in line for the ferry."

Qwilleran helped Nick carry the hurricane shutters out of the basement, and then he helped carry the porch furniture indoors. By that time his laundry would be finished, and he walked up to Vacation Helpers. Shelley had two neat packages of folded clothing waiting for him, plus a foil-wrapped brick of something that looked all too familiar.

She said, "This is your Thursday meatloaf, just out of the oven. Would you like to take it with you? It may not be as good as before, because it's all-beef. Do you mind? Midge's regular recipe calls for two parts beef and one part rabbit, but she couldn't get any rabbit meat today."

"I can live with that," Qwilleran said agreeably.

He had a hunch, and it proved to be correct. As soon as he returned to his suite at the inn, he gave the Siamese a taste of rabbitless meatloaf, and they gobbled it, yowling for more.

"Cats!" he said in exasperation. "Who can understand them?"

They were adjusting to their new environment readily. It was the bridal suite. The furniture was new, the chairs luxuriously cushiony, the colors soft. There was none of the overscaled, bargain-priced fabric that decorated the rest of the inn. There were too many knickknacks for Qwilleran's taste, and the pictures on the wall were Victorian Romantic; he removed two of them over the sofa and substituted the gilded leather masks. He had also brought the maroon velvet box from Four Pips.

"How would you guys like to play the numbers?" he asked.

Koko was in good form. The first dominoes he swished off the table spelled *gale*. Next came one of his favorites: *lake*, which could be shuffled to spell *leak*.

Qwilleran said to him, "If the weatherman is correct, there's going to be a leak in the plumbing of Mount Olympus tomorrow."

After that the words were ordinary: *idea, blade, gable, hack, deaf* (or *fade)* and *deal* (or *lead)*. Then five of Koko's favorite dominoes landed on the floor: 3-3, 2-2, 6-6, 2-3, and 4-5. As usual, Qwilleran was able to spell *field*. There was no particular significance to *field* until the next draw, which consisted of 2-4, 1-3, 6-3, 6-6, and 0-5. Although the pips were different, they reduced to the same digits, which corresponded to the same letters: *field*. It had been one of the cat's favorites from the start. A tremor rippled across Qwilleran's upper lip. For the first time it occurred to him that *field* could be shuffled to spell *filed*. He hurried from the room and ran downstairs to have a look at the porch. The crawl space underneath was ventilated with panels of wood lattice. He found Nick hanging shutters on the south side of the building. "How do we get under the porch?" he asked. "I'd like to put Koko on a leash and have him look at the underside of the steps."

"There are removable panels at each end. You need a high-powered flashlight—maybe two. I'll go with you."

Qwilleran never traveled with the Siamese without taking their harnesses. Yum Yum abhorred the idea, but Koko always liked to be buckled up.

Downstairs Nick had removed the access panel and had two battery-operated lanterns.

Qwilleran said, "This is a wild shot, but we might find evidence of tampering." First he let Koko wander about the porch, now empty of swings and chairs. The cat sniffed in desultory fashion for a few minutes and then went directly to the third step from the top. In a low voice Qwilleran said, "He knows the trouble spot. Let's crawl underneath."

He went first, with Koko leading. Nick followed with the second lantern. It was a long crawl through damp sand, detritus, and skeletons of small animals. They made slow progress, as Koko was distracted by many items of catly interest. When they reached the steps, Nick flashed his lantern up at the new construction—treated wood, solidly braced and nailed—but the cat was interested only in the sand below. There were sawed-off remnants of lumber and new galvanized nails dropped by the carpenter. There were also fragments of old rusty nails and something else half-buried in the sand. Koko was digging for it—an old hack saw blade. Qwilleran's moustache bristled as he remembered the dominoes: *hack* and *blade* and *filed.*

He said to Nick, "Do you see what I see?"

"A couple of swipes with that thing would cut through a rusty nail like a piece of cake."

"Don't touch it. It's our evidence," Qwilleran said. "You know, Nick, when my barn was being converted, there were rusty nails in the hundred-year-old timbers, and the carpenter whacked them with a metal file. They broke like breadsticks."

"So now the question is: Who whacked the nails under our steps?"

"Let's get out of here."

They crawled out, dragging a reluctant cat. Nick wanted to finish the shuttering. Qwilleran wanted another look at the domino records he had been keeping. He also wanted to check the post office before it closed.

Upstairs, Yum Yum greeted the returning hero with assorted reactions; he brought with him the scent of untold mysteries. Koko, when divested of his leather trappings, took a half hour to launder his fur thoroughly. Qwilleran checked the records for words and numbers that would trigger a thought process.

Lead, depending on how it was pronounced, could refer to a metal with chemically poisonous properties, or it could be another name for *leash.* Words with K, L, and J reflected Koko's preference for high-pip dominoes: 5-6, 6-6, and 5-5. In general he favored doubles—like 1-1, 2-2, 3-3, and 4-4—suggesting a sense of order or balance.

Next Qwilleran examined his own shuffling of letters: *Field* became *filed; idle* could be *lied; lake* and *leak* appeared on the list every day. Why? Because Koko liked 5-6 and 6-6? The letters, Qwilleran now realized, could also spell *kale,* a kind of cabbage of which he was not fond, or the name of a local family. There were Kales, Beadles, and Lawsons all over the island, someone had said.

"Yow!" said Koko in a tone that made Qwilleran's moustache bristle again.

He glanced at his watch. There was no time to lose. "Be right back," he said to the Siamese, who gazed at him with their so-what? expression.

The postal clerk at General Delivery, who had disappointed him so many times, was pleased to hand him two pieces of mail. The postcard he read immediately. It was written in Polly's usual telegraphic style:

> Wonderful country. Good birding. Sarah is fun! She's helped me make a very important decision. Details later. Arrive airport 7:35 Friday. Love, Polly

Qwilleran's suspicions were confirmed. So be it! He huffed into his moustache with resignation. It would make some changes in his life. It would never be the same without Polly.

The other piece of mail was a letter in a Pear Island Hotel envelope, with "D.S." inked above the return address. He put it in his pocket. At the moment, and under the circumstances, what did he care about Noisette's last name?

Seventeen

Qwilleran was somewhat subdued as he helped shutter the windows of the inn. Nick said, "They darken the rooms completely, so we'll leave one window uncovered in each room—until the last minute. After that, we live with artificial light, like prison inmates—unless there's a power failure. That means no lights, no water, no refrigeration. We're filling the bathtub with water—and also some five-gallon jugs for drinking. Lori has a campstove that's all right for heating canned food and boiling coffee, but that's about all. The radios operate on batteries, and we have plenty of oil lamps and flashlights, but it won't be fun. If you don't want to stay, Qwill, I'll understand. I'll take you back to the mainland while the lake's still calm."

"I'll stay," Qwilleran said.

"Okay, but don't say I didn't warn you. If you want to phone anyone on the mainland, tell them we're on high ground, and the building is solid, constructed with huge timbers and thick planks. No shortcuts or substitutions or imitations."

Qwilleran took the suggestion and phoned the newspaper office, leaving a message with the secretary. It was a relief to find that Riker was out of the building. The editor would have tried to harangue him into changing his mind. Whatever Qwilleran proposed to do, his old friend insisted that it was too reckless, too impractical, too frivolous, or too expensive.

Now he was suffering from lack of sleep and the exertion of ladder climbing, and Polly's postcard had induced a state of numb indifference. He flopped on his bed, narrowly missing two dormant lumps of fur, and slept until he was disturbed by two active cats, who were themselves disturbed by noises in the corridor. There were voices, and sounds of luggage handling, and the opening and closing of doors. Someone was moving in! In the groggy state of first awakening, he wondered why anyone would move into the Domino Inn at a time like this, when everyone else was moving out.

He roused himself, combed his hair, washed his face, and went downstairs, where he was met by a wide-eyed Lori. "You'll never guess!" she said. "A new guest just registered! She has beautiful luggage, and she was brought here in a splendid carriage! She says she knows you!"

"What's her name?" he asked warily.

"Elizabeth Cage. I wanted to ask why she'd check into a place with shuttered windows, but then . . ." Lori looked at Qwilleran slyly. "I thought it might be something private between you two."

"Where is she now?"

"Upstairs, unpacking. She's in the Lakeview Suite across from you."

"This comes as a total surprise. Do we have any meatloaf sandwiches left over from the fire?"

"That's about all—including the whole meatloaf you gave us. I'm not prepared to serve dinner guests, you know."

"She doesn't eat much, so don't fuss and don't apologize. I'll go upstairs," he said irritably, "to see what this is all about."

The young woman who opened the door was dressed in a caftan and seemed very glad to see him.

"Liz! What the devil are you doing here?" he demanded.

"My family left this noon, taking both boats, and I told Mother I didn't wish to go. I told her I'm moving to Pickax City."

"You're a very impulsive young woman! You don't know anything about Pickax." He was thinking, Arch is right; I should mind my own business.

"Will you come in? I'd offer you tea, but I suppose there's no room service today."

"Not today, and not ever! And if the storm hits hard, there may be no lights, no water, and no ferries to the mainland. The only boat left in the downtown marina belongs to Domino Inn, and the storm could reduce it to splinters. Have all the boats left the Grand Island Club?"

"Yes, but . . . if I may use the telephone, I think I can arrange something."

"Go down and tell Mrs. Bamba what you have in mind. She'll let you use the office phone . . . And now, if you'll excuse me, I have an errand to do."

He wanted to walk away from the situation and consider the complications involved if Liz should move to Pickax. Could she handle her own living arrangements, face responsibility, make wise decisions? Or would she require and expect a full-time guardian? That was a role he was not prepared to play. He had come to the island to help Nick, and he had stepped into . . . the peat bog, so to speak.

Qwilleran walked to Harriet's Family Café, not expecting it to be open but hoping to follow up their previous conversation. Two men—who proved to be her cousins from the village—were shuttering the windows, while she supervised with tough authority. When she saw Qwilleran, she walked toward him with a solemn step and an anguished face.

"Isn't it terrible about the fire?" she moaned. "We had to notify the fire marshal. He comes up from Down Below if anyone dies—or if the chief suspects arson."

"But you and the other volunteers did a heroic job, Harriet. It could have been much worse."

"I know, but I feel bad *because I knew her!* I knew June Kale all her life, and I know her pa."

"June Kale? I thought her name was Halliburton."

"She got married once. It didn't last long. Yep, she grew up on the island and went to high school on the mainland, like I did, but she was really bright. Never took piano lessons till ninth grade, and next thing we knew, she was teaching music and playing the piano in big halls. She got kinda stuck-up then—didn't want anybody to know she came from Providence Island, but she visited her ma and pa a lot, and I give her credit for that! . . . My! They were so proud of their daughter! Her ma's dead now, and her pa must be all broke up. I feel terribly sorry for him. He's the caretaker at The Pines."

"Does he live in the gatehouse?"

"Yep, as far back as I can remember. June grew up there—with electric light, a bathroom, telephone, and all that."

Qwilleran was asking himself questions, and answering them. Did June want to live in the north country to be near her parents? *She was too brittle, too worldly for that kind of sentiment.* Did she really rent Five Pips to avoid disturbing her elderly neighbors? . . . Or so her father could steal in to visit her via the nature trail? *Neither. The voices drifting across the yard after dark weren't those of father and daughter. They were young, bantering, teasing, laughing voices. The parties didn't sound like auditions either.*

"Do you want some coffee or ice cream?" Harriet asked.

"No, thanks. I just came to see how you are. You must be exhausted after being up all night. Do you plan to stay here during the storm?"

"Nope. I'll be sitting with my ma in the village. It's gonna be a bad one! My cousins are putting up the shutters to save the glass."

Qwilleran turned away as if to leave and then added as an afterthought, "The fire is the sixth incident in less than three weeks, and the fourth to result in a death. If you have any idea who's involved, now is the time to come forward."

Harriet's face became flushed, and she clenched and unclenched her fists. "The fire was an accident! How could it be anything else? She was smoking in bed. She always smoked a lot. Her ma and pa tried to stop her, but they couldn't."

"Okay, leave the fire out of it," Qwilleran said. "You told me you knew something about the other incidents. You knew someone who was responsible."

"I was wrong. That was a mistake. It was just village gossip," she said, walking away and shouting to the cousins who were shuttering the windows.

Qwilleran walked away, too, thinking, Once an islander, always an islander. Harriet had decided to remain loyal. Actually, her transparent denials only confirmed his suspicions.

* * *

The WPKX announcer said, "A storm watch is now in effect for all shoreline communities. The Disaster Center has issued evacuation directives for all occupants of beach property. Two fronts are approaching at the rate of five miles an hour and could converge over northern Moose County and adjoining lake areas by midnight. Severe thunderstorms, winds of seventy to a hundred miles an hour, and rising lake levels are expected."

The storm was indeed closing in on all sides, as four persons gathered around the kitchen table at the Domino Inn. Nick had installed the last of the shutters and had nailed planks across the front and back doors to prevent them from bursting open. He also nailed a towel-wrapped two-by-four across the bottom of each door to keep the rain from pouring across the threshold.

Lori served a pickup supper in the kitchen, around a big square table with piano legs and scarred top. There were meatloaf sandwiches, and there was a homemade soup that was thick and grayish in color, but it tasted good. The only recognizable ingredient was alphabet pasta. She explained, "It's full of chicken broth and veggies, but I puree them so the kids won't know what they're eating, and the alphabet letters keep them from thinking about it too much."

Since the pasta alphabet contained all twenty-six letters—as opposed to twelve in the domino game—Qwilleran was able to spell *papilionaceous,* a word that had once won him a spelling championship and a trip to Washington. Liz had the good manners to be amused by the soup and tolerant of the sandwiches.

Lori said, "Ms. Cage arranged for us to dock the *Double-Six* at the Grand Island Club."

"Yeah, it worked out great!" Nick said. "I took the boat up there, and they rolled it into a concrete boathouse. Then one of the guys drove me home in a snappy little cart. He said he'd always wanted to see the four big tree trunks inside our lodge."

Liz told them that the west beach had never experienced much damage from summer storms. "We might lose a few tree branches or shingles, but we've never been inconvenienced by loss of power, because we have generators. So it surprised me that Mother wanted to leave this time."

It was no surprise to Qwilleran. The queen mother, he guessed, wanted to whisk her daughter away from his radical influence. Thinking the Bambas deserved an explanation, he said, "Ms. Cage has been wanting to relocate in Pickax, and she thought this would be an appropriate time, storm or no storm."

Lori expressed surprise and pleasure. "You'll like Pickax," she said. "The population is only three thousand, but the town has some good things going for it, including a very good theater club. Also, they're getting a community college." She turned and looked brightly and expectantly at Qwilleran, who had authorized the Klingenschoen Foundation to underwrite the new institution. He had no intention of picking up the cue, however, and said not a word about the college or the theater club or anything else in Pickax. He was not going to encourage this impulsive and eager and reputedly flaky young woman to move into his backyard. Instead he said to her, "You might prefer Lockmaster in the adjoining county. They have horse farms and carriage collectors and driving clubs."

"I've never cared about joining clubs," she said. "What I enjoy is a leisurely drive down a country lane. I would have my favorite horse shipped to Pickax; I suppose he could be stabled there. And my brother William would let me have the physician's phaeton."

Lori said, "If you like country lanes, you'll love Moose County. It has very picturesque countryside."

Shut up, Lori, Qwilleran thought. He said, "I don't know whether picturesque is the right word. The terrain has a ravaged look because of the strip mining and overcutting of forests earlier in the century. Abandoned mines and abandoned quarries are everywhere. They can be an eyesore."

"Yes, but the abandoned shafthouses are like romantic monuments to the past," said Lori, her eyes sparkling. He wanted to kick her under the table, but even his long legs couldn't reach.

Nick, noticing his scowl and sensing his purpose, said, "There's a lot of industry coming into Pickax—like plastics, auto parts, and electronics—but the major industry is the federal prison covering hundreds of acres and housing ten thousand convicted felons."

Lori said, "Yes, but the prison is famous for its flower gardens, tended by inmates. People come from all over to photograph them."

Oh, God! Qwilleran thought. He said, "Does anyone play dominoes? We may have to play a lot of dominoes before this storm is over."

Thunder claps were coming closer, and lightning bolts made themselves felt like electric shocks. Even the solid wood shutters couldn't keep the flashes from outlining the windows like blue neon.

After dessert—ice cream on a stick—Qwilleran excused himself and went upstairs to the bridal suite, intending to remain in seclusion until the rains came. Then he would go downstairs to offer help and moral support to the Bambas and the uninvited guest. He tried to read, but thoughts of the present dilemma crowded the words from the page. He felt burdened with a sense of failure. In his search for clues and evidence he had nothing to show but hunches, suspicions, and a hack saw blade.

The air was heavy with portent, and the cats, huddled close to him, kept looking at the ceiling. Suddenly there was a clap of thunder directly overhead, like the crack of doom. Koko jumped two feet in the air and went into orbit. Circling madly around the suite he kicked a table lamp, sent knickknacks flying, terrorized Yum Yum, and sideswiped one of the leather masks over the sofa.

"Stop!" Qwilleran bellowed as he rescued the expensive artwork—it was the tragedy mask—but Koko was wound up and continued the rampage until his internal springs ran down. Then he flicked his tongue nonchalantly over random patches of fur. At one point he stopped and, with tongue hanging out and one hind leg held aloft, he stared at Qwilleran's forehead.

"Let's play dominoes," Qwilleran said, stroking his moustache.

At the same moment there was another shattering thunderbolt. The rain slammed into the building, and the lights flickered momentarily, but they played the game. Koko's penchant for white spots resulted in words like *click, balked, jack, deckle, ilk* and the ubiquitous *lake*. Just as Qwilleran was trying to make a word out of 4-4, 5-6, 3-5, 0-1, 5-5, 3-6, 6-6, and 2-3, there was a light tap on the door.

There stood Liz in her caftan, carrying an oil lamp. "I'm sorry to trouble you," she said, "but would you show me how to light this lamp, in case there's a power failure?" She handed him a box of kitchen matches. "These were with the lamp."

"Come in," he said brusquely, "and close the door to keep the cats from escaping. In stormy weather they sometimes go berserk." He removed the glass chimney, turned up the wick, and tried to strike a match. "These are no good. They're damp. Let's try mine. Islands are always damp. Shoes mildew, nails rust, crackers get soggy, and matches don't strike. You should know about that; you've spent summers here."

"There was never any problem," she said. "The air-conditioning controlled the humidity."

The matches in the bridal suite were equally damp. "It will be a joke," he said, "if there are thirty oil lamps on the premises and no matches."

"Would anyone have a cigarette lighter?"

"Not at the Domino Inn! No cigarette lighters, no automatic

weapons, and no illegal drugs. Did you hear about the fire last night?"

Liz nodded sadly. "The woman who died was the daughter of our steward. The poor man is almost out of his mind. When we were growing up, she was like my big sister, and I heard something this morning that was very upsetting." She moistened her lips and lowered her eyes.

"Please sit down," Qwilleran said. "Would you like a glass of water? That's all I can offer."

She perched on the edge of a chair and took a dainty sip.

"Where did you hear this upsetting news?"

"I was in the stable, giving Skip his daily dose of affection in his stall. He's such a loving animal! And I heard two men in the tack room, having a very heated argument. I knew the voices. One was my brother, and the other was our steward. They've always been friendly, and it was a shock to hear them shouting at each other. I know it's bad form to eavesdrop, but Jack has never had any respect for me, so I didn't feel guilty about listening."

"Did you learn what the trouble was?"

Before she could reply, there was another violent crack of thunder overhead. A purple flash seeped into the room, and the lights went out! Liz uttered an involuntary cry.

"Well, I guess that's it!" he said. "We'd better go downstairs. I have a flashlight. We'll go across the hall and get the one in your room—and hope the Bambas have dry matches."

Nick met them at the foot of the stairs. "Come into the family room. We're lighting lamps. Sorry about this. We should have a generator, but there've been so many other things to do and buy."

"Qwill," Lori called from the office door, "why don't you bring Koko and Yum Yum down?"

For the next five hours, four persons and two animal companions huddled together as sheets of rain assaulted the building and the wind screamed through the treetops like a hundred harmonicas. At the storm's apex, when the turbulence was directly over the island, the thunder was a series of explosions, each louder than the last, making the ground shudder. There were moments when the building quaked enough to rattle glasses and tilt pictures. At such moments Lori sat quietly with eyes closed and lips moving as she hugged Koko for security. Qwilleran held Yum Yum, mumbling reassurances. Both cats were wide-eyed, and their ears swiveled wildly.

Nick produced a jug of red wine, saying, "We might as well be drunk as the way we are."

Qwilleran had to exercise intense willpower to refuse. "How long can it last?" he shouted above the din.

"It's passing over."

Now there were several seconds or even a full minute between thunderclaps, and the purple flashes were weaker, but the rain still bombarded the building. Occasionally there was a loud crack as a tree limb snapped off, followed by a jarring thump as it landed on the roof. No one mentioned it, but all must have been thinking, What if a tree comes through the roof? What if tons of water pour into the building?

Now at least it was possible to talk and be heard, awas no conversation as such—merely spoken thoughts:

"It still sounds like a locomotive roaring past!"

"The ancient gods of the island are snarling and gnashing their teeth."

"Thank God we sent the kids to the mainland."

"They'll be getting it over there, too."

"Have you ever seen one as bad as this?"

"The cats are very good. Koko is tense, though."

"Yum Yum has been trembling nonstop."

"Did you look at the wind gauge, Nick?"

"It broke the gauge. Must've reached a hundred."

"Wonder how high the lake is."

"If it reaches road-level, we could have a washout."

"Did anyone ever read *High Wind in Jamaica?*"

Sometimes the wind stopped for one blessed moment, then resumed its attack from another direction. When, in the small hours of the morning, the tumult ceased, there was stunned silence in the small room. Everyone claimed to be weary.

"Anyone hungry?" Lori asked.

It was sleep that everyone craved. The oil lamps were extinguished, and flashlights guided the survivors through the black rooms.

Eighteen

No daylight filtered through the shuttered windows the day after the storm; even the Siamese didn't know it was breakfast time. Only the sound of the sheriff's helicopter assessing the damage and the sound of Nick removing shutters suggested that it was time to get up.

Lori offered Qwilleran hot coffee, cold cereal, and an orange from the fruit basket. "Look out the front door," she said. "You won't believe it."

The sun was shining; the flood waters were rapidly receding; and a workmanlike breeze was drying the drenched building and terrain.

"We were lucky." Lori said. "Wait'll you hear the eleven o'clock newscast!" The WPKX announcer said:

> The worst storm in forty years has done its dirty work in Moose County. Beach homes and fisheries on the shore sustained minor damage, but the storm vented its greatest fury on the south end of Pear Island, commonly called Breakfast Island. The Pear Island Hotel was virtually leveled during the five-hour onslaught, which has been officially recorded as a northern hurricane. Winds up to a hundred miles an hour, plus a lake surge, made mincemeat of a structure that was completed less than two months ago. Uprooted trees of tremendous height fell on the flat-roofed building and adjoining strip malls. Sections of the boardwalk and piers were hurled into the wreckage. All personnel had been evacuated from the complex, and no casualties have been reported. The developers, XYZ Enterprises, could not be reached for comment at this hour, but observers estimate that the damage will be in the high millions. Elsewhere on the island, buildings that have survived almost a century of storms continued to withstand the elements with only minor damage.

Qwilleran asked Lori, "Has Ms. Cage been down?"

"No, but I took some tea upstairs. I was worried about her. She's so fragile for a young woman, and so thin! I'm a perfect fourteen, but she makes me feel fat. She's okay, but tired and a little stunned. Aren't we all? You can't use your shaver, Qwill, but you can take a pitcher of water upstairs for washing. I hear the cats yowling. Do you want to let them out?"

"Let them stay where they are. If I open the door, they'll stick their heads out, think about it for five minutes, and then go back in."

"I'll keep them company," said a small voice from the stairs. "We'll play dominoes." It was Liz, wearing another caftan.

Qwilleran helped Nick with the shutters and porch furniture, while Lori tackled the indoor cleanup as well as she could without water or electricity. Rain and sand had blown into the building through invisible cracks, along with black soot from the charred remains of Five Pips.

Nick said, "Did you hear about the hotel? That should tell you something about modern technology. They laugh at our four big tree trunks and birchbark siding, but we didn't blow away, did we? Sorry about the power and phones being out. If you want to go back to the mainland, say when. Any time."

"Well . . ." said Qwilleran, thinking fast, "there's a lot of work here that I could help you with . . . and Polly's plane doesn't come in until tomorrow evening . . . so why don't I stay until then? *But you might ferry Ms. Cage over today.* I'm sure she'd appreciate it. She's not accustomed to discomforts and inconveniences."

"Be glad to, and I can drive her to the airport, if she's flying out."

"Uh . . . she hasn't quite decided. Just deliver her to the hotel in Mooseville. She can stay there a few days until she makes up her mind."

"Sure. Tell her to let me know when she wants to leave. Lori will be more comfortable, I know, if she doesn't have a guest to worry about while the place is such a mess."

Qwilleran found Liz on the porch, reading a book on the preservation of wetlands, and he was only too glad to relay Nick's offer.

"When are *you* leaving, Qwill?" she asked.

"Tomorrow evening."

"I'm in no hurry," she said. "Being here in the aftermath of a hurricane is rather exciting. I'd prefer to wait until tomorrow evening and save Mr. Bamba a trip. And since I'm going to Pickax—and you live there—perhaps you'll let me ride into the city with you."

"Well . . . yes . . . of course," Qwilleran said, "but there's another consideration: It embarrasses Mrs. Bamba when she's unable to produce decent meals."

"Don't let her worry about that! I'm not particular about food. She's a lovely person, and I'm enjoying my stay. Koko and Yum Yum and I are quite compatible, and I'll keep them entertained while you're helping Mr. Bamba," Liz assured him.

She stayed. Qwilleran cleaned up the storm debris. Lori served canned beans and canned corned beef. Finally, at departure time on Friday, Qwilleran accompanied Liz to the Grand Island Club on foot, and they returned with a dogcart. The luggage was stowed in the dog box, and the two men and two cats perched high on the seat above, while Liz, wearing travel clothes and her Gauguin hat, took the driver's seat. At the last minute Lori ran out with a maroon velvet box. "A souvenir of your vacation, Qwill!"

Aboard the *Double-Six* it was a smooth voyage to the mainland on a lake that had been raging the previous night. At the municipal pier in Mooseville, Nick helped carry the luggage to Qwilleran's small four-door: two suitcases, typewriter, some cartons, the cat carrier, and the turkey roaster—plus five pieces of luggage belonging to Liz. The uninvited guest was busy photographing the *Double-Six* and the seagulls on the waterfront.

"The cats and their commode go in the backseat," Qwilleran told Nick. Even so, the engineer's skill was required to fit everything into the trunk. Polly's luggage, they concluded, would have to go inside the car.

"Qwill, I don't know how to thank you," Nick said. "Sorry the weather was so lousy."

"I wish I could have come up with more answers, Nick, but I'm not through yet. I want to kick it around with Brodie when I get back to Pickax. I know you suspect troublemakers from Lockmaster, but I say the blame lies closer to home. Both the natives and the summer people resent the resort, and something tells me the crimes are being committed by a coalition. The sharpies from Down Below have the brains to organize a harassment campaign, and the islanders have the personnel to sneak around and poison the gumbo or plant a bomb. They're everywhere on the island, in low-level jobs where they can be virtually invisible."

"Gosh, you've really been thinking, Qwill."

"Tell you why I think the summer people are involved. They're angry enough to want to sue the resort, but it's a no-win case, and if they can't do it legally, they'll do it illegally. They're used to exercising their power, and they don't like to be thwarted." Qwilleran lowered his voice. "My immediate problem is: what to do with *this woman!*"

"Don't ask me. She's your woman!" Nick said with a grin.

"Like hell she is! She blew in with the hurricane, and I don't know what she expects . . . Well, never mind, I'll figure something out."

The *Double-Six* chugged back to the island, and Qwilleran faced Liz squarely. "Are you sure you want to go to Pickax and not to this charming town of Mooseville with its quaint Northern Lights Hotel? There's a maritime museum and a mall in a fish cannery and a good little restaurant called the Nasty Pasty."

"No, I find Pickax City more appealing," she said.

Huffing unobtrusively into his moustache, Qwilleran opened the passenger door for her. "We have to stop at the airport to pick up my friend, who's coming in on the seven-thirty-five shuttle. And now that you're here, Liz, what are your plans?"

"I'm going to drop 'Appelhardt.' I like 'Cage' better. It was the maiden name of my paternal grandmother."

"I mean, where do you want to live? What kind of people would you like to meet? How long do you think you'll stay? What do you want to do while you're here?"

"I don't know. Do you have any suggestions?"

He groaned inwardly. He should never have gone to tea at The Pines. "You might take an apartment in Indian Village. They have a clubhouse and golf course, and a lot of young people live there."

"I prefer older people," she said, looking at him appreciatively.

"A lot of older people live there, too. Do you play bridge?"

"No, cards don't appeal to me."

"Wherever you live, you'll need a car. It's a necessity in Moose County. There are no taxis."

"Would there be any objection to a horse and carriage? I could have Skip shipped over here, and William would let me have the physician's phaeton."

"In order to stable a horse, you'd have to live in the country, and you'd still need a car. I assume you have a driver's license."

"I'm afraid it's expired. Mother didn't want me to drive."

"Well, you'll have to renew it."

"Is there a foreign car dealer in Pickax? I'd like a Bentley. William has a Bentley."

Nothing had been settled by the time they reached the airport. Qwilleran parked at the passenger-pickup curb and told Liz to sit tight while he made a phone call and picked up his friend's luggage.

In the terminal he called Fran Brodie, the interior designer. "Fran! Have I got a client for you! She's loaded! She's young! She wants to live in Pickax! . . . Don't ask questions. Just listen. She's checking into the Pickax Hotel in half an hour, and I want you to take her under your wing and see that she gets a good apartment, furniture, a car, knives and forks, everything! Her name is Elizabeth Cage. Call her early tomorrow, or even tonight, before she does something impulsive. I've gotta hang up. I'm at the airport. I'm meeting a plane."

When the shuttle taxied to the terminal, eight passengers deplaned, and Qwilleran—in a state of preoccupation—greeted Polly with less enthusiasm than she probably expected. He took her carry-on tote and a long roll of something, saying, "You have one other bag to claim, don't you?"

"That and two cartons. I bought a few things."

While trundling the luggage cart to the curb, he said casually, "I have a hitchhiker who wants to be dropped at the Pickax Hotel."

"Really? I thought you never picked up hitchhikers, Qwill."

"This one is different. I'll explain later."

He introduced Ms. Cage to Mrs. Duncan, and Polly looked at the Gauguin hat and said a stiff how-do-you-do. She was automatically jealous of any woman younger and thinner than she. To his relief, the younger woman had the good manners to relinquish her seat. "Let me sit with the cats," she said.

Polly requested, "When you put my impedimenta in the trunk, Qwill, be careful with that long roll." It looked as if it might be a wall map of the United States.

"I'm sorry, but all your luggage will have to go inside the car," he explained. "The trunk is jam-packed."

As they drove away from the airport, Polly half-turned and asked the other passenger politely, "Did you fly in?"

"No," said Liz in her ingenuous way, "Qwill and I came over on a boat from Grand Island. We were trapped in a strange inn during the hurricane—with no windows or lights or water. It was quite an adventure!"

"Really?" Polly looked at Qwilleran questioningly. "I'm not familiar with Grand Island."

"How was your flight?" he asked forcefully.

"Tolerable. Were you covering the hurricane for the paper?"

"Not officially. *Did you see any puffin birds in Oregon?"*

On the way into town the conversation struggled through a quagmire of bewilderment, evasion, awkwardness, and non sequiturs until they reached Goodwinter Boulevard. Then Qwilleran said, "If you don't mind, Polly, I'll drop you off first. We have a luggage problem to contend with in the trunk, and I know you're tired and want to get home."

Her second-floor apartment occupied a carriage house behind an old mansion, and she rushed upstairs to hug Bootsie, her adored animal companion, while Qwilleran brought up her luggage. Then she turned to him and said crisply, "*Who is she?*"

"It's a long story, but I'll make it brief," he said, talking fast and inventing half-truths. "After you left, the paper sent me to Breakfast Island on assignment . . . and I stayed at the Bambas' B-and-B . . . and I happened to meet a wealthy family from Chicago . . . whose daughter is relocating in Pickax. She's a friend of Fran Brodie's. I think she has some interest in the new college."

"Well!" Polly seemed unconvinced.

"And may I ask the nature of the important decision mentioned on your postcard?"

"That's a long story, too. We can talk about it later."

Downstairs, Liz had moved into the front seat again and was enthusing about the neighborhood. "I'd love to live here," she said.

"All these buildings are part of the new college campus," he explained, as he turned back onto Main Street. At Park Circle he pointed out the courthouse, the public library, and the K Theater, originally a mansion that was gutted by fire. *Fire!* His mind did a flashback to Breakfast Island: the fire in Five Pips, the death of June Halliburton, the revelation that she was the caretaker's daughter . . . Liz had known her . . . Liz had heard something upsetting in connection with the fire and was about to relate it when the power failed.

Qwilleran turned the wheel quickly and stopped the car in a parking lot. "Just before the lights went out, Liz, you were about to tell me something you overheard in the stable."

"Yes . . . yes . . ." she said moodily. "It haunts me, but I don't know whether I should talk about it or not."

"Tell it. You'll feel better."

"I'm afraid it's incriminating."

"If it's the truth, it should be told."

At that moment their conversation was interrupted by a tap on the car window, driver's side. "Hi, Mr. Q! Are you back?"

Qwilleran lowered the window but replied curtly. "Yes, I'm back."

An incredibly tall young man peered into the car, regarding the passenger with interest. "I've got my job back at the Old Stone Mill," he said.

"Good for you!"

The fellow was looking speculatively at Liz, and she leaned forward with a half-smile that gave Qwilleran a brilliant idea. He said, "Liz, this is Derek Cuttlebrink—you saw him in the Corsair Room—a prominent man-about-Pickax . . . Derek, Elizabeth Cage is a newcomer from Chicago."

"Hi! I like your crazy hat!" he said with uninhibited honesty.

Qwilleran added congenially, "We'll have to get her interested in the theater club, won't we?"

"Sure will!" Derek said with enthusiasm.

A scenario of the young man's future unreeled in Qwilleran's mind . . . *Exit: the ecologist with camping equipment. Enter: the amateur botanist with trust fund. Botanist and ex-pirate enroll in the new college.*

Derek ambled away, and Liz repeated what she had said in the hotel lobby: "He's so tall!" Her eyes were lively with admiration.

"Nice young man," Qwilleran said. "Good personality. Lots of talent . . . Now, where were we? You overheard your brother arguing with the steward in the stable."

"Yes, I was in the stall with Skip, and they were in the tack room and didn't see me. I couldn't believe my ears! The steward accused Jack of starting the fire that killed his daughter! Elijah said, 'You were married to two women, and you had to get rid of one! You're a murderer! I'm going to the sheriff!' And Jack said, 'You stupid peasant! No one will believe you! And don't forget, I've got the goods on you—enough to put you away for life. You say one word to anyone, and I'll tell them about the explosion . . . and the shooting . . . and the poisoning! That's enough to hang you twice!' Then Elijah screamed at him, 'You're the one told me to do it! You murderer!' And in between they were shouting obscenities that I couldn't repeat . . . Just then, Skip whinnied! There was sudden silence. I almost died!"

She paused to recollect the crucial moment, and Qwilleran urged her to continue.

"The arguing stopped then, and I heard Jack leave the stable, still shouting nasty names at the old man who had been like an uncle to him when we were all growing up. After that, Elijah banged things around in the tack room for a while, and then he left, too. When it was safe, I slipped out the back door and walked all around the poolhouse and croquet court before going home. That's when I discovered that Mother was giving evacuation orders. She said it was going to be the storm of the century. But I think it was Jack's idea to—"

"Leave the scene of the crime?" Qwilleran suggested.

"If it's true what Elijah said."

"Elijah Kale? Is that his name?" Mentally Qwilleran spelled it: 5-12-9-10-1-8 and then 11-1-12-5. "Were you aware that Jack had married his daughter?"

"Well, when we were young we spent summers together at The Pines, you know, and she always had a crush on Jack. Mother didn't like him to go sailing with the steward's daughter, but he always got his own way. Then June went away to school, and that was the end of it—until last summer. She spent the whole season on the island, playing the piano at the club, and Jack spent all his time there. Mother had William investigate, and it was true: June was Wife Number Four! William told me. Mother never tells me anything."

"Did you have any suspicion of a Wife Number Five?"

"William says Jack met a French woman in Florida and wanted Mother to settle with June, but the *steward's daughter* didn't want money; she wanted Jack Appelhardt." Liz said it with scorn.

As soon as Liz was safely registered at the Pickax Hotel, Qwilleran took the shortcut to his apple barn—through the theater parking lot and the dense patch of woods that separated his orchard from urban Pickax. He unloaded the Siamese, put fresh water in their bowl, and unpacked only enough to find his record of the domino games.

The last entry included 4-4, 5-6, 6-6, 2-3, 3-6, 5-5, 0-1, and 3-5—pips that he had translated into H, K, L, E, I, J, A, and another H. He had been trying to unscramble them when Liz knocked on his door, wearing a caftan and carrying an oil lamp like a vestal of Roman myth.

Now the letters fell into place. Discarding the K and one H, he spelled *Elijah*. In that same game Koko had produced dominoes that spelled *Jack* and *Kale*. (Although Qwilleran had thought it was *lake* or *leak*.) Reviewing that final game, he pounded his forehead with his fist and muttered, "Dumb! Dumb!"

Koko, he admitted once again, was amazing. He couldn't spell; neither could he add or subtract. He bypassed the three Rs because he knew everything instinctively. He was psychic! Qwilleran often asked himself, How did I happen to adopt the only psychic cat in captivity? It never occurred to him that Koko may have made it happen, just as he had engineered Qwilleran's presence on the nature trail at a vital moment.

Without further unpacking, Qwilleran phoned the police chief at home. "Andy, I got your phone message, and now I have some information—"

"Where are you?"

"Back at the apple barn, but I was on the island during the storm."

"How was it?"

"Halfway between terrifying and boring. Want to run over for a confidential chat and a nip of the good stuff?"

"Be there in three minutes."

Galloping paws were thundering up the ramps, around the balconies, across the beams, back down to the mezzanine level, from which they swooped to a cushioned chair on the main floor. After two weeks of confinement, they had rediscovered SPACE. Qwilleran said to them, "I swear never to subject you guys to that ordeal again!"

While waiting for Brodie he took another look at the note from Dwight Somers:

> Didn't want to give you this dope over the phone (I used Watergate tactics to get it) and I'm leaving the island on the next ferry. I quit this crummy job! Have an appointment with a firm in Lockmaster—sounds good. Noisette's last name is duLac. Permanent residence: Lake Worth FL. Hope this helps.

Almost immediately a vehicle could be seen weaving through the woods and bouncing on the rutted road. It was an occurrence that always excited Koko. "It's the law!" Qwilleran warned him. "*Please,* no catfits!"

Andy parked at the back door and came blustering through the kitchen. "This had better be good! You pulled me away from a TV special on Edinburgh."

"If it isn't good enough to take to the prosecutor, I'll buy you and your wife dinner at the Old Stone Mill."

Andy's Scotch was ready—with a little water and no ice—and the two men took their glasses into the lounge, where the chief sank into the cushions of an oversize chair. "I hear the hotel got hit bad, just as I predicted."

"The ancient gods of the island have had a curse on the Pear Island resort from the beginning."

"You can't fight nature . . . any more than you can fight City Hall. So what have you got? Hard evidence or soft clues?"

"I've got a hack saw blade, some signals from Koko (who's never wrong), and enough two-and-two to put together and make a case of sabotage, bigamy, arson, murder, and several counts of attempted murder. Everyone tried to explain them away as accidents, but I maintain they were the result of two criminal plots, both masterminded by the black sheep of a wealthy family from Chicago. Finding himself married to June Halliburton and Noisette duLac at the same time, he got rid of one wife and helped the other wife to get rid of her husband. I'd guess that both murders were accomplished by drugging the drinks of the victims. Then June's mattress was set afire, and George duLac fell into the hotel pool, probably with a gentle assist.

"Both of these incidents," Qwilleran pointed out, "made unfavorable publicity for the resort but were actually subplots. The major campaign to harass the resort and undermine its tourist business was engineered by the bigamist and an employee at his family's estate. I'll name names when I talk to the prosecutor."

"How much of this is guesswork on your part?" the chief asked.

"You can call it what you like, but it's deduction based on observation, reports from witnesses, and tips from Koko." Qwilleran went into a few details regarding the gumbo poisoning, the finding of the hack saw blade, and the argument in the stable. He thought it best not to mention the dominoes. Brodie's admiration for Koko's occult talents had its limits. "Freshen your drink, Andy?"

"Just a wee dram."

On Saturday all three of them—the man and his two animal companions—found themselves in a post-vacation, post-hurricane lethargy. The Siamese curled up in their old familiar places; Qwilleran lolled around and refused to answer the telephone. Later, when he checked his answering machine, there were these messages:

From Fran Brodie: "Thanks for sending me Ms. Cage. I'm doing an apartment for her at Indian Village."

From Polly Duncan: "Sorry I was snippy last night. I was travel-weary. I'm dying to tell you about my big decision."

From Mildred Riker: "If you'll invite us for drinks tomorrow, I'll bring a casserole and a salad. Want to hear about the hurricane and Polly's vacation."

On Sunday evening the Rikers arrived with food and bad news: The high winds had damaged the new addition to their beach house. Polly arrived with her roll of papers and good news. "When I told my friend in Oregon that I intended to keep my carriage house apartment in the new college complex, she convinced me I should own my own home. She's an architect, and we spent the whole time planning a house—two stories high, so Bootsie can run up and down stairs. All I need to do is find a piece of land that's not too remote and not too expensive." She unrolled the architect's sketches and spread them on the coffee table.

Riker applauded. Mildred was thrilled. Qwilleran felt much relieved. He said, "There are two acres at the far end of the orchard, where the Trevelyan farmhouse used to be. I'll sell them for a dollar." Then everyone applauded.

When they asked him about the hurricane, he shrugged it off. "When you've seen one hurricane, you've seen 'em all." He captivated them, however, with the tale of the missing lightkeepers.

Mildred said, "Why is everyone mystified? It's perfectly obvious that the men were plucked off the island by a UFO."

No one applauded, but Koko said "Yow-ow-ow" in what seemed to be an authoritative affirmative.

Glibly Qwilleran explained, "He smells the casserole in the oven."

"Okay, Qwill," said Riker. "What was your real reason for going to Breakfast Island? You didn't fool me for one minute, and you've filed only one piece of copy in two weeks."

"Well, you know, Nick Bamba was concerned about the series of accidents on the island, and he wanted me to go over there and poke around for evidence of foul play; but . . . there were three plainclothes detectives from the state police on the scene, so I told myself, Why get involved?"

"Now you're getting smart," the editor said. "I've always told you to mind your own business."

The Rikers left fairly early. Qwilleran drove Polly home and returned to the barn fairly late. He gave the Siamese their bedtime snack, and then the three of them enjoyed their half-hour of propinquity before retiring: Qwilleran sprawled in his big chair, Yum Yum curled on his lap with chin on paw, and Koko on the arm of the chair, condensing himself into an introspective bundle of fur. Satisfied with his treat and contemplating lights-out, Koko looked like anyone's pampered pet, and yet . . .

Qwilleran asked himself the questions that would never be fully answered:

When Koko tore the month of June off the calendar, did he know that June Halliburton would lose her life next door?

When he ruined my good clothes and stopped me from visiting

the merry widows, did he know what lay ahead on the nature trail? Otherwise, I would never have met the royal family or heard their daughter's story of royal intrigue. Or was it all coincidence?

When Koko threw his catfit and dislodged the tragedy mask, was it because it looked like the dissipated Jack Appelhardt?

And how about his raid on the nutbowl? Did he know that the French word for hazelnut is *noisette?*

And how about the dominoes? "Level with me, Koko," Qwilleran said to the sleepy cat at his elbow. "Do you get a kick out of swishing your tail and sending them flying off the table? Or do you know what you're doing?"

Koko squeezed his eyes and opened his mouth in a cavernous yawn—showing his fangs, exposing a pink gullet, and breathing a potent reminder of his bedtime snack.